# BRITISH WOMEN OF MYSTERY

**Three Novels Penned by Women of the Golden Age of Mysteries**

## Edited by Greg Fowlkes

# BRITISH WOMEN
## OF MYSTERY

© 2015 Resurrected Press
www.ResurrectedPress.com

## Published by Resurrected Press

This classic book was handcrafted by Resurrected Press. Resurrected Press is dedicated to bringing high quality classic books back to the readers who enjoy them. These are not scanned versions of the originals, but, rather, quality checked and edited books meant to be enjoyed!

Please visit ResurrectedPress.com to view our entire catalogue!

**Like us on Facebook to stay up-to-date on all of our latest releases: http://www.facebook.com/ResurrectedPress**

ISBN 13: 978-1-943403-12-7

Printed in the United States of America

# FOREWORD

Before World War I, British detective fiction was almost exclusively a male enclave. This was to change dramatically in the period between the two wars, an era that has rightly come to be known the "Golden Age of British Detective Fiction." A whole series of young women writers, many of whom were university educated or who had served in France as nurses or ambulance drivers, joined the profession, and indeed came to dominate it. This group of women, which was led by the Grande Dame of the all, Agatha Christie, also included in their numbers Dorothy Sayers, Ngaio Marsh, and Marjorie Allingham as well as a host of lesser known writers.

The reasons for this influx of women into the genre were many. The Great War, as it was known at the time, had drawn many women into previously male occupations so as to free up those men for military service. The dislocations and destruction of the war also altered the economic balance between country and town in ways that provided new freedoms for women even as it added new uncertainties to life. At the same time, new educational opportunities were also opening up for women. There was also a change in culture as it became acceptable for young women to lead a life outside the home and to even pursue a career.

Whatever the reasons behind it, the introduction of so many women writers into detective fiction altered the genre forever. The puzzle element, while still present during the era, began to take second place to the psychological apsect. The mysteries penned by these authors were much more concerned with the motives and the interactions of the characters than they were in producing a more clever way to murder someone.

The scene of the crime also underwent a change. These new women authors were primarily middle-class in origin, and it shows in their mysteries. The grand country houses with their large weekend parties began to give way to the smaller cottages of the village and the apartment blocks of London as the backdrop for the story. Murder became a small scale affair, less concerned with the theft of fabulous jewels and more likely to involve a small inheritance from a distant uncle.

The three authors that have been chosen for this collection couldn't be more different. Dorothy L. Sayers was extremely well known, not just for her mysteries, but for her serious work as a classicist and a translator of Dante's *Divine Comedy*. Her major character, introduced in *Whose Body?* is Lord Peter Wimsey, an aristocratic detective of the old school complete to the monocle he wears. Yet, even Wimsey reflects the changing of the times. One of Sayers' best mysteries, *Murder Must Advertise,* is set not in the manor house, but in an advertising agency. In later books in the series, his sister would marry a police detective and he himself became romantically involved with an Oxford University woman.

Elaine Hamilton is much more of a new woman, though actually little information on her is available. The typical character in her novel is a young woman, middle class in origins, but fallen on hard times. The detective in the series is Inspector Reynolds, a man with no aristocratic pretensions. He is happily married, but other than that, he seems to be tied to his work which he carries out in a determined but unflamboyant manner. The book presented here, *The Westminster Mystery*, is the first book of the series.

Not much is known about A. E. Fielding, though her American publisher described her as a middle-aged woman who enjoyed gardening and lived in a London suburb, coincidentally, the same one where Agatha Christie resided. Her detective is Chief Inspector Pointer of Scotland Yard, a man of humble roots, though well educated and fluent in several languages. In the books, he has almost no social life outside of work, though we are informed that he makes time for a week or two of mountain climbing on the continent each year. *The Clifford Affair*, the novel in this volume, is fairly early in the series, and, as with a number of the Pointer books, features a bit of international intrigue as well as simple murder.

All three of these mysteries involve the unexpected discovery of a body in an apartment, two in bathrooms and one in the dining room, but other than that similarity, they take the reader in completely different directions.

While Sayers has maintained a reputation as a writer of detective stories over the years, Hamilton and Fielding, though obviously popular at the time, have faded into obscurity along with too much of the mystery literature of the time. This collection is an attempt to try to correct that fact and introduce a new generation of readers to these three women of mystery.


Greg Fowlkes
Editor-In-Chief
Resurrected Press
www.ResurrectedPress.com

# RESURRECTED PRESS CLASSIC
# MYSTERY CATALOGUE

**E. C. Bentley**
*Trent's Last Case: The Woman in Black*

**Ernest Bramah**
*Max Carrados Resurrected:
The Detective Stories of Max Carrados*

**Agatha Christie**
*The Secret Adversary
The Mysterious Affair at Styles*

**Octavus Roy Cohen**
*Midnight*

**Freeman Wills Croft**
*The Ponson Case
The Pit Prop Syndicate*

**J. S. Fletcher**
*The Herapath Property
The Rayner-Slade Amalgamation
The Chestermarke Instinct
The Paradise Mystery
Dead Men's Money
The Middle of Things
Ravensdene Court
Scarhaven Keep
The Orange-Yellow Diamond
The Middle Temple Murder
The Tallyrand Maxim
The Borough Treasurer
In the Mayor's Parlour
The Saftey Pin*

## R. Austin Freeman

*The Mystery of 31 New Inn from the Dr. Thorndyke Series*
*John Thorndyke's Cases from the Dr. Thorndyke Series*
*The Red Thumb Mark from The Dr. Thorndyke Series*
*The Eye of Osiris from The Dr. Thorndyke Series*
*A Silent Witness from the Dr. John Thorndyke Series*
*The Cat's Eye from the Dr. John Thorndyke Series*
*Helen Vardon's Confession: A Dr. John Thorndyke Story*
*As a Thief in the Night: A Dr. John Thorndyke Story*
*Mr. Pottermack's Oversight: A Dr. John Thorndyke Story*
*Dr. Thorndyke Intervenes: A Dr. John Thorndyke Story*
*The Singing Bone: The Adventures of Dr. Thorndyke*
*The Stoneware Monkey: A Dr. John Thorndyke Story*
*The Great Portrait Mystery, and Other Stories: A Collection of Dr.
John Thorndyke and Other Stories*
*The Penrose Mystery: A Dr. John Thorndyke Story*
*The Uttermost Farthing: A Savant's Vendetta*

## Arthur Griffiths

*The Passenger From Calais*
*The Rome Express*

## Fergus Hume

*The Mystery of a Hansom Cab*
*The Green Mummy*
*The Silent House*
*The Secret Passage*

## Edgar Jepson

*The Loudwater Mystery*

## A. E. W. Mason

*At the Villa Rose*

## A. A. Milne

*The Red House Mystery*

## Baroness Emma Orczy

*The Old Man in the Corner*

## Edgar Allan Poe

*The Detective Stories of Edgar Allan Poe*

## Arthur J. Rees
*The Hampstead Mystery*
*The Shrieking Pit*
*The Hand In The Dark*
*The Moon Rock*
*The Mystery of the Downs*

## Mary Roberts Rinehart
*Sight Unseen and The Confession*

## Dorothy L. Sayers
*Whose Body?*

## Sir William Magnay
*The Hunt Ball Mystery*

## Mabel and Paul Thorne
*The Sheridan Road Mystery*

## Louis Tracy
*The Strange Case of Mortimer Fenley*
*The Albert Gate Mystery*
*The Bartlett Mystery*
*The Postmaster's Daughter*
*The House of Peril*
*The Sandling Case: What Would You Have Done?*

## Charles Edmonds Walk
*The Paternoster Ruby*

## John R. Watson
*The Mystery of the Downs*
*The Hampstead Mystery*

## Edgar Wallace
*The Daffodil Mystery*
*The Crimson Circle*

# TABLE OF CONTENTS

# WHOSE BODY?
## BY DOROTHY L. SAYERS

Whose Body?
*by* Dorothy L. Sayers

R. P.

A Resurrected Press Mystery

## ORIGINALLY PUBLISHED 1923

Editor's Notes:

# Whose Body?

### By Dorothy L. Sayers

*Whose Body?* is the first work of Sayers featuring one of the most memorable detectives of the Golden Age of British detective fiction, Lord Peter Wimsey. Brother of a peer, the Duke of Denver, Lord Peter exhibits all of the traits of the idle rich of the period, expensive clothes, fast cars, a taste for all the finer things of life, he even sports a monocle. As a member of an old and prominent family, he knows everyone who is anyone and has access to the best clubs and country houses. He also has a taste for solving crime, much to the chagrin of his brother, the duke. Lord Peter was to appear in a further ten novels and two collections of short stories.

Depending on the critics viewpoint, Sayers is either loved or hated. As Julian Symons put it in *Bloody Murder*, "For her whole-hearted admirers she is the finest detective story writer of the twentieth century, to those less enthusiastic her work is long winded and ludicrously snobbish." No one, however, can deny that she was not an influential writer, and that she did not help to bring a certain literary respectability to the genre.

She is considered to be one of the four leading writers of detective fiction in the period between the two world wars, the so called "Golden Age" of detective fiction, along with Agatha Christie, Anthony Berkeley, and S. S. Van Dine. She was well educated and widely read both within and outside of the genre. Having worked on several highly successful advertising campaigns as a copywriter, she was able to craft clear and concise prose when she so wished. She also had a talent for devising interesting plots that involved original and well researched means of murder. It is, therefore, not surprising that her works were immensely popular at the time.

In the 70's the character of Lord Peter experienced a revival of sorts when Masterpiece Theatre produced a series of TV episodes based on several of the original novels. This series introduced a whole new generation to the works of Dorothy L. Sayers and resulted in the reissue of the books in paperback form.

Anyone who wishes to know more about detective fiction must read Dorothy L. Sayers to have a complete understanding of the genre. Therefore, Resurrected Press is happy to offer this new edition of *Whose Body?*

## About the Author

Dorothy L. Sayers (June 13, 1893-December 17, 1957) was a British writer, playwright, essayist and translator. She was one of the "big four" mystery writers during the "Golden Age" of British detective fiction, the period between the two world wars. Oxford educated, Sayers later worked in advertising working as the copywriter for campaigns for Coleman's mustard and Guinness, before turning to detective fiction full time. Later in life she did a translation of Dante's *Divine Comedy*.

# WHOSE BODY

## CHAPTER I

"Oh, damn!" said Lord Peter Wimsey at Piccadilly Circus. "Hi, driver!

The taxi man, irritated at receiving this appeal while negotiating the intricacies of turning into Lower Regent Street across the route of a 19 'bus, a 38-B and a bicycle, bent an unwilling ear.

"I've left the catalogue behind," said Lord Peter deprecatingly, "uncommonly careless of me. D'you mind puttin' back to where we came from?"

"To the Savile Club, sir?"

"No—110 Piccadilly—just beyond—thank you."

"Thought you was in a hurry," said the man, overcome with a sense of injury.

"I'm afraid it's an awkward place to turn in," said Lord Peter, answering the thought rather than the words. His long, amiable face looked as if it had generated spontaneously from his top hat, as white maggots breed from Gorgonzola.

The taxi, under the severe eye of a policeman, revolved by slow jerks, with a noise like the grinding of teeth.

The block of new, perfect and expensive flats in which Lord Peter dwelt upon the second floor, stood directly opposite the Green Park, in a spot for many years occupied by the skeleton of a frustrate commercial enterprise. As Lord Peter let himself in he heard his man's voice in the library, uplifted in that throttled stridency peculiar to well-trained persons using the telephone.

"I believe that's his lordship just coming in again—if your Grace would kindly hold the line a moment."

"What is it, Bunter?"

"Her Grace has just called up from Denver, my lord. I was just saying your lordship had gone to the sale when I heard your lordship's latchkey."

"Thanks," said Lord Peter; "and you might find me my catalogue, would you? I think I must have left it in my bedroom, or on the desk."

He sat down to the telephone with an air of leisurely courtesy, as though it were an acquaintance dropped in for a chat.

"Hullo, Mother—that you?"

"Oh, there you are, dear," replied the voice of the Dowager Duchess. "I was afraid I'd just missed you."

"Well, you had, as a matter of fact. I'd just started off to Brocklebury's sale to pick up a book or two, but I had to come back for the catalogue. What's up?"

"Such a quaint thing," said the Duchess. "I thought I'd tell you. You know little Mr. Thipps?"

"Thipps?" said Lord Peter. "Thipps? Oh, yes, the little architect man who's doing the church roof. Yes. What about him?"

"Mrs. Throgmorton's just been in, in quite a state of mind."

"Sorry, Mother, I can't hear. Mrs. Who?"

"Throgmorton—Throgmorton—the vicar's wife."

"Oh, Throgmorton, yes?"

"Mr. Thipps rang them up this morning. It was his day to come down, you know."

"Yes?"

"He rang them up to say he couldn't. He was so upset, poor little man. He'd found a dead body in his bath."

"Sorry, Mother, I can't hear; found what, where?"

"A dead body, dear, in his bath."

"What?—no, no, we haven't finished. Please don't cut us off. Hullo! Hullo! Is that you, Mother? Hullo!—Mother!—Oh, yes—sorry, the girl was trying to cut us off. What sort of body?"

"A dead man, dear, with nothing on but a pair of pince-nez. Mrs. Throgmorton positively blushed when she was telling me. I'm afraid people do get a little narrow-minded in country vicarages."

"Well, it sounds a bit unusual. Was it anybody he knew?"

"No, dear, I don't think so, but, of course, he couldn't give her many details. She said he sounded quite distracted. He's such a respectable little man—and having the police in the house and so on, really worried him."

"Poor little Thipps! Uncommonly awkward for him. Let's see, he lives in Battersea, doesn't he?"

"Yes, dear; 59 Queen Caroline Mansions; opposite the Park. That big block just around the corner from the Hospital. I thought perhaps you'd like to run round and see him and ask if there's anything we can do. I always thought him a nice little man."

"Oh, quite," said Lord Peter, grinning at the telephone. The Duchess was always of the greatest assistance to his hobby of criminal investigation, though she never alluded to it, and maintained a polite fiction of its non-existence.

"What time did it happen, Mother?"

"I think he found it early this morning, but, of course, he didn't think of telling the Throgmortons just at first. She came up to me just before lunch—so tiresome, I had to ask her to stay. Fortunately, I was alone. I don't mind being bored myself, but I hate having my guests bored."

"Poor old Mother! Well, thanks awfully for tellin' me. I think I'll send Bunter to the sale and toddle round to Battersea now an' try and console the poor little beast. So-long."

"Good-bye, dear."

"Bunter!"

"Yes, my lord."

"Her Grace tells me that a respectable Battersea architect has discovered a dead man in his bath."

"Indeed, my lord? That's very gratifying."

"Very, Bunter. Your choice of words is unerring. I wish Eton and Balliol had done as much for me. Have you found the catalogue?"

"Here it is, my lord."

"Thanks. I am going to Battersea at once. I want you to attend the sale for me. Don't lose time—I don't want to miss the Folio Dante* nor the de Voragine—here you are—see? 'Golden Legend'—Wynkyn de Worde, 1493—got that?—and, I say, make a special effort for the Caxton folio of the 'Four Sons of Aymon'—it's the 1489 folio and unique. Look! I've marked the lots I want, and put my outside offer against each. Do your best for me. I shall be back to dinner."

"Very good, my lord."

"Take my cab and tell him to hurry. He may for you; he doesn't like me very much. Can I," said Lord Peter, looking at himself in the eighteenth-century mirror over the mantelpiece, "can I have the heart to fluster the flustered Thipps further—that's very difficult to say quickly—by appearing in a top-hat and frock-coat? I think not. Ten to one he will overlook my trousers and mistake me for the undertaker. A grey suit, I fancy, neat but not gaudy, with a hat to tone, suits my other self better. Exit the amateur of first editions; new motif introduced by solo bassoon; enter Sherlock Holmes, disguised as a walking gentleman. There goes Bunter. Invaluable fellow—never offers to do his job when you've told him to do somethin' else. Hope he doesn't miss the 'Four Sons of Aymon.' Still, there is another copy of that—in the Vatican.** It might become available, you never know—if the Church of Rome went to pot or Switzerland invaded Italy—whereas a strange corpse doesn't turn up in a suburban bathroom more than once in a lifetime—at least, I should think not—at any rate, the number of times it's happened, with a pince-nez, might be counted on the fingers of one hand, I imagine. Dear me! it's a dreadful mistake to ride two hobbies at once."

He had drifted across the passage into his bedroom, and was changing with a rapidity one might not have expected from a man of his mannerisms. He selected a dark-green tie to match his socks and tied it accurately without hesitation or the slightest compression of his lips; substituted a pair of brown shoes for his black ones, slipped a monocle into a breast pocket, and took up a beautiful Malacca walking-stick with a heavy silver knob.

"That's all, I think," he murmured to himself. "Stay—I may as well have you—you may come in useful—one never knows." He added a flat silver matchbox to his equipment, glanced at his watch, and seeing that it was already a quarter to three, ran briskly downstairs, and, hailing a taxi, was carried to Battersea Park.

Mr. Alfred Thipps was a small, nervous man, whose flaxen hair was beginning to abandon the unequal struggle with destiny. One might say that his only really marked feature was a large bruise over the left eyebrow, which gave him a faintly dissipated air incongruous with the rest of his appearance. Almost in the same breath with his first greeting, he made a self-conscious apology for it, murmuring something about having run against the dining-room door in the dark. He was touched almost to tears by Lord Peter's thoughtfulness and condescension in calling.

"I'm sure it's most kind of your lordship," he repeated for the dozenth time, rapidly blinking his weak little eyelids. "I appreciate it very deeply, very deeply, indeed, and so would Mother, only she's so deaf, I don't like to trouble you with making her understand. It's been very hard all day," he added, "with the policemen in the house and all this commotion. It's what Mother and me have never been used to, always living very retired, and it's most distressing to a man of regular habits, my lord, and really, I'm almost thankful Mother doesn't understand, for I'm sure it would worry her terribly if she was to know about it. She was upset at first, but she's made up some idea of her own about it now, and I'm sure it's all for the best."

The old lady who sat knitting by the fire nodded grimly in response to a look from her son.

"I always said as you ought to complain about that bath, Alfred," she said suddenly, in the high, piping voice peculiar to the deaf, "and it's to be 'oped the landlord'll see about it now; not but what I think you might have managed without having the police in, but there! you always were one to make a fuss about a little thing, from chicken-pox up."

"There now," said Mr. Thipps apologetically, "you see how it is. Not but what it's just as well she's settled on that, because she understands we've locked up the bathroom and don't try to go in there. But it's been a terrible shock to me, sir—my lord, I should say, but there! my nerves are all to pieces. Such a thing has never 'appened—happened to me in all my born days. Such a state I was in this morning—I didn't know if I was on my head or my heels—I really didn't, and my heart not being too strong, I hardly knew how to get out of that horrid room and telephone for the police. It's affected me, sir, it's affected me, it really has—I couldn't touch a bit of breakfast, nor lunch neither, and what with telephoning and putting off clients and interviewing people all morning, I've hardly known what to do with myself?"

"I'm sure it must have been uncommonly distressin'," said Lord Peter, sympathetically, "especially comin' like that before breakfast. Hate anything tiresome happenin' before breakfast. Takes a man at such a confounded disadvantage, what?"

"That's just it, that's just it," said Mr. Thipps, eagerly, "when I saw that dreadful thing lying there in my bath, mother-naked, too, except for a pair of eyeglasses, I assure you, my lord, it regularly turned my stomach, if you'll excuse the expression. I'm not very strong, sir, and I get that sinking feeling sometimes in the morning, and what with one thing and another I 'ad—had to send the girl for a stiff brandy or I don't know what mightn't have happened. I felt so queer, though I'm anything but partial to spirits as a rule. Still, I make it a rule never to be without brandy in the house, in case of emergency, you know?"

"Very wise of you," said Lord Peter, cheerfully, "you're a very far-seein' man, Mr. Thipps. Wonderful what a little nip'll do in case of need, and the less you're used to it the more good it does you. Hope your girl is a sensible young woman, what? Nuisance to have women faintin' and shriekin' all over the place."

"Oh, Gladys is a good girl," said Mr. Thipps, "very reasonable indeed. She was shocked, of course, that's very understandable. I was shocked myself, and it wouldn't be proper in a young woman not to be shocked under the circumstances, but she is really a helpful, energetic girl in a crisis, if you understand me. I consider myself very fortunate these days to have got a good, decent girl to do for me and Mother, even though she is a bit careless and forgetful about little things, but that's only natural. She was very sorry indeed about having left the bathroom window open, she really was, and though I was angry at first, seeing what's come of it, it wasn't anything to speak of, not in the ordinary way, as you might say. Girls will forget things, you know, my lord, and really she was so distressed I didn't like to say too much to her. All I said was, 'It might have been burglars,' I said, 'remember that, next time you leave a window open all night; this time it was a dead man,' I said, 'and that's unpleasant enough, but next time it might be burglars,' I said, 'and all of us murdered in our beds.' But the police-inspector—Inspector Sugg, they called him, from the Yard—he was very sharp with her, poor girl. Quite frightened her, and made her think he suspected her of something, though what good a body could be to her, poor girl, I can't imagine, and so I told the inspector. He was quite rude to me, my lord—I may say I didn't like his manner at all. 'If

you've got anything definite to accuse Gladys or me of, Inspector,' I said
to him, 'bring it forward, that's what you have to do,' I said, 'but I've yet
to learn that you're paid to be rude to a gentleman in his own 'ouse—
house.' Reely," said Mr. Thipps, growing quite pink on the top of his
head, "he regularly roused me, regularly roused me, my lord, and I'm a
mild man as a rule."

"Sugg all over," said Lord Peter, "I know him. When he don't know
what else to say, he's rude, Stands to reason you and the girl wouldn't
go collectin' bodies. Who'd want to saddle himself with a body?
Difficulty's usually to get rid of 'em. Have you got rid of this one yet, by
the way?"

"It's still in the bathroom," said Mr. Thipps. "Inspector Sugg said
nothing was to be touched till his men came in to move it. I'm expecting
them at any time. If it would interest your lordship to have a look at
it—"

"Thanks awfully," said Lord Peter, "I'd like to very much, if I'm not
puttin' you out."

"Not at all," said Mr. Thipps. His manner as he led the way along
the passage convinced Lord Peter of two things—first, that, gruesome
as his exhibit was, he rejoiced in the importance it reflected upon
himself and his flat, and secondly, that Inspector Sugg had forbidden
him to exhibit it to anyone. The latter supposition was confirmed by
the action of Mr. Thipps, who stopped to fetch the doorkey from his
bedroom, saying that the police had the other, but that he made it a
rule to have two keys to every door, in case of accident.

The bathroom was in no way remarkable. It was long and narrow,
the window being exactly over the head of the bath. The panes were of
frosted glass; the frame wide enough to admit a man's body. Lord Peter
stepped rapidly across to it, opened it and looked out.

The flat was the top one of the building and situated about the
middle of the block. The bathroom window looked out upon the
backyards of the flats, which were occupied by various small
outbuildings, coal-holes, garages, and the like. Beyond these were the
back gardens of a parallel line of houses. On the right rose the
extensive edifice of St. Luke's Hospital, Battersea, with its grounds,
and, connected with it by a covered way, the residence of the famous
surgeon, Sir Julian Freke, who directed the surgical side of the great
new hospital, and was, in addition, known in Harley Street as a
distinguished neurologist with a highly individual point of view.

This information was poured into Lord Peter's ear at considerable
length by Mr. Thipps, who seemed to feel that the neighbourhood of
anybody so distinguished shed a kind of halo of glory over Queen
Caroline Mansions.

"We had him round here himself this morning," he said, "about this horrid business. Inspector Sugg thought one of the young medical gentlemen at the hospital might have brought the corpse round for a joke, as you might say, they always having bodies in the dissecting-room. So Inspector Sugg went round to see Sir Julian this morning to ask if there was a body missing. He was very kind, was Sir Julian, very kind indeed, though he was at work when they got there, in the dissecting-room. He looked up the books to see that all the bodies were accounted for, and then very obligingly came round here to look at this"—he indicated the bath—"and said he was afraid he couldn't help us—there was no corpse missing from the hospital, and this one didn't answer to the description of any they'd had."

"Nor to the description of any of the patients, I hope," suggested Lord Peter casually.

At this grisly hint Mr. Thipps turned pale.

"I didn't hear Inspector Sugg enquire," he said, with some agitation. "What a very horrid thing that would be—God bless my soul, my lord, I never thought of it."

"Well, if they had missed a patient they'd probably have discovered it by now," said Lord Peter. "Let's have a look at this one."

He screwed his monocle into his eye, adding: "I see you're troubled here with the soot blowing in. Beastly nuisance, ain't it? I get it, too—spoils all my books, you know. Here, don't you trouble, if you don't care about lookin' at it."

He took from Mr. Thipps's hesitating hand the sheet which had been flung over the bath, and turned it back.

The body which lay in the bath was that of a tall, stout man of about fifty. The hair, which was thick and black and naturally curly, had been cut and parted by a master hand, and exuded a faint violet perfume, perfectly recognizable in the close air of the bathroom. The features were thick, fleshy and strongly marked, with prominent dark eyes, and a long nose curving down to a heavy chin. The clean-shaven lips were full and sensual, and the dropped jaw showed teeth stained with tobacco. On the dead face the handsome pair of gold pince-nez mocked death with grotesque elegance; the fine gold chain curved over the naked breast. The legs lay stiffly stretched out side by side; the arms reposed close to the body; the fingers were flexed naturally. Lord Peter lifted one arm, and looked at the hand with a little frown.

"Bit of a dandy, your visitor, what?" he murmured. "Parma violet and manicure." He bent again, slipping his hand beneath the head. The absurd eyeglasses slipped off, clattering into the bath, and the noise put the last touch to Mr. Thipps's growing nervousness.

"If you'll excuse me," he murmured, "it makes me feel quite faint, it really does."

He slipped outside, and he had no sooner done so than Lord Peter, lifting the body quickly and cautiously, turned it over and inspected it with his head on one side, bringing his monocle into play with the air of the late Joseph Chamberlain approving a rare orchid. He then laid the head over his arm, and bringing out the silver matchbox from his pocket, slipped it into the open mouth. Then making the noise usually written "Tut-tut," he laid the body down, picked up the mysterious pince-nez, looked at it, put it on his nose and looked through it, made the same noise again, readjusted the pince-nez upon the nose of the corpse, so as to leave no traces of interference for the irritation of Inspector Sugg; rearranged the body; returned to the window and, leaning out, reached upwards and sideways with his walking-stick, which he had somewhat incongruously brought along with him. Nothing appearing to come of these investigations, he withdrew his head, closed the window, and rejoined Mr. Thipps in the passage.

Mr. Thipps, touched by this sympathetic interest in the younger son of a duke, took the liberty, on their return to the sitting-room, of offering him a cup of tea. Lord Peter, who had strolled over to the window and was admiring the outlook on Battersea Park, was about to accept, when an ambulance came into view at the end of Prince of Wales Road. Its appearance reminded Lord Peter of an important engagement, and with a hurried "By Jove!" he took his leave of Mr. Thipps.

"My mother sent kind regards and all that," he said, shaking hands fervently; "hopes you'll soon be down at Denver again. Good-bye, Mrs. Thipps," he bawled kindly into the ear of the old lady. "Oh, no, my dear sir, please don't trouble to come down."

He was none too soon. As he stepped out of the door and turned towards the station, the ambulance drew up from the other direction, and Inspector Sugg emerged from it, with two constables. The Inspector spoke to the officer on duty at the Mansions, and turned a suspicious gaze on Lord Peter's retreating back.

"Dear old Sugg," said that nobleman, fondly, "dear, dear old bird! How he does hate me, to be sure."

* This is the first Florence edition, 1481, by Niccolo di Lorenzo. Lord Peter's collection of printed Dantes is worth inspection. It includes, besides the famous Aldine 8vo. of 1502, the Naples folio of 1477—"edizione rarissima," according to Colomb. This copy has no history, and Mr. Parker's private belief is that its present owner conveyed it away by stealth from somewhere or other. Lord Peter's own account is that he "picked it up in a little place in the hills," when making a walking-tour through Italy.

** *Lord Peter's wits were wool-gathering. The book is in the possession of Earl Spencer. The Brockelbury copy is incomplete, the five last signatures being altogether missing, but is unique in possessing the colophon.*

# CHAPTER 2

"Excellent, Bunter," said Lord Peter, sinking with a sigh into a luxurious armchair. "I couldn't have done better myself. The thought of the Dante makes my mouth water—and the 'Four Sons of Aymon.' And you've saved me £60—that's glorious. What shall we spend it on, Bunter? Think of it—all ours, to do as we like with, for as Harold Skimpole so rightly observes, £60 saved is £60 gained, and I'd reckoned on spending it all. It's your saving, Bunter, and properly speaking, your £60. What do we want? Anything in your department? Would you like anything altered in the flat?"

"Well, my lord, as your lordship is so good"—the man-servant paused, about to pour an old brandy into a liqueur glass.

"Well, out with it, my Bunter, you imperturbable old hypocrite. It's no good talking as if you were announcing dinner—you're spilling the brandy. The voice is Jacob's voice, but the hands are the hands of Esau. What does that blessed darkroom of yours want now?"

"There's a Double Anastigmat with a set of supplementary lenses, my lord," said Bunter, with a note almost of religious fervour. "If it was a case of forgery now—or footprints—I could enlarge them right up on the plate. Or the wide-angled lens would be useful. It's as though the camera had eyes at the back of its head, my lord. Look—I've got it here."

He pulled a catalogue from his pocket, and submitted it, quivering, to his employer's gaze.

Lord Peter perused the description slowly, the corners of his long mouth lifted into a faint smile.

"It's Greek to me," he said, "and £50 seems a ridiculous price for a few bits of glass. I suppose, Bunter, you'd say £750 was a bit out of the way for a dirty old book in a dead language, wouldn't you?"

"It wouldn't be my place to say so, my lord."

"No, Bunter, I pay you £200 a year to keep your thoughts to yourself. Tell me, Bunter, in these democratic days, don't you think that's unfair?"

"No, my lord."

"You don't. D'you mind telling me frankly why you don't think it unfair?"

"Frankly, my lord, your lordship is paid a nobleman's income to take Lady Worthington in to dinner and refrain from exercising your lordship's undoubted powers of repartee."

Lord Peter considered this.

"That's your idea, is it, Bunter? Noblesse oblige—for a consideration. I daresay you're right. Then you're better off than I am, because I'd have to behave myself to Lady Worthington if I hadn't a penny. Bunter, if I sacked you here and now, would you tell me what you think of me?"

"No, my lord."

"You'd have a perfect right to, my Bunter, and if I sacked you on top of drinking the kind of coffee you make, I'd deserve everything you could say of me. You're a demon for coffee, Bunter—I don't want to know how you do it, because I believe it to be witchcraft, and I don't want to burn eternally. You can buy your cross-eyed lens."

"Thank you, my lord."

"Have you finished in the dining-room?"

"Not quite, my lord."

"Well, come back when you have. I have many things to tell you. Hullo! who's that?"

The doorbell had rung sharply.

"Unless it's anybody interestin' I'm not at home."

"Very good, my lord."

Lord Peter's library was one of the most delightful bachelor rooms in London. Its scheme was black and primrose; its walls were lined with rare editions, and its chairs and Chesterfield sofa suggested the embraces of the houris. In one corner stood a black baby grand, a wood fire leaped on a wide old-fashioned hearth, and the Sevres vases on the chimneypiece were filled with ruddy and gold chrysanthemums. To the eyes of the young man who was ushered in from the raw November fog it seemed not only rare and unattainable, but friendly and familiar, like a colourful and gilded paradise in a medieval painting.

"Mr. Parker, my lord."

Lord Peter jumped up with genuine eagerness.

"My dear man, I'm delighted to see you. What a beastly foggy night, ain't it? Bunter, some more of that admirable coffee and another glass and the cigars. Parker, I hope you're full of crime—nothing less than arson or murder will do for us to-night. 'On such a night as this—' Bunter and I were just sitting down to carouse. I've got a Dante, and a Caxton folio that is practically unique, at Sir Ralph Brocklebury's sale. Bunter, who did the bargaining, is going to have a lens which does all kinds of wonderful things with its eyes shut, and

We both have got a body in a bath,
We both have got a body in a bath—
For in spite of all temptations
To go in for cheap sensations
We insist upon a body in a bath—

Nothing less will do for us, Parker. It's mine at present, but we're going shares in it. Property of the firm. Won't you join us? You really must put something in the jack-pot. Perhaps you have a body. Oh, do have a body. Every body welcome.

Gin a body meet a body
Hauled before the beak,
Gin a body jolly well knows who murdered a body and that old Sugg is on the wrong tack,
Need a body speak?

Not a bit of it. He tips a glassy wink to yours truly and yours truly reads the truth."

"Ah," said Parker, "I knew you'd been round to Queen Caroline Mansions. So've I, and met Sugg, and he told me he'd seen you. He was cross, too. Unwarrantable interference, he calls it."

"I knew he would," said Lord Peter, "I love taking a rise out of dear old Sugg, he's always so rude. I see by the *Star* that he has excelled himself by taking the girl, Gladys What's-her-name, into custody. Sugg of the evening, beautiful Sugg! But what were you doing there?"

"To tell you the truth," said Parker, "I went round to see if the Semitic-looking stranger in Mr. Thipps's bath was by any extraordinary chance Sir Reuben Levy. But he isn't."

"Sir Reuben Levy? Wait a minute, I saw something about that. I know! A headline: 'Mysterious disappearance of famous financier.' What's it all about? I didn't read it carefully."

"Well, it's a bit odd, though I daresay it's nothing really—old chap may have cleared for some reason best known to himself. It only happened this morning, and nobody would have thought anything about it, only it happened to be the day on which he had arranged to attend a most important financial meeting and do some deal involving millions—I haven't got all the details. But I know he's got enemies who'd just as soon the deal didn't come off, so when I got wind of this fellow in the bath, I buzzed round to have a look at him. It didn't seem likely, of course, but unlikelier things do happen in our profession. The funny thing is, old Sugg has got bitten with the idea it is him, and is wildly telegraphing to Lady Levy to come and identify him. However, as Sir Reuben is a pious Jew of pious parents, and the chap in the bath obviously isn't, I'm not going to waste my time. One thing is, the man would be really extraordinarily like Sir Reuben if he had a beard, and as Lady Levy is abroad with the family, somebody may say it's him, and Sugg will build up a lovely theory, like the Tower of Babel, and destined so to perish."

"You're certain of your facts, I suppose."

"Positive. Sugg, of course, says he doesn't take account of fancy religions—"

"Sugg's a beautiful, braying ass," said Lord Peter. "He's like a detective in a novel. Well, I don't know anything about Levy, but I've seen the body, and I should say the idea was preposterous upon the face of it. What do you think of the brandy?"

"Unbelievable, Wimsey—sort of thing makes one believe in heaven. But I want your yarn."

"D'you mind if Bunter hears it, too? Invaluable man, Bunter—amazin' fellow with a camera. And the odd thing is, he's always on the spot when I want my bath or my boots. I don't know when he develops things—I believe he does 'em in his sleep. Bunter!"

"Yes, my lord."

"Stop fiddling about in there, and get yourself the proper things to drink and join the merry throng."

"Certainly, my lord."

"Mr. Parker has a new trick: The Vanishing Financier. Absolutely no deception. Hey, presto, pass! and where is he? Will some gentleman from the audience kindly step upon the platform and inspect the cabinet? Thank you, sir. The quickness of the 'and deceives the heye."

"I'm afraid mine isn't much of a story," said Parker. "It's just one of those simple things that offer no handle. Sir Reuben Levy dined last night with three friends at the Ritz. After dinner the friends went to the theatre. He refused to go with them on account of an appointment. I haven't yet been able to trace the appointment, but anyhow, he returned home to his house—9 Park Lane—at twelve o'clock."

"Who saw him?"

"The cook, who had just gone up to bed, saw him on the doorstep and heard him let himself in. He walked upstairs, leaving his greatcoat on the hall peg and his umbrella in the stand—you remember how it rained last night. He undressed and went to bed. Next morning he wasn't there. That's all," said Parker abruptly, with a wave of the hand.

"It isn't all, it isn't all. Daddy, go on, that's not half a story," pleaded Lord Peter.

"But it is all. When his man came to call him he wasn't there. The bed had been slept in. His pyjamas and all his clothes were there, the only odd thing being that they were thrown rather untidily on the ottoman at the foot of the bed, instead of being neatly folded on a chair, as is Sir Reuben's custom—looking as though he had been rather agitated or unwell. No clean clothes were missing, no suit, no boots—nothing. The boots he had worn were in his dressing-room as usual. He had washed and cleaned his teeth and done all the usual things. The housemaid was down cleaning the hall at half-past six, and can swear that nobody came in or out after that. So one is forced to suppose that a respectable middle-aged Hebrew financier either went mad between twelve and six a. m. and walked quietly out of the house in his birthday suit on a November night, or else was spirited away like the lady in the 'Ingoldsby Legends,' body and bones, leaving only a heap of crumpled clothes behind him."

"Was the front door bolted?"

"That's the sort of question you would ask, straight off; it took me an hour to think of it. No; contrary to custom, there was only the Yale lock on the door. On the other hand, some of the maids had been given leave to go to the theatre, and Sir Reuben may quite conceivably have left the door open under the impression they had not come in. Such a thing has happened before."

"And that's really all?"

"Really all. Except for one very trifling circumstance."

"I love trifling circumstances," said Lord Peter, with childish delight; "so many men have been hanged by trifling circumstances. What was it?"

"Sir Reuben and Lady Levy, who are a most devoted couple, always share the same room. Lady Levy, as I said before, is in Mentone at the moment for her health. In her absence, Sir Reuben sleeps in the double bed as usual, and invariably on his own side—the outside—of the bed. Last night he put the two pillows together and slept in the middle, or, if anything, rather closer to the wall than otherwise. The housemaid, who is a most intelligent girl, noticed this when she went up to make the bed, and, with really admirable detective instinct, refused to touch the bed or let anybody else touch it, though it wasn't till later that they actually sent for the police."

"Was nobody in the house but Sir Reuben and the servants?"

"No; Lady Levy was away with her daughter and her maid. The valet, cook, parlourmaid, housemaid and kitchenmaid were the only people in the house, and naturally wasted an hour or two squawking and gossiping. I got there about ten."

"What have you been doing since?"

"Trying to get on the track of Sir Reuben's appointment last night, since, with the exception of the cook, his 'appointer' was the last person who saw him before his disappearance. There may be some quite simple explanation, though I'm dashed if I can think of one for the moment. Hang it all, a man doesn't come in and go to bed and walk away again 'mid nodings on' in the middle of the night."

"He may have been disguised."

"I thought of that—in fact, it seems the only possible explanation. But it's deuced odd, Wimsey. An important city man, on the eve of an important transaction, without a word of warning to anybody, slips off in the middle of the night, disguised down to his skin, leaving behind his watch, purse, cheque-book, and—most mysterious and important of all—his spectacles, without which he can't see a step, as he is extremely short-sighted. He—"

"That is important," interrupted Wimsey. "You are sure he didn't take a second pair?"

"His man vouches for it that he had only two pairs, one of which was found on his dressing-table, and the other in the drawer where it is always kept."

Lord Peter whistled.

"You've got me there, Parker. Even if he'd gone out to commit suicide he'd have taken those."

"So you'd think—or the suicide would have happened the first time he started to cross the road. However, I didn't overlook the possibility. I've got particulars of all to-day's street accidents, and I can lay my hand on my heart and say that none of them is Sir Reuben. Besides, he took his latchkey with him, which looks as though he'd meant to come back."

"Have you seen the men he dined with?"

"I found two of them at the club. They said that he seemed in the best of health and spirits, spoke of looking forward to joining Lady Levy later on—perhaps at Christmas—and referred with great satisfaction to this morning's business transaction, in which one of them—a man called Anderson of Wyndham's—was himself concerned."

"Then up till about nine o'clock, anyhow, he had no apparent intention or expectation of disappearing."

"None—unless he was a most consummate actor. Whatever happened to change his mind must have happened either at the mysterious appointment which he kept after dinner, or while he was in bed between midnight and 5:30 a. m."

"Well, Bunter," said Lord Peter, "what do you make of it?"

"Not in my department, my lord. Except that it is odd that a gentleman who was too flurried or unwell to fold his clothes as usual should remember to clean his teeth and put his boots out. Those are two things that quite frequently get overlooked, my lord."

"If you mean anything personal, Bunter," said Lord Peter, "I can only say that I think the speech an unworthy one. It's a sweet little problem, Parker mine. Look here, I don't want to butt in, but I should dearly love to see that bedroom to-morrow. 'Tis not that I mistrust thee, dear, but I should uncommonly like to see it. Say me not nay— take another drop of brandy and a Villar Villar, but say not, say not nay!"

"Of course you can come and see it—you'll probably find lots of things I've overlooked," said the other, equably, accepting the proffered hospitality.

"Parker, acushla, you're an honor to Scotland Yard. I look at you, and Sugg appears a myth, a fable, an idiot-boy, spawned in a moonlight hour by some fantastic poet's brain. Sugg is too perfect to be possible. What does he make of the body, by the way?"

"Sugg says," replied Parker, with precision, "that the body died from a blow on the back of the neck. The doctor told him that. He says it's been dead a day or two. The doctor told him that, too. He says it's the body of a well-to-do Hebrew of about fifty. Anybody could have told him that. He says it's ridiculous to suppose it came in through the window without anybody knowing anything about it. He says it probably walked in through the front door and was murdered by the household. He's arrested the girl because she's short and frail-looking and quite unequal to downing a tall and sturdy Semite with a poker. He'd arrest Thipps, only Thipps was away in Manchester all yesterday and the day before and didn't come back till late last night—in fact, he wanted to arrest him till I reminded him that if the body had been a day or two dead, little Thipps couldn't have done him in at 10:30 last night. But he'll arrest him to-morrow as an accessory—and the old lady with the knitting, too, I shouldn't wonder."

"Well, I'm glad the little man has so much of an alibi," said Lord Peter, "though if you're only gluing your faith to cadaveric lividity, rigidity, and all the other quiddities, you must be prepared to have some sceptical beast of a prosecuting counsel walk slap-bang through the medical evidence. Remember Impey Biggs defending in that Chelsea tea-shop affair? Six bloomin' medicos contradictin' each other in the box, an' old Impey elocutin' abnormal cases from Glaister and Dixon Mann till the eyes of the jury reeled in their heads! 'Are you prepared to swear, Dr. Thingumtight, that the onset of *rigor mortis* indicates the hour of death without the possibility of error?' 'So far as my experience goes, in the majority of cases,' says the doctor, all stiff. 'Ah!' says Biggs, 'but this is a Court of Justice, Doctor, not a Parliamentary election. We can't get on without a minority report. The law, Dr. Thingumtight, respects the rights of the minority, alive or dead.' Some ass laughs, and old Biggs sticks his chest out and gets impressive. 'Gentlemen, this is no laughing matter. My client—an upright and honourable gentleman—is being tried for his life—for his life, gentlemen—and it is the business of the prosecution to show his guilt—if they can—without a shadow of doubt. Now, Dr. Thingumtight, I ask you again, can you solemnly swear, without the least shadow of doubt—probable, possible shadow of doubt—that this unhappy woman met her death neither sooner nor later than Thursday evening? A probable opinion? Gentlemen, we are not Jesuits, we are straightforward Englishmen. You cannot ask a British-born jury to convict any man on the authority of a probable opinion.' Hum of applause."

"Biggs's man was guilty all the same," said Parker.

"Of course he was. But he was acquitted all the same, an' what you've just said is libel." Wimsey walked over to the bookshelf and took down a volume of Medical Jurisprudence. "'*Rigor mortis*—can only be stated in a very general way—many factors determine the result.' Cautious brute. 'On the average, however, stiffening will have begun—neck and jaw—5 to 6 hours after death'—m'm—'in all likelihood have passed off in the bulk of cases by the end of 36 hours. Under certain circumstances, however, it may appear unusually early, or be retarded unusually long!' Helpful, ain't it, Parker? 'Brown-Squared states ... 3 1/2 minutes after death.... In certain cases not until lapse of 16 hours after death ... present as long as 21 days thereafter.' Lord! 'Modifying factors—age—muscular state—or febrile diseases—or where temperature of environment is high'—and so on and so on—any bloomin' thing. Never mind. You can run the argument for what it's worth to Sugg. He won't know any better." He tossed the book away. "Come back to facts. What did you make of the body?"

"Well," said the detective, "not very much—I was puzzled—frankly. I should say he had been a rich man, but self-made, and that his good fortune had come to him fairly recently."

"Ah, you noticed the calluses on the hands—I thought you wouldn't miss that."

"Both his feet were badly blistered—he had been wearing tight shoes."

"Walking a long way in them, too," said Lord Peter, "to get such blisters as that. Didn't that strike you as odd, in a person evidently well off?"

"Well, I don't know. The blisters were two or three days old. He might have got stuck in the suburbs one night, perhaps—last train gone and no taxi—and had to walk home."

"Possibly."

"There were some little red marks all over his back and one leg I couldn't quite account for."

"I saw them."

"What did you make of them?"

"I'll tell you afterwards. Go on."

"He was very long-sighted—oddly long-sighted for a man in the prime of life; the glasses were like a very old man's. By the way, they had a very beautiful and remarkable chain of flat links chased with a pattern. It struck me he might be traced through it."

"I've just put an advertisement in the *Times* about it," said Lord Peter. "Go on."

"He had had the glasses some time—they had been mended twice."

"Beautiful, Parker, beautiful. Did you realize the importance of that?"

"Not specially, I'm afraid—why?"

"Never mind—go on."

"He was probably a sullen, ill-tempered man—his nails were filed down to the quick as though he habitually bit them, and his fingers were bitten as well. He smoked quantities of cigarettes without a holder. He was particular about his personal appearance."

"Did you examine the room at all? I didn't get a chance."

"I couldn't find much in the way of footprints. Sugg & Co. had tramped all over the place, to say nothing of little Thipps and the maid, but I noticed a very indefinite patch just behind the head of the bath, as though something damp might have stood there. You could hardly call it a print."

"It rained hard all last night, of course."

"Yes; did you notice that the soot on the window-sill was vaguely marked?"

"I did," said Wimsey, "and I examined it hard with this little fellow, but I could make nothing of it except that something or other had rested on the sill." He drew out his monocle and handed it to Parker.

"My word, that's a powerful lens."

"It is," said Wimsey, "and jolly useful when you want to take a good squint at somethin' and look like a bally fool all the time. Only it don't do to wear it permanently—if people see you full-face they say, 'Dear me! how weak the sight of that eye must be!' Still, it's useful."

"Sugg and I explored the ground at the back of the building," went on Parker, "but there wasn't a trace."

"That's interestin'. Did you try the roof?"

"No."

"We'll go over it to-morrow. The gutter's only a couple of feet off the top of the window. I measured it with my stick—the gentleman-scout's vade-mecum, I call it—it's marked off in inches. Uncommonly handy companion at times. There's a sword inside and a compass in the head. Got it made specially. Anything more?"

"Afraid not. Let's hear your version, Wimsey."

"Well, I think you've got most of the points. There are just one or two little contradictions. For instance, here's a man wears expensive gold-rimmed pince-nez and has had them long enough to be mended twice. Yet his teeth are not merely discoloured, but badly decayed and look as if he'd never cleaned them in his life. There are four molars missing on one side and three on the other and one front tooth broken right across. He's a man careful of his personal appearance, as witness his hair and his hands. What do you say to that?"

"Oh, these self-made men of low origin don't think much about teeth, and are terrified of dentists."

"True; but one of the molars has a broken edge so rough that it had made a sore place on the tongue. Nothing's more painful. D'you mean to tell me a man would put up with that if he could afford to get the tooth filed?"

"Well, people are queer. I've known servants endure agonies rather than step over a dentist's doormat. How did you see that, Wimsey?"

"Had a look inside; electric torch," said Lord Peter. "Handy little gadget. Looks like a matchbox. Well—I daresay it's all right, but I just draw your attention to it. Second point: Gentleman with hair smellin' of Parma violet and manicured hands and all the rest of it, never washes the inside of his ears. Full of wax. Nasty."

"You've got me there, Wimsey; I never noticed it. Still—old bad habits die hard."

"Right oh! Put it down at that. Third point: Gentleman with the manicure and the brilliantine and all the rest of it suffers from fleas."

"By Jove, you're right! Flea-bites. It never occurred to me."

"No doubt about it, old son. The marks were faint and old, but unmistakable."

"Of course, now you mention it. Still, that might happen to anybody. I loosed a whopper in the best hotel in Lincoln the week before last. I hope it bit the next occupier!"

"Oh, all these things might happen to anybody—separately. Fourth point: Gentleman who uses Parma violet for his hair, etc., etc., washes his body in strong carbolic soap—so strong that the smell hangs about twenty-four hours later."

"Carbolic to get rid of the fleas."

"I will say for you, Parker, you've an answer for everything. Fifth point: Carefully got-up gentleman, with manicured, though masticated, finger-nails, has filthy black toe-nails which look as if they hadn't been cut for years."

"All of a piece with habits as indicated."

"Yes, I know, but such habits! Now, sixth and last point: This gentleman with the intermittently gentlemanly habits arrives in the middle of a pouring wet night, and apparently through the window, when he has already been twenty-four hours dead, and lies down quietly in Mr. Thipps's bath, unseasonably dressed in a pair of pince-nez. Not a hair on his head is ruffled—the hair has been cut so recently that there are quite a number of little short hairs stuck on his neck and the sides of the bath—and he has shaved so recently that there is a line of dried soap on his cheek—"

"Wimsey!"

"Wait a minute—and dried soap in his mouth."

Bunter got up and appeared suddenly at the detective's elbow, the respectful man-servant all over.

"A little more brandy, sir?" he murmured.

"Wimsey," said Parker, "you are making me feel cold all over." He emptied his glass—stared at it as though he were surprised to find it empty. set it down, got up, walked across to the bookcase, turned round, stood with his back against it and said:

"Look here, Wimsey—you've been reading detective stories, you're talking nonsense."

"No, I ain't," said Lord Peter, sleepily, "uncommon good incident for a detective story, though, what? Bunter, we'll write one, and you shall illustrate it with photographs."

"Soap in his—Rubbish!" said Parker. "It was something else—some discoloration—"

"No," said Lord Peter, "there were hairs as well. Bristly ones. He had a beard."

He took his watch from his pocket, and drew out a couple of longish, stiff hairs, which he had imprisoned between the inner and the outer case.

Parker turned them over once or twice in his fingers, looked at them close to the light, examined them with a lens, handed them to the impassible Bunter, and said:

"Do you mean to tell me, Wimsey, that any man alive would"—he laughed harshly—"shave off his beard with his mouth open, and then go and get killed with his mouth full of hairs? You're mad."

"I don't tell you so," said Wimsey. "You policemen are all alike—only one idea in your skulls. Blest if I can make out why you're ever appointed. He was shaved after he was dead. Pretty, ain't it? Uncommonly jolly little job for the barber, what? Here, sit down, man, and don't be an ass, stumpin' about the room like that. Worse things happen in war. This is only a blinkin' old shillin' shocker. But I'll tell you what, Parker, we're up against a criminal—the criminal—the real artist and blighter with imagination—real, artistic, finished stuff. I'm enjoyin' this, Parker."

# CHAPTER 3

Lord Peter finished a Scarlatti sonata, and sat looking thoughtfully at his own hands. The fingers were long and muscular, with wide, flat joints and square tips. When he was playing, his rather hard grey eyes softened, and his long, indeterminate mouth hardened in compensation. At no other time had he any pretensions to good looks, and at all times he was spoilt by a long, narrow chin, and a long, receding forehead, accentuated by the brushed-back sleekness of his tow-coloured hair. Labour papers, softening down the chin, caricatured him as a typical aristocrat.

"That's a wonderful instrument," said Parker.

"It ain't so bad," said Lord Peter, "but Scarlatti wants a harpsichord. Piano's too modern—all thrills and overtones. No good for our job, Parker. Have you come to any conclusion?"

"The man in the bath," said Parker, methodically, "was not a well-off man careful of his personal appearance. He was a labouring man, unemployed, but who had only recently lost his employment. He had been tramping about looking for a job when he met with his end. Somebody killed him and washed him and scented him and shaved him in order to disguise him, and put him into Thipps's bath without leaving a trace. Conclusion: the murderer was a powerful man, since he killed him with a single blow on the neck, a man of cool head and masterly intellect, since he did all that ghastly business without leaving a mark, a man of wealth and refinement, since he had all the apparatus of an elegant toilet handy, and a man of bizarre, and almost perverted imagination, as is shown in the two horrible touches of putting the body in the bath and of adorning it with a pair of pince-nez."

"He is a poet of crime," said Wimsey. "By the way, your difficulty about the pince-nez is cleared up. Obviously, the pince-nez never belonged to the body."

"That only makes a fresh puzzle. One can't suppose the murderer left them in that obliging manner as a clue to his own identity."

"We can hardly suppose that; I'm afraid this man possessed what most criminals lack—a sense of humour."

"Rather macabre humour."

"True. But a man who can afford to be humourous at all in such circumstances is a terrible fellow. I wonder what he did with the body between the murder and depositing it chez Thipps. Then there are more questions. How did he get it there? And why? Was it brought in at the door, as Sugg of our heart suggests? or through the window, as we think, on the not very adequate testimony of a smudge on the window-sill? Had the murderer accomplices? Is little Thipps really in it, or the girl? It don't do to put the notion out of court merely because Sugg inclines to it. Even idiots occasionally speak the truth accidentally. If not, why was Thipps selected for such an abominable practical joke? Has anybody got a grudge against Thipps? Who are the people in the other flats? We must find out that. Does Thipps play the piano at midnight over their heads or damage the reputation of the staircase by bringing home dubiously respectable ladies? Are there unsuccessful architects thirsting for his blood? Damn it all, Parker, there must be a motive somewhere. Can't have a crime without a motive, you know."

"A madman—" suggested Parker, doubtfully.

"With a deuced lot of method in his madness. He hasn't made a mistake—not one, unless leaving hairs in the corpse's mouth can be called a mistake. Well, anyhow, it's not Levy—you're right there. I say, old thing, neither your man nor mine has left much clue to go upon, has he? And there don't seem to be any motives knockin' about, either. And we seem to be two suits of clothes short in last night's work. Sir Reuben makes tracks without so much as a fig-leaf, and a mysterious individual turns up with a pince-nez, which is quite useless for purposes of decency. Dash it all! If only I had some good excuse for takin' up this body case officially—"

The telephone bell rang. The silent Bunter, whom the other two had almost forgotten, padded across to it.

"It's an elderly lady, my lord," he said, "I think she's deaf—I can't make her hear anything, but she's asking for your lordship."

Lord Peter seized the receiver, and yelled into it a "Hullo!" that might have cracked the vulcanite. He listened for some minutes with an incredulous smile, which gradually broadened into a grin of delight. At length he screamed, "All right! all right!" several times, and rang off.

"By Jove!" he announced, beaming, "sportin' old bird! It's old Mrs. Thipps. Deaf as a post. Never used the 'phone before. But determined. Perfect Napoleon. The incomparable Sugg has made a discovery and arrested little Thipps. Old lady abandoned in the flat. Thipps's last shriek to her, 'Tell Lord Peter Wimsey.' Old girl undaunted. Wrestles with telephone book. Wakes up the people at the exchange. Won't take no for an answer (not bein' able to hear it), gets through, says, 'Will I do what I can?' Says she would feel safe in the hands of a real gentleman. Oh, Parker, Parker! I could kiss her, I really could, as Thipps says. I'll write to her instead—no, hang it, Parker, we'll go round. Bunter, get your infernal machine and the magnesium. I say, we'll all go into partnership—pool the two cases and work 'em out together. You shall see my body to-night, Parker, and I'll look for your wandering Jew to-morrow. I feel so happy, I shall explode. O Sugg, Sugg, how art thou suggified! Bunter, my shoes. I say, Parker, I suppose yours are rubber-soled. Not? Tut, tut, you mustn't go out like that. We'll lend you a pair. Gloves? Here. My stick, my torch, the lampblack, the forceps, knife, pill-boxes—all complete?"

"Certainly, my lord."

"Oh, Bunter, don't look so offended. I mean no harm. I believe in you, I trust you—what money have I got? That'll do. I knew a man once, Parker, who let a world-famous poisoner slip through his fingers, because the machine on the Underground took nothing but pennies. There was a queue at the booking office and the man at the barrier stopped him, and while they were arguing about accepting a five-pound-note (which was all he had) for a twopenny ride to Baker Street, the criminal had sprung into a Circle train, and was next heard of in Constantinople, disguised as an elderly Church of England clergyman touring with his niece. Are we all ready? Go!"

They stepped out, Bunter carefully switching off the lights behind them.

\* \* \*

As they emerged into the gloom and gleam of Piccadilly, Wimsey stopped short with a little exclamation.

"Wait a second," he said, "I've thought of something. If Sugg's there he'll make trouble. I must short-circuit him."

He ran back, and the other two men employed the few minutes of his absence in capturing a taxi.

Inspector Sugg and a subordinate Cerberus were on guard at 59, Queen Caroline Mansions, and showed no disposition to admit unofficial enquirers. Parker, indeed, they could not easily turn away, but Lord Peter found himself confronted with a surly manner and what Lord Beaconsfield described as a masterly inactivity. It was in vain that Lord Peter pleaded that he had been retained by Mrs. Thipps on behalf of her son.

"Retained!" said Inspector Sugg, with a snort, "she'll be retained if she doesn't look out. Shouldn't wonder if she wasn't in it herself, only she's so deaf, she's no good for anything at all."

"Look here, Inspector," said Lord Peter, "what's the use of bein' so bally obstructive? You'd much better let me in—you know I'll get there in the end. Dash it all, it's not as if I was takin' the bread out of your children's mouths. Nobody paid me for finding Lord Attenbury's emeralds for you."

"It's my duty to keep out the public," said Inspector Sugg, morosely, "and it's going to stay out."

"I never said anything about your keeping out of the public," said Lord Peter, easily, sitting down on the staircase to thrash the matter out comfortably, "though I've no doubt pussyfoot's a good thing, on principle, if not exaggerated. The golden mean, Sugg, as Aristotle says, keeps you from bein' a golden ass. Ever been a golden ass, Sugg? I have. It would take a whole rose-garden to cure me, Sugg—

"You are my garden of beautiful roses,

My own rose, my one rose, that's you!"

"I'm not going to stay any longer talking to you," said the harassed Sugg, "it's bad enough—hullo, drat that telephone. Here, Cawthorn, go and see what it is, if that old catamaran will let you into the room. Shutting herself up there and screaming," said the Inspector, "it's enough to make a man give up crime and take to hedging and ditching."

The constable came back:

"It's from the Yard, sir," he said, coughing apologetically, "the Chief says every facility is to be given to Lord Peter Wimsey, sir. Um!" He stood apart noncommittally, glazing his eyes.

"Five aces," said Lord Peter, cheerfully. "The Chief's a dear friend of my mother's. No go, Sugg, it's no good buckin' you've got a full house. I'm goin' to make it a bit fuller."

He walked in with his followers.

The body had been removed a few hours previously, and when the bathroom and the whole flat had been explored by the naked eye and the camera of the competent Bunter, it became evident that the real problem of the household was old Mrs. Thipps. Her son and servant had both been removed, and it appeared that they had no friends in town, beyond a few business acquaintances of Thipps's, whose very addresses the old lady did not know. The other flats in the building were occupied respectively by a family of seven, at present departed to winter abroad, an elderly Indian colonel of ferocious manners, who lived alone with an Indian man-servant, and a highly respectable family on the third floor, whom the disturbance over their heads had outraged to the last degree. The husband, indeed, when appealed to by Lord Peter, showed a little human weakness, but Mrs. Appledore, appearing suddenly in a warm dressing-gown, extricated him from the difficulties into which he was carelessly wandering.

"I am sorry," she said, "I'm afraid we can't interfere in any way. This is a very unpleasant business, Mr.—I'm afraid I didn't catch your name, and we have always found it better not to be mixed up with the police. Of course, if the Thippses are innocent, and I am sure I hope they are, it is very unfortunate for them, but I must say that the circumstances seem to me most suspicious, and to Theophilus too, and I should not like to have it said that we had assisted murderers. We might even be supposed to be accessories. Of course you are young, Mr.—"

"This is Lord Peter Wimsey, my dear," said Theophilus mildly.

She was unimpressed.

"Ah, yes," she said, "I believe you are distantly related to my late cousin, the Bishop of Carisbrooke. Poor man! He was always being taken in by impostors; he died without ever learning any better. I imagine you take after him, Lord Peter."

"I doubt it," said Lord Peter. "So far as I know he is only a connection, though it's a wise child that knows its own father. I congratulate you, dear lady, on takin' after the other side of the family. You'll forgive my buttin' in upon you like this in the middle of the night, though, as you say, it's all in the family, and I'm sure I'm very much obliged to you, and for permittin' me to admire that awfully fetchin' thing you've got on. Now, don't you worry, Mr. Appledore. I'm thinkin' the best thing I can do is to trundle the old lady down to my mother and take her out of your way, otherwise you might be findin' your Christian feelin's gettin' the better of you some fine day, and there's nothin' like Christian feelin's for upsettin' a man's domestic comfort. Good-night, sir—good-night, dear lady—it's simply rippin' of you to let me drop in like this."

"Well!" said Mrs. Appledore, as the door closed behind him.

And—

"I thank the goodness and the grace

That on my birth have smiled,"

said Lord Peter, "and taught me to be bestially impertinent when I choose. Cat!"

Two a. m. saw Lord Peter Wimsey arrive in a friend's car at the Dower House, Denver Castle, in company with a deaf and aged lady and an antique portmanteau.

\* \* \*

"It's very nice to see you, dear," said the Dowager Duchess, placidly. She was a small, plump woman, with perfectly white hair and exquisite hands. In feature she was as unlike her second son as she was like him in character; her black eyes twinkled cheerfully, and her manners and movements were marked with a neat and rapid decision. She wore a charming wrap from Liberty's, and sat watching Lord Peter eat cold beef and cheese as though his arrival in such incongruous circumstances and company were the most ordinary event possible, which with him, indeed, it was.

"Have you got the old lady to bed?" asked Lord Peter.

"Oh, yes, dear. Such a striking old person, isn't she? And very courageous. She tells me she has never been in a motor-car before. But she thinks you a very nice lad, dear—that careful of her, you remind her of her own son. Poor little Mr. Thipps—whatever made your friend the inspector think he could have murdered anybody?"

"My friend the inspector—no, no more, thank you, Mother—is determined to prove that the intrusive person in Thipps's bath is Sir Reuben Levy, who disappeared mysteriously from his house last night. His line of reasoning is: We've lost a middle-aged gentleman without any clothes on in Park Lane; we've found a middle-aged gentleman without any clothes on in Battersea. Therefore they're one and the same person, Q.E.D., and put little Thipps in quod."

"You're very elliptical, dear," said the Duchess, mildly. "Why should Mr. Thipps be arrested even if they are the same?"

"Sugg must arrest somebody," said Lord Peter, "but there is one odd little bit of evidence come out which goes a long way to support Sugg's theory, only that I know it to be no go by the evidence of my own eyes. Last night at about 9:15 a young woman was strollin' up the Battersea Park Road for purposes best known to herself, when she saw a gentleman in a fur coat and top-hat saunterin' along under an umbrella, lookin' at the names of all the streets. He looked a bit out of place, so, not bein' a shy girl, you see, she walked up to him, and said, 'Good-evening.' 'Can you tell me, please,' says the mysterious stranger, 'whether this street leads into Prince of Wales Road?' She said it did, and further asked him in a jocular manner what he was doing with himself and all the rest of it, only she wasn't altogether so explicit about that part of the conversation, because she was unburdenin' her heart to Sugg, d'you see, and he's paid by a grateful country to have very pure, high-minded ideals, what? Anyway, the old boy said he couldn't attend to her just then as he had an appointment. 'I've got to go and see a man, my dear,' was how she said he put it, and he walked on up Alexandra Avenue towards Prince of Wales Road. She was starin' after him, still rather surprised, when she was joined by a friend of hers, who said, 'It's no good wasting your time with him—that's Levy—I knew him when I lived in the West End, and the girls used to call him Pea-green Incorruptible'—friend's name suppressed, owing to implications of story, but girl vouches for what was said. She thought no more about it till the milkman brought news this morning of the excitement at Queen Caroline Mansions; then she went round, though not likin' the police as a rule, and asked the man there whether the dead gentleman had a beard and glasses. Told he had glasses but no beard, she incautiously said: 'Oh, then, it isn't him,' and the man said, 'Isn't who?' and collared her. That's her story. Sugg's delighted, of course, and quodded Thipps on the strength of it."

"Dear me," said the Duchess, "I hope the poor girl won't get into trouble."

"Shouldn't think so," said Lord Peter. "Thipps is the one that's going to get it in the neck. Besides, he's done a silly thing. I got that out of Sugg, too, though he was sittin' tight on the information. Seems

Thipps got into a confusion about the train he took back from Manchester. Said first he got home at 10:30. Then they pumped Gladys Horrocks, who let out he wasn't back till after 11:45. Then Thipps, bein' asked to explain the discrepancy, stammers and bungles and says, first that he missed the train. Then Sugg makes enquiries at St. Pancras and discovers that he left a bag in the cloakroom there at ten. Thipps, again asked to explain, stammers worse an' says he walked about for a few hours—met a friend—can't say who—didn't meet a friend—can't say what he did with his time—can't explain why he didn't go back for his bag—can't say what time he did get in—can't explain how he got a bruise on his forehead. In fact, can't explain himself at all. Gladys Horrocks interrogated again. Says, this time, Thipps came in at 10:30. Then admits she didn't hear him come in. Can't say why she didn't hear him come in. Can't say why she said first of all that she did hear him. Bursts into tears. Contradicts herself. Everybody's suspicion roused. Quod 'em both."

"As you put it, dear," said the Duchess, "it all sounds very confusing, and not quite respectable. Poor little Mr. Thipps would be terribly upset by anything that wasn't respectable."

"I wonder what he did with himself," said Lord Peter thoughtfully. "I really don't think he was committing a murder. Besides, I believe the fellow has been dead a day or two, though it don't do to build too much on doctors' evidence. It's an entertainin' little problem."

"Very curious, dear. But so sad about poor Sir Reuben. I must write a few lines to Lady Levy; I used to know her quite well, you know, dear, down in Hampshire, when she was a girl. Christine Ford, she was then, and I remember so well the dreadful trouble there was about her marrying a Jew. That was before he made his money, of course, in that oil business out in America. The family wanted her to marry Julian Freke, who did so well afterwards and was connected with the family, but she fell in love with this Mr. Levy and eloped with him. He was very handsome, then, you know, dear, in a foreign-looking way, but he hadn't any means, and the Fords didn't like his religion. Of course we're all Jews nowadays and they wouldn't have minded so much if he'd pretended to be something else, like that Mr. Simons we met at Mrs. Porchester's, who always tells everybody that he got his nose in Italy at the Renaissance, and claims to be descended somehow or other from La Bella Simonetta—so foolish, you know, dear—as if anybody believed it; and I'm sure some Jews are very good people, and personally I'd much rather they believed something, though of course it must be very inconvenient, what with not working on Saturdays and circumcising the poor little babies and everything depending on the new moon and that funny kind of meat they have with such a slang-sounding name, and never being able to have bacon for breakfast. Still, there it was, and it was much better for the girl to marry him if she was really fond of him, though I believe young Freke was really devoted to her, and they're still great friends. Not that there was ever a real engagement, only a sort of understanding with her father, but he's never married, you know, and lives all by himself in that big house next to the hospital, though he's very rich and distinguished now, and I know ever so many people have tried to get hold of him—there was Lady Mainwaring wanted him for that eldest girl of hers, though I remember saying at the time it was no use expecting a surgeon to be taken in by a figure that was all padding—they have so many opportunities of judging, you know, dear."

"Lady Levy seems to have had the knack of makin' people devoted to her," said Peter. "Look at the pea-green incorruptible Levy."

"That's quite true, dear; she was a most delightful girl, and they say her daughter is just like her. I rather lost sight of them when she married, and you know your father didn't care much about business people, but I know everybody always said they were a model couple. In fact it was a proverb that Sir Reuben was as well loved at home as he was hated abroad. I don't mean in foreign countries, you know, dear—just the proverbial way of putting things—like 'a saint abroad and a devil at home'—only the other way on, reminding one of the *Pilgrim's Progress*."

"Yes," said Peter, "I daresay the old man made one or two enemies."

"Dozens, dear—such a dreadful place, the City, isn't it? Everybody Ishmaels together—though I don't suppose Sir Reuben would like to be called that, would he? Doesn't it mean illegitimate, or not a proper Jew, anyway? I always did get confused with those Old Testament characters."

Lord Peter laughed and yawned.

"I think I'll turn in for an hour or two," he said. "I must be back in town at eight—Parker's coming to breakfast."

The Duchess looked at the clock, which marked five minutes to three.

"I'll send up your breakfast at half past six, dear," she said. "I hope you'll find everything all right. I told them just to slip a hot-water bottle in; those linen sheets are so chilly; you can put it out if it's in your way."

# CHAPTER 4

"—So there it is, Parker," said Lord Peter, pushing his coffee-cup aside and lighting his after-breakfast pipe; "you may find it leads you to something, though it don't seem to get me any further with my bathroom problem. Did you do anything more at that after I left?"

"No; but I've been on the roof this morning."

"The deuce you have—what an energetic devil you are! I say, Parker, I think this co-operative scheme is an uncommonly good one. It's much easier to work on someone else's job than one's own—gives one that delightful feelin' of interferin' and bossin' about, combined with the glorious sensation that another fellow is takin' all one's own work off one's hands. You scratch my back and I'll scratch yours, what? Did you find anything?"

"Not very much. I looked for any footmarks of course, but naturally, with all this rain, there wasn't a sign. Of course, if this were a detective story, there'd have been a convenient shower exactly an hour before the crime and a beautiful set of marks which could only have come there between two and three in the morning, but this being real life in a London November, you might as well expect footprints in Niagara. I searched the roofs right along—and came to the jolly conclusion that any person in any blessed flat in the blessed row might have done it. All the staircases open on to the roof and the leads are quite flat; you can walk along as easy as along Shaftesbury Avenue. Still, I've got some evidence that the body did walk along there."

"What's that?"

Parker brought out his pocketbook and extracted a few shreds of material, which he laid before his friend.

"One was caught in the gutter just above Thipps's bathroom window, another in a crack of the stone parapet just over it, and the rest came from the chimney-stack behind, where they had caught in an iron stanchion. What do you make of them?"

Lord Peter scrutinized them very carefully through his lens.

"Interesting," he said, "damned interesting. Have you developed those plates, Bunter?" he added, as that discreet assistant came in with the post.

"Yes, my lord."

"Caught anything?"

"I don't know whether to call it anything or not, my lord," said Bunter, dubiously. "I'll bring the prints in."

"Do," said Wimsey. "Hallo! here's our advertisement about the gold chain in the *Times*—very nice it looks: 'Write, 'phone or call 110,

Piccadilly.' Perhaps it would have been safer to put a box number, though I always think that the franker you are with people, the more you're likely to deceive 'em; so unused is the modern world to the open hand and the guileless heart, what?"

"But you don't think the fellow who left that chain on the body is going to give himself away by coming here and enquiring about it?"

"I don't, fathead," said Lord Peter, with the easy politeness of the real aristocracy, "that's why I've tried to get hold of the jeweler who originally sold the chain. See?" He pointed to the paragraph. "It's not an old chain—hardly worn at all. Oh, thanks, Bunter. Now, see here, Parker, these are the finger-marks you noticed yesterday on the window-sash and on the far edge of the bath. I'd overlooked them; I give you full credit for the discovery, I crawl, I grovel, my name is Watson, and you need not say what you were just going to say, because I admit it all. Now we shall—Hullo, hullo, hullo!"

The three men stared at the photographs.

"The criminal," said Lord Peter, bitterly, "climbed over the roofs in the wet and not unnaturally got soot on his fingers. He arranged the body in the bath, and wiped away all traces of himself except two, which he obligingly left to show us how to do our job. We learn from a smudge on the floor that he wore india rubber boots, and from this admirable set of fingerprints on the edge of the bath that he had the usual number of fingers and wore rubber gloves. That's the kind of man he is. Take the fool away, gentlemen."

He put the prints aside, and returned to an examination of the shreds of material in his hand. Suddenly he whistled softly.

"Do you make anything of these, Parker?"

"They seemed to me to be ravellings of some coarse cotton stuff—a sheet, perhaps, or an improvised rope."

"Yes," said Lord Peter—"yes. It may be a mistake—it may be our mistake. I wonder. Tell me, d'you think these tiny threads are long enough and strong enough to hang a man?"

He was silent, his long eyes narrowing into slits behind the smoke of his pipe.

"What do you suggest doing this morning?" asked Parker.

"Well," said Lord Peter, "it seems to me it's about time I took a hand in your job. Let's go round to Park Lane and see what larks Sir Reuben Levy was up to in bed last night."

\* \* \*

"And now, Mrs. Pemming, if you would be so kind as give me a blanket," said Mr. Bunter, coming down into the kitchen, "and permit of me hanging a sheet across the lower part of this window, and drawing the screen across here, so—so as to shut off any reflections, if you understand me, we'll get to work."

Sir Reuben Levy's cook, with her eye upon Mr. Bunter's gentlemanly and well-tailored appearance, hastened to produce what was necessary. Her visitor placed on the table a basket, containing a water-bottle, a silver-backed hairbrush, a pair of boots, a small roll of linoleum, and the "Letters of a Self-made Merchant to His Son," bound in polished morocco. He drew an umbrella from beneath his arm and added it to the collection. He then advanced a ponderous photographic machine and set it up in the neighbourhood of the kitchen range; then, spreading a newspaper over the fair, scrubbed surface of the table, he began to roll up his sleeves and insinuate himself into a pair of surgical gloves. Sir Reuben Levy's valet, entering at the moment and finding him thus engaged, put aside the kitchenmaid, who was staring from a front-row position, and inspected the apparatus critically. Mr. Bunter nodded brightly to him, and uncorked a small bottle of grey powder.

"Odd sort of fish, your employer, isn't he?" said the valet, carelessly.

"Very singular, indeed," said Mr. Bunter. "Now, my dear," he added, ingratiatingly, to the parlourmaid, "I wonder if you'd just pour a little of this grey powder over the edge of the bottle while I'm holding it—and the same with this boot—here, at the top—thank you, Miss—what is your name? Price? Oh, but you've got another name besides Price, haven't you? Mabel, eh? That's a name I'm uncommonly partial to—that's very nicely done, you've a steady hand, Miss Mabel—see that? That's the finger marks—three there, and two here, and smudged over in both places. No, don't you touch 'em, my dear, or you'll rub the bloom off. We'll stand 'em up here till they're ready to have their portraits taken. Now then, let's take the hairbrush next. Perhaps, Mrs. Pemming, you'd like to lift him up very carefully by the bristles."

"By the bristles, Mr. Bunter?"

"If you please, Mrs. Pemming—and lay him here. Now, Miss Mabel, another little exhibition of your skill, if you please. No—we'll try lampblack this time. Perfect. Couldn't have done it better myself. Ah! there's a beautiful set. No smudges this time. That'll interest his lordship. Now the little book—no, I'll pick that up myself—with these gloves, you see, and by the edges—I'm a careful criminal, Mrs. Pemming, I don't want to leave any traces. Dust the cover all over, Miss Mabel; now this side—that's the way to do it. Lots of prints and no smudges. All according to plan. Oh, please, Mr. Graves, you mustn't touch it—it's as much as my place is worth to have it touched."

"D'you have to do much of this sort of thing?" enquired Mr. Graves, from a superior standpoint.

"Any amount," replied Mr. Bunter, with a groan calculated to appeal to Mr. Graves's heart and unlock his confidence. "If you'd kindly hold one end of this bit of linoleum, Mrs. Pemming, I'll hold up this end while Miss Mabel operates. Yes, Mr. Graves, it's a hard life, valeting by day and developing by night—morning tea at any time from 6:30 to 11, and criminal investigation at all hours. It's wonderful, the ideas these rich men with nothing to do get into their heads."

"I wonder you stand it," said Mr. Graves. "Now there's none of that here. A quiet, orderly, domestic life, Mr. Bunter, has much to be said for it. Meals at regular hours; decent, respectable families to dinner—none of your painted women—and no valeting at night, there's much to be said for it. I don't hold with Hebrews as a rule, Mr. Bunter, and of course I understand that you may find it to your advantage to be in a titled family, but there's less thought of that these days, and I will say, for a self-made man, no one could call Sir Reuben vulgar, and my lady at any rate is county—Miss Ford, she was, one of the Hampshire Fords, and both of them always most considerate."

"I agree with you, Mr. Graves—his lordship and me have never held with being narrow-minded—why, yes, my dear, of course it's a footmark, this is the washstand linoleum. A good Jew can be a good man, that's what I've always said. And regular hours and considerate habits have a great deal to recommend them. Very simple in his tastes, now, Sir Reuben, isn't he? for such a rich man, I mean."

"Very simple indeed," said the cook, "the meals he and her ladyship have when they're by themselves with Miss Rachel—well, there now—if it wasn't for the dinners, which is always good when there's company, I'd be wastin' my talents and education here, if you understand me, Mr. Bunter."

Mr. Bunter added the handle of the umbrella to his collection, and began to pin a sheet across the window, aided by the housemaid.

"Admirable," said he. "Now, if I might have this blanket on the table and another on a towel-horse or something of that kind by way of a background—you're very kind, Mrs. Pemming.... Ah! I wish his lordship never wanted valeting at night. Many's the time I've sat up till three and four, and up again to call him early to go off Sherlocking at the other end of the country. And the mud he gets on his clothes and his boots!"

"I'm sure it's a shame, Mr. Bunter," said Mrs. Pemming, warmly. "Low, I calls it. In my opinion, police-work ain't no fit occupation for a gentleman, let alone a lordship."

"Everything made so difficult, too," said Mr. Bunter, nobly sacrificing his employer's character and his own feelings in a good cause; "boots chucked into a corner, clothes hung up on the floor, as they say—"

"That's often the case with these men as are born with a silver spoon in their mouths," said Mr. Graves. "Now, Sir Reuben, he's never lost his good old-fashioned habits. Clothes folded up neat, boots put out in his dressing-room, so as a man could get them in the morning, everything made easy."

"He forgot them the night before last, though."

"The clothes, not the boots. Always thoughtful for others, is Sir Reuben. Ah! I hope nothing's happened to him."

"Indeed, no, poor gentleman," chimed in the cook, "and as for what they're sayin', that he'd 'ave gone out surrepshous-like to do something he didn't ought, well, I'd never believe it of him, Mr. Bunter not if I was to take my dying oath upon it."

"Ah!" said Mr. Bunter, adjusting his arc-lamps and connecting them with the nearest electric light, "and that's more than most of us could say of them as pays us."

   * * *

"Five foot ten," said Lord Peter, "and not an inch more." He peered dubiously at the depression in the bed clothes, and measured it a second time with the gentleman-scout's vade-mecum. Parker entered this particular in a neat pocketbook.

"I suppose," he said, "a six-foot-two man might leave a five-foot-ten depression if he curled himself up."

"Have you any Scotch blood in you, Parker?" enquired his colleague, bitterly.

"Not that I know of," replied Parker. "Why?"

"Because of all the cautious, ungenerous, deliberate and cold-blooded devils I know," said Lord Peter, "you are the most cautious, ungenerous, deliberate and cold-blooded. Here am I, sweating my brains out to introduce a really sensational incident into your dull and disreputable little police investigation, and you refuse to show a single spark of enthusiasm."

"Well, it's no good jumping at conclusions."

"Jump? You don't even crawl distantly within sight of a conclusion. I believe if you caught the cat with her head in the cream-jug you'd say it was conceivable that the jug was empty when she got there."

"Well, it would be conceivable, wouldn't it?"

"Curse you," said Lord Peter. He screwed his monocle into his eye, and bent over the pillow, breathing hard and tightly through his nose.

"Here, give me the tweezers," he said presently. "good heavens, man, don't blow like that, you might be a whale." He nipped up an almost invisible object from the linen.

"What is it?" asked Parker.

"It's a hair," said Wimsey grimly, his hard eyes growing harder. "Let's go and look at Levy's hats, shall we? And you might just ring for that fellow with the churchyard name, do you mind?"

Mr. Graves, when summoned, found Lord Peter Wimsey squatting on the floor of the dressing-room before a row of hats arranged upside-down before him.

"Here you are," said that nobleman cheerfully, "now, Graves, this is a guessin' competition—a sort of three-hat trick, to mix metaphors. Here are nine hats, including three top-hats. Do you identify all these hats as belonging to Sir Reuben Levy? You do? Very good. Now I have three guesses as to which hat he wore the night he disappeared, and if I guess right, I win; if I don't, you win. See? Ready? Go. I suppose you know the answer yourself, by the way."

"Do I understand your lordship to be asking which hat Sir Reuben wore when he went out on Monday night, your lordship?"

"No, you don't understand a bit," said Lord Peter. "I'm asking if you know—don't tell me, I'm going to guess."

"I do know, your lordship," said Mr. Graves, reprovingly.

"Well," said Lord Peter, "as he was dinin' at the Ritz he wore a topper. Here are three toppers. In three guesses I'd be bound to hit the right one, wouldn't I? That don't seem very sportin'. I'll take one guess. It was this one."

He indicated the hat next the window.

"Am I right, Graves—have I got the prize?"

"That is the hat in question, my lord," said Mr. Graves, without excitement.

"Thanks," said Lord Peter, "that's all I wanted to know. Ask Bunter to step up, would you?"

Mr. Bunter stepped up with an aggrieved air, and his usually smooth hair ruffled by the focussing cloth.

"Oh, there you are, Bunter," said Lord Peter; "look here—"

"Here I am, my lord," said Mr. Bunter, with respectful reproach, "but if you'll excuse me saying so, downstairs is where I ought to be, with all those young women about—they'll be fingering the evidence, my lord."

"I cry you mercy," said Lord Peter, "but I've quarrelled hopelessly with Mr. Parker and distracted the estimable Graves, and I want you to tell me what finger-prints you have found. I shan't be happy till I get it, so don't be harsh with me, Bunter."

"Well, my lord, your lordship understands I haven't photographed them yet, but I won't deny that their appearance is interesting, my lord. The little book off the night table, my lord, has only the marks of one set of fingers—there's a little scar on the right thumb which makes them easy recognized. The hairbrush, too, my lord, has only the same set of marks. The umbrella, the toothglass and the boots all have two sets: the hand with the scarred thumb, which I take to be Sir Reuben's, my lord, and a set of smudges superimposed upon them, if I may put it that way, my lord, which may or may not be the same hand in rubber gloves. I could tell you better when I've got the photographs made, to measure them, my lord. The linoleum in front of the washstand is very gratifying indeed, my lord, if you will excuse my mentioning it. Besides the marks of Sir Reuben's boots which your lordship pointed out, there's the print of a man's naked foot—a much smaller one, my lord, not much more than a ten-inch sock, I should say if you asked me."

Lord Peter's face became irradiated with almost a dim, religious light.

"A mistake," he breathed, "a mistake, a little one, but he can't afford it. When was the linoleum washed last, Bunter?"

"Monday morning, my lord. The housemaid did it and remembered to mention it. Only remark she's made yet, and it's to the point. The other domestics—"

His features expressed disdain.

"What did I say, Parker? Five-foot-ten and not an inch longer. And he didn't dare to use the hairbrush. Beautiful. But he had to risk the top-hat. Gentleman can't walk home in the rain late at night without a hat, you know, Parker. Look! what do you make of it? Two sets of finger-prints on everything but the book and the brush, two sets of feet on the linoleum, and two kinds of hair in the hat!"

He lifted the top-hat to the light, and extracted the evidence with tweezers.

"Think of it, Parker—to remember the hairbrush and forget the hat—to remember his fingers all the time, and to make that one careless step on the telltale linoleum. Here they are, you see, black hair and tan hair—black hair in the bowler and the panama, and black and tan in last night's topper. And then, just to make certain that we're on the right track, just one little auburn hair on the pillow, on this pillow, Parker, which isn't quite in the right place. It almost brings tears to my eyes."

"Do you mean to say—" said the detective, slowly.

"I mean to say," said Lord Peter, "that it was not Sir Reuben Levy whom the cook saw last night on the doorstep. I say that it was another man, perhaps a couple of inches shorter, who came here in Levy's clothes and let himself in with Levy's latchkey. Oh, he was a bold, cunning devil, Parker. He had on Levy's boots, and every stitch of Levy's clothing down to the skin. He had rubber gloves on his hands which he never took off, and he did everything he could to make us think that Levy slept here last night. He took his chances, and won. He walked upstairs, he undressed, he even washed and cleaned his teeth, though he didn't use the hairbrush for fear of leaving red hairs in it. He had to guess what Levy did with boots and clothes; one guess was wrong and the other right, as it happened. The bed must look as if it had been slept in, so he gets in, and lies there in his victim's very pyjamas. Then, in the morning sometime, probably in the deadest hour between two and three, he gets up, dresses himself in his own clothes that he has brought with him in a bag, and creeps downstairs. If anybody wakes, he is lost, but he is a bold man, and he takes his chance. He knows that people do not wake as a rule—and they don't wake. He opens the street door which he left on the latch when he came in—he listens for the stray passer-by or the policeman on his beat. He slips out. He pulls the door quietly to with the latchkey. He walks brisky away in rubber-soled shoes—he's the kind of criminal who isn't complete without rubber-soled shoes. In a few minutes he is at Hyde Park Corner. After that—"

He paused, and added:

"He did all that, and unless he had nothing at stake, he had everything at stake. Either Sir Reuben Levy has been spirited away for some silly practical joke, or the man with the auburn hair has the guilt of murder upon his soul."

"Dear me!" ejaculated the detective, "you're very dramatic about it."

Lord Peter passed his hand rather wearily over his hair.

"My true friend," he murmured, in a voice surcharged with emotion, "you recall me to the nursery rhymes of my youth—the sacred duty of flippancy:

'There was an old man of Whitehaven
Who danced a quadrille with a raven,
But they said: It's absurd
To encourage that bird—
So they smashed that old man of Whitehaven.'

That's the correct attitude, Parker. Here's a poor old buffer spirited away—such a joke—and I don't believe he'd hurt a fly himself—that makes it funnier. D'you know, Parker, I don't care frightfully about this case after all."

"Which, this or yours?"

"Both. I say, Parker, shall we go quietly home and have lunch and go to the Coliseum?"

"You can if you like," replied the detective; "but you forget I do this for my bread and butter."

"And I haven't even that excuse," said Lord Peter; "well, what's the next move? What would you do in my case?"

"I'd do some good, hard grind," said Parker. "I'd distrust every bit of work Sugg ever did, and I'd get the family history of every tenant of every flat in Queen Caroline Mansions. I'd examine all their boxrooms and rooftraps, and I would inveigle them into conversations and suddenly bring in the words 'body' and 'pince-nez,' and see if they wriggled, like those modern psycho-what's-his-names."

"You would, would you?" said Lord Peter with a grin. "Well, we've exchanged cases, you know, so just you toddle off and do it. I'm going to have a jolly time at Wyndham's."

Parker made a grimace.

"Well," he said, "I don't suppose you'd ever do it, so I'd better. You'll never become a professional till you learn to do a little work, Wimsey. How about lunch?"

"I'm invited out," said Lord Peter, magnificently. "I'll run round and change at the club. Can't feed with Freddy Arbuthnot in these bags; Bunter!"

"Yes, my lord."

"Pack up if you're ready, and come round and wash my face and hands for me at the club."

"Work here for another two hours, my lord. Can't do with less than thirty minutes' exposure. The current's none too strong."

"You see how I'm bullied by my own man, Parker? Well, I must bear it, I suppose. Ta-ta!"

He whistled his way downstairs.

The conscientious Mr. Parker, with a groan, settled down to a systematic search through Sir Reuben Levy's papers, with the assistance of a plate of ham sandwiches and a bottle of Bass.

Lord Peter and the Honourable Freddy Arbuthnot, looking together like an advertisement for gents' trouserings, strolled into the dining-room at Wyndham's.

"Haven't seen you for an age," said the Honourable Freddy, "what have you been doin' with yourself?"

"Oh, foolin' about," said Lord Peter, languidly.

"Thick or clear, sir?" enquired the waiter of the Honourable Freddy.

"Which'll you have, Wimsey?" said that gentleman, transferring the burden of selection to his guest, "they're both equally poisonous."

"Well, clear's less trouble to lick out of the spoon," said Lord Peter.

"Clear," said the Honourable Freddy.

"Consommé Polonais," agreed the waiter. "Very nice, sir."

Conversation languished until the Honourable Freddy found a bone in the filleted sole, and sent for the head waiter to explain its presence. When this matter had been adjusted Lord Peter found energy to say:

"Sorry to hear about your gov'nor, old man."

"Yes, poor old buffer," said the Honourable Freddy; "they say he can't last long now. What? Oh! the Montrachet '08. There's nothing fit to drink in this place," he added gloomily.

After this deliberate insult to a noble vintage there was a further pause, till Lord Peter said: "'How's 'Change?"

"Rotten," said the Honourable Freddy.

He helped himself gloomily to salmis of game.

"Can I do anything?" asked Lord Peter.

"Oh, no, thanks—very decent of you, but it'll pan out all right in time."

"This isn't a bad salmis," said Lord Peter.

"I've eaten worse," admitted his friend.

"What about those Argentines?" enquired Lord Peter. "Here, waiter, there's a bit of cork in my glass."

"Cork?" cried the Honourable Freddy, with something approaching animation; "you'll hear about this, waiter. It's an amazing thing a fellow who's paid to do the job can't manage to take a cork out of a bottle. What you say? Argentines? Gone all to hell. Old Levy bunkin' off like that's knocked the bottom out of the market."

"You don't say so," said Lord Peter; "what d'you suppose has happened to the old man?"

"Cursed if I know," said the Honourable Freddy; "knocked on the head by the bears, I should think."

"P'r'aps he's gone off on his own," suggested Lord Peter. "Double life, you know. Giddy old blighters, some of these City men."

"Oh, no," said the Honourable Freddy, faintly roused; "no, hang it all, Wimsey, I wouldn't care to say that. He's a decent old domestic bird, and his daughter's a charmin' girl. Besides, he's straight enough—he'd do you down fast enough, but he wouldn't let you down. Old Anderson is badly cut up about it."

"Who's Anderson?"

"Chap with property out there. He belongs here. He was goin' to meet Levy on Tuesday. He's afraid those railway people will get in now, and then it'll be all U. P."

"Who's runnin' the railway people over here?" enquired Lord Peter.

"Yankee blighter, John P. Milligan. He's got an option, or says he has. You can't trust these brutes."

"Can't Anderson hold on?"

"Anderson isn't Levy. Hasn't got the shekels. Besides, he's only one. Levy covers the ground—he could boycott Milligan's beastly railway if he liked. That's where he's got the pull, you see."

"B'lieve I met the Milligan man somewhere," said Lord Peter, thoughtfully; "ain't he a hulking brute with black hair and a beard?"

"You're thinkin' of somebody else," said the Honourable Freddy. "Milligan don't stand any higher than I do, unless you call five-feet-ten hulking—and he's bald, anyway."

Lord Peter considered this over the Gorgonzola. Then he said:

"Didn't know Levy had a charmin' daughter."

"Oh, yes," said the Honourable Freddy, with an elaborate detachment. "Met her and Mamma last year abroad. That's how I got to know the old man. He's been very decent. Let me into this Argentine business on the ground floor, don't you know?"

"Well," said Lord Peter, "you might do worse. Money's money, ain't it? And Lady Levy is quite a redeemin' point. At least, my mother knew her people."

"Oh, she's all right," said the Honourable Freddy, "and the old man's nothing to be ashamed of nowadays. He's self-made, of course, but he don't pretend to be anything else. No side. Toddles off to business on a 96 'bus every morning. 'Can't make up my mind to taxis, my boy,' he says. 'I had to look at every halfpenny when I was a young man, and I can't get out of the way of it now.' Though, if he's takin' his family out, nothing's too good. Rachel—that's the girl—always laughs at the old man's little economies."

"I suppose they've sent for Lady Levy," said Lord Peter.

"I suppose so," agreed the other. "I'd better pop round and express sympathy or somethin', what? Wouldn't look well not to, d'you think? But it's deuced awkward. What am I to say?"

"I don't think it matters much what you say," said Lord Peter, helpfully. "I should ask if you can do anything."

"Thanks," said the lover, "I will. Energetic young man. Count on me. Always at your service. Ring me up any time of the day or night. That's the line to take, don't you think?"

"That's the idea," said Lord Peter.

\* \* \*

Mr. John P. Milligan, the London representative of the great Milligan railroad and shipping company, was dictating code cables to his secretary in an office in Lombard Street, when a card was brought up to him, bearing the simple legend:

LORD PETER WIMSEY

*Marlborough Club*

Mr. Milligan was annoyed at the interruption, but, like many of his nation, if he had a weak point, it was the British aristocracy. He postponed for a few minutes the elimination from the map of a modest but promising farm, and directed that the visitor should be shown up.

"Good-afternoon," said that nobleman, ambling genially in, "it's most uncommonly good of you to let me come round wastin' your time like this. I'll try not to be too long about it, though I'm not awfully good at comin' to the point. My brother never would let me stand for the county, y'know—said I wandered on so nobody'd know what I was talkin' about."

"Pleased to meet you, Lord Wimsey," said Mr. Milligan. "Won't you take a seat?"

"Thanks," said Lord Peter, "but I'm not the Duke, you know—that's my brother Denver. My name's Peter. It's a silly name, I always think, so old-world and full of homely virtue and that sort of thing, but my godfathers and godmothers in my baptism are responsible for that, I suppose, officially—which is rather hard on them, you know, as they didn't actually choose it. But we always have a Peter, after the third duke, who betrayed five kings somewhere about the Wars of the Roses, though come to think of it, it ain't anything to be proud of. Still, one has to make the best of it."

Mr. Milligan, thus ingeniously placed at that disadvantage which attends ignorance, maneuvered for position, and offered his interrupter a Corona.

"Thanks, awfully," said Lord Peter, "though you really mustn't tempt me to stay here barblin' all afternoon. By Jove, Mr. Milligan, if you offer people such comfortable chairs and cigars like these, I wonder they don't come an' live in your office." He added mentally: "I wish to goodness I could get those long-toed boots off you. How's a man to know the size of your feet? And a head like a potato. It's enough to make one swear."

"Say now, Lord Peter," said Mr. Milligan, "can I do anything for you?"

"Well, d'you know," said Lord Peter, "I'm wonderin' if you would. It's damned cheek to ask you, but fact is, it's my mother, you know. Wonderful woman, but don't realize what it means, demands on the time of a busy man like you. We don't understand hustle over here, you know, Mr. Milligan."

"Now don't you mention that," said Mr. Milligan; "I'd be surely charmed to do anything to oblige the Duchess."

He felt a momentary qualm as to whether a duke's mother were also a duchess, but breathed more freely as Lord Peter went on:

"Thanks—that's uncommonly good of you. Well, now, it's like this. My mother—most energetic, self-sacrificin' woman, don't you see, is thinkin' of gettin' up a sort of a charity bazaar down at Denver this winter, in aid of the church-roof, y'know. Very sad case, Mr. Milligan— fine old antique—early English windows and decorated angel roof, and all that—all tumblin' to pieces, rain pourin' in and so on—vicar catchin' rheumatism at early service, owin' to the draught blowin' in over the altar—you know the sort of thing. They've got a man down startin' on it—little beggar called Thipps—lives with an aged mother in Battersea—vulgar little beast, but quite good on angel roofs and things, I'm told."

At this point, Lord Peter watched his interlocutor narrowly, but finding that this rigmarole produced in him no reaction more startling than polite interest tinged with faint bewilderment, he abandoned this line of investigation, and proceeded:

"I say, I beg your pardon, frightfully—I'm afraid I'm bein' beastly long-winded. Fact is, my mother is gettin' up this bazaar, and she thought it'd be all awfully interestin' side-show to have some lectures— sort of little talks, y'know—by eminent business men of all nations. 'How I did it' kind of touch, y'know—'A Drop of Oil with Mr. Rockefeller'—'Cash and Conscience' by Cadbury's Cocoa and so on. It would interest people down there no end. You see, all my mother's friends will be there, and we've none of us any money—not what you'd call money, I mean—I expect our incomes wouldn't pay your telephone calls, would they?—but we like awfully to hear about the people who can make money. Gives us a sort of uplifted feelin', don't you know. Well, anyway, I mean, my mother'd be frightfully pleased and grateful to you, Mr. Milligan, if you'd come down and give us a few words as a representative American. It needn't take more than ten minutes or so, y'know, because the local people can't understand much beyond shootin' and huntin', and my mother's crowd can't keep their minds on anythin' more than ten minutes together, but we'd really appreciate it very much if you'd come and stay a day or two and just give us a little breezy word on the almighty dollar."

"Why, yes," said Mr. Milligan, "I'd like to, Lord Peter. It's kind of the Duchess to suggest it. It's a very sad thing when these fine old antiques begin to wear out. I'll come with great pleasure. And perhaps you'd be kind enough to accept a little donation to the Restoration Fund."

This unexpected development nearly brought Lord Peter up all standing. To pump, by means of an ingenious lie, a hospitable gentleman whom you are inclined to suspect of a peculiarly malicious murder, and to accept from him in the course of the proceedings a large cheque for a charitable object, has something about it unpalatable to any but the hardened Secret Service agent. Lord Peter temporized.

"That's awfully decent of you," he said. "I'm sure they'd be no end grateful. But you'd better not give it to me, you know. I might spend it, or lose it. I'm not very reliable, I'm afraid. The vicar's the right person—the Rev. Constantine Throgmorton, St. John-before-the-Latin-Gate Vicarage, Duke's Denver, if you like to send it there."

"I will," said Mr. Milligan. "Will you write it out now for a thousand pounds, Scoot, in case it slips my mind later?"

The secretary, a sandy-haired young man with a long chin and no eyebrows, silently did as he was requested. Lord Peter looked from the bald head of Mr. Milligan to the red head of the secretary, hardened his heart and tried again.

"Well, I'm no end grateful to you, Mr. Milligan, and so'll my mother be when I tell her. I'll let you know the date of the bazaar—it's not quite settled yet, and I've got to see some other business men, don't you know. I thought of askin' Lord Northcliffe to represent English newspapers, you know, and a friend of mine promises me a leadin' German—very interestin' if there ain't too much feelin' against it down in the country, and I'd better get Rothschild, I suppose, to do the Hebrew point of view. I thought of askin' Levy, y'know, only he's floated off in this inconvenient way."

"Yes," said Mr. Milligan, "that's a very curious thing, though I don't mind saying, Lord Peter, that it's a convenience to me. He had a cinch on my railroad combine, but I'd nothing against him personally, and if he turns up after I've brought off a little deal I've got on, I'll be happy to give him the right hand of welcome."

A vision passed through Lord Peter's mind of Sir Reuben kept somewhere in custody till a financial crisis was over. This was exceedingly possible, and far more agreeable than his earlier conjecture; it also agreed better with the impression he was forming of Mr. Milligan.

"Well, it's a rum go," said Lord Peter, "but I daresay he had his reasons. Much better not enquire into people's reasons, y'know, what? Specially as a police friend of mine who's connected with the case says the old johnnie dyed his hair before he went."

Out of the tail of his eye, Lord Peter saw the red-headed secretary add up five columns of figures simultaneously and jot down the answer.

"Dyed his hair, did he?" said Mr. Milligan.

"Dyed it red," said Lord Peter. The secretary looked up. "Odd thing is," continued Wimsey, "they can't lay hands on the bottle. Somethin' fishy there, don't you think, what?"

The secretary's interest seemed to have evaporated. He inserted a fresh sheet into his loose-leaf ledger, and carried forward a row of digits from the preceding page.

"I daresay there's nothin' in it," said Lord Peter, rising to go. "Well, it's uncommonly good of you to be bothered with me like this, Mr. Milligan, my mother'll be no end pleased. She'll write you about the date."

"I'm charmed," said Mr. Milligan, "very pleased to have met you."

Mr. Scoot rose silently to open the door, uncoiling as he did so a portentous length of thin leg, hitherto hidden by the desk. With a mental sigh Lord Peter estimated him at six-foot-four.

"It's a pity I can't put Scoot's head on Milligan's shoulders," said Lord Peter, emerging into the swirl of the city, "and what will my mother say?"

# CHAPTER 5

Mr. Parker was a bachelor, and occupied a Georgian but inconvenient flat at No. 12 Great Ormond Street, for which he paid a pound a week. His exertions in the cause of civilization were rewarded, not by the gift of diamond rings from empresses or munificent cheques from grateful Prime Ministers, but by a modest, though sufficient, salary, drawn from the pockets of the British taxpayer. He awoke, after a long day of arduous and inconclusive labour, to the smell of burnt porridge. Through his bedroom window, hygienically open top and bottom, a raw fog was rolling slowly in, and the sight of a pair of winter pants, flung hastily over a chair the previous night, fretted him with a sense of the sordid absurdity of the human form. The telephone bell rang, and he crawled wretchedly out of bed and into the sitting-room, where Mrs. Munns, who did for him by the day, was laying the table, sneezing as she went.

Mr. Bunter was speaking.

"His lordship says he'd be very glad, sir, if you could make it convenient to step round to breakfast."

If the odour of kidneys and bacon had been wafted along the wire, Mr. Parker could not have experienced a more vivid sense of consolation.

"Tell his lordship I'll be with him in half an hour," he said, thankfully, and plunging into the bathroom, which was also the kitchen, he informed Mrs. Munns, who was just making tea from a kettle which had gone off the boil, that he should be out to breakfast.

"You can take the porridge home for the family," he added, viciously, and flung off his dressing-gown with such determination that Mrs. Munns could only scuttle away with a snort.

A 19 'bus deposited him in Piccadilly only fifteen minutes later than his rather sanguine impulse had prompted him to suggest, and Mr. Bunter served him with glorious food, incomparable coffee, and the *Daily Mail* before a blazing fire of wood and coal. A distant voice singing the "et iterum venturus est" from Bach's Mass in B minor proclaimed that for the owner of the flat cleanliness and godliness met at least once a day, and presently Lord Peter roamed in, moist and verbena-scented, in a bathrobe cheerfully patterned with unnaturally variegated peacocks.

"Mornin', old dear," said that gentleman; "beast of a day, ain't it? Very good of you to trundle out in it, but I had a letter I wanted you to see, and I hadn't the energy to come round to your place. Bunter and I've been makin' a night of it."

chewing-gum hand the card to the secretary, and when I got into the inner shrine I saw John P. Milligan standing with it in his hand, so it's one or the other, and for the moment it's immaterial to our purpose which is which. I boned the card from the table when I left.

"Well, now, Parker, here's what's been keeping Bunter and me up till the small hours. I've measured and measured every way backwards and forwards till my head's spinnin', and I've stared till I'm nearly blind, but I'm hanged if I can make my mind up. Question 1. Is C identical with B? Question 2. Is D or E identical with B? There's nothing to go on but the size and shape, of course, and the marks are so faint—what do you think?"

Parker shook his head doubtfully.

"I think E might almost be put out of the question," he said, "it seems such an excessively long and narrow thumb. But I think there is a decided resemblance between the span of B on the water-bottle and C on the bath. And I don't see any reason why D shouldn't be the same as B, only there's so little to judge from."

"Your untutored judgment and my measurements have brought us both to the same conclusion—if you can call it a conclusion," said Lord Peter, bitterly.

"Another thing," said Parker. "Why on earth should we try to connect B with C? The fact that you and I happen to be friends doesn't make it necessary to conclude that the two cases we happen to be interested in have any organic connection with one another. Why should they? The only person who thinks they have is Sugg, and he's nothing to go by. It would be different if there were any truth in the suggestion that the man in the bath was Levy, but we know for a certainty he wasn't. It's ridiculous to suppose that the same man was employed in committing two totally distinct crimes on the same night, one in Battersea and the other in Park Lane."

"I know," said Wimsey, "though of course we mustn't forget that Levy was in Battersea at the time, and now we know he didn't return home at twelve as was supposed, we've no reason to think he ever left Battersea at all."

"True. But there are other places in Battersea besides Thipps's bathroom. And he wasn't in Thipps's bathroom. In fact, come to think of it, that's the one place in the universe where we know definitely that he wasn't. So what's Thipps's bath got to do with it?"

"I don't know," said Lord Peter. "Well, perhaps we shall get something better to go on today."

He leaned back in his chair and smoked thoughtfully for some time over the papers which Bunter had marked for him.

"They've got you out in the limelight," he said. "Thank Heaven, Sugg hates me too much to give me any publicity. What a dull Agony

Column! 'Darling Pipsey—Come back soon to your distracted Popsey'—
and the usual young man in need of financial assistance, and the usual
injunction to 'Remember thy Creator in the days of thy youth.' Hullo!
there's the bell. Oh, it's our answer from Scotland Yard."

The note from Scotland Yard enclosed an optician's specification
identical with that sent by Mr. Crimplesham, and added that it was an
unusual one, owing to the peculiar strength of the lenses and the
marked difference between the sight of the two eyes.

"That's good enough," said Parker.

"Yes," said Wimsey. "Then Possibility No. 3 is knocked on the head.
There remain Possibility No. 1: Accident or Misunderstanding, and No.
2: Deliberate Villainy, of a remarkably bold and calculating kind—of a
kind, in fact, characteristic of the author or authors of our two
problems. Following the methods inculcated at that University of
which I have the honour to be a member, we will now examine
severally the various suggestions afforded by Possibility No. 2. This
Possibility may be again subdivided into two or more Hypotheses. On
Hypothesis 1 (strongly advocated by my distinguished colleague
Professor Snupshed), the criminal, whom we may designate as X, is not
identical with Crimplesham, but is using the name of Crimplesham as
his shield. This hypothesis may be further subdivided into two
alternatives. Alternative A: Crimplesham is an innocent and
unconscious accomplice, and X is in his employment. X writes in
Crimplesham's name on Crimplesham's office-paper and obtains that
the object in question, i.e., the eyeglasses, be despatched to
Crimplesham's address. He is in a position to intercept the parcel
before it reaches Crimplesham. The presumption is that X is
Crimplesham's charwoman, office-boy, clerk, secretary or porter. This
offers a wide field of investigation. The method of enquiry will be to
interview Crimplesham and discover whether he sent the letter, and if
not, who has access to his correspondence. Alternative B: Crimplesham
is under X's influence or in his power, and has been induced to write
the letter by (a) bribery, (b) misrepresentation or (c) threats. X may in
that case be a persuasive relation or friend, or else a creditor,
blackmailer or assassin; Crimplesham, on the other hand, is obviously
venal or a fool. The method of enquiry in this case, I would tentatively
suggest, is again to interview Crimplesham, put the facts of the case
strongly before him, and assure him in the most intimidating terms
that he is liable to a prolonged term of penal servitude as an accessory
after the fact in the crime of murder— Ah-hem! Trusting, gentlemen,
that you have followed me thus far, we will pass to the consideration of
Hypothesis No. 2, to which I personally incline, and according to which
X is identical with Crimplesham.

"In this case, Crimplesham, who is, in the words of an English classic, a man-of-infinite-resource-and-sagacity, correctly deduces that, of all people, the last whom we shall expect to find answering our advertisement is the criminal himself. Accordingly, he plays a bold game of bluff. He invents an occasion on which the glasses may very easily have been lost or stolen, and applies for them. If confronted, nobody will be more astonished than he to learn where they were found. He will produce witnesses to prove that he left Victoria at 5:45 and emerged from the train at Balham at the scheduled time, and sat up all Monday night playing chess with a respectable gentleman well known in Balham. In this case, the method of enquiry will be to pump the respectable gentleman in Balham, and if he should happen to be a single gentleman with a deaf housekeeper, it may be no easy matter to impugn the alibi, since, outside detective romances, few ticket-collectors and 'bus-conductors keep an exact remembrance of all the passengers passing between Balham and London on any and every evening of the week.

"Finally, gentlemen, I will frankly point out the weak point of all these hypotheses, namely: that none of them offers any explanation as to why the incriminating article was left so conspicuously on the body in the first instance."

Mr. Parker had listened with commendable patience to this academic exposition.

"Might not X," he suggested, "be an enemy of Crimplesham's, who designed to throw suspicion upon him?"

"He might. In that case he should be easy to discover, since he obviously lives in close proximity to Crimplesham and his glasses, and Crimplesham in fear of his life will then be a valuable ally for the prosecution."

"How about the first possibility of all, misunderstanding or accident?"

"Well! Well, for purposes of discussion, nothing, because it really doesn't afford any data for discussion."

"In any case," said Parker, "the obvious course appears to be to go to Salisbury."

"That seems indicated," said Lord Peter.

"Very well," said the detective, "is it to be you or me or both of us?"

"It is to be me," said Lord Peter, "and that for two reasons. First, because, if (by Possibility No. 2, Hypothesis 1, Alternative A) Crimplesham is an innocent catspaw, the person who put in the advertisement is the proper person to hand over the property. Secondly, because, if we are to adopt Hypothesis 2, we must not overlook the sinister possibility that Crimplesham-X is laying a careful trap to rid himself of the person who so unwarily advertised in the daily press his interest in the solution of the Battersea Park mystery."

"That appears to me to be an argument for our both going," objected the detective.

"Far from it," said Lord Peter. "Why play into the hands of Crimplesham-X by delivering over to him the only two men in London with the evidence, such as it is, and shall I say the wits, to connect him with the Battersea body?"

"But if we told the Yard where we were going, and we both got nobbled," said Mr. Parker, "it would afford strong presumptive evidence of Crimplesham's guilt, and anyhow, if he didn't get hanged for murdering the man in the bath he'd at least get hanged for murdering us."

"Well," said Lord Peter, "if he only murdered me you could still hang him—what's the good of wasting a sound, marriageable young male like yourself? Besides, how about old Levy? If you're incapacitated, do you think anybody else is going to find him?"

"But we could frighten Crimplesham by threatening him with the Yard."

"Well, dash it all, if it comes to that, I can frighten him by threatening him with you, which, seeing you hold what evidence there is, is much more to the point. And, then, suppose it's a wild-goose chase after all, you'll have wasted time when you might have been getting on with the case. There are several things that need doing."

"Well," said Parker, silenced but reluctant, "why can't I go, in that case?"

"Bosh!" said Lord Peter. "I am retained (by old Mrs. Thipps, for whom I entertain the greatest respect) to deal with this case, and it's only by courtesy I allow you to have anything to do with it."

Mr. Parker groaned.

"Will you at least take Bunter?" he said.

"In deference to your feelings," replied Lord Peter, "I will take Bunter, though he could be far more usefully employed taking photographs or overhauling my wardrobe. When is there a good train to Salisbury, Bunter?"

"There is an excellent train at 10:50, my lord."

"Kindly make arrangements to catch it," said Lord Peter, throwing off his bathrobe and trailing away with it into his bedroom. "And Parker—if you have nothing else to do you might get hold of Levy's secretary and look into that little matter of the Peruvian oil."

Lord Peter took with him, for light reading in the train, Sir Reuben Levy's diary. It was a simple, and in the light of recent facts, rather a pathetic document. The terrible fighter of the Stock Exchange, who could with one nod set the surly bear dancing, or bring the savage bull to feed out of his hand, whose breath devastated whole districts with famine or swept financial potentates from their seats, was revealed in private life as kindly, domestic, innocently proud of himself and his belongings, confiding, generous and a little dull. His own small economies were duly chronicled side by side with extravagant presents to his wife and daughter. Small incidents of household routine appeared, such as: "Man came to mend the conservatory roof," or "The new butler ( Simpson) has arrived, recommended by the Goldbergs. I think he will be satisfactory." All visitors and entertainments were duly entered, from a very magnificent lunch to Lord Dewsbury, the Minister for Foreign Affairs, and Dr. Jabez K. Wort, the American plenipotentiary, through a series of diplomatic dinners to eminent financiers, down to intimate family gatherings of persons designated by Christian names or nicknames. About May there came a mention of Lady Levy's nerves, and further reference was made to the subject in subsequent months. In September it was stated that "Freke came to see my dear wife and advised complete rest and change of scene. She thinks of going abroad with Rachel." The name of the famous nerve-specialist occurred as a diner or luncher about once a month, and it came into Lord Peter's mind that Freke would be a good person to consult about Levy himself. "People sometimes tell things to the doctor," he murmured to himself. "And, by Jove! if Levy was simply going round to see Freke on Monday night, that rather disposes of the Battersea incident, doesn't it?" He made a note to look up Sir Julian and turned on further. On September 18th, Lady Levy and her daughter had left for the south of France. Then suddenly, under the date October 5th, Lord Peter found what he was looking for: "Goldberg, Skriner and Milligan to dinner."

There was the evidence that Milligan had been in that house. There had been a formal entertainment—a meeting as of two duellists shaking hands before the fight. Skriner was a well-known picture-dealer; Lord Peter imagined an after-dinner excursion upstairs to see the two Corots in the drawing-room, and the portrait of the eldest Levy girl, who had died at the age of sixteen. It was by Augustus John, and hung in the bedroom. The name of the red-haired secretary was nowhere mentioned, unless the initial S., occurring in another entry, referred to him. Throughout September and October, Anderson (of Wyndham's) had been a frequent visitor.

Lord Peter shook his head over the diary, and turned to the consideration of the Battersea Park mystery. Whereas in the Levy affair it was easy enough to supply a motive for the crime, if crime it were, and the difficulty was to discover the method of its carrying out and the whereabouts of the victim, in the other case the chief obstacle to enquiry was the entire absence of any imaginable motive. It was odd that, although the papers had carried news of the affair from one end of the country to the other and a description of the body had been sent to every police station in the country, nobody had as yet come forward to identify the mysterious occupant of Mr. Thipps's bath. It was true that the description, which mentioned the clean-shaven chin, elegantly cut hair and the pince-nez, was rather misleading but on the other hand, the police had managed to discover the number of molars missing, and the height, complexion and other data were correctly enough stated, as also the date at which death had presumably occurred. It seemed, however, as though the man had melted out of society without leaving a gap or so much as a ripple. Assigning a motive for the murder of a person without relations or antecedents or even clothes is like trying to visualize the fourth dimension—admirable exercise for the imagination, but arduous and inconclusive. Even if the day's interview should disclose black spots in the past or present of Mr. Crimplesham, how were they to be brought into connection with a person apparently without a past, and whose present was confined to the narrow limits of a bath and a police mortuary?

"Bunter," said Lord Peter, "I beg that in the future you will restrain me from starting two hares at once. These cases are gettin' to be a strain on my constitution. One hare has nowhere to run from, and the other has nowhere to run to. It's a kind of mental D.T., Bunter. When this is over I shall turn pussyfoot, forswear the police news, and take to an emollient diet of the works of the late Charles Garvice."

* * *

It was its comparative proximity to Milford Hill that induced Lord Peter to lunch at the Minster Hotel rather than at the White Hart or some other more picturesquely situated hostel. It was not a lunch calculated to cheer his mind; as in all Cathedral cities, the atmosphere of the Close pervades every nook and corner of Salisbury, and no food in that city but seems faintly flavoured with prayer-books. As he sat sadly consuming that impassive pale substance known to the English as "cheese" unqualified (for there are cheeses which go openly by their names, as Stilton, Camembert, Gruyere, Wensleydale or Gorgonzola, but "cheese" is cheese and everywhere the same), he enquired of the waiter the whereabouts of Mr. Crimplesham's office.

The waiter directed him to a house rather further up the street on the opposite side, adding, "But anybody'll tell you, sir; Mr. Crimplesham's very well known hereabouts."

"He's a good solicitor, I suppose?" said Lord Peter.

"Oh, yes, sir," said the waiter, "you couldn't do better than trust to Mr. Crimplesham, sir. There's folk say he's old-fashioned, but I'd rather have my little bits of business done by Mr. Crimplesham than by one of these fly-away young men. Not but what Mr. Crimplesham'll be retiring soon, sir, I don't doubt, for he must be close on eighty, sir, if he's a day, but then there's young Mr. Wicks to carry on the business, and he's a very nice, steady-like young gentleman."

"Is Mr. Crimplesham really as old as that?" said Lord Peter. "Dear me! He must be very active for his years. A friend of mine was doing business with him in town last week."

"Wonderful active, sir," agreed the waiter, "and with his game leg, too, you'd be surprised. But there, sir, I often think, when a man's once past a certain age, the older he grows the tougher he gets, and women the same or more so."

"Very likely," said Lord Peter, calling up and dismissing the mental picture of a gentleman of eighty with a game leg carrying a dead body over the roof of a Battersea flat at midnight. "'He's tough, sir, tough, is old Joey Bagstock, tough and devilish sly,' " he added, thoughtlessly.

"Indeed, sir?" said the waiter. "I couldn't say, I'm sure."

"I beg your pardon," said Lord Peter, "I was quoting poetry. Very silly of me. I got the habit at my mother's knee and I can't break myself of it."

"No, sir," said the waiter, pocketing a liberal tip. "Thank you very much, sir. You'll find the house easy. Just afore you come to Penny-farthing Street, sir, about two turnings off, on the right hand side opposite."

"Afraid that disposes of Crimplesham-X," said Lord Peter. "I'm rather sorry; he was a fine sinister figure as I had pictured him. Still, his may yet be the brain behind the hands—the aged spider sitting invisible in the centre of the vibrating web, you know, Bunter."

"Yes, my lord," said Bunter. They were walking up the street together.

"There is the office over the way," pursued Lord Peter. "I think, Bunter, you might step into this little shop and purchase a sporting paper, and if I do not emerge from the villain's lair—say within three-quarters of an hour, you may take such steps as your perspicuity may suggest."

Mr. Bunter turned into the shop as desired, and Lord Peter walked across and rang the lawyer's bell with decision.

"The truth, the whole truth and nothing but the truth is my long suit here, I fancy," he murmured, and when the door was opened by a clerk he delivered over his card with an unflinching air.

He was ushered immediately into a confidential-looking office, obviously furnished in the early years of Queen Victoria's reign, and never altered since. A lean, frail-looking old gentleman rose briskly from his chair as he entered and limped forward to meet him.

"My dear sir," exclaimed the lawyer, "how extremely good of you to come in person! Indeed, I am ashamed to have given you so much trouble. I trust you were passing this way, and that my glasses have not put you to any great inconvenience. Pray take a seat, Lord Peter." He peered gratefully at the young man over a pince-nez obviously the fellow of that now adorning a dossier in Scotland Yard.

Lord Peter sat down. The lawyer sat down. Lord Peter picked up a glass paper-weight from the desk and weighed it thoughtfully in his hand. Subconsciously he noted what an admirable set of finger-prints he was leaving upon it. He replaced it with precision on the exact centre of a pile of letters.

"It's quite all right," said Lord Peter. "I was here on business. Very happy to be of service to you. Very awkward to lose one's glasses, Mr. Crimplesham."

"Yes," said the lawyer, "I assure you I feel quite lost without them. I have this pair, but they do not fit my nose so well—besides, that chain has a great sentimental value for me. I was terribly distressed on arriving at Balham to find that I had lost them. I made enquiries of the railway, but to no purpose. I feared they had been stolen. There were such crowds at Victoria, and the carriage was packed with people all the way to Balham. Did you come across them in the train?"

"Well, no," said Lord Peter, "I found them in rather an unexpected place. Do you mind telling me if you recognized any of your fellow-travellers on that occasion?"

The lawyer stared at him.

"Not a soul," he answered. "Why do you ask?"

"Well," said Lord Peter, "I thought perhaps the—the person with whom I found them might have taken them for a joke."

The lawyer looked puzzled.

"Did the person claim to be an acquaintance of mine?" he enquired. "I know practically nobody in London, except the friend with whom I was staying in Balham, Dr. Philpots, and I should be very greatly surprised at his practising a jest upon me. He knew very well how distressed I was at the loss of the glasses. My business was to attend a meeting of shareholders in Medlicott's Bank, but the other gentlemen present were all personally unknown to me, and I cannot think that any of them would take so great a liberty. In any case," he added, "as the glasses are here, I will not enquire too closely into the manner of their restoration. I am deeply obliged to you for your trouble."

Lord Peter hesitated.

"Pray forgive my seeming inquisitiveness," he said, "but I must ask you another question. It sounds rather melodramatic, I'm afraid, but it's this. Are you aware that you have any enemy—anyone, I mean, who would profit by your—er—decease or disgrace?"

Mr. Crimplesham sat frozen into stony surprise and disapproval.

"May I ask the meaning of this extraordinary question?" he enquired stiffly.

"Well," said Lord Peter, "the circumstances are a little unusual. You may recollect that my advertisement was addressed to the jeweller who sold the chain."

"That surprised me at the time," said Mr. Crimplesham, "but I begin to think your advertisement and your behaviour are all of a piece."

"They are," said Lord Peter. "As a matter of fact I did not expect the owner of the glasses to answer my advertisement. Mr. Crimplesham, you have no doubt read what the papers have to say about the Battersea Park mystery. Your glasses are the pair that was found on the body, and they are now in the possession of the police at Scotland Yard, as you may see by this." He placed the specification of the glasses and the official note before Crimplesham.

"Good God!" exclaimed the lawyer. He glanced at the paper, and then looked narrowly at Lord Peter.

"Are you yourself connected with the police?" he enquired.

"Not officially," said Lord Peter. "I am investigating the matter privately, in the interests of one of the parties."

Mr. Crimplesham rose to his feet.

"My good man," he said, "this is a very impudent attempt, but blackmail is an indictable offence, and I advise you to leave my office before you commit yourself." He rang the bell.

"I was afraid you'd take it like that," said Lord Peter. "It looks as though this ought to have been my friend Detective Parker's job, after all." He laid Parker's card on the table beside the specification, and added: "If you should wish to see me again, Mr. Crimplesham, before to-morrow morning, you will find me at the Minster Hotel."

Mr. Crimplesham disdained to reply further than to direct the clerk who entered to "show this person out."

In the entrance Lord Peter brushed against a tall young man who was just coming in, and who stared at him with surprised recognition. His face, however, aroused no memories in Lord Peter's mind, and that baffled nobleman, calling out Bunter from the newspaper shop, departed to his hotel to get a trunk-call through to Parker.

Meanwhile, in the office, the meditations of the indignant Mr. Crimplesham were interrupted by the entrance of his junior partner.

"I say," said the latter gentleman, "has somebody done something really wicked at last? What ever brings such a distinguished amateur of crime on our sober doorstep?"

"I have been the victim of a vulgar attempt at blackmail," said the lawyer; "an individual passing himself off as Lord Peter Wimsey—"

"But that is Lord Peter Wimsey," said Mr. Wicks, "there's no mistaking him. I saw him give evidence in the Attenbury emerald case. He's a big little pot in his way, you know, and goes fishing with the head of Scotland Yard."

"Oh, dear," said Mr. Crimplesham.

Fate arranged that the nerves of Mr. Crimplesham should be tried that afternoon. When, escorted by Mr. Wicks, he arrived at the Minster Hotel, he was informed by the porter that Lord Peter Wimsey had strolled out, mentioning that he thought of attending Evensong. "But his man is here, sir," he added, "if you like to leave a message."

Mr. Wicks thought that on the whole it would be well to leave a message. Mr. Bunter, on enquiry, was found to be sitting by the telephone, waiting for a trunk-call. As Mr. Wicks addressed him the bell rang, and Mr. Bunter, politely excusing himself, took down the receiver.

"Hullo!" he said. "Is that Mr. Parker? Oh, thanks! Exchange! Exchange! Sorry, can you put me through to Scotland Yard? Excuse me, gentlemen, keeping you waiting.—Exchange! all right—Scotland Yard—Hullo! Is that Scotland Yard?—Is Detective Parker round there?—Can I speak to him?—I shall have done in a moment, gentlemen.—Hullo! is that you, Mr. Parker? Lord Peter would be much obliged if you could find it convenient to step down to Salisbury, sir. Oh, no, sir, he's in excellent health, sir—just stepped round to hear Evensong, sir—oh, no, I think to-morrow morning would do excellently, sir, thank you, sir."

* Apollonios Rhodios. Lorenzobodi Alopa. Firenze. 1496. (4to.) The excitement attendant on the solution of the Battersea Mystery did not prevent Lord Peter from securing this rare work before his departure for Corsica.

# CHAPTER 6

It was, in fact, inconvenient for Mr. Parker to leave London. He had had to go and see Lady Levy towards the end of the morning, and subsequently his plans for the day had been thrown out of gear and his movements delayed by the discovery that the adjourned inquest of Mr. Thipps's unknown visitor was to be held that afternoon, since nothing very definite seemed forthcoming from Inspector Sugg's enquiries. Jury and witnesses had been convened accordingly for three o'clock. Mr. Parker might altogether have missed the event, had he not run against Sugg that morning at the Yard and extracted the information from him as one would a reluctant tooth. Inspector Sugg, indeed, considered Mr. Parker rather interfering; moreover, he was hand-in-glove with Lord Peter Wimsey, and Inspector Sugg had no words for the interferingness of Lord Peter. He could not, however, when directly questioned, deny that there was to be an inquest that afternoon, nor could he prevent Mr. Parker from enjoying the inalienable right of any interested British citizen to be present. At a little before three, therefore, Mr. Parker was in his place, and amusing himself with watching the efforts of those persons who arrived after the room was packed to insinuate, bribe or bully themselves into a position of vantage. The coroner, a medical man of precise habits and unimaginative aspect, arrived punctually, and looking peevishly round at the crowded assembly, directed all the windows to be opened, thus letting in a stream of drizzling fog upon the heads of the unfortunates on that side of the room. This caused a commotion and some expressions of disapproval, checked sternly by the coroner, who said that with the influenza about again an unventilated room was a deathtrap; that anybody who chose to object to open windows had the obvious remedy of leaving the court, and further, that if any disturbance was made he would clear the court. He then took a Formamint lozenge, and proceeded, after the usual preliminaries, to call up fourteen good and lawful persons and swear them diligently to enquire and a true presentment make of all matters touching the death of the gentleman with the pince-nez and to give a true verdict according to the evidence, so help them God. When an expostulation by a woman juror—an elderly lady in spectacles who kept a sweetshop, and appeared to wish she was back there—had been summarily quashed by the coroner, the jury departed to view the body. Mr. Parker gazed round again and identified the unhappy Mr. Thipps and the girl Gladys led into an adjoining room under the grim guard of the police. They were soon followed by a gaunt old lady in a bonnet and mantle. With her, in a wonderful fur coat and a motor bonnet of fascinating construction, came the Dowager Duchess of Denver, her quick, dark eyes darting hither and thither about the crowd. The next moment they had lighted on Mr. Parker, who had several times visited the Dower House, and she nodded to him, and spoke to a policeman. Before long, a way opened magically through the press, and Mr. Parker found himself accommodated with a front seat just behind the Duchess, who greeted him charmingly, and said: "What's happened to poor Peter?" Parker began to explain, and the coroner glanced irritably in their direction. Somebody went up and whispered in his ear, at which he coughed, and took another Formamint.

"We came up by car," said the Duchess—"so tiresome—such bad roads between Denver and Gunbury St. Walters—and there were people coming to lunch—I had to put them off—I couldn't let the old lady go alone, could I? By the way, such an odd thing's happened about the Church Restoration Fund—the Vicar—oh, dear, here are these people coming back again; well, I'll tell you afterwards—do look at that woman looking shocked, and the girl in tweeds trying to look as if she sat on undraped gentlemen every day of her life—I don't mean that—corpses of course—but one finds oneself being so Elizabethan nowadays—what an awful little man the coroner is, isn't he? He's looking daggers at me—do you think he'll dare to clear me out of the court or commit me for what-you-may-call-it?"

The first part of the evidence was not of great interest to Mr. Parker. The wretched Mr. Thipps, who had caught cold in gaol, deposed in an unhappy croak to having discovered the body when he went in to take his bath at eight o'clock. He had arrived at St. Pancras at ten o'clock. He sent the girl for brandy. He had never seen the deceased before. He had no idea how he came there.

Yes, he had been in Manchester the day before. He had arrived at St. Pancras at ten o'clock. He had cloak-roomed his bag. At this point Mr. Thipps became very red, unhappy and confused, and glanced nervously about the court.

"Now, Mr. Thipps," said the Coroner, briskly, "we must have your movements quite clear. You must appreciate the importance of the matter. You have chosen to give evidence, which you need not have done, but having done so, you will find it best to be perfectly explicit."

"Yes," said Mr. Thipps faintly.

"Have you cautioned this witness, officer?" inquired the Coroner, turning sharply to Inspector Sugg.

The Inspector replied that he had told Mr. Thipps that anything he said might be used again' him at his trial. Mr. Thipps became ashy, and said in a bleating voice that he 'adn't—hadn't meant to do anything that wasn't right.

This remark produced a mild sensation, and the Coroner became even more acidulated in manner than before.

"Is anybody representing Mr. Thipps?" he asked, irritably. "No? Did you not explain to him that he could—that he ought to be represented? You did not? Really, Inspector! Did you not know, Mr. Thipps, that you had a right to be legally represented?"

Mr. Thipps clung to a chair-back for support, and said "No" in a voice barely audible.

"It is incredible," said the Coroner, "that so-called educated people should be so ignorant of the legal procedure of their own country. This places us in a very awkward position. I doubt, Inspector, whether I should permit the prisoner—Mr. Thipps—to give evidence at all. It is a delicate position."

The perspiration stood on Mr. Thipps's forehead.

"Save us from our friends," whispered the Duchess to Parker. "If that cough-drop-devouring creature had openly instructed those fourteen people—and what unfinished-looking faces they have—so characteristic, I always think, of the lower middle-class, rather like sheep, or calves' head (boiled, I mean), to bring in wilful murder against the poor little man, he couldn't have made himself plainer."

"He can't let him incriminate himself, you know," said Parker.

"Stuff!" said the Duchess. "How could the man incriminate himself when he never did anything in his life? You men never think of anything but your red tape."

Meanwhile Mr. Thipps, wiping his brow with a handkerchief, had summoned up courage. He stood up with a kind of weak dignity, like a small white rabbit brought to bay.

"I would rather tell you," he said, "though it's reelly very unpleasant for a man in my position. But I reelly couldn't have it thought for a moment that I'd committed this dreadful crime. I assure you, gentlemen, I couldn't bear that. No. I'd rather tell you the truth, though I'm afraid it places me in rather a—well, I'll tell you."

"You fully understand the gravity of making such a statement, Mr. Thipps," said the Coroner.

"Quite," said Mr. Thipps. "It's all right—I—might I have a drink of water?"

"Take your time," said the Coroner, at the same time robbing his remark of all conviction by an impatient glance at his watch.

"Thank you, sir," said Mr. Thipps. "Well, then, it's true I got to St. Pancras at ten. But there was a man in the carriage with me. He'd got in at Leicester. I didn't recognize him at first, but he turned out to be an old schoolfellow of mine."

"What was this gentleman's name?" enquired the Coroner, his pencil poised.

Mr. Thipps shrank together visibly.

"I'm afraid I can't tell you that," he said. "You see—that is, you will see—it would get him into trouble, and I couldn't do that—no, I reelly couldn't do that, not if my life depended on it. No!" he added, as the ominous pertinence of the last phrase smote upon him, "I'm sure I couldn't do that."

"Well, well," said the Coroner.

The Duchess leaned over to Parker again. "I'm beginning quite to admire the little man," she said.

Mr. Thipps resumed.

"When we got to St. Pancras I was going home, but my friend said no. We hadn't met for a long time and we ought to—to make a night of it, was his expression. I fear I was weak, and let him overpersuade me to accompany him to one of his haunts. I use the word advisedly," said Mr. Thipps, "and I assure you, sir, that if I had known beforehand where we were going I never would have set foot in the place.

"I cloak-roomed my bag, for he did not like the notion of our being encumbered with it, and we got into a taxicab and drove to the corner of Tottenham Court Road and Oxford Street. We then walked a little way, and turned into a side street (I do not recollect which) where there was an open door, with the light shining out. There was a man at a counter, and my friend bought some tickets, and I heard the man at the counter say something to him about 'Your friend,' meaning me, and my friend said, 'Oh, yes, he's been here before, haven't you, Alf?' (which was what they called me at school), though I assure you, sir"—here Mr. Thipps grew very earnest—"I never had, and nothing in the world should induce me to go to such a place again.

"Well, we went down into a room underneath, where there were drinks, and my friend had several, and made me take one or two— though I am an abstemious man as a rule—and he talked to some other men and girls who were there—a very vulgar set of people, I thought them, though I wouldn't say but what some of the young ladies were nice-looking enough. One of them sat on my friend's knee and called him a slow old thing, and told him to come on—so we went into another room, where there were a lot of people dancing all these up-to-date dances. My friend went and danced, and I sat on a sofa. One of the young ladies came up to me and said, didn't I dance, and I said 'No,' so she said wouldn't I stand her a drink then. 'You'll stand us a drink then, darling,' that was what she said, and I said, 'Wasn't it after hours?' and she said that didn't matter. So I ordered the drink—a gin and bitters it was—for I didn't like not to, the young lady seemed to expect it of me and I felt it wouldn't be gentlemanly to refuse when she asked. But it went against my conscience—such a young girl as she was—and she put her arm round my neck afterwards and kissed me just like as if she was paying for the drink—and it reelly went to my 'eart," said Mr. Thipps, a little ambiguously, but with uncommon emphasis.

Here somebody at the back said, "Cheer-oh!" and a sound was heard as of the noisy smacking of lips.

"Remove the person who made that improper noise," said the Coroner, with great indignation. "Go on, please, Mr. Thipps."

"Well," said Mr. Thipps, "about half past twelve, as I should reckon, things began to get a bit lively, and I was looking for my friend to say good-night, not wishing to stay longer, as you will understand, when I saw him with one of the young ladies, and they seemed to be getting on altogether too well, if you follow me, my friend pulling the ribbons off her shoulder and the young lady laughing—and so on," said Mr. Thipps, hurriedly, "so I thought I'd just slip quietly out, when I heard a scuffle and a shout—and before I knew what was happening there were half a dozen policemen in, and the lights went out, and everybody stampeding and shouting—quite horrid, it was. I was knocked down in the rush, and hit my head a nasty knock on a chair—that was where I got that bruise they asked me about—and I was dreadfully afraid I'd never get away and it would all come out, and perhaps my photograph in the papers, when someone caught hold of me—I think it was the young lady I'd given the gin and bitters to—and she said, 'This way,' and pushed me along a passage and out at the back somewhere. So I ran through some streets, and found myself in Goodge Street, and there I got a taxi and came home. I saw the account of the raid afterwards in the papers, and saw my friend had escaped, and so, as it wasn't the sort of thing I wanted made public and I didn't want to get him into difficulties, I just said nothing. But that's the truth."

"Well, Mr. Thipps," said the Coroner, "we shall be able to substantiate a certain amount of this story. Your friend's name—"

"No," said Mr. Thipps, stoutly, "not on any account."

"Very good," said the Coroner. "Now, can you tell us what time you did get in?"

"About half past one, I should think. Though reelly, I was so upset—"

"Quite so. Did you go straight to bed?"

"Yes, I took my sandwich and glass of milk first. I thought it might settle my inside, so to speak," added the witness, apologetically, "not being accustomed to alcohol so late at night and on an empty stomach, as you may say."

"Quite so. Nobody sat up for you?"

"Nobody."

"How long did you take getting to bed first and last?"

Mr. Thipps thought it might have been half an hour.

"Did you visit the bathroom before turning in?"

"No."

"And you heard nothing in the night?"

"No. I fell fast asleep. I was rather agitated, so I took a little dose to make me sleep, and what with being so tired and the milk and the dose, I just tumbled right off and didn't wake till Gladys called me."

Further questioning elicited little from Mr. Thipps. Yes, the bathroom window had been open when he went in in the morning, he was sure of that, and he had spoken very sharply to the girl about it. He was ready to answer any questions; he would be only too 'appy— happy to have this dreadful affair sifted to the bottom.

Gladys Horrocks stated that she had been in Mr. Thipps's employment about three months. Her previous employers would speak to her character. It was her duty to make the round of the flat at night, when she had seen Mrs. Thipps to bed at ten. Yes, she remembered doing so on Monday evening. She had looked into all the rooms. Did she recollect shutting the bathroom window that night? Well, no, she couldn't swear to it, not in particular, but when Mr. Thipps called her into the bathroom in the morning it certainly was open. She had not been into the bathroom before Mr. Thipps went in. Well, yes, it had happened that she had left that window open before, when anyone had been 'aving a bath in the evening and 'ad left the blind down. Mrs. Thipps 'ad 'ad a bath on Monday evening, Mondays was one of her regular bath nights. She was very much afraid she 'adn't shut the window on Monday night, though she wished her 'ead 'ad been cut off afore she'd been so forgetful.

Here the witness burst into tears and was given some water, while the Coroner refreshed himself with a third lozenge.

Recovering, witness stated that she had certainly looked into all the rooms before going to bed. No, it was quite impossible for a body to be 'idden in the flat without her seeing of it. She 'ad been in the kitchen all evening, and there wasn't 'ardly room to keep the best dinner service there, let alone a body. Old Mrs. Thipps sat in the drawing-room. Yes, she was sure she'd been into the dining-room. How? Because she put Mr. Thipps's milk and sandwiches there ready for him. There had been nothing in there,—that she could swear to. Nor yet in her own bedroom, nor in the 'all. Had she searched the bedroom cupboard and the box-room? Well, no, not to say searched; she wasn't used to searchin' people's 'ouses for skelintons every night. So that a man might have concealed himself in the box-room or a wardrobe? She supposed he might.

In reply to a woman juror—well, yes, she was walking out with a young man. Williams was his name, Bill Williams—well, yes, William Williams, if they insisted. He was a glazier by profession. Well, yes, he 'ad been in the flat sometimes. Well, she supposed you might say he was acquainted with the flat. Had she ever—no, she 'adn't, and if she'd thought such a question was going to be put to a respectable girl she wouldn't 'ave offered to give evidence. The vicar of St. Mary's would speak to her character and to Mr. Williams's. Last time Mr. Williams was at the flat was a fortnight ago.

Well, no, it wasn't exactly the last time she 'ad seen Mr. Williams. Well, yes, the last time was Monday—well, yes, Monday night. Well, if she must tell the truth, she must. Yes, the officer had cautioned her, but there wasn't any 'arm in it, and it was better to lose her place than to be 'ung, though it was a cruel shame a girl couldn't 'ave a bit of fun without a nasty corpse comin' in through the window to get 'er into difficulties. After she 'ad put Mrs. Thipps to bed, she 'ad slipped out to go to the Plumbers' and Glaziers' Ball at the "Black Faced Ram." Mr. Williams 'ad met 'er and brought 'er back. 'E could testify to where she'd been and that there wasn't no 'arm in it. She'd left before the end of the ball. It might 'ave been two o'clock when she got back. She'd got the keys of the flat from Mrs. Thipps's drawer when Mrs. Thipps wasn't looking. She 'ad asked leave to go, but couldn't get it, along of Mr. Thipps bein' away that night. She was bitterly sorry she 'ad be'aved so, and she was sure she'd been punished for it. She had 'eard nothing suspicious when she came in. She had gone straight to bed without looking round the flat. She wished she were dead.

No, Mr. and Mrs. Thipps didn't 'ardly ever 'ave any visitors; they kep' themselves very retired. She had found the outside door bolted that morning as usual. She wouldn't never believe any 'arm of Mr. Thipps. Thank you, Miss Horrocks. Call Georgiana Thipps, and the Coroner thought we had better light the gas.

The examination of Mrs. Thipps provided more entertainment than enlightenment, affording as it did an excellent example of the game called "cross questions and crooked answers." After fifteen minutes' suffering, both in voice and temper, the Coroner abandoned the struggle, leaving the lady with the last word.

"You needn't try to bully me, young man," said that octogenarian with spirit, "settin' there spoilin' your stomach with them nasty jujubes."

At this point a young man arose in court and demanded to give evidence. Having explained that he was William Williams, glazier, he was sworn, and corroborated the evidence of Gladys Horrocks in the matter of her presence at the "Black Faced Ram" on the Monday night. They had returned to the flat rather before two, he thought, but certainly later than 1:30. He was sorry that he had persuaded Miss Horrocks to come out with him when she didn't ought. He had observed nothing of a suspicious nature in Prince of Wales Road at either visit.

Inspector Sugg gave evidence of having been called in at about half past eight on Monday morning. He had considered the girl's manner to be suspicious and had arrested her. On later information, leading him to suspect that the deceased might have been murdered that night, he had arrested Mr. Thipps. He had found no trace of breaking into the flat. There were marks on the bathroom window-sill which pointed to somebody having got in that way. There were no ladder marks or foot-marks in the yard; the yard was paved with asphalt. He had examined the roof, but found nothing on the roof. In his opinion the body had been brought into the flat previously and concealed till the evening by someone who had then gone out during the night by the bathroom window, with the connivance of the girl. In that case, why should not the girl have let the person out by the door? Well, it might have been so. Had he found traces of a body or a man or both having been hidden in the flat? He found nothing to show that they might not have been so concealed. What was the evidence that led him to suppose that the death had occurred that night?

At this point Inspector Sugg appeared uneasy, and endeavoured to retire upon his professional dignity. On being pressed, however, he admitted that the evidence in question had come to nothing.

*One of the jurors:* Was it the case that any finger-marks had been left by the criminal?

Some marks had been found on the bath, but the criminal had worn gloves.

*The Coroner:* Do you draw any conclusion from this fact as to the experience of the criminal?

*Inspector Sugg:* Looks as if he was an old hand, sir.

*The Juror:* Is that very consistent with the charge against Alfred Thipps, Inspector?

The Inspector was silent.

*The Coroner:* In the light of the evidence which you have just heard, do you still press the charge against Alfred Thipps and Gladys Horrocks?

*Inspector Sugg:* I consider the whole set-out highly suspicious. Thipps's story isn't corroborated, and as for the girl Horrocks, how do we know this Williams ain't in it as well?

*William Williams:* Now, you drop that. I can bring a 'undred witnesses—

*The Coroner:* Silence, if you please. I am surprised, Inspector, that you should make this suggestion in that manner. It is highly improper. By the way, can you tell us whether a police raid was actually carried out on the Monday night on any Night Club in the neighbourhood of St. Giles's Circus?

*Inspector Sugg (sulkily):* I believe there was something of the sort.

*The Coroner:* You will, no doubt, enquire into the matter. I seem to recollect having seen some mention of it in the newspapers. Thank you, Inspector, that will do.

Several witnesses having appeared and testified to the characters of Mr. Thipps and Gladys Horrocks, the Coroner stated his intention of proceeding to the medical evidence.

"Sir Julian Freke."

There was considerable stir in the court as the great specialist walked up to give evidence. He was not only a distinguished man, but a striking figure, with his wide shoulders, upright carriage and leonine head. His manner as he kissed the Book presented to him with the usual deprecatory mumble by the Coroner's officer, was that of a St. Paul condescending to humour the timid mumbo-jumbo of superstitious Corinthians.

"So handsome, I always think," whispered the Duchess to Mr. Parker, "just exactly like William Morris, with that bush of hair and beard and those exciting eyes looking out of it—so splendid, these dear men always devoted to something or other—not but what I think socialism is a mistake—of course it works with all those nice people, so good and happy in art linen and the weather always perfect—Morris, I mean, you know—but so difficult in real life. Science is different—I'm sure if I had nerves I should go to Sir Julian just to look at him—eyes like that give one something to think about, and that's what most of these people want, only I never had any—nerves, I mean. Don't you think so?"

"You are Sir Julian Freke," said the Coroner, "and live at St. Luke's House, Prince of Wales Road, Battersea, where you exercise a general direction over the surgical side of St. Luke's Hospital?"

Sir Julian assented briefly to this definition of his personality.

"You were the first medical man to see the deceased?"

"I was."

"And you have since conducted an examination in collaboration with Dr. Grimbold of Scotland Yard?"

"I have."

"You are in agreement as to the cause of death?"

"Generally speaking, yes."

"Will you communicate your impressions to the jury?"

"I was engaged in research work in the dissecting room at St. Luke's Hospital at about nine o'clock on Monday morning, when I was informed that Inspector Sugg wished to see me. He told me that the dead body of a man had been discovered under mysterious circumstances at 59 Queen Caroline Mansions. He asked me whether it could be supposed to be a joke perpetrated by any of the medical students at the hospital. I was able to assure him, by an examination of the hospital's books, that there was no subject missing from the dissecting room."

"Who would be in charge of such bodies?"

"William Watts, the dissecting-room attendant."

"Is William Watts present?" enquired the Coroner of the officer.

William Watts was present, and could be called if the Coroner thought it necessary.

"I suppose no dead body would be delivered to the hospital without your knowledge, Sir Julian?"

"Certainly not."

"Thank you. Will you proceed with your statement?"

"Inspector Sugg then asked me whether I would send a medical man round to view the body. I said that I would go myself."

"Why did you do that?"

"I confess to my share of ordinary human curiosity, Mr. Coroner."

Laughter from a medical student at the back of the room.

"On arriving at the flat I found the deceased lying on his back in the bath. I examined him, and came to the conclusion that death had been caused by a blow on the back of the neck, dislocating the fourth and fifth cervical vertebra, bruising the spinal cord and producing internal hemorrhage and partial paralysis of the brain. I judged the deceased to have been dead at least twelve hours, possibly more. I observed no other sign of violence of any kind upon the body. Deceased was a strong, well-nourished man of about fifty to fifty-five years of age."

"In your opinion, could the blow have been self-inflicted?"

"Certainly not. It had been made with a heavy, blunt instrument from behind, with great force and considerable judgment. It is quite impossible that it was self-inflicted."

"Could it have been the result of an accident?"

"That is possible, of course."

"If, for example, the deceased had been looking out of window, and the sash had shut violently down upon him?"

"No; in that case there would have been signs of strangulation and a bruise upon the throat as well."

"But deceased might have been killed through a heavy weight accidentally falling upon him?"

"He might."

"Was death instantaneous, in your opinion?"

"It is difficult to say. Such a blow might very well cause death instantaneously, or the patient might linger in a partially paralyzed condition for some time. In the present case I should be disposed to think that deceased might have lingered for some hours. I base my decision upon the condition of the brain revealed at the autopsy. I may say, however, that Dr. Grimbold and I are not in complete agreement on the point."

"I understand that a suggestion has been made as to the identification of the deceased. You are not in a position to identify him?"

"Certainly not. I never saw him before. The suggestion to which you refer is a preposterous one, and ought never to have been made. I was not aware until this morning that it had been made; had it been made to me earlier I should have known how to deal with it, and I should like to express my strong disapproval of the unnecessary shock and distress inflicted upon a lady with whom I have the honour to be acquainted."

The Coroner: It was not my fault, Sir Julian; I had nothing to do with it; I agree with you that it was unfortunate you were not consulted.

The reporters scribbled busily, and the court asked each other what was meant, while the jury tried to look as if they knew already.

"In the matter of the eyeglasses found upon the body, Sir Julian. Do these give any indication to a medical man?"

"They are somewhat unusual lenses; an oculist would be able to speak more definitely, but I will say for myself that I should have expected them to belong to an older man than the deceased."

"Speaking as a physician, who has had many opportunities of observing the human body, did you gather anything from the appearance of the deceased as to his personal habits?"

"I should say that he was a man in easy circumstances, but who had only recently come into money. His teeth are in a bad state, and his hands show signs of recent manual labor."

"An Australian colonist, for instance, who had made money?"

"Something of that sort; of course, I could not say positively."

"Of course not. Thank you, Sir Julian."

Dr. Grimbold, called, corroborated his distinguished colleague in every particular, except that, in his opinion, death had not occurred for several days after the blow. It was with the greatest hesitancy that he ventured to differ from Sir Julian Freke, and he might be wrong. It was difficult to tell in any case, and when he saw the body, deceased had been dead at least twenty-four hours, in his opinion.

Inspector Sugg, recalled. Would he tell the jury what steps had been taken to identify the deceased?

A description had been sent to every police station and had been inserted in all the newspapers. In view of the suggestion made by Sir Julian Freke, had inquiries been made at all the seaports? They had. And with no results? With no results at all. No one had come forward to identify the body? Plenty of people had come forward; but nobody had succeeded in identifying it. Had any effort been made to follow up the clue afforded by the eyeglasses? Inspector Sugg submitted that, having regard to the interests of justice, he would beg to be excused from answering that question. Might the jury see the eyeglasses? The eyeglasses were handed to the jury.

William Watts, called, confirmed the evidence of Sir Julian Freke with regard to dissecting-room subjects. He explained the system by which they were entered. They usually were supplied by the workhouses and free hospitals. They were under his sole charge. The young gentlemen could not possibly get the keys. Had Sir Julian Freke, or any of the house surgeons, the keys? No, not even Sir Julian Freke. The keys had remained in his possession on Monday night? They had. And, in any case, the enquiry was irrelevant, as there was no body missing, nor ever had been. That was the case.

The Coroner then addressed the jury, reminding them with some asperity that they were not there to gossip about who the deceased could or could not have been, but to give their opinion as to the cause of death. He reminded them that they should consider whether, according to the medical evidence, death could have been accidental or self-inflicted or whether it was deliberate murder, or homicide. If they considered the evidence on this point insufficient, they could return an open verdict. In any case, their verdict could not prejudice any person; if they brought it in "murder," all the whole evidence would have to be gone through again before the magistrate. He then dismissed them, with the unspoken adjuration to be quick about it.

Sir Julian Freke, after giving his evidence, had caught the eye of the Duchess, and now came over and greeted her.

"I haven't seen you for an age," said that lady. "How are you?"

"Hard at work," said the specialist. "Just got my new book out. This kind of thing wastes time. Have you seen Lady Levy yet?"

"No, poor dear," said the Duchess. "I only came up this morning, for this. Mrs. Thipps is staying with me—one of Peter's eccentricities, you know. Poor Christine! I must run round and see her. This is Mr. Parker," she added, "who is investigating that case."

"Oh," said Sir Julian, and paused. "Do you know," he said in a low voice to Parker, "I am very glad to meet you. Have you seen Lady Levy yet?"

"I saw her this morning."

"Did she ask you to go on with the inquiry?"

"Yes," said Parker; "she thinks," he added, "that Sir Reuben may be detained in the hands of some financial rival or that perhaps some scoundrels are holding him to ransom."

"And is that your opinion?" asked Sir Julian.

"I think it very likely," said Parker, frankly.

Sir Julian hesitated again.

"I wish you would walk back with me when this is over," he said.

"I should be delighted," said Parker.

At this moment the jury returned and took their places, and there was a little rustle and hush. The Coroner addressed the foreman and enquired if they were agreed upon their verdict.

"We are agreed, Mr. Coroner, that deceased died of the effects of a blow upon the spine, but how that injury was inflicted we consider that there is not sufficient evidence to show."

Mr. Parker and Sir Julian Freke walked up the road together.

"I had absolutely no idea until I saw Lady Levy this morning," said the doctor, "that there was any idea of connecting this matter with the disappearance of Sir Reuben. The suggestion was perfectly monstrous, and could only have grown up in the mind of that ridiculous police officer. If I had had any idea what was in his mind I could have disabused him and avoided all this."

"I did my best to do so," said Parker, "as soon as I was called in to the Levy case—"

"Who called you in, if I may ask?" enquired Sir Julian.

"Well, the household first of all, and then Sir Reuben's uncle, Mr. Levy of Portman Square, wrote to me to go on with the investigation."

"And now Lady Levy has confirmed those instructions?"

"Certainly," said Parker in some surprise.

Sir Julian was silent for a little time.

"I'm afraid I was the first person to put the idea into Sugg's head," said Parker, rather penitently. "When Sir Reuben disappeared, my first step, almost, was to hunt up all the street accidents and suicides and so on that had turned up during the day, and I went down to see this Battersea Park body as a matter of routine. Of course, I saw that the thing was ridiculous as soon as I got there, but Sugg froze on to the idea—and it's true there was a good deal of resemblance between the dead man and the portraits I've seen of Sir Reuben."

"A strong superficial likeness," said Sir Julian. "The upper part of the face is a not uncommon type, and as Sir Reuben wore a heavy beard and there was no opportunity of comparing the mouths and chins, I can understand the idea occurring to anybody. But only to be dismissed at once. I am sorry," he added, "as the whole matter has been painful to Lady Levy. You may know, Mr. Parker, that I am an old, though I should not call myself an intimate, friend of the Levys."

"I understood something of the sort."

"Yes. When I was a young man I—in short, Mr. Parker, I hoped once to marry Lady Levy." (Mr. Parker gave the usual sympathetic groan.) "I have never married, as you know," pursued Sir Julian. "We have remained good friends. I have always done what I could to spare her pain."

"Believe me, Sir Julian," said Parker, "that I sympathize very much with you and with Lady Levy, and that I did all I could to disabuse Inspector Sugg of this notion. Unhappily, the coincidence of Sir Reuben's being seen that evening in the Battersea Park Road—"

"Ah, yes," said Sir Julian. "Dear me, here we are at home. Perhaps you would come in for a moment, Mr. Parker, and have tea or a whisky-and-soda or something."

Parker promptly accepted this invitation, feeling that there were other things to be said.

The two men stepped into a square, finely furnished hall with a fireplace on the same side as the door, and a staircase opposite. The dining-room door stood open on their right, and as Sir Julian rang the bell a man-servant appeared at the far end of the hall.

"What will you take?" asked the doctor.

"After that dreadfully cold place," said Parker, "what I really want is gallons of hot tea, if you, as a nerve specialist, can bear the thought of it."

"Provided you allow of a judicious blend of China with it," replied Sir Julian in the same tone, "I have no objection to make. Tea in the library at once," he added to the servant, and led the way upstairs.

"I don't use the downstairs rooms much, except the dining-room," he explained, as he ushered his guest into a small but cheerful library on the first floor. "This room leads out of my bedroom and is more convenient. I only live part of my time here, but it's very handy for my research work at the hospital. That's what I do there, mostly. It's a fatal thing for a theorist, Mr. Parker, to let the practical work get behindhand. Dissection is the basis of all good theory and all correct diagnosis. One must keep one's hand and eye in training. This place is far more important to me than Harley Street, and some day I shall abandon my consulting practice altogether and settle down here to cut up my subjects and write my books in peace. So many things in this life are a waste of time, Mr. Parker."

Mr. Parker assented to this.

"Very often," said Sir Julian, "the only time I get for any research work—necessitating as it does the keenest observation and the faculties at their acutest—has to be at night, after a long day's work and by artificial light, which, magnificent as the lighting of the dissecting room here is, is always more trying to the eyes than daylight. Doubtless your own work has to be carried on under even more trying conditions."

"Yes, sometimes," said Parker; "but then you see," he added, "the conditions are, so to speak, part of the work."

"Quite so, quite so," said Sir Julian; "you mean that the burglar, for example, does not demonstrate his methods in the light of day, or plant the perfect footmark in the middle of a damp patch of sand for you to analyze."

"Not as a rule," said the detective, "but I have no doubt many of your diseases work quite as insidiously as any burglar."

"They do, they do," said Sir Julian, laughing, "and it is my pride, as it is yours, to track them down for the good of society. The neuroses, you know, are particularly clever criminals—they break out into as many disguises as—"

"As Leon Kestrel, the Master-Mummer," suggested Parker, who read railway-stall detective stories on the principle of the 'busman's holiday.

"No doubt," said Sir Julian, who did not, "and they cover up their tracks wonderfully. But when you can really investigate, Mr. Parker, and break up the dead, or for preference the living body with the scalpel, you always find the footmarks—the little trail of ruin or disorder left by madness or disease or drink or any other similar pest. But the difficulty is to trace them back, merely by observing the surface symptoms—the hysteria, crime, religion, fear, shyness, conscience, or whatever it may be; just as you observe a theft or a murder and look for the footsteps of the criminal, so I observe a fit of hysterics or an outburst of piety and hunt for the little mechanical irritation which has produced it."

"You regard all these things as physical?"

"Undoubtedly. I am not ignorant of the rise of another school of thought, Mr. Parker, but its exponents are mostly charlatans or self-deceivers. '*Sie haben sich so weit darin eingeheimnisst*' that, like Sludge the Medium, they are beginning to believe their own nonsense. I should like to have the exploring of some of their brains, Mr. Parker; I would show you the little faults and landslips in the cells—the misfiring and short-circuiting of the nerves, which produce these notions and these books. At least," he added, gazing sombrely at his guest, "at least, if I could not quite show you to-day, I shall be able to do so to-morrow—or in a year's time—or before I die."

He sat for some minutes gazing into the fire, while the red light played upon his tawny beard and struck out answering gleams from his compelling eyes.

Parker drank tea in silence, watching him. On the whole, however, he remained but little interested in the causes of nervous phenomena, and his mind strayed to Lord Peter, coping with the redoubtable Crimplesham down in Salisbury. Lord Peter had wanted him to come: that meant, either that Crimplesham was proving recalcitrant or that a clue wanted following. But Bunter had said that to-morrow would do, and it was just as well. After all the Battersea affair was not Parker's case; he had already wasted valuable time attending an inconclusive inquest, and he really ought to get on with his legitimate work. There was still Levy's secretary to see and the little matter of the Peruvian Oil to be looked into. He looked at his watch.

"I am very much afraid—if you will excuse me—" he murmured.

Sir Julian came back with a start to the consideration of actuality.

"Your work calls you?" he said smiling. "Well, I can understand that. I won't keep you. But I wanted to say something to you in connection with your present inquiry—only I hardly know—I hardly like—"

Parker sat down again, and banished every indication of hurry from his face and attitude.

"I shall be very grateful for any help you can give me," he said.

"I'm afraid it's more in the nature of hindrance," said Sir Julian, with a short laugh. "It's a case of destroying a clue for you, and a breach of professional confidence on my side. But since—accidentally— a certain amount has come out, perhaps the whole had better do so."

Mr. Parker made the encouraging noise which, among laymen, supplies the place of the priest's insinuating, "Yes, my son?"

"Sir Reuben Levy's visit on Monday night was to me," said Sir Julian.

"Yes?" said Mr. Parker, without expression.

"He found cause for certain grave suspicions concerning his health," said Sir Julian, slowly, as though weighing how much he could in honour disclose to a stranger. "He came to me, in preference to his own medical man, as he was particularly anxious that the matter should be kept from his wife. As I told you, he knew me fairly well, and Lady Levy had consulted me about a nervous disorder in the summer."

"Did he make an appointment with you?" asked Parker.

"I beg your pardon," said the other, absently.

"Did he make an appointment?"

"An appointment? Oh, no! He turned up suddenly in the evening after dinner when I wasn't expecting him. I took him up here and examined him, and he left me somewhere about ten o'clock, I should think."

"May I ask what was the result of your examination?"

"Why do you want to know?"

"It might illuminate—well, conjecture as to his subsequent conduct," said Parker, cautiously. This story seemed to have little coherence with the rest of the business, and he wondered whether coincidence was alone responsible for Sir Reuben's disappearance on the same night that he visited the doctor.

"I see," said Sir Julian. "Yes. Well, I will tell you in confidence that I saw grave grounds of suspicion, but as yet, no absolute certainty of mischief."

"Thank you. Sir Reuben left you at ten o'clock?"

"Then or thereabouts. I did not at first mention the matter as it was so very much Sir Reuben's wish to keep his visit to me secret, and there was no question of accident in the street or anything of that kind, since he reached home safely at midnight."

"Quite so," said Parker.

"It would have been, and is, a breach of confidence," said Sir Julian, "and I only tell you now because Sir Reuben was accidentally seen, and because I would rather tell you in private than have you ferreting round here and questioning my servants, Mr. Parker. You will excuse my frankness."

"Certainly," said Parker. "I hold no brief for the pleasantness of my profession, Sir Julian. I am very much obliged to you for telling me this. I might otherwise have wasted valuable time following up a false trail."

"I am sure I need not ask you, in your turn, to respect this confidence," said the doctor. "To publish the matter abroad could only harm Sir Reuben and pain his wife, besides placing me in no favourable light with my patients."

"I promise to keep the thing to myself," said Parker, "except of course," he added hastily, "that I must inform my colleague."

"You have a colleague in the case?"

"I have."

"What sort of person is he?"

"He will be perfectly discreet, Sir Julian."

"Is he a police officer?"

"You need not be afraid of your confidence getting into the records at Scotland Yard."

"I see that you know how to be discreet, Mr. Parker."

"We also have our professional etiquette, Sir Julian."

On returning to Great Ormond Street, Mr. Parker found a wire awaiting him, which said: "Do not trouble to come. All well. Returning to-morrow. Wimsey."

# CHAPTER 7

On returning to the flat just before lunch-time on the following morning, after a few confirmatory researches in Balham and the neighbourhood of Victoria Station, Lord Peter was greeted at the door by Mr. Bunter (who had gone straight home from Waterloo) with a telephone message and a severe and nursemaid-like eye.

"Lady Swaffham rang up, my lord, and said she hoped your lordship had not forgotten you were lunching with her."

"I have forgotten, Bunter, and I mean to forget. I trust you told her I had succumbed to lethargic encephalitis suddenly, no flowers by request."

"Lady Swaffham said, my lord, she was counting on you. She met the Duchess of Denver yesterday—"

"If my sister-in-law's there I won't go, that's flat," said Lord Peter.

"I beg your pardon, my lord, the elder Duchess."

"What's she doing in town?"

"I imagine she came up for the inquest, my lord."

"Oh, yes—we missed that, Bunter."

"Yes, my lord. Her Grace is lunching with Lady Swaffham."

"Bunter, I can't. I can't, really. Say I'm in bed with whooping cough, and ask my mother to come round after lunch."

"Very well, my lord. Mrs. Tommy Frayle will be at Lady Swaffham's, my lord, and Mr. Milligan—"

"Mr. Who?"

"Mr. John P. Milligan, my lord, and—"

"Good God, Bunter, why didn't you say so before? Have I time to get there before he does? All right. I'm off. With a taxi I can just—"

"Not in those trousers, my lord," said Mr. Bunter, blocking the way to the door with deferential firmness.

"Oh, Bunter," pleaded his lordship, "do let me—just this once. You don't know how important it is."

"Not on any account, my lord. It would be as much as my place is worth."

"The trousers are all right, Bunter."

"Not for Lady Swaffham's, my lord. Besides, your lordship forgets the man that ran against you with a milk can at Salisbury."

And Mr. Bunter laid an accusing finger on a slight stain of grease showing across the light cloth.

"I wish to God I'd never let you grow into a privileged family retainer, Bunter," said Lord Peter, bitterly, dashing his walking-stick into the umbrella-stand. "You've no conception of the mistakes my mother may be making."

Mr. Bunter smiled grimly and led his victim away.

When an immaculate Lord Peter was ushered, rather late for lunch, into Lady Swaffham's drawing-room, the Dowager Duchess of Denver was seated on a sofa, plunged in intimate conversation with Mr. John P. Milligan of Chicago.

"I'm vurry pleased to meet you, Duchess," had been that financier's opening remark, "to thank you for your exceedingly kind invitation. I assure you it's a compliment I deeply appreciate."

The Duchess beamed at him, while conducting a rapid rally of all her intellectual forces.

"Do come and sit down and talk to me, Mr. Milligan," she said. "I do so love talking to you great business men—let me see, is it a railway king you are or something about puss-in-the-corner—at least, I don't mean that exactly, but that game one used to play with cards, all about wheat and oats, and there was a bull and a bear, too—or was it a horse?—no, a bear, because I remember one always had to try and get rid of it and it used to get so dreadfully crumpled and torn, poor thing, always being handed about, one got to recognize it, and then one had to buy a new pack—so foolish it must seem to you, knowing the real thing, and dreadfully noisy, but really excellent for breaking the ice with rather stiff people who didn't know each other—I'm quite sorry it's gone out."

Mr. Milligan sat down.

"Well, now," he said, "I guess it's as interesting for us business men to meet British aristocrats as it is for Britishers to meet American railway kings, Duchess. And I guess I'll make as many mistakes talking your kind of talk as you would make if you were tryin' to run a corner in wheat in Chicago. Fancy now, I called that fine lad of yours Lord Wimsey the other day, and he thought I'd mistaken him for his brother. That made me feel rather green."

This was an unhoped-for lead. The Duchess walked warily.

"Dear boy," she said, "I am so glad you met him, Mr. Milligan. Both my sons are a great comfort to me, you know, though, of course, Gerald is more conventional—just the right kind of person for the House of Lords, you know, and a splendid farmer. I can't see Peter down at Denver half so well, though he is always going to all the right things in town, and very amusing sometimes, poor boy."

"I was very much gratified by Lord Peter's suggestion," pursued Mr. Milligan, "for which I understand you are responsible, and I'll surely be very pleased to come any day you like, though I think you're flattering me too much."

"Ah, well," said the Duchess, "I don't know if you're the best judge of that, Mr. Milligan. Not that I know anything about business myself," she added. "I'm rather old-fashioned for these days, you know, and I can't pretend to do more than know a nice man when I see him; for the other things I rely on my son."

The accent of this speech was so flattering that Mr. Milligan purred almost audibly, and said:

"Well, Duchess, I guess that's where a lady with a real, beautiful, old-fashioned soul has the advantage of these modern young blatherskites—there aren't many men who wouldn't be nice—to her, and even then, if they aren't rock-bottom she can see through them."

"But that leaves me where I was," thought the Duchess. "I believe," she said aloud, "that I ought to be thanking you in the name of the vicar of Duke's Denver for a very munificent cheque which reached him yesterday for the Church Restoration Fund. He was so delighted and astonished, poor dear man."

"Oh, that's nothing," said Mr. Milligan, "we haven't any fine old crusted buildings like yours over on our side, so it's a privilege to be allowed to drop a little kerosene into the worm-holes when we hear of one in the old country suffering from senile decay. So when your lad told me about Duke's Denver I took the liberty to subscribe without waiting for the Bazaar."

"I'm sure it was very kind of you," said the Duchess. "You are coming to the Bazaar, then?" she continued, gazing into his face appealingly.

"Sure thing," said Mr. Milligan, with great promptness. "Lord Peter said you'd let me know for sure about the date, but we can always make time for a little bit of good work anyway. Of course I'm hoping to be able to avail myself of your kind invitation to stop, but if I'm rushed, I'll manage anyhow to pop over and speak my piece and pop back again."

"I hope so very much," said the Duchess. "I must see what can be done about the date—of course, I can't promise—"

"No, no," said Mr. Milligan heartily. "I know what these things are to fix up. And then there's not only me—there's Nat Rothschild and Cadbury, and all the other names your son mentioned, to be consulted."

The Duchess turned pale at the thought that any one of these illustrious persons might some time turn up in somebody's drawing-room, but by this time she had dug herself in comfortably, and was even beginning to find her range.

"I can't say how grateful we are to you," she said, "it will be such a treat. Do tell me what you think of saying."

"Well—" began Mr. Milligan.

Suddenly everybody was standing up and a penitent voice was heard to say:

"Really, most awfully sorry, y'know—hope you'll forgive me, Lady Swaffham, what? Dear lady, could I possibly forget an invitation from you? Fact is, I had to go an' see a man down in Salisbury—absolutely true, 'pon my word, and the fellow wouldn't let me get away. I'm simply grovellin' before you, Lady Swaffham. Shall I go an' eat my lunch in the corner?"

Lady Swaffham gracefully forgave the culprit.

"Your dear mother is here," she said.

"How do, Mother?" said Lord Peter, uneasily.

"How are you, dear?" replied the Duchess. "You really oughtn't to have turned up just yet. Mr. Milligan was just going to tell me what a thrilling speech he's preparing for the Bazaar, when you came and interrupted us."

Conversation at lunch turned, not unnaturally, on the Battersea inquest, the Duchess giving a vivid impersonation of Mrs. Thipps being interrogated by the Coroner.

" 'Did you hear anything unusual in the night?' says the little man, leaning forward and screaming at her, and so crimson in the face and his ears sticking out so—just like a cherubim in that poem of Tennyson's—or is a cherub blue?—perhaps it's seraphim I mean—anyway, you know what I mean, all eyes, with little wings on its head. And dear old Mrs. Thipps saying, 'Of course I have, any time these eighty years,' and such a sensation in court till they found out she thought he'd said, 'Do you sleep without a light?' and everybody laughing, and then the Coroner said quite loudly, 'Damn the woman,' and she heard that, I can't think why, and said: 'Don't you get swearing, young man, sitting there in the presence of Providence, as you may say. I don't know what young people are coming to nowadays'—and he's sixty if he's a day, you know," said the Duchess.

By a natural transition, Mrs. Tommy Frayle referred to the man who was hanged for murdering three brides in a bath.

"I always thought that was so ingenious," she said, gazing soulfully at Lord Peter, "and do you know, as it happened, Tommy had just made me insure my life, and I got so frightened, I gave up my morning bath and took to having it in the afternoon when he was in the House—I mean, when he was not in the house—not at home, I mean."

"Dear lady," said Lord Peter, reproachfully, "I have a distinct recollection that all those brides were thoroughly unattractive. But it was an uncommonly ingenious plan—the first time of askin'—only he shouldn't have repeated himself."

"One demands a little originality in these days, even from murderers," said Lady Swaffham. "Like dramatists, you know—so much easier in Shakespeare's time, wasn't it? Always the same girl dressed up as a man, and even that borrowed from Boccaccio or Dante or somebody. I'm sure if I'd been a Shakespeare hero, the very minute I saw a slim-legged young page-boy I'd have said: 'Ods-bodikins! There's that girl again!'"

"That's just what happened, as a matter of fact," said Lord Peter. "You see, Lady Swaffham, if ever you want to commit a murder, the thing you've got to do is to prevent people from associatin' their ideas. Most people don't associate anythin'—their ideas just roll about like so many dry peas on a tray, makin' a lot of noise and goin' nowhere, but once you begin lettin' 'em string their peas into a necklace, it's goin' to be strong enough to hang you, what?"

"Dear me!" said Mrs. Tommy Frayle, with a little scream, "what a blessing it is none of my friends have any ideas at all!"

"Y'see," said Lord Peter, balancing a piece of duck on his fork and frowning, "it's only in Sherlock Holmes and stories like that, that people think things out logically. Or'nar'ly, if somebody tells you somethin' out of the way, you just say, 'By Jove!' or 'How sad!' an' leave it at that, an' half the time you forget about it, 'nless somethin' turns up afterwards to drive it home. F'r instance, Lady Swaffham, I told you when I came in that I'd been down to Salisbury, 'n' that's true, only I don't suppose it impressed you much; 'n' I don't suppose it'd impress you much if you read in the paper to-morrow of a tragic discovery of a dead lawyer down in Salisbury, but if I went to Salisbury again next week 'n' there was a Salisbury doctor found dead the day after, you might begin to think I was a bird of ill omen for Salisbury residents; and if I went there again the week after, 'n' you heard next day that the see of Salisbury had fallen vacant suddenly, you might begin to wonder what took me to Salisbury, an' why I'd never mentioned before that I had friends down there, don't you see, an' you might think of goin' down to Salisbury yourself, an' askin' all kinds of people if they'd happened to see a young man in plum-coloured socks hangin' round the Bishop's Palace."

"I daresay I should," said Lady Swaffham.

"Quite. An' if you found that the lawyer and the doctor had once upon a time been in business at Poggleton-on-the-Marsh when the Bishop had been vicar there, you'd begin to remember you'd once heard of me payin' a visit to Poggleton-on-the-Marsh a long time ago, an' you'd begin to look up the parish registers there an' discover I'd been married under an assumed name by the vicar to the widow of a wealthy farmer, who'd died suddenly of peritonitis, as certified by the doctor, after the lawyer'd made a will leavin' me all her money, and then you'd begin to think I might have very good reasons for gettin' rid of such promisin' blackmailers as the lawyer, the doctor an' the bishop.

Only, if I hadn't started an association in your mind by gettin' rid of 'em all in the same place, you'd never have thought of goin' to Poggleton-on-the-Marsh, 'n' you wouldn't even have remembered I'd ever been there."

"Were you ever there, Lord Peter?" enquired Mrs. Tommy, anxiously.

"I don't think so," said Lord Peter, "the name threads no beads in my mind. But it might, any day, you know."

"But if you were investigating a crime," said Lady Swaffham, "you'd have to begin by the usual things, I suppose—finding out what the person had been doing, and who'd been to call, and looking for a motive, wouldn't you?"

"Oh, yes," said Lord Peter, "but most of us have such dozens of motives for murderin' all sorts of inoffensive people. There's lots of people I'd like to murder, wouldn't you?"

"Heaps," said Lady Swaffham. "There's that dreadful—perhaps I'd better not say it, though, for fear you should remember it later on."

"Well, I wouldn't if I were you," said Peter, amiably. "You never know. It'd be beastly awkward if the person died suddenly to-morrow."

"The difficulty with this Battersea case, I guess," said Mr. Milligan, "is that nobody seems to have any associations with the gentleman in the bath."

"So hard on poor Inspector Sugg," said the Duchess. "I quite felt for the man, having to stand up there and answer a lot of questions when he had nothing at all to say."

Lord Peter applied himself to the duck, having got a little behindhand. Presently he heard somebody ask the Duchess if she had seen Lady Levy.

"She is in great distress," said the woman who had spoken, a Mrs. Freemantle, "though she clings to the hope that he will turn up. I suppose you knew him, Mr. Milligan—know him, I should say, for I hope he's still alive somewhere."

Mrs. Freemantle was the wife of an eminent railway director, and celebrated for her ignorance of the world of finance. Her faux pas in this connection enlivened the tea parties of city men's wives.

"Well, I've dined with him," said Mr. Milligan, good-naturedly. "I think he and I've done our best to ruin each other, Mrs. Freemantle. If this were the States," he added, "I'd be much inclined to suspect myself of having put Sir Reuben in a safe place. But we can't do business that way in your old country; no, ma'am."

"It must be exciting work doing business in America," said Lord Peter.

"It is," said Mr. Milligan. "I guess my brothers are having a good time there now. I'll be joining them again before long, as soon as I've fixed up a little bit of work for them on this side."

"Well, you mustn't go till after my bazaar," said the Duchess.

Lord Peter spent the afternoon in a vain hunt for Mr. Parker. He ran him down eventually after dinner in Great Ormond Street.

Parker was sitting in an elderly but affectionate armchair, with his feet on the mantelpiece, relaxing his mind with a modern commentary on the Epistle to the Galatians. He received Lord Peter with quiet pleasure, though without rapturous enthusiasm, and mixed him a whisky-and-soda. Peter took up the book his friend had laid down and glanced over the pages.

"All these men work with a bias in their minds, one way or other," he said; "they find what they are looking for."

"Oh, they do," agreed the detective, "but one learns to discount that almost automatically, you know. When I was at college, I was all on the other side—Conybeare and Robertson and Drews and those people, you know, till I found they were all so busy looking for a burglar whom nobody had ever seen, that they couldn't recognize the footprints of the household, so to speak. Then I spent two years learning to be cautious."

"Hum," said Lord Peter, "theology must be good exercise for the brain then, for you're easily the most cautious devil I know. But I say, do go on reading—it's a shame for me to come and root you up in your off-time like this."

"It's all right, old man," said Parker.

The two men sat silent for a little, and then Lord Peter said:

"D'you like your job?"

The detective considered the question, and replied:

"Yes—yes, I do. I know it to be useful, and I am fitted to it. I do it quite well—not with inspiration, perhaps, but sufficiently well to take a pride in it. It is full of variety and it forces one to keep up to the mark and not get slack. And there's a future to it. Yes, I like it. Why?"

"Oh, nothing," said Peter. "It's a hobby to me, you see. I took it up when the bottom of things was rather knocked out for me, because it was so damned exciting, and the worst of it is, I enjoy it—up to a point. If it was all on paper I'd enjoy every bit of it. I love the beginning of a job—when one doesn't know any of the people and it's just exciting and amusing. But if it comes to really running down a live person and getting him hanged, or even quodded, poor devil, there don't seem as if there was any excuse for me buttin' in, since I don't have to make my livin' by it. And I feel as if I oughtn't ever to find it amusin'. But I do."

Parker gave this speech his careful attention.

"I see what you mean," he said.

"There's old Milligan, fr instance," said Lord Peter. "On paper, nothin' would be funnier than to catch old Milligan out. But he's rather a decent old bird to talk to. Mother likes him. He's taken a fancy to me. It's awfully entertainin' goin' and pumpin' him with stuff about a bazaar for church expenses, but when he's so jolly pleased about it and that, I feel a worm. S'pose old Milligan has cut Levy's throat and plugged him into the Thames. It ain't my business."

"It's as much yours as anybody's," said Parker; "it's no better to do it for money than to do it for nothing."

"Yes, it is," said Peter stubbornly. "Havin' to live is the only excuse there is for doin' that kind of thing."

"Well, but look here!" said Parker. "If Milligan has cut poor old Levy's throat for no reason except to make himself richer, I don't see why he should buy himself off by giving £1,000 to Duke's Denver church roof, or why he should be forgiven just because he's childishly vain, or childishly snobbish."

"That's a nasty one," said Lord Peter.

"Well, if you like, even because he has taken a fancy to you."

"No, but—"

"Look here, Wimsey—do you think he has murdered Levy?"

"Well, he may have."

"But do you think he has?"

"I don't want to think so."

"Because he has taken a fancy to you?"

"Well, that biases me, of course—"

"I daresay it's quite a legitimate bias. You don't think a callous murderer would be likely to take a fancy to you?"

"Well—besides, I've taken rather a fancy to him."

"I daresay that's quite legitimate, too. You've observed him and made a subconscious deduction from your observations, and the result is, you don't think he did it. Well, why not? You're entitled to take that into account."

"But perhaps I'm wrong and he did do it."

"Then why let your vainglorious conceit in your own power of estimating character stand in the way of unmasking the singularly cold-blooded murder of an innocent and lovable man?"

"I know—but I don't feel I'm playing the game somehow."

"Look here, Peter," said the other with some earnestness, "suppose you get this playing-fields-of-Eton complex out of your system once and for all. There doesn't seem to be much doubt that something unpleasant has happened to Sir Reuben Levy. Call it murder, to strengthen the argument. If Sir Reuben has been murdered, is it a game? and is it fair to treat it as a game?"

"That's what I'm ashamed of, really," said Lord Peter. "It is a game to me, to begin with, and I go on cheerfully, and then I suddenly see that somebody is going to be hurt, and I want to get out of it."

"Yes, yes, I know," said the detective, "but that's because you're thinking about your attitude. You want to be consistent, you want to look pretty, you want to swagger debonairly through a comedy of puppets or else to stalk magnificently through a tragedy of human sorrows and things. But that's childish. If you've any duty to society in the way of finding out the truth about murders, you must do it in any attitude that comes handy. You want to be elegant and detached? That's all right, if you find the truth out that way, but it hasn't any value in itself, you know. You want to look dignified and consistent— what's that got to do with it? You want to hunt down a murderer for the sport of the thing and then shake hands with him and say, 'Well played—hard luck—you shall have your revenge to-morrow!' Well, you can't do it like that. Life's not a football match. You want to be a sportsman. You can't be a sportsman. You're a responsible person."

"I don't think you ought to read so much theology," said Lord Peter. "It has a brutalizing influence."

He got up and paced about the room, looking idly over the bookshelves. Then he sat down again, filled and lit his pipe, and said:

"Well, I'd better tell you about the ferocious and hardened Crimplesham."

He detailed his visit to Salisbury. Once assured of his bona fides, Mr. Crimplesham had given him the fullest details of his visit to town.

"And I've substantiated it all," groaned Lord Peter, "and unless he's corrupted half Balham, there's no doubt he spent the night there. And the afternoon was really spent with the bank people. And half the residents of Salisbury seem to have seen him off on Monday before lunch. And nobody but his own family or young Wicks seems to have anything to gain by his death. And even if young Wicks wanted to make away with him, it's rather far-fetched to go and murder an unknown man in Thipps's place in order to stick Crimplesham's eyeglasses on his nose."

"Where was young Wicks on Monday?" asked Parker.

"At a dance given by the Precentor," said Lord Peter, wildly. "David—his name is David—dancing before the ark of the Lord in the face of the whole Cathedral Close."

There was a pause.

"Tell me about the inquest," said Wimsey.

Parker obliged with a summary of the evidence.

"Do you believe the body could have been concealed in the flat after all?" he asked. "I know we looked, but I suppose we might have missed something."

"We might. But Sugg looked as well."

"Sugg!"

"You do Sugg an injustice," said Lord Peter; "if there had been any signs of Thipps's complicity in the crime, Sugg would have found them."

"Why?"

"Why? Because he was looking for them. He's like your commentators on Galatians. He thinks that either Thipps, or Gladys Horrocks, or Gladys Horrocks's young man did it. Therefore he found marks on the window sill where Gladys Horrocks's young man might have come in or handed something in to Gladys Horrocks. He didn't find any signs on the roof, because he wasn't looking for them."

"But he went over the roof before me."

"Yes, but only in order to prove that there were no marks there. He reasons like this: Gladys Horrocks's young man is a glazier. Glaziers come on ladders. Glaziers have ready access to ladders. Therefore Gladys Horrocks's young man had ready access to a ladder. Therefore Gladys Horrocks's young man came on a ladder. Therefore there will be marks on the window sill and none on the roof. Therefore he finds marks on the window sill but none on the roof. He finds no marks on the ground, but he thinks he would have found them if the yard didn't happen to be paved with asphalt. Similarly, he thinks Mr. Thipps may have concealed the body in the box-room or elsewhere. Therefore you may be sure he searched the box-room and all the other places for signs of occupation. If they had been there he would have found them, because he was looking for them. Therefore, if he didn't find them it's because they weren't there."

"All right," said Parker, "stop talking. I believe you."

He went on to detail the medical evidence.

"By the way," said Lord Peter, "to skip across for a moment to the other case, has it occurred to you that perhaps Levy was going out to see Freke on Monday night?"

"He was; he did," said Parker, rather unexpectedly, and proceeded to recount his interview with the nerve-specialist.

"Humph!" said Lord Peter. "I say, Parker, these are funny cases, ain't they? Every line of enquiry seems to peter out. It's awfully exciting up to a point, you know, and then nothing comes of it. It's like rivers getting lost in the sand."

"Yes," said Parker. "And there's another one I lost this morning."

"What's that?"

"Oh, I was pumping Levy's secretary about his business. I couldn't get much that seemed important except further details about the Argentine and so on. Then I thought I'd just ask 'round in the City about those Peruvian Oil shares, but Levy hadn't even heard of them, so far as I could make out. I routed out the brokers, and found a lot of mystery and concealment, as one always does, you know, when somebody's been rigging the market, and at last I found one name at the back of it. But it wasn't Levy's."

"No? Whose was it?"

"Oddly enough, Freke's. It seems mysterious. He bought a lot of shares last week, in a secret kind of way, a few of them in his own name, and then quietly sold 'em out on Tuesday at a small profit—a few hundreds, not worth going to all that trouble about, you wouldn't think."

"Shouldn't have thought he ever went in for that kind of gamble."

"He doesn't as a rule. That's the funny part of it."

"Well, you never know," said Lord Peter; "people do these things, just to prove to themselves or somebody else that they could make a fortune that way if they liked. I've done it myself in a small way."

He knocked out his pipe and rose to go.

"I say, old man," he said suddenly, as Parker was letting him out, "does it occur to you that Freke's story doesn't fit in awfully well with what Anderson said about the old boy having been so jolly at dinner on Monday night? Would you be, if you thought you'd got anything of that sort?"

"No, I shouldn't," said Parker; "but," he added with his habitual caution, "some men will jest in the dentist's waiting-room. You, for one."

"Well, that's true," said Lord Peter, and went downstairs.

# CHAPTER 8

Lord Peter reached home about midnight, feeling extraordinarily wakeful and alert. Something was jigging and worrying in his brain; it felt like a hive of bees, stirred up by a stick. He felt as though he were looking at a complicated riddle, of which he had once been told the answer but had forgotten it and was always on the point of remembering.

"Somewhere," said Lord Peter to himself, "somewhere I've got the key to these two things. I know I've got it, only I can't remember what it is. Somebody said it. Perhaps I said it. I can't remember where, but I know I've got it. Go to bed, Bunter, I shall sit up a little. I'll just slip on a dressing-gown."

Before the fire he sat down with his pipe in his mouth and his jazz-coloured peacocks gathered about him. He traced out this line and that line of investigation—rivers running into the sand. They ran out from the thought of Levy, last seen at ten o'clock in Prince of Wales Road. They ran back from the picture of the grotesque dead man in Mr. Thipps's bathroom—they ran over the roof, and were lost—lost in the sand. Rivers running into the sand—rivers running underground, very far down—

Where Alph, the sacred river, ran
Through caverns measureless to man
Down to a sunless sea.

By leaning his head down, it seemed to Lord Peter that he could hear them, very faintly, lipping and gurgling somewhere in the darkness. But where? He felt quite sure that somebody had told him once, only he had forgotten.

He roused himself, threw a log on the fire, and picked up a book which the indefatigable Bunter, carrying on his daily fatigues amid the excitements of special duty, had brought from the Times Book Club. It happened to be Sir Julian Freke's "Physiological Bases of the Conscience," which he had seen reviewed two days before.

"This ought to send one to sleep," said Lord Peter; "if I can't leave these problems to my subconscious I'll be as limp as a rag to-morrow."

He opened the book slowly, and glanced carelessly through the preface.

"I wonder if that's true about Levy being ill," he thought, putting the book down; "it doesn't seem likely. And yet— Dash it all, I'll take my mind off it."

He read on resolutely for a little.

"I don't suppose Mother's kept up with the Levys much," was the next importunate train of thought. "Dad always hated self-made people and wouldn't have 'em at Denver. And old Gerald keeps up the tradition. I wonder if she knew Freke well in those days. She seems to get on with Milligan. I trust Mother's judgment a good deal. She was a brick about that bazaar business. I ought to have warned her. She said something once—"

He pursued an elusive memory for some minutes, till it vanished altogether with a mocking flicker of the tail. He returned to his reading.

Presently another thought crossed his mind, aroused by a photograph of some experiment in surgery.

"If the evidence of Freke and that man Watts hadn't been so positive," he said to himself, "I should be inclined to look into the matter of those shreds of lint on the chimney."

He considered this, shook his head and read with determination.

Mind and matter were one thing, that was the theme of the physiologist. Matter could erupt, as it were, into ideas. You could carve passions in the brain with a knife. You could get rid of imagination with drugs and cure an outworn convention like a disease. "The knowledge of good and evil is an observed phenomenon, attendant upon a certain condition of the brain-cells, which is removable." That was one phrase; and again:

"Conscience in man may, in fact, be compared to the sting of a hive-bee, which, so far from conducing to the welfare of its possessor, cannot function, even in a single instance, without occasioning its death. The survival-value in each case is thus purely social; and if humanity ever passes from its present phase of social development into that of a higher individualism, as some of our philosophers have ventured to speculate, we may suppose that this interesting mental phenomenon may gradually cease to appear; just as the nerves and muscles which once controlled the movements of our ears and scalps have, in all save a few backward individuals, become atrophied and of interest only to the physiologist."

"By Jove!" thought Lord Peter, idly, "that's an ideal doctrine for the criminal. A man who believed that would never—"

And then it happened—the thing he had been half-unconsciously expecting. It happened suddenly, surely, as unmistakably as sunrise. He remembered—not one thing, nor another thing, nor a logical succession of things, but everything—the whole thing, perfect, complete, in all its dimensions as it were and instantaneously; as if he stood outside the world and saw it suspended in infinitely dimensional space. He no longer needed to reason about it, or even to think about it. He knew it.

There is a game in which one is presented with a jumble of letters and is required to make a word out of them, as thus:

C O S S S S R I

The slow way of solving the problem is to try out all the permutations and combinations in turn, throwing away impossible conjunctions of letters, as:

S S S I R C

or

S C S R S O

Another way is to stare at the incoŝrdinate elements until, by no logical process that the conscious mind can detect, or under some adventitious external stimulus, the combination

S C I S S O R S

presents itself with calm certainty. After that, one does not even need to arrange the letters in order. The thing is done.

Even so, the scattered elements of two grotesque conundrums, flung higgledy-piggledy into Lord Peter's mind, resolved themselves, unquestioned henceforward. A bump on the roof of the end house—Levy in a welter of cold rain talking to a prostitute in the Battersea Park Road—a single ruddy hair—lint bandages—Inspector Sugg calling the great surgeon from the dissecting-room of the hospital—Lady Levy with a nervous attack—the smell of carbolic soap—the Duchess's voice—"not really an engagement, only a sort of understanding with her father"—shares in Peruvian Oil—the dark skin and curved, fleshy profile of the man in the bath—Dr. Grimbold giving evidence, "In my opinion, death did not occur for several days after the blow"—india-rubber gloves—even, faintly, the voice of Mr. Appledore, "He called on me, sir, with an anti-vivisectionist pamphlet"—all these things and many others rang together and made one sound, they swung together like bells in a steeple, with the deep tenor booming through the clamour:

"The knowledge of good and evil is a phenomenon of the brain, and is removable, removable, removable. The knowledge of good and evil is removable."

Lord Peter Wimsey was not a young man who habitually took himself very seriously, but this time he was frankly appalled. "It's impossible," said his reason, feebly; "*credo quia impossibile*," said his interior certainty with impervious self-satisfaction. "All right," said conscience, instantly allying itself with blind faith, "what are you going to do about it?"

Lord Peter got up and paced the room: "Good Lord!" he said. "Good Lord!" He took down "Who's Who" from the little shelf over the telephone, and sought comfort in its pages.

FREKE, Sir Julian. Kt. *er.* 1916; G. C. V. O. *er.* 1919; K.C.V.O. 1917; K.C.B. 1918; M.D., F.R.C.P., F.R.C.S., Dr. en MŽd. Paris; D. Sci. Cantab.; Knight of Grace of the Order of S. John of Jerusalem; Consulting Surgeon of St. Luke's Hospital, Battersea. *b.* Gryllingham, 16 March 1872, only son, of Edward Curzon Freke Esq. of Gryll Court, Gryllingham. Educ. Harrow and Trinity Coll. Cambridge; Col. A.M.S.; late Member of the Advisory Board of the Army Medical Service. *Publications*: Some Notes on the Pathological Aspects of Genius, 1892; Statistical Contributions to the Study of Infantile Paralysis in England and Wales, 1894; Functional Disturbances of the Nervous System, 1899; Cerebro-Spinal Diseases, 1904; The Borderland of Insanity, 1906; An Examination into the Treatment of Pauper Lunacy in the United Kingdom, 1906; Modern Developments in Psycho-Therapy: A Criticism, 1910; Criminal Lunacy, 1914; The Application of Psycho-Therapy to the Treatment of Shell-Shock, 1917; An Answer to Professor Freud, with a Description of Some Experiments Carried Out at the Base Hospital at Amiens, 1919; Structural Modifications Accompanying the More Important Neuroses, 1920. *Clubs*: White's; Oxford and Cambridge; Alpine, etc. *Recreations*: Chess, Mountaineering, Fishing. *Address*: 82, Harley Street and St. Luke's House, Prince of Wales Road, Battersea Park, S.W. 11."

He flung the book away. "Confirmation!" he groaned. "As if I needed it!"

He sat down again and buried his face in his hands. He remembered quite suddenly how, years ago, he had stood before the breakfast table at Denver Castle—a small, peaky boy in blue knickers, with a thunderously beating heart. The family had not come down; there was a great silver urn with a spirit lamp under it, and an elaborate coffee-pot boiling in a glass dome. He had twitched the corner of the tablecloth—twitched it harder, and the urn moved ponderously forward and all the teaspoons rattled. He seized the tablecloth in a firm grip and pulled his hardest—he could feel now the delicate and awful thrill as the urn and the coffee machine and the whole of a Sevres breakfast service had crashed down in one stupendous ruin—he remembered the horrified face of the butler, and the screams of a lady guest.

A log broke across and sank into a fluff of white ash. A belated motor-lorry rumbled past the window.

Mr. Bunter, sleeping the sleep of the true and faithful servant, was aroused in the small hours by a hoarse whisper, "Bunter!"

"Yes, my lord," said Bunter, sitting up and switching on the light.

"Put that light out, damn you!" said the voice. "Listen—over there—listen—can't you hear it?"

"It's nothing, my lord," said Mr. Bunter, hastily getting out of bed and catching hold of his master; "it's all right, you get to bed quick and I'll fetch you a drop of bromide. Why, you're all shivering—you've been sitting up too late."

"Hush! no, no—it's the water," said Lord Peter with chattering teeth, "it's up to their waists down there, poor devils. But listen! can't you hear it? Tap, tap, tap—they're mining us—but I don't know where—I can't hear—I can't. Listen, you! There it is again—we must find it—we must stop it . . . Listen! Oh, my God! I can't hear—I can't hear anything for the noise of the guns. Can't they stop the guns?"

"Oh, dear!" said Mr. Bunter to himself. "No, no—it's all right, Major—don't you worry."

"But I hear it," protested Peter.

"So do I," said Mr. Bunter stoutly; "very good hearing, too, my lord. That's our own sappers at work in the communication trench. Don't you fret about that, sir."

Lord Peter grasped his wrist with a feverish hand.

"Our own sappers," he said; "sure of that?"

"Certain of it," said Mr. Bunter, cheerfully.

"They'll bring down the tower," said Lord Peter.

"To be sure they will," said Mr. Bunter, "and very nice, too. You just come and lay down a bit, sir—they've come to take over this section."

"You're sure it's safe to leave it?" said Lord Peter.

"Safe as houses, sir," said Mr. Bunter, tucking his master's arm under his and walking him off to his bedroom.

Lord Peter allowed himself to be dosed and put to bed without further resistance. Mr. Bunter, looking singularly un-Bunterlike in striped pyjamas, with his stiff black hair ruffled about his head, sat grimly watching the younger man's sharp cheekbones and the purple stains under his eyes.

"Thought we'd had the last of these attacks," he said. "Been overdoin' of himself. Asleep?" He peered at him anxiously. An affectionate note crept into his voice. "Bloody little fool!" said Sergeant Bunter.

# CHAPTER 9

Mr. Parker, summoned the next morning to 110 Piccadilly, arrived to find the Dowager Duchess in possession. She greeted him charmingly.

"I am going to take this silly boy down to Denver for the week-end," she said, indicating Peter, who was writing and only acknowledged his friend's entrance with a brief nod. "He's been doing too much—running about to Salisbury and places and up till all hours of the night—you really shouldn't encourage him, Mr. Parker, it's very naughty of you—waking poor Bunter up in the middle of the night with scares about Germans, as if that wasn't all over years ago, and he hasn't had an attack for ages, but there! Nerves are such funny things, and Peter always did have nightmares when he was quite a little boy—though very often of course it was only a little pill he wanted; but he was so dreadfully bad in 1918, you know, and I suppose we can't expect to forget all about a great war in a year or two, and, really, I ought to be very thankful with both my boys safe. Still, I think a little peace and quiet at Denver won't do him any harm."

"Sorry you've been having a bad turn, old man," said Parker, vaguely sympathetic; "you're looking a bit seedy."

"Charles," said Lord Peter, in a voice entirely void of expression, "I am going away for a couple of days because I can be no use to you in London. What has got to be done for the moment can be much better done by you than by me. I want you to take this"—he folded up his writing and placed it in an envelope—"to Scotland Yard immediately and get it sent out to all the workhouses, infirmaries, police stations, Y. M. C. A.'s and so on in London. It is a description of Thipps's corpse as he was before he was shaved and cleaned up. I want to know whether any man answering to that description has been taken in anywhere, alive or dead, during the last fortnight. You will see Sir Andrew Mackenzie personally, and get the paper sent out at once, by his authority; you will tell him that you have solved the problems of the Levy murder and the Battersea mystery"—Mr. Parker made an astonished noise to which his friend paid no attention—"and you will ask him to have men in readiness with a warrant to arrest a very dangerous and important criminal at any moment on your information. When the replies to this paper come in, you will search for any mention of St. Luke's Hospital, or of any person connected with St. Luke's Hospital, and you will send for me at once.

"Meanwhile you will scrape acquaintance—I don't care how—with one of the students at St. Luke's. Don't march in there blowing about murders and police warrants, or you may find yourself in Queer Street. I shall come up to town as soon as I hear from you, and I shall expect to find a nice ingenuous Sawbones here to meet me." He grinned faintly.

"D'you mean you've got to the bottom of this thing?" asked Parker.

"Yes. I may be wrong. I hope I am, but I know I'm not."

"You won't tell me?"

"D'you know," said Peter, "honestly I'd rather not. I say I may be wrong—and I'd feel as if I'd libelled the Archbishop of Canterbury."

"Well, tell me—is it one mystery or two?"

"One."

"You talked of the Levy murder. Is Levy dead?"

"God—yes!" said Peter, with a strong shudder.

The Duchess looked up from where she was reading the *Tatler*.

"Peter," she said, "is that your ague coming on again? Whatever you two are chattering about, you'd better stop it at once if it excites you. Besides, it's about time to be off."

"All right, Mother," said Peter. He turned to Bunter, standing respectfully in the door with an overcoat and suitcase. "You understand what you have to do, don't you?" he said.

"Perfectly, thank you, my lord. The car is just arriving, your Grace."

"With Mrs. Thipps inside it," said the Duchess. "She'll be delighted to see you again, Peter. You remind her so of Mr. Thipps. Good-morning, Bunter."

"Good-morning, your Grace."

Parker accompanied them downstairs.

When they had gone he looked blankly at the paper in his hand—then, remembering that it was Saturday and there was need for haste, he hailed a taxi.

"Scotland Yard!" he cried.

Tuesday morning saw Lord Peter and a man in a velveteen jacket swishing merrily through seven acres of turnip-tops, streaked yellow with early frosts. A little way ahead, a sinuous undercurrent of excitement among the leaves proclaimed the unseen yet ever-near presence of one of the Duke of Denver's setter pups. Presently a partridge flew up with a noise like a police rattle, and Lord Peter accounted for it very creditably for a man who, a few nights before, had been listening to imaginary German sappers. The setter bounded foolishly through the turnips, and fetched back the dead bird.

"Good dog," said Lord Peter.

Encouraged by this, the dog gave a sudden ridiculous gambol and barked, its ear tossed inside out over its head.

"Heel," said the man in velveteen, violently. The animal sidled up, ashamed.

"Fool of a dog, that," said the man in velveteen; "can't keep quiet. Too nervous, my lord. One of old Black Lass's pups."

"Dear me," said Peter, "is the old dog still going?"

"No, my lord; we had to put her away in the spring."

Peter nodded. He always proclaimed that he hated the country and was thankful to have nothing to do with the family estates, but this morning he enjoyed the crisp air and the wet leaves washing darkly over his polished boots. At Denver things moved in an orderly way; no one died sudden and violent deaths except aged setters—and partridges, to be sure. He sniffed up the autumn smell with appreciation. There was a letter in his pocket which had come by the morning post, but he did not intend to read it just yet. Parker had not wired; there was no hurry.

\* \* \*

He read it in the smoking-room after lunch. His brother was there, dozing over the *Times*—a good, clean Englishman, sturdy and conventional, rather like Henry VIII in his youth; Gerald, sixteenth Duke of Denver. The Duke considered his cadet rather degenerate, and not quite good form; he disliked his taste for police-court news.

The letter was from Mr. Bunter.

110, Piccadilly,

W.I.

My Lord:

I write (Mr. Bunter had been carefully educated and knew that nothing is more vulgar than a careful avoidance of beginning a letter with the first person singular) as your lordship directed, to inform you of the result of my investigations.

I experienced no difficulty in becoming acquainted with Sir Julian Freke's man-servant. He belongs to the same club as the Hon. Frederick Arbuthnot's man, who is a friend of mine, and was very willing to introduce me. He took me to the club yesterday (Sunday) evening, and we dined with the man, whose name is John Cummings, and afterwards I invited Cummings to drinks and a cigar in the flat. Your lordship will excuse me doing this, knowing that it is not my habit, but it has always been my experience that the best way to gain a man's confidence is to let him suppose that one takes advantage of one's employer.

("I always suspected Bunter of being a student of human nature," commented Lord Peter.)

I gave him the best old port ("The deuce you did," said Lord Peter), having heard you and Mr. Arbuthnot talk over it. ("Hum!" said Lord Peter.)

Its effects were quite equal to my expectations as regards the principal matter in hand, but I very much regret to state that the man had so little understanding of what was offered to him that he smoked a cigar with it (one of your lordship's Villar Villars). You will understand that I made no comment on this at the time, but your lordship will sympathize with my feelings. May I take this opportunity of expressing my grateful appreciation of your lordship's excellent taste in food, drink and dress? It is, if I may say so, more than a pleasure—it is an education, to valet and buttle your lordship.

Lord Peter bowed his head gravely.

"What on earth are you doing, Peter, sittin' there noddin' an' grinnin' like a what-you-may-call-it?" demanded the Duke, coming suddenly out of a snooze. "Someone writin' pretty things to you, what?"

"Charming things," said Lord Peter.

The Duke eyed him doubtfully.

"Hope to goodness you don't go and marry a chorus beauty," he muttered inwardly, and returned to the *Times*.

Over dinner I had set myself to discover Cummings's tastes, and found them to run in the direction of the music-hall stage. During his first glass I drew him out in this direction, your lordship having kindly given me opportunities of seeing every performance in London, and I spoke more freely than I should consider becoming in the ordinary way in order to make myself pleasant to him. I may say that his views on women and the stage were such as I should have expected from a man who would smoke with your lordship's port.

With the second glass I introduced the subject of your lordship's enquiries. In order to save time I will write our conversation in the form of a dialogue, as nearly as possible as it actually took place.

*Cummings:* You seem to get many opportunities of seeing a bit of life, Mr. Bunter.

*Bunter:* One can always make opportunities if one knows how.

*Cummings:* Ah, it's very easy for you to talk, Mr. Bunter. You're not married, for one thing.

*Bunter:* I know better than that, Mr. Cummings.

*Cummings:* So do I—now, when it's too late. (He sighed heavily, and I filled up his glass.)

*Bunter:* Does Mrs. Cummings live with you at Battersea?

*Cummings:* Yes; her and me we do for my governor. Such a life! Not but what there's a char comes in by the day. But what's a char? I can tell you it's dull all by ourselves in that d—d Battersea suburb.

*Bunter:* Not very convenient for the Halls, of course.

*Cummings:* I believe you. It's all right for you, here in Piccadilly, right on the spot as you might say. And I daresay your governor's often out all night, eh?

*Bunter:* Oh, frequently, Mr. Cummings.

*Cummings:* And I daresay you take the opportunity to slip off yourself every so often, eh?

*Bunter:* Well, what do you think, Mr. Cummings?

*Cummings:* That's it; there you are! But what's a man to do with a nagging fool of a wife and a blasted scientific doctor for a governor, as sits up all night cutting up dead bodies and experimenting with frogs?

*Bunter:* Surely he goes out sometimes.

*Cummings:* Not often. And always back before twelve. And the way he goes on if he rings the bell and you ain't there. I give you my word, Mr. Bunter.

*Bunter:* Temper?

*Cummings:* No-o-o—but looking through you, nasty-like, as if you was on that operating table of his and he was going to cut you up. Nothing a man could rightly complain of, you understand, Mr. Bunter, just nasty looks. Not but what I will say he's very correct. Apologizes if he's been inconsiderate. But what's the good of that when he's been and gone and lost you your nights rest?

*Bunter:* How does he do that? Keeps you up late, you mean?

*Cummings:* Not him; far from it. House locked up and household to bed at half past ten. That's his little rule. Not but what I'm glad enough to go as a rule, it's that dreary. Still, when I do go to bed I like to go to sleep.

*Bunter:* What does he do? Walk about the house?

*Cummings:* Doesn't he? All night. And in and out of the private door to the hospital.

*Bunter:* You don't mean to say, Mr. Cummings, a great specialist like Sir Julian Freke does night work at the hospital?

*Cummings:* No, no; he does his own work—research work, as you may say. Cuts people up. They say he's very clever. Could take you or me to pieces like a clock, Mr. Bunter, and put us together again.

*Bunter:* Do you sleep in the basement, then, to hear him so plain?

*Cummings:* No; our bedroom's at the top. But, Lord! what's that? He'll bang the door so you can hear him all over the house.

*Bunter:* Ah, many's the time I've had to speak to Lord Peter about that. And talking all night. And baths.

*Cummings:* Baths? You may well say that, Mr. Bunter. Baths? Me and my wife sleep next to the cistern-room. Noise fit to wake the dead. All hours. When d'you think he chose to have a bath, no later than last Monday night, Mr. Bunter?

*Bunter:* I've known them to do it at two in the morning, Mr. Cummings.

*Cummings:* Have you, now? Well, this was at three. Three o'clock in the morning we was waked up. I give you my word.

*Bunter:* You don't say so, Mr. Cummings.

*Cummings:* He cuts up diseases, you see, Mr. Bunter, and then he don't like to go to bed till he's washed the bacilluses off, if you understand me. Very natural, too, I daresay. But what I say is, the middle of the night's no time for a gentleman to be occupying his mind with diseases.

*Bunter:* These great men have their own way of doing things.

*Cummings:* Well, all I can say is, it isn't my way.

(I could believe that, your lordship. Cummings has no signs of greatness about him, and his trousers are not what I would wish to see in a man of his profession.)

*Bunter:* Is he habitually as late as that, Mr. Cummings?

*Cummings:* Well, no, Mr. Bunter, I will say, not as a general rule. He apologized, too, in the morning, and said he would have the cistern seen to—and very necessary, in my opinion, for the air gets into the pipes, and the groaning and screeching as goes on is something awful. Just like Niagara, if you follow me, Mr. Bunter, I give you my word.

*Bunter:* Well, that's as it should be, Mr. Cummings. One can put up with a great deal from a gentleman that has the manners to apologize. And, of course, sometimes they can't help themselves. A visitor will come in unexpectedly and keep them late, perhaps.

*Cummings:* That's true enough, Mr. Bunter. Now I come to think of it, there was a gentleman come in on Monday evening. Not that he came late, but he stayed about an hour, and may have put Sir Julian behindhand.

*Bunter:* Very likely. Let me give you some more port, Mr. Cummings. Or a little of Lord Peter's old brandy.

*Cummings:* A little of the brandy, thank you, Mr. Bunter. I suppose you have the run of the cellar here. (He winked at me.)

"Trust me for that," I said, and I fetched him the Napoleon. I assure your lordship it went to my heart to pour it out for a man like that. However, seeing we had got on the right tack, I felt it wouldn't be wasted.

"I'm sure I wish it was always gentlemen that come here at night," I said. (Your lordship will excuse me, I am sure, making such a suggestion.)

("Good God," said Lord Peter, "I wish Bunter was less thorough in his methods.")

*Cummings:* Oh, he's that sort, his lordship, is he? (He chuckled and poked me. I suppress a portion of his conversation here, which could not fail to be as offensive to your lordship as it was to myself. He went on:) No, it's none of that with Sir Julian. Very few visitors at night, and always gentlemen. And going early as a rule, like the one I mentioned.

*Bunter:* Just as well. There's nothing I find more wearisome, Mr. Cummings, than sitting up to see visitors out.

*Cummings:* Oh, I didn't see this one out. Sir Julian let him out himself at ten o'clock or thereabouts. I heard the gentleman shout "Good-night" and off he goes.

*Bunter:* Does Sir Julian always do that?

*Cummings:* Well, that depends. If he sees visitors downstairs, he lets them out himself; if he sees them upstairs in the library, he rings for me.

*Bunter:* This was a downstairs visitor, then?

*Cummings:* Oh, yes. Sir Julian opened the door to him, I remember. He happened to be working in the hall. Though now I come to think of it, they went up to the library afterwards. That's funny. I know they did, because I happened to go up to the hall with coals, and I heard them upstairs. Besides, Sir Julian rang for me in the library a few minutes later. Still, anyway, we heard him go at ten, or it may have been a bit before. He hadn't only stayed about three-quarters of an hour. However, as I was saying, there was Sir Julian banging in and out of the private door all night, and a bath at three in the morning, and up again for breakfast at eight—it beats me. If I had all his money, curse me if I'd go poking about with dead men in the middle of the night. If it was a nice live girl, now, Mr. Bunter—

I need not repeat any more of his conversation, as it became unpleasant and incoherent, and I could not bring him back to the events of Monday night. I was unable to get rid of him till three. He cried on my neck, and said I was the bird, and you were the governor for him. He said that Sir Julian would be greatly annoyed with him for coming home so late, but Sunday night was his night out and if anything was said about it he would give notice. I think he will be ill-advised to do so, as I feel he is not a man I could conscientiously recommend if I were in Sir Julian Freke's place. I noticed that his boot-heels were slightly worn down.

I should wish to add, as a tribute to the great merits of your lordship's cellar, that, although I was obliged to drink a somewhat large quantity both of the Cockburn '68 and the 1800 Napoleon I feel no headache or other ill effects this morning.

Trusting that your lordship is deriving real benefit from the country air, and that the little information I have been able to obtain will prove satisfactory, I remain,

With respectful duty to all the family, their ladyships,

Obediently yours,

MERVYN BUNTER.

"Y'know," said Lord Peter thoughtfully to himself, "I sometimes think Mervyn Bunter's pullin' my leg. What is it, Soames?"

"A telegram, my lord."

"Parker," said Lord Peter, opening it. It said:

"Description recognized Chelsea Workhouse. Unknown vagrant injured street accident Wednesday week. Died workhouse Monday. Delivered St. Luke's same evening by order Freke. Much puzzled. Parker."

"Hurray!" said Lord Peter, suddenly sparkling. "I'm glad I've puzzled Parker. Gives me confidence in myself. Makes me feel like Sherlock Holmes. 'Perfectly simple, Watson.' Dash it all, though! this is a beastly business. Still, it's puzzled Parker."

"What's the matter?" asked the Duke, getting up and yawning.

"Marching orders," said Peter, "back to town. Many thanks for your hospitality, old bird—I'm feelin' no end better. Ready to tackle Professor Moriarty or Leon Kestrel or any of 'em."

"I do wish you'd keep out of the police courts," grumbled the Duke. "It makes it so dashed awkward for me, havin' a brother makin' himself conspicuous."

"Sorry, Gerald," said the other, "I know I'm a beastly blot on the 'scutcheon."

"Why can't you marry and settle down and live quietly, doin' something useful?" said the Duke unappeased.

"Because that was a wash-out as you perfectly well know," said Peter; "besides," he added cheerfully, "I'm bein' no end useful. You may come to want me yourself, you never know. When anybody comes blackmailin' you, Gerald, or your first deserted wife turns up unexpectedly from the West Indies, you'll realize the pull of havin' a private detective in the family. 'Delicate private business arranged with tact and discretion. Investigations undertaken. Divorce evidence a specialty. Every guarantee!' Come, now."

"Ass!" said Lord Denver, throwing the newspaper violently into his armchair. "When do you want the car?"

"Almost at once. I say, Jerry, I'm taking Mother up with me."

"Why should she be mixed up in it?"

"Well, I want her help."

"I call it most unsuitable," said the Duke.

The Dowager Duchess, however, made no objection.

"I used to know her quite well," she said, "when she was Christine Ford. Why, dear?"

"Because," said Lord Peter, "there's a terrible piece of news to be broken to her about her husband."

"Is he dead, dear?"

"Yes; and she will have to come and identify him."

"Poor Christine."

"Under very revolting circumstances, Mother."

"I'll come with you, dear."

"Thank you, Mother, you're a brick. D'you mind gettin' your things on straight away and comin' up with me? I'll tell you about it in the car."

# CHAPTER 10

   Mr. Parker, a faithful though doubting Thomas, had duly secured his medical student: a large young man like an overgrown puppy, with innocent eyes and a freckled face. He sat on the Chesterfield before Lord Peter's library fire, bewildered in equal measure by his errand, his surroundings and the drink which he was absorbing. His palate, though untutored, was naturally a good one, and he realized that even to call this liquid a drink—the term ordinarily used by him to designate cheap whisky, post-war beer or a dubious glass of claret in a Soho restaurant—was a sacrilege; this was something outside normal experience: a genie in a bottle.

   The man called Parker, whom he had happened to run across the evening before in the public-house at the corner of Prince of Wales Road, seemed to be a good sort. He had insisted on bringing him round to see this friend of his, who lived splendidly in Piccadilly. Parker was quite understandable; he put him down as a government servant, or perhaps something in the City. The friend was embarrassing; he was a lord, to begin with, and his clothes were a kind of rebuke to the world at large. He talked the most fatuous nonsense, certainly, but in a disconcerting way. He didn't dig into a joke and get all the fun out of it; he made it in passing, so to speak, and skipped away to something else before your retort was ready. He had a truly terrible manservant—the sort you read about in books—who froze the marrow in your bones with silent criticism. Parker appeared to bear up under the strain, and this made you think more highly of Parker; he must be more habituated to the surroundings of the great than you would think to look at him. You wondered what the carpet had cost on which Parker was carelessly spilling cigar ash; your father was an upholsterer—Mr. Piggott, of Piggott & Piggott, Liverpool—and you knew enough about carpets to know that you couldn't even guess at the price of this one. When you moved your head on the bulging silk cushion in the corner of the sofa, it made you wish you shaved more often and more carefully. The sofa was a monster—but even so, it hardly seemed big enough to contain you. This Lord Peter was not very tall—in fact, he was rather a small man, but he didn't look undersized. He looked right; he made you feel that to be six-foot-three was rather vulgarly assertive; you felt like Mother's new drawing-room curtains—all over great, big blobs. But everybody was very decent to you, and nobody said anything you couldn't understand, or sneered at you. There were some frightfully deep-looking books on the shelves all round, and you had looked into a great folio Dante which was lying on the table, but your hosts were talking

quite ordinarily and rationally about the sort of books you read
yourself—clinking good love stories and detective stories. You had read
a lot of those, and could give an opinion, and they listened to what you
had to say, though Lord Peter had a funny way of talking about books,
too, as if the author had confided in him beforehand, and told him how
the story was put together, and which bit was written first. It reminded
you of the way old Freke took a body to pieces.

"Thing I object to in detective stories," said Mr. Piggott, "is the way
fellows remember every bloomin' thing that's happened to 'em within
the last six months. They're always ready with their time of day and
was it rainin' or not, and what were they doin' on such an' such a day.
Reel it all off like a page of poetry. But one ain't like that in real life,
d'you think so, Lord Peter?" Lord Peter smiled, and young Piggott,
instantly embarrassed, appealed to his earlier acquaintance. "You
know what I mean, Parker. Come now. One day's so like another, I'm
sure I couldn't remember—well, I might remember yesterday, p'r'aps,
but I couldn't be certain about what I was doin' last week if I was to be
shot for it."

"No," said Parker, "and evidence given in police statements sounds
just as impossible. But they don't really get it like that, you know. I
mean, a man doesn't just say, 'Last Friday I went out at ten o'clock a.
m. to buy a mutton chop. As I was turning into Mortimer Street I
noticed a girl of about twenty-two with black hair and brown eyes,
wearing a green jumper, check skirt, Panama hat and black shoes
riding a Royal Sunbeam Cycle at about ten miles an hour turning the
corner by the Church of St. Simon and St. Jude on the wrong side of
the road riding towards the market place!' It amounts to that, of
course, but it's really wormed out of him by a series of questions."

"And in short stories," said Lord Peter, "it has to be put in
statement form, because the real conversation would be so long and
twaddly and tedious, and nobody would have the patience to read it.
Writers have to consider their readers, if any, y'see."

"Yes," said Mr. Piggott, "but I bet you most people would find it
jolly difficult to remember, even if you asked 'em things. I should—of
course, I know I'm a bit of a fool, but then, most people are, ain't they?
You know what I mean. Witnesses ain't detectives, they're just average
idiots like you and me."

"Quite so," said Lord Peter, smiling as the force of the last phrase
sank into its unhappy perpetrator; "you mean, if I were to ask you in a
general way what you were doin'—say, a week ago to-day, you wouldn't
be able to tell me a thing about it offhand."

"No—I'm sure I shouldn't." He considered. "No. I was in at the
Hospital as usual, I suppose, and, being Tuesday, there'd be a lecture
on something or the other—dashed if I know what—and in the evening

I went out with Tommy Pringle—no, that must have been Monday—or was it Wednesday? I tell you, I couldn't swear to anything."

"You do yourself an injustice," said Lord Peter gravely. "I'm sure, for instance, you recollect what work you were doing in the dissecting-room on that day, for example."

"Lord, no! not for certain. I mean, I daresay it might come back to me if I thought for a long time, but I wouldn't swear to it in a court of law."

"I'll bet you half a crown to sixpence," said Lord Peter, "that you'll remember within five minutes."

"I'm sure I can't."

"We'll see. Do you keep a notebook of the work you do when you dissect? Drawings or anything?"

"Oh, yes."

"Think of that. What's the last thing you did in it?"

"That's easy, because I only did it this morning. It was leg muscles."

"Yes. Who was the subject?"

"An old woman of sorts; died of pneumonia."

"Yes. Turn back the pages of your drawing-book in your mind. What came before that?"

"Oh, some animals—still legs; I'm doing motor muscles at present. Yes. That was old Cunningham's demonstration on comparative anatomy. I did rather a good thing of a hare's legs and a frog's, and rudimentary legs on a snake."

"Yes. Which day does Mr. Cunningham lecture?"

"Friday."

"Friday; yes. Turn back again. What comes before that?"

Mr. Piggott shook his head.

"Do your drawings of legs begin on the right-hand page or the left-hand page? Can you see the first drawing?"

"Yes—yes—I can see the date written at the top. It's a section of a frog's hind leg, on the right-hand page."

"Yes. Think of the open book in your mind's eye. What is opposite to it?"

This demanded some mental concentration.

"Something round—coloured—oh, yes—it's a hand."

"Yes. You went on from the muscles of the hand and arm to leg- and foot-muscles?"

"Yes; that's right. I've got a set of drawings of arms."

"Yes. Did you make those on the Thursday?"

"No; I'm never in the dissecting-room on Thursday."

"On Wednesday, perhaps?"

"Yes; I must have made them on Wednesday. Yes; I did. I went in there after we'd seen those tetanus patients in the morning. I did them on Wednesday afternoon. I know I went back because I wanted to finish 'em. I worked rather hard—for me. That's why I remember."

"Yes; you went back to finish them. When had you begun them, then?"

"Why, the day before."

"The day before. That was Tuesday, wasn't it?"

"I've lost count—yes, the day before Wednesday—yes, Tuesday."

"Yes. Were they a man's arms or a woman's arms?"

"Oh, a man's arms."

"Yes; last Tuesday, a week ago to-day, you were dissecting a man's arms in the dissecting-room. Sixpence, please."

"By Jove!"

"Wait a moment. You know a lot more about it than that. You've no idea how much you know. You know what kind of man he was."

"Oh, I never saw him complete, you know. I got there a bit late that day, I remember. I'd asked for an arm specially, because I was rather weak in arms, and Watts—that's the attendant—had promised to save me one."

"Yes. You have arrived late and found your arm waiting for you. You are dissecting it—taking your scissors and slitting up the skin and pinning it back. Was it very young, fair skin?"

"Oh, no—no. Ordinary skin, I think—with dark hairs on it—yes, that was it."

"Yes. A lean, stringy arm, perhaps, with no extra fat anywhere?"

"Oh, no—I was rather annoyed about that. I wanted a good, muscular arm, but it was rather poorly developed and the fat got in my way."

"Yes; a sedentary man who didn't do much manual work."

"That's right."

"Yes. You dissected the hand, for instance, and made a drawing of it. You would have noticed any hard calluses."

"Oh, there was nothing of that sort."

"No. But should you say it was a young man's arm? Firm young flesh and limber joints?"

"No—no."

"No. Old and stringy, perhaps."

"No. Middle-aged—with rheumatism. I mean, there was a chalky deposit in the joints, and the fingers were a bit swollen."

"Yes. A man about fifty."

"About that."

"Yes. There were other students at work on the same body."

"Oh, yes."

"Yes. And they made all the usual sort of jokes about it."

"I expect so—oh, yes!"

"You can remember some of them. Who is your local funny man, so to speak?"

"Tommy Pringle."

"What was Tommy Pringle doing?"

"Can't remember."

"Whereabouts was Tommy Pringle working?"

"Over by the instrument-cupboard—by sink C."

"Yes. Get a picture of Tommy Pringle in your mind's eye."

Piggott began to laugh.

"I remember now. Tommy Pringle said the old Sheeny—"

"Why did he call him a Sheeny?"

"I don't know. But I know he did."

"Perhaps he looked like it. Did you see his head?"

"No."

"Who had the head?"

"I don't know—oh, yes, I do, though. Old Freke bagged the head himself, and little Bouncible Binns was very cross about it, because he'd been promised a head to do with old Scrooger."

"I see; what was Sir Julian doing with the head?"

"He called us up and gave us a jaw on spinal hemorrhage and nervous lesions."

"Yes. Well, go back to Tommy Pringle."

Tommy Pringle's joke was repeated, not without some embarrassment.

"Quite so. Was that all?"

"No. The chap who was working with Tommy said that sort of thing came from overfeeding."

"I deduce that Tommy Pringle's partner was interested in the alimentary canal."

"Yes; and Tommy said, if he'd thought they'd feed you like that he'd go to the workhouse himself."

"Then the man was a pauper from the workhouse."

"Well, he must have been, I suppose."

"Are workhouse paupers usually fat and well-fed?"

"Well, no—come to think of it, not as a rule."

"In fact, it struck Tommy Pringle and his friend that this was something a little out of the way in a workhouse subject?"

"Yes."

"And if the alimentary canal was so entertaining to these gentlemen, I imagine the subject had come by his death shortly after a full meal."

"Yes—oh, yes—he'd have had to, wouldn't he?"

"Well, I don't know," said Lord Peter. "That's in your department, you know. That would be your inference, from what they said."

"Oh, yes. Undoubtedly."

"Yes, you wouldn't, for example, expect them to make that observation if the patient had been ill for a long time and fed on slops."

"Of course not."

"Well, you see, you really know a lot about it. On Tuesday week you were dissecting the arm muscles of a rheumatic middle-aged Jew, of sedentary habits, who had died shortly after eating a heavy meal, of some injury producing spinal hemorrhage and nervous lesions, and so forth, and who was presumed to come from the workhouse."

"Yes."

"And you could swear to those facts, if need were?"

"Well, if you put it that way, I suppose I could."

"Of course you could."

Mr. Piggott sat for some moments in contemplation.

"I say," he said at last, "I did know all that, didn't I?"

"Oh, yes—you knew it all right—like Socrates's slave."

"Who's he?"

"A person in a book I used to read as a boy."

"Oh—does he come in 'The Last Days of Pompeii'?"

"No—another book—I daresay you escaped it. It's rather dull."

"I never read much except Henty and Fenimore Cooper at school.... But—have I got rather an extra good memory, then?"

"You have a better memory than you credit yourself with."

"Then why can't I remember all the medical stuff? It all goes out of my head like a sieve."

"Well, why can't you?" said Lord Peter, standing on the hearthrug and smiling down at his guest.

"Well," said the young man, "the chaps who examine one don't ask the same sort of questions you do."

"No?"

"No—they leave you to remember all by yourself. And it's beastly hard. Nothing to catch hold of, don't you know? But, I say—how did you know about Tommy Pringle being the funny man and—"

"I didn't, till you told me."

"No; I know. But how did you know he'd be there if you did ask? I mean to say—I say," said Mr. Piggott, who was becoming mellowed by influences themselves not unconnected with the alimentary canal—"I say, are you rather clever, or am I rather stupid?"

"No, no," said Lord Peter, "it's me. I'm always askin' such stupid questions, everybody thinks I must mean somethin' by 'em."

This was too involved for Mr. Piggott.

"Never mind," said Parker, soothingly, "he's always like that. You mustn't take any notice. He can't help it. It's premature senile decay, often observed in the families of hereditary legislators. Go away, Wimsey, and play us the 'Beggar's Opera,' or something."

"That's good enough, isn't it?" said Lord Peter, when the happy Mr. Piggott had been despatched home after a really delightful evening.

"I'm afraid so," said Parker. "But it seems almost incredible."

"There's nothing incredible in human nature," said Lord Peter; "at least, in educated human nature. Have you got that exhumation order?"

"I shall have it to-morrow. I thought of fixing up with the workhouse people for to-morrow afternoon. I shall have to go and see them first."

"Right you are; I'll let my mother know."

"I begin to feel like you, Wimsey, I don't like this job."

"I like it a deal better than I did."

"You are really certain we're not making a mistake?"

Lord Peter had strolled across to the window. The curtain was not perfectly drawn, and he stood gazing out through the gap into lighted Piccadilly. At this he turned round:

"If we are," he said, "we shall know to-morrow, and no harm will have been done. But I rather think you will receive a certain amount of confirmation on your way home. Look here, Parker, d'you know, if I were you I'd spend the night here. There's a spare bedroom; I can easily put you up."

Parker stared at him.

"Do you mean—I'm likely to be attacked?"

"I think it very likely indeed."

"Is there anybody in the street?"

"Not now; there was half an hour ago."

"When Piggott left?"

"Yes."

"I say—I hope the boy is in no danger."

"That's what I went down to see. I don't think so. Fact is, I don't suppose anybody would imagine we'd exactly made a confidant of Piggott. But I think you and I are in danger. You'll stay?"

"I'm damned if I will, Wimsey; why should I run away?"

"Bosh!" said Peter, "you'd run away all right if you believed me, and why not? You don't believe me. In fact, you're still not certain I'm on the right tack. Go in peace, but don't say I didn't warn you."

"I won't; I'll dictate a message with my dying breath to say I was convinced."

"Well, don't walk—take a taxi."

"Very well, I'll do that."

"And don't let anybody else get into it."

"No."

It was a raw, unpleasant night. A taxi deposited a load of people returning from the theatre at the block of flats next door, and Parker secured it for himself. He was just giving the address to the driver, when a man came hastily running up from a side street. He was in evening dress and an overcoat. He rushed up, signalling frantically.

"Sir—sir!—dear me! why, it's Mr. Parker! How fortunate! If you would be so kind—summoned from the club—a sick friend—can't find a taxi—everybody going home from the theatre—if I might share your cab—you are returning to Bloomsbury? I want Russell Square—if I might presume—a matter of life and death."

He spoke in hurried gasps, as though he had been running violently and far. Parker promptly stepped out of the taxi.

"Delighted to be of service to you, Sir Julian," he said; "take my taxi. I am going down to Craven Street myself, but I'm in no hurry. Pray make use of the cab."

"It's extremely kind of you," said the surgeon. "I am ashamed—"

"That's all right," said Parker, cheerily. "I can wait." He assisted Freke into the taxi. "What number? 24 Russell Square, driver, and look sharp."

The taxi drove off. Parker remounted the stairs and rang Lord Peter's bell.

"Thanks, old man," he said. "I'll stop the night, after all."

"Come in," said Wimsey.

"Did you see that?" asked Parker.

"I saw something. What happened exactly?"

Parker told his story. "Frankly," he said, "I've been thinking you a bit mad, but now I'm not quite so sure of it."

Peter laughed.

"Blessed are they that have not seen and yet have believed. Bunter, Mr. Parker will stay the night."

"Look here, Wimsey, let's have another look at this business. Where's that letter?"

Lord Peter produced Bunter's essay in dialog. Parker studied it for a short time in silence.

"You know, Wimsey, I'm as full of objections to this idea as an egg is of meat."

"So'm I, old son. That's why I want to dig up our Chelsea pauper. But trot out your objections."

"Well—"

"Well, look here, I don't pretend to be able to fill in all the blanks myself. But here we have two mysterious occurrences in one night, and a complete chain connecting the one with another through one particular person. It's beastly, but it's not unthinkable."

"Yes, I know all that. But there are one or two quite definite stumbling-blocks."

"Yes, I know. But, see here. On the one hand, Levy disappeared after being last seen looking for Prince of Wales Road at nine o'clock. At eight next morning a dead man, not unlike him in general outline, is discovered in a bath in Queen Caroline Mansions. Levy, by Freke's own admission, was going to see Freke. By information received from Chelsea workhouse a dead man, answering to the description of the Battersea corpse in its natural state, was delivered that same day to Freke. We have Levy with a past, and no future, as it were; an unknown vagrant with a future (in the cemetery) and no past, and Freke stands between their future and their past."

"That looks all right—"

"Yes. Now, further: Freke has a motive for getting rid of Levy—an old jealousy."

"Very old—and not much of a motive."

"People have been known to do that sort of thing.* You're thinking that people don't keep up old jealousies for twenty years or so. Perhaps not. Not just primitive, brute jealousy. That means a word and a blow. But the thing that rankles is hurt vanity. That sticks. Humiliation. And we've all got a sore spot we don't like to have touched. I've got it. You've got it. Some blighter said hell knew no fury like a woman scorned. Stickin' it on to women, poor devils. Sex is every man's loco spot—you needn't fidget, you know it's true—he'll take a disappointment, but not a humiliation. I knew a man once who'd been turned down—not too charitably—by a girl he was engaged to. He spoke quite decently about her. I asked what had become of her. 'Oh,' he said, 'she married the other fellow.' And then burst out—couldn't help himself. 'Lord, yes!' he cried. 'I think of it—jilted for a Scotchman!' I don't know why he didn't like Scots, but that was what got him on the raw. Look at Freke. I've read his books. His attacks on his antagonists are savage. And he's a scientist. Yet he can't bear opposition, even in his work, which is where any first-class man is most sane and open-minded. Do you think he's a man to take a beating from any man on a side-issue? On a man's most sensitive side-issue? People are opinionated about side-issues, you know. I see red if anybody questions my judgment about a book. And Levy—who was nobody twenty years ago—romps in and carries off Freke's girl from under his nose. It isn't the girl Freke would bother about—it's having his aristocratic nose put out of joint by a little Jewish nobody.

"There's another thing. Freke's got another side-issue. He likes crime. In that criminology book of his he gloats over a hardened murderer. I've read it, and I've seen the admiration simply glaring out between the lines whenever he writes about a callous and successful criminal. He reserves his contempt for the victims or the penitents or the men who lose their heads and get found out. His heroes are Edmond de la Pommerais, who persuaded his mistress into becoming an accessory to her own murder, and George Joseph Smith of Brides-in-a-bath fame, who could make passionate love to his wife in the night and carry out his plot to murder her in the morning. After all, he thinks conscience is a sort of vermiform appendix. Chop it out and you'll feel all the better. Freke isn't troubled by the usual conscientious deterrent. Witness his own hand in his books. Now again. The man who went to Levy's house in his place knew the house: Freke knew the house; he was a red-haired man, smaller than Levy, but not much smaller, since he could wear his clothes without appearing ludicrous: you have seen Freke—you know his height—about five-foot-eleven, I suppose, and his auburn mane; he probably wore surgical gloves: Freke is a surgeon; he was a methodical and daring man: surgeons are obliged to be both daring and methodical. Now take the other side. The man who got hold of the Battersea corpse had to have access to dead bodies. Freke obviously had access to dead bodies. He had to be cool and quick and callous about handling a dead body. Surgeons are all that. He had to be a strong man to carry the body across the roofs and dump it in at Thipps's window. Freke is a powerful man and a member of the Alpine Club. He probably wore surgical gloves and he let the body down from the roof with a surgical bandage. This points to a surgeon again. He undoubtedly lived in the neighbourhood. Freke lives next door. The girl you interviewed heard a bump on the roof of the end house. That is the house next to Freke's. Every time we look at Freke, he leads somewhere, whereas Milligan and Thipps and Crimplesham and all the other people we've honoured with our suspicion simply led nowhere."

"Yes; but it's not quite so simple as you make out. What was Levy doing in that surreptitious way at Freke's on Monday night?"

"Well, you have Freke's explanation."

"Rot, Wimsey. You said yourself it wouldn't do."

"Excellent. It won't do. Therefore Freke was lying. Why should he lie about it, unless he had some object in hiding the truth?"

"Well, but why mention it at all?"

"Because Levy, contrary to all expectation, had been seen at the corner of the road. That was a nasty accident for Freke. He thought it best to be beforehand with an explanation—of sorts. He reckoned, of course, on nobody's ever connecting Levy with Battersea Park."

"Well, then, we come back to the first question: Why did Levy go there?"

"I don't know, but he was got there somehow. Why did Freke buy all those Peruvian Oil shares?"

"I don't know," said Parker in his turn.

"Anyway," went on Wimsey, "Freke expected him, and made arrangement to let him in himself, so that Cummings shouldn't see who the caller was."

"But the caller left again at ten."

"Oh, Charles! I did not expect this of you. This is the purest Suggery! Who saw him go? Somebody said 'Good-night' and walked away down the street. And you believe it was Levy because Freke didn't go out of his way to explain that it wasn't."

"D'you mean that Freke walked cheerfully out of the house to Park Lane, and left Levy behind—dead or alive—for Cummings to find?"

"We have Cummings's word that he did nothing of the sort. A few minutes after the steps walked away from the house, Freke rang the library bell and told Cummings to shut up for the night."

"Then—"

"Well—there's a side door to the house, I suppose—in fact, you know there is—Cummings said so—through the hospital."

"Yes—well, where was Levy?"

"Levy went up into the library and never came down. You've been in Freke's library. Where would you have put him?"

"In my bedroom next door."

"Then that's where he did put him."

"But suppose the man went in to turn down the bed?"

"Beds are turned down by the housekeeper, earlier than ten o'clock."

"Yes... But Cummings heard Freke about the house all night."

"He heard him go in and out two or three times. He'd expect him to do that, anyway."

"Do you mean to say Freke got all that job finished before three in the morning?"

"Why not?"

"Quick work."

"Well, call it quick work. Besides, why three? Cummings never saw him again till he called him for eight o'clock breakfast."

"But he was having a bath at three."

"I don't say he didn't get back from Park Lane before three. But I don't suppose Cummings went and looked through the bathroom keyhole to see if he was in the bath."

Parker considered again.

"How about Crimplesham's pince-nez?" he asked.

"That is a bit mysterious," said Lord Peter.

"And why Thipps's bathroom?"

"Why, indeed? Pure accident, perhaps—or pure devilry."

"Do you think all this elaborate scheme could have been put together in a night, Wimsey?"

"Far from it. It was conceived as soon as that man who bore a superficial resemblance to Levy came into the workhouse. He had several days."

"I see."

"Freke gave himself away at the inquest. He and Grimbold disagreed about the length of the man's illness. If a small man (comparatively speaking) like Grimbold presumes to disagree with a man like Freke, it's because he is sure of his ground."

"Then—if your theory is sound—Freke made a mistake."

"Yes. A very slight one. He was guarding, with unnecessary caution, against starting a train of thought in the mind of anybody— say, the workhouse doctor. Up till then he'd been reckoning on the fact that people don't think a second time about anything (a body, say) that's once been accounted for."

"What made him lose his head?"

"A chain of unforeseen accidents. Levy's having been recognized— my mother's son having foolishly advertised in the *Times* his connection with the Battersea end of the mystery—Detective Parker (whose photograph has been a little prominent in the illustrated press lately) seen sitting next door to the Duchess of Denver at the inquest. His aim in life was to prevent the two ends of the problem from linking up. And there were two of the links, literally side by side. Many criminals are wrecked by over-caution."

Parker was silent.

* *Lord Peter was not without authority for his opinion: "With respect to the alleged motive, it is of great importance to see whether there was a motive for committing such a crime, or whether there was not, or whether there is an improbability of its having been committed so strong as not to be overpowered by positive evidence. But if there be any motive which can be assigned, I am bound to tell you that the inadequacy of that motive is of little importance. We know, from the experience of criminal courts, that atrocious crimes of this sort have been committed from very slight motives; not merely from malice and revenge, but to gain a small pecuniary advantage, and to drive off for a time pressing difficulties."—L. C. J. Campbell, summing up in Reg. v. Palmer, Shorthand Report, p. 308 C. C. C., May, 1856, Sess. Pa. 5. (Italics mine. D. L. S.)*

# CHAPTER 11

"A regular pea-souper, by Jove," said Lord Peter.

Parker grunted, and struggled irritably into an overcoat.

"It affords me, if I may say so, the greatest satisfaction," continued the noble lord, "that in a collaboration like ours all the uninteresting and disagreeable routine work is done by you."

Parker grunted again.

"Do you anticipate any difficulty about the warrant?" enquired Lord Peter.

Parker grunted a third time.

"I suppose you've seen to it that all this business is kept quiet?"

"Of course."

"You've muzzled the workhouse people?"

"Of course."

"And the police?"

"Yes."

"Because, if you haven't, there'll probably be nobody to arrest."

"My dear Wimsey, do you think I'm a fool?"

"I had no such hope."

Parker grunted finally and departed.

Lord Peter settled down to a perusal of his Dante. It afforded him no solace. Lord Peter was hampered in his career as a private detective by a public-school education. Despite Parker's admonitions, he was not always able to discount it. His mind had been warped in its young growth by "Raffles" and "Sherlock Holmes," or the sentiments for which they stand. He belonged to a family which had never shot a fox.

"I am an amateur," said Lord Peter.

Nevertheless, while communing with Dante, he made up his mind.

In the afternoon he found himself in Harley Street. Sir Julian Freke might be consulted about one's nerves from two till four on Tuesdays and Fridays. Lord Peter rang the bell.

"Have you an appointment, sir?" enquired the man who opened the door.

"No," said Lord Peter, "but will you give Sir Julian my card? I think it possible he may see me without one."

He sat down in the beautiful room in which Sir Julian's patients awaited his healing counsel. It was full of people. Two or three fashionably dressed women were discussing shops and servants together, and teasing a toy griffon. A big, worried-looking man by himself in a corner looked at his watch twenty times a minute. Lord Peter knew him by sight. It was Wintrington, a millionaire, who had tried to kill himself a few months ago. He controlled the finances of five countries, but he could not control his nerves. The finances of five countries were in Sir Julian Freke's capable hands. By the fireplace sat a soldierly-looking young man, of about Lord Peter's own age. His face was prematurely lined and worn; he sat bolt upright, his restless eyes darting in the direction of every slightest sound. On the sofa was an elderly woman of modest appearance, with a young girl. The girl seemed listless and wretched; the woman's look showed deep affection, and anxiety tempered with a timid hope. Close beside Lord Peter was another, younger woman, with a little girl, and Lord Peter noticed in both of them the broad cheekbones and beautiful, grey, slanting eyes of the Slav. The child, moving restlessly about, trod on Lord Peter's patent-leather toe, and the mother admonished her in French before turning to apologize to Lord Peter.

"Mais je vous en prie, madame," said the young man, "it is nothing."

"She is nervous, pauvre petite," said the young woman.

"You are seeking advice for her?"

"Yes. He is wonderful, the doctor. Figure to yourself, monsieur, she cannot forget, poor child, the things she has seen." She leaned nearer, so that the child might not hear. "We have escaped—from starving Russia—six months ago. I dare not tell you—she has such quick ears, and then, the cries, the tremblings, the convulsions—they all begin again. We were skeletons when we arrived—mon Dieu!—but that is better now. See, she is thin, but she is not starved. She would be fatter but for the nerves that keep her from eating. We who are older, we forget—enfin, on apprend ˆ ne pas y penser—but these children! When one is young, monsieur, tout a impressionne trop."

Lord Peter, escaping from the thraldom of British good form, expressed himself in that language in which sympathy is not condemned to mutism.

"But she is much better, much better," said the mother, proudly, "the great doctor, he does marvels."

"C'est un homme precieux," said Lord Peter.

"Ah, monsieur, c'est un saint qui opre des miracles! Nous prions pour lui, Natasha et moi, tous les jours. N'est-ce pas, cherie? And consider, monsieur, that he does it all, ce grand homme, cet homme illustre, for nothing at all. When we come here, we have not even the clothes upon our backs—we are ruined, famished. Et avec a que nous sommes de bonne famille—mais helas! monsieur, en Russie, comme vous savez, a ne vous vaut que des insultes—des atrocites. Enfin! the great Sir Julian sees us, he says—'Madame, your little girl is very interesting to me. Say no more. I cure her for nothing—pour ses beaux yeux,' a-t-il ajoute en riant. Ah, monsieur, c'est un saint, un veritable saint! and Natasha is much, much better."

"Madame, je vous en felicite."

"And you, monsieur? You are young, well, strong—you also suffer? It is still the war, perhaps?"

"A little remains of shell-shock," said Lord Peter.

"Ah, yes. So many good, brave, young men—"

"Sir Julian can spare you a few minutes, my lord, if you will come in now," said the servant.

Lord Peter bowed to his neighbour, and walked across the waiting-room. As the door of the consulting-room closed behind him, he remembered having once gone, disguised, into the staff-room of a German officer. He experienced the same feeling—the feeling of being caught in a trap, and a mingling of bravado and shame.

He had seen Sir Julian Freke several times from a distance, but never close. Now, while carefully and quite truthfully detailing the circumstances of his recent nervous attack, he considered the man before him. A man taller than himself, with immense breadth of shoulder, and wonderful hands. A face beautiful, impassioned and inhuman; fanatical, compelling eyes, bright blue amid the ruddy bush of hair and beard. They were not the cool and kindly eyes of the family doctor, they were the brooding eyes of the inspired scientist, and they searched one through.

"Well," thought Lord Peter, "I shan't have to be explicit, anyhow."

"Yes," said Sir Julian, "yes. You had been working too hard. Puzzling your mind. Yes. More than that, perhaps—troubling your mind, shall we say?"

"I found myself faced with a very alarming contingency."

"Yes. Unexpectedly, perhaps."

"Very unexpected indeed."

"Yes. Following on a period of mental and physical strain."

"Well—perhaps. Nothing out of the way."

"Yes. The unexpected contingency was—personal to yourself?"

"It demanded an immediate decision as to my own actions yes, in that sense it was certainly personal."

"Quite so. You would have to assume some responsibility, no doubt."

"A very grave responsibility."

"Affecting others besides yourself?"

"Affecting one other person vitally, and a very great number indirectly."

"Yes. The time was night. You were sitting in the dark?"

"Not at first. I think I put the light out afterwards."

"Quite so—that action would naturally suggest itself to you. Were you warm?"

"I think the fire had died down. My man tells me that my teeth were chattering when I went in to him."

"Yes. You live in Piccadilly?"

"Yes."

"Heavy traffic sometimes goes past during the night, I expect."

"Oh, frequently."

"Just so. Now this decision you refer to—you had taken that decision."

"Yes."

"Your mind was made up?"

"Oh, yes."

"You had decided to take the action, whatever it was."

"Yes."

"Yes. It involved perhaps a period of inaction."

"Of comparative inaction—yes."

"Of suspense, shall we say?"

"Yes—of suspense, certainly."

"Possibly of some danger?"

"I don't know that that was in my mind at the time."

"No—it was a case in which you could not possibly consider yourself."

"If you like to put it that way."

"Quite so. Yes. You had these attacks frequently in 1918?"

"Yes—I was very ill for some months."

"Quite. Since then they have recurred less frequently?"

"Much less frequently."

"Yes—when did the last occur?"

"About nine months ago."

"Under what circumstances?"

"I was being worried by certain family matters. It was a question of deciding about some investments, and I was largely responsible."

"Yes. You were interested last year, I think in some police case?"

"Yes—in the recovery of Lord Attenbury's emerald necklace."

"That involved some severe mental exercise?"

"I suppose so. But I enjoyed it very much."

"Yes. Was the exertion of solving the problem attended by any bad results physically?"

"None."

"No. You were interested, but not distressed."

"Exactly."

"Yes. You have been engaged in other investigations of the kind?"

"Yes. Little ones."

"With bad results for your health?"

"Not a bit of it. On the contrary. I took up these cases as a sort of distraction. I had a bad knock just after the war, which didn't make matters any better for me, don't you know."

"Ah! you are not married?"

"No."

"No. Will you allow me to make an examination? Just come a little nearer to the light. I want to see your eyes. Whose advice have you had till now?"

"Sir James Hodges'."

"Ah! yes—he was a sad loss to the medical profession. A really great man—a true scientist. Yes. Thank you. Now I should like to try you with this little invention."

"What's it do?"

"Well—it tells me about your nervous reactions. Will you sit here?"

The examination that followed was purely medical. When it was concluded, Sir Julian said:

"Now, Lord Peter, I'll tell you about yourself in quite untechnical language—"

"Thanks," said Peter, "that's kind of you. I'm an awful fool about long words."

"Yes. Are you fond of private theatricals, Lord Peter?"

"Not particularly," said Peter, genuinely surprised. "Awful bore as a rule. Why?"

"I thought you might be," said the specialist, drily. "Well, now. You know quite well that the strain you put on your nerves during the war has left its mark on you. It has left what I may call old wounds in your brain. Sensations received by your nerve-endings sent messages to your brain, and produced minute physical changes there—changes we are only beginning to be able to detect, even with our most delicate instruments. These changes in their turn set up sensations; or I should say, more accurately, that sensations are the names we give to these changes of tissue when we perceive them: we call them horror, fear, sense of responsibility and so on."

"Yes, I follow you."

"Very well. Now, if you stimulate those damaged places in your brain again, you run the risk of opening up the old wounds. I mean, that if you get nerve-sensations of any kind producing the reactions which we call horror, fear, and sense of responsibility, they may go on to make disturbance right along the old channel, and produce in their turn physical changes which you will call by the names you were accustomed to associate with them—dread of German mines, responsibility for the lives of your men, strained attention and the inability to distinguish small sounds through the overpowering noise of guns."

"I see."

"This effect would be increased by extraneous circumstances producing other familiar physical sensations—night, cold or the rattling of heavy traffic, for instance."

"Yes."

"Yes. The old wounds are nearly healed, but not quite. The ordinary exercise of your mental faculties has no bad effect. It is only when you excite the injured part of your brain."

"Yes, I see."

"Yes. You must avoid these occasions. You must learn to be irresponsible, Lord Peter."

"My friends say I'm only too irresponsible already."

"Very likely. A sensitive nervous temperament often appears so, owing to its mental nimbleness."

"Oh!"

"Yes. This particular responsibility you were speaking of still rests upon you?"

"Yes, it does."

"You have not yet completed the course of action on which you have decided?"

"Not yet."

"You feel bound to carry it through?"

"Oh, yes—I can't back out of it now."

"No. You are expecting further strain?"

"A certain amount."

"Do you expect it to last much longer?"

"Very little longer now."

"Ah! Your nerves are not all they should be."

"No?"

"No. Nothing to be alarmed about, but you must exercise care while undergoing this strain, and afterwards you should take a complete rest. How about a voyage in the Mediterranean or the South Seas or somewhere?"

"Thanks. I'll think about it."

"Meanwhile, to carry you over the immediate trouble I will give you something to strengthen your nerves. It will do you no permanent good, you understand, but it will tide you over the bad time. And I will give you a prescription."

"Thank you."

Sir Julian got up and went into a small surgery leading out of the consulting-room. Lord Peter watched him moving about—boiling something and writing. Presently he returned with a paper and a hypodermic syringe.

"Here is the prescription. And now, if you will just roll up your sleeve, I will deal with the necessity of the immediate moment."

Lord Peter obediently rolled up his sleeve. Sir Julian Freke selected a portion of his forearm and anointed it with iodine.

"What's that you're goin' to stick into me. Bugs?"

The surgeon laughed.

"Not exactly," he said. He pinched up a portion of flesh between his finger and thumb. "You've had this kind of thing before, I expect."

"Oh, yes," said Lord Peter. He watched the cool fingers, fascinated, and the steady approach of the needle. "Yes—I've had it before—and, d'you know—I don't care frightfully about it."

He had brought up his right hand, and it closed over the surgeon's wrist like a vise.

The silence was like a shock. The blue eyes did not waver; they burned down steadily upon the heavy white lids below them. Then these slowly lifted; the grey eyes met the blue—coldly, steadily—and held them.

When lovers embrace, there seems no sound in the world but their own breathing. So the two men breathed face to face.

"As you like, of course, Lord Peter," said Sir Julian, courteously.

"Afraid I'm rather a silly ass," said Lord Peter, "but I never could abide these little gadgets. I had one once that went wrong and gave me a rotten bad time. They make me a bit nervous."

"In that case," replied Sir Julian, "it would certainly be better not to have the injection. It might rouse up just those sensations which we are desirous of avoiding. You will take the prescription, then, and do what you can to lessen the immediate strain as far as possible."

"Oh, yes—I'll take it easy, thanks," said Lord Peter. He rolled his sleeve down neatly. "I'm much obliged to you. If I have any further trouble I'll look in again."

"Do—do—" said Sir Julian. cheerfully. "Only make an appointment another time. I'm rather rushed these days. I hope your mother is quite well. I saw her the other day at that Battersea inquest. You should have been there. It would have interested you."

# CHAPTER 12

The vile, raw fog tore your throat and ravaged your eyes. You could not see your feet. You stumbled in your walk over poor men's graves.

The feel of Parker's old trench-coat beneath your fingers was comforting. You had felt it in worse places. You clung on now for fear you should get separated. The dim people moving in front of you were like Brocken spectres.

"Take care, gentlemen," said a toneless voice out of the yellow darkness, "there's an open grave just hereabouts."

You bore away to the right, and floundered in a mass of freshly turned clay.

"Hold up, old man," said Parker.

"Where is Lady Levy?"

"In the mortuary; the Duchess of Denver is with her. Your mother is wonderful, Peter."

"Isn't she?" said Lord Peter.

A dim blue light carried by somebody ahead wavered and stood still.

"Here you are," said a voice.

Two Dantesque shapes with pitchforks loomed up.

"Have you finished?" asked somebody.

"Nearly done, sir." The demons fell to work again with the pitchforks—no, spades.

Somebody sneezed. Parker located the sneezer and introduced him.

"Mr. Levett represents the Home Secretary. Lord Peter Wimsey. We are sorry to drag you out on such a day, Mr. Levett."

"It's all in the day's work," said Mr. Levett, hoarsely. He was muffled to the eyes.

The sound of the spades for many minutes. An iron noise of tools thrown down. Demons stooping and straining.

A black-bearded spectre at your elbow. Introduced. The Master of the Workhouse.

"A very painful matter, Lord Peter. You will forgive me for hoping you and Mr. Parker may be mistaken."

"I should like to be able to hope so too."

Something heaving, straining, coming up out of the ground.

"Steady, men. This way. Can you see? Be careful of the graves— they lie pretty thick hereabouts. Are you ready?"

"Right you are, sir. You go on with the lantern. We can follow you."

Lumbering footsteps. Catch hold of Parker's trench-coat again. "That you, old man? Oh, I beg your pardon, Mr. Levett—thought you were Parker."

"Hullo, Wimsey—here you are."

More graves. A headstone shouldered crookedly aslant. A trip and jerk over the edge of the rough grass. The squeal of gravel under your feet.

"This way, gentlemen, mind the step."

The mortuary. Raw red brick and sizzling gas-jets. Two women in black, and Dr. Grimbold. The coffin laid on the table with a heavy thump.

"'Ave you got that there screw-driver, Bill? Thank 'ee. Be keerful wi' the chisel now. Not much substance to these 'ere boards, sir."

Several long creaks. A sob. The Duchess's voice, kind but peremptory.

"Hush, Christine. You mustn't cry."

A mutter of voices. The lurching departure of the Dante demons— good, decent demons in corduroy.

Dr. Grimbold's voice—cool and detached as if in the consulting-room.

"Now—have you got that lamp, Mr. Wingate? Thank you. Yes, here on the table, please. Be careful not to catch your elbow in the flex, Mr. Levett. It would be better, I think, if you came on this side. Yes—yes— thank you. That's excellent."

The sudden brilliant circle of an electric lamp over the table. Dr. Grimbold's beard and spectacles. Mr. Levett blowing his nose. Parker bending close. The Master of the Workhouse peering over him. The rest of the room in the enhanced dimness of the gas-jets and the fog.

A low murmur of voices. All heads bent over the work.

Dr. Grimbold again—beyond the circle of the lamplight.

"We don't want to distress you unnecessarily, Lady Levy. If you will just tell us what to look for-the—? Yes, yes, certainly—and—yes— stopped with gold? Yes—the lower jaw, the last but one on the right? Yes—no teeth missing—no—yes? What kind of a mole? Yes—just over the left breast? Oh, I beg your pardon, just under—yes—appendicitis? Yes—a long one—yes—in the middle? Yes, I quite understand—a scar on the arm? Yes, I don't know if we shall be able to find that—yes—any little constitutional weakness that might—? Oh, yes—arthritis—yes— thank you, Lady Levy—that's very clear. Don't come unless I ask you to. Now, Wingate."

A pause. A murmur. "Pulled out? After death, you think—well, so do I. Where is Dr. Colegrove? You attended this man in the workhouse? Yes. Do you recollect—? No? You're quite certain about that? Yes—we mustn't make a mistake, you know. Yes, but there are reasons why Sir

Julian can't be present; I'm asking you, Dr. Colegrove. Well, you're certain—that's all I want to know. Just bring the light closer, Mr. Wingate, if you please. These miserable shells let the damp in so quickly. Ah! what do you make of this? Yes—yes—well, that's rather unmistakable, isn't it? Who did the head? Oh, Freke—of course. I was going to say they did good work at St. Luke's. Beautiful, isn't it, Dr. Colegrove? A wonderful surgeon—I saw him when he was at Guy's. Oh, no, gave it up years ago. Nothing like keeping your hand in. Ah—yes, undoubtedly that's it. Have you a towel handy, sir? Thank you. Over the head, if you please—I think we might have another here. Now, Lady Levy—I am going to ask you to look at a scar, and see if you recognize it. I'm sure you are going to help us by being very firm. Take your time—you won't see anything more than you absolutely must."

"Lucy, don't leave me."

"No, dear."

A space cleared at the table. The lamplight on the Duchess's white hair.

"Oh, yes—oh, yes! No, no—I couldn't be mistaken. There's that funny little kink in it. I've seen it hundreds of times. Oh, Lucy—Reuben!"

"Only a moment more, Lady Levy. The mole—"

"I—I think so—oh, yes, that is the very place."

"Yes. And the scar—was it three-cornered, just above the elbow?"

"Yes, oh, yes."

"Is this it?"

"Yes—yes—"

"I must ask you definitely, Lady Levy. Do you, from these three marks identify the body as that of your husband?"

"Oh! I must, mustn't I? Nobody else could have them just the same in just those places? It is my husband. It is Reuben. Oh—"

"Thank you, Lady Levy. You have been very brave and very helpful."

"But—I don't understand yet. How did he come here? Who did this dreadful thing?"

"Hush, dear," said the Duchess, "the man is going to be punished."

"Oh, but—how cruel! Poor Reuben! Who could have wanted to hurt him? Can I see his face?"

"No, dear," said the Duchess. "That isn't possible. Come away—you mustn't distress the doctors and people."

"No—no—they've all been so kind. Oh, Lucy!"

'We'll go home, dear. You don't want us any more, Dr. Grimbold?"

'No, Duchess, thank you. We are very grateful to you and to Lady Levy for coming."

There was a pause, while the two women went out, Parker, collected and helpful, escorting them to their waiting car. Then Dr. Grimbold again:

"I think Lord Peter Wimsey ought to see—the correctness of his deductions—Lord Peter—very painful—you may wish to see—yes, I was uneasy at the inquest—yes—Lady Levy—remarkably clear evidence—yes—most shocking case—ah, here's Mr. Parker—you and Lord Peter Wimsey entirely justified—do I really understand—? Really? I can hardly believe it—so distinguished a man—as you say, when a great brain turns to crime—yes—look here! Marvellous work—marvellous—somewhat obscured by this time, of course—but the most beautiful sections—here, you see, the left hemisphere—and here—through the corpus striatum—here again—the very track of the damage done by the blow—wonderful—guessed it—saw the effect of the blow as he struck it, you know—ah, I should like to see his brain, Mr. Parker—and to think that—heavens, Lord Peter, you don't know what a blow you have struck at the whole profession—the whole civilized world! Oh, my dear sir! Can you ask me? My lips are sealed of course—all our lips are sealed."

The way back through the burial ground. Fog again, and the squeal of wet gravel.

"Are your men ready, Charles?"

"They have gone. I sent them off when I saw Lady Levy to the car."

"Who is with them?"

"Sugg."

"Sugg?"

"Yes—poor devil. They've had him up on the mat at headquarters for bungling the case. All that evidence of Thipps's about the night club was corroborated, you know. That girl he gave the gin-and-bitters to was caught, and came and identified him, and they decided their case wasn't good enough, and let Thipps and the Horrocks girl go. Then they told Sugg he had overstepped his duty and ought to have been more careful. So he ought, but he can't help being a fool. I was sorry for him. It may do him some good to be in at the death. After all, Peter, you and I had special advantages."

"Yes. Well, it doesn't matter. Whoever goes won't get there in time. Sugg's as good as another."

But Sugg—an experience rare in his career—was in time.

Parker and Lord Peter were at 110 Piccadilly. Lord Peter was playing Bach and Parker was reading Origen when Sugg was announced.

"We've got our man, sir," said he.

"Good God!" said Peter. "Alive?"

"We were just in time, my lord. We rang the bell and marched straight up past his man to the library. He was sitting there doing some writing. When we came in, he made a grab for his hypodermic, but we were too quick for him, my lord. We didn't mean to let him slip through our hands, having got so far. We searched him thoroughly and marched him off."

"He is actually in gaol, then?"

"Oh, yes—safe enough—with two warders to see he doesn't make away with himself."

"You surprise me, Inspector. Have a drink."

"Thank you, my lord. I may say that I'm very grateful to you—this case was turning out a pretty bad egg for me. If I was rude to your lordship—"

"Oh, it's all right, Inspector," said Lord Peter, hastily. "I don't see how you could possibly have worked it out. I had the good luck to know something about it from other sources."

"That's what Freke says." Already the great surgeon was a common criminal in the inspector's eyes—a mere surname. "He was writing a full confession when we got hold of him, addressed to your lordship. The police will have to have it, of course, but seeing it's written for you, I brought it along for you to see first. Here it is."

He handed Lord Peter a bulky document.

"Thanks," said Peter. "Like to hear it, Charles?"

"Rather."

Accordingly Lord Peter read it aloud.

# CHAPTER 13

Dear Lord Peter—When I was a young man I used to play chess with an old friend of my father's. He was a very bad, and a very slow, player, and he could never see when a checkmate was inevitable, but insisted on playing every move out. I never had any patience with that kind of attitude, and I will freely admit now that the game is yours. I must either stay at home and be hanged or escape abroad and live in an idle and insecure obscurity. I prefer to acknowledge defeat.

If you have read my book on "Criminal Lunacy," you will remember that I wrote: "In the majority of cases, the criminal betrays himself by some abnormality attendant upon this pathological condition of the nervous tissues. His mental instability shows itself in various forms: an overweening vanity, leading him to brag of his achievement; a disproportionate sense of the importance of the offence, resulting from the hallucination of religion, and driving him to confession; egomania, producing the sense of horror or conviction of sin, and driving him to headlong flight without covering his tracks; a reckless confidence, resulting in the neglect of the most ordinary precautions, as in the case of Henry Wainwright, who left a boy in charge of the murdered woman's remains while he went to call a cab, or on the other hand, a nervous distrust of apperceptions in the past, causing him to revisit the scene of the crime to assure himself that all traces have been as safely removed as his own judgment knows them to be. I will not hesitate to assert that a perfectly sane man, not intimidated by religious or other delusions, could always render himself perfectly secure from detection, provided, that is, that the crime were sufficiently premeditated and that he were not pressed for time or thrown out in his calculations by purely fortuitous coincidence.

You know as well as I do, how far I have made this assertion good in practice. The two accidents which betrayed me, I could not by any possibility have foreseen. The first was the chance recognition of Levy by the girl in the Battersea Park Road, which suggested a connection between the two problems. The second was that Thipps should have arranged to go down to Denver on the Tuesday morning, thus enabling your mother to get word of the matter through to you before the body was removed by the police and to suggest a motive for the murder out of what she knew of my previous personal history. If I had been able to destroy these two accidentally forged links of circumstance, I will venture to say that you would never have so much as suspected me, still less obtained sufficient evidence to convict.

Of all human emotions, except perhaps those of hunger and fear, the sexual appetite produces the most violent and, under some circumstances, the most persistent reactions; I think, however, I am right in saying that at the time when I wrote my book, my original sensual impulse to kill Sir Reuben Levy had already become profoundly modified by my habits of thought. To the animal lust to slay and the primitive human desire for revenge, there was added the rational intention of substantiating my own theories for the satisfaction of myself and the world. If all had turned out as I had planned, I should have deposited a sealed account of my experiment with the Bank of England, instructing my executors to publish it after my death. Now that accident has spoiled the completeness of my demonstration, I entrust the account to you, whom it cannot fail to interest, with the request that you will make it known among scientific men, in justice to my professional reputation.

The really essential factors of success in any undertaking are money and opportunity, and as a rule, the man who can make the first can make the second. During my early career, though I was fairly well-off, I had not absolute command of circumstance. Accordingly I devoted myself to my profession, and contented myself with keeping up a friendly connection with Reuben Levy and his family. This enabled me to remain in touch with his fortunes and interests, so that, when the moment for action should arrive, I might know what weapons to use.

Meanwhile, I carefully studied criminology in fiction and fact—my work on "Criminal Lunacy" was a side-product of this activity—and saw how, in every murder, the real crux of the problem was the disposal of the body. As a doctor, the means of death were always ready to my hand, and I was not likely to make any error in that connection. Nor was I likely to betray myself on account of any illusory sense of wrongdoing. The sole difficulty would be that of destroying all connection between my personality and that of the corpse. You will remember that Michael Finsbury, in Stevenson's entertaining romance, observes: "What hangs people is the unfortunate circumstance of guilt." It became clear to me that the mere leaving about of a superfluous corpse could convict nobody, provided that nobody was guilty in connection with that particular corpse. Thus the idea of substituting the one body for the other was early arrived at, though it was not till I obtained the practical direction of St. Luke's Hospital that I found myself perfectly unfettered in the choice and handling of dead bodies. From this period on, I kept a careful watch on all the material brought in for dissection.

My opportunity did not present itself until the week before Sir Reuben's disappearance, when the medical officer at the Chelsea workhouse sent word to me that an unknown vagrant had been injured that morning by the fall of a piece of scaffolding, and was exhibiting some very interesting nervous and cerebral reactions. I went round and saw the case, and was immediately struck by the man's strong superficial resemblance to Sir Reuben. He had been heavily struck on the back of the neck, dislocating the fourth and fifth cervical vertebra and heavily bruising the spinal cord. It seemed highly unlikely that he could ever recover, either mentally or physically, and in any case there appeared to me to be no object in indefinitely prolonging so unprofitable an existence. He had obviously been able to support life until recently, as he was fairly well nourished, but the state of his feet and clothing showed that he was unemployed, and under present conditions he was likely to remain so. I decided that he would suit my purpose very well, and immediately put in train certain transactions in the City which I had already sketched out in my own mind. In the meantime, the reactions mentioned by the workhouse doctor were interesting, and I made careful studies of them, and arranged for the delivery of the body to the hospital when I should have completed my preparations.

On the Thursday and Friday of that week I made private arrangements with various brokers to buy the stock of certain Peruvian oil-fields, which had gone down almost to waste-paper. This part of my experiment did not cost me very much, but I contrived to arouse considerable curiosity, and even a mild excitement. At this point I was of course careful not to let my name appear. The incidence of Saturday and Sunday gave me some anxiety lest my man should after all die before I was ready for him, but by the use of saline injections I contrived to keep him alive and, late on Sunday night, he even manifested disquieting symptoms of at any rate a partial recovery.

On Monday morning the market in Peruvians opened briskly. Rumours had evidently got about that somebody knew something, and this day I was not the only buyer in the market. I bought a couple of hundred more shares in my own name, and left the matter to take care of itself. At lunch time I made my arrangements to run into Levy accidentally at the corner of the Mansion House. He expressed (as I expected) his surprise at seeing me in that part of London. I simulated some embarrassment and suggested that we should lunch together. I dragged him to a place a bit off the usual beat, and there ordered a good wine and drank of it as much as he might suppose sufficient to induce a confidential mood. I asked him how things were going on 'Change. He said, "Oh, all right," but appeared a little doubtful, and asked me whether I did anything in that way. I said I had a little flutter occasionally, and that, as a matter of fact, I'd been put on to rather a good thing. I glanced round apprehensively at this point, and shifted my chair nearer to his.

"I suppose you don't know anything about Peruvian Oil, do you?" he said.

I started and looked round again, and leaning across to him, said, dropping my voice:

"Well, I do, as a matter of fact, but I don't want it to get about. I stand to make a good bit on it."

"But I thought the thing was hollow," he said; "it hasn't paid a dividend for umpteen years."

"No," I said, "it hasn't, but it's going to. I've got inside information." He looked a bit unconvinced, and I emptied off my glass, and edged right up to his ear.

"Look here," I said, "I'm not giving this away to everyone, but I don't mind doing you and Christine a good turn. You know, I've always kept a soft place in my heart for her, ever since the old days. You got in ahead of me that time, and now it's up to me to heap coals of fire on you both."

I was a little excited by this time, and he thought I was drunk.

"It's very kind of you, old man," he said, "but I'm a cautious bird, you know, always was. I'd like a bit of proof."

And he shrugged up his shoulders and looked like a pawnbroker.

"I'll give it to you," I said, "but it isn't safe here. Come round to my place to-night after dinner, and I'll show you the report."

"How d'you get hold of it?" said he.

"I'll tell you to-night," said I. "Come round after dinner—any time after nine, say."

"To Harley Street?" he asked, and I saw that he meant coming.

"No," I said, "to Battersea—Prince of Wales Road; I've got some work to do at the hospital. And look here," I said, "don't you let on to a soul that you're coming. I bought a couple of hundred shares to-day, in my own name, and people are sure to get wind of it. If we're known to be about together, someone'll twig something. In fact, it's anything but safe talking about it in this place."

"All right," he said, "I won't say a word to anybody. I'll turn up about nine o'clock. You're sure it's a sound thing?"

"It can't go wrong," I assured him. And I meant it.

We parted after that, and I went round to the workhouse. My man had died at about eleven o'clock. I had seen him just after breakfast, and was not surprised. I completed the usual formalities with the workhouse authorities, and arranged for his delivery at the hospital about seven o'clock.

In the afternoon, as it was not one of my days to be in Harley Street, I looked up an old friend who lives close to Hyde Park, and found that he was just off to Brighton on some business or other. I had tea with him, and saw him off by the 5:35 from Victoria. On issuing from the barrier it occurred to me to purchase an evening paper, and I thoughtlessly turned my steps to the bookstall. The usual crowds were rushing to catch suburban trains home, and on moving away I found myself involved in a contrary stream of travellers coming up out of the Underground, or bolting from all sides for the 5:45 to Battersea Park and Wandsworth Common. I disengaged myself after some buffeting and went home in a taxi; and it was not till I was safely seated there that I discovered somebody's gold-rimmed pince-nez involved in the astrachan collar of my overcoat. The time from 6:15 to seven I spent concocting something to look like a bogus report for Sir Reuben.

At seven I went through to the hospital, and found the workhouse van just delivering my subject at the side door. I had him taken straight up to the theatre, and told the attendant, William Watts, that I intended to work there that night. I told him I would prepare the body myself—the injection of a preservative would have been a most regrettable complication. I sent him about his business, and then went home and had dinner. I told my man that I should be working in the hospital that evening, and that he could go to bed at 10:30 as usual, as I could not tell whether I should be late or not. He is used to my erratic ways. I only keep two servants in the Battersea house—the man-servant and his wife, who cooks for me. The rougher domestic work is done by a charwoman, who sleeps out. The servants' bedroom is at the top of the house, overlooking Prince of Wales Road.

As soon as I had dined I established myself in the hall with some papers. My man had cleared dinner by a quarter past eight, and I told him to give me the siphon and tantalus; and sent him downstairs. Levy rang the bell at twenty minutes past nine, and I opened the door to him myself. My man appeared at the other end of the hall, but I called to him that it was all right, and he went away. Levy wore an overcoat with evening dress and carried an umbrella. "Why, how wet you are!" I said. "How did you come?" "By 'bus," he said, "and the fool of a conductor forgot to put me down at the end of the road. It's pouring cats and dogs and pitch-dark—I couldn't see where I was." I was glad he hadn't taken a taxi, but I had rather reckoned on his not doing so. "Your little economies will be the death of you one of these days," I said. I was right there, but I hadn't reckoned on their being the death of me as well. I say again, I could not have foreseen it.

I sat him down by the fire, and gave him a whisky. He was in high spirits about some deal in Argentines he was bringing off the next day. We talked money for about a quarter of an hour and then he said:

"Well, how about this Peruvian mare's-nest of yours?"

"It's no mare's-nest," I said; "come and have a look at it."

I took him upstairs into the library, and switched on the centre light and the reading lamp on the writing table. I gave him a chair at the table with his back to the fire, and fetched the papers I had been faking, out of the safe. He took them, and began to read them, poking over them in his short-sighted way, while I mended the fire. As soon as I saw his head in a favourable position I struck him heavily with the poker, just over the fourth cervical. It was delicate work calculating the exact force necessary to kill him without breaking the skin, but my professional experience was useful to me. He gave one loud gasp, and tumbled forward on to the table quite noiselessly. I put the poker back, and examined him. His neck was broken, and he was quite dead. I carried him into my bedroom and undressed him. It was about ten minutes to ten when I had finished. I put him away under my bed, which had been turned down for the night, and cleared up the papers in the library. Then I went downstairs, took Levy's umbrella, and let myself out at the hall door, shouting "Good-night" loudly enough to be heard in the basement if the servants should be listening. I walked briskly away down the street, went in by the hospital side door, and returned to the house noiselessly by way of the private passage. It would have been awkward if anybody had seen me then, but I leaned over the back stairs and heard the cook and her husband still talking in the kitchen. I slipped back into the hall, replaced the umbrella in the stand, cleared up my papers there, went up into the library and rang the bell. When the man appeared I told him to lock up everything except the private door to the hospital. I waited in the library until he had done so, and about 10:30 I heard both servants go up to bed. I waited a quarter of an hour longer and then went through to the dissecting-room. I wheeled one of the stretcher-tables through the passage to the house door, and then went to fetch Levy. It was a nuisance having to get him downstairs, but I had not liked to make away with him in any of the ground-floor rooms, in case my servant should take a fancy to poke his head in during the few minutes that I was out of the house, or while locking up. Besides, that was a flea-bite to what I should have to do later. I put Levy on the table, wheeled him across to the hospital and substituted him for my interesting pauper. I was sorry to have to abandon the idea of getting a look at the latter's brain, but I could not afford to incur suspicion. It was still rather early, so I knocked down a few minutes getting Levy ready for dissection. Then I put my pauper on the table and trundled him over to the house. It was now five past eleven, and I thought I might conclude that the servants were in bed. I carried the body into my bedroom. He was rather heavy, but less so than Levy, and my Alpine experience had taught me how to handle bodies. It is as much a matter of knack as of strength, and I am, in any case, a powerful man for my height. I put the body into the bed—not that I expected anyone to look in during my absence, but if they should they might just as well see me apparently asleep in bed. I drew the clothes a little over his head, stripped, and put on Levy's clothes, which were fortunately a little big for me everywhere, not forgetting to take his spectacles, watch and other oddments. At a little before half past eleven I was in the road looking for a cab. People were just beginning to come home from the theatre, and I easily secured one at the corner of Prince of Wales Road. I told the man to drive me to Hyde Park Corner. There I got out, tipped him well, and asked him to pick me up again at the same place in an hour's time. He assented with an understanding grin, and I walked on up Park Lane. I had my own clothes with me in a suitcase, and carried my own overcoat and Levy's umbrella. When I got to No. 9 there were lights in some of the top windows. I was very nearly too early, owing to the old man's having sent the servants to the theatre. I waited about for a few minutes, and heard it strike the quarter past midnight. The lights were extinguished shortly after, and I let myself in with Levy's key.

It had been my original intention, when I thought over this plan of murder, to let Levy disappear from the study or the dining-room, leaving only a heap of clothes on the hearth-rug. The accident of my having been able to secure Lady Levy's absence from London, however, made possible a solution more misleading, though less pleasantly fantastic. I turned on the hall light, hung up Levy's wet overcoat and placed his umbrella in the stand. I walked up noisily and heavily to the bedroom and turned off the light by the duplicate switch on the landing. I knew the house well enough, of course. There was no chance of my running into the man-servant. Old Levy was a simple old man, who liked doing things for himself. He gave his valet little work, and never required any attendance at night. In the bedroom I took off Levy's gloves and put on a surgical pair, so as to leave no telltale finger-prints. As I wished to convey the impression that Levy had gone to bed in the usual way, I simply went to bed. The surest and simplest method of making a thing appear to have been done is to do it. A bed that has been rumpled about with one's hands, for instance, never looks like a bed that has been slept in. I dared not use Levy's brush, of course, as my hair is not of his colour, but I did everything else. I supposed that a thoughtful old man like Levy would put his boots handy for his valet, and I ought to have deduced that he would fold up his clothes. That was a mistake, but not an important one. Remembering that well-thought-out little work of Mr. Bentley's, I had examined Levy's mouth for false teeth, but he had none. I did not forget, however, to wet his toothbrush.

At one o'clock I got up and dressed in my own clothes by the light of my own pocket torch. I dared not turn on the bedroom lights, as there were light blinds to the windows. I put on my own boots and an old pair of galoshes outside the door. There was a thick Turkey carpet on the stairs and hall-floor, and I was not afraid of leaving marks. I hesitated whether to chance the banging of the front door, but decided it would be safer to take the latchkey. (It is now in the Thames. I dropped it over Battersea Bridge the next day.) I slipped quietly down, and listened for a few minutes with my ear to the letter-box. I heard a constable tramp past. As soon as his steps had died away in the distance I stepped out, and pulled the door gingerly to. It closed almost soundlessly, and I walked away to pick up my cab. I had an overcoat of much the same pattern as Levy's, and had taken the precaution to pack an opera hat in my suitcase. I hoped the man would not notice that I had no umbrella this time. Fortunately the rain had diminished for the moment to a sort of drizzle, and if he noticed anything he made no observation. I told him to stop at 50 Overstrand Mansions, and I paid him off there, and stood under the porch till he had driven away. Then I hurried round to my own side door and let myself in. It was about a quarter to two, and the harder part of my task still lay before me.

My first step was so to alter the appearance of my subject as to eliminate any immediate suggestion either of Levy or of the workhouse vagrant. A fairly superficial alteration was all I considered necessary, since there was not likely to be any hue-and-cry after the pauper. He was fairly accounted for, and his deputy was at hand to represent him. Nor, if Levy was after all tracted to my house, would it be difficult to show that the body in evidence was, as a matter of fact, not his. A clean shave and a little hair-oiling and manicuring seemed sufficient to suggest a distinct personality for my silent accomplice. His hands had been well washed in hospital, and though calloused, were not grimy. I was not able to do the work as thoroughly as I should have liked, because time was getting on. I was not sure how long it would take me to dispose of him, and, moreover, I feared the onset of *rigor mortis*, which would make my task more difficult. When I had him barbered to my satisfaction, I fetched a strong sheet and a couple of wide roller bandages, and fastened him up carefully, padding him with cotton wool wherever the bandages might chafe or leave a bruise.

Now came the really ticklish part of the business. I had already decided in my own mind that the only way of conveying him from the house was by the roof. To go through the garden at the back in this soft wet weather was to leave a ruinous trail behind us. To carry a dead man down a suburban street in the middle of the night seemed outside the range of practical politics. On the roof, on the other hand, the rain, which would have betrayed me on the ground, would stand my friend.

To reach the roof, it was necessary to carry my burden to the top of the house, past my servants' room, and hoist him out through the trapdoor in the box-room roof. Had it merely been a question of going quietly up there myself, I should have had no fear of waking the servants, but to do so burdened by a heavy body was more difficult. It would be possible, provided that the man and his wife were soundly asleep, but if not, the lumbering tread on the narrow stair and the noise of opening the trapdoor would be only too plainly audible. I tiptoed delicately up the stair and listened at their door. To my disgust I heard the man give a grunt and mutter something as he moved in his bed.

I looked at my watch. My preparations had taken nearly an hour, first and last, and I dared not be too late on the roof. I determined to take a bold step and, as it were, bluff out an alibi. I went without precaution against noise into the bathroom, turned on the hot and cold water taps to the full and pulled out the plug.

My household has often had occasion to complain of my habit of using the bath at irregular night hours. Not only does the rush of water into the cistern disturb any sleepers on the Prince of Wales Road side of the house, but my cistern is afflicted with peculiarly loud gurglings and thumpings, while frequently the pipes emit a loud groaning sound. To my delight, on this particular occasion, the cistern was in excellent form, honking, whistling and booming like a railway terminus. I gave the noise five minutes' start, and when I calculated that the sleepers would have finished cursing me and put their heads under the clothes to shut out the din, I reduced the flow of water to a small stream and left the bathroom, taking good care to leave the light burning and lock the door after me. Then I picked up my pauper and carried him upstairs as lightly as possible.

The box-room is a small attic on the side of the landing opposite to the servants' bedroom and the cistern-room. It has a trapdoor, reached by a short, wooden ladder. I set this up, hoisted up my pauper and climbed up after him. The water was still racing into the cistern, which was making a noise as though it were trying to digest an iron chain, and with the reduced flow in the bathroom the groaning of the pipes had risen almost to a hoot. I was not afraid of anybody hearing other noises. I pulled the ladder through on to the roof after me.

Between my house and the last house in Queen Caroline Mansions there is a space of only a few feet. Indeed, when the Mansions were put up, I believe there was some trouble about ancient lights, but I suppose the parties compromised somehow. Anyhow, my seven-foot ladder reached well across. I tied the body firmly to the ladder, and pushed it over till the far end was resting on the parapet of the opposite house. Then I took a short run across the cistern-room and the box-room roof, and landed easily on the other side, the parapet being happily both low and narrow.

The rest was simple. I carried my pauper along the flat roofs, intending to leave him, like the hunchback in the story, on someone's staircase or down a chimney. I had got about half way along when I suddenly thought, "Why, this must be about little Thipps's place," and I remembered his silly face, and his silly chatter about vivisection. It occurred to me pleasantly how delightful it would be to deposit my parcel with him and see what he made of it. I lay down and peered over the parapet at the back. It was pitch-dark and pouring with rain again by this time, and I risked using my torch. That was the only incautious thing I did, and the odds against being seen from the houses opposite were long enough. One second's flash showed me what I had hardly dared to hope—an open window just below me.

I knew those flats well enough to be sure it was either the bathroom or the kitchen. I made a noose in a third bandage that I had brought with me, and made it fast under the arms of the corpse. I twisted it into a double rope, and secured the end to the iron stanchion of a chimney-stack. Then I dangled our friend over. I went down after him myself with the aid of a drain-pipe and was soon hauling him in by Thipps's bathroom window.

By that time I had got a little conceited with myself, and spared a few minutes to lay him out prettily and make him shipshape. A sudden inspiration suggested that I should give him the pair of pince-nez which I had happened to pick up at Victoria. I came across them in my pocket while I was looking for a penknife to loosen a knot, and I saw what distinction they would lend his appearance, besides making it more misleading. I fixed them on him, effaced all traces of my presence as far as possible, and departed as I had come, going easily up between the drain-pipe and the rope.

I walked quietly back, re-crossed my crevasse and carried in my ladder and sheet. My discreet accomplice greeted me with a reassuring gurgle and thump. I didn't make a sound on the stairs. Seeing that I had now been having a bath for about three-quarters of an hour, I turned the water off, and enabled my deserving domestics to get a little sleep. I also felt it was time I had a little myself.

First, however, I had to go over to the hospital and make all safe there. I took off Levy's head, and started to open up the face. In twenty minutes his own wife could not have recognized him. I returned, leaving my wet galoshes and mackintosh by the garden door. My trousers I dried by the gas stove in my bedroom, and brushed away all traces of mud and brick-dust. My pauper's beard I burned in the library.

I got a good two hours' sleep from five to seven, when my man called me as usual. I apologized for having kept the water running so long and so late, and added that I thought I would have the cistern seen to.

I was interested to note that I was rather extra hungry at breakfast, showing that my night's work had caused a certain wear-and-tear of tissue. I went over afterwards to continue my dissection. During the morning a peculiarly thickheaded police inspector came to inquire whether a body had escaped from the hospital. I had him brought to me where I was, and had the pleasure of showing him the work I was doing on Sir Reuben Levy's head. Afterwards I went round with him to Thipps's and was able to satisfy myself that my pauper looked very convincing.

As soon as the Stock Exchange opened I telephoned my various brokers, and by exercising a little care, was able to sell out the greater part of my Peruvian stock on a rising market. Towards the end of the day, however, buyers became rather unsettled as a result of Levy's death, and in the end I did not make more than a few hundreds by the transaction.

Trusting I have now made clear to you any point which you may have found obscure, and with congratulations on the good fortune and perspicacity which have enabled you to defeat me, I remain, with kind remembrances to your mother,

Yours very truly,
JULIAN FREKE.

*Post-Scriptum:* My will is made, leaving my money to St. Luke's Hospital, and bequeathing my body to the same institution for dissection. I feel sure that my brain will be of interest to the scientific world. As I shall die by my own hand, I imagine that there may be a little difficulty about this. Will you do me the favour, if you can, of seeing the persons concerned in the inquest, and obtaining that the brain is not damaged by an unskillful practitioner at the post-mortem, and that the body is disposed of according to my wish?

By the way, it may be of interest to you to know that I appreciated your motive in calling this afternoon. It conveyed a warning, and I am acting upon it. In spite of the disastrous consequences to myself, I was pleased to realize that you had not underestimated my nerve and intelligence, and refused the injection. Had you submitted to it, you would, of course, never have reached home alive. No trace would have been left in your body of the injection, which consisted of a harmless preparation of strychnine, mixed with an almost unknown poison, for which there is at present no recognized test, a concentrated solution of sn—

At this point the manuscript broke off.

"Well, that's all clear enough," said Parker.

"Isn't it queer?" said Lord Peter. "All that coolness, all those brains—and then he couldn't resist writing a confession to show how clever he was, even to keep his head out of the noose."

"And a very good thing for us," said Inspector Sugg, "but Lord bless you, sir, these criminals are all alike."

"Freke's epitaph," said Parker, when the Inspector had departed. "What next, Peter?"

"I shall now give a dinner party," said Lord Peter, "to Mr. John P. Milligan and his secretary and to Messrs. Crimplesham and Wicks. I feel they deserve it for not having murdered Levy."

"Well, don't forget the Thippses," said Mr. Parker.

"On no account," said Lord Peter, "would I deprive myself of the pleasure of Mrs. Thipps's company. Bunter!"

"My lord?"

"The Napoleon brandy."

THE END

# The Westminster Mystery
## BY ELAINE HAMILTON

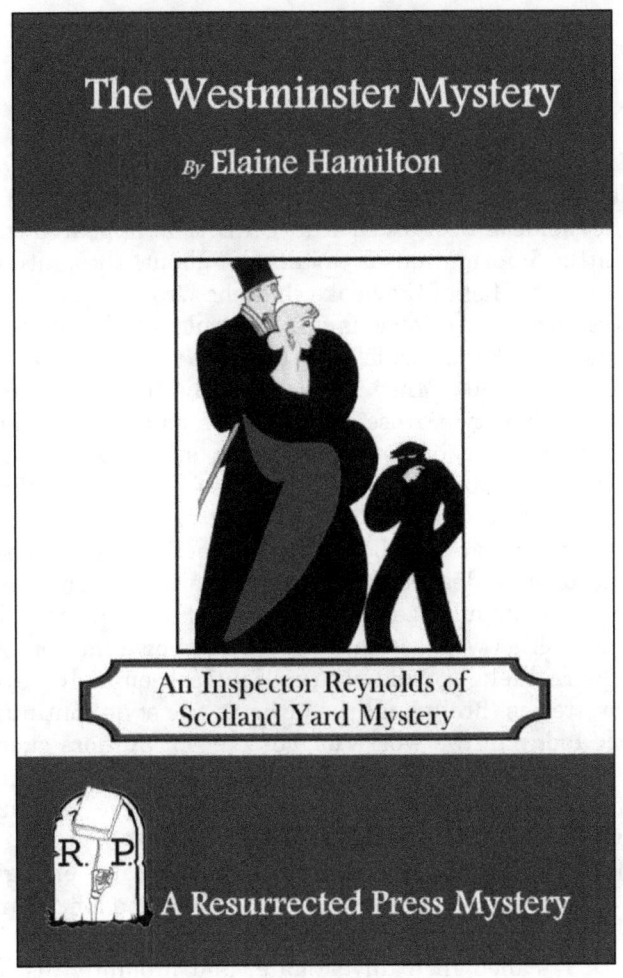

The Westminster Mystery

*By* Elaine Hamilton

An Inspector Reynolds of
Scotland Yard Mystery

R. P.

A Resurrected Press Mystery

## ORIGINALLY PUBLISHED IN 1930

EDITOR'S NOTES:
# THE WESTMINSTER MYSTERY
## BY ELAINE HAMILTON

*The Westminster Mystery* also published as *Some Unknown Hand* was published in 1930, the first of a series of mysteries featuring Inspector Reynolds of Scotland Yards' C.I.D. that appeared through the 1930's. Little information is available about the author, Elaine Hamilton, beyond a list of the books that she wrote.

*The Westminster Mystery* is an example of the style that has become known as "Hum Drum" not because the books are lacking in excitement, but because they try to portray the reality of a police investigation. This style arose in the 1930's as a reaction against the more flamboyant style of detective fiction as epitomized by Agatha Christie's Hercule Poirot or Dorothy Sayers' Lord Peter Wimsey. In place of the eccentricities of these amateur detectives, this style revolves around rather somber police detectives who achieve their results by hard work, dogged attention to details and common sense.

The style was popularized by writers such as Freeman Wills Croft and Ngaio Marsh as well as many less well known authors such John Bude and A. E. Fielding who churned out a seemingly never ending stream of mysteries throughout the period. The style continues to have an influence today in the works of more recent authors such as P. D. James and Colin Dexter who still emphasize the routine aspects of police work, though their detectives may have acquired more personality.

*The Westminster Mystery* begins in a dramatic enough fashion when a popular actress comes home to her London apartment to discover a body in her dining room. Inspector Reynolds of Scotland Yards' C.I.D. is called in to investigate, and promptly discovers that everyone involved in the case seems to be hiding something including the dead man. Much of the rest of the story revolves around Reynolds' efforts to unravel these secrets and place them in context as they relate to the murdered man.

*The Westminster Mystery* was the first novel by Elaine Hamilton to feature Detective Inspector Reynolds, and as such it does exhibit some of the flaws of a first effort. There is perhaps an over reliance on coincidences and disguises, but the story does move on at a nice pace as one fact after another is revealed to the reader.

Elaine Hamilton is today a nearly forgotten author, but during the 1930's at least nine of her novels were published though they are today hard to find. It is with pleasure the Resurrected Press offers this new edition of *The Westminster Mystery*.

## About the Author

Not much is known about Elaine Hamilton other than the fact that she wrote a series of mysteries in the 1930's featuring Inspector Reynolds of Scotland Yard. *The Westminster Mystery*, published in 1930 was the first of these. Other titles in the series include *Murder in the Fog* (1931), *The Green Death* (1932), *The Chelsea Mystery* (1932), *The Silent Bell* (1933), *Peril at Midnight* (1934), *Tragedy in the Dark* (1935), *The Casino Mystery* (1936) and *Murder Before Tuesday* (1937).

## Other Resurrected Press books in Elaine Hamilton's *Inspector Reynolds of Scotland Yard* Series

*The Westminster Mystery  (1930)*
*Peril at Midnight  (1934)*
*Tragedy in the Dark  (1935)*
*The Casino Mystery  (1936)*
*Murder Before Tuesday  (1937)*

# Like us on Facebook to stay up-to-date on all of our latest releases: http://www.facebook.com/ResurrectedPress

# THE WESTMINSTER MYSTERY

## I. THE DRAMA OPENS

BENTLEY, P. C, caught a flash of pink and silver, of golden hair above a girl's laughing face as the taxi came round the corner and drew up at the block of flats fifty yards away.

Maybe there were a thousand pink cloaks, but there was only one golden head like that and Bentley felt sure he knew to whom it belonged. Perhaps his luck would be in again to-night.

Last week she had given him a smile as he picked up the key she had dropped. It wasn't every one who had that favor from Laureen, the revue artist London was raving about.

Police Constable Bentley was very young. He jerked his belt down a shade and, measuring his stride nicely, arrived in time to hear her invitation to her companion—a distinguished-looking man in the forties.

"Come up for ten minutes and share my chocolate. My maid always waits up for me with that stodgy beverage."

The constable heard the man's courteous acceptance, and then what he had greatly hoped for happened.

Laureen glanced over her shoulder and smiled.

"Good night, officer."

The policeman saluted, conscious of a blush that he prayed was invisible.

"Good night, miss," he replied and strolled on.

"You are nothing if not a coquette," said the girl's escort.

"Not at all," she retorted. "You never know when you may be glad of his services in these cat-burglar times."

There was no night porter and the hall was empty at that hour, the tenants operating the lift for themselves.

"Which floor?" Laureen's friend asked, his finger on the switch.

"Second," Laureen, her gray eyes speculative, replied mechanically. Her mind was concentrated on the fact that Ivan Lansberg, the mysterious financial power behind so many theatrical productions was actually beside her, going to share her chocolate. She chuckled at the thought. The man of reputed millions, whose nationality every one guessed at and nobody knew; the friend of every well-known celebrity in Europe—and hot chocolate.

Several times they had met at suppers or night clubs. To-night— Sunday, June 30th—at a gay studio party. And for the first time Lansberg seemed to have recognized that she had an existence apart from the stage. Sallow, strong-featured to the point of ugliness, she decided him to be, but a man who could not be overlooked or forgotten in a crowd.

Laureen led the way to her apartment at right angles to the lift, and pressed the bell.

"My maid always waits up for me. Isn't it respectable! But actresses are the only women careful of their reputations nowadays."

"Well, for once yours would seem to be at stake," he answered as the door remained closed. "Have you a key?"

The girl produced it from her handbag and started to fit it in the lock; but before she could turn the key, at the slight pressure of her hand the door yielded—it opened on to a hall dark but for the light in the corridor.

She drew back with a startled exclamation.

"The latch must have been fastened up! How extraordinary! And where on earth is Bertha?"

"Even the most perfect of maids will run out to post a letter at times," Lansberg suggested lightly.

Laureen's expression relaxed at his casual tone.

"Perhaps that's it, but it would have been awkward if I'd forgotten my key. I so rarely carry it. Shall we chance our reputations and go in?"

Lansberg nodded. "Mine went long ago, my child; there's only yours to consider. But remember I was promised some nourishment."

Laureen switched on the light in the little square hall. The man followed her in, released the catch of the lock and closed the door behind him.

She paused with her hand on the knob of the door facing her and sniffed.

"Oof! What a queer smell. Disinfectant or something. I'm a nervous idiot! Bertha has probably been cleaning my gloves with benzine, so that's that."

The man noticed that her lips trembled slightly. He tucked his arm into hers and led her into the drawing-room, switching on the lights as he passed. She dropped on to the couch with a sigh of relief, glancing about uneasily.

"Look here, my girl, what you need is a stiff drink. Have you any whisky?"

"In the dining-room," she pointed to a half-open door opposite. "Hello, that benzine smell is stronger here," she whispered.

He pulled back the curtains and opened the window.

"Yes, Bertha seems to have been pretty active," he agreed drily. "I'll get you a toddy. Don't move."

As he was crossing the room Laureen called him back.

"No, I hate spirit; it's a last resource. I'm all right now. By the way, perhaps my maid went off her dot. To-night in Dick Spencer's studio I was handed a parcel. Somebody said it had been left for me by my maid! I thought it was a joke and that I'd spoil their trick by not opening it. Well, they crowded round and insisted, so I pulled off the paper and found a pair of black satin shoes! They were mine, too; I recognized the maker's name and the buckles. I left them in the studio—forgot to bring them back with me. Did you ever hear of anything so idiotic as bringing me a pair of slippers I'd never asked for?"

Lansberg drew out his cigarette-case, his eyes narrowed thoughtfully.

"Have a cigarette? Perhaps the girl fancied you might, like Cinderella, drop a slipper at midnight. Where's that promised chocolate? Let's have it while we're waiting for her and her explanation." He shot a quick glance at Laureen. "Or would you like me to look round the flat?"

"We'll do that if Bertha isn't here in a minute." Rising, she fetched a covered tray with a thermos bottle on it from a table in the corner.

"Now this is becoming really interesting, Mr. Lansberg. This thermos is only used if Bertha has gone to bed—a blue moon occurrence! When she is here naturally she heats the stuff in the kitchen. I'm going to see if she's in her room."

Lansberg put out his hand to check her. "Let me—" he began and broke off at her breathed "Hush! Listen!"

In the tense silence they heard something rustle on the carpet, and then the door into the dining-room slammed suddenly.

Laureen gave a nervous jump.

"A piece of paper blown by a sudden gust of wind which also caused the door to slam." Lansberg spoke in slow, reassuring tones to calm the girl.

But her previous nervousness had gone. She picked up the paper fluttering near the window and held it with steady fingers.

She scanned it through quickly in silence, and then turned to the man with a puzzled air.

"Listen! This is a copy made by Bertha of a telephone call she received at eight thirty this evening. Long ago I insisted that she must write down every call that came through, giving the time, in case she forgot a message."

Over her shoulder Lansberg saw that the paper was evidently a sheet torn from a pad intended for recording telephone messages.

Laureen read it aloud slowly:

*Miss Laureen wishes you to take her black satin shoes with paste buckles to Mr. Spencer's studio, 4 Clarence Road, Chelsea, at ten o'clock to-night certain. Don't ask for her but leave parcel with the servant. Also Miss Laureen says she may not return to-night and that you are to sleep out as usual and return to flat at noon to-morrow.*

Below this was written a note, which Laureen also read:

*Miss Gilbert telephoned this message at 8:15.*
*BERTHA*

"The instructions seem clear and definite," Lansberg remarked.

Laureen folded the paper carefully but absent-mindedly and laid it on the tray.

"Exactly, but who sent them?" she said sharply. "I didn't. I don't know any 'Miss Gilbert.'"

The man regarded her in surprise. This was not the gay laughing girl he had met in the studio, nor the overstrung individual of five minutes ago. Alert and wide-eyed she faced him now with no trace of fear.

"Would you mind going through the flat, Mr. Lansberg?" she asked. "This door," indicating the one behind her, "leads to my bedroom. Beyond it is the bathroom with another door into the hall. You'll find on the left a tiny corridor with two rooms—kitchen and my maid's bedroom. Coming back from her room you'll find the dining-room door in front of you and that will lead you through to this room. A kind of circular tour," she added with a short laugh.

Lansberg bowed, responding immediately to her changed decisive attitude.

"You'll stay here or come with me?" he inquired.

She seated herself on the couch again and poured out the steaming chocolate.

"I'll wait here," she decided. "You'll find switches inside each door. Bring an extra cup and saucer from the kitchen. Please close the doors as you go or they may bang and—and startle me again."

The man saw her composedly add sugar to the chocolate in her cup and stir it. With a shrug as if he cast aside all hope of comprehending a woman's moods, he stepped into the bedroom.

The girl turned as the door closed, listened for his footsteps, then rose and went swiftly to the door that led into the dining-room—the room Lansberg would visit last—opened it noiselessly and slipped inside.

A minute or two later a scream rang through the flat—a scream high-pitched and filled with terror.

Lansberg rushed from the hall into the drawing-room and saw

Laureen standing there, holding on to the handle of the closed dining-room door as if that support alone kept her from falling.

He caught her by the shoulders.

"What is it?"

Her breath came in shuddering gasps as she clung to his arm.

"I—don't—know—exactly. A man asleep—drunk —dead perhaps. I only looked in from the door-way."

"Dead!" he repeated blankly as he drew her back to the couch. "Why did you go in there?" he demanded. "You sent me to search the place."

"It seemed ages waiting. I felt I had to go. What are we to do?" She was fighting for self-control now.

Lansberg's face was like a mask as he answered quietly.

"Sit still, Laureen. You'll need all your strength later. First I'm going into that room and then I shall ring up the police station—if necessary."

The girl shivered as he opened the dining-room door and clicked on the light.

He reappeared in a few seconds.

"Dead!" he snapped out. "Chloroform, I fancy. That accounts for the smell. Where's the telephone?"

She indicated a pink crinolined doll on the bureau, heard the man's crisp tones demanding Scotland Yard.

"What is the exact address of this place, Laureen?" he asked while waiting for the number.

"Flat ten, forty-nine Beresford Street, Westminster," she informed him.

"An inspector and police surgeon will come round at once," he told her a moment later, hanging up the receiver.

"And then?" Laureen's voice was calm again.

Lansberg smiled ruefully.

"Well, then I'm afraid the trouble begins—for somebody. A certain amount for you, possibly, as the scene of action is in your flat. The inspector will ask questions, take possession of the place and search it."

"Search it?" she questioned with a frown. "How —how queer."

Lansberg drummed his fingers on the table a moment. Then: "Did you know this man, Laureen?" he asked sharply.

The girl's eyes wavered.

"Of course not," she replied at once. Then, seeing her mistake, hesitatingly added, "I mean—"

The man laid his hand on hers gently.

"Better make up your mind what you mean before the police arrive," he suggested.

## II. SCOTLAND YARD AT WORK

LAUREEN stared at the closed dining-room door. Mechanically she took a fresh cigarette from a box on the table. Lansberg lighted it, lighted one for himself. For a second his fingers—the fingers that had lain on hers—were held near his face as the match flickered.

"Go and wash your hands quickly, Laureen, and spray some perfume on your dress." Fear flashed across her face as he added, "I smell chloroform there and so may the inspector."

She obeyed, still with that withdrawn air of mental indecision.

He heard her moving about the bedroom for several minutes, opening drawers, splashing water.

"Laureen," he called. And again . . . after a few moments, "Laureen."

Something in the steady sound of the water made him walk into the hall. The bathroom door was open, the light burning, taps turned full on. He turned them off automatically, stood there frowning. Three shrill blasts on a police whistle came suddenly from outside, then soft light steps on the stairs.

Lansberg's hand was on the hall door when it opened against him and Laureen slipped in, her frock gleaming, gray eyes ablaze, triumphant. She held out a police whistle.

"I ran down to see if that nice policeman would come," she explained breathlessly. "Quick, let's go to the drawing-room window and call him up if he comes along the street."

The man followed her to the open window.

"Equally I might have whistled from here and saved you a journey," he remarked, "if you particularly wanted him."

She leaned her bare arms on the window ledge and thrust back her hair with a tired gesture. "He seemed friendly and," she laughed mirthlessly, "I look like needing a friend."

"How far is the pillar-box from here?" he asked irrelevantly.

"At the end of the street," was her instant reply, "quite a hundred yards away. Look, there he is." She pointed to a helmeted figure hurrying along, scanning every house. "Call him."

Lansberg leaned out. "Here, officer," he shouted. "Second floor, right."

"Please," her voice trembled, "I want to speak to you alone before the others arrive."

She heard Lansberg open the outer door, heard the policeman's "Anything wrong, sir? I hope the lady is all right?"

"Something is very wrong. We have found a man dead in there.

I've telephoned Scotland Yard and the inspector will be here any minute. The lady is naturally somewhat distressed. After you've had a look around you might wait in the hall until they come."

"Certainly, sir." Bentley, P. C, removed his helmet with alacrity, as Laureen appeared in the doorway, a less radiant, paler Laureen than had wished him "good night," but no less beautiful.

"Thank you for coming," she said in her soft, clear voice.

In the drawing-room Lansberg took her hands in his.

"Regard me as your friend, my child, not your enemy," he urged.

Her gray eyes were misty, her lips curved in a tremulous smile.

"There may be limits even to what one can impose on friends," she whispered.

"It's you who make those boundaries; not I." She glanced round the room wearily.

"Well, you've had a messy half-hour, Mr. Lansberg. It might have strained an older friendship than ours." She bit her lip.

He tightened his grasp on her hands, as if he would steady her, give her courage.

"Did you know that man, Laureen?"

"Will *they* ask me that?"

"Of course. Why should a stranger be found dead in your flat? But if you know him—well, you are a beautiful and famous actress and it would not be the first time a foolish youth took his life for such a cause." He paused and looked closely at her. "You went close to that man, maybe you even touched him."

Her lips parted.

"What makes you think that?"

"Because as you could not have seen his face from the doorway, you must have gone near him, and, judging from the strong smell of chloroform on your hands, perhaps touched him."

The girl drooped her head and something splashed on his hand.

"Yes," she admitted. "I know him. I—I bent over him to see his face."

"Who is he?"

"A film actor called Delmond. Once I played in a movie with him—years ago," she added hurriedly. The man caught his lower lip between his teeth.

"Is there any reason why you don't want to acknowledge that acquaintance?" he questioned.

For a second she paused. Then:

"Yes," she said desperately. "The usual reason a woman tries to conceal."

Surprise crossed the man's face.

"He was your lover?" he asked incredulously.

"Yes."

Lansberg released her hands, walked to the window and back.

"I see," he said at last, thoughtfully. "Now, about Bertha, your maid. Quick, that's the taxi with the inspector and the doctor, I expect. Do you know who could have sent that extraordinary telephone message?"

"I do not." Her reply was quick and definite. She was evidently concealing nothing there, he felt.

"That phrase about your possibly not returning and the maid to sleep out—what did it mean?"

"That's the curious part," was her answer. "The woman who sent that message knew my arrangements with Bertha intimately. You see, my maid is terrified to sleep here alone, and we have an understanding that any night I may be away I always telephone or send a telegram warning her I shall not come back. On those occasions she goes to some friends."

They heard the bell ring, and a murmur of voices in the hall.

Lansberg bent swiftly to her.

"Leave as much of the talking to me as you can," he warned. "Tell them you once acted in a film with this man and can only suppose—if you're asked—that he might have come here to ask help to get a job. Of the rest, you know nothing. I hope it will be unnecessary to mention your other relationship to the dead man."

The drawing-room door was opened by the policeman and two men entered. They gave a casual glance round the room and the older man of the two spoke to Lansberg.

"You telephoned the Yard, sir, I believe, saying you had found a dead man here just over half an hour ago. I'm Detective Inspector Reynolds. This is Dr. Tempest," he indicated his companion.

Lansberg bowed gravely.

"That is quite correct, Inspector. First of all you'll both want to see the body, I expect."

"Yes, please. Nothing has been touched, of course?"

"Nothing."

Lansberg opened the door into the dining-room and switched on the light, standing aside to allow the inspector and doctor to pass in.

"Miss Laureen is distressed by the tragedy, Inspector," he said in a low voice. "This is her flat. Unless you wish me to remain here while you make your examination I will stay in the next room with her, and tell you all I know when you have finished."

"Certainly," the C. I. D. man agreed. "She will, of course, be able to identify the deceased?"

Lansberg made a dubious gesture.

"That ordeal awaits her, I'm afraid," he said. "I went in alone, and immediately telephoned to Scotland Yard."

He went toward Laureen, leaving the door between the two rooms open and holding up a warning finger to her to be silent.

Presently both men returned.

"And now, sir," said the inspector, "I shall be glad to hear all you can tell me. First, did you know this man?"

"No," replied Lansberg definitely. "My name is Lansberg," he went on; drawing out a thin case, he laid a card on the table. "That is my address. I escorted this lady back from a studio party we had both attended to-night at—" He turned to the girl: "Have you the slightest idea what time we arrived here?"

She shook her head. "I'm afraid not."

Bentley from the background spoke promptly. "It was exactly one twelve A. M., sir, as you paid off the taxi."

Laureen's mouth twitched faintly at the constable's answer.

"Miss Laureen asked me if I would come up and share her chocolate," Lansberg explained. He glanced at the policeman. "Possibly you heard the lady's remark, officer?"

"I did, sir. She also said her maid always waited up for her," he replied sturdily.

Inspector Reynolds wrote something in his note-book. Then he looked up. "You both walked upstairs to the flat, Mr. Lansberg?"

"No," corrected the latter. "We came up by lift. At the door we rang the bell and as there was no answer Miss Laureen was going to put her key in the lock when the hall door opened at the touch of her fingers. The hall was in darkness. The latch was fastened back."

For the first time Inspector Reynolds looked steadily at Laureen— a seemingly vacant gaze as if his thoughts were elsewhere.

"The lady was alarmed?" he questioned.

"Not exactly alarmed. Puzzled and uneasy, perhaps, because her maid, she said, had never done such a thing before. I suggested the maid might have gone out to post a letter and that we might as well go in and wait for her return. The next thing was a curious odor. That worried her a little until she thought perhaps the maid had been cleaning gloves with benzine." Lansberg paused. "Please tell me if I am being too detailed, Inspector."

"You are giving me exactly the information I need, thank you, Mr. Lansberg. Later on some of these memories may be blurred. To-night they are fresh in your mind. Omit no small point: it may be of the highest importance. By the way, you have frequently been to this flat?" The detective's dull gaze swept over Lansberg's imperturbable face.

"Never until to-night, Inspector. We came straight into this room and as the smell was very strong I opened the window. Miss Laureen looked pale and uneasy and I wanted her to have whisky, but she refused."

The inspector let his eyes drift idly over the pink and silver diamante frock the girl was wearing. He turned again to Lansberg. "And after that, sir?"

Lansberg puckered his brows in an endeavor to recall things consecutively, and then detailed the slipper episode.

"They were hers—she recognized the maker's name, and ornaments—but she had not told her maid to bring them there," Lansberg concluded.

"You have the slippers here, madam?" the inspector asked.

"No," replied the girl. "I forgot them. They are at Mr. Spencer's studio."

Inspector Reynolds took up his pencil again. "What is his address, please?"

"Mr. Richard Spencer, four Clarence Road, Chelsea," Lansberg interposed. He waited for the address to be written and then handed Bertha's copy of the telephone message to the inspector, who read it frowningly.

Lansberg turned to the doctor.

"May I ask if you know the cause of death yet, Dr. Tempest?"

"Probably chloroform," the medical man replied guardedly. "One cannot be sure until after the autopsy. He has been dead two or three hours—maybe a little longer."

Lansberg nodded his thanks.

"Who is this Miss Gilbert who telephoned?" asked the detective.

The girl shook her head. Her face was set in a stillness foreign to her usual animation, Lansberg noticed, noticed too that the doctor was studying her.

"I have no idea. I know no one of that name. But, as I told Mr. Lansberg, it must have been sent by some one who knows my arrangements very well," she continued evenly. "Bertha will not sleep here alone at night, so, if unexpectedly I decide not to return, I always send her a message and she goes to friends of hers for the night."

"Where do these friends live?" Reynolds asked.

"At Clapham, I think. I have never needed the address as she has a key and always returns next morning."

The inspector tapped his pencil on the book.

"Um! In that case, madam, she may be there to-night and will return here," he referred to the written message, "at noon, following out your presumed instructions."

Laureen raised her hands in a helpless gesture. "I suppose so, since she has faithfully followed out the first part of them."

The inspector stroked his chin pensively a moment. "When you read this message," he said, "you had no idea there had been a tragedy?"

Lansberg caught Laureen's eyes in one steadying glance and then his calm voice answered for her:

"I think we were both certain by that time that something was wrong and she asked me to search the flat. I began here," Lansberg pointed to the bedroom door, "and went through to the bathroom which led from it."

"The lady accompanied you," suggested the inspector idly.

"No, she remained here."

The C. I. D. man turned swiftly to the girl, pointing an accusing finger.

"And while Mr. Lansberg was out of hearing, you went in and looked at the dead man, madam."

## III. THE TINSELED TRAIL

THE words formed a statement more than a question, and Lansberg felt a pulse beat hard in his neck as they waited for the girl's reply.

She raised puzzled gray eyes to the inspector's stolid countenance.

"Yes," she admitted readily. "That is true. Though I can't think how you knew."

Inspector Reynolds frowned, slightly nonplussed by her unhesitating answer.

"Why did you not go with Mr. Lansberg, or wait until his return, as arranged?" he said crisply to the girl.

She shrugged her shoulders lightly.

"Impulse made me change my mind, I suppose, Inspector. I suddenly felt I could bear the suspense no longer and must do something. It was my fault Mr. Lansberg did not tell you this."

Reynolds switched round to Lansberg again.

"You found no signs of disorder in the bedroom or bathroom, Mr. Lansberg?"

"No. All appeared to be normal. As I say, nothing has been touched since. I had just reached the hall and was about to visit the maid's room and kitchen when I heard a scream. I hurried into this room and found Miss Laureen standing over there," he pointed to the dining-room door. "She looked so ill that I feared she was going to faint."

He paused and glanced from Inspector Reynolds to the doctor, who had been a silent listener to the cross-examination. Something curiously sympathetic in Dr. Tempest's expression induced Lansberg to address him directly.

"I suppose a sudden shock like that, following a series of unusual happenings at one o'clock in the morning, would unnerve any woman, Doctor?"

"I can assure you, Mr. Lansberg," Dr. Tempest replied, "that most women would have been in hysterics for less. Miss Laureen has shown remarkable composure."

Reynolds detected a note of admiration in the doctor's voice and interrupted with a touch of asperity. This was no time for compliments.

"No need to waste any more of your time, Doctor," he said bluntly. "You've seen all you want to in there, I suppose?"

"Quite!"

Dr. Tempest rose, and bade good night to Lansberg and Laureen. At the door he stopped, and, calling the inspector outside, said something to him in an undertone.

"She looks all right," grumbled the inspector.

"Very well, do as you please, but don't blame me afterwards," Dr. Tempest warned him. "That girl has had a bad shock and is fighting pluckily—too pluckily—to prevent herself from breaking down. She needs rest. Where is she going to sleep tonight?"

Reynolds looked aggrieved. "That's not my funeral. A hotel, I suppose. Wherever she goes I shall have an eye kept on her, of course."

The doctor's lips tightened. "She'd be better with friends or relatives than alone in a hotel in her over-strung condition," he retorted curtly. "Better defer your third degree methods on her or she'll be ill. Good night."

He glanced round once more at the girl whose eyes rested on his face wistfully as though she would have wished him to stay. "Good night, Miss Laureen," he said again. "Take a couple of aspirin before you go to bed."

"Thank you, Doctor, I will," she answered gratefully.

Dr. Tempest walked to his home with cold rage in his heart. He and the inspector were on excellent terms, but it was not the first time they had crossed swords over Reynolds's ruthless methods.

As the door closed behind the doctor the inspector spoke almost genially.

"I'm going to look through the flat now. You'd better come too, Mr. Lansberg. The constable can stay in this room in case the lady feels nervous."

The two men went into the bedroom and began their search. In the bathroom the C. I. D. man paused and glanced at the window which was open at the top.

"Did you open that, sir?" he asked.

Lansberg shook his head.

"No. I noticed the bedroom window was open too when I came through earlier."

Reynolds peered through a pane of glass, shading his eyes.

"Umph! Fire-escape staircase just outside, too. All nice and handy!" His eyes wandered vaguely round the tiled walls, came back to the wash-basin with its shining taps. He bent down.

"Some one has just used this," he announced. "The soap is wet."

Lansberg felt a grudging admiration for the man's deductive powers. Evidently he knew his job.

"Yes. Miss Laureen washed her hands here recently, I believe."

Inspector Reynolds seemed to be on the point of asking a question. Then changed his mind and stalked out.

Laureen could hear their footsteps but no sound of conversation reached her ears. Apparently the inspector was saving himself up for her cross-examination, she decided.

She leaned her throbbing head back on the cushions of the chesterfield and closed her eyes. Oh, if only she dare relax! But she knew quite well that any such weakness would mean a flood of tears. Some people could weep with their eyes easily. With Laureen, who cried rarely, it was a crashing down of all control and she knew she would need every ounce of intelligence she possessed presently, when that stony-eyed inspector began his process of dissection.

Police Constable Bentley from his seat just inside the room regarded the lady's white face with consternation. He ventured on a slight cough and, as she looked across at him, he spoke in a voice husky but sympathetic.

"I'm afraid this unpleasant business has upset you, miss. Can I get you anything?"

She regarded his kindly, honest face, reddened slightly now by confusion at the smile she turned on him.

"Thank you, officer, no. One doesn't find a dead man in one's flat every night, you know, or probably one would get used to it and take the matter lightly."

Reynolds at the door, saw the smile and overheard her remark as he was about to enter. He attributed it to flippancy, and registered a decision to ignore Dr. Tempest's advice to go gently with her.

"Tempest's a nervous old maid," he decided. "This girl's as hard as nails; brazenly making eyes at the constable directly my back's turned. I'll put her through it before she has time to make up her story. She knows a deal more than she'll admit."

Aloud he said:

"And now, madam, I'd like you to follow me, please."

He strode firmly across the room and turned on the lights inside the dining-room door.

Lansberg slipped his arm through that of the girl as she rose a little unsteadily. He could feel her body trembling and the fingers that touched his hand were cold as ice. With instinctive kindliness he laid his other hand on hers and gripped it hard just as the inspector swung round with one of his quick gestures.

Reynolds abruptly turned his back again but he had seen the clasped hands, and interpreted it in his own way. His was not a profession that called for sentiment, and personal ambition played a far larger part in his life than devotion to the gentle woman he had married and to whom he had been doggedly faithful ever since.

His voice cut in coldly as Lansberg led the girl toward a big chair which was beside the fireplace, its back toward them.

"Please stand here, madam, *where you stood before*." There was an ominous note in his voice. "Do you recognize the deceased?"

Laureen moistened her dry lips, gazed fearfully at the sagging figure almost hidden in the depths of the big chair. The head was flung back, the face—that of a dark, clean-shaven man about thirty— turned upward. She shuddered and Lansberg felt her lean heavily against him.

"Yes," she said with difficulty. "Yes, I knew him years ago." She swallowed and went on like a child repeating a lesson. "He was a cinema actor, his name was Leslie Delmond. We acted in a film together four years ago. I haven't seen him since and don't know why he came here. We were not on friendly terms. Can I go in the other room now and answer the rest of your questions there?" she finished tremulously.

The inspector turned, bent over the dead man slightly and indicated something on the dark waistcoat, something that glistened.

"Half an hour ago," he said sternly, "you were not afraid to come in here alone and bend over this man, maybe to look more closely at him." He paused for deliberate effect before driving home his thrust. "Even to search his pockets for letters that might be incriminating. This," his finger pointed accusingly at the shining speck on the dead man's waistcoat, "this dropped from the dress you are now wearing. There are other traces of them right across this room. Also—" He checked himself as Laureen covered her face with her hands and gave a choking cry.

Lansberg felt a queer emotion surge in his heart at that cry of pain, an overwhelming pity for the girl who had been broken by the skilled questions of this official. He curbed his anger, realizing the futility of it, indeed the danger of losing any measure of control.

He drew the girl's arm more firmly into his and addressed the inspector with dignity.

"This interview must be continued in the next room, Inspector, otherwise I shall telephone for the lady's doctor to come immediately." There was authority in his voice.

Reynolds was a cautious man. Dr. Tempest's words of warning came back to him. He glanced at the girl anxiously as she stood pale and rigid.

"Certainly, Mr. Lansberg," he agreed hastily. "I can defer questioning the lady further until tomorrow."

Laureen lifted her head proudly.

"No," she said coldly. "I prefer no delay." She spoke to Lansberg, who still held her arm, as they went back to the drawing-room. "It was stupid of me to break down like that. One would think I was already convicted of the crime! I'll have some of that chocolate now; I can drink it cold. Ah, and a cigarette, please."

She extended the box toward Inspector Reynolds as he stood biting his lip, thrown a little out of his stride by this volte-face. "Will you have one, Inspector?"

There was something of challenge in her casual tone, almost a gamin smile on her face as if she tempted him to do his worst with her now.

Reynolds interpreted that glance as one of daring impudence. "Pretending to be hysterical to get my sympathy," he decided, "and when that failed, now thinks she'll try her wiles instead."

Abruptly he declined to smoke.

"I must ring up the Yard at once. Where is your telephone, please?" he demanded.

Laureen pointed.

"Under that frivolous pink thing. I'm sure you disapprove of it, Inspector, nearly as much as you do of me."

She crinkled her nose and made a moue at his stiff back as he issued curt orders through the instrument.

Then he strode into the hall and instructed Bentley to stay there until the men with the ambulance arrived. He returned presently, and choosing the hardest chair he could find, took out his note-book.

Laureen was curled up on the couch, one white arm above her head, blowing smoke rings nonchalantly. From an easy chair opposite Lansberg watched her with anxious eyes. Her present mood was a dangerous one, he realized, for she was keyed up to heights of bravado that might have serious consequences.

"And now, Inspector, I am at your service," she observed sweetly.

"Have you any idea where the deceased lived, or if he has any relatives?" Reynolds began.

"I have no knowledge whatever," she replied, "either of his movements, his relatives or his address."

"Your name, age and occupation, please."

She flashed an impish glance at Lansberg. "Marjorie Laureen; age—well, shall we say twenty-five? Occupation, when lucky, actress."

"Better say revue artist," supplemented Lansberg. "Miss Laureen is very well known, Inspector. In fact one might say she is famous."

Inspector Reynolds licked his pencil and applied himself to his note-book. Spelling had never been one of his strong points and he was by no means sure how to spell the girl's name or exactly what was the technical difference between an actress and a revue artist.

Just then the bell echoed and in a moment Bentley announced that the police photographer and a sergeant had arrived.

"Show them into the dining-room," snapped Reynolds. "I want photographs of all the finger-prints they can find." He turned to the girl again.

"So this is your flat?"

"Yes, I took over the rest of the lease from the last tenant and bought some of his furniture ten months ago. And after this episode he can buy it back from me at his own price as soon as he likes."

She flicked the ash from her cigarette and faced the inspector brightly, waiting for his next question with a look of pleased interest.

Reynolds gnawed his lip but refused to be drawn.

"Please confine yourself to the facts we are now concerned with, madam," he said in his earlier dull tone. "You live here alone?"

"With my maid."

"Her name, please."

"Bertha Mackie." She pronounced it in the Scottish way, accenting the last syllable, and lowered one eyelid in Lansberg's direction as she watched the inspector struggle three times to write the name.

"How do you spell it?" he rapped at last.

Laureen spelled it, waiting patiently for him to write each letter.

"Thank you. At what time did you leave the flat this evening, madam?"

She reflected for a moment. "I think it was ten or twelve minutes past seven."

"Wearing that dress?" He waved his hand at her shining frock.

"Yes—with a cloak over it, naturally."

"You walked downstairs?" he asked.

"No, I pressed the automatic 'ascent' button for the lift to come up, and went down in it."

"You did not return to the flat again until you came here with Mr. Lansberg at one twelve a.m.?"

"I did not," Laureen answered, still with that encouraging look on her face.

Inspector Reynolds lifted his eyes and stared at her.

"Then, Miss Laureen," he said with careful emphasis, "if you went down in the lift at seven twelve P. M., did not return to the flat in the interval, and came up in the lift with Mr. Lansberg at one ten A. M., how is it that I saw tiny glass crystals, like those on your frock, on several stairs when I walked up to-night?"

Laureen's lips parted and terror crept into her eyes as instinctively her mind darted back to the thing she wished to conceal.

"Oh, yes, of course," she added breathlessly, "I—I ran down to whistle for the policeman."

## IV. SHADOWED

AGAIN the bell echoed through the flat, and low voices sounded in the hall.

Bentley appeared and whispered something to the inspector.

"All right, I'll come," he said irritably, fully conscious that this interruption gained time for Laureen, whereas experience had proved to him that an examination taken at top speed reduced the victim to the desired pulp. "The ambulance men, Mr. Lansberg," he explained.

Lansberg leaned toward the girl as the detective went out.

"Listen, my child, I don't want to pry into your secrets, but you're involving yourself in a bad tangle. Won't you trust me? Why did you really run downstairs?"

Her gray eyes had the tragic look, her lips the forlorn droop of a lost child.

"I'll explain that—later," she whispered. "Thank you for wanting to help me. What had I better do?"

"Well, although I detest the idea, you'll be safer if you tell the inspector how much"—he hesitated—"I mean about you and Delmond."

She seemed curiously relieved.

"Oh, about *him*. Very well, I will. What's that?" She twisted round toward the closed bedroom and listened to stealthy sounds. "Some one is opening my wardrobe," she breathed. "I know the squeak of the hinge."

Lansberg's lips set in a grim line.

"They're having a preliminary canter through your things, probably," he said with disgust. "Of course one might protest, but, as you've managed to get yourself in rather a corner, I think it's wiser to ignore it. Unless—Laureen," he asked anxiously, "there's something in there you don't want them to find."

She smiled faintly. "Nothing, you kind man."

"No recent letters from Delmond?"

"Not a line," she assured him.

His tense expression relaxed.

"Thank Heaven for that. Where will you sleep to-night? Of course you can't stay here. Have you any relatives or friends near? I don't like your being in a hotel alone."

She puckered her brows whimsically.

"My dear man, I look like spending a large part of my life alone if this mess doesn't get cleared up satisfactorily." She made a grimace as another creak came from the room behind. "They're at my little desk where I've piles of love letters: most of them from men I've never seen!

What a fool I was to keep them. Indeed, the righteous Reynolds will think I'm an abandoned woman now."

Lansberg clenched his fist, and drew in his breath. "If it would not make things worse for you I'd go in and stop him," he declared. "As it is, I'm helpless. Think where you can sleep to-night."

She was silent for a moment.

"I know," she said with decision. "Top floor in this building. A nice girl and her mother live there: the girl's in the box-office at our theater. The mother's away on a holiday so I know Betty Marden will let me have her room."

The surreptitious creakings in the bedroom ceased, and from the dining-room opposite heavy shuffling sounds came as the ambulance men performed their task.

"Remember, you'll probably be shadowed from this moment onward until the mystery is cleared up, Laureen," Lansberg warned her. "So be careful; to-morrow particularly. And don't antagonize that detective any more to-night."

Suddenly she snatched up her handbag with an exclamation and from it drew out a sheet of thin paper covered with handwriting. She read its contents as if memorizing it, then swiftly struck a match and held it in the flame until the last corner was destroyed, mixing the ashes with the cigarette ends in the ash-tray.

"Light a cigarette," whispered Lansberg, "or he may smell paper has been burnt."

He was holding the match for her as Reynolds entered with his stolid, noiseless tread. The detective's glance traveled round with its usual vague stare, but this time both Lansberg and the girl knew he was missing no detail.

"You left the flat at seven ten p.m. to-night." The C. I. D. man glanced at his watch as he addressed the girl. "Where did you dine?"

"The Regina Grill Room."

"With whom?"

"Two women I knew years ago." She pulled a card out of her bag and tossed it across the table. "You can verify the statement. That is their address. They have only just gone there to live, hence the card to remind me."

The C. I. D. man took the card and carefully slipped it into his note-book.

"You left the Grill Room at what time?"

Laureen frowned.

"Possibly the waiter may know. About eight forty-five."

"And when did you leave those friends?" asked Reynolds as if the matter had lost interest for him.

"They remained in the restaurant when I came away."

"Where did you go then?"

The girl flushed, hesitated and finally spoke in a quick flurry of words.

"I went for a little walk round that neighborhood. It was a lovely night and the restaurant was airless, so I wandered about a bit as it was too early to go to the party. After"—she gave a nervous laugh—"oh yes, after that I took a taxi to Mr. Spencer's studio."

The detective walked across, picked up the pink brocaded wrap on the couch beside her, and scrutinized it minutely. Even its black satin lining did not escape his attention and the pocket cleverly and almost invisibly made. He patted it lightly and laid it down with approval.

"You were wearing this when you were walking?"

"Yes."

"Quite practical, too, in a way, with that black lining," he observed conversationally.

"Yes," amiably agreed Laureen. "It is made to be reversible," and paled instantly at the change in his face.

"Which side were you wearing outward when you wandered about from eight forty-five until you took the taxi to Mr. Spencer's studio?" the C. I. D. man demanded harshly.

Laureen pressed her hand to her cheek. "I—I forget. Oh, the pink side."

"I see." He resumed his seat and pulled at his chin. "So you wish me to believe that you strolled about the West End streets alone to-night from eight forty-five for an hour; hatless, attired in evening dress, covered by a pink evening cloak and wearing thin black slippers."

"Yes," she murmured. Then with a flush of spirit she looked into his face that was expressionless but for the steely eyes. "At least I don't expect you to believe it. I have merely told you what happened."

"I suggest you called somewhere in the interval—at your flat for instance, madam?"

She flung her bag on the table and stood up, erect, proud.

"And may I suggest, Inspector, that three a.m. is the time limit for this interview? I have my work at the theater to-morrow, and Mr. Lansberg can tell you I don't merely show my teeth and smile at the audience. You doubtless will take the precaution of seeing I don't bolt before morning. What time and just where do you wish to renew my acquaintance?"

A vein stood out like a cord on the detective's forehead but he reined in his anger. Overstrung to the breaking-point, was she? Well, later on, he'd see whether Dr. Tempest was right.

"In this room at eleven to-morrow morning, please," he answered. "I want you to be here before your maid returns—if she does."

Laureen bowed coldly. "I shall be here punctually. Do you wish me to appear in this dress, or am I allowed to go to my room now for some more suitable garments?"

Inspector Reynolds swallowed.

"You may, of course, get what you need for the night and during the day. Where do you propose to sleep?" His eyes scanned the fragile frock she wore, making sure its slim outlines left no room for the concealment of important documents.

"Mr. Lansberg can tell you that while I am putting my things together. Is there anything else?"

"Yes," he snapped. "Give me your key to this flat, please."

She pointed to her handbag.

"You may take it for yourself," she remarked contemptuously, and turned her back on him.

Alone with the C. I. D. man Lansberg ventured to placate him.

"Miss Laureen has had a terrific shock and ordeal, Inspector. You must make allowances for her nervous condition and irritation. She feels you are accusing her in some way of concealing something of grave importance. Any girl with her temperament might react in the same way."

The inspector was a little mollified by Lansberg's quiet voice.

"Her answers lack straightforwardness. She runs on smoothly for a while, gets confused suddenly and becomes either frightened or—" he bit back the word "insolent" and substituted "pert." "Where is she going to sleep?"

Lansberg explained what Laureen had thought of doing.

"Very well, sir," Reynolds assented. "She'll be handy if I want her. Tell her to say as little as possible about this affair." He drummed his fingers on his note-book. "I'd like to get at the truth of when she saw Delmond last."

"Ask her," urged Lansberg quickly, remembering his advice to her.

"You know this lady well?" questioned the C. I. D. man.

Lansberg stiffened noticeably, but his reply was courteous.

"Up to this evening she was an acquaintance, a beautiful and witty girl I had admired on the stage. I had met her casually at various parties, but I had never been alone with her until she allowed me to escort her here to-night. After this, however, I hope she will permit me to call her my friend," he said stanchly.

The detective's back was toward the bedroom door and as Lansberg spoke, he looked up and saw her framed in the doorway, gray eyes blurred, her fingers blowing him a mute kiss. And Lansberg was too wise a man to misinterpret that action for other than gratitude.

In a few moments she returned in a black walking-dress and hat. Lansberg took her dressing-case from her hand.

"Tell Inspector Reynolds about Delmond, will you?"

Her eyes flickered, evading the detective's gaze, but she replied in an even voice.

"Leslie Delmond was my lover—while we were at Nice. We quarreled, finally and definitely, and parted there. Do you want to know any more?" she asked wearily.

The inspector metaphorically rubbed his hands. At last he was getting some sense out of her. He could see a speck of daylight. She and Delmond had disagreed, she had become famous and he had wanted to make it up.

"That accounts for a great deal, madam. Why didn't you tell me before?"

"Yes, why didn't I?" echoed the girl tonelessly.

"Nobody likes to rake up such episodes, naturally," continued the detective rather pompously, "but in a case of murder or suicide there must be no concealment. Maybe one need not use that information publicly."

"Good night," said Laureen, as if the publicity or privacy of her statement were all one to her.

"I'll take you up to the top floor and see if you will be all right there before I leave," Lansberg announced.

Inspector Reynolds looked up from writing something.

"By the way, sir, what is your profession? I think I've heard your name."

The man of millions smiled faintly.

"Maybe you have, Inspector. As to my job—well, my interests are varied and a little difficult to enumerate and explain off-hand. Good night. I'll be here at eleven A.M. sharp."

After seeing Laureen admitted to Miss Marden's flat, Lansberg walked slowly downstairs, thinking hard.

On the two bottom flights he noticed at intervals the diamante specks glistening on several steps.

In the empty hall he glanced round, still engrossed in his thoughts. Then, his eyes followed the track of crystals; he gave an exclamation and stared at something fixed to the wall in a recess behind the stairs. Pulling out his handkerchief he flicked aside that damaging trail of shining specks, fervently hoping that Reynolds had not noticed it led to that spot.

Outside the front door stood what was evidently a plain-clothes officer.

"Want a taxi, sir?" the man asked.

"Thanks, no. I think I'll walk," Lansberg replied and strolled up the street.

At the corner he fancied he heard light regular footsteps at some distance behind.

In the next street as he paused to light a cigarette and shot a swift look round, he no longer "fancied"—he knew.

The plain-clothes man was discreetly but surely trailing him, and for the first time that night Lansberg was conscious of lurking fear.

# V. THE MAID'S SECRET

INSPECTOR REYNOLDS was telephoning when Lansberg arrived at the flat two or three minutes before eleven next morning.

The detective nodded in response to Lansberg's greeting and continued to rap sharp orders through the instrument.

"You understand: I want the telephone clerk found who was on duty at eight fifteen last night and any information he or she can give on the subject. If he is off duty, get his address and hunt him up. Send round those prints the minute they're ready."

There was suppressed irritation in the inspector's manner. Usually he could sleep solidly no matter what had happened. But in the few hours at his disposal last night he had tossed restlessly, his mind turning over and over the points of the case.

An hour ago he had arrived and searched minutely through Laureen's rooms for any fresh clue. Beyond the silver specks from the girl's frock, and fingerprints which the photographs would presently show, there was nothing. Temporarily baffled, he felt annoyed, disturbed.

The door-bell rang and Laureen walked into the room as the clock struck eleven. Reynolds felt sure she had deliberately waited for the first stroke of the hour.

She gave him a formal bow and extended her hand to Lansberg. He held it a moment while he studied her face, framed in a small black hat with a smooth wave of her golden hair showing at one side.

"Did you sleep?" he asked her.

"Excellently," adding under her breath, "thanks to the aspirin."

Pale and composed, clad in a soft black-silk suit, she appeared totally different from the temperamental creature of the night before. It was as though she had put on a new personality with her change of dress.

"Splendid," said the man, and thought to himself it would take a wider vision than that of Reynolds to see more than Laureen intended he should see that morning. In other circumstances Lansberg might even have enjoyed the rapier thrusts of her wit against the detective's trained deductions, of instinct against reasoning.

Outside the newsboys were shouting the first editions of the Evening News.

"Mysterious death in Westminster, in famous revue artist's flat."

"Do you hear that?" she asked. "Well, they've got a nice day for it!"

She shrugged her shoulders and settled herself comfortably on the couch, pushing aside the tray of chocolate and the overflowing ash-tray with disgust.

Reynolds was still talking on the telephone, his voice more controlled now.

"Dr. Tempest asked me to say that he hopes you have had some sleep, madam," he announced stiffly as he hung up the receiver.

"Thank you," she replied with equal coldness. "Is there any chance of seeing a newspaper, Mr. Lansberg?"

Lansberg passed her a copy of one just issued.

"I bought it coming along here. Not much more than the bare statement, of course, but I'm afraid they've 'starred' your name pretty prominently."

The inspector interrupted.

"One minute, please, Miss Laureen. Are you married?"

"No," she answered demurely.

"Is Marjorie Laureen your real or stage name?" the detective questioned.

"On the stage and in private life I am known solely as 'Laureen.' I never use the name of Marjorie, which was inflicted upon me when I was too young to protest."

"One name only—I never heard of such a thing," snapped Reynolds.

The girl raised her eyebrows. "Well, you mustn't blame me for that," she flashed back.

"Do you consider the one name legal?"

Laureen's lips twitched. "It seems to have answered that purpose fairly well up to now, considering that I sign all my checks and contracts that way. Shall I consult my lawyer?" she asked with a gentle anxiety that made the tell-tale vein on Reynolds' forehead—sure sign in him of repressed temper—again show clearly.

"Why," he asked, "did you run downstairs to whistle for the policeman? You could have done that from the window."

She smiled sweetly.

"Of course. But in case he was in sight I thought I could have told him what was wrong more quickly."

Her answer had reason but it failed somehow to convince Reynolds entirely.

"And how long did this journey up and down stairs take?" he questioned.

"Not more than three or four minutes. I ran both ways."

"What time did you arrive at Mr. Spencer's studio last night? I want the exact time, please," he rasped, changing the theme.

"One doesn't 'clock in' at a party," she explained patiently. "I can't tell you to half an hour. About ten fifteen, perhaps. Although it might have been later."

"Mr. Spencer will know, of course," he commented, "as you must have spoken to him on arrival."

"You can ask him," she remarked indifferently. "There were crowds of people there. It's a largish flat and every room was packed."

"Had you been there long when the parcel containing your slippers was given you?"

She glanced at Lansberg. "I believe you were there then. Do you remember the time?"

Lansberg reflected.

"About eleven o'clock, I should think, but it's a rough guess."

Inspector Reynolds tapped his pencil on the table impatiently.

Fencing with these "abouts" annoyed him. Of course the girl knew when she arrived there and at what time the parcel was given to her. He could not possibly visualize that Laureen had been surrounded by a delighted circle of friends the moment she came. A gay laughing crowd with no thought of time, whose one idea was to squeeze the last drop of pleasure from any diversion.

"Where did you pick up the taxi in which you went to the studio?"

Laureen hesitated an instant.

"Regent Street—near Oxford Circus," she replied slowly.

The detective made a note reminding him to trace that vehicle.

She watched his face, knowing he was mentally measuring the distance between that spot and the restaurant at which she had dined.

The telephone bell jarred. Before the girl could move to answer it Reynolds was at the instrument.

They heard his curt monosyllables. Presently he banged down the receiver and walked back to the table. But he did not sit down.

Laureen looked up at him and was startled to see the stern expression on his face.

"I have just ascertained, madam, that you left the restaurant at eight twenty-five P.M. Two waiters agreed as to that point, which has also been confirmed by the ladies with whom you dined."

"How nice for you," Laureen remarked flippantly. "You have quite enough trouble with me without my friends adding to it. I really must try to start a time chart of all I do. So much simpler—"

"Miss Laureen," the inspector checked her, "do you realize that a man was murdered in this flat last night and that you are hampering the course of justice by these"—he choked back the word he longed to use—"idle jests?" he substituted.

And even he was surprised at the result of his rebuke.

"I don't think I had fully realized that, Inspector," she said at once, gently. "I'm sorry."

It was a difficult remark for the C. I. D. man to grapple. Her swift apology disarmed him.

"Damned clever little actress," he told himself.

But Laureen had meant exactly what she had said. With the warm, impulsive generosity that characterized her, she was honest enough to see the justice of his words, reasonable enough to express immediate regret. She saw now, however, that he doubted her sincerity, and in her pride almost wished she could recall that apology.

Following a ring of the door a sergeant brought in a parcel and left it at the inspector's elbow.

Reynolds sat down heavily, opened the package and engrossed himself in the contents.

"Will you play to-night, Laureen?" asked Lansberg.

"Why not?" she demanded.

"An Irishman's answer!" he smiled. "I only wondered if you would feel fit."

"It's my job," she said casually. "What right have I to let down my manager and fellow artists?"

"To say nothing of the audience. The theater won't have standing room to-night after that publicity." He pointed to the newspaper on the table.

"Notoriety, you mean," she retorted with that delicious little crinkling up of her nose and mouth that expressed so much. A critic had once said of her that she had reduced restraint in gesture to the last point of economy, which was doubtless why every movement of her hands, every change of expression indicated so much.

"I've reserved a box for to-night. Will you have supper with me afterward?" Lansberg asked her.

She nodded.

"Yes, I'd like to. Anybody else coming?"

"I thought of asking Spencer and that Dr. Tempest who was here last night. I'd met Tempest before but we discreetly ignored that fact. Will they please you and would you like any one else? Any women friends?"

She flicked the newspaper with her fingers.

"After those head-lines I'm not likely to have women coveting my society."

"Nonsense," said Lansberg. "We'll arrange that later."

With a mischievous glance toward the detective's bent head she raised her hand to her mouth and whispered:

"Couldn't ask my nice policeman, I suppose?"

"You could not," asserted Lansberg with twitching lips.

"Ah me," she sighed. "Well, I'll console myself with a cigarette. May I smoke, Inspector?" she asked as Lansberg held the match for her to light it.

The C. I. D. man nodded permission and drew a piece of brown paper thoughtfully over what he had been scrutinizing so closely. Then he looked at Lansberg.

Last night the detective had not had much time to study this man. Briefly he had noted that he was well-dressed, had a cultured voice and manner as of one used to command and be obeyed; forty-ish, a fraction over the medium height and firmly built though slim.

Now he noticed the strength of the jaw, the firm mouth and alert eyes with tired lines round them, the thick smoothly brushed black hair parted in the middle, graying at the temples.

But the C. I. D. man studied more particularly Lansberg's hands. Strong, thin, beautifully shaped hands with fine sunburnt skin.

Hands were the detective's fetish. He often declared there was far more to be learnt from a hand than a face, and he never forgot a man's hands, as many a criminal behind bars knew to his sorrow.

As far as movement went, there was little to be learnt from Lansberg's hands. He had more than the usual English lack of gesture. When he did make a rare movement, however, it had decision and determination in it.

There were a lot of things Inspector Reynolds wanted to know about Lansberg, but that would have to wait until later. He glanced at his watch and set the door leading into the hall ajar.

"Twenty to twelve," he said aloud. "If your maid comes, where is she likely to go first when she arrives, madam?"

"Probably to her bedroom to take off her hat, providing your sergeant in the hall doesn't scare her to flight."

"I've already seen to that. He is in the dining-room and that door into the hall is locked. I'm anxious to know if she has a key or will have to ring. Mr. Lansberg, I should like to have a talk with you alone this afternoon," he added.

"Choose your time and place, Inspector," Lansberg replied calmly.

"Two thirty," the detective paused deliberately for the fraction of a second, "at your apartment."

Whatever effect he hoped to gain by that slight hesitation produced no result in the courteous mask, of Lansberg's face as he assented.

But the inspector's eyes were watching Lansberg's hands, recording the slight tension in those slim fingers.

Suddenly there was the click of a key being turned in the lock, the hall door opened and closed firmly, and a woman's voice was heard humming some melody.

"She hasn't heard the news," breathed Laureen.

The inspector gave a sharp glance of approval. Yes, this girl had a quick brain right enough.

The humming ceased, giving way to two loud sniffs.

Laureen pointed to her cigarette silently and raised her eyes in mock despair.

"Are you in, miss?" came from the hall.

Laureen glanced at Reynolds for instructions.

"Call her," he whispered.

"Yes: in the drawing-room. Come in here, Bertha."

A woman of about thirty-five entered the doorway.

"I smelt tobacco and guessed—" she began and broke off in startled surprise to see the two men.

"Don't be alarmed, Bertha," said Laureen quietly. "Something rather tragic happened here last night and these gentlemen are inquiring into it." She looked at Reynolds. "I'll leave the matter in your hands now."

The detective let his glance slide over the woman as he told her to sit down.

"I want to ask you a few questions," he began in a soothing way. He was anxious not to frighten this woman too soon.

"My name is Reynolds, Inspector Reynolds. That gentleman you already know, I expect," he waved his hand toward Lansberg.

The maid looked as directed.

"No," she said definitely. "I don't know him."

"You mean you don't know him personally, or that you've never seen him in this flat before?"

"Both," came the brief retort. Bertha had lived long enough with Laureen to admire and imitate her mistress's crisp style of repartee, and was rather pleased at the chance of showing off her powers now. All this back-chat with an inspector, indeed! What did he want with her? Had there been a burglary?

"You swear you never saw this gentleman before?" the inspector asked.

"I didn't say so," replied the maid unexpectedly.

Reynolds sat back and stared at her, then glanced swiftly at Lansberg, whose countenance showed faint surprise.

"Didn't you tell me you'd never seen this gentleman before?" he questioned in astonishment. Bertha folded her hands calmly.

"Certainly not. I told you I didn't know him personally, and had never seen him in this flat. That's all you asked and that's all I answered." She turned to her mistress. "Excuse me, miss, but have I got to reply to all these questions? I've my work to do."

"The work can wait, Bertha," Laureen told her. "You must answer anything Inspector Reynolds wishes to ask you."

"Very well, miss, but please tell me what has happened." She peered round nervously. "Have there been burglars here?"

Laureen gave a tired sigh. "I'm afraid you'll know soon enough, Bertha."

The C. I. D. man had an opportunity to observe and sum up the maid while she was speaking to her mistress. Scottish accent, not bad-looking, he decided; neat, probably honest, loyal, reserved with that extraordinary faculty for surrender that only the reserved possess; obstinate, proud of her mistress—his sharp ear had already detected the unconscious imitation in her crisp replies. Altogether a harder nut to crack than he had imagined. However, he had resources with which to break down most defenses. Servants usually had a healthy fear of the law. He would try a little more force.

"Your full name, please, and correct age," he demanded bruskly.

The maid barely suppressed a snort. "Bertha Ellen Mackie, age thirty-five," flushing a little as she caught her mistress's amused eyes. Well, she didn't *look* more than twenty-eight, so what did it matter if she had given that as her age when she had been engaged.

"You are English?" went on the detective.

"Born in Aberdeen, as my father was."

"When did you become Miss Laureen's maid?"

"Ten months ago when she took this flat."

"You sleep here?"

"I do, unless my mistress is going to be away and then she lets me know and I sleep out." She turned suddenly to Laureen. "You got your slippers in time, miss?"

Laureen repressed a smile.

"Yes, thank you, Bertha."

"I left the telephone message from a Miss Gilbert written down, miss."

"Yes, I saw it, thank you."

"Didn't you think it strange that your mistress should send orders for a pair of slippers when you knew she had gone out wearing a pair?" Reynolds asked in his mildest tones.

"It's not my business to think about my mistress's affairs. She pays me to do the work and carry out her instructions. She pays me well, too," the maid added loyally.

"Pays you well, eh," the inspector ruminated. Then, pointing his finger at the woman suddenly, he rasped, *"Why?"*

"Got her," he exulted to himself as he saw her jump.

"As I said, to do the work and obey orders," she replied in a dogged voice.

"And keep your mouth shut?"

"Nothing of the sort," she retorted indignantly. "Miss Laureen is as open as the day. And I don't believe you've any right to insult me, inspector or no inspector."

Bertha was angry now, which was all to the good for Reynolds. People were off their guard then.

"How many keys are there to this flat?" he asked. The maid hesitated for the first time.

"There were three. The one my mistress has, one I have and a third that was kept in a drawer in the hall table." She looked a little shamefacedly at her mistress. "I'm sorry I never told you, miss, but I must have dropped mine from my bag a week ago. You let me in when I came back next morning and I just took the other key from the drawer and said nothing about it."

"It doesn't matter, Bertha," Laureen assured her gently.

"No idea where you lost it?" pursued the inspector.

"No," she replied promptly. "I probably pulled it out in the street with my handkerchief." She faced her mistress. "I left the chocolate ready, miss, in case you returned after all. I'm glad you had it."

The chocolate! Laureen's eyes met those of Lansberg ruefully for a second. If it had not been for that invitation she might have come up alone last night. She shivered at the thought.

"Yes," she replied. "It was a good thing you made it, Bertha."

"Where and when did you see this gentleman and by what name do you know him?" the inspector demanded of the maid.

"I don't know him by any name," she answered. "I saw him last night half an hour after I'd left Mr. Spencer's studio."

"Where?"

"Getting on a bus near Victoria."

"And what made you notice him—a stranger—particularly?" asked Reynolds blandly.

"I'd seen him twice before in Miss Laureen's theater in a box: she often gives me a pass. Last night I remembered his face and thought in his evening dress he looked more suited to a Rolls-Royce than an omnibus."

Lansberg's eyes twinkled.

"It's quite correct that I took a bus to the studio, Inspector. I couldn't find a taxi. I wasn't aware I had made myself so conspicuous."

The inspector paused to make a note.

"And after you saw this gentleman get on a bus, what did you do?"

Bertha gave the nearest thing to tossing her head that her standard of manners permitted.

"Then I took a walk before going to my friends at Clapham."

"It seems to have been a night for taking exercise," observed the inspector. "Made you a bit late in getting to Clapham, didn't it?"

"My friends never go to bed until midnight. I got there before that."

"What is their name, address and business?"

"Mrs. and Miss Dean, fifteen Garfield Road, Clapham. They own the house and let apartments. She's an Aberdeen woman. I pay for my room," Bertha added shortly.

"Any particular reason why you took a walk? Any friend you wanted to see?" questioned Reynolds casually.

"I thought I might meet a friend, but they didn't turn up."

"H'm. 'They' being a young man, I suppose?"

The maid reddened, showed signs of losing her temper.

"That's no affair of anybody's but my own," she retorted with heat.

The inspector slipped his hand under the brown paper and drew out a photograph. Sometimes a chance shot brought unexpected results.

"Ever seen that man before?" he asked, swiftly putting the print before her.

The maid stared speechlessly, her hands clutching the sides of the chair.

"That man was found dead in the dining-room here last night," the inspector said slowly and ruthlessly.

But even he was startled at the result of his words, for the color drained from the maid's face and with a gasp she slipped fainting to the floor.

## VI. THE LETTER

THE inspector's face showed neither elation at the success of his manoeuver nor regret at the collapse of the girl.

"Sergeant," he called, "help me to carry this woman to her room. Don't worry, madam," he said to Laureen, who was bending over Bertha in consternation. "The sergeant's a 'first aid' man. She'll come round presently."

As they conveyed the woman out there came from the street below a piercing cry, followed by a crash. Lansberg darted to the open window and leaned out.

"Oh, what is it now?" Laureen asked anxiously, pressing her hands to her head.

"A girl has been knocked down by a motor-car," he answered.

"Is she hurt?"

"I don't know. The men have lifted her into the car and driven off."

Lansberg spoke casually; Laureen had had enough shocks in the last twelve hours. "Is the maid recovering, Inspector?" he added as the detective reentered the room.

"Yes, she'll be all right soon, sir. My man's looking after her." "In more senses of the word than one," he supplemented inwardly. There was a great deal more he wanted to know about Bertha's acquaintance with the dead man.

"What were her duties here, Miss Laureen?" the inspector went on. "Please tell me her daily routine."

The girl reflected.

"When I wake she brings me my tea, prepares my bath, gets out any clothes I require, tidies my room and makes the bed. Then Mrs. Carter—"

"Mrs. Carter," interjected the C. I. D. man.

"Who is she?"

"The wife of the caretaker. They live in the basement and Mrs. Carter works in the different flats, by the hour, as she is required."

Reynolds wrote something hurriedly in his notebook.

"Go on, please," he urged.

"Mrs. Carter comes in and cleans my bedroom and bathroom and I suppose these sitting-rooms and the hall. Bertha dusts them, arranges the flowers and so on, does light washing and mends and looks after my clothes. She was a dressmaker once."

"That occupies all her time?" Reynolds questioned. "What about meals?"

"Bertha does the shopping in the afternoons usually and she and

Mrs. Carter prepare the few meals I have here. During the evenings she is always free to go out, but I don't think she avails herself of her freedom very often."

"How do you know?" he demanded.

"When I've telephoned her from the theater I don't think I've ever failed to get an answer. Except perhaps within the last week or two."

"Oh, been going out more in the evenings lately, has she?"

Laureen raised her eyebrows. "I've already told you she was at liberty to do so, Inspector. It is no business of mine what the maid does on her own time," she said distantly.

Reynolds thumped the table in exasperation. "I daresay, madam, but it happens to be very much my business what she did, where and when she went and with whom. That woman knows a great deal about Delmond."

*"Impossible."* The word shot from the girl forcefully, inadvertently, and the color rose to her pale face as she realized her slip.

The detective's eyes narrowed a little, though his voice was silky and persuasive.

"And what makes you think your maid—after recognizing the dead man's photograph and fainting at the news of his death—could know nothing about him?"

But Laureen had herself in hand this time.

"I was thinking of my own—episode, of course. How could Bertha have known of it?" she fenced coolly.

"I see," the detective replied. "How about this Mrs. Carter? If she works here daily how is it she hasn't turned up this morning?"

"Whenever I'm sleeping out—as Bertha presumed I was last night—my maid calls down the speaking-tube and informs her, and Mrs. Carter doesn't come up next day until Bertha tells her. I believe that is their arrangement."

"Speaking-tube?" Reynolds looked blankly round the room. "I didn't know you had one. Where is it?"

"In the hall, just outside the dining-room door. It's in a dark corner, rather hidden by some coats that hang there. It was installed by the previous tenant, I believe."

The inspector stamped out, annoyed at having overlooked anything.

"Yes, it's there," he announced glumly. "If I blow down the thing, will Mrs. Carter answer?"

"Probably, unless she's working in one of the other flats. In which case her husband will possibly reply and fetch her if you wish."

"I certainly do wish," he said with finality, and again went into the hall.

"What a morning!" sighed Laureen, raising her hands wearily.

"After such a night, too, you poor child," Lansberg softly replied. "And now we're to have more witnesses and more questions."

Panic came to the girl's heart as she remembered a visitor who *might* call. There indeed would be a witness in whom the inspector would revel. Laureen prayed fervently that no one would come.

They listened to Reynolds shouting urgent instructions for Mrs. Carter to be fetched at once.

"You come up too," he demanded through the tube.

In a few moments a thin, anxious woman appeared, wiping her hands nervously on her apron.

"Are you Mrs. Carter?" Reynolds began.

"Yes, sir. My husband will be here in a minute," she said in a frightened voice. "He's just dressing."

"Dressing!" ejaculated the detective. "Isn't the man up yet?"

"He's only been in bed an hour or two, sir. He's a night-watchman."

The C. I. D. man smiled.

"Oh, I see. Sorry to have to disturb him. I'm Inspector Reynolds from Scotland Yard. By the way, have you seen any newspapers at all this morning, Mrs. Carter?"

The woman looked surprised at his question.

"Me, sir? I've no time to read newspapers weekdays. Why, has anything happened?"

"Yes," Reynolds told her briefly. "A man was found dead in here last night." He pointed to the dining-room.

The woman glanced with an awed expression at the door he indicated.

"Well, I don't know anything about it, sir," she assured him.

Reynolds looked at her kindly.

"There's nothing for you to be alarmed about. I only want you to answer my questions truthfully and clearly."

"I'll try, sir," she murmured.

"Very good. Now tell me why you didn't come up here as usual this morning?"

"Miss Laureen's maid called down to me last night that she and her mistress would be away for the night and that she'd let me know when she wanted me this morning." She turned her tired face to Laureen. "I'm sorry if you wanted me earlier, miss, but I've been working in the flats above and when Joe's asleep—my husband, that is—he don't always hear the speaking-tube."

"You've done exactly as my maid told you, Mrs. Carter. She didn't want you sooner," Laureen replied.

"Have you ever seen this gentleman before?" the detective by a gesture drew the woman's attention to Lansberg.

"No, sir. The maid always opens the door to visitors."

Lansberg turned towards Reynolds with amused eyes.

"You'll soon have evidence enough to force you to believe my statement that I was never in this flat until last night, Inspector," he remarked.

The detective looked uneasy.

"We are obliged to verify everything, sir," he said in conciliating tones, and bent over his note-book.

"Rather an endless chain, but of course you have your own methods," Lansberg returned indifferently as he offered his cigarette case to Laureen.

She took a cigarette, bent forward to light it from the match he held and pointed to the ash-tray, unemptied of last night's stubs and ashes.

"Might we have that unpleasantness removed, Inspector?" she asked, "or are you preserving it as an important exhibit?"

Reynolds raised his torpid eyes to the tray Lansberg was just about to tip into the coal-scuttle. He rose suddenly.

"Allow me," he said with heavy politeness, and taking it from Lansberg's hand he walked into the hall.

Laureen's brows went up in comical surprise. "Well, well," she murmured. "Quite the little gentleman, isn't he?"

But Lansberg's eyes were serious. Burnt paper, even crushed, never achieves the fine powder of cigarette ash, and he was pretty sure Reynolds's action had been neither accidental nor merely courteous.

They heard a knock on the hall door and a moment later the detective returned, followed by a sleepy-eyed man with tumbled sandy hair, and coat collar turned up to hide the fact that he had had no time to put on a collar.

Carter glared around irritably and centered his indignation on his wife as being the only person on whom he dared vent his anger.

"You'd better get along with your work upstairs," he jerked his head sideways toward the door. "Disturbing a respectable man just as he's got to sleep," he grumbled generally, sending a hostile look in Laureen's direction. He didn't hold with play actresses and wasn't at all surprised there was something wrong in her flat. "Wot's all this about?" he demanded of Reynolds aggressively.

The inspector signed to Mrs. Carter, who was obediently making for the door, to sit down.

"Keep a civil tongue in your head, my man," he said peremptorily, "or you may be sorry for it. I'm from Scotland Yard. There was a mysterious death in this flat last night. Answer my questions carefully. What's your name?"

The bluster died out of the man's tone.

"Death?" he repeated with awe. And then seeing the detective's stern face, swallowed and automatically replied, "Albert Joseph Carter."

"How long have you and your wife acted as caretakers of this house?"

"Five years come Michaelmas, sir." He cast another infuriated glance at Laureen. "And never had anything go wrong until now. First time we've ever had an actress for a 'let.' Very genteel people live here who go to work and come back at reasonable hours."

The girl smiled demurely. "I'm sorry my work brings me back at unreasonable hours, Inspector."

"Work!" interposed Carter with a snort.

"Silence!" The detective thundered. "Answer my questions without insults or comment, Carter. You're a night-watchman, I believe. Where?"

"Garland's garage, Oxford Street," came the sullen reply.

"What are your hours there?"

"Nine at night to six in the morning. Sundays included, more's the shame," he added bitterly.

"Joe's 'chapel,' sir, and feels he ought to have his Sundays free," Mrs. Carter interpreted.

"Ah, I understand. Just what duties have you here?"

"A jolly lot of work and five shillings a week rent to pay besides," muttered the man.

Inspector Reynolds fixed him with a steely eye.

"Don't beat about the bush. What do you do each morning when you return? This morning, for instance?"

"Same as every other morning. Opened the front door—"

"Stop a minute." The inspector held up his hand. "Is that door locked at night?"

Carter shook his head.

"Never is now. Tenants were always forgetting their hall door key and ringing me up."

"Ringing *me* up, Joe," put in his wife. "You're not there at night."

"Well, same thing," Joe continued. "So the landlord said the door need only be shut. Often it stays wide open all night."

The C. I. D. man drummed his fingers on the table.

"Right. Continue your list of duties. You open the front door," he prompted.

"Beat the mats, sweep down five blessed flights of stairs—"

"Oh, I always help you with the stairs, Joe," reproached his wife. "We wash them down once a week, sir."

"Go on," encouraged the inspector. "What next after the stairs, Carter?"

"After I've done the stairs," the man went on doggedly, ignoring his wife's interruption, "I sweep and wash the hall and steps, take the milk bottles and newspapers up outside the different flats, and go down to my breakfast and then to bed."

"Nothing more?" queried the detective.

"The post-box, Joe," prompted Mrs. Carter in an awed whisper behind her hand.

"Post-box?" Inspector Reynolds sat up abruptly.

"A new-fangled box for the tenants to put their letters in," Carter replied. "The pillar-box is a good way from here, so the landlord had this box screwed up in the hall and I've got orders to clear it night and morning. One more job for me just because folks are too lazy to post their own letters."

"Where's the box fixed?"

"In a recess, round by the lift and stairs, sir."

The detective stroked his chin, visualizing the staircase and hall, remembering the track of those glittering beads.

"Now think very carefully, Carter. If any one entered by the hall door and came up here by lift or stairs, need they pass near the post-box?"

The man answered promptly.

"Certainly not, sir. The box is behind the stairs. They'd be going out of their way up or down to go near it."

The C. I. D. man looked speculatively at Laureen. If she had been near that box when she rushed downstairs to whistle for a policeman it was obviously to post something.

"It's very handy if it's wet weather, sir," Mrs. Carter put in. "Very few people use it if it's fine."

"As if that mattered," growled her husband. "Full or empty I got to clear it all the same."

"Who keeps the key?" questioned the C. I. D. man.

"I do, sir," Carter answered.

"Many letters there this morning?" Reynolds asked in his dullest tone, sharpening his pencil as though nothing else interested him.

"Four or five."

"None you noticed a bit different in any way?"

Carter aired his grievance again. "I got too much to do when I've been up all night to bother about other people's letters, sir."

"Quite so," agreed Reynolds, regarding his beautifully pointed pencil with pride. "But you're a smart-brained man and it occurred to me you might have seen something unusual this morning that might have helped me. Caught sight of an address for instance."

Carter preened at the compliment.

"I remember one was a bit heavy, sir, and I sort of weighed it in my hand going up the street to the pillar-box thinking somebody might have to pay extra on it."

Inspector Reynolds turned a fond eye on him.

"Now didn't I say you had a smart brain, Carter? I suppose it's too much to hope for that you noticed any part of the address?"

Carter began to enjoy himself. He screwed himself up to violent mental effort. This inspector evidently recognized intelligence when he saw it.

"I remember looking to see whether it had more than a three ha'penny stamp on it."

"Now that was really bright," appreciated the inspector. "Was the handwriting large or small?"

"Very large. Looked as if a child had scribbled it in a hurry. It was addressed to 'Miss Valerie Somebody,' but I can't remember the surname or the address."

Reynolds handed the man an envelope and flashed a casual glance at Laureen's long lashes as she sat absorbed in the newspaper.

"Just scribble down roughly what it looked like for length of the name, how many lines of address, etc. Do you think it was for London?"

"Yes, sir," said the man promptly. "I remember the W.1. The surname was shortish."

"Like Smith?"

The man nodded.

"Well," said Reynolds pleasantly, handing Carter his pencil, "it's wonderful you should have recalled all that. Half the people in this world go along with their eyes shut. Whereas you—" Eloquence seemed to fail him when he dealt with Carter's gift of observation. "Make that envelope look as much like the other as possible. Fill in crosses to get the length of the words approximately."

The man worked laboriously for a while, conscious of the Inspector's admiring regard.

"That's as near as I can get it, sir," he said at last, pushing the envelope across the table. It was inscribed as follows:

Miss Valerie XXXXX,
XXXX XXXXX xxxxxxx
London, W. 1.

The inspector regarded it slowly. "Splendid!" he said. "You've done exactly what I wanted." He pulled a crumpled piece of paper from his pocket and smoothed it out. It bore the address of the flat in one corner and was evidently a letter for some reason unfinished. Reynolds loved a wastepaper basket as a cat loves canaries.

"Was the writing anything like this, Carter?" he asked, indicating the crumpled paper.

"Yes, it was, rather, sir, only written larger."

Reynolds put the papers carefully into his pocket.

"Excellent," he said with a pleased air, and found Laureen's eyes peering at him curiously.

"Is it necessary to waste Mr. Lansberg's morning listening to these trivial questions? He is a busy man with many engagements. To say nothing of mine," she interposed.

"It's not only necessary but imperative, madam," the inspector assured her. "At any moment I may need your or Mr. Lansberg's help, and for your sakes it's wiser for you both to be present to hear the evidence."

"That's all right, Inspector," assented Lansberg. "Of course we must remain. My appointments are unimportant compared with this. Have you as yet learned of the precise cause of death?" he asked in a low voice.

The detective shook his head.

"Can't know that until latish this afternoon, sir." He turned to Carter. "Well, I think you can go back to bed, Carter, and your wife to her work. You've both given very honest and helpful replies. I'll call either of you again if necessary."

"Thank you, sir." Carter touched his forehead and rose to go. "Come on," he said roughly to his wife.

But a change had come over Mrs. Carter.

Maybe she resented Laureen's slighting remark about "trivial questions," maybe she was envious of the limelight thrown on her husband's performance compared to her own colorless statements.

Suddenly she stood up in front of the inspector.

"Perhaps I ought to mention that I heard men's voices talking loudly here in this flat soon after the maid went last night, sir," she said and folded her hands, placidly waiting for the effect of her words.

## VII.  THE SPEAKING TUBE

MRS. CARTER created all the interest she expected. Each member of her audience reacted differently.

Laureen leaned forward amusedly, chin cupped in her hand.

Lansberg's face set into graver lines, while Carter glared stonily at his wife for stealing his thunder.

Into the detective's eyes crept the hazy look that drew his victims on to a sense of false security.

"What business had you got listening at the doors of flats at night?" demanded Carter.

His wife gave him a withering look. "I wasn't listening at any doors," she retorted. "If Bertha leaves the stopper out of the speaking-tube is that my fault? She often does, and then if I pass close to the tube in my kitchen I can hear if people are talking near it up here."

"What time was this, Mrs. Carter?" asked the detective gently. "About ten to half past?"

"That's right, sir. I didn't look at the clock but it was about half an hour after the maid went out, and I went to bed at quarter to eleven, so it must have been as you said."

Reynolds made a hurried note.

"Hear anything? Just tell me what happened."

Mrs. Carter put her head on one side meditatively.

"Well, sir, Joe had gone to work and I was having a quiet read of the Sunday papers when I heard men's voices. Two or three men, I should think."

She paused a minute, then continued. "Yes, I'm sure I heard three different voices altogether. For a minute I was startled. Then I remembered the tube was right beside me and I'd left my stopper out when the maid called me."

"This is all highly important, Mrs. Carter," the detective said. "I only hope you listened," he added, urgently, in case ill-judged reticence might keep her from admitting that fact and all she had heard.

She twisted her apron and colored. "Yes, sir, I did, because after the maid said she and Miss Laureen would be out for the night it seemed queer that men should be up there talking."

"Very queer," agreed Reynolds. "Could you hear what was said?"

Mrs. Carter shook her head. "Not clearly. But I'm sure they were quarreling. They must have been in the hall. First I heard men's voices. Then they faded away, probably the men went into another room."

"And you couldn't distinguish a word they said?" asked Reynolds eagerly.

"No, sir. I only wish I had."

"You didn't think of coming up to see who those men were in Miss Laureen's flat when you knew she and her maid were out? They might have been burglars." The C.I.D. man's tone was curt.

The woman bristled. After all her help, for this detective to turn round on her like that!

"Burglars, indeed!" she said scornfully. "They wouldn't make a row, would they? They'd be as quiet as they could. Actresses do queer things. It was no business of mine if Miss Laureen pretended she'd be away for the night and sent her maid off, and then brought back some men to gamble. That's my belief if you ask me."

Nobody did, and Mrs. Carter added viciously: "She's got a roulette wheel. I asked the maid what it was once and she said it was a Monte Carlo gambling machine."

Laureen bit her lip to hide her amusement. "It's over there, Inspector," she pointed to a low table, "under a pile of magazines. Somebody gave it me ages ago, but it has a bias, so has not been used."

The inspector lifted the books off and scanned the "gambling machine" carefully.

"It's covered with dust and has evidently not been used for months," he observed. "Sergeant," he called to his man in the hall, "go downstairs with Mrs. Carter and sit where she was last night. Blow up the tube when you're ready. I want to test this speaking-tube."

Presently they heard a whistle and the detective spoke in a loud voice some feet away from the pipe.

"You, too, Mr. Lansberg," the detective requested. "Will you please come here and talk to me in an angry manner?"

Lansberg's eyes twinkled as he caught Laureen's muttered "I wish he'd ask me to talk to him in an angry manner. It would come so naturally!"

"Hear anything, Sergeant?" Reynolds asked a few moments later when his man returned from the basement.

"Yes, sir," came the reply. "Just as Mrs. Carter said. I could hear a voice, yours, I think, sir, but couldn't hear a word distinctly."

The inspector heaved a sigh of relief.

"That's one point proved, anyhow, in this case. Most unusual one I've had for a long time. Anybody could have walked in and killed that man. Every door open, no hall porter, nobody about, windows open, fire-escape outside. Everything handy for the murderer to escape."

"Now who were those people who were here talking?" he meditated. Then with one of his swift moves he turned to the girl.

"Have *you* any idea who the men were, Miss Laureen?" he rasped.

"Presumably Delmond was one. Other than that, I certainly do not know. Neither do I know how, why or when they entered my flat," she replied firmly.

"Sergeant, if that maid has recovered from her fainting fit, fetch her in. I want to ask her a question or two."

Declining the help of the sergeant who offered her his arm, Bertha came in a little unsteadily and took the chair indicated by the inspector.

She looked pale, but obstinate and a little defiant as she sat waiting for Reynolds to open fire. "Going to try and brazen it out," he decided to himself.

The detective began gently, willing to give her a chance.

"About these black satin shoes, Bertha. How could the sender of that telephone message know your mistress had such a pair?"

The maid drew a breath of relief. This was going to be easier than she thought. As long as he only wanted to talk about shoes, she didn't mind.

"I couldn't tell, sir, unless she had been seen in them?"

"May I interrupt, Inspector?" ventured Laureen. She was anxious to help the maid all she could. "It has just occurred to me that may have been a chance shot, because, you see, practically every woman possesses a pair of black satin slippers with paste buckles. Why, I'm sure I have two, maybe three pairs." She looked inquiringly at Bertha.

"You have three pairs, miss," confirmed the maid.

"Thank you," Reynolds responded. "You may be right on that point." He stared vaguely across the room.

"Have you been wearing any of those black satin shoes lately, madam?"

Laureen reflected and shook her head helplessly.

"I'm afraid I really can't remember, Inspector." She smiled at the maid. "Can you, Bertha? You've a wonderful memory for what I wear. I used a black brocaded pair last night, I'm sure."

The compliment produced a flow of eloquence from the maid. She started off volubly.

"It comes easy to me, miss, and I've got to remind you or you'd be wearing the same clothes over and over again. You've not used any of those black satin slippers since you wore your black lace dress at Lady Wentworth's dance the end of April."

"Indeed, an excellent memory," murmured Reynolds with a satisfied smile which made Laureen frown.

Bertha ran on unsuspectingly, pleased at the inspector's tribute.

"Then you said one black pair were a little shabby, another pair hurt you a bit," she ticked them off on her fingers, "and the third pair had the lining torn inside."

"Your maid must be a treasure," Reynolds remarked to Laureen, whose face expressed cold disdain as she met his glance. "Did you notice which pair you took to the studio?" he asked the maid in smooth tones. "I'll guess it was the shabby pair, because the one pair hurt and the other pair had a broken lining."

"Of course I noticed which pair, sir. I take great pride in looking after my mistress's things. But you're wrong. I chose the ones that had had the lining repaired."

"So you'd remembered to have that done," admired the inspector. "When was that?"

"Last week, sir. I took them to Hanbury's myself and—" She stopped abruptly and a flood of color swept over her face.

Instantly Reynolds pounced at an obvious point.

"Who was with you," he demanded, "when you went on that errand?"

Lansberg shifted his position as though he wanted to break the tension in the room.

But Reynolds relentlessly repeated his question.

*"Who was it?"*

Bertha hesitated, looked piteously at her mistress, and back at Reynolds's stern face, as if hypnotized.

"My friend," she whispered, "Mr. Jackson."

"Jackson!" murmured Laureen in astonishment.

The inspector hushed her with a warning finger.

"You mean the dead man whose photograph I showed you?" he questioned more kindly.

The maid nodded, tears running down her cheeks. "Yes, sir," she sobbed. "It's dreadful to think we had words on Saturday night and the very next night he must have got in here somehow and been killed."

Over her bent head the two men looked at each other in amazement. Poor deluded woman caught in the toils of her own vanity! But Laureen's eyes were wet as she heard the pitiful sobs, though there was something akin to terror in her heart.

"Tell me, Bertha, when and how did you meet Jackson?" the detective asked.

The maid fought back her distress.

"Three weeks ago, sir. I was going out one evening when he stopped and asked me where the nearest tube station was. I told him but he said he was a stranger and would I be so kind as to show him the way." She sighed at the remembrance of her brief romance.

"And then?" suggested Reynolds quietly.

"Well, sir, I'm the last to pick up with any man like that, but he—he was so different. He was so grateful to me for walking along to the tube with him. He told me he was a single man and had no friends in London. He was here on business for a while."

"Did he say what his business was, Bertha?"

"Oh yes, sir, he was very frank. He was a traveler."

"Did he mention the name of his employers?"

Bertha shook her head. "No, sir; he just said he dealt in soft goods."

The inspector's hand went up to hide his mouth quickly.

"I see," he remarked in a stifled voice, ashamed to see that Lansberg and Laureen had controlled their expression better. "And after that first walk you naturally met him often by his wish?"

Bertha wrung her hands nervously.

"It sounds dreadfully bold to talk about it, but he was such a gentleman and so devoted to me. It seemed like love at first sight for both of us. We used to go for walks or to the cinema and once we went to Miss Laureen's theater when she gave me tickets."

The detective drew little patterns on a piece of paper.

"Must have been during one of those walks that you lost your key, I suppose," he hinted.

"It was the night we went to a cinema, sir. My bag fell down. It must have opened and the key dropped out."

"Mr. Jackson was concerned probably to know you'd lost it," stated the inspector.

"I never told him, sir. I didn't miss it until next morning when I got up to the flat, and then as my mistress was there she let me in. I took the other key and said nothing about it until this morning."

"Did Jackson often come to this flat to see you?" the inspector asked.

The maid flushed indignantly.

"Never," she exclaimed emphatically. "That is, until last Saturday night. I was to meet him outside, but he said as he was a bit early he thought he'd call for me. I asked him inside the hall while I put on my hat, and was annoyed to find him in here when I came back ready to go out."

"As any honorable maid would in her mistress's absence," agreed Reynolds. "Is that what began the quarrel?"

Bertha's face had a tortured expression as she responded: "Yes, sir. I found him in this room at that bureau opening the drawers and turning over some letters;"

Laureen made an involuntary sound. Reynolds glanced at her speculatively before he again addressed the maid.

"You were angry?"

"I was; very angry. More than I ought to have been perhaps, for Mr. Jackson explained that he often did a bit of society reporting and as Miss Laureen was a very famous revue artist all the world was interested in her."

"This is very interesting, Bertha," commented Reynolds. "What was your answer to that?"

"Well, sir, I understood a bit better, though I was still annoyed. Then he said he'd heard rumors that my mistress was giving a special surprise party here on Sunday night, June 30th, and probably a member of some royal family was coming."

"And you replied?" the detective questioned eagerly.

"That he'd heard entirely wrong as I happened to know my mistress was going to a studio party at Mr. Spencer's and would be there from ten o'clock that night."

"I see." Reynolds tapped his pencil on the table aimlessly. "Did he ask what time she would return?"

"Yes, sir, he did. That made me angry again. I said, 'Some time after midnight, but I always wait up for her, so it's no use your trying to crawl in here and interview her when she's tired.' Then he fired up and said some horrible things about Miss Laureen. We quarreled dreadfully and at last he went away alone and I had a good cry."

"And you never saw him again, Bertha?"

"No, sir. I walked along to Victoria last night and back hoping to meet him as usual and make it up. But he didn't come and now it's too late." Again her self-control gave way and the inspector signaled to Laureen to take the maid to her room.

Lansberg looked at his watch and rose as he saw Reynolds putting his papers together.

"I'll go and get some luncheon, Inspector, and be at my rooms ready for you at two thirty. Wonderful how the pieces are fitting into the puzzle, isn't it?"

"It will be," corrected Reynolds grimly, "when I can force open the fingers that hold on to some of those pieces."

"Inspector," asked Laureen from the doorway, "can my maid pack up some of our clothes and remove them to St. Andrew's Hotel near by? With your permission I propose to take rooms there for Bertha and myself."

"Certainly. Your maid can stay for an hour or so. The sergeant will be here on guard. And you, madam?"

"I must get some luncheon. Then I'll go to the theater and lie down in my dressing-room for an hour or so," she said quickly. She turned to Lansberg. "It will be quieter than the hotel and after last night I need rest or what will my work be like to-night?"

The inspector nodded and led them to the hall door.

"For God's sake be careful, Laureen," warned Lansberg in a swift undertone as they walked downstairs together. "Reynolds will have a man watching every step you take to-day."

She screwed up her face impishly.

"What's the betting that I elude the creature?" she whispered.

But Lansberg's face was serious, his mind on the ordeal before him that afternoon.

# VIII. BUTTERFLIES

DOWNSTAIRS the front door was closed.

"Press photographers and reporters outside, sir," explained the officer in plain clothes, who was on guard. "I'll take you and the lady out the back way if you like."

"Thank you," Lansberg replied.

The man unlocked a door behind the staircase that led through a walled-in yard, opened another door and conducted them through a narrow alley into the street behind.

Lansberg put Laureen into a passing taxi, raised his hat and strolled away in the opposite direction.

Upstairs in the flat Reynolds turned back for a last word with Bertha, who was on her knees packing a trunk.

"Do you know any one of the name of Valerie?" he asked.

The maid bent over the garments she was deftly folding. "No, sir," she responded firmly.

"Any of your mistress's friends called by that name?"

"Not that I'm aware of."

Some latent obstinacy in her tone made Reynolds tap her on the shoulder.

"Don't conceal anything," he warned. "You've heard that name recently. Who mentioned it?"

The woman hesitated; then said reluctantly:

"My friend, Mr. Jackson, asked me once if any lady of that name had ever been to the flat. I said no.

"Did 'Jackson' give his reason for asking?"

Bertha thought a minute. "I'm not quite sure, sir, but I believe he said this Valerie—he didn't give her other name—had once known Miss Laureen, acted with her or something, he'd been told. And I said maybe that was before my time as I'd only worked for my mistress for ten months."

"He never mentioned the subject again?"

"Oh, no, sir. It was only asked casually, I think."

"About this Miss Gilbert who rang you up last night with the message. Have you ever heard her voice before or seen her?"

"No, sir. And I'm sure no one of that name has been here. I never admit any one who won't give her name because my mistress is always being bothered by all kinds of people."

"H'm. Anything peculiar about this woman's voice over the telephone? Could you recognize it?"

Bertha tried conscientiously to describe it.

"I *think* I'd know it again, sir, as it was a very clear, rather high voice."

"Thank you," said the inspector. "That's all I need bother you with now. Good morning."

He was walking away when the maid timidly called him back.

"Please, sir," she clasped her hands nervously, her eyes swimming with tears, "do you think I might have a photo of my friend? One like you showed me this morning. I should be so grateful."

"Yes, you shall," he said with rough kindliness, foreign to a man alleged to be without a heart.

With a word to the sergeant on duty, he strode heavily downstairs and thrust aside impatiently the eager newspaper men awaiting him.

By the pillar-box at the corner of the street the inspector stopped and glanced at the tablet indicating the hours of clearance. Afterward he walked the short distance to Scotland Yard, revolving in his mind the facts he had elucidated and the huge gaps remaining to be bridged in this problem.

One or two things had gone very smoothly. The photograph of Leslie Delmond, for instance. Early that morning he'd sent a man out to try all the film agencies for pictures of the dead man, and within an hour one had been obtained. An excellent portrait, too, judging by Bertha Mackie's instant recognition of it.

In his office he ordered coffee and sandwiches and began sifting out reports that had come in on investigations for which he had previously given instructions.

A thin, scholarly-looking man came in. Reynolds gave him a rapid summary of the facts up to date and then asked:

"Found that telephone clerk yet, Jenkins?"

"Not yet. But I'll have news presently."

"That film agency where you picked up the photo of Delmond. Did they know his address?"

"No. Hadn't seen or heard of him for ages. That photo is two or three years old."

The inspector ticked off those items on his list.

"You saw the women Miss Laureen dined with last night. Did they observe anything unusual in her manner?"

Jenkins shook his head.

"Nothing noticeable, they said. But, after a bit of trouble, I got them to admit she'd seemed in a hurry to get away. Kept looking at her watch, they said."

The inspector's mouth tightened.

"She did, eh! Funny she couldn't remember what time she left there when I asked her last night, or rather early this morning. What about the waiters in the restaurant? Nothing fresh there?"

"Only what I told you on the telephone, sir. Two waiters were positive Miss Laureen left at eight twenty-five, and the porter outside said the lady wore a pink cloak and wouldn't have a taxi."

Reynolds stroked his chin.

"That bit agrees with what she said. But, Jenkins, that cloak is lined with black and is reversible. She let that out. And in the pocket was a black scarf or maybe a little black cap. Doesn't take much to cover a woman's head in these days."

Jenkins pondered. "Reversible, eh!"

"Nothing remarkable in a *black* cloak and hat," went on Reynolds, "whereas in a pink cloak, bareheaded, and with her golden hair, she'd have been marked wandering about before going to Spencer's studio."

"I called at Spencer's address," Jenkins added, "and got hold of the caretaker. Richard Spencer is a bachelor and a bit sweet on Laureen, the woman who cleans his flat told me. She says he's got sketches of her all over the place."

The inspector whistled softly.

"So Spencer's keen on this girl, is he?"

Jenkins laughed.

"Dozens like him from all I can hear, sir. I don't wonder. She's as clever as she's good-looking. I went to see her show last week. Lansberg's got money in it, they say."

The detective made a sudden decision.

"Ring up and book me a seat in her theater for tonight. I'll go and see her myself and find out why people rave about her."

"You'll know all right once you've seen her," predicted Jenkins. "Back of the stalls, side seat will be best, I expect. Not too conspicuous. You needn't dress up, you know, sir," he added.

But the inspector had finished with that theme.

"Get copies of this photograph of the dead man sent to all the newspapers and tell them we want information about him," he ordered. "And while you're about it, get an extra copy for me."

"I'll see to that at once," promised Jenkins.

"Also," went on Reynolds, "I must have news about this girl or woman called Valerie."

He briefly outlined all he knew and showed Jenkins the envelope Carter had worked on with the address. "Get them to reproduce that and ask any one who saw or received that letter to call here immediately."

"Pillar-box cleared at seven fifteen A. M.," mused Jenkins. "Letter for W.1. district. H'm. It would get delivered any time after two P.M., I suppose."

"About that," agreed the inspector, looking at his watch. "I must be off to my appointment. I shall be at Lansberg's flat if you want me. It's somewhere near the Adelphi. Look up his number and ring me if the report of the post-mortem comes in."

"Curious that no key of the flat was found on the dead man," observed Jenkins. "No letters either, or papers. The other oddments we found in his pockets are in this box."

"All right. Within twenty-four hours we may get some light on this Leslie Delmond from his landlady or wherever he lived."

"Do you want me to comb through all the flats in forty-nine Beresford Street and ask the tenants if they posted a letter addressed to some one called Valerie?" asked Jenkins.

The inspector considered the question.

"No," he said at last. "That maid, Bertha Mackie, says the dead man asked her if a girl called Valerie ever came to see her mistress. So it's long odds the letter came from somebody in that flat, and I'd give something to know what was in it."

"You're having Laureen watched?" questioned Jenkins.

"You bet I am," Reynolds assured him emphatically as he jammed on his hat. "Get on with that newspaper business at once."

Inside the spacious hall of Lansberg's apartment the inspector, against his will, felt impressed. His duties often carried him into palatial mansions, but in the silence and dignity of this place there was something quite apart from anything he had seen before.

It occupied the whole of the first floor and the interior had evidently been reconstructed to suit its owner's taste. Doorways had been widened and hung with rich draperies. Thick carpets deadened all sound. Even Reynolds's untrained eye could realize beauty in the two or three exquisite pieces of statuary that gleamed with color filtering through a large stained-glass window.

He tried to shake off the feeling of awed respect that was creeping over him. Firmly he told himself that this type of furnishing wasn't English, and that the olive-hued, sloe-eyed man-servant who had taken in his card, was a dago.

Almost he started as he found the man at his elbow announcing with a strong foreign accent:

"Mr. Lansberg will see you, sir."

"See me, indeed!" murmured the detective to himself. "He certainly will."

Hat in hand, the inspector followed the man through the portiere, across a lofty room decorated in a style neither ornate nor austere, into a library.

From a huge writing table at an angle to the window, Lansberg rose, dismissed the man-servant with a few words in a language unknown to the detective, and bowed with grave courtesy.

"Where would you like to sit, Inspector? With your permission I will stay where I am." His eyes twinkled. "As you see, I face the light nicely here."

And again Reynolds had that uneasy sense of being out of his depths. Was this the man he had badgered and kept at heel with his commands and questions last night and this morning? Also Reynolds felt he would give quite a lot to know what his superior officers in conference that morning had in mind when they urged he must not annoy Mr. Lansberg unduly.

Lansberg opened a carved ebony box and twisted it toward the detective, who had chosen a hard chair with its back to the window.

"Will you smoke?" Lansberg asked. It was almost as if he were trying to put an awkward guest at his ease.

The inspector selected a cigarette with an effort at being casual, striving for equally composed manners.

"Thank you," he said, repressing the "sir" which rose to his lips almost mechanically, and bending forward for the lighted match Lansberg offered.

Leaning back calmly, Lansberg awaited the detective's opening, one hand idly fingering an ivory paper-knife.

On the little finger Reynolds noticed a heavy gold ring engraved with armorial bearings unlike any he had seen before. He wished—

But even a Scotland Yard man has limits, and he had no adequate excuse for asking leave to examine that ring. Anyhow he could hunt up Lansberg's pedigree later.

He pulled himself together with a frown. "I should like your full name, age, occupation, please," he began formally.

Lansberg pushed a card across to him.

"Anticipating those questions, I wrote the answers down for you, Inspector, as my names are lengthy and a little complicated to spell."

The detective glanced up under his eyebrows as he took the card and read it slowly to gain time. That inability of his to spell! Was Lansberg making fun of him?

But there was no hint of anything except well-bred attention in Lansberg's face.

"Like a blooming Sphinx," the detective muttered to himself. "He'll answer my questions but give nothing away voluntarily."

Aloud he said:

"A good way to avoid any mistakes. Now, Mr. Lansberg, before I go back to the events of last evening, will you tell me what your business is?"

Lansberg smiled faintly, flicked one finger toward the card Reynolds held.

"It is clearly stated there, Inspector. I have many interests that cannot possibly affect this affair; interests," he added icily, "that I am not at liberty to reveal. It will be sufficient for your purposes if I tell you—what you probably already know—that I have considerable money invested in the theatrical world, including the theater in which Miss Laureen acts."

"That I suppose is your hobby," said the detective with a heavy attempt at sarcasm.

"It's quite a good name. Call it that by all means, if you like," Lansberg agreed genially.

"What is your staff here?" the inspector asked.

"This is a service flat. I rarely take any meals here. The only resident servant of my own is the man you saw, who acts as butler and valet."

"Does he speak English?"

Lansberg shook his head.

"About a dozen words. I have a secretary, an English ex-officer, who comes daily," he added, almost as though he wished to change the subject. "Knowing you were coming, I sent him off for the afternoon."

"Why?" asked the C. I. D. man bluntly.

"Only so that we should be undisturbed," was the quiet answer. He wrote something rapidly on a card and passed it to Reynolds.

"There is his name and private address if you care to call on him."

The inspector tucked the address into his pocket-book.

"We'll now deal with your movements last night, Mr. Lansberg. Where did you dine and with whom?"

"At my club and alone. That address too you will find both on my visiting card and the supplementary card I gave you just now," he added. Reynolds verified the remark, slightly irritated to realize Lansberg was getting the better of him in some vague way.

"I suppose the hall porter or waiters at your club can confirm that statement?"

Lansberg raised his hand indifferently in one of his rare gestures.

"Possibly. That is your affair, Inspector."

Something in that gesture prompted Reynolds to ask another question.

"Are you English?"

"By birth, no. My origin is rather cosmopolitan since my mother was English and my father was from one of the Balkan States. I was born in Paris, and am a nationalized Englishman."

"And subject to English law," commented the inspector inwardly with a grim satisfaction.

"Please outline what you did, Mr. Lansberg," he added aloud, "from the time you left here and went to your club until you reached Mr. Spencer's studio."

Lansberg reflected.

"I left here about seven thirty last night, strolled along to my club, found one or two letters and read them while dinner was being served."

"Many people dining there?" interpolated the detective.

"Very few. On Sunday nights there rarely are many. That is one reason why I like to dine at my club then."

"Do you remember conversing with any particular member?"

"No, or I should remember it. I dined alone, nodded to one or two men, smoked a cigar and looked at the papers for a while, and then about half past nine I set out for the studio."

"By taxi, or your own car?"

"Neither. It was a fine evening, I had plenty of time, and I walked as far as Victoria, where you have proof from Miss Laureen's maid that I took a bus to Chelsea."

For one wild second the detective felt almost hysterical. Yet another of them who took a walk after dinner! There seemed to have been a passionate wave of pedestrian exercise last night.

But *was* it all as straightforward as it appeared to be? Mentally he measured the distance between Lansberg's club and Victoria.

A glint came to his dull eyes as he worked out that Laureen's flat was midway and could easily have been visited in the time.

"You had no reason to pass through Beresford Street and call at Miss Laureen's flat during that walk?"

"No," he said, "I had no reason for doing so, and it would have been out of my way."

Lansberg's reply was unhesitating, his face composed. But Reynolds's eyes were not on Lansberg's face. Once before he had seen the man's hands tighten as they tightened now on that paper-knife, which he still fingered unconsciously.

The detective had at last got a lead. Those sensitive fingers made him positive Lansberg knew more than he meant to tell. Reynolds's mind plowed through the events of last night as he endeavored to reconstruct the situation if Lansberg had called at that flat before going to the studio.

On the supposition that there might have been a struggle he swiftly tried his old means of lightning attack.

"I should like to see the garments you wore last night, please. Including the shirt," he added.

Lansberg's face expressed nothing more than the ordinary surprise, tinged with good-natured amusement, that any man might exhibit if called upon to produce his wardrobe.

He pressed a bell. "Certainly, if you wish, Inspector."

The man-servant appeared, but before Lansberg could give him any orders Reynolds addressed him.

"*Est-ce-que vous parlez franqais?*" he demanded rapidly.

*"Oui, monsieur,"* the man replied.

Continuing to speak French fluently but with a harsh accent, Reynolds asked the man:

"You have been many years with your master?"

The man darted a glance at Lansberg before replying, as if asking permission. Lansberg nodded assentingly and the servant answered:

"I and my people we have served for many years with— monsieur"—Reynolds noted he hesitated before the name—"and his family before him," the servant said proudly.

The inspector turned to Lansberg.

"Please tell your man to answer any questions I ask him."

Lansberg did so, speaking in French—a degree of tact and courtesy which the detective appreciated.

"What time did your master leave here last night to go out to dinner?" Reynolds went on.

"At seven thirty or not more than seven thirty-five."

Although the replies were coldly polite, Reynolds felt the servant's disdain of him as a being of common clay who dared to intrude into his master's life.

"At what hour did he return here last night?" questioned the inspector inexorably.

This time the servant's gaze flickered in quick supplication to Lansberg, who calmly interposed:

"My servant—his name is Neron—does not wait up for me with chocolate, Inspector. He was in bed when I returned about three fifteen a.m. after our late interview last night."

But he had spoken in French! Was that to give the man his cue, Reynolds wondered.

"Bring me the evening suit and shirt your master wore last night," he commanded.

The man turned instantly and went out of the room.

"Did you return here before going to Mr. Spencer's party, Mr. Lansberg?"

Before he could reply, the telephone on the desk rang and Lansberg lifted off the receiver.

"Mr. Lansberg speaking." He passed over the instrument. "It's for you, Inspector."

Reynolds took the receiver, and after a curt monosyllable listened attentively for a few minutes.

"All right, I shall be back very shortly," he said, and ended the conversation.

He looked at Lansberg meditatively.

"The result of the post-mortem on Leslie Delmond has just come in. He died from the effects of —in fact was undoubtedly murdered with—chloroform."

*"Chloroform!"* There was amazement in Lansberg's face. "Is that certain?"

"Our pathologists are fairly reliable," commented the inspector drily. He paused, his eyes narrowed. "Have you any reason to think there should be another cause for this man's death?" he demanded harshly.

"No," Lansberg replied calmly, "none whatever. Only it seemed an unusual weapon. Surely it takes a large—an awkwardly large— quantity of chloroform to murder a man?"

"Somewhere about half a pint, probably," Reynolds impatiently glanced round the room, again baffled by Lansberg's explanation of his surprise. A natural surprise, he agreed. Chloroform was an unusual weapon and a bulky one.

What was that servant doing? Probably examining his master's suit carefully.

The inspector scrutinized the book-lined walls, noticed a huge safe skilfully built into one corner, a case of vividly colored butterflies above it.

Reynolds longed to get a peep into that safe; maybe it could tell him more than its owner would. Just then the servant entered silently and deposited a pile of clothes on a table.

Reynolds rose, looked the garments over mechanically and without interest; picked up the shirt, stared at it abstractedly and laid it down again. He took his hat from the chair beside him.

"Thank you, Mr. Lansberg. Good day."

But as he walked back to Scotland Yard his mind was not on the shirt he had just seen—in one second he knew it was not the same one as that worn last night, although the cuffs had obviously had studs in them. The one Lansberg had worn last night, the detective remembered, had a smear of cigarette ash on it, and a bulge at one side of the front incompatible with Lansberg's immaculate attire.

Reynolds decided to solve that problem later. For the moment his thoughts curiously turned on butterflies.

## IX. A HIDING PLACE

LAUREEN had luncheon in a little tea-shop that was nearly empty. From her seat in the window she could catch glimpses of a man who alternately was absorbed in a newspaper or thoughtfully propping up the wall.

She slid back the curtain considerately so that he could more easily see she was there. Her brain was busy on a plan in which she hoped the faithful hound, as she mentally dubbed him, would play no part.

Presently her eyes twinkled. She hurriedly wrote something on a card, folded it over and called the waitress.

"Take this note across to that poor man standing over there," she indicated him to the girl. "He looks as if he's out of work and needs a meal. Give me his bill if he comes in and orders something."

From the window she watched the shadow unfold the visiting card and read the message:

Why not come in and have luncheon? You can see better and will find it less tiring. I shall be here some time yet.

For a second the man hesitated, then he swung round and entered the tea-room. Raising his hat without looking in Laureen's direction, he chose a table as far from hers as possible, but one that gave him an excellent view of the door.

She heard him give his order.

"Anything you have ready and coffee, please."

When the waitress came to her table again Laureen said in an undertone:

"Ask. the gentleman if he will kindly lend me his newspaper for a few minutes, as I'm interested in sport." She slid a shilling into the girl's hand. "Don't forget the last sentence."

Scenting romance, the waitress obediently gave the message and returned with the newspaper, but not before Laureen had seen the man quickly bend his head to hide a smile.

"Really, I'm getting quite fond of that nice little fellow," she told herself as she handed the girl a pound note.

"Take the money for both bills from that without mentioning it to him, or his pride may be hurt," she warned the waitress.

Laureen knew that only a sense of humor would keep her from screaming to-day.

After her ordeal of last night followed by the inspector's examination, her nerves were screwed up almost to snapping point. And there were things she had to do with a cold brain, as well as get through her work in the theater to-night.

The newspaper she had borrowed from the faithful hound was the mid-day sporting edition. Its front page was emblazoned with huge headlines:

WESTMINSTER
MYSTERY
Film Actor Found Dead
In Famous Revue
Artist's Flat

So far, apparently, Inspector Reynolds had spared her reputation, she noticed, inasmuch as no reference was made to her statement that the dead man had been her lover. But she had a growing conviction that that was about all Reynolds would spare her before he had finished.

She shrugged her shoulders as she gathered up her change. Well, she could look after herself. She was used to publicity, and what did a little more or less matter to one who had fought and kicked her way by sheer hard work up to the position she now held? Reached there unaided too, disdaining the easier and speedier methods.

From the other end of the tea-shop came sounds of distress from an embarrassed man struggling to get his bill from a loyal and sentimental waitress.

Laureen smothered a giggle, laid the newspaper on her table and walked slowly to her theater.

The stage-door entrance was in an alley at the side of the theater. There, in the doorway, Laureen paused and in clear tones asked Minnis, the door porter, how he was, how his wife was and his garden; this to give the hound time to get within earshot.

Taking her letters, she yawned audibly and remarked, "Well, Minnis, after last night's ghastly affair in my flat I'm going up to my dressing-room to get some sleep and write a few letters. Don't let any reporters get by you, I don't want to be disturbed." She lowered her voice. "The man now in the alley outside is a detective. If he likes to come in and sit in your office where he can watch this door, let him."

Minnis stared. He admired Laureen very much.

"A detective, miss!" he gasped. "But they can't suspect—?"

She shook her finger to and fro.

"Suspect me? Of course not. He's only taking a kindly interest in me to see I come to no harm. If he speaks to you say I hope he enjoyed his lunch. He'll understand."

She pushed open the swing door and walked up the stone staircase leading to the dressing-rooms.

Half-way up she paused to look closely at a small iron door fastened by two heavy bolts. It was the door that led to the theater. Gently she wriggled the bolts and found they slid easily in their sockets. Then contentedly she went on to her dressing-room.

Except when there was a matinee, at this hour of the day—it was twenty past two—she knew the place would be deserted, save for stage-hands.

About an hour later, a neat old lady, with gray hair and bent shoulders, called at a house in Bloomsbury and asked to see one of the lodgers.

The slovenly maid servant stared at the patient figure clad in an old-fashioned brown coat, and then called over her shoulder:

"Missus. Somebody wants Miss Baird."

"If you'll please tell me where her room is, I will go up," interrupted the old lady. "There is no need to disturb your mistress."

But before the maid could reply heavy steps along the passage heralded the landlady.

"I want to see Miss Baird," repeated the caller.

"So do I," sniffed the owner of the house indignantly. "She went out at six o'clock last night. Said she was going to church, and I haven't seen her since. Church, indeed! This is a respectable house for respectable people," the woman added fiercely.

"Yes, yes, I'm sure it is," murmured the old lady. She seemed taken aback by the landlady's words. "Probably Miss Baird stayed the night with friends and will be back soon," she ventured hopefully.

The landlady, looking at the pathetic, stooping figure, withheld what she longed to say and substituted:

"Will you call again or leave a message?"

"Thank you, thank you," the caller said nervously, "I'm only in town for the day. Tell Miss Baird her old governess left her love."

The landlady watched the shabbily dressed old lady go down the steps, and called out warningly as she passed the railings:

"Mind, that paint's wet. I'll give your message when she conies back."

Once again in Oxford Street the old lady climbed nimbly on a bus, her face, shaded by its out-of-date mushroom hat, worried and abstracted.

"Not been back since six o'clock last night!" she repeated over and over again to herself.

At Piccadilly Circus she got out and threaded her way to a large imposing hotel. Inside the entrance hall she passed through the crowds to the letter bureau. A man was already there asking for his mail and she overheard the conversation.

"Have you a room, sir?" asked the clerk.

"Not yet," was the man's reply.

"Please register for your room first, sir. That is our rule."

The old lady faded away from that department, and going across to the reception clerk asked for a single room.

"Number 420. Ten and sixpence. Sign your name here, please. Luggage?" The clerk ripped off the formula automatically.

The elderly client signed in a thin cramped handwriting without removing her glove.

"My luggage is at the station. Shall I pay in advance?" she offered timidly.

The clerk cast a practised eye down the old figure, saw faded gentility written all over it, said it didn't matter and handed over the ticket giving the number of the room.

Back at the letter bureau again, the old lady produced the ticket and asked if there were any letters.

The clerk glanced through the file.

"Nothing, madam."

The old lady looked so disappointed that he added, "Wait a minute. I've not had time to sort through this last lot yet." His fingers rapidly dealt with a large stack of letters beside him. "What name did you say?"

The old lady repeated it, watching anxiously as the pile grew less.

"Ah, here you are!" He handed her a thickish envelop, glanced at her casually, and went on with his task.

Twenty minutes later an old lady went unobtrusively in at the front entrance of a theater, slid past the big crowd near the box office and pushing open the door leading into the back of the stalls, found herself once more in the dark, empty auditorium. Silently she made her way to the corridor behind the stage box, opened a small iron door in the wall and vanished.

"Joe," called Miss Laureen presently to one of the carpenters, "you might slip out and get me some cigarettes."

Joe looked approvingly at the dainty negligee the lady was wearing. He liked women to wear pretty feminine things.

"Certainly, miss," he said eagerly. All the staff liked doing jobs for Miss Laureen, and not only because she rewarded them liberally. "I'm doing a bit of papering in number four," he added. "The guv'nor thinks he'll turn it into an extra office as it's not wanted as a dressing-room. What'll you have, miss? Turkish or Egyptian?"

"Virginian, and get some for yourself at the same time, Joe."

The cigarette shop was some distance from the theater. Laureen thought she could reckon on eight minutes before Joe returned.

Silently she went along the passage from her room to number four where Joe had been working. Her breath came quickly as her eyes searched the bare room for some hiding place. It had the usual paper-hanger's table, steps and bucket of paste.

Joe had evidently been hanging a strip of wallpaper when she called him. With a gleam of hope she noticed the baseboard had warped out slightly from the wall and that he had stuck the paper over it to hide the opening.

Bending down she gently raised the bottom edge of the paper. The paste was still wet and the paper lifted easily. Yes, there was ample space behind the board.

In a moment she had slipped a thin white packet between the baseboard and the plaster, thrust it down and delicately pressed the edges of the wallpaper over it again, adding a little more paste to make it firm. Even if Joe lifted the paper he could not possibly see the packet behind the woodwork.

She was in her dressing-room lying on her couch, white arms curved above her head, when the man returned.

"Thank you, Joe," she said, holding out her hand for the cigarettes and yawning.

"It's a wonder you're not ill, miss, after all you went through last night," he remarked sympathetically. "'Orrible affair. Shall I tell Minnis to order tea for you?"

She glanced at her watch.

"Quarter past four. Yes, I'd like some."

Minnis appeared with a tray in a few minutes, obtained from a café near the stage-door. He set it down on a table beside her and said in a low voice:

"That fellow down in the passage has been asking me questions." He grinned. "He didn't get much change out of me though, miss."

Laureen poured out a cup of tea and dropped in some sugar.

"I'm sure he didn't, Minnis. But he's a nice little fellow and very attached to me, so I hope you treated him kindly and asked him into your office."

Minnis looked up under his shaggy eyebrows, not quite sure if Miss Laureen was serious.

"No, miss, not exactly, but he's been leaning against my door ever since you came, trying to pump me as to everybody's movements here. I'm getting sick of the sight of him."

"So he's been leaning against your door all the time, has he?" The lady smiled to herself. "Well, well, that's something. Did you say I hoped he'd enjoyed his lunch, Minnis?"

"I did, miss. He got red."

Laureen put down her cup and chuckled.

"He'll be purple before I've finished with him," she predicted. "Wait a minute while I write a letter."

She scribbled a note rapidly, addressed the envelop, fastened it insecurely, and handed it to the porter with fun dancing in her eyes.

"Like to help me in a joke, Minnis?" she questioned.

Minnis nodded, with a grin.

"Rather, miss."

"Good. You can go down and casually mention I'm going to my hotel to get some dinner before the show to-night. Say I told you to post this letter as I've no stamps. You can grumble and say 'She thinks I can run out at all hours and leave this office, to do her fool errands.' Something like that. Being kind-hearted, he'll offer to post it for you— *which is just what I want.* D'you understand?"

"Exactly, miss," beamed the man.

"I shall just give you time to get that off your chest," Laureen added with a smile, "and then I'll come down."

The man retired with the letter and within three minutes Laureen had hurriedly dressed and strolled downstairs singing.

Minnis was in his office alone. As she was passing out he whispered and pointed with his thumb.

"All gone nicely. He's outside waiting for you, and he's got your letter."

Laureen went up the alley slowly, beckoned a taxi and told the man to drive to her hotel, without troubling to see whether the hound was trailing her. She had had a most successful afternoon from her point of view, with only one anxiety.

In the hotel where she had reserved rooms, she found Bertha had unpacked and was sewing placidly. The maid was paler than usual, but did not allude to the morning's proceedings.

"I've ordered the porter to send up the evening newspapers as soon as they arrive," she informed her mistress, who had gone at once to the telephone.

"Is Mr. Spencer there?" Laureen asked when her call was answered. And seemed staggered by the reply.

"You think he's gone to Paris!" she repeated.

Swiftly she demanded particulars of the caretaker at the other end of the wire, and learned that Mr. Spencer had gone out about eleven thirty that morning with a suitcase, saying he didn't know when he'd be back, and that she—the caretaker—was to clean up the studio, which was "in a nice mess after the party," lock it up and keep the keys. No, he had left no address but she had heard him ring up Croydon and ask about aeroplanes to Paris when she was doing the bedroom. There had been two men there since asking about him, and one of them—a detective—had taken away a pair of black satin slippers. "Belonging to you, miss. Was that all right?"

"Yes," assented Laureen. It was all right. But about the only thing that was right, she felt at the moment.

Dick Spencer dashing off to Paris like that? What did it mean? Was it accidental? Had he read the news of the murder in the papers before he left? If so, surely he would have telephoned to her. *Or had he not needed the newspapers to tell him that news?*

Laureen's head whirled as she lay back and tried to face this new difficulty. She might have been cheered could she have heard a little conversation at Scotland Yard.

Her sleuth—Bradley by name—had reported there after he had seen her deposited at her hotel door.

"I want to see Inspector Reynolds," he told Jenkins importantly. "I've got hold of a letter Miss Laureen wanted to have posted."

It was addressed to one of the women Laureen had dined with last night, the inspector noticed as he delicately raised the flap of the envelop.

He read the note and looked at Bradley.

"You may like to read it," he remarked. "That young woman seems to have a sense of humor."

Bradley's face indeed grew purple as he read:

*Dearest Eileen,*
*So sorry you're being drawn into this mess of mine. I'd come round and see you, only I'm no longer alone and fear you don't like dogs. He's a very faithful hound, extremely attached to me, though rather an ugly brute and not over-bright. One of these days when he's had a bath I must bring him along to see you. We lunched together to-day and I found his table manners are not all one would like; I must really teach him not to put his feet in the plate. Still, one can't have everything in this life, and as I say he comes to heel most obediently.*
*Yours,*
*Laureen*

"I suppose it must be posted, sir," said Bradley disgustedly as he handed it back to his chief with a brief explanation of this luncheon.

"It certainly must," the inspector replied firmly as he re-sealed the envelope and put it with other letters for the post.

"I hoped I'd get something out of her by going into that tea-shop," Bradley explained.

"It will take a brighter lad than you to get that young woman to tell you what she doesn't wish you to know. I'll have to put somebody else on to her. If she's fooled you in this she'll fool you in something else. If she has not already done so," he added with tightened lips.

"She was in her dressing-room resting all the afternoon," apologized Bradley meekly. "I never left the stage-door."

"Humph!" grunted the inspector. "Well, cut along back to her hotel now and to-morrow I'll make fresh plans."

As the man went out crestfallen Reynolds remembered his arrangement to go to the theater that night, and rang for Jenkins.

"Fixed up that seat?" he demanded.

Jenkins nodded.

"Bit of luck to get one, sir. Just what you want, too. Wall end of stalls, eighth row. No need for you to doll up."

"You said that before," said Reynolds tersely. "I shall know what to do." Already he was beginning to look forward to a thoroughly enjoyable evening of business combined with pleasure.

"Maybe I'll get a little light there on this murder," he told himself hopefully.

Motive in this affair seemed to pivot round Laureen, and he had an urgent desire to see more of this girl on her native heath, as it were; find out why men circled round, apparently willing to risk their necks for her.

# X. THE MISSING LODGER

THE last editions of the evening papers had done full justice to the information meted out to them by Scotland Yard.

Huge head-lines screamed of the Westminster flat mystery. Photographs of the murdered man, Leslie Delmond, appeared with a brief account of his career. Photographs of Laureen with a lengthy and, mostly, inaccurate description of her career followed. There was a reproduction of the address drawn by Carter, "Miss Valerie XXXXX, etc.," together with a request for information concerning that letter. News was also demanded about Valerie and Leslie Delmond.

The Star had featured the letter episode and its chief head-line read:

WHO IS VALERIE?

The earlier editions of the evening papers had caused every reserved seat to be booked in the theater, and an enormous crowd had queued up for the cheaper seats, willing to pay any price if only to stand in order to see the revue actress on whom the limelight of a murder drama was playing fiercely.

From his secluded seat in the stalls Inspector Reynolds felt the peculiar thrill surging through the packed theater. With his opera glasses he carefully scanned the house, dwelling particularly on the boxes.

There was a stir in the audience as a distinguished looking man with hair graying at the temples entered the stage box, followed a moment later by two women and another man whose face was invisible from Reynolds's angle.

The first man was Lansberg. No mistaking that calm dignified face with its dominant, lustrous eyes. He placed the ladies in their seats, and then with a casual glance round the crowded theater, stood talking with the other man who was in the background.

"That's the Countess of Warnham and her niece, Lady Avice Garth," Reynolds heard a woman behind him say. "Who's the distinguished foreign-looking man with them? He looks worlds above this sort of thing."

"That's Lansberg, a millionaire and Heaven knows what besides," her companion replied. "They say Lady Avice is setting her cap at him. She and her family are poor as church mice and heavily in debt."

Both women in the box had a curiously deferential manner toward

Lansberg, urging him to take a seat at the front. Presently he yielded with that aloof, calm way the inspector was beginning to know, and as the other man came into view Reynolds recognized him.

It was Dr. Tempest, the pathologist, and Reynolds's keen eyes noticed that Lansberg paid almost more attention to the doctor than to the ladies in his party.

The curtain rose on the opening numbers which were received with keen enthusiasm.

About a quarter of an hour later there was a strange keyed-up lull in the audience, the chorus divided to form an opening in the middle of the stage, limelights centered, and Laureen darted straight down, a radiant being so full of vitality that the chorus seemed as wax dummies.

Instantly there was a wild crash of applause, drowning the orchestra and preventing all stage action for some time. People stood, waved their programs and shouted, "Laureen, Laureen," disregarding cries of "Sit down."

Without hesitation Laureen raised one hand imperiously for silence, then, both arms akimbo, she leaned across the footlights.

"'Ush!" she said sternly.

There was a roar of laughter and then the house settled down.

Reynolds was amazed at the versatility of the girl. She could sing and dance, but his interest was not in those more ordinary talents. It was her character sketches and quick humor that fascinated him. Her extraordinary changes of voice, age, nationality, language, as in turn she was a Cockney flower-girl, an American tourist, a French tragedienne, an elderly English spinster alcoholically lively at a birthday party, an Italian street singer stabbed by her lover.

No wonder she could deceive him in her flat last night, past mistress as she was of every art of mimicry.

Inspector Reynolds's seat was at the end of the row, an aisle only between him and an exit door, over which the attendant had jerked a heavy velvet curtain when the performance began.

Suddenly, just before the interval, his eye caught a tremor of movement behind that curtain, which was almost facing the stage box on the opposite side of the theater. Presently the tips of a man's fingers stealthily drew aside the folds of the velvet, though the man's face was out of sight.

There was nothing abnormal in any one peeping through to get a glimpse of the stage. It might have been the attendant anxious to see how near the interval was, or some one searching for friends in the stalls.

But in a moment the curtain swayed back a little and he caught sight of a man's hand—a hand that lacked a thumb!

An unusual mutilation which sent Reynolds to his feet. For among the fingerprints that had been photographed in Laureen's dining room was the clear impress of a man's hand showing a stump where the thumb should have been. The photograph had been taken from the dining-room table beside the dead man.

The C. I. D. man made a swift dive across the passageway, but tripped over a cloak that was trailing from the seat in front of him.

That slight delay lost him his chance. When he snatched back the curtain there was nobody there.

Pushing open the exit door he found himself in the corridor, equally empty. On the left it ran down behind two boxes and ended in a cul-de-sac; the right side, up which Reynolds hurried, led round to the back of the auditorium.

Two attendants were there and the detective spoke to them.

"Seen a man just go out?"

"No, sir," both replied.

Reynolds's worried expression made one of them add: "Perhaps you'll find him in the bar, sir. Down there to the left."

The detective searched as directed with no result. There were four youngish men in the bar, laughing together, and not one had a mutilated hand.

He retraced his steps to the corridor and found himself behind the stage box which Lansberg occupied with his party. A roar of applause indicated that the first part of the revue was over and the intermission had begun.

For a moment the detective hesitated whether to knock and ask to speak to Lansberg when his attention was caught by a small iron door in the wall at the end of the corridor. He pulled, found it unfastened and opened it far enough to see that it gave on to a stone staircase.

"Come away from that door, sir, please," said an attendant from behind him.

Reynolds closed it carefully and turned round.

"I wanted a little air," he observed in conciliating tones. "Isn't it an exit door?"

"No, sir, the exit door is farther back. That's a private door leading to the dressing-rooms and greenroom."

"I see," the detective said thoughtfully. A door that led from the dressing-rooms to the front of the theater, while the stage-door was in a side alley!

Suddenly the door of the stage box opened and Lansberg and Dr. Tempest came out.

The two men showed amiable surprise at seeing the detective.

"Hello, Inspector," Lansberg greeted, "are you here to see the show or do you want me for anything?"

Reynolds smiled pleasantly.

"Both, sir, if you can spare me a moment."

Dr. Tempest broke in.

"I'll leave you to talk. Come along to the bar when you've finished, Inspector, and have a drink. Good show, isn't it?"

"Excellent, Doctor. Thank you, I'll join you in two minutes if I can."

The detective twisted round swiftly to Lansberg.

"Do you know a man with a missing thumb, Mr. Lansberg?" he asked.

Even in the half light of the corridor he could see Lansberg recoil and his mask-like face stiffen to severe lines.

"A missing thumb!" he repeated aghast.

"Yes, the right hand. It's a noticeable mutilation."

"Where have you seen this man?" Lansberg demanded agitatedly. "Not here?"

Reynolds nodded, perplexed. There was no mistake about Lansberg's grave concern.

"Hiding behind the curtain over the exit door opposite your box ten minutes ago," he explained definitely. "Who is he?"

"That I cannot tell you, Inspector. But if he's lucky he probably will be my executioner," Lansberg observed grimly. "He made two excellent efforts a year or so ago in Paris. This time he may succeed."

The inspector's eyes were watchful as he put his next questions.

"What has this man against you, sir? And what makes you think he'll make a third attempt on your life? Please answer me clearly. I can't afford to waste a second longer."

"I can only imagine he wishes to steal certain valuable—" He paused and Reynolds fancied changed his word. "—articles that are in my possession. I can think of no other reason. I do not know his name, his business or his nationality. And I think he may again attempt my life because he has so far not succeeded in obtaining what he desired."

"You've not seen him lately?"

"Not for about a year."

Reynolds turned on his heel. "Thank you sir. I must be off at once."

A hurried search of the corridors and foyer proving hopeless, he telephoned for men to be sent to watch all exits and went back to the Yard, bewildered and annoyed at the new tangle.

That Lansberg was concealing much, he was sure. But he was equally sure that Lansberg was acting within his rights and knew the limits of the detective's power to question him.

Well, Reynolds decided, Lansberg must be forced to open his hand. Some damaging clue might yet come to light.

"Jenkins," he called, when he arrived at his office, "I want another look at the photographs of the impression of a man's thumbless right hand."

A moment later he was staring at them—two excellent prints, each showing clearly four fingers, the palm and the stump of the thumb.

"Humph," grunted Reynolds. "Got any news?"

"Yes. Spencer—that Chelsea artist—has gone to Paris. Left no address, his caretaker says."

"I'll start on him to-morrow. Had no time to-day," grunted the inspector. "Anything else?"

"Yes. There's a hotel clerk waiting to see you. He thinks he handed over that Valerie letter this afternoon."

*"What!"* the detective roared. "Show him in at once."

Reynolds could scarcely wait for the man whom Jenkins ushered in.

"Tell me your story as precisely as you can," he urged.

"Right, sir. I'm one of the clerks in the mail department at the Hotel Imperial," the man began. "I read in the Evening News at seven to-night that you wished immediate information concerning a letter, so directly I was off duty I came along here."

"I've already taken his name and address, sir, to save time," Jenkins interposed.

"This afternoon at three twenty-five or three thirty," the clerk continued, "an elderly lady asked if I had any letters for Miss Valerie Baird."

*"Baird!"* exclaimed Reynolds with triumph. "Yes, go on."

"She showed me her room ticket, number four twenty, otherwise I should have asked her for it or for her key."

"What's the reason?"

"Hundreds of people began using our letter bureau as a *poste restante*, so the only way we could reserve it for hotel residents was by making that rule."

Reynolds nodded.

"Well," the man continued, "I looked through the file and there was nothing for her. She seemed anxious and disappointed so I told her to wait while I looked through the mail that had just come in. That's how I fixed the time as three twenty-five or three thirty: the mail arrives at three fifteen."

The inspector rubbed his hands contentedly. This was the type of statement he reveled in, clear, matter-of-fact, concise.

"Excellent," he commented. "Take your time, and don't forget any trifling detail."

"I'll do my best, sir," promised the clerk. "The old lady thanked me. She seemed a patient soul of about seventy though I couldn't see much of her face because she had a drooping brim to her hat and a veil."

"How did you guess her age then?" asked the C. I. D. man.

"She had white hair at the sides and some showing at the back of her hat. Also she stooped like an elderly woman and had a thin quavering voice."

"Well, you sorted the letters?" prompted the inspector.

"Yes, sir, and I found one for the name she had given. A thickish white envelope addressed in big writing to Miss Valerie Baird, care of Hotel Imperial, London, W.1. I handed it to her and she thanked me again and went away."

Inspector Reynolds turned over his papers and found the envelope which the caretaker at Laureen's flat had drafted. He wrote out the address he now knew, compared it with the one Carter had reproduced from memory and showed it to Jenkins.

"Carter wasn't far out, you see," he commented. Then turning to the clerk:

"Can you possibly recall what this woman wore?"

"I thought it was a long dark coat, but was not *quite* sure. So I went at once to the reception clerk and he was positive the woman wore a dark brown coat, rather old-fashioned, a black hat and veil. Also he was sure she was round-shouldered or bent with age."

"Why didn't you bring him along?" asked Reynolds.

"He's on duty until midnight, sir, but you can verify this on the telephone. His name is Foster."

"Did you or Foster notice this woman's hands?" Reynolds questioned eagerly.

"I didn't, sir, but Foster is certain she signed the register with her gloves on. I couldn't bring the hotel register away—besides you can always see it there if you wish—but," he produced an envelope from his pocket and laid it on the table, "Foster and I made a tracing of her signature."

Reynolds scrutinized the slip of paper carefully.

"You and Foster are too intelligent for your jobs," he stated with an approving smile. "You ought to be in this line."

"Thank you, sir. But we've got to use our eyes where we are, too. This isn't so wonderful."

"Isn't it?" The detective cast a look at Jenkins. "We should be glad to have all our witnesses as intelligent, eh?"

"We should," Jenkins agreed with emphasis.

"Anything else you can remember?" Reynolds asked the clerk.

The telephone bell rang before the man could answer. Jenkins took up the receiver.

"A woman's just arrived from Bloomsbury: thinks she has some information concerning this Valerie business," he announced to his chief.

"Tell them to send her up here immediately," the inspector

ordered.

"Shall I go, sir?" the hotel clerk asked.

"No, no. I shall be glad to compare what this woman has to say with your story. Possibly she knows nothing at all. And now before she comes, have you thought of any other detail about this Valerie Baird?"

"It's only a trifle, sir, but Foster says he thinks there was a smear of red plaster or paint on the woman's sleeve. I didn't see it."

The door opened before he finished speaking and the inspector looked up to see a rather untidy, out-of-breath woman enter with Jenkins.

She was obviously ill at ease. The inspector tactfully offered her a chair and thanked her for coming, before beginning to question her.

Jenkins, always a master of method and time-saving, placed a slip giving the woman's name and address before his chief. The inspector read it carefully, found the woman more composed and began his work in easy tones.

"Now, Mrs. Hornett, will you tell me what you know of Miss Valerie Baird, please?"

The woman opened her eyes in astonishment.

"Why, that's what I'm here for you to tell me, sir," she said in a puzzled voice, "considering I've not set eyes on her since she went out at six o'clock last night. Told me she was going to *church!*" she added indignantly.

The inspector raised his eyebrows and gave a humorous glance at the hotel clerk and began again patiently. He knew this rambling type only too well.

"How came Miss Baird to be in your house, Mrs. Hornett?"

"Same way as all my other lodgers. I keep an apartment house and she took a room, fourth floor front, twelve days ago. Very little luggage she had, and a week's rent owing come Wednesday. I might have guessed!" She sighed heavily.

"Guessed what?" Reynolds demanded.

"I suppose she had no money and just walked out leaving her few things. And they're not worth much," Mrs. Hornett added with disgust.

"So as the old lady didn't return last night you looked through her luggage to-day," Reynolds remarked blandly.

"Well and what if I did, sir. I've been cheated that way before." Then, remembering his sentence, she added sharply, "But what do you mean about an *old* lady? I'm talking about Miss Baird."

The detective shot a warning glance at the hotel clerk, who had started at the woman's last remark.

"Ah," he said, "that was just a slip of mine. About how old should you say this Miss Baird was, Mrs. Hornett?"

She looked at him a little suspiciously. She hadn't come here at ten o'clock of the night for this detective to make fun of her, she decided.

"I don't know what age *your* Miss Baird was," she said heavily, "but Miss Valerie Baird who took my room and walked out last night to go to church, so she said, was not a day more than twenty-four. If that!"

"Thank you, Mrs. Hornett. That's a great help to me," commended Reynolds graciously. "Please describe her."

"Thin, pale, fair, blue eyes, medium height or a bit shorter, dressed nearly always in navy blue or black and hadn't got much else so far as I could see.

"What did she do for a living?"

"Well, sir, she was very reserved and stand-offish if I ever asked her a few questions," Mrs. Hornett bridled at the memory of being rebuffed by her lodger, "but I saw a lot of drawings of dresses done in ink in her suit—I mean, in her room."

"Did she receive any correspondence?"

"Never saw a letter and I see all that come to the house."

"I'll bet you do," said Reynolds to himself.

"Any visitors?" he asked aloud.

"None till Saturday night—day before yesterday," she added importantly. "Some girl called to see her but Miss Baird was out."

"Did you answer the bell?"

"Certainly not," Mrs. Hornett replied. "I've a servant to do that, but I heard voices and went up immediately."

"What did this girl wear? I'm sure you've a good memory for a lady's clothes, Mrs. Hornett," said Reynolds, hoping flattery would help a little.

"There wasn't much to remember, sir. A small black hat and a black cape. It was about half past nine and nearly dark. I couldn't see her face. She'd had her answer from my servant and was turning to go down the steps as I came."

"Did you notice her hands or feet?" the inspector asked.

"No, I didn't. Well, as I was saying when you interrupted me, there was that girl came Saturday night, and this afternoon some old lady called to see her."

Reynolds's eyes glinted with excitement, but he asked casually:

"Did she give her name?"

Mrs. Hornett shook her head.

"She said she was only in town for the day and I was to give Miss Baird her love and say it was her old governess who had called."

"Did you happen to mention Miss Baird's surprising absence since the night before?"

"Yes, I mentioned it," she replied, "and the old soul seemed quite upset at first. Then she said probably Miss Baird had unexpectedly stayed the night with friends. Do you know where she is, sir?"

"Not at the moment," the inspector admitted. "Can you describe this old lady's appearance?"

"Black hat, mushroom brim, and veil, dark brown coat, out of date. White hair, very stooping shoulders, shaky old person."

A long brown coat! Reynolds reflected to himself.

"Sounds like the same woman, eh?" he said in an undertone to the hotel clerk, who had listened to the conversation with the deepest interest.

"It certainly does, sir," he replied emphatically.

"Well, I think that's all for to-night, Mrs. Hornett, thank you. Directly I have news of Miss Baird I'll let you know. Meanwhile, lock her room up. I shall come along to-morrow and examine it, so don't touch or remove anything," he warned her. "Good night."

She rose, offended at his warning, and smoothed the folds out of her coat.

"Drat that paint," she said softly, rubbing a piece of the cloth.

Reynolds's head shot up, alertly.

*"Paint?"* he demanded. "Where?"

The woman pointed to her coat where a red mark showed.

"Off my railings. They were only painted this morning, and I came out in such a hurry—"

The inspector signaled to Jenkins to get her away, his mind intent on linking up details rapidly.

"And Foster saw red paint on the coat of the old lady who called for that letter to-day?" he demanded of the hotel clerk.

"Yes, sir."

"Thank you. Good night," said Reynolds absently.

For suddenly he remembered where he had seen a brown coat on an old lady, a coat that had had a red mark on the shoulder.

Laureen had worn it in her impersonation of the inebriated elderly spinster on the stage that night!

## XI. THE MYSTERIOUS VOICE

THE next morning, Tuesday, found Inspector Reynolds in his office at nine as usual. Nearly an hour before that, however, he had paid an early call in Bloomsbury, to the surprise of an indignant Mrs. Hornett.

A thorough inspection of her lodger's modest belongings had revealed little except that Valerie Baird had left no clue to her identity there. Not one of her simple garments bore any initial, not even a laundry mark with the inevitable red cotton. There were no letters, no papers. Only a few half-finished pen and ink sketches of frocks, executed with the fineness of an engraving.

These Reynolds took away with him, after again locking the door and instructing Mrs. Hornett to open it for no one but himself or its owner.

"Telephone me at once," he ordered, "if Miss Baird returns, and say nothing to her of my visit."

"What's she been up to?" questioned the landlady curiously after giving the required promise.

"We have no reason to think she has been 'up to' anything, madam," Reynolds replied as he left the house.

At the Yard he learned that Bertha's statements had been verified as to the time of her arrival at Clapham on the Sunday night; that the porters and waiters at Lansberg's club agreed he had arrived, dined and left there at the hours he had said.

"What about those ashes from Miss Laureen's flat? Had them examined?" he asked Jenkins.

"Yes. Paper undoubtedly had been burnt, but there wasn't a vestige of it left. The cigarette stubs corresponded to the kind Lansberg used, and others that were found in her cigarette-box."

Reynolds frowned. Another dead end, he grunted to himself.

"Show me the contents of Delmond's pockets again, Jenkins."

A little despondently the C. I. D. man turned over the articles which Jenkins spread before him. An ordinary penknife, two stubs of pencils, three Treasury notes and some odd silver, four small keys on a ring, a cheap wrist-watch and a colored silk handkerchief.

There was no pocket-book or letters of any kind; only a plain crumpled half sheet of note-paper such as might have been torn from a letter. Thick pale blue paper of an expensive make.

Reynolds smoothed it and held it up to the light.

"Hand-made," he mused. "Might be possible to trace it."

Jenkins preened himself.

"I've already done so, sir," he remarked nonchalantly.

"Eh!" Reynolds sat forward abruptly. "Where?"

"In Miss Laureen's flat. I found three notes in her bureau, asking her to dinner or luncheon, all written on this paper. Also I found out she often stays the night with this girl—they're great friends. Laureen even leaves some of her clothes there so that she need not bother with a dressing-case each time."

"What's the girl's name and address?" demanded Reynolds.

"Lady Avice Garth, Warnham House, Curzon Street," the man replied, handing the chief the written address, together with the notes he had found in Laureen's bureau.

Reynolds drummed his fingers on the desk a moment, thinking hard. Then he reached for the telephone book.

"Mayfair five eight X two," Jenkins said quietly.

The inspector smiled.

"Bright lad," he said, as he picked up the instrument and repeated the number.

"Is that Warnham House? Good. I want to speak to Lady Avice Garth, please. I'm Inspector Reynolds of Scotland Yard," he said over the wire. He listened to the reply with a grim expression.

"Did she give any address or reason for this sudden journey?" he asked.

Presently he hung up the receiver and stared blankly at Jenkins.

"Lady Avice has just left for Paris, the butler says. He doesn't know the reason but says her ladyship usually stays at the Continental and only took a dressing-bag, so evidently doesn't mean to stay long."

"That makes two of them who have had a sudden desire for gay Paree," announced Jenkins. "Spencer went yesterday morning, you remember, sir."

The inspector's lips tightened.

"Ring up Croydon and book me a seat by aeroplane as soon as you can. I've a fancy to make a third who'll pay a visit to Paris. With luck I can get there in time to meet her train."

"Do you know her by sight?" Jenkins asked in surprise.

Reynolds nodded.

"She and her aunt were in Lansberg's box at the theater last night. I'll know her again easily."

"Yes, she lives with her aunt, the Countess of Warnham, and how they keep that establishment going is a mystery. I learned they're in very low water financially."

"Well, among other things, I hope to find out how they manage it," announced the detective firmly. "Get through to Croydon as quick as you can. Come in," he called, hearing a knock on the door.

Dr. Tempest put his head inside.

"Good morning, Inspector. Am I disturbing you?"

Reynolds beamed amiably.

"Not a bit, Doctor. Come in. I'm off to Paris in an hour or two."

The doctor sat down and filled his pipe.

"Indeed," he remarked. "A flying visit?"

"In every sense of the word," the detective responded with a touch of pride in what was to him an adventure.

Dr. Tempest glanced through the window at the cloudless sky.

"You'll have a good trip. I almost envy you. The inquest on Delmond is at ten thirty this morning, I hear. Will you be there?"

The inspector nodded.

"Only formal evidence will be given, and there will be an adjournment, of course. I shan't be needed more than ten minutes. It won't delay you long either."

"Good. By the way, Inspector, you didn't join me for that drink in the theater bar last night."

Reynolds blew out a cloud of smoke and leaned back in his chair with a tired sigh.

"No, I had to rush off directly I'd seen Lansberg. I say, Doctor, what do you know about that man?"

"Lansberg? Much less than you, I'm afraid, Inspector. I've met him twice casually before seeing him in Miss Laureen's flat the night before last."

"I didn't know that. You met there, I thought, as strangers."

Dr. Tempest smiled quizzically. He had a charming easy manner and cultured voice that Reynolds at times tried to imitate.

"It seemed scarcely the moment to remind Mr. Lansberg that he and I had twice been fellow guests at dinner parties and had exchanged a few commonplaces. I was in an official capacity at the flat as a doctor investigating the cause of death."

"You were quite right, Doctor, of course," agreed the detective hastily. Nobody loved the delicacy of etiquette more than he.

"I was even surprised when Lansberg rang me up yesterday," the doctor went on, "inviting me to join his party in the stage box last night and afterward have supper with them. Laureen was there after the show. By gad, that girl's clever!"

"She is," Reynolds avowed with bitter emphasis. "Do you mind telling me if you knew her before or anything about her."

The doctor laughed.

"My dear chap, ask me anything you like. I met her for the first time on Sunday night, June thirtieth, or rather one thirty A.M. Monday, July first, to be precise, in her flat. You were badgering her like the brute you are."

The detective grinned.

"And," continued the doctor, "seeing her over-strung condition, I warned you. As it happens, all is well. She was in marvelous spirits after the theater last night."

"I can believe that," Reynolds thought.

"Oh, I say, Doctor," he asked, "what sort of a girl is Lady Avice Garth? I hear she's a friend of Laureen's."

"They're great friends, I believe," supplemented the doctor. "I was introduced to her and her aunt last night and found them both intelligent and amusing. Lady Avice has a fearless personality, chooses her friends as she pleases and sticks to them."

"I've just heard she's gone abroad this morning," remarked Reynolds. "Did she happen to mention it last night?"

"Gone abroad?" Tempest raised his eyebrows. "Far from saying so last night I overheard her telling Laureen to be sure to come to tea with her this afternoon."

"Is that so?" the inspector observed indifferently, tapping out his pipe. "No fresh details about the post-mortem on Leslie Delmond, I suppose, Doctor?"

The pathologist shook his head, his expression at once grave.

"Nothing since my report, signed by my colleague and myself. Death by chloroform which could not have been self-administered. Delmond's heart was pretty groggy, so it probably took less than half a pint to kill him. An extraordinary murder," he mused. "What do you make of it, Inspector?"

"Rather early yet to answer that," said Reynolds. "It was good of you to come along with me on Sunday night, Doctor. One doesn't often get the services of a distinguished pathologist on such a case," he added pompously.

Dr. Tempest's thin, serious face lighted with amusement at the inspector's deferential remark.

"It's not often we poor post-mortem individuals get the chance of seeing the *mise en scene.* I'm glad I called in here on Sunday night. Good luck to your trip. You're really very likeable when you're not cross-examining, you know," he bantered.

Dr. Tempest's post of assistant pathologist to Scotland Yard often drew him there on business. Frequently he had been present at Inspector Reynolds's examinations of witnesses and nearly always objected to what he considered a lack of humane treatment. But he was not a detective.

Jenkins entered as the doctor went out.

"I've fixed you up, sir. Car will be here at noon. I'll see your bag is put in. You'll get to Paris in plenty of time to meet the boat train."

The inspector nodded his thanks and handed the man a written list of inquiries to be made. Then he urged:

"And particularly I want Lansberg's laundry found and his dress shirts that were sent this week looked at. You understand?"

Jenkins nodded. The inspector picked up the telephone again and gave the number of his home address.

"That you, Agnes? I'm off to France for a day or two. Starting in an hour. . . . Yes, I've all I need here in my bag. . . . You've had a wire from whom? . . . Oh, Bill? . . . When did his boat get in? . . . Well, make him stay over Sunday, then. . . . Oh, I'll be back by Thursday probably. . . . Good-by, my dear."

He had only just replaced the receiver when the bell tinkled.

"Hello!" he replied. "Who? . . . Of course I've got time," he snapped over the wire. "Send her up immediately."

A constable presently ushered in a nervous-looking girl of about twenty-four or five, who was obviously in a condition bordering on panic.

Inspector Reynolds knew the symptoms quite well. A witness had something to tell that might be dangerous to conceal, yet also realized that the revelation might be prejudicial to her reputation or position.

He glanced at his watch anxiously. These cases often took time to deal with. "Wrigglers" he dubbed them.

"Sit down, please, Miss —" he looked up questioningly.

"Perring. May Perring." She sat down timidly, her eyes lowered.

"You're a telephone operator, I hear," Reynolds began in conversational tones, "employed at the exchange which connects Beresford Street and therefore Miss Laureen's flat." So much he had learned on the telephone a moment before.

The girl swallowed.

"Yes, sir. I was on duty Sunday night from four until ten thirty."

The inspector bent across his desk.

"What are you worried about?" he asked in kindly fashion.

She raised her anxious face and hesitated a moment.

"Because, sir, we have no right to listen to conversations when we connect up, and if I tell you, I may lose my job. And I can't afford to be out of work."

Reynolds smiled reassuringly.

"Miss Perring, if, as I think possible, your information proves valuable to me, I'll promise you shall not lose your job because you were plucky enough to come here and tell the truth. And if your evidence is useless, nobody shall be a penny the wiser. Does that console you?"

The girl sighed with relief.

"Yes, sir, thank you. Sunday evening is usually rather dull in the office and I'm afraid Miss Laureen's telephone calls always interest us—me," she substituted loyally.

Seeing the inspector's bewilderment she added:

"You see, sir, she's such a popular actress and all sorts of interesting people put calls through to her and when there's time I love to hear what is said. We're all crazy about her in the office and she's so clever and witty on the telephone."

"Know the names of any of these callers, Miss Perring?"

"Several, sir. But of course Laureen—everybody calls her that— has dozens of strangers, men, ring her up and oh! how she snaps at them when they invite her out."

"I'm beginning to understand why you want to listen in," the inspector smiled. "What calls went through on Sunday?"

"The maid replied each time," the telephone clerk said. "She said her mistress was out or engaged, to every call."

"That certainly was tiresome," agreed Reynolds. "There was a call at eight thirty P. M., wasn't there?"

The girl referred to a piece of paper. "From a Miss Gilbert in a call box in Piccadilly, ordering some shoes to be taken to a certain address and saying the maid was to sleep out as Laureen would not be back that night."

"Could you recognize that voice again, Miss Perring?"

The girl's eyes opened with astonishment. "Why, of course, sir. We get to know voices like you know faces. This was easily remembered: high and clear and—queer, somehow."

"Ever heard Miss Gilbert's voice since?" the inspector inquired.

"No, sir," replied the telephone girl promptly. "Never since those two calls."

Reynolds looked up quickly.

"*Two* calls?"

"Yes, sir, that's why I came here. Miss Gilbert gave the message from Piccadilly Circus at eight thirty saying the maid was to go out and leave this parcel at ten P.M. at Chelsea where her mistress would be. So it seemed strange that when at nine fifty a Mr. Spencer rang up Laureen's flat this Miss Gilbert's voice should answer, this time, and say her mistress had already started for the studio!"

Inspector Reynolds felt a pulse of excitement race through him.

"You're quite sure it was the same voice that first spoke from Piccadilly and then spoke from Miss Laureen's flat?" he asked eagerly.

"Quite sure," the girl replied. "When I read of the man found dead there I thought it was a woman who had telephoned first to get the maid away and then had gone there to burgle the flat with some man who died suddenly."

"Do you happen to remember why this Mr. Spencer called up Laureen?"

The girl nodded.

"Yes, he wanted to know if he could come and fetch her. He adores her and is always ringing her up.

The detective rose.

"Your evidence is very valuable, Miss Perring," he assured her. "Don't worry about the consequences *this* time. I'll let you know if I need you again. Good morning."

"Two calls in the same voice and one of them from Laureen's flat," he repeated to himself as he hurried off to-the inquest. "And Laureen is a marvelous mimic! She left the restaurant at eight twenty-five P.M. I wonder . . ."

## XII. THE MAIMED HAND

MRS. DE GROOT glanced restlessly at her diamond wrist-watch and for the sixth time that afternoon compared it with the ornate clock on the mantelpiece, which at that moment chimed the hour. She counted its strokes eagerly. Five o'clock at last!

"Therese," she called to her maid.

A serious-faced, neatly clad Frenchwoman of about thirty five came from the adjoining bedroom at her mistress's summons.

"Yes, madame."

Mrs. de Groot spoke irritably:

"Lady Avice ought to be here any moment now. This room's insufferably hot. Open the windows or something, and do try to make the place look a little less ghastly. Push those hideous vases in a cupboard."

Mrs. de Groot glared round at the offending red plush and gilt furnishings. Her suite of rooms was in one of the most expensive hotels in Paris, and, she reflected, evidently the only taste its designer had was in his mouth. She flung herself back on the chaise-longue impatiently.

Therese opened a window, started an electric fan and deftly placed bowls of lilies in place of the ugly vases she put away.

"Shall I ring for tea, madame, or will you wait for her ladyship?"

"I'll wait until she comes," Mrs. de Groot answered.

She pressed her forehead with thick heavily jeweled fingers. "My headache is worse. Give me another aspirin and some eau de Cologne."

Therese obeyed and brushed her mistress's shingled hair that had been rumpled by the cushions on which she had been tossing. She was a faithful maid who knew and liked her mistress and her duties, but she sighed inwardly as she looked down at the squat figure and clumsy features of her lady. Not even the exquisite negligee Mrs. de Groot was wearing, nor all the artifices of cosmetic delicately and skilfully applied, could turn this ugly duckling into a swan.

Mrs. de Groot smiled good-naturedly as the maid dusted a powder-puff lightly across her face.

"That will do, thank you, Therese. I look a hag and feel a wreck to-day, and touching me up won't hide the facts. I'm forty-five and that's too old for these all-night parties. Got back here at five this morning, didn't I?"

"Half past five, madame," corrected the maid.

"Where are the English papers?" demanded her mistress, turning over a pile of journals beside her. "I don't see the Continental Daily Mail either."

Therese made some confused excuse about sending for them and left the room.

The widow of an American "tobacco king," Mrs. de Groot found existence more agreeable in Europe, and passed her life scouring the fashionable "season" resorts in search of gaiety.

It was on the Riviera four years ago, in a Nice hotel, that she had met Lady Avice Garth. At first Mrs. de Groot's love of a title had led her to court the girl's society, but as she grew to know her, the wealthy American found in Avice a true generous heartedness and loved her.

"Another of Avice's weird friends," the girl's circle had said. But Avice had recognized a certain pathos in this lonely rich woman and the two had become warm friends.

There was a quick double knock on the outer door of Mrs. de Groot's suite, and Therese went hurriedly to open it, closing the sitting-room door carefully behind her.

A tall, slim, dark-haired girl entered the little hall and spoke in rapid French to the maid.

"You had the telegram I sent to-you as well as the one to Mrs. de Groot, Therese?" she questioned anxiously.

"Yes, my lady, and I managed to keep the English papers out of sight as you ordered. My mistress was delighted to know you were coming. May I take your wrap?"

The girl slipped her arms from the loose light traveling coat she wore, and stood as one accustomed to such service, while the maid smoothed out a crease from her frock.

She thanked the maid with a gesture.

"Where is Mrs. de Groot?"

"In here, my lady. She had a late night and has a bad headache."

Therese opened the sitting room door and announced with pride, "Lady Avice Garth."

Mrs. de Groot held out her arms.

"Avice, you're an angel to come over and see me in this dreadful heat wave. I was tickled to death to get your wire this morning, my dear."

The girl kissed her warmly, sat down on the couch beside her, regarding her with a serious face.

Something in the girl's grave expression warned the older woman of trouble.

"Is anything wrong?"

Avice nodded; and as if to gain time, took her hat off and smoothed her hair back with her slender ringless hand.

Mrs. de Groot squeezed the girl's arm affectionately.

"Tony?" she questioned. And as Avice did not reply, she went on, "Well, whatever it is, you know you can count on me to the last ditch."

The girl turned to her with troubled eyes.

"Mary, what I'm going to say will hurt you. It's —it's about Leslie Delmond."

The older woman's lips parted in a startled gasp.

"Leslie!" she breathed. "Where is he? I've not seen him since—he left me."

Avice Garth took her friend's hands in hers and held them tightly as if she would impart courage to the woman on whom she was going to inflict suffering by her news.

"Try to be plucky, Mary dear. Leslie Delmond is dead."

The color drained from Mrs. de Groot's face, leaving the patches of rouge standing out.

"Leslie—dead," she repeated blankly.

The girl looked at her pityingly, knowing the worst of the ordeal was to come for this poor foolish woman who had idolized and been discarded by this struggling film artist.

"Yes," Avice continued steadily. "Two nights ago, June thirtieth. It—it was chloroform caused his death, Mary."

The older woman raised her haggard face.

"Suicide?" she whispered.

The girl shook her head.

"He was murdered," she replied slowly.

"Murdered!" Mrs. de Groot closed her eyes and caught her breath in anguish.

Avice Garth waited until that first terrible moment of knowledge had passed, then she went on gently:

"He was found dead in Laureen's flat. She is a great friend of mine. You remember meeting her in Nice. I can't believe Delmond was there by Laureen's invitation," she added loyally. "No details are known yet but I couldn't let you learn it from the newspapers, so this morning I decided to come over to you."

Slow tears forced themselves from under Mary de Groot's eyelids. For a minute she was silent, then she caught Avice to her.

"Thank you, my dear. He was a worthless scoundrel, but—I loved him. He had me in his clutches because I cared so much."

"He had me in his clutches also in another way," the girl said bitterly. "Tony, too."

Suddenly Mrs. de Groot sat erect, horror-stricken.

"Avice," she gasped, "who murdered Leslie? Oh, my God, you can't mean—" She broke off as she saw the tragic fear on the girl's quivering face.

"I don't know what to think," the girl said. "Tony was in London on Sunday. Dick Spencer saw him and told me so: I was at a party in Dick's studio on Sunday. Oh, Mary, I'm terrified!"

The older woman slid her arm round the girl and held her comfortingly.

"My poor darling," she murmured. "And with all your own worry you took this journey to break this ghastly news tenderly to me."

"Not entirely for that," Avice replied honestly. "Dick Spencer told me that Tony was half mad with drink or rage or both, and said he was going back to Paris when he'd done his job! Dick laughed at him and said he looked more fit for an ambulance than a job. He begged Tony to go to the studio with him, but Tony rushed off. And that very night Leslie Delmond was murdered!"

The sight of the girl's suffering helped Mrs. de Groot to recover from her own shock.

"Avice dear, money can do a lot. We can find Tony and get him away. Do you know where he is in Paris?"

"He wrote me a month ago saying he couldn't bear to meet me— yet. I understood. But now I must find him. I think possibly he may be in his old rooms in— What was that?" the girl broke off. "I heard a creaking sound from over there." She pointed to a door behind her friend.

Mary de Groot twisted round to see what it was.

"No, dear, your nerves are on edge. It's probably the waiter bringing our tea."

"Where does that door lead to?" demanded Avice.

"Into the bedroom of the next suite, which is vacant. All the rooms seem to communicate in this hotel. I knew the woman there; she went away this morning."

Lady Avice stood up, not quite satisfied.

"I'm going to look for myself," she announced.

Crossing the room she pushed back the bolt fastening the door and pulled it open swiftly. In front of her—six inches away—was a second door which she tried to open but failed.

Which was just as well for Inspector Reynolds, who had only a moment before bolted it, and now was crouched closely on the other side, listening.

He had reached the Gare du Nord ten minutes before the boat train was due, after a wild half-hour in a Paris taxi—a journey he had found infinitely more of an adventure than his placid flight from Croydon.

At the train his task was made easier by the fact that Lady Avice Garth did not know him, so there was no need for concealment. There was not a large crowd of passengers. The tourist season had scarcely begun and the intense heat Paris was undergoing had kept away many casual visitors.

In a few minutes Inspector Reynolds had picked out the tall graceful figure of the girl he wanted. Her face appeared wan and pale and he thought there was a strained look in her eyes.

He had half expected that Spencer, whom he had never seen, would meet her, thereby allowing him to kill two birds with one stone. But giving her dressing bag to a porter, she had walked at once to a taxi, looking neither to right nor left.

Reynolds managed to brush past her as she was giving the address, and was lucky enough to hear it as he had hoped. On arrival at the hotel he walked into the hall immediately behind his quarry and straight to the bureau, where he heard her ask for Mrs. de Groot's suite.

"Number 54, madame, first floor. The lift is there." The reception clerk waved a highly manicured hand vaguely and turned to Reynolds as the lady went in the direction indicated.

"I want a quiet room," the detective said. "First floor preferably. Perhaps you have a suite that would suit me."

The clerk referred to his chart.

"We have three suites vacant on the first floor, sir. You shall see them." He touched a bell and to the attendant who appeared said, "Show this gentleman numbers twenty-seven, thirty-eight and fifty-three."

Within a few minutes Reynolds had settled on Number 53, which was next to the suite occupied by Mrs. de Groot.

He locked himself in, and taking off his shoes, crept to the communicating door between the two suites, unbolted it and placed his ear against the panel of the second door in good time to hear virtually the beginning of the conversation, every nerve strained to the effort of missing no word that passed between the two women.

So now he had another hitherto unknown quantity to reckon with in "Tony," whoever he was. Maybe the fiancé, brother or lover of Lady Avice. And "Tony" had been in London mad with rage or drink on Sunday, and both Lady Avice and Spencer were alarmed.

Ah! thought the inspector, so that is why Spencer is in Paris. He has come over to get "Tony," who is probably a close friend, out of danger. No wonder Spencer and Lady Avice had become infected with this sudden fancy to come to France.

Reynolds was devoutly thankful that he had caught the same malady.

If he could only get hold of "Tony's" address! He blocked up one ear and forced the other even tighter against the communicating door in his keen anxiety to hear the address. And that pressure was his undoing. The door gave an ominous creak and Lady Avice stopped abruptly in the middle of the sentence that was most vital—for Inspector Reynolds.

Instantly he darted back and silently closed and bolted his door only a moment before the girl opened the other and tried his.

He held his breath as he crouched there with beating heart. Sick with disappointment he heard her shut the door and go back to her friend.

But they talked in undertones after that, and though he again ventured to open his door and repeat his former performance, the only phrase he heard was Mrs. de Groot insisting on her friend staying the night there.

Apparently Lady Avice agreed for he heard the American woman order Therese to get the bed prepared in the dressing-room.

Inspector Reynolds rubbed his chin. He was in for a dose of tiresome surveillance during which time he dared not leave his room to get food, dared not even smoke there.

Bitterly he regretted his office in Scotland Yard where, at a touch of the bell, he could despatch trained men to do his present detestable job. But generally he preferred to play a lone hand, with Jenkins as assistant. And his work had been such at the Yard that those in authority over him gave him a fairly loose rope.

Just then three things happened in quick succession in Mrs. de Groot's sitting-room—things which cheered the detective considerably.

Lady Avice asked if she could have a bath, which Reynolds thought would place her safely for half an hour.

Mrs. de Groot announced that they would have a light dinner sent up at seven o'clock and go out afterward.

The telephone bell rang and Mrs. de Groot, being called by her maid, answered:

"Yes, this is Mrs. de Groot speaking," the detective heard her say. "Who are you? . . . Well, that's the best news I've heard to-day. We were going to hunt you up after dinner. You'd better come along here at once and dine with us. Seven o'clock. My suite is Number 54 . . . Who do I mean by 'we'? . . . Oh, I forgot you didn't know Avice was here. . . . Lady Avice Garth," she repeated distinctly. "Yes, she's just arrived. Came to tell me the—the news. . . . Have you found him? . . . Oh, dear, well, we can't do anything by telephone. You come right along."

The detective heard her slam down the receiver and could guess she had gone into the bedroom to tell Lady Avice. He got up from his cramped position and stretched himself.

In the corridor, not far from his door and at the other side of the lift, was an alcove with big chairs. He would order some sandwiches to be brought there at once and keep his eye on Mrs. de Groot's suite for the coming visitor. He expected Spencer, but hoped for "Tony."

Settled in a comfortable armchair in a shaded corner of the alcove, his light meal concluded, Inspector Reynolds lighted a cigar, held a newspaper up to screen his face and gave himself up to patient waiting. He was not sorry for this interlude, for his future plan of action demanded careful thought.

There were many things he needed to ask Lady Avice. The half-sheet of her note-paper found in the dead man's pocket and the conversation he had just overheard, proved she had known Leslie Delmond. Probably knew where he had been staying in London.

Should he wait until Mrs. de Groot's guest arrived, then boldly knock at their door and demand an interview? In which case, he feared, they might deny any knowledge of the mysterious "Tony." Or should he to-night follow Mrs. de Groot, Lady Avice and the man—probably Spencer?

He had just decided on this course when the lift gates opened and the attendant conducted a gentleman along the corridor to Number 54.

Reynolds could not see the man's face, but guessed him to be about thirty years of age. The attendant knocked at the door and then went farther along the corridor and around a corner, leaving the lift gates open. Presently Mrs. de Groot's maid opened the door and the visitor entered.

There was nothing to be done for an hour and Reynolds was continuing his mental resume when some sixth sense made him aware he was no longer alone in the corridor.

The lift gates were still wide open but creeping up the stairs was a man in a light dust coat carrying a suitcase. He turned and walked stealthily to Mrs. de Groot's suite, stooped, and putting his hand to his ear, listened at the door.

The detective inadvertently let the newspaper he held crackle as he tried to rise silently.

The man heard it, turned, and in a second divined that he was being watched. He made a sudden dive for the lift, which was nearer him than it was to the detective, slammed the gates and let it glide upward.

Reynolds dashed for the stairs which circled round the lift, watching as he ran to see at which floor the car stopped.

At the sixth floor! He heard the gates open as he raced up two steps at a time. Half-way up the sixth flight he heard the gates crash again, and saw the lift shoot down past him to the ground, leaving him more angry than he had been for years. Fooled at his age, he growled to himself, by the simplest of tricks!

Rapidly he ran down to the crowded hall, asking two or three porters if they had seen a man in a light dust coat go out. A hopeless question, he knew, as he received negative replies from each person.

Furious and baffled, he went back to his post in the alcove, his interest in Mrs. de Groot's two visitors lessened by the incident of the last few minutes.

For as the man in the dust coat had put his hand to his ear Reynolds had seen that it lacked a thumb!

# XIII. ESCAPE!

THE girl opened her eyes dazedly, blinked at the sunlight that peeped through cracks of the curtained window, and lapsed into queer dreams again.

Presently she was aware of voices near.

"Is she conscious yet, nurse?" some one was saying.

"No, she hasn't moved," was the answer.

The girl could feel the bedclothes being adjusted round her, but had no wish to see who was doing it. In a few moments her heavy lids lifted again and, with clearer consciousness, she stared at the screens round her bed, realizing that she must be in a hospital. On the far side of the screen she heard a continuous murmur of conversation, probably visitors to the other patients.

Bit by bit she tried to piece things together. She remembered attempting to cross the road hurriedly in front of a car that morning, and had felt a terrible blow. It must be afternoon, now, hours since her accident. Or was it even the next day? If only she could find out!

There was a bandage round her head which throbbed painfully, some plaster on her cheek, and her right shoulder felt stiff and sore. Gently she tried each limb in turn, trying to assess the damage, raised her head from the pillow and laid it back languidly again. No bones were broken, she was sure. Apparently the car had hit her shoulder, knocking her down, and she had cut her cheek and been stunned in the fall.

Who had brought her here, she wondered? Probably the people whose car had caused the accident. She closed her eyes in case any one should look in on her and strained every nerve to hear what was being said to the patient on the other side of the screen. At all costs she must lie still until she could find out more and decide what to do. Suppose they demanded her name and an account of her accident was made public!

The visitor on the other side of the screen was evidently reading aloud from a newspaper. Then as a light firm step sounded on the wooden floor she heard a whining voice—presumably that of the patient in the next bed—ask:

"How's that pore young girl, nurse? She's been moaning a lot."

"Just the same, Mrs. Rookes," replied the crisp tones of the nurse.

"Found out her name and address yet?" By diligent listening Mrs. Rookes had overheard the nurse inform Sister that there was nothing to indicate who the unconscious girl was. "Her friends must be anxious about her," Mrs. Rookes added mournfully.

"They'll know in good time," responded the nurse. "Don't let me find that your visitors have brought you in ham sandwiches this time, Mrs. Rookes, or I shall have to report it," she warned as she walked on through the ward.

Mrs. Rookes chuckled, supremely conscious of a greasy packet now reposing snugly under her pillow.

"Crool hard they are here. No feelin' at all," she remarked to her visitor. "Did you bring me that shawl you promised?"

"Hadn't time to fetch it to-day. I'll bring it in on Sunday," replied her friend.

The girl behind the screens caught at the remark. "Bring it in on Sunday." Hospital visiting days were usually twice a week, she knew, so that probably meant to-day was Wednesday or Thursday. And she had been knocked down on Monday, at least two days ago!

"Go on reading, dearie," said Mrs. Rookes. "Is there any more about that Beresford Street flat murder? That actress knows something about it, I'll bet. Actresses are never up to much good," she sniffed.

"Beresford Street." The name roused some link of memory in the girl. Laureen lived in that street, and was an actress! But of course other actresses might live in the same street, she reflected.

"Well," went on Mrs. Rookes's friend obligingly, picking out the most thrilling bits, "I think this other girl did it. The one who bolted from her lodgings in Bloomsbury on Sunday night and hasn't been back since."

"What was the name of the man she murdered?" asked Mrs. Rookes.

"Leslie Delmond, a film artist. Between you and me," the friend answered, reconstructing the drama, "I believe he was potty on this Laureen and went to her flat to see her. This other girl followed and murdered him. He'd probably cast her off," she added unctuously.

"What do the papers say about her?" demanded Mrs. Rookes, impressed but cautious in passing judgment.

"They're all demanding news of this Valerie Somebody." Her visitor searched down the columns. "Valerie Baird," she announced. "They've found her landlady and they'll scour London until they get this girl."

"The police'll find her all right for sure," Mrs. Rookes said contentedly, as a bell thundered in the corridor. "That's four o'clock. You must go. Don't forget my shawl, and give my love to Nellie. Good-by."

Behind the screen the girl lay trembling, bathed in a cold

perspiration. Leslie Delmond murdered in Laureen's flat and all London being searched to find Valerie! Oh, if she could only see that newspaper, learn more about it all. What was she to do, she thought distractedly.

Perhaps even now the police knew where she was and were waiting to pounce directly she came round. She must lie perfectly still, pretend to be semi-conscious, and moan a little as Mrs. Rookes said she had been doing.

Were her clothes here? Stealthily she raised the lid of the locker and was comforted to see them folded inside. How soon would she be strong enough to stand? And how could she steal away from this place where for her lurked that ghastly fear of detection, of arrest, of a possible trial for murder?

Yes, she must escape, plan it cunningly and watch her chance. For the moment she must concentrate all her will-power on getting well enough to slip away, given the opportunity.

Would they give her any food? she asked herself. A hysterical desire came over her for Mrs. Rookes's ham sandwiches, now being slipped into that lady's locker she judged by the crackling of paper. The locker was quite close—she could see the edge of it as she lay—and if only Mrs. Rookes went to sleep before eating the sandwiches Valerie vowed desperately she would have a shot at securing them that night.

She dozed off and awoke to find some liquid, broth she fancied, being administered from a feeding cup.

Allowing her eyes to open half-way for a second she saw a young, fresh-faced nurse beside her, so intent on preventing the broth from being spilled that she did not observe the girl's swift glance. Evidently *she* didn't suspect her patient was fully conscious, Valerie decided, as the nurse covered her carefully and went away leaving the screen open a little at the foot.

Opposite Valerie's bed, which was against the wall on one side, was a pantry, and leading from that apparently was a back staircase, for at intervals through her half-closed eyes she could see nurses coming up or going down.

She determined to sleep now and wake about three in the morning to watch the routine as a guide for the moment when she could get free. She knew she would not physically be able to attempt it tonight. Even at the risk of being found out the next day, she must lie still.

Fortunately most of her luggage was in the cloakroom at Victoria. She had only taken suitcases to her room in Bloomsbury and, not trusting the inquisitive landlady, had never left any letters or papers there.

For a second her heart almost stopped beating as she remembered the cloak-room ticket.

Days ago she had ripped the lining of her handbag, slipped the cloak-room check inside and sewn up the slit carefully for fear of losing it. Had they discovered it in the hospital when they searched her things? Was her handbag in the locker with her clothes?

Well, she dared not look until the middle of the night when she hoped the staff would be considerably diminished and the patients asleep. Definitely she must rest now.

Just as she was becoming drowsy she heard the stealthy crackling of paper from the next bed. Mrs. Rookes getting ready to attack the sandwiches, Valerie thought angrily; and then almost smiled, for the nurse's quick step was heard coming along the ward and Mrs. Rookes with a muttered "Drat the woman" thrust the forbidden food in her locker.

Valerie woke at three o'clock to the sound of faint snoring. One shaded light burned at a table in the middle of the ward, and she could hear the scratching of a pen. Presently a nurse walked quietly down the ward, spoke softly to the writer at the table, and Valerie heard the reply:

"Yes, I'm coming now."

A moment later the night sister passed through the ward with a glance at each bed and went out.

Valerie sat up quickly, her heart beating fast, and opening her locker felt for her handbag. It was not there! Nearly sick with disappointment she twisted round and saw it underneath a towel on the top of the locker. With breathless eagerness she opened it and searched for the cloak-room ticket. To her joy she felt it safely at the side of her bag inside the lining. In the dim light she examined her face and head with her tiny mirror.

There was a huge purple bruise on her forehead and a slight scar at the side. Lifting the plaster a little she discovered a few scratches on one side of her face. She replaced her bag and sliding out of bed, moved the screen an inch or two to get at Mrs. Rookes's sandwiches from which she was thankful the crackling paper had been removed.

Sitting on the edge of her bed a trifle dizzily, she munched the thick sandwiches with a wary eye for the return of the nurse. There was one thing more to be accomplished before she settled down to the long twenty-four hours of pretended unconsciousness which must pass before she dared attempt flight. She *must* see where those stairs led from the pantry. Suppose they terminated at the floor below!

Staggering a little, she opened the screens and crept across the ward on bare feet.

The pantry contained cups and saucers and so on, and in a cupboard she found bread, butter and cake and a large jug of milk. With her mind on the necessity for gaining strength, she drank a large cup of milk and took a piece of cake to eat, if possible, during the long day ahead of her. A clock on the wall showed the hour to be three fifteen; a fact to be remembered in to-morrow's adventure.

Leaning over, she could see the well of the narrow stone staircase which, she decided, certainly went to the ground floor. She could do no more to-night.

Her head was swimming as she reached her bed, and hiding the cake in her locker, she lay down after winding and setting the little wrist watch in her handbag and hoping its ticking would not give her away.

Carefully she timed the length of the night sister's absence from the ward. Forty minutes! And no other sound from the corridors outside. With luck that would be the routine to-morrow night.

The long day passed more quickly than she had dared hope. She slept through most of it, taking the broth at intervals and trying to keep herself limp and apparently helpless while being fed. The doctor's visit was brief. He was exceptionally busy, she heard him tell Sister, and seemed content with a report that the patient was not yet fully conscious.

She awoke at three A.M. feeling much stronger, and the pain in her head was bearable. Again the nurse came in, spoke to the night sister, who surveyed the ward and they went out.

Now for it, thought the girl. As swiftly as her trembling fingers allowed, she dressed herself, took off the bandage and plaster, and pulled her black felt hat well down over her face.

Taking her shoes in her hand, she stole lightly across the ward to the pantry. There she stopped a second to select three newspapers from a pile—she must read about what had happened in Laureen's flat— folded them tightly and crept noiselessly down the stone stairs.

Two flights lower she paused, terrified at the sound of voices from a room near by, the door being ajar. The night staff having a meal, perhaps.

She fled shakily down two more flights and found herself in the hospital basement near the furnaces, which in this summer weather were not alight, otherwise she knew men would have been there on duty.

Stumbling weakly around, she at last found a door bolted on the inside, which when unfastened led to the foot of the area steps.

It took her some time to reach Charing Cross, as buses were infrequent. With the pretense of waiting for an early train she spent some hours on the platform, where she studied the newspapers, and afterward entered a near-by all-night café. Before nine o'clock she took a bus to Victoria, bought a thin black coat and long black scarf, and went to the cloak-room where she claimed a trunk and suitcase.

"Boat train, ma'am?" the porter questioned. "If so, better hurry up."

She nodded.

In the train, the morning papers beside her, she arranged her gauze scarf over her hat like a widow's veil and felt fairly secure from detection. At last she knew the day: it was Friday, July 5th.

From the suitcase she took her passport, thankful she had left it there and not taken it to her lodgings. Yes, there was nothing for her but flight and long months of terrible loneliness: a hunted creature, hiding until the chase had died down.

It was an ordeal which seemed the only way out of this impasse. For on opening the morning newspaper huge head-lines had met her eye.

WHERE IS
VALERIE?
Scotland Yard Finds
a Fresh Clue

Then followed an excellent description of her height, coloring and the clothes she had last been wearing.

# XIV: ALADDIN'S CAVE

INSPECTOR REYNOLDS often laughingly said of Jenkins that he had a woman's eye for detail and the instincts of a burglar. However true that summing up of Jenkins's character was it would have been incomplete without adding his almost slavish adoration of his chief.

The inspector had the broad vision that could fathom motives. Jenkins, having no imaginative qualities, could concentrate intensively on the more trifling links in the chain, plodding through seemingly irrelevant masses of evidence in the hope of extracting one useful point to pass on to his beloved chief.

Directly Reynolds had left for Paris on this Tuesday after the brief opening of the inquest, Jenkins dealt patiently with various commissions and reports, and then gave himself up to an ambitious idea of his own that was rapidly developing into clarity. It was not the first time he had worked out a plan and succeeded in giving the inspector some pleasant surprise.

Jenkins couldn't forget a remark his chief had made about Lansberg.

"I'd give something to have a quiet hour alone in his rooms, Jenkins," he had confessed. "But it just can't be done. I've not enough against him to justify a search-warrant. He's a big man apparently, and not to be disturbed unnecessarily, I'm informed. All the same I'd like to know a lot more about him."

Jenkins's thoughts were interrupted by the telephone bell. Answering, he discovered its summons was from the detective who was trailing Lansberg.

"Lansberg," came the voice, "has just gone off in his Rolls. His secretary's with him. They've got golf-clubs and a black tin case. There was no taxi about so I couldn't follow, and anyhow their car would go too fast."

"Any idea where they are going?" Jenkins demanded.

"Crowborough. That's near Tunbridge Wells. What am I to do?" asked the man.

"Report here now, and pick him up on his return. I can easily phone the golf house later, and find out if he's been there. It's a pity, but you couldn't help it."

Crowborough and golf, Jenkins reflected with satisfaction! Lansberg couldn't get back for some hours.

A little later a young man, wearing horn-rimmed spectacles and carrying a small bag, rang the caretaker's bell in the basement of a block of flats. He pulled at the brim of his hat without raising it and smiled amiably at the buxom woman who opened the door.

"And phwat may ye be wantin'?" she demanded with a brogue that clearly indicated her origin.

"Shure and it's thinkin' we come from the same old counthry," responded the young man with as unmistakable an accent as her own.

"Waterford was me home and yours was not far away by your voice," replied the Irishwoman.

"Tipperary," the young man said with a sigh. "It's nice to hear a friendly voice in these foreign parts. Ah well, I mustn't be after wastin' your time, Mrs.—"

"Milligan," she supplied. "Me husband's Irish too, and a good enough man when he's not in drink. Can I be helpin' you in any way?"

The young man produced a note-book and pencil timidly.

"I'm workin' for a firm who are bringing out a new directory of this district. I've to be gettin' the names and addresses of all the tenants and an awful job it is," he confided, "for if you go to each flat most of the tenants are out, and if you go to the caretakers you get your head snapped off. They're not all like you, Mrs. Milligan."

She beamed at the compliment.

"Ye'll not be gettin' that treatment here. Come inside and I'll show ye the list of tenants in this house and you can copy it off quick. I've just finished me dinner and was makin' a cup of tea. Perhaps ye'll be joinin' me in one?" she invited hospitably as he followed her round a screen into the kitchen and sat down in a wicker chair which she pulled forward.

"I'll keep my hat on, ma'am, if you'll excuse me, as I've a bit of a chill on me," he explained. "And that reminds me," he added, fishing in his bag and producing a bottle, "a friend gave me this to-day for my cold. I think a dose of it would do us both good and be even better than a cup of tea. Help yourself," he laughed.

"Good whisky's the finest medicine in the world," she announced solemnly as she drew the cork and produced glasses. "There's the list of tenants, me boy; you get on and copy 'em out."

The young man wrote with amazing rapidity, passing brief comments occasionally while she sipped at her whisky.

"This Mr. Lansdown?" he asked. "Has he any family?"

"*Lansberg*," corrected the woman. "No, he's a bachelor, very rich; shure he's got all the first floor. Furnished like a palace too."

"Fancy that now," said the young man in an awed tone. "Lots of servants for certain?"

Mrs. Milligan shook her head and set down her empty glass.

"You're wrong. He's only got one really, a valet. A regular heathen and such a queer name he's got—Neron. Me and me husband do all the cleanin' there as Mr. Lansberg nearly always has his meals out. He's after going off in his motor to-day with his secretary to play golf."

The young man gazed at her admiringly as he refilled her tumbler generously.

"Shows how this gentleman must trust you," he murmured.

Mrs. Milligan sniffed complacently and picked up her full glass.

"Well, Milligan and me knows our work. Butler and parlor maid in the best Irish families we was before we came here. But as for trustin'—that heathen servant is always sneakin' round there of a mornin' when we're cleanin' the place."

"Shure and couldn't you do your work when he goes out?" suggested the young man. "Or perhaps he rarely leaves the flat."

Mrs. Milligan withdrew her lips reluctantly from the tumbler.

"Oh, that Neron goes out every afternoon for hours," she asserted, "but me husband likes to get his work done in the mornin' and go off. He's gone to Brighton for the afternoon. That's why I'm alone. Good thing, too," she giggled nervously, "and me drinkin' all this fine whisky of yours."

"Suppose there was a fire or anything in this Mr. Lansberg's flat and his servant out," her guest said as he again tilted the bottle over her glass.

The Irishwoman's face assumed a pompous air.

"And haven't I got duplicate keys of all the flats in case of em— em," she suppressed a hiccough delicately and finished the word with care, "—emergency."

"I believe you're jokin'," chaffed the young man. But his eyes watched her keenly as she opened a small cupboard where hung rows of keys on hooks with a name over each.

"I'd take ye through the flats to prove it," she remarked indistinctly as she lurched back to her chair, "but I've got a bit of a headache and think I'll have forty winks."

"No, no, I don't want to see the flats, of course, Mrs. Milligan. You drink up and get a bit of rest while you can, and I'll be off to the next house and hope for as good luck as I've had here. Now one nice little drink to ould Ireland before I go and then off you go to bye-byes."

She smiled at him fondly over the rim of her glass.

"Ould Oireland!" she repeated fervently, "Ye might shut the door as you go out. I'm that sleepy!" And she closed her eyes.

The young man regarded her for a second, then opened the door to the area and slammed it, thoughtfully remaining on the inside behind the screen.

Jenkins waited there until Mrs. Milligan's heavy snoring assured him that he could move with safety. Then slipping a pair of cotton gloves on his hands he stole noiselessly across to the key cupboard in his rubber-soled shoes.

Outside the first-floor flat he pressed the bell several times without response. His heart was beating quickly as he inserted the key, entered the spacious entrance hall and stood listening.

Not a sound broke the silence save the ticking of a clock.

He made a hurried preliminary search through the apartment to make certain no one was there before beginning a methodical scrutiny of each room. Painstakingly he opened drawers and cupboards in what was evidently Mr. Lansberg's bedroom and dressing-room, turning over the linen.

In a smaller bedroom—the heathen servant's, he guessed—between the mattresses he found two things that sent a pleased glint to his eyes. He tucked them both into the handbag he carried and returned to the library.

There he made a tour of the room, memorizing every detail, glanced through some letters on the writing table and investigated the drawers and waste-paper basket.

On the desk was a case which he opened and shut swiftly as his fingers touched something soft inside and a faint smell came to his nose. His eyes narrowed speculatively as he saw a case on the wall and some tall rods in a corner.

Then he gave his attention to the large old-fashioned safe. Jenkins knew as much about safes as most experts. This one had a combination lock, which his fingers twisted and swung, his ear pressed closely to it, listening for the faint almost indiscernible fall of the tumblers. The perspiration was standing on his forehead when at last the heavy door opened on well-oiled hinges.

The safe was more than four feet high, with shelves and drawers inside. These contained sealed documents which he could not unfasten and dared not take.

The shelves had black velvet coverings draped over some objects which could be seen bulging beneath them. He lifted up the cloths quickly and drew back with a gasp of surprise. The shelves were spread with jewels of an amazing kind.

Breathlessly he gazed upon magnificent tiaras blazing with huge stones, a pile of rings, at least two diamond necklaces, ropes of gleaming pearls and pendants set in strange design.

Was this the Aladdin's cave of a rich connoisseur or had he stumbled upon the hiding place of some super-thief? Half dazed, he regarded the astonishing collection but was afraid to touch them. This job was beyond him.

With a start, he heard a clock chime and decided it was wiser to go. Gently he pushed the door of the safe and strove to close it.

Something prevented it from shutting, some unseen spring, perhaps. He struggled hard, feeling all round for the obstruction, but it obstinately resisted his efforts. The sweat was pouring down his face as he decided he must leave it open and get out quickly.

Picking up his bag he was walking toward the library door when there was a faint sound from the hall. Some one was putting a key in the lock!

Scrambling hurriedly behind the velvet curtains that concealed the huge doors, he flattened himself.

If he were seen by Lansberg or his servant, they would have even less mercy upon him than he would get from Inspector Reynolds, he knew.

It was not the first time he had made a burglarious trip and found undeniably useful information. But each time his chief had warned him of the risk he ran, a risk in which, if discovered, he would get no help from Scotland Yard.

Crouched there with every sense alert, he heard the entrance door open and close, and soft steps on the carpet in the hall. In an agony of fear he waited to find out whether they were coming to this room. After a tension that seemed to last hours he cautiously opened the library door an inch and peered into the hall. It was empty!

Gathering his courage he crept out and listened again. To his ears there came a faint grinding sound which at first puzzled him.

Then he recognized it as a coffee-mill. The heathen was evidently preparing coffee, Jenkins thought with relief, as he stepped warily along the hall. With trembling fingers he let himself out and inserting the key outside, closed the entrance door silently.

Mrs. Milligan was still snoring as he replaced the key.

# XV. A NIGHT HUNT IN PARIS

MONEY plays a good speaking part in most civilized countries, but perhaps in France it has a louder voice than in many others. Inspector Reynolds remembered this fact with comfort as he felt the thick packet of thousand franc notes in his pocket-book.

For ten minutes, after the man with the missing thumb had eluded him in the hotel lift he gave himself up to bitterness as he sat in the alcove watching the door of Mrs. de Groot's suite.

Then he became galvanized into action, and his face resumed its usual blank mask.

Near his hand was a telephone. Still keeping his eye on the door of Number 54 he picked up the instrument and asked for the hotel manager.

"I want you," he said, "to send up at once to the alcove near my suite, Number 53, your most intelligent porter. Choose carefully. I may need his services for some hours. Don't send a boy; my business is important. I am willing to pay both the hotel and the man well if he can carry out my instructions."

The Gallic voice at the other end had almost a lilt of joy as it replied:

"Of course, monsieur! Immediately!"

Clients like this were indeed rare and refreshing fruit, the hotel manager reflected, as he proceeded to his task of selection.

In two or three minutes an alert young man stood at Reynolds's elbow reporting for action.

The inspector looked him up and down, asked him his name and a few ordinary questions in concise French, and was satisfied with the porter's swift interested replies.

"Good!" commented the inspector, handing him two thousand-franc notes. "Get these cables off at once. Send them yourself, Pierre. Do you understand English?"

The man's face gleamed to a smile as he replied in that language. "I was a clerk in a shipping office in London for three years after the war, sir. But when I got married my wife wanted to live in Paris where she was born."

"Right!" said Reynolds. "Now, after you've despatched the cables, call at a reliable garage and hire a small, high-powered closed car with a driver who knows his job. I don't want a breakdown. See there's plenty of petrol put in," he added, recalling a previous incident when he had lost his quarry through a car running out of fuel at a critical moment.

"I understand, monsieur. Have you dined?"

"Why do you ask that?"

"The manager indicated you may need me for some hours, monsieur. If you've not had dinner I could bring some food in the car, in case we have a long journey or a long wait."

Reynolds clapped his hand on the man's shoulder.

"Splendid!" he said approvingly. "You've not only got a brain, but it works. Bring enough for the chauffeur as well as ourselves, a bottle of wine, cigars and cigarettes." He studied his watch and glanced keenly at a tray which a waiter was carrying to Mrs. de Groot's suite. "I can give you not more than half an hour." He hesitated a second. "I'm from Scotland Yard. A big jewel theft is expected," he added briefly. "I want to follow another car to-night from this hotel to an unknown destination."

"In that case, monsieur, I will select a car as nearly resembling a taxi as possible. It will be less conspicuous. You will wish the driver to remain near the hotel entrance?"

Reynolds assented.

"Choose the best spot, Pierre, and report here to me."

He pored earnestly over a cross-word puzzle in the newspaper as the man vanished on his errands, in case any one from Mrs. de Groot's rooms remarked his presence in the alcove.

But save for the waiters, no one entered or came out of that suite until Pierre returned. Handing the inspector a list of his expenses and a pile of change, he announced that the car was waiting outside.

"I've changed into an ordinary suit, monsieur, lest my hotel uniform be noticed," Pierre remarked eagerly. It was evident the man not only intended to earn his money but was bringing to the task a vivid intelligence which Reynolds felt to be magnetic.

The inspector's mental barometer was rising. An hour before he had felt lonely and baffled. Now, with this bright-eyed young lieutenant beside him, he was keyed up, equal to any situation.

He gave the man a cigarette. Up to a point he must confide in Pierre if he wished to get his best assistance, he knew.

"Sit there and talk to me," he ordered. "And be ready for my signal. I'm tracking two ladies and a gentleman from Suite 54 in the hope that they will lead me to the man I want."

Pierre's dark eyes flashed with pleasure at the inspector's confidence. "I understand perfectly," he replied. "Also I promise to respect monsieur's trust in me. I will be back in one moment." He ran down the stairs and had only just returned to the inspector when there was a click of a door opening behind them and they heard Mrs. de Groot's voice instructing her maid not to wait up.

Reynolds did not dare to raise his head from the newspaper until they were at the lift. Then he ventured a keen glance.

Both ladies wore small hats well over their eyes: Lady Avice, tall and slender in her traveling wrap, Mrs. de Groot short and square-figured in a black coat with the collar turned up. Their companion was standing with his back toward the alcove and Reynolds could not see his face.

The instant the lift vanished Pierre and the inspector tore down the stairs and made for the car outside. As they entered it Mrs. de Groot and her friends came from the hotel and, ignoring the row of taxis, walked up the street.

"Tell the chauffeur to follow slowly," urged Reynolds in an agony of fear lest he miss his trio in the crowded streets. Pierre picked up the speaking-tube and gave swift instructions.

"He understands, monsieur," consoled Pierre as their car crawled slowly along.

At the corner of the street the man with Mrs. de Groot beckoned a passing taxi and gave his orders. Apparently the driver demurred, for Mrs. de Groot suddenly pressed some money into his hand, which reassured him. The three entered the cab and drove off.

Reynolds's car followed at a discreet distance, dodging in and out of the traffic skilfully.

"I've taken the number of the taxi," Pierre said, "but we shall not lose sight of it."

The inspector leaned forward anxiously watching the taxi in front as it swirled along the streets.

"We're making for Montmartre," remarked Pierre.

"What I would give to know his name!" Reynolds muttered aloud.

"If monsieur means the gentleman in the taxi with the ladies, his name is Deek.'"

The inspector started with astonishment. "Dick!" he interpreted. "How in the world did you learn that, Pierre?"

"I left monsieur a moment, caught the waiter serving the dinner in Number 54, and asked him if he knew the names of Madame de Groot's guests, in case monsieur was interested."

"Monsieur certainly is!" Reynolds avowed. "Well, Pierre, what could he tell you?"

Pierre shook his head sadly. "Very little, monsieur. Only that the tall young lady had just arrived from England, that two cablegrams came this morning, one for Madame de Groot and one for her maid, and that the ladies had both addressed the gentleman during dinner as Deek. The waiter had never seen either Mademoiselle or Monsieur Deek before."

The inspector sighed with relief. "That's excellent work of yours,

Pierre." "Dick" was undoubtedly Richard Spencer, which proved that they were searching for "Tony."

They were now racing through dingy streets in Montmartre. Suddenly the taxi in front stopped outside a small café and Spencer, as the inspector now knew him to be, hurried inside, returning almost immediately.

That performance was repeated at several cafés. Presently the taxi stopped at a dark shuttered house and Spencer getting out, helped the ladies to descend and paid off the cab.

At Pierre's suggestion Reynolds's car had turned up a small street nearly opposite the house. Through the window at the back of the car Reynolds eagerly watched the door, outside which the three were waiting.

"Shall I get out and walk past the house?" asked the Frenchman eagerly. "I may hear something."

Reynolds nodded quickly.

It was fully two minutes before Spencer could get any answer to his repeated ringing, but at length the door opened a little, and the inspector could see he was arguing with some one inside. An argument which Mrs. de Groot again ended by an offering of money.

Then the three entered and the door was closed.

"Well?" inquired the inspector as Pierre returned to the car.

"I think it's a private gambling house. There are many in this quarter. Would you like to see if we can get in, monsieur?"

Reynolds considered the suggestion. Very badly indeed he wanted to go inside that house, but by doing so he might miss his goal. Lady Avice and her friends would recognize he was English if they were in the same room and saw him. And if they were not in the same room, it would be fatally easy for them to slip away with this Tony.

No, he concluded, he would have to remain here on guard.

"It's a pity to lose the chance, but I must stay in the car prepared to follow them," he told the Frenchman. "We'll have something to eat."

Pierre produced his purchases and passing some to the chauffeur, they began their al-fresco meal.

Presently the Frenchman spoke, his eyes flashing as an idea struck him. "Monsieur, may *I* try to go in? I'm French and they would not suspect me."

"Go to it, my lad!" agreed Reynolds.

The Frenchman laughed gaily and sprang out of the car. "If your people come out of the house before I do," he said, "follow them and don't trouble about me. I will see you at the hotel later."

Reynolds watched him stroll along to the house and ring for admittance. There was a little colloquy, and then Pierre vanished inside.

The inspector looked at his watch. A quarter past ten. Settling himself sideways on the seat, he kept guard through the back window of the car.

It was long after midnight when he woke the sleeping chauffeur and told him to turn the car to save time.

The car was scarcely in its new position before Reynolds saw Pierre stagger out from the house. Up the street he rolled and swayed in the opposite direction from the car, while Reynolds sat in a fever of anxiety to know whether he ought to follow him or remain where he was. Suppose Pierre had been drugged or wounded!

Then suddenly he noticed an old woman's head peering out from the door, and guessed the Frenchman's maneuver.

As the woman withdrew, apparently satisfied, and shut the door, Pierre darted into a doorway, stood still a second listening, and then rapidly retraced his steps to the car. He was barely inside, assuring Reynolds all was well with him, when a taxi drove down the street and stopped at the house.

The cab must have been expected for again the door opened, and the two ladies came out and entered it.

"Quick, tell me," Reynolds demanded of Pierre, "have you found out anything?"

"Yes, there's a big gambling room on the first floor, monsieur. A rough crowd. Your people were not there but I had to stay and play and drink."

He laughed reminiscently. "Oh, the good wine I spilled on the floor! As soon as I dared I slipped out of the room and crept upstairs."

"Plucky but risky," commented the inspector, his eye still on the waiting taxi across the road.

"I heard English voices in a back room on the third floor. The man you look for is there, but is either drunk or ill. He seemed to be very excited, shouting he would not go with them. At last he became calmer and I heard Monsieur Deek say he would telephone for a taxi. Then I crept downstairs and pretending to be drunk, came out. Voila!" He spread his hands deprecatingly.

"You're a jewel, my boy!" remarked the inspector warmly. "Hello! They've called their taxi driver inside the house."

The tall slim figure of Lady Avice suddenly stepped out of the taxi. She glanced anxiously up and down the street.

The detective and Pierre ducked their heads, though there was little risk of their being seen in the narrow dark side street.

"Here they come," said Pierre's voice excitedly as the cabman and Spencer appeared supporting the drooping form of a man clad in a long dark coat that came nearly to his heels. Probably borrowed for the occasion, the inspector surmised. The newcomer was helped inside the cab. Spencer pushed two suitcases in with him, afterward climbing beside the driver. Then the cab started up the street.

The inspector's car pursued at a prudent range; the taxi going at an exceptionally moderate pace.

"This is a queer route!" murmured Pierre.

"Queer?" questioned the detective.

"They're zigzagging up one street and back another. Do you think they've seen us following, monsieur?"

The detective frowned. "I sincerely hope not," he replied uneasily.

"Ah, now we're making for somewhere definite," the Frenchman decided as the taxi in front gathered speed.

It stopped in a few minutes at a small corner hotel near the Louvre. The taxi man and Spencer got down and almost lifted out the helpless man in the long dark coat.

Instantly Reynolds slipped out of his car. He strolled casually along, as near as he dared, and concealed himself in a doorway.

He watched the two men assist the sagging form of "Tony" into the dark hall, saw Mrs. de Groot follow them and the driver run back for the suitcases. Lady Avice evidently intended remaining in the taxi, Reynolds decided.

Presently Mrs. de Groot and Spencer returned. But only Spencer got into the cab.

"I'll be back as quickly as possible," Reynolds heard him say. "Don't leave him."

Mrs. de Groot was turning back into the hotel when she called out: "Avice, you know where to find my keys. Don't forget you'll find that packet in the left pocket of my dressing-case. And for mercy's sake, hurry."

Reynolds hurried back to the car. "I'm going into this hotel," he announced decisively. "The others are evidently coming back here. You can push off now, Pierre. I'll see you to-morrow at the hotel. Good night, my boy, and thank you."

"You won't follow the taxi?" questioned Pierre with a worried expression.

"No, no," said Reynolds impatiently. "The main object is here." He flicked his thumb towards the hotel. "Tony" was all he cared about at the moment, and in the man's present helpless condition Spencer and Lady Avice were bound to come back to him.

Of the sleepy night porter in the hall he demanded the number of the room of his friends who had just entered, and also asked if there was another exit to the hotel.

The room of Monsieur "Spencaire" was Number 19, second floor, he was informed. No, there was no other exit.

The detective thanked the man, said he could find the room by himself, and ran up the narrow circular staircase with a grim joy in his heart.

This "Tony" certainly had some grave thing to conceal, Reynolds reflected, otherwise why this journey from London of Lady Avice and Spencer, the frantic conversation he had overheard in Mrs. de Groot's room and this subsequent wild search in the Paris cafes?

He listened at the door of Number 19, but hearing nothing except indistinct sounds of some one moving about the room, he stood near an angle of the corridor where he could watch the door and stairs at the same time.

Fully half an hour he remained there. At last he heard soft movements on the stairs.

Some one was stealthily creeping up!

Then as an anticlimax Reynolds heard a whispered "Monsieur," and saw—Pierre!

The Frenchman was pale and breathless. "What is it now?" demanded Reynolds hastily.

Pierre raised his hands in despair.

"I thought, monsieur, you would like me to telephone to your hotel to see if those two had arrived and gone to Mrs. de Groot's suite."

"That was very smart of you," agreed the detective. "Well?"

"The clerk on duty is a friend of mine, monsieur. I asked him to make certain himself. He telephones up and Therese, the maid, answered. She said she had not gone to bed and that no one had entered the suite since her mistress with her friends had left it just after eight o'clock."

"Either they hadn't arrived or they had been and gone without the maid's knowledge," commented the detective.

The Frenchman shook his head. "Impossible, monsieur," he urged insistently. "The maid had decided to wait up for Mrs. de Groot, who had had a bad headache all day, in case her mistress needed something. And Therese had bolted the entrance door to the suite." He paused. "Monsieur, the hotel is not five minutes by taxi from here and they have been gone forty minutes!"

Reynolds clapped his hands to his head with an exclamation, and then started to go along the corridor to Number 19.

"Wait, monsieur," implored Pierre. "There is something more, but my friend is nervous that he may get into trouble for telling me. Can you keep his name out of it if I tell you?"

The detective bit his lip and cogitated a moment. "Pierre," he said with decision, "this is more than a suspected robbery. It is a murder case. I *must* know all you can tell me, and I promise no harm can befall your friend."

"Murder!" the Frenchman gasped. "*Eh alors,* monsieur, indeed you must be told. My friend came on duty at seven to-night and has been in charge of the telephone department ever since. At seven thirty-five a gentleman—this Monsieur Deek, of course— from Mrs. de Groot's suite demanded a number and was given it. After he had finished speaking the person he had called up rang the hotel and wished to speak to the manager. The manager, who was busy, instructed my friend to take the message. He did so. It was to ask if Mrs. de Groot of Suite 54 was financially reliable as she, or the gentleman acting for her, had ordered a private aeroplane to be ready to start at any moment after midnight."

"An aeroplane!" repeated Reynolds—amazed. Pierre nodded.

"Yes, monsieur. The call was from the big aerodrome at Le Bourget. The manager returned an answer to the effect that Mrs. de Groot was very wealthy and entirely to be trusted."

The inspector's lips tightened grimly.

"Well, their little joy ride will be a bit delayed, I think. Stay here, Pierre. I'm going to interview this man in Number Nineteen, whether he's ill or drunk or both."

He strode along the corridor and knocked firmly at the door. It was opened at once by Mrs. de Groot, who puckered her brows in surprise as the detective walked past her into the room. He glanced round quickly. There was only one other occupant of the room.

Sitting on the bed, smoking a cigarette, with a long dark coat thrown back from her shoulders, was Lady Avice Garth, regarding him with cold, amused eyes.

# XVI. A NEW FEAR

LAUREEN awoke from troubled dreams to the sound of the telephone bell ringing. Sleepily she punched her pillow into a more comfortable position, and, without opening her eyes, felt for the electric bell push suspended over the head of her bed. Her fingers groped lazily about for a moment, encountering at last a strange knob, which roused her to consciousness.

She looked round blankly at the unfamiliar room, and her brow puckered as gradual remembrance came to her that she was in the St. Andrew's Hotel. She thrust away the memory of why she was there. It was too early in the day to let that horrible shadow creep over her, haunting every hour, as it had, since Sunday night. Could this only be Tuesday morning? It seemed an eternity.

Resolutely she raised herself on her elbow and called her maid.

"Bertha! I'm awake. Do you make tea or shall I ring for it?"

From the adjoining room the maid came in, her face a little drawn. "Good morning, miss. Please don't ring. Hotel tea is awful stuff. I brought our electric kettle with me and it's nearly boiling."

Laureen stretched her arms and yawned. "Now isn't that thoughtful of you! Did you sleep, Bertha?"

The maid averted her head and drew back the curtains. "Not very well, miss, thank you. I hope you did. After all you've been through—"

Her mistress extended a warning hand.

"No," she said sternly. "We won't talk about that yet, please. It's bad for both of us. Who rang me up just now?"

"Mr. Lansberg, miss. I said you were asleep. He told me he would be glad if you would telephone him as soon as you awoke." Bertha added with importance: "Two lots of flowers have come this morning— roses and orchids. Mr. Lansberg sent the roses."

"H'm," commented Laureen to herself with a grimace. "Very devoted after all the bother I've let the poor man in for." She clapped her hands. "Tea, letters, newspapers, quick, Bertha! Oh, the letters will be at the flat, though."

"No, miss. Carter brought them round ten minutes ago. It's a quarter past nine. Shall I bring the telephone in? There's a plug by your bed."

Laureen nodded, her mind on her letters. The mail was delivered at seven thirty at the flats. Had that wretched inspector spent an hour looking over her correspondence first?

She glanced swiftly through the little pile Bertha brought in, throwing one  envelope aside after another with a sigh of relief.

Suppose Valerie had written and Inspector Reynolds had got hold of it! Oh, if only she could talk to somebody, ask advice.

The maid returned with a tray and an armful of red roses which she laid on the bed. The orchids could wait, she surmised.

Laureen picked up the flowers, burying her nose in the cool scented petals for a moment.

"Ring up Mr. Lansberg, please, Bertha," she asked, knowing quite well how the maid adored doing these little intimate things for her.

Bertha obeyed, her heart warm with gratitude. Her mistress was ignoring the fact that this dreadful tragedy might never have happened but for her —Bertha's—fatal weakness for the dead man.

The maid's lips quivered as she demanded the number and silently passed over the receiver.

Laureen laid her hand on the woman's arm, noticed the brimming eyes, and with an impulsive gesture drew her down and kissed her.

"Don't worry," she said gently. "I'm not blaming you in any way."

"It was all my fault, miss," the maid sobbed. "Look at the trouble I've brought on you."

"I hate looking at unpleasant things," replied her mistress with a smile. She pulled the telephone toward her as a voice came over the wire.

"Speaking," she replied. "Good morning, Mr. Lansberg. Thank you for the marvelous roses. I'm embedded in them. Yes indeed, the reporters would say that I live in the lap of luxury could they but see me now, which thank goodness they can't."

"Two of them tried to half an hour ago, miss," whispered Bertha. "I cleared them off," she added grimly.

Laureen repeated Bertha's rejoinder over the telephone delightedly. Her face grew grave as Lansberg told her the inquest on Leslie Delmond was fixed for ten thirty that morning.

"Very well," she answered, "I'll be punctual."

She listened attentively to a request of Lansberg's and reflected a moment before she replied.

"Thank you, yes, I'd love to come. I believe it's just what I need and there's no matinee to-day. May I telephone Avice and ask her to come? Lady Avice Garth. . . . Thanks so much. Good-by."

She hung up the receiver and announced to her maid:

"The inquest is at ten thirty, Bertha. After it's over I'm going to motor to Crowborough with Mr. Lansberg and his secretary and play a round of golf. In case Inspector Reynolds wants to know where I am, you can explain."

The maid brought her mistress's dressing-gown and held it for her.

"Your bath's ready, miss," she temporized, secretly determined to tell the inspector nothing. What right had he to pry into Laureen's movements?

"Ring up Lady Avice, Bertha, while I have my bath, and ask her if she's disengaged to-day. If so, will she come with Mr. Lansberg and myself to Crowborough for golf. Say we'll call for her about noon. Explain I'm in a hurry because of the inquest."

In a few minutes the maid came to the bathroom with the reply.

"The butler says that Lady Avice left for Paris unexpectedly early this morning, miss," she reported. "He has no idea of her address or when she will return."

"Oh, ho," sang out Laureen. Then to herself she said, "Gone to Paris indeed! Funny she never mentioned it last night! Why, she even asked me to come to tea to-day!"

The inquest was brevity itself. Laureen and Lansberg deposed to finding the man dead in her flat; she identified him and the coroner then adjourned the proceedings.

After luncheon and a foursome on the links at Crowborough they strolled back across the crisp scented turf, under a blue and gold sky that Lansberg felt was reflected in the eyes and hair of the girl beside him. A soft breeze beat lightly against their faces, cooling the heat of the sun.

"A perfect day," sighed Laureen. "If only one need never leave this heavenly spot for the crowds and noise of London!"

Lansberg bent toward her. "If you're so happy here, why go back?" he questioned.

Her eyes gazed wistfully round the panoramic view before them. "I don't know. Ambition, I suppose. Having worked so hard to get where I am, it seems foolish to abandon it all. Also," she waved her hand toward the landscape, "this won't always be like it is to-day, and London is always London, whatever the weather or season."

They were almost at the Club House when the man stopped and put his hand on her shoulder.

"Laureen, forgive me if I spoil to-day by such a subject, but I've grown to know you very well since Sunday night and," he spoke with diffidence, "I find it difficult to believe that Leslie Delmond was ever your lover."

She raised frank gray eyes to his grave face.

"So do I," she said whimsically.

"You mean—?" he asked.

She shrugged her shoulders and the shadow of a smile drifted over her expression. "When one is in a desperate hole, even a soiled ladder is not to be despised to clamber out by. I wish I could explain, *mon ami*, but I can't, and that's all there is to it."

Some acquaintances seized Laureen as they reached the big veranda, and Lansberg left her.

"I have an—appointment," he said a trifle formally. "May I fetch you in an hour?" He turned to his secretary. "Lyall, please wait here for me and see to Miss Laureen's comfort."

He bowed to her and to her friends with an almost foreign grace, in which there was nothing effeminate. Indeed, Laureen thought, as she watched him stroll off to the car, she had never seen any man with such extraordinary dignity. He was invariably courteous; yet when he spoke, men listened; when he commanded, he was obeyed. He neither strained after effect, nor sought to impress himself on others.

A beautiful revue actress of her attainments could have been a favorite in any circle. But one reason for her success was that hers was not merely a theatrical personality. Her private life was her own, she had long ago decided, and half-way up the ladder she had kicked herself free from those social invitations which most girls in her sphere would have grasped tenaciously. She did not fawn on a duchess to be asked to her ball, nor expect that duchess's husband to fawn on her! Many acquaintances said she was hard and cold; her friends found her warm and generous.

A little tired and listless after her game—she had played well and Lansberg badly for some reason—she leaned back in the low wicker chair and listened idly to the conversation. Her attention turned to Lansberg's secretary, and subconsciously she began to sum him up. Rather characterless, amiable, honest, probably efficient at his job. A man with no particular ambition, was her decision.

"Don't you golf, Captain Lyall?" she asked, accepting the cigarette and light he offered her. "I thought you were going to play in our foursome to-day."

"Yes, I often play," he replied, "but Mr. Lansberg wanted me to do something else this afternoon."

He lifted a black tin case from the floor beside him and opened it cautiously.

"I went after these," he explained. "Had quite a bit of luck, too. Those are golden Emperors, not very rare, but rather nice specimens which Mr. Lansberg wanted."

He raised the lid of the box and Laureen glanced in carelessly, her thoughts elsewhere. There were about half a dozen large butterflies inside. A curious hobby it seemed to her for a man of Lansberg's type.

Then a faint odor came to her senses. She sniffed it and frowned. Where had she known that smell before? What did it remind her of?

Suddenly she remembered in one horrified flash. She forced herself to ask a question.

"How do you kill them, Captain Lyall?"

He shut the lid and fastened it carefully. "Oh, just a few drops of chloroform on cotton wool," he answered. "They die quickly."

Chloroform! The world seemed to spin round her. Dimly she heard the light babel of conversation near and strove desperately to fight back a terrible fear.

Was it only a minute since she had been so happy, able for a time to forget the tragedy of two nights ago? And now everything had crashed! Stumbling she rose to her feet, murmuring some excuse, and walked round the veranda—almost into Lansberg's arms.

He surveyed her closely. "You look tired, my child. Get your wrap and let me take you back at once."

"No, no, I'm all right," she protested.

"It has been too long a day for you," he blamed himself reproachfully. "You must rest before the theater to-night. Lyall ought to have looked after you better."

"He—he was very thoughtful. He showed me your butterflies," she jerked out with a nervous laugh. And fled toward the coat room.

## XVII. EVASION

FOR the second time that evening in Paris, Inspector Reynolds knew he had been fooled. The next trick, however, might yet be his, since he had cabled instructions to have all channel ports watched for the man with the missing thumb.

The ruse played on him by Lady Avice Garth was of a complicated nature. It would call for much bluffing on his part, and he was afraid, judging from this evening's escapade, that the young lady might beat him at his own game, the cards being certainly in her hands up to now. Well, he would take his lead from her.

But apparently Lady Avice knew the value of silence.

She regarded the inspector slowly from head to foot with as detached and impersonal a look as though he were a piece of furniture not entirely to her taste.

Then, as if he did not exist, she flicked the ash from her cigarette and turned to her friend.

"Yes, in a measure I agree with you, Mary," she remarked casually. "Climate does affect temperament enormously. The Italian becomes indolent and warbles grand opera more or less well, but none of those Latin races can be compared to the Russians for temperament and mentality. Look at the Russian ballet for instance. . . ."

Mrs. de Groot appeared incapable of looking at anything but her friend. Her heavy jaw had dropped in astonishment as Avice had begun this rambling monologue of nonsense, ignoring the sudden appearance of a man. Who was he? Why had he forced his way in here? How much did he know? Why had Avice played this sudden trick? Why indeed had Avice sent her back to the taxi to call, through the window, that stupid message about her keys?

All these questions flooded through the elder woman's mind as she endeavored to follow her friend's cue.

"Of course they are—" she began valiantly.

But whatever they were was left unrecorded.

Inspector Reynolds stepped forward briskly, and forced himself into the conversation. A tired and irritable man, he had no intention of being defeated at this hour. He addressed the girl who sat curled up on the foot of the bed, one slender arm dangling negligently over the rail.

"Lady Avice Garth?" he began questioningly.

She twisted round a little in his direction as if she had suddenly become aware of his presence, and gave the faintest inclination of her head.

"You have entered this room, unasked by my friend or myself, to see Mr. Spencer, I suppose," she remarked frigidly. "The procedure seems a little unusual."

"Quite a good card, my Lady," said Reynolds to himself in grim admiration, "but I'll trump it."

"That is correct, madam," he replied with deliberation. "What time will Mr. Spencer return from the aerodrome or is he crossing too?"

If the girl flinched inwardly at his questions she showed no outward indication, as she tossed her cigarette end in the grate and stretched her hand toward Mrs. de Groot.

"Give me a cigarette, Mary. Egyptian, please."

Mrs. de Groot eagerly opened her case and passed it to Avice.

The girl selected and lit a cigarette with studied leisure before she replied to the detective. But she roused no sign of annoyance or impatience on his expressionless face. Stolidly he awaited her answer.

"There is no reason why I should discuss Mr. Spencer's movements with you," Lady Avice hedged.

The C. I. D. man almost smiled. Indeed she had played into his hands. He drew a card from his pocket and gave it to her.

"Detective Inspector Reynolds, Criminal Investigation Department, Scotland Yard," the girl read out slowly, with a steadying glance at Mrs. de Groot, who had visibly paled. She twirled the card in her fingers. "What does this mean, Inspector?"

"I am investigating the murder of Leslie Delmond," Reynolds explained patiently, perfectly aware that a lady of her proved intelligence already knew this. Then with a touch of his old manner he rapped out: "When did you last see Delmond, Lady Avice?"

This time it was Mrs. de Groot who caused a delay. With a faint sigh she leaned back in her chair, cheeks blanched to an alarming pallor.

The girl went swiftly to her side, sat on the arm of the chair and pulled the elder woman's head on her shoulder protectingly.

"It's all right, Mary," she murmured. "Inspector Reynolds must ask these questions," she said with a reasonableness that surprised the detective.

Still holding her friend closely she answered the detective with calm frankness.

"I have not seen Leslie Delmond for more than four years, Inspector."

"It might save time," Reynolds suggested, "if you would explain how and why your friendship with the dead man ceased."

Lady Avice drew her fine brows together with a puzzled air. "But he never was my friend," she announced in surprise.

"Acquaintance, if you prefer," conceded Reynolds.

The girl looked a little troubled, then bent toward Mrs. de Groot. "Mary dear, I'm afraid one of us must tell the inspector. Will you do so or do you prefer that I should?"

The elder woman opened her eyes and spoke in a trembling voice. "Leslie Delmond was my friend. I loved him, foolishly, although Lady Avice warned me against him over and over again. She had nothing whatever to do with him in any way."

"Then, Mrs. de Groot—" Both women started slightly as the man spoke the name with emphasis, for it had not been mentioned since he entered. To them it indicated that he knew more than they imagined. "Then, Mrs. de Groot, if Leslie Delmond was never Lady Avice Garth's friend, will you tell me why she wrote him a letter just before he was murdered?"

The girl's face was blank, but the inspector's eyes flickered to her fingers which had suddenly clenched.

"Wrote him a letter?" gasped Mrs. de Groot. There was almost suspicion in the hurt gaze she turned to her friend. "Avice, you never told me—" she began.

The detective metaphorically rubbed his hands with joy.

"Perhaps Lady Avice would explain better herself," he volunteered mildly.

But that was what Lady Avice did not intend to do. "Are you asking a question or stating a fact, Inspector?" she demanded.

Reynolds's eyes hardened.

"Both," he replied. And decided to make a chance shot. That plain crumpled half sheet of note-paper had undoubtedly been torn from a letter she had written. "A part of a letter of yours was found in Leslie Delmond's pocket after he was murdered, Lady Avice."

The girl faced him without a tremor, her voice clear and firm.

"Then in that case you know the contents and do not need me to repeat them," she retorted.

"Undoubtedly your trick, my Lady," he thought, "but I've not finished yet."

"Nevertheless, Lady Avice," he urged doggedly, "I must ask you the reason for that letter."

The girl drew a quick breath of relief. It was quite obvious this detective had not read the letter and was bluffing. "Inspector Reynolds, if you have read the letter you say you found on Leslie Delmond, then you know the reason. If you have not read it, then I cannot at this stage tell you anything about it."

Reynolds frowned slightly. The girl had courage and the restraint of her class, and added to that, a vivid intelligence.

"Are you reserving your statement, Lady Avice, because it involves some one else? The man you call Tony, for instance?" he chanced.

His question had a different effect on the two women. Mrs. de Groot clutched her friend's hand in quick sympathy. Reynolds heard her whisper, "What are we to do, Avice?"

The girl's fine features set as if they were chiseled in marble and she stared blankly at the C. I. D. man.

There was a silence, broken by footsteps in the corridor outside. At the sound Reynolds slipped immediately behind the door, hoping to overhear at least one unsuspecting sentence from the newcomer.

The door opened suddenly. A young man burst in and announced breathlessly: "Well, of all the surprising adventures. That boy has grit and deserves—" He broke off, alarmed at the startled faces of the two women.

Lady Avice was the first to regain her poise. "Inspector Reynolds of Scotland Yard is waiting to see you, Dick. This is Mr. Spencer, Inspector," she introduced him tranquilly, with an air of leaving the matter to the two men.

Dick Spencer wheeled round. The inspector saw a frank good-humored face, rumpled brown hair, and merry eyes that were gazing at him in bewilderment.

Before the detective could speak the younger man shot a mischievous glance at Mrs. de Groot. "Mary, I'm surprised at you!" he remarked sternly. "What have you been up to now?" He turned to the detective with a friendly smile. "Well, it's a bit late or early for a call, Inspector, but you've had a long journey, so do sit down and let's hear what it's all about."

"The murder of Leslie Delmond in Laureen's apartment," replied the inspector crisply, taking the chair Spencer pulled forward.

Spencer nodded understandingly.

"Of course, I might have guessed," he replied. "Jolly rough on Laureen," he flushed as he mentioned her name, "having a tragedy like that in her flat. And I suppose, as her pals, we're all more or less suspected until we can prove our innocence, what?"

"More or less," agreed Reynolds, his eyes twinkling a little at his own thoughts.

Spencer grinned. "Well, I'm going to propose we have a useful little drink all round. Mary, you look as if you need one."

He dug up a bottle of whisky, found glasses and prepared the drinks, keeping up a cheery patter all the time that made even Lady Avice smile.

"Here you are, Inspector." Reynolds shook his head. "Well, well, I suppose you know best. Mary, you drink up yours quickly. Your face reminds me of a bad channel crossing."

Somehow this young man with his disarming friendliness was very likeable, Reynolds felt, particularly after the frosty reception he had

had from Lady Avice. Of all the many classes the detective had to deal with, he invariably disliked contact with that into which Lady Avice had been born. Their cold poise baffled him.

Therefore he welcomed this more Bohemian temperament of Spencer's. Quickly he summed him up as a wealthy young dilettante, who dabbled in painting, had no great talent or intelligence, was impulsive and amiable, and had tumbled across to Paris like an eager school-boy to help Tony—evidently a scapegoat pal—at the request of either Laureen or Lady Avice. The detective decided it would not be difficult to find out all this volatile young man knew.

Spencer was perched on the bed near Lady Avice, his long legs swinging to and fro.

"I say, we are making hay of my bye-byes, aren't we?" he remarked ruefully. "Thank goodness I'll be in London to-morrow night in the good old studio. I never can sleep in these stuffy hotel bedrooms." He grimaced. "Maybe I'll not be so lucky as that, though. I say, Inspector, do I sleep on a box-spring mattress or a plank at Pentonville or wherever you propose to dump me?"

Reynolds was thankful he had refused a drink. He was conscious that a long and exhausting day, following previous sleepless nights, was taking the desire for battle out of him. And outside in the corridor Pierre was waiting for instructions.

Spencer glanced at Mrs. de Groot, whose weariness was apparent, lowered an eyelid at the girl beside him, and said: "Look here, Inspector. My friends are pretty well tired. Shall we call it a day and go to our respective stables? I'll give you my parole to meet you when and where you like in the morning."

The detective fought back the haze of drowsiness and reflected. He was entirely at a loss, he knew. There was no reason to believe Spencer had actually committed the murder. "Very well, Mr. Spencer," he agreed. "I have a car outside and can take these ladies to their hotel, where I also am staying. Will you please meet me in Mrs. de Groot's sitting-room in her suite at nine thirty A. M.?"

"I'll be there, Inspector," promised Spencer, as he wished the ladies good night.

Pierre was standing beside the car, now drawn up outside the hotel. Hat in hand, the Frenchman assisted the ladies and murmured a quick offer to Reynolds, who shook his head.

"No, no, my boy. You've done good work. Get off to bed and come to my room in the morning if you can. It's no use cabling every air-port when I don't know what this man they call Tony is like, or the name he's got on his passport. He's beaten me this time."

At the door of Mrs. de Groot's suite the inspector left her and Lady Avice, reminding them he would be there at half past nine. But he did not mention that he was their neighbor in the adjoining suite.

Singing in his bath was not a vice of Inspector Reynolds's, but at nine o'clock next morning he splashed and hummed cheerfully, reveling in the unusual luxury of his private suite. His sleep had refreshed his optimism. After all if Tony had got away, he could be traced through Lady Avice sooner or later.

Reynolds contemplated with satisfaction all that the forthcoming interview might disclose. He looked at his wrist watch as he wrestled with his collar stud: twenty past nine. Nine minutes more in which to plan a course of action. There were four questions he meant to put before he was much older, questions to which Lady Avice could and should give the answers.

Who was Tony?

Where was he now?

Where was he at the time of the murder?

What had Lady Avice written to Delmond?

Replies to those questions would carry him a long way.

There was a soft tapping at his outer door, and wondering who his visitor could be, Reynolds flung it open.

Pierre, now in his hotel uniform again, slipped inside quickly, an uneasy expression on his face.

"Monsieur," he said urgently, "she has gone!"

The C. I. D. man started back with a frown. "Gone! *Who?*"

The Frenchman spread his hands deprecatingly. "The young lady 'Aveese,' monsieur. I came on duty at nine this morning and as soon as I could, went to the telephone bureau to learn if any calls came through from or to Mrs. de Groot's room last night. I had previously asked my friend to get a record of all calls made even when he went off duty."

"Lady Avice Garth!" Reynolds groaned. "Go on, Pierre."

"Less than half an hour after you went to bed last night, or rather early this morning, monsieur, Lady Avice telephoned the aerodrome and asked if the gentleman had arrived for whom Mrs. de Groot had ordered a private aeroplane to be ready after midnight. She was told he was there waiting and would speak to her himself."

A vein stood out on Reynolds's forehead.

The Frenchman went on: "The gentleman came to the telephone, monsieur, but, alas, my friend in the telephone bureau was off duty and the operator who replaced him knew very little English. All he could understand was that the lady said, 'Wait for me.'

"'Wait for me!' " repeated the detective bitterly to himself.

"The young lady left the hotel in a taxi a few minutes after that, monsieur. About two fifteen A. M. it must have been. I'm very sorry I did not know earlier."

The inspector held out his hand kindly.

"I can't thank you enough, Pierre. This is a bit of bad luck but we'll get through. I'll see you again before I leave the hotel. I'm going at once to Mrs. de Groot's suite."

Outside in the corridor he met Spencer coming from the lift.

The young man waved his stick and sang out cheerily: "Hello, Inspector. Had a good night?"

Reynolds studied him a moment. Was this young man as innocent as he appeared, or was he a remarkably good actor?

"Thank you, yes," the detective replied calmly. Then with a keen glance: "Are the ladies all right?"

Spencer gave his boyish grin. "I dunno. Lady Avice should be, but my bet is that Mrs. de Groot's still in bed weeping over her black sheep—" He broke off. "I say, I'm talking too much. Let's go in and see 'em."

The maid admitted them to the salon, her face inscrutable. "I will tell madame," she responded to their request for Mrs. de Groot and Lady Avice Garth.

Spencer lighted a cigarette and strolled about the room, the inspector grimly watching him.

In about five minutes Mrs. de Groot entered the room wrapped in a negligee, her face bearing the signs of recent tears. She was trembling obviously as she greeted the two men and sank into an armchair.

"Mrs. de Groot, where is Lady Avice?" the detective demanded of her, though his eyes were on Spencer.

Mrs. de Groot's lips quivered. "I—don't know," she said in a terrified whisper. "I begged her not to go but she is very impulsive. Please don't be angry, Inspector. She didn't do it to annoy you."

Spencer's face showed nothing but blank bewilderment. "What on earth are you talking about, Mary?" he demanded. "Where's Avice?"

Mrs. de Groot gazed up at him piteously.

"Gone!" she said. "Last night she sent me to bed and then came in with her hat and cloak on and kissed me good-by. She left a message for you, Inspector." Mrs. de Groot pressed a hand to her forehead. "I was to tell you she would be at your service to-night or to-morrow at her London address. That's all I know." She raised her hands despairingly.

"Avice gone!" Spencer's jaw dropped. "Well, of all the prize lunatics!"

It was evident the news had been a surprise to him, the detective decided. "Mr. Spencer," he remarked sternly, "I shall be glad if you will tell me exactly who and where 'Tony' is, and why you came to Paris suddenly to get him safely away?"

Spencer's face was still placid and amiable, but there was a determined glint in his eye as he drawled:

"And that, my dear Inspector, is precisely what I *cannot* tell you—anyhow until I've seen Lady Avice. Y'see, some of it I don't know, some of it I don't want to know, and some of it I couldn't tell you because—er—well, because it's not my business. You can lock me up as hostage or any jolly old thing you like, and that's that."

And that certainly *was* that, as far as opening Spencer's mouth was concerned. After a rather unfruitful conversation with Mrs. de Groot, Reynolds and the young man traveled back to England together that day.

They were nearing London when the detective had a bright idea. In a measure he appreciated and understood this young man's reticence concerning Lady Avice's affairs which appeared to include Tony. Well, Reynolds decided, he could obtain all his information—insist upon getting it too—from her later. Meanwhile there was one question that had nothing to do with her.

"Mr. Spencer, do you remember telephoning to Miss Laureen's flat on Sunday night at nine fifty P.M.?"

"I do," replied that young man promptly, "though I'm hazy as to the exact time."

"Will you tell me all the conversation that took place?"

"Certainly." Spencer thought a moment. "I asked if Miss Laureen had started for my studio yet and the reply was that she was on her way. That was every word so far as I can remember."

"Was it her maid's voice that you heard?" Reynolds asked.

Spencer shot a glance at the detective. "That's the funny part of it," he declared. "I'll swear it wasn't Bertha's voice." He reddened slightly. "You see, I'm absolutely crazy on Laureen and often ring her up, and I know the maid's voice very well. No, it was high and clear, I wondered who the woman was. If it *was* a woman," he added.

"If it *was* a woman!" caught up the inspector sharply. "What do you mean?"

"Well, it might have been a man's falsetto just as easily," explained Spencer with no particular interest. He peered through the carriage window. "Ah, here we are. Good old Charing Cross."

But the detective's mind was echoing "It might have been a man's falsetto." Why hadn't he thought of that before?

## XVIII. THE KNIFE

LAUREEN had proved an unusually silent companion on the journey back from Crowborough with Lansberg. From his seat at the wheel he glanced at her several times as she stared ahead with a troubled expression.

He had over-tired her, he feared. After the tension she had endured since Sunday night this journey down and back, the heat on a shadeless golf-links and a strenuous game had all been too much. And to-night she had her work in the theater!

He metaphorically kicked himself for his thoughtlessness as the big car slid silently along.

Suddenly she relaxed, and leaned back with a little gurgle of laughter as she noticed Lansberg's worried face. "Did you think I'd developed motor nerves or had become 'mental'?" she asked.

Lansberg smiled down into her gray eyes with relief. "Neither," he affirmed. "But I do know you are a very tired girl, thanks to my selfishness. I ought not to have asked you to come on this long exhausting trip after—"

Laureen interrupted him. "I shall scream if you say, as my maid does, 'after all you've been through.'"

There was an extraordinary mixture of tenderness and self-reproach in the look he bent upon her. For one second he took one hand from the wheel as though he would touch hers lying on the light rug. Then his face resumed its accustomed stillness and he drove on steadily with tightened lips.

"If only you need not act to-night!" The words seemed forced from him.

"That's my job," she stated simply. "I'm paid well for it too."

"Yes, but on top—" He stopped like a naughty child as her finger went up with a warning gesture.

"Be careful or my scream will outdo your Klaxon." Her mouth had crinkled comically, but there was a soft radiance in her eyes that sent a sudden fire through the man's veins.

"Mr. Lansberg," she began softly.

"One of my several hideous Christian names is Ivan," he suggested with diffidence.

"Ivan," she repeated tentatively. "It's not at all hideous, though, whatever the others may be."

"Then it's yours to use, if you will. What were you going to say when I interrupted you?"

Her fingers twisted a corner of the rug nervously. "You offered to show me your rooms once. If you're not engaged or tired of the sight of me, might I come to tea when we get back, please—Ivan?"

This time his hand dropped over her fingers and held them closely. "You will make me very happy, my child."

She peeped mischievously over her shoulder at the secretary, who was discreetly studying the streets they were now gliding through. "That very correct person will blush presently," she predicted.

But Lansberg was in a dream that made him oblivious of trivialities, as automatically he guided the car through the traffic and a little later pulled up before his house.

Lansberg put his key in the lock and stood aside for Laureen to pass into the impressive entrance hall of his apartment. She looked round wonderingly, appreciating its dignity and beauty, all enhanced now by the sunlight drifting in iridescent coloring through the old stained window.

"This isn't a flat: it's a fairy palace, Ivan," she said softly.

"Sometimes a palace can be only a dungeon when it lacks a princess," he replied as he led her to the large double doors that opened into his library. "I think you may like this room where I work. If you will go in I'll find my servant and order tea."

Laureen drew back the heavy curtains and entered the room. For a moment, coming from the subdued light of the hall, she was dazzled by the glare.

Then she distinguished a dark menacing figure rising from a crouching position, and gave an involuntary cry that brought Lansberg quickly to her.

"What is it?" he asked.

With a shaking hand she pointed. "That man—he—he was kneeling with his forehead bent over to the floor, I think. He startled me."

Lansberg drew her to the couch.

"That's my servant, Neron. At his prayers, I expect."

He addressed the man in a language the girl did not understand. She saw the servant indicate the open door of a huge safe in the corner and caught a glimpse of marvelous flashing gems on the shelves within.

There followed a rapid conversation between the two men— agitated on the servant's part, coldly angry on Lansberg's. Then he ordered the man from the room, and hurriedly examining the contents of the safe, closed and locked it.

Laureen noticed his face was whiter and more set than usual as he sat down beside her.

"I'm so sorry you were alarmed," he said gently. "My servant found the safe open and hasn't yet got over it. Nothing has been touched so I must have left the thing unfastened this morning," he added reassuringly.

Laureen shivered a little as the thought flashed through her mind that Lansberg had not left that safe open, that he knew it and had only said so to avoid exciting her.

She glanced slowly round the lofty room, noticing subconsciously the different things, until she saw a large case of butterflies.

"Do you collect butterflies?" she asked with apparent casualness. "I see a case of them there, and your secretary showed me some he had caught today." She bit on her lip to still the shudder that passed through her.

But there was no trace of embarrassment in Lansberg's frank answer. "I used to have quite a fine collection," he admitted. "Then I became too busy or lost interest. Now I've started again because a young twelve-year-old god-son of mine has begun to collect and I'm sending all I find to him. He wrote asking for a variety—common enough—to be found in Sussex. That's why Lyall went a-hunting for me to-day."

His explanation was so natural that the girl almost laughed at her previous fears. Absurd to imagine that a man of Lansberg's type and wealth could have any connection with Leslie Delmond or any motive for murdering him.

They had finished tea and were smoking cigarettes when suddenly Lansberg leaned toward her, idly twisting the long string of pearls that dangled from her neck.

"I've often meant to ask you if you had any sisters or brothers, Laureen."

"My father died a few months after I was born," she replied. "He and my mother believed in a small but good family. I'm *it*," she added with a quaint little smile.

"My dear, forgive these questions, but I'm very worried," he said presently. "Did you write a letter to the girl—I thought maybe it was your sister—called Valerie the night we discovered the murder?"

Laureen shook her head, her eyes on his slim fingers nervously toying with her pearls.

"No," she said definitely.

"Then, Laureen, if you wrote no letter, what was in the envelope you dropped into the hall letter box when you ran down to whistle for the policeman?"

There was a curiously speculative look on Laureen's face. Was it merely his keen interest in her that made him ask these questions, or was there some deeper reason?

She drew away from him sharply before he could release his fingers from her necklace. There was a snap and two of the pearls rolled on the ground.

She caught up the broken thing and tucked it into her hand bag, together with one pearl that had fallen beside her on the couch.

"I'm so sorry," Lansberg murmured with vexation.

"It doesn't matter. Only one has dropped. It is there under your desk."

Lansberg knelt to find it. As he stooped, a tiny article fell from one of his pockets and rolled along the ground close to the girl's feet, unnoticed by him. Something in its appearance made her bend down and examine it closely, turning it over in her fingers. Then with an ashen face she silently rolled it along the carpet away from her and rose.

"Please don't trouble any more," she urged. "It will be found to-morrow. I must get back to my hotel now."

Her lips framed the words mechanically. Lansberg stood up, obviously much annoyed at his carelessness.

"Yes, my man will find it, I'm sure. You must let me get the pearls re-strung for you, Laureen. They're valuable."

"An actress's bank," she managed to say lightly.

As they walked across the room his foot touched the small article he had dropped. Deftly he picked it up and slipped it into his pocket. It was only after she had gone that he remembered she had not answered his question.

But in her mind now there was no question whether he knew Delmond. For, with wildly beating heart, in one instant she had recognized that the small thing dropped from Lansberg's pocket was a seal which Leslie Delmond had worn four years ago in Nice.


It was just after eleven o'clock that same night—Tuesday—when Inspector Reynolds's wife and her brother-in-law came out of a cinema house in Highgate. She blinked a little in the jostling crowds.

"There's our tram, Bill, but we shall have to wait for the next. It's full."

"Trams be blowed!" exclaimed her brother-in-law. "When I take a lady out I like to do things properly. Hi, taxi, ahoy!" he shouted vigorously to a passing cab.

Remonstrating gently at his extravagance she allowed Bill to help her into the vehicle. She adored her husband's bluff-mannered brother—a sea captain.

Bill had not been in England for two years, and early this morning he had telegraphed saying he would arrive that afternoon for a short visit.

"Got any idea when Tom will be back, Agnes?" Captain Reynolds asked as their taxi jolted up the hill.

She shook her head. "Not exactly," she sighed. "He telephoned me this morning from the Yard, as I told you, saying he had to go to France at once, and expected he'd be back by Thursday. He said I was to be sure and make you stay over Sunday."

Captain Reynolds lighted his pipe and blew out a heavy cloud of smoke contentedly. He was very fond of his brother and sister-in-law and nothing pleased him better than to potter about their house and garden when he was ashore.

"Of course I'll stay," he said in his bluff tones. "Couldn't go away without a sight of the old chap. I say, Agnes, what's he gone to France about?"

Mrs. Reynolds looked important.

"He's in charge of a big case that happened two nights ago. Some film actor found murdered with chloroform in Laureen's flat. She's that famous revue artist. I shouldn't be surprised if Tom's tracking a clue in Paris."

The taxi pulled up at the gate of the semi-detached house and Captain Reynolds helped his sister-in-law out.

"A beautiful film," she murmured as he unfastened the door, "but very sad. Thank you, Bill, for taking me. I've enjoyed my evening so much."

"Give me Charlie Chaplin and a good laugh for my money. You put on a kettle for some toddy. Do you good after crying your eyes out over that blessed film."

Mrs. Reynolds entered the house, switched on the lights and obediently put water on to boil. Then hastened to remove the traces of tears still remaining after her evening's enjoyment. She had laid supper and the kettle was singing before she realized Bill had not yet come into the house.

"Smoking that horrible old pipe outside because he knows his tobacco makes me cough," she decided.

Opening the front door she called him. "Kettle's boiling, supper's ready, Bill."

There was no answer. Probably he was walking up and down the road in his restless way.

She went to the gate.

"Bill!" she called again. From somewhere near in the garden she heard a faint choking sound.

As she listened, fearful, she heard it once more, saw something dragging itself heavily, slowly along the ground toward her.

A wild scream came to her lips but she suppressed it. Inspector Reynolds's wife was no coward.

Deliberately she opened the hall door so that the light should fall on this object, whatever it was, and seized a heavy stick from the umbrella-stand.

But the weapon dropped from her hand as the crawling thing drew nearer to the circle of light and she recognized it to be her brother-in-law. Before she could reach him, he rolled on his back and, with a shuddering groan, lay still.

She knelt on the path beside him, slipping her arm beneath his neck to raise his head. Could he have had a heart attack or a seizure?

"Bill," she cried, "it's all right I'm here." And then sank back trembling, for her fingers felt something warm and moist. Protruding from the man's left shoulder was the handle of a knife.

# XIX. FINGERPRINTS

INSPECTOR REYNOLDS felt like a horse nearing its stables as he stepped out of the boat train that Wednesday evening with Spencer.

"You'll find me at my studio to-night, Inspector," said the painter, "or I'll come along to the Yard now if you prefer."

"I'll ring you up probably to-morrow morning," replied the detective, out of his abstraction.

He had more important interviews ahead than the one with this young man who had unwittingly thrown a new light on the problem. A falsetto voice might be the solution of that telephone call. If so, whose? Was it Delmond's before he was murdered? Mrs. Carter had overheard men's voices through the speaking tube. Was it one of those men who had spoken on the telephone?

Thrusting aside the newspaper boys calling up their "six-thirty finals" the detective jumped into a taxi and ordered the man to drive to Scotland Yard. He was eager to see Jenkins and hear all his faithful assistant had discovered. Then he would call on Lady Avice Garth and wring from her the truth about Tony.

Reynolds marched into his office with a jaunty air as if a thirty-six hour trip to Paris and back was an ordinary occurrence.

"Well, Jenkins, get my cables? Had any luck anywhere?" he asked.

Jenkins rose, his face somber, hands fidgeting with a pen. "I'm afraid I've got some rather bad news for you, sir," he began.

The inspector glanced at him with a frown. "Lady Avice Garth not turned up at her house?" he questioned sharply.

Jenkins shook his head. "It's your brother, sir. He was stabbed about eleven thirty last night in the front garden of your house. Mrs. Reynolds found him and telephoned here at once. He's alive but unconscious."

"Bill!" exclaimed Reynolds in amazement. "Why, he hadn't an enemy in the world." Then as a light broke on him, "I suppose somebody was after me and got him instead. We are very much the same build."

He sat down at his desk and rested his head on his hands. At that moment he bitterly regretted his profession.

"Where is he?" the C. I. D. man asked Jenkins dejectedly.

"Highgate Infirmary, private ward, sir. The Yard sent down two specialists and Dr. Tempest was there most of last night with him and twice to-day. Dr. Tempest told me to ring up directly you arrived. Shall I do so?"

The detective nodded, his face drawn with pain. Poor defenseless old Bill, knifed in his own brother's home by some malicious fiend.

Reynolds's fist clenched. If he had to scour Europe he'd get that brute and make him suffer for it!

Jenkins passed over the receiver. "Dr. Tempest is waiting, sir."

"That you, Inspector?"

"Yes, I've only just heard the news," Reynolds replied. "Thank you for all you've done, Doctor. Is there any hope?"

At Dr. Tempest's words the strain on the detective's face relaxed.

"You think he has a chance," he repeated eagerly. "Conscious for a few minutes and now sleeping. . . . A clean wound, missed the lungs by half an inch. . . . Do whatever you think best. Don't spare any money so long as you save him. . . . No, I won't try to see him until you say I may. . . . Thank you again, Doctor."

Reynolds turned from the instrument joyfully. "Did you hear that, Jenkins? The doctor says my brother has a chance now."

He put through a call to his home and waited impatiently.

"Yes, Agnes, I've just got back and heard about Bill," he told his wife, and then gave her the gist of his conversation with Dr. Tempest. "Don't worry too much. I'll be with you as soon as I can."

The inspector hung up the receiver and drummed his fingers on the desk. "I'll find out the scoundrel who did this or change my job," he announced sternly.

His assistant looked uneasy. "I suppose it couldn't have been any one connected with this murder case," he suggested.

His chief reflected a moment, running over the principals in his mind. Certainly no woman could have done it. Bill was a remarkably strong man. Lansberg he dismissed at once as being unlikely. Spencer, Tony and the man with the missing thumb were definitely in Paris at the time.

"No," Reynolds replied slowly. "I shouldn't think it probable. Besides, how would they know my house address? There are dozens of Reynoldses in the telephone book, and my official position is not shown there."

Jenkins stared at his chief aghast. Sweeping over him was the dreadful knowledge of a confession he had to make: of over-zealous efforts that possibly had had tragically far-reaching effects. For he remembered that on Lansberg's desk he had seen Inspector Reynolds's private address written on a slip of paper.

The detective regarded Jenkins's haggard face with a puzzled air. What on earth was the matter with the man? It wasn't his brother who had been stabbed!

"Have we got the knife that was used?" Reynolds asked.

Jenkins pulled out a drawer and produced a cardboard box.

"It's in there, sir. The doctor was very careful not to touch the handle."

Lifting the lid, the inspector gazed at the weapon —a blade, curved on one side like a French table-knife, hinged and set in a wooden handle.

"A most unusual type," muttered Reynolds as he pushed the box away with a shiver. "I've never seen anything quite like it. What about fingerprints?"

Jenkins replaced the cover and put the box back in the drawer before he answered.

"Three different sets were found. Overlapping a bit, but distinct and identifiable. Right hand in each case. Two sets have been identified," Jenkins announced.

Reynolds sprang up with excitement. "One set has a thumb missing?" he demanded eagerly. Adding as Jenkins shook his head, "No, of course he was in Paris at the time, but he might have handled the knife previously." Suddenly he observed his assistant's worried manner, noticed the perspiration standing on his forehead.

"What's wrong? Are you ill?"

Jenkins drew a long breath and raised his eyes. "No, sir. I'm in a mess. Yesterday when you went to Paris—I—tried to be clever, thinking I could help you. You warned me before and now I'm afraid I'm responsible for this—this stabbing affair."

"You, responsible!" The detective echoed the words blankly, surveying his assistant with a frown. Was the man demented? Then he added quietly, "Sit down, Jenkins, and tell me what the trouble is."

The man sank to a chair and moistened his lips, eyes resting piteously on his chief's face as if asking at least for understanding.

Inspector Reynolds's countenance was inscrutable as the man poured out the story of how he had gained admission to Lansberg's apartment, the trick he had played on the caretaker to get the key, his search in the apartment, the opening of the safe and the amazing collections of jewels on the shelves.

The detective interrupted him.

"That's queer," he returned. "Bachelors don't usually hoard tiaras and necklaces and rings such as you describe, in a private safe. Unless they're connoisseurs or jewel thieves. Lansberg seems too austere to be the former and too wealthy, I should have thought, for the latter. However, go on with your story, Jenkins. You locked the safe," he prompted, "and got out without any one seeing you, I hope."

The man mopped his brow.

"That's the mischief, sir. I could not close the darned safe, let alone lock it. There was some catch keeping it open and I'd just decided I daren't stay any longer when I heard some one enter the flat."

He described hiding behind the curtain, creeping out while the servant was grinding coffee, and replacing the keys in the basement cupboard.

"How do you know it was the servant? It might have been Mr. Lansberg or the secretary."

Jenkins negatived the suggestion firmly. "No, sir. They drove up with Miss Laureen about four thirty. The secretary carried in the golf-clubs and a tin case and then took the car to the garage. Laureen and Mr. Lansberg entered the flat and she drove off alone in a taxi at five forty. I had our man watching them. They'd been to Crowborough all right: I telephoned the Club House to make that certain."

Inspector Reynolds pushed back his chair and tramped up and down the room, his features set. Jenkins watched him, expecting a torrent of bitter reproach for his unauthorized adventure.

To his surprise, none came. He felt a hand on his shoulder and heard Reynolds's voice say mildly: "Well, you took a big risk."

The younger man fumbled with a parcel a moment and then opening it, exhibited to the astonished inspector a dress shirt and a silk vest.

"I found this under the mattress in the servant's room, sir," he stated. He pointed silently to a gash in the linen at the side of the starched front, and a corresponding slit in the undergarment.

Reynolds's eyes gleamed as he examined both cuts with a magnifying glass.

"The gash on the vest has not cut quite through the silk, so apparently never reached the flesh," he announced.

Jenkins played his ace bravely although he knew also he condemned himself thereby.

"On the bottom shelf of Mr. Lansberg's safe, sir, was the knife which stabbed your brother," he said slowly.

And then indeed, Inspector Reynolds was aroused as the probabilities unfolded before him. He could picture Lansberg's servant finding the safe open and guessing it was the inspector who had been there searching the flat. The detective's face hardened as he recalled the scarcely veiled antagonism to him in the servant's eye when he was ordered to bring his master's clothes. His devotion to Lansberg was obvious. Why else had he hidden that shirt and vest under his own mattress?

When the servant discovered that these had been taken it was easy to link up their disappearance with the detective's previous visit, easier still to imagine that fanatical creature bent on revenge, seizing the weapon in the safe and watching outside Reynolds's house in the dark.

Then another vital point occurred to the detective.

How had that knife come to be in Lansberg's safe? From whom had *he* taken it and when?

Aloud he demanded swiftly, "Whose fingerprints were on the handle of that knife?"

"Those of Lansberg were there. Also those of Delmond, the murdered man."

*"Lansberg!"* shouted the detective. "How can you be sure they're his?"

"We got some from the cigarette-box left in Laureen's flat," Jenkins replied, "and fresh ones to-day from the driving wheel of Lansberg's car."

Reynolds thumped his clenched fist on his desk.

"D'you see what all this means, Jenkins? That knife must have belonged to Delmond, and he evidently struck at Lansberg the night he was murdered, as this slashed shirt proves. So Lansberg was in Laureen's flat, after all. He must have seized the knife after he or his accomplices had chloroformed Delmond, and locked it up in his safe. Butterflies!" commented the detective grimly. "In this case a butterfly with golden hair and a pretty face! He'll have a job to explain away this evidence, I fancy."

"You would like the fingerprints of Lansberg's servant, sir?" asked Jenkins.

"Like?" snorted the inspector. "I mean to have them. They're an indispensable link in the chain."

Then his animation flickered a little. Was not all this merely circumstantial, a trifle too simple and easy? Why should a man of Lansberg's position commit murder and risk its consequences? Certainly not to obtain Laureen, who, if Reynolds could read character, disliked the dead man and liked Lansberg.

Also, in that case, where did Tony and Spencer, Lady Avice and Mrs. de Groot fit in? What about Valerie Baird and the packet of letters? And who was the man with the missing thumb who had undoubtedly been in Laureen's flat, as his fingerprints on the table proved?

No, Reynolds decided, he wasn't out of the woods yet, even if there was a glimmer of daylight.

"What about those cabled orders I sent to watch the ports?" he asked suddenly.

Jenkins's face clouded. "No luck, sir," he reported. "No man minus a thumb was seen anywhere."

His chief, however, showed no signs of disappointment.

"H'm, well, I didn't expect any. It was a forlorn hope, but worth trying. Ring up Lady Avice Garth, Warnham House, and if she has arrived say I want to speak to her."

Jenkins gave the number and presently passed over the receiver.

"Inspector Reynolds of Scotland Yard speaking. . . . Left a message.

Well, repeat it exactly, please." He put his hand over the mouthpiece and turned to Jenkins hurriedly. "Take down this conversation," he whispered. "Lady Avice Garth arrived at four o'clock and said she would call at Scotland Yard at eleven to-morrow, Thursday morning, and see Inspector Reynolds," he repeated. "Was her ladyship alone when she arrived? . . . She was? . . . Where has she gone now? Her ladyship did not say."

He banged down the receiver angrily.

"If I go off my head with this confounded case, Jenkins, it will be through the tangle of women mixed up in it. They've tied the men's tongues nicely. Chivalry, I suppose, would be their fancy name for it. Concealment of facts hindering the course of justice, that's what I call it."

The inspector was thoroughly irritated by this postponement of the interview with Lady Avice. Jenkins wisely tried to change the subject.

"No news of this Valerie Baird has come in yet, sir. Funny how she seems to have vanished."

"There are a lot of funny things in this case," agreed the inspector gloomily. "Come in," he called as a knock sounded on the door.

"A man to see you, sir," announced a constable. "Says he thinks Delmond was his lodger."

"Show him up at once," ordered Reynolds.

A short narrow-chested man with furtive darting eyes entered and sat down at the inspector's invitation.

"What makes you think the murdered man was your lodger?" demanded Reynolds bluntly. He had already sized up his visitor and knew the best way of tackling him.

"I recognized the photo in the paper and thought it might be the same man who'd had a room in my private hotel up to last Sunday."

The inspector gazed at him with steely eyes.

"This is Wednesday evening," he commented. "The photographs were printed in Tuesday's morning papers. It took you two days to decide whether you recognized it or not, eh?"

The man shuffled uneasily in his chair. "A murder case isn't nice to be mixed up in when you've got your business to consider," he whined.

"And where is this hotel of yours?"

"Near Euston station," replied the man, adding the address reluctantly. "Besides, I never knew he was called Delmond. Mr. Leslie Jackson he said was his name. The room's locked—he has the key."

"I shall be there to see it to-morrow," promised the inspector. "How long had he lodged at your house?"

"Going on for a month. Always paid well too and gave no trouble," replied the man sullenly. "Out all day. So as I didn't know anything against him, I thought I'd wait and see if he came back."

"Although by the photograph you knew he'd been murdered!" commented the detective. "Had he any visitors or letters?"

"No letters ever came for him. But once I found a torn envelope and addressed to L. Delmond, Poste Restante, Charing Cross, so his mail went there in that name probably. As to his visitors, I mind my own affairs so long as my rent is paid and my lodgers behave themselves."

"Answer my question," said the inspector sharply. "Did you ever see any visitors?"

"Well, once I believe a lady went up to his room, but I'm not sure. Might have been to see somebody else. I don't pry into other folk's affairs."

"A slim young lady, fair or dark?" suggested the inspector.

"Neither," affirmed the man. "I'm not certain which room she went to but I know what the lady was like. She was elderly, with gray hair and wore handsome clothes. A real lady, too."

"You're sure she was elderly?" questioned the inspector. "It might have been a young woman disguised."

"Well, it wasn't," said the man definitely. "What's more, I know who the old lady is," he added with a touch of triumph at scoring over the detective. "I've seen her since then."

"Where?"

"I was in the pit of Laureen's theater on Monday night and a lot of swells were in the stage box. I recognized the old party who'd been to my hotel a few days before and I asked the program girl who she was. That's how I know."

The detective bit back his impatience.

"And the program girl knew her name?" he asked mildly.

"Yes. The Countess of Warnham, and with her in the box was her niece, Lady Something Garth."

## XX. THE THIRD KEY

"THE Countess of Warnham!" echoed the detective after Delmond's landlord had gone. "Do you hear that, Jenkins? Another woman to deal with. Will you tell me what was Delmond's attraction that all these females hung round him?"

Jenkins shrugged his shoulders.

"From the photographs he seemed a good-looking fellow," he conceded. "And of course a film actor, successful or no, always has a certain glamour."

"Glamour!" Reynolds sniffed disdainfully.

"Surely a woman of the Countess of Warnham's age and social standing—she must be over seventy—was not dazzled. What about that American woman, Mrs. de Groot? She's an astute bird in the early forties. Yet she fell for him."

"Has he some hold on them, do you think, sir?" Jenkins suggested.

"It's an idea, but Mrs. de Groot's feeling for Leslie Delmond was sincere. There is no doubt she really loved him. And I tell you, Jenkins, her grief was pitiful when she knew he was dead. Love! Why she was almost jealous of her friend Lady Avice when it came out that Lady Avice had written Delmond recently!"

The inspector had outlined the whole history of his Paris trip to his assistant. He often did this kind of thing: it arranged the pattern of events in his own mind and often drew valuable suggestions from Jenkins.

Jenkins pondered.

"It seems to me you did fine work in Paris, sir. You've definitely established the fact that this man with the missing thumb knows Mrs. de Groot and Lady Avice. You've discovered the *liaison* between Mrs. de Groot and Delmond, and that Tony is mixed up with them all. Shall I look up Lady Avice's pedigree?" he inquired.

"Look up any darned thing you can about her and her family," he said bitterly. "All *I* know is that they're nearly broke and Lady Avice's father, the Earl of Brentshire, is a dissolute old gambler who lives chiefly by his wits on the Riviera."

Presently Jenkins looked up from the big red book he was poring over.

"Lady Avice has three brothers," he announced, "and one of the younger brother's names is *Anthony*. They've got about five apiece!"

"Aha!" the inspector ejaculated. "Tony is short for Anthony." He picked up the telephone receiver and gave a number.

After a short conversation he hung it up with a look of satisfaction.

"Lady Avice's eldest brother is in India with his regiment. Both the younger ones are abroad and have not been seen for years. One was in the diplomatic service but resigned. The other dabbled in art a bit and then is supposed to have gone into a bank in Paris. That's our precious Tony, I'll lay any odds."

He glanced at his watch.

"Well, I'm through for to-night. If Highgate Infirmary says there's any change in my brother's condition call me at my home. Good night."

The street was deserted as a man came round a corner. Only a few seconds before he had seen the policeman on duty stalk slowly ahead flashing his lantern at each doorway conscientiously.

The man walked along with rapid steps until he reached the building he sought. Still no one in sight. He gave one furtive glance up and down, then vanished inside, his rubber-shod feet making no sound on the stairs.

Outside the door of a flat he paused, listened carefully and gave one light touch to the bell. His heart beat a little faster as he heard that faint summons tinkle distantly inside. A minute, perhaps two, he waited, but no one came.

One glance he bent toward the empty staircase before inserting a key in the lock. Quickly he entered, closed the door and again stood listening in the darkness. Save for the distant faint roar of traffic, there was absolute silence.

He crept through the flat to be sure it was unoccupied. Then satisfied he was alone, he began his work.

At first he searched with method and deliberation, going through drawers and cupboards patiently. But as time passed and still he was unsuccessful, beads of perspiration stood on his brow. He tore frantically at carpets, cut open the cushions and chair coverings with a knife taken from the kitchen, muttering to himself in a frenzy of rage. Pictures he ripped from their frames and flung down, as if lost to all fear of being discovered.

One room was locked, but he forced it easily with his shoulder. Inside was a large leather arm-chair before which he knelt, slashing the arms and seat wildly and inserting his hand amongst the padding. At one side of the seat the springs had sagged a little, leaving a gap between it and the arm.

With a gleam of hope on his white face he pushed his hand down, feeling carefully. But the thing he sought was not there.

Holding his head, he staggered out into the hall, reeling as if drunk, and regardless now of being seen or heard, shut the door behind him and went downstairs.

Walking blindly he came at last to the Embankment and sank on a seat shivering, although the night was warm and dry. Mechanically he moved along if a policeman came in sight, slinking back again when he had passed.

Haggard, the man's frenzy calmed to despair with the dawn, he crossed the nearest bridge and ambled off to his room in one of the murky streets on the south side of the Thames.

Early on Thursday morning Inspector Reynolds telephoned the hospital and learned that Bill had passed a fair night. A little comforted he set out for Euston to inspect the murdered man's room.

"Tell me," he said to the hotel proprietor who had called on him the evening before, "where were you when the Countess of Warnham called that day?"

"I was coming downstairs as she was going up."

"She might have been going to visit some one on the first or second floor perhaps," hinted the C. I. D. man.

The landlord looked at him skeptically. "Then what was she doing half-way up the third flight, where I met her?" he objected.

Reynolds nodded meditatively.

"Who else lives on the third and upper floors?" he demanded.

"A man and his wife, who are always out at business all day, have the next room to Mr. Leslie Jackson's or Delmond's. The only other room on that floor has been vacant for weeks. On the top floor live four shop assistants who have been here for three years."

"So you know quite well that this lady must have been going to call on Delmond as the other lodgers were out."

"I don't know for certain. I only guess," said the man sulkily.

The inspector raised an admonishing finger. "Look here, my man," he warned sharply, "if you do not answer my questions clearly and civilly I shall force your hand in a way you won't like. Go upstairs and show me the room."

"The door's fastened, sir. Mr. Jackson—I mean Delmond—always locked it when he went out."

"We'll try this. It was found in Delmond's pocket."

On the landing of the third floor the man paused and indicated a door.

"That was his room, sir," he said politely. "I can show you the other two on this floor as well if you like."

He opened the other two doors. One room was obviously unoccupied, and the other was as obviously in use but the tenants were out.

"The man and his wife I told you of," he explained. "They've got a little lock-up tobacco shop in the Euston Road."

The landlord was now as anxious to please the inspector as before he had been insolently secretive.

Reynolds inserted the key that had been found on the dead man and went into a good-sized room. He looked round eagerly, receptive always to atmosphere. The furniture told him nothing, but the articles on dressing-table and mantelpiece clearly showed the type of man Delmond had been.

There was a bottle of perfume and also a spray, a box of face-powder, nail polishing pad, brilliantine highly scented on the toilet table, together with two ornate silver-backed hair brushes. A pile of old paper-covered novels and out-of-date film journals were lying on a chair.

The mantelpiece held several photographs of film stars, all dated two to four years ago. There were also half a dozen pictures of the dead man in various attitudes and costumes, probably from the films he had played in.

The wardrobe and chest of drawers showed Delmond's taste in clothes to have been florid.

Reynolds searched the pockets deftly, finding nothing more interesting than old bus tickets.

"Where is his luggage?" the detective asked the landlord.

The man lifted the bed valance and dragged out two suitcases. One was unfastened and empty. The other the detective opened with one of Delmond's keys which he had brought with him.

Inside the suitcase was a small locked compartment. This too Reynolds unfastened with another key and quickly closed again when he saw it contained papers.

"I shall take this with me," he told the man. "The room will be locked again and no one must enter without my permission."

"Very well, sir," agreed the landlord, as they went downstairs to the hall.

"Do you remember which day that elderly lady called on Delmond?" asked the detective.

"Yes, I do," the man replied promptly. "Last Friday afternoon about three o'clock. That was June twenty-eighth, two days before Mr. Delmond was murdered."

"Why should you recollect that so clearly?" the inspector questioned suspiciously.

"Because it had rained heavily all the night before and that morning the lodgers who sleep on the top floor said the roof was leaking. I was too busy to go up and see about it until after I'd had my dinner. Then I remembered and went up."

"Quite so. But that might have happened any night or day." Reynolds was anxious to test the accuracy of this man's statements.

"No, sir, it was Friday, I'm positive, for when I saw the ceiling so wet, I was vexed, knowing Saturday was a half-day and I'd not get any work done on the roof until Monday."

"Have you a telephone here?" the inspector asked.

The man pointed to an alcove behind the hall door.

"Did you ever hear Delmond telephone to any one?"

The landlord shook his head.

"He never called any one up so far as I know, but once or twice I fetched him to the telephone. Each time it was a lady speaking—a haughty kind of voice—a youngish lady, I think."

"Can you remember when those calls were made?"

The man thought a minute.

"Within the last few days that Delmond was here I'm sure, as before that I scarcely saw him except when he paid his bill!" He puckered his forehead in an effort to recall something.

"Ah, now I've got it, sir. One call was last Thursday or Friday. It was a lady speaking. The second call—in the same voice, I fancy—was last Sunday about half past one when I was having my dinner in there." He indicated the room next the telephone.

The detective's eyes gleamed.

"Go on!" he urged.

"I ran up and called Mr. Delmond. He came down at once but I couldn't hear what was said except I think he replied, 'Oh, you've nothing to add to your letter, eh? We'll see about that.' He pushed open my door and thanked me and said, 'Your dinner smells good.' I laughed and replied, 'You'd better have some with me.' His answer was that he'd only just got up and had to go out on business. I never saw him again," the man added, "but I think he went out soon after."

"H'm. A telephone call in a lady's voice about Thursday. The Countess of Garth at three thirty on Friday to see him, and another telephone call about one thirty on Sunday, June thirtieth in the same voice," checked up the inspector.

"That's right, sir," agreed the man.

"Who answers the telephone when you're out?"

The landlord smiled. "Nobody: it just rings. My wife's deaf as a post and the old charwoman doesn't understand it."

In his office, Reynolds opened the compartment in the suitcase and scrutinized the contents carefully.

He found several letters signed "Mary" couched in terms of deepest affection, some indicating that money had been sent with them—without doubt from Mrs. de Groot. A few insignificant trinkets, such as links and tie pins. Three pictures of Laureen, cut out of current magazines, on one of which the address of her flat was penciled. A few other notes and bills.

Three pawn-tickets in his haul pleased Reynolds most of all and he decided to have these investigated at once.

Of passport, bank or check book, or addressed envelops there was no trace. To the detective it suggested that the dead man had much to conceal, and trusted nobody.

Also, Delmond might have been near the end of his resources, as his total cash appeared to be the money found in his pockets.

Again the detective's mind went back to the scene in Laureen's flat when he had questioned Carter the caretaker, about the letter to Valerie which he had posted.

What did that letter contain and where was it now? Could Laureen, or Lansberg, acting either separately or in collusion, have taken papers from the dead man's pocket, and fearing a personal search, posted them in the hall box?

And then at the bottom of the case, tucked inside the tattered manuscript of a scenario, he found a snapshot. Holding it under a magnifying-glass he peered at it intently, knowing that here was another tiny link.

He was still staring at it when Jenkins came in and handed him a note. It bore the address of the hotel Laureen had moved to. He read:

*Dear Sir,*
*I thank you most sincerely for the photograph you so kindly sent me of Mr. Jackson. In spite of all people may say against him, I shall always think of him the same.*
*Yours respectfully,*
*Bertha E. Mackie.*

Poor Bertha, he reflected, duped but tenaciously faithful to the memory of this man who had used her merely as a tool. And he thought of that other woman, Mary de Groot, whom Delmond had treated in the same heartless fashion.

Jenkins recalled him from his reverie. "Miss Laureen would like to speak to you on the telephone, sir."

"Good morning, Inspector," Reynolds heard her across the wire cheerfully. "I hate hotels, and couldn't possibly return to that flat even if you allowed me to do so. Have I your permission to remove my own furniture and possessions to another flat which I have been offered? Of course you can leave the dining-room as it is. I never want to see any of that furniture again."

After a moment's reflection the inspector gave the required permission, adding, "Let me know when you wish to get your things."

"I must," came the quick retort, "since you have the keys."

"By the way, Miss Laureen, I meant to ask you before, have you any family living?"

Over the wire he heard a gurgle of laughter. "Inspector Reynolds,

I'm surprised at you. I told you I was as yet unmarried."

The detective thanked his stars that television was not yet universal as he suppressed a smile.

"I referred to parents and possible brothers and sisters," he said.

"That's funny," she replied. "You're the second person in two days who has shown interest in my family-tree. I will give you the same reply I gave to—the other person. Which was to the effect that my father and mother believed in a small but good family and I'm *it*. My father died when I was a baby," she added.

"Thank you," replied Reynolds. "May I ask for the name of the other person interested in your family history?"

"Certainly," she answered casually. "It was Mr. Lansberg. Good morning, Inspector. Thank you for permission to get my belongings."

So Lansberg asked Laureen that question, Reynolds mused, as he hung up the receiver. Which meant that the man knew little of Laureen's past, or wished to verify the knowledge he had.

He turned to Jenkins. "Any one likely to be in Laureen's flat if I ring up?"

"Yes, sir. The photographers have gone round again to see if they can pick up any more fingerprints. They must be there now."

"Well, ring 'em up. I want them to get everything they can before Miss Laureen has her furniture removed. The dining-room of course must not be touched, until after the inquest."

Jenkins gave the number and waited for a reply. Presently he turned to his chief with a startled expression.

"Our men have just arrived, sir, and say they are certain the flat has been burgled. Everything is in disorder; drawers turned upside down, clothes all over the floor, carpets torn up and even chairs and cushions slashed open."

Reynolds snatched the receiver from him and asked a dozen swift questions. "Was the lock of the flat broken or the door open when you arrived?" he demanded.

"No," was the reply. "The lock is in perfect order and the door was fastened properly."

"The third key!" the detective snapped. "The person who entered that flat last night had the missing key and got it from Delmond—alive or dead."

The clock chimed the hour and reminded him that his interview with Lady Avice Garth was due. His bet was that she would not keep her appointment.

"A lady to see you, sir," said a constable at the door.

"Show her in," ordered Reynolds. So she *had* come after all.

But he was astounded to hear the constable announce:

"The Countess of Warnham."

# XXI. REVELATIONS

INSPECTOR REYNOLDS felt a tremor of excitement pass through him as he rose deferentially to greet the elderly lady who entered. It was not a rare thing for him to come into contact with titled people, but it was certainly the first time a countess, and one of an old and distinguished family, had sought an interview with him.

Or, better still, obeyed a summons by proxy in place of her niece. A subtle distinction with an infinite difference, decided Reynolds, knowing perfectly well that he was at heart a thorough snob.

A little uneasily he sought in his memory for the correct mode of address.

"Will your ladyship be seated?" he invited, drawing forward a chair to face the light.

The old woman surveyed him and the room impartially through her lorgnette.

"Thank you," she said briefly, and seated herself in another chair with her back to the window, resuming her research work on the office.

"I am indebted to your ladyship for calling, but it was your niece—" began Reynolds heavily.

The woman withdrew her gaze from the mantelpiece and turned it on him. "It will be simpler if you address me as Lady Warnham," she interrupted. "I presume you are Inspector Reynolds." Her tone was peremptory.

The detective bowed, momentarily nonplussed by the inadequacy of his social knowledge.

"My niece, Lady Avice Garth, is ill. She insisted that I should keep her appointment with you and explain."

The detective smiled inwardly. These aristocrats imagined they could bluff the law, did they? Ill, indeed!

"Lady Avice seemed in perfect health last night in Paris when I saw her," he remarked blandly.

"And this Leslie Delmond was probably in perfect health on Sunday afternoon, yet he was dead by midnight," retorted Lady Warnham unexpectedly.

"There is no reason to imagine that Lady Avice will meet with such an untimely end," Reynolds observed, cynically.

"Indeed!" his visitor remarked coldly. "Perhaps this note will stimulate your imagination, Inspector."

Reynolds took the envelope she offered him, determined not to be beguiled by any plea of fatigue as a cause for postponing an interview.

Opening it he saw the inclosure was a medical certificate. Persuaded their tame doctor to come in on the job, he murmured to himself.

But his eyes widened as he read the few lines certifying that Lady Avice Garth was suffering from shock and loss of blood owing to a bullet wound in the left shoulder.

"A bullet wound!" he exclaimed. "What does this mean, your— Lady Warnham?"

"Probably just what it says," his visitor remarked indifferently. "I am not a medical man, but should say it also means considerable pain and fever for at least several days."

The inspector swallowed his temper and longed to give vent to a few ungentlemanly words not usually employed when conversing with a countess. Exasperating old woman, sitting there at insolent ease as if she had the whip hand over him. In his own office too!

Controlling his feelings with difficulty, he said quietly, "Please tell me how and when this happened, Lady Warnham."

"At five minutes to ten, just over an hour ago. My niece's friend, Laureen, called to see her at nine thirty, asking Avice to go with her to look over some flat she had been offered."

"Excuse me a moment," Reynolds interrupted. "What time was it, Jenkins, when Miss Laureen rang me up?"

"About ten thirty, sir," replied Jenkins from the far corner of the room.

"Thank you. Please continue, Lady Warnham."

"My niece said she could not do so as she had an appointment with you at eleven o'clock. After a short conversation Laureen went. She was driving herself in her new two-seater car and my niece went down to look at it. They stood by the car for a moment. Then Laureen got in, pressed the self-starter and drove off."

"Where were you at the time, Lady Warnham?"

"Reading the *Times* in the dining-room, on the ground floor. With my back to the window, as I am now," the lady remarked pointedly. "I heard a bang but thought it was the back-fire of the engine. Then a minute later Avice staggered in, holding her shoulder. She looked ghastly. I thought she was going to faint."

"Were you alone? I mean, were there any servants in the hall or dining-room?" the inspector asked.

"Nobody was in the hall, but as my niece came into the dining-room the parlor-maid came to clear away the breakfast. She saw the blood pouring from my niece's shoulder and, of course, screamed."

Inspector Reynolds frowned.

"And you mean to say that Miss Laureen calmly motored away knowing her friend had been shot?" he questioned sternly.

"Nonsense, my good man, I mean nothing of the kind. Laureen motored calmly away not dreaming what had happened. If she heard anything, she probably thought, as I did, that it was an engine back-firing."

"How long after Miss Laureen's departure was the shot fired?"

"I should say at the second she started."

The inspector weighed the matter a moment. No, it was quite evident Laureen had not known her friend had been shot when she telephoned to him so light-heartedly at ten thirty. Then a point struck him. That shot, might it not equally well have been intended for Laureen? If so, who fired it?

"Did you see any one in Curzon Street near your house?" he asked.

"I have already told you, Inspector, that I was reading the newspaper with my back to the window and knew nothing of the incident until my niece entered the room and the idiotic maid screamed."

"Of course you immediately sent for the police."

"Of course I immediately sent for the *doctor*," Lady Warnham corrected caustically.

"The police also should have been informed," he told her.

"Well, I'm informing them now. There was no time before. My niece was my first concern. Directly the doctor had arrived and dressed her wound—a clean flesh wound, the bullet having passed straight through—Lady Avice insisted that you should be sent for. She said you would not believe in the accident unless you actually saw the wound."

The detective reddened.

"I didn't know my previous behavior had been so inhuman, Lady Warnham."

The lady raised her eyebrows.

"One doesn't expect humanity from a detective," she responded with blunt indifference. "*Ce n'est pas son metier.* Also, my niece hasn't forgotten that she evaded her appointment with you in Paris yesterday morning."

"She also promised to see me last night in London and then left a message saying she would call this morning," he offered in extenuation of his apparent disbelief.

Lady Warnham gave him an amiable smile.

"Ah well, we mustn't be too severe on the erratic younger generation, Inspector. The war bred a new type, you know."

The friendly "we" was as balm to the detective after the rankling "my good man" of a few moments before. But it did not blind him to the fallacy of the lady's diplomatic words.

"Perhaps you would like to call at 'Warnham House,' Inspector. The doctor may give you permission to see my niece, even if you may not question her to-day."

"I shall most certainly call there this morning," Reynolds assured her gravely.

He turned to Jenkins and gave him some rapid instructions. His visitor rose, gathering her cloak round her. The detective raised his hand detaining her. "One moment, please, Lady Warnham. There is something I should like to ask you."

The lady's face expressed bored surprise as she resumed her seat.

"I have told you all I know of this shooting affair, Inspector. This morning I have an important engagement."

"Madam," Reynolds said seriously, "there can be no more important engagement than the one you are now keeping. I am concerned with a deeper matter than the unfortunate accident to Lady Avice Garth."

He paused, well aware it would add tension to his next question, hoping to rouse comment from Lady Warnham.

"I am waiting," she remarked imperturbably, lifting her lorgnette and regarding him as though he were a new species of insect under a microscope.

But this time she aroused no irritation in the inspector. The moment he had worked for had arrived, and he used it dramatically.

Leaning across his desk he spoke slowly. "Lady Warnham, what was the object of your visit to Leslie Delmond or Jackson in his hotel on Friday afternoon, June twenty-eighth, two days before he was murdered?"

His visitor lowered her glasses calmly, but her fingers tightened on the handle.

"Are you suggesting *I* killed the man?" she demanded.

The detective waved aside her remark with a gesture of impatience.

"I am suggesting nothing, madam. I am asking a question."

He watched her closely but could detect no sign of fear. Her vague gaze wandered past him as though she were deciding how much or little she should reveal.

"If I hesitate, Inspector, it is because one does not willingly wash soiled linen in public," she explained. "Especially when it involves the honor of a member of one's own family."

"I'm afraid the law does not consider niceties of that kind," the C. I. D. man said in a warning tone.

The lady raised her head proudly. "There is yet another law that my family has obeyed for centuries, Inspector. Its members even endured torture in the observance of it—but they held their tongues." She was silent for a second. Then she said clearly, "I have said this to prove to you that I am not to be frightened into speech. I am old now, but alive to the duty I owe to those of my own blood."

"Even though you protect a criminal by your silence, Lady

Warnham?" His voice was toneless but in his heart was a deep respect for this courageous old woman who faced him now.

"Thank God I am not called upon to decide on so serious a matter as that, Inspector," she replied fervently. "No, my problem is purely a matter of family honor and nothing more. Please let me think a moment."

She leaned her head on her thin, finely-veined hand while Reynolds regarded her compassionately. Deeply attached to his own mother—she was about the same age as Lady Warnham, he reflected—how would *he* feel if some man were roughly urging her to speak against some member of her family. But thrusting sentiment aside, he reminded himself that possibly on Lady Warnham's frankness rested the detection of a murder.

"Two years ago last February I went to Nice, Inspector," she began suddenly. "My niece, Lady Avice Garth, was then living with her father, who is my brother."

"The Earl of Brentshire," put in the detective.

"Yes. My brother had been gambling as usual, but with worse than the usual results. I am a childless widow and very fond of Avice. She was leading an unhappy existence; a very undignified one too, for, thanks to her father, they were in debt everywhere. At great personal inconvenience I paid what they owed, stipulating that my niece should be allowed in future to live with me. My brother agreed. He still spends his winters there and gambles wildly, I believe, though where he gets the money is a mystery I've never solved."

Inspector Reynolds thought he could guess, remembering the many company prospectuses on which the Earl of Brentshire's name figured as enticing bait.

"And you met Delmond that winter in Nice," he suggested.

Lady Warnham nodded.

"He was acting in some film and a scene was taken on the terrace of my hotel. The guests were invited to figure in the scene, seated at little tables, and some of them did so. My niece among them. She was very excited about it and became so attracted to Laureen—who was the heroine of this film, that we drove out to the studios and visited the place next day, on Laureen's invitation."

"Was Mrs. de Groot, an American lady, by any chance staying in your hotel?"

His visitor's expression altered slightly.

"She was. A floridly dressed, be-jeweled woman, very wealthy but good-natured. She apparently had few or no friends and my niece with her warm impulsiveness promptly adopted Mrs. de Groot and insisted on taking her in our party everywhere. I was against it at first, but I must admit that Mary de Groot has sterling qualities, even if—" She broke off a trifle confused.

"Even if she became infatuated with Delmond," supplemented Reynolds with a reassuring smile.

Lady Warnham looked relieved.

"Oh, you know about that affair. Yes, Mrs. de Groot was of our party. That is how she met Delmond. After that he spent all his spare time with her while Laureen and my niece became great friends and have remained so ever since."

"You raised no objection to their friendship?" asked the detective.

"Certainly not," the lady replied firmly. "Apart from the fact that Laureen is as charming as she looks, I had no right to interfere. One of the lessons age has to learn is not to antagonize youth by applying ancient rules to these modern times. I love my niece and wish to keep her affection and friendship. Therefore I leave her absolutely free."

"Possibly too free," thought the inspector, remembering that midnight escapade in Paris.

"Were Laureen and Delmond very friendly?" he asked.

*"Never,"* declared the countess emphatically. "She despised and disliked the man for taking Mary de Groot's money and gifts and laughing about her behind her back. He and Laureen quarreled bitterly about it."

"Maybe Laureen was jealous?" the detective surmised.

Lady Warnham scorned the idea.

"Jealous? Of what? She was the star, while he played a small part. The film director told me that Laureen detested Delmond the first day she was introduced to him. He attempted to kiss her in public and she ridiculed him—also in public. After that, it was war to the knife. She tried very hard to save Mrs. de Groot from a vain, unworthy man."

So Laureen had detested Delmond from the first day! Yet only last Sunday night she said he had been her lover and they had quarreled. Why had she lied? Whom was she protecting? For that her statement was untrue the detective was fully convinced.

"And now I come to the part I dislike, Inspector. My jewels are valuable; a few of them are heirlooms, the rest I have the right to dispose of." Her lips twitched. "And I have exercised that right through force of circumstances in regard to a part of them.

"One day my brother came to me at my hotel in Nice in great trouble," she continued. "Financial, of course! He had gambled and lost and borrowed to such an extent that he owed several hundreds of pounds. He implored me to sell some jewels to help him. I refused and he actually struggled with me to obtain my keys! We were on the hotel terrace and Delmond and Mrs. de Groot came along. Delmond pretended not to have seen or heard anything and Mrs. de Groot introduced him to my brother. To my astonishment my brother and

Delmond became friendly and were often together after that."

A tinge of shame crept over the old lady's pale cheeks. "About a fortnight later I discovered accidentally that all my brother's debts had been paid. Discovered—" She stopped and faced the detective steadily.

"I am afraid, Inspector," she went on, "in spite of all you can do to me, that this is where my story must end abruptly. I have no right to tell you more," she said with dignity.

"Since others are involved," finished Reynolds to himself. He changed the subject deftly. "Lady Warnham, where is Tony?" he asked swiftly.

The old lady appeared puzzled or disturbed. He could not decide which.

"Tony!" she repeated blankly.

"Yes. One of Lady Avice's brothers—the youngest, I believe—is called Anthony. Abbreviated, that would be Tony, wouldn't it?"

"Lady Avice's youngest brother was generally known as 'Stinker.'" The old lady's eyes twinkled with amusement. "I never heard him called anything so refined as 'Tony.' I have no idea where he is at the moment. 'Stinker' was painting, or trying to, in Paris when last I heard of him. We are not a particularly communicative family so far as letter writing goes, though we have rather a weakness for loyalty," she added with gentle sarcasm.

Reynolds switched the former subject back adroitly.

"Forgive me, Lady Warnham, for again dragging up this painful question. Your story lacked completion, you see. Can you not explain to me why you called on Delmond two days before he was murdered?"

Lady Warnham rose and drew herself up, eyes tragic with grief. "Inspector Reynolds, you think of Delmond as a murdered film artist to be avenged by the law. I knew him to be a blackmailer." Her voice faltered and she put her hand on the table to support herself. "At this moment I can tell you no more."

# XXII. TIGHTENING THE NET

IN Laureen's flat, to which Inspector Reynolds went immediately the Countess of Warnham had left him, there was utter chaos. The photographers and a policeman awaited him.

He addressed the constable sharply. "You were in charge here?"

"Yes, sir. I locked up at six last night after looking round as I've done each evening by your instructions. Everything was in order then."

"What time did you get here this morning?"

"With the photographers, sir, about ten thirty."

Reynolds walked from room to room, and thought a tornado might have produced much the same effect. Surely this could not have been done by a sane person. Was it the result of madness, malice or panic? The answer to that might help considerably, he realized.

The dining-room doors had been locked the evening before. Now the one leading into the hall was open, the lock roughly forced.

Before the big leather chair in which Delmond had been found dead the inspector paused, with pursed lips. For the first time he noticed the space between the seat and the arm, and thought how easy it would have been for something to have slipped from Delmond's hand or pocket and lain concealed. Had the searcher of last night found what he wanted there? Reynolds was inclined to believe not. He slid his hand along the lining but there was nothing there now.

"Lock the place up again, and have it watched. The burglar may come back, but I doubt it."

In Curzon Street, almost opposite the Countess of Warnham's house, he took out a cigarette and asked a man for a match. It was the same constable who had trailed Laureen unsuccessfully three days before.

"Well?" demanded Reynolds abruptly.

"Nobody round here heard the shot or noticed any one loitering before it happened. The bullet struck the wall by Warnham House visitors' bell. You can see the mark. I picked up the bullet, sir. No visitors to the house since I came."

Reynolds slipped the leaden ball in his pocket.

"All right. Hang round," he said.

As the inspector crossed the road a small car driven by Laureen pulled up at Warnham House and its occupant jumped out hurriedly. The actress was about to ring the bell when she saw Reynolds beside her.

"Of course you've heard about Lady Avice?" she said. "I've just rushed back to see how she is."

The inspector eyed her keenly. "When did you learn about the accident, Miss Laureen?" he asked pointedly.

She frowned as she pressed the button. "Ten minutes ago. Lady Warnham telephoned to my hotel and my maid rang me up at the new flat I was looking at. I came here immediately."

The butler opened the door and admitted them at once.

"How is Lady Avice, Mason?" Laureen asked anxiously.

"I hear there is no danger, miss, but her ladyship has lost a lot of blood and must be kept quiet, the doctor says." He cast a frigid eye at the C. I. D. man.

"This is an inspector from Scotland Yard. Lady Warnham expects him," Laureen explained.

"I should like to see the butler alone a moment," Reynolds told her.

Turning to the man, he asked him where he was when the accident occurred.

"In my pantry at the back of the house, sir."

"Any of the other servants see or hear anything?"

The butler shook his head. "I questioned them, but only the parlor-maid knew anything about it. And all she saw was Lady Avice stagger into the dining-room."

"Who closed the front door behind Lady Avice as she came in from the street?"

"The parlor-maid says she shut it. That was only a few seconds before she entered the dining-room," he added.

A dead end there, decided the inspector, though he patiently questioned the staff one by one.

None had heard the shot or been near the front of the house at the time.

"The doctor has just called again, sir," said the butler. "He says he will see you when he comes down from her ladyship's room, if you wish. If you will wait here I will bring him to you."

An elderly man was presently shown into the dining-room where Reynolds was standing at the window, visualizing the shooting affair.

"You signed the medical certificate I received this morning, Doctor?" asked Reynolds.

The doctor assented curtly. "I did; at Lady Avice's express wish. She seemed more distressed at being unable to keep her appointment with you than by the unfortunate cause."

Reynolds sensed the sting in his words. "How is she now?" he asked.

"In no danger, but in considerable pain and very weak," the doctor announced.

The C. I. D. man held something out on his hand. "Here is the bullet," he said.

The medical man took it to the light and regarded it with interest.

"A little lower and the wound would have been serious," he declared, returning the thing to Reynolds. "I suppose you wish to know when you can see Lady Avice?"

"It would help me considerably, Doctor."

"Well, you may see her now, and nothing more. I greatly disapprove, but again it is her particular wish. Perhaps to-morrow afternoon she can talk to you a little, but on no account must she be agitated," he said severely.

"I understand perfectly. Why does she wish me to see her now if I may not speak?" Reynolds asked in a puzzled voice.

The doctor laughed. "Don't ask me to explain the mental processes of a woman. I'm far too busy. Please come with me. Miss Laureen is sitting with Lady Avice. I allowed her to go in on the understanding that she does not permit her friend to speak."

Hat in hand, Reynolds followed the doctor up the wide shallow staircase to a room on the first floor, feeling perhaps more awkward than he had for years.

He stood in the darkened room gazing at the pale face of the girl who lay propped against pillows. She raised one hand in greeting and smiled faintly.

The detective saw her lips move, and Laureen bent quickly over her friend.

"Lady Avice wishes me to say she is so sorry, but this time it is not her fault, Inspector," Laureen repeated.

"Please believe how deeply I regret that you should be suffering like this, Lady Avice," Reynolds said in a low voice. "Thank you for allowing me to come in."

There was a queer sensation in his throat as he went downstairs. There was grit and fineness in that girl, and with all his heart he wished she had not been mixed up in this business.

"Don't be anxious," he assured the doctor as they stood in the hall. "I shall not do anything to worry your patient to-morrow. If you wish I'll leave it until a day later."

But apparently the medical man was satisfied with Reynolds's discretion.

"Oh, you can have half an hour with her tomorrow if she's had a good night," he conceded. "I don't want to hinder you in your duty. Good day."

Laureen came downstairs as Reynolds was leaving. "I'll give you a lift, Inspector, if you care to risk your neck with me."

"Thank you," he accepted. "Your life is as precious as mine. I'll chance it, Miss Laureen. Just one moment and I'll join you."

He turned aside to speak to the butler.

"Did Lady Avice come here alone yesterday on her return from

Paris?" he asked.

"Yes, sir."

"What time?"

The butler reflected. "About four o'clock," he answered.

"Did any gentleman call on her either last evening or this morning?"

"Mr. Spencer called just before dinner, but as her ladyship was out he did not enter the house. He is calling later, I believe."

There was cold reserve in the man's voice, although he replied unhesitatingly. His mistress had given him instructions to answer the detective's questions, but Reynolds realized that the man resented it when Lady Avice was ill and defenseless. Ah well, he thought, his was a ruthless, indelicate job.

Outside, Laureen sat in her car waiting for him. He went out to her.

"I want you to put the car, as nearly as you can remember, in the exact position it was in this morning when you were talking to Lady Avice," Reynolds requested.

The girl measured the distance with her eye and then reversed for about a yard.

"Just here," she said. "I left it where it could be seen from the dining-room. Avice stood there," she pointed to a spot immediately in front of the bell marked "Visitors."

Across the road was a narrow alley running between two houses, where it was obvious that any one could have remained fairly well concealed.

"From the position you were in the bullet might easily have hit you instead, Miss Laureen," he remarked as he got into her car.

"Why, of course," she said, staring at him in astonishment. "It was *meant* for me," and bit her lip quickly as she pressed the self-starter. "Where shall I drop you, Inspector? I'm going back to my hotel."

"Anywhere near there will do for me," he answered vaguely. "Meant for you, eh!" he thought to himself. "That was a slip, young lady."

"Have you any enemy that you know of?" the C. I. D. man asked quietly, admiring the sure way she guided the car through the busy traffic.

"Dozens, I should think," she replied lightly, her eyes dancing with fun. "But I can't believe they would willingly risk their necks for the pleasure of shooting me."

"Yet you thought that shot was meant for you," persisted Reynolds.

"Well, who could possibly have wanted to hurt Avice?" she fenced. "Whereas I—maybe I've an unknown foe more venturesome than those I know of."

"Among those enemies, known or unknown, do you think there is a man who lacks a thumb?" Reynolds watched her intently and was certain that she started.

"Is it a conundrum?" she demanded. "If so, I can't tell you the answer. My unknown enemy may even lack a nose or ears, Inspector." She pulled into the curb by her hotel. "Here we are, but here I shall not be for many days, thanks to your permission to get my furniture and belongings."

Reynolds got out of the car and stood with his hand resting on the wind screen, a position that gave him a good angle from which to watch her face.

"That reminds me," he said. "I've news for you. Your flat was broken into last night."

"What? With a real live policeman of your own choice on guard!" she mocked.

"He does not stay there all night," the detective told her.

"Well, unless they wanted my clothing or the chairs and tables there wasn't much to interest them. My jewelry is in the hotel."

"Nothing apparently was taken. The intruder seems to have been searching for something and in the process to have gone berserker. He slashed open the padding of chairs and cushions, tore down the pictures and ripped up the carpets."

A look of relief, almost of triumph, crossed her face. "There was nothing there—I mean," she added hurriedly, "nothing of value."

"Have you a matinee this afternoon, Miss Laureen?"

The girl shook her head.

"Not on Thursdays. Matinees are Wednesdays and Saturdays."

"I may need to ring you up," Reynolds explained.

"I shall be at Mr. Spencer's studio all this afternoon. He's doing a portrait of me. You might tell that little pet of yours who is on guard. He lost me twice yesterday and I saw him trotting round like a stray rabbit. I felt sorry for him. Good-by. I'm going to the garage."

She slipped in the gear and slid off, her eyes twinkling. Inspector Reynolds amused her with his stolidity. But he had asked questions that she dared not answer just now. Yet she found something likeable in him, and her heart had warmed with quick sympathy when Bertha showed her the photograph of her quondam lover which Reynolds had not forgotten to send.

"A nice man with a nasty job, Bertha," she had replied, when Bertha had said the inspector was very kind.

The C. I. D. man walked slowly back to Scotland Yard deep in thought and fully aware that Laureen had avoided a reply.

There were so many things to sift out in this case. His chief difficulty lay in deciding which to work at first. Every hour that passed now was that much to the good for the murderer.

Rarely had he come across so, apparently, simple a murder case involving three people that had opened out into one that enmeshed at least a dozen. In his office he found Lansberg and Dr. Tempest waiting to see him.

The doctor greeted him hurriedly. "I can wait, Inspector. Your brother's doing nicely. I'll tell you all details when you've seen Mr. Lansberg."

"Thank you, Doctor. Will you have a hurried luncheon with me?"

The doctor assented. "I'll wait downstairs," he added. "Good-by, Lansberg."

"Can you dine with me to-night, Doctor? Eight o'clock at the club?" Lansberg asked.

Dr. Tempest smiled. "That will make two free meals in one day," he remarked. "Thanks very much, Lansberg. I'll be there."

Lansberg turned to the detective as Dr. Tempest went out. "Dr. Tempest has just told me of this murderous attack on your brother, Inspector. I'm very sorry to hear of it. It was a senseless, cruel act."

The detective sat down at his desk and began slowly to fill his pipe.

"That's very kind of you, Mr. Lansberg," he replied. "I suppose the attack appeared to be senseless, but no more so than the one made on Lady Avice Garth this morning." He seemed to be only occupied with pressing in the tobacco but for one second his swift glance shot to Lansberg's face.

It expressed utter surprise and consternation.

"An attack on Lady Avice!" Lansberg repeated.

Suspense was always a favorite card with Reynolds. He lighted a match and drew several leisurely puffs at his pipe to make sure it was well alight before he answered.

"Yes. She was shot outside Warnham House this morning. Happily only a flesh wound in the shoulder."

Lansberg uttered an exclamation. "She might have been killed," he said indignantly.

"Easily," agreed Reynolds. "Or her companion. They were both within the same range. It's possibly a parallel case with that of my brother."

"I don't understand."

The inspector watched a curl of smoke fade upward. Then he brought his gaze back to the man opposite him.

"It's quite simple," he replied. "The man who struck down my brother mistook him for me. The man who shot Lady Avice," he paused, "was possibly—I only say *possibly*—aiming at her companion."

"And that was?"

"Laureen!" The inspector replied ominously, keenly alive to the pallor that swept at once over Lansberg's face and to the fine fingers clenched tightly.

Now was the time to follow up that blow and Reynolds knew it. Leaning across his desk, he said firmly:

"Mr. Lansberg, there is not only mystery in this murder case, there is undoubtedly grave danger surrounding others. If you value Miss Laureen's life you will be frank and help me all you can—before it is too late."

The lines of Lansberg's face seemed graven with suffering as he sat there, staring blindly at the detective.

"I promise to help you," he said with difficulty. He passed a hand across his face as if he were striving to clear away the memory of what he had heard. Laureen's life in danger! Yes, he would have to speak—but not now. He must have time to think.

"There was something you wanted to see me about," reminded the detective.

The dazed look faded from Lansberg's eyes. "Yes, of course. The shock of your news made me forget. On Tuesday afternoon I motored to Crowborough for golf, with Miss Laureen and my secretary."

"I am aware of that," said Reynolds succinctly.

"On returning to my apartment at four thirty I found some one had got in during my servant's absence and managed to open my safe. Miss Laureen was with me."

"And maybe that's why you're reporting this," thought the detective shrewdly. "Indeed," he replied aloud. "Was anything missing?"

Lansberg shook his head.

"Nothing of value, although the safe contained some valuable things. It seemed purely a voyage of discovery."

The inspector forebore from asking if any article of no intrinsic value had been taken.

"You are sure you locked the safe before going out?" he questioned mildly.

The color was gradually coming back to Lansberg's face now, as he replied in a troubled tone. "I could have sworn I did, only memory plays strange tricks at times. Because of that I might even not have troubled to report this to you but for an extraordinary occurrence."

The detective glanced up curiously. "What's that?"

"My servant Neron—you saw him the previous day—went out that evening and has not returned. He is absolutely faithful and devoted to my interests. I'm afraid something may have happened to him."

The detective regarded his visitor speculatively.

"I remember the man perfectly. He certainly behaved as if you were a minor deity, Mr. Lansberg. But you say he went out on Tuesday evening. This is Thursday morning," he reminded. "Why this delay on your part?"

Lansberg's expression stiffened a little at the implied reproach. "There was no particular reason for informing Scotland Yard at once," he remarked frigidly. "But becoming uneasy yesterday afternoon I telephoned to you and learned you were away. I rang again later last night and heard you had returned but would not be in the office until this morning."

"That's quite correct," agreed Reynolds. "I was informed you had telephoned twice. The news of the attack on my brother sent me home earlier than usual."

"Naturally. Well, this morning I had important business to transact and came here as soon as I could."

The inspector knocked out his pipe and put it in his pocket. "You've no idea in your mind, Mr. Lansberg, to account for your servant's absence?"

"None. Unless he has met with an accident. Perhaps you could get into touch with the hospitals for me.

"I could—if necessary," Reynolds replied meditatively. "You've no reason to suspect foul play?"

Lansberg made a faint gesture. "To my knowledge he had neither friends nor foes in London."

"Nor reason to suspect his flight?" Reynolds's voice had a clearer, harder tone now.

"Flight!" Lansberg echoed looking puzzled.

"Flight," repeated the detective. "Self-preservation is the first law."

"I don't understand you, Inspector."

"No?" queried Reynolds mildly. He drew a box from a drawer beside him and laid it on the table. "Perhaps this will explain."

He whipped off the lid and exhibited a long curved knife within.

"This knife, Mr. Lansberg, was taken"—he paused a second—"from my brother's shoulder. I think it may account for your servant's absence."

## XXIII. BEHIND THE STAGE

LANSBERG looked at the ugly weapon, its curving blade dulled with ominous spots. His face was like a mask, the color again driven from it by the sheer horror this thing had conjured up.

"Mr. Lansberg, this damnable concealment of fact and evasion of frankness has to come to an end," the detective thundered, banging his fist on the desk. "It has already caused suffering to two innocent people. My brother at least is entirely guiltless of complicity. Of Lady Avice Garth's part in this conspiracy of silence I have yet to judge. Her worst crime is shielding some one else, I think."

The ghost of a smile flickered across Lansberg's face, giving it an extraordinary sweetness.

"You may be quite sure of that, Inspector. I know her to be a loyal, courageous and honorable woman. As for my own case, maybe you will not think so harshly of me by this time to-morrow, if I may ask for so much grace to decide my course of action. One hesitates to involve others, you see."

Reynolds was taken aback by Lansberg's obvious sincerity. Before he could speak, Lansberg continued:

"I am neither contemplating flight nor suicide," he remarked with a whimsical twist of his mouth. "And I am quite sure you will be satisfied—when I *do* speak."

"Delays complicate our duties more than the lay mind understands," said Reynolds. He was not unwilling to grant Lansberg the time he asked for because there were many points that urgently needed his attention that afternoon. And also there was the memory that those in authority over him had urged the utmost delicacy in dealing with Mr. Lansberg.

"Very well," he agreed. "Shall we say noon tomorrow in this office?"

Lansberg bowed. "At noon to-morrow," he promised.

On the desk near him was a photograph. Lansberg's eyes fell on it unconsciously as he rose, then his forehead wrinkled in perplexity and he bent over it a moment.

"Leslie Delmond," explained the inspector. "It was taken at Nice two and a half years ago, I believe. I've had it copied for the newspapers."

"Yes," murmured Lansberg, almost as if he hadn't heard. "May I look at it through your glass?"

Reynolds pushed the lens across and watched intently. Lansberg had said he had never met the dead man. Why this sudden interest?

"You did not know him?" the detective questioned.

Lansberg raised his head abstractedly.

"No," he replied. "But he resembles a woman who twice came to me in queer circumstances; once about a couple of years ago, and once more recently. The likeness is so extraordinary that she might be his twin sister," he added as he laid the picture back on the desk.

"Will you tell me about it?" The inspector tried to speak idly and cloak his curiosity.

Lansberg hesitated. "It can have nothing to do with this case and the woman asked me to tell no one." He smiled. "A promise to a mysterious unknown—it sounds quite romantic."

"You don't know her name and address?"

"Neither. She was thickly veiled each time but her features were unmistakable. After all, as the incident is finished, maybe there is no harm in telling you the rough outline. She asked me the first time to lock something up for her as her husband might steal it. And recently she called to claim it. That's all."

"I see," Reynolds nodded, his eyes bent on his writing pad. "Had she a husky contralto voice by any chance?"

"The very reverse," stated Lansberg definitely. "It was clear, very clear, and rather high." He rose. "I must be off or Tempest will be tired of waiting for you. I'll see you to-morrow, Inspector."

A high, clear voice, reflected Reynolds as he stumped solidly downstairs. Oh, undoubtedly he'd got a very nice little clue that suggested many possibilities.

He was rather distrait over luncheon. Dr. Tempest studied him thoughtfully. "You need not worry about your brother, Inspector. You can see him when you like. Your wife was there this morning. He's enjoying poor health, he says, thanks to a pretty nurse who happens to be looking after him. This morning he informed me he didn't mind how long he was ill."

The inspector roared with laughter. "Bill's at his old games then. He's a rascal; flirts desperately with every good-looking girl he meets."

The doctor's thin face brightened with amusement. "I can promise you he's losing no time now. Insists on kissing the hand that feeds him, as he puts it. He'll pull through all right."

"I'm deeply grateful to you," Reynolds said sincerely.

Dr. Tempest brushed aside the remark. "Your brother says he has no idea who struck him. He saw and heard nothing. Just felt a terrible pain and went down unconscious."

Reynolds's face was grim.

"I've a pretty good idea, though." He peered at his companion closely. "I say, Doctor, you're eating nothing and look like a ghost. What's wrong?"

"Working a bit too hard possibly."

"And probably up all night with Bill. I shall always feel you saved his life."

"Nonsense," said Tempest bruskly. "Well, I must be off. I've a lot to do."

The inspector was in his office a little later when the telephone bell rang. His wife's voice answered him. "I've seen Bill," she said. "He's getting on well. By the way, the matron told me that Dr. Tempest insisted on blood transfusion at once last night, and he unselfishly offered to be the donor. Couldn't get any one else at that hour. Wasn't it splendid of him? I thought he looked very ill this morning."

So that was why Tempest seemed so wan and tired, thought Reynolds as he put back the receiver. Indeed he owed him a debt of gratitude. A pang of remorse touched the detective as he remembered how he and Dr. Tempest had crossed swords more than once. He had thought the doctor was inclined to be nervous and weak, though clever at his job. Now he realized there was a fine, quiet courage underlying those aloof, gentle manners.

"I've determined to find out something about that Valerie Baird, Jenkins," he said. "Ring up the hospitals again and at the same time ask if a man answering to the description of Lansberg's servant has been brought in. Hang it all, it's ridiculous to think of two people disappearing, both mixed up in this Delmond case."

Reynolds walked up Whitehall in a troubled frame of mind. The murder had been committed on Sunday night. This was Thursday afternoon and he was as far off laying his hands on the culprit as he had ever been.

True, he had discovered many important details, and proved that several people, in a more or less indirect way, were linked up with the affair. Dozens of little irritating clues leading to no real issue. Motive was the main thing to search for, but he could not trace a sufficient reason why any of these people should risk their own lives to put Leslie Delmond out of the way.

Always the detective liked to see a background to the leading actors in a murder drama. It helped him tremendously. Now in the cases of the Countess of Warnham and her niece, of Dick Spencer, even of Mrs. de Groot, it was easy to see more than the bare picture. Their environment stood out around them clearly. But with Laureen, Lansberg, and the valet, he had nothing but the barest silhouette. Of their previous life and surroundings he knew practically nothing.

And three others who undoubtedly played a big part in the affair, Valerie, Tony and the man with the missing thumb, had never really materialized. They were merely shadows. And who was the woman who had intrusted something to Lansberg's care years ago and had claimed it recently? Was she implicated in this case? *Was* it a woman?

There was a big theatrical agency near, the manager of which he knew well. Presently Reynolds was in that manager's office, refusing a large cigar.

"Can you tell me anything about this man?" he asked, showing him Delmond's photograph.

The manager grinned. "I know he was murdered in Laureen's flat last Sunday and that he'd been doing film work off and on—chiefly off—for the past few years. You probably know all that too, Inspector."

"I meant before that," Reynolds explained patiently. "Film actors often start on the stage."

The manager picked up a desk telephone and talked rapidly for a few minutes. Presently he turned to the detective. "Am afraid I can't help you much. My man says Delmond was doing a turn on the halls for a bit several years ago, but was a failure so he turned to film work. That's all he can tell and he'd know if any one did."

Reynolds got up, a little disappointed. "Thanks very much. You've done your best. Oh, by the way, do you happen to know what Delmond's turn consisted of?"

The manager picked up the instrument again and asked the question.

"Female impersonator," he announced.

The detective wondered whether it was Delmond, dressed as a woman, who had twice called on Lansberg. A high, clear voice! Yes, and that telephone operator said it was a high, clear voice that had answered Spencer's telephone call at nine fifty last Sunday night, and that same voice had called Bertha at eight thirty and sent her out of the flat on a false errand. Suppose *that* was Delmond too! Not too bad a jump so far as guesses went.

Outside the theater, where each night Laureen's name blazed on huge electric signs, he slowed his pace and at the main entrance mixed with the crowd waiting at the box-office.

In a moment, keeping a wary eye on the commissionaire in uniform on the front steps, he slipped out of the queue. Glancing at the photographs on the walls, gradually he edged his way to the darkest end of the lobby where swinging doors led into the theater itself.

Watching his opportunity he tried the door. It was not locked, and going in, he found himself in the corridors leading right and left to the stalls. The same corridors along which he had raced last Monday night searching for the man with the mutilated hand. How easy it was for any one to enter that way and even get to the little iron door in the wall by the stage box, which opened on to the stone staircase by the dressing-rooms.

He retraced his steps to the foyer, attracting no attention from the eager clients at the box-office.

The commissionaire was still looking up and down the street.

Well, Reynolds decided, that showed how easily one could get to and from the dressing-rooms, unseen from the front entrance.

He walked out of the theater and up the alley by the side. Minnis, the stage-door keeper, sat on a high stool studying a racing paper. He raised his eyes as Reynolds appeared and scanned him from head to toe.

Minnis always swore he could tell what a man wanted in half a minute. Out-of-work actors, hangers-on after the chorus girls, more elegantly attired men wanting Laureen, authors with manuscripts of plays they wanted read—Minnis knew them by heart and could classify them before they opened their mouths.

But the detective puzzled him. There was no category into which he quite fitted. Minnis had another good look: he hated to be baffled.

He saw a stolidly built man of about forty with rather a heavy face and dull eyes. His clothes were neat and well-cut without a touch of flashiness. He carried neither flowers for chorus girls nor a parcel of manuscript. By his assured bearing he was not a betting tout. There was no tinge of nervousness in his manner, no hint that he wanted to curry favor with Minnis, as most of them did.

"What d'you want?" he demanded of the stranger, with a faint touch of aggressiveness. "Whoever you wish to see, they aren't here. There isn't a matinee to-day."

Reynolds glanced round the tiny cupboard of an office as he leaned negligently against the door frame.

"I know there's nobody here. That's why I came," he observed mildly. His sole interest apparently was in the signed portraits, chiefly of actresses, with effusive dedications to their dear Minnis scrawled in large handwriting, decorating the walls.

The detective strolled inside now and gazed at one photograph, which appeared to be chiefly an exhibition of arms and legs, with an intentness his wife might have misunderstood.

Minnis stood up indignant at the intrusion. "Well, you've got no business on these premises," he said with authority.

The detective swung round and transferred his gaze—no longer dull, Minnis noted—to the door-keeper.

"On the contrary, I have quite a lot of business here and every right to be doing it," he contradicted as he handed a card to the man.

Minnis read it, his indignation fading into nervous civility. He had been warned to expect this visit and told how to behave.

"I beg your pardon, sir, but how was I to know? We've got to be pretty strict with strangers."

"That's all right," agreed the detective. "I just want to have a look round the place undisturbed. And don't mention my visit to any one. Understand?"

If there was one weak spot in Inspector Reynolds it was a love of the dramatic. To lead witnesses unsuspectingly "up the garden," and then thrust suddenly upon them the knowledge of who he was, and see them collapse, was sheer joy to him who had sometimes long intervals of dreary routine work with no glimmer of interest to brighten it. He glowed now to see the instant respect in the man's attitude.

"Certainly, sir. There's nobody up there but Joe. He does the odd jobs when the place is quiet."

Half-way up the darkish staircase the detective noticed the iron door leading through into the theater. Along the corridor there was a sound of cheery whistling.

Following the direction of it the inspector came on a shirt-sleeved workman on a step-ladder, painting a door. He laid down his brush as Reynolds approached.

"Good afternoon, sir," the man said politely.

"Good afternoon," the detective responded in his pleasantest tones. "I'm an inspector from Scotland Yard. I just want to have a glance round the rooms."

Joe looked a trifle apprehensive. Strangers going through the dressing-rooms! Still, that was up to Minnis. If he allowed this detective here, it must be all right.

"Hope there's nothing wrong, sir," he ventured. Had one of those giddy chorus-girls been up to something? The Delmond murder case never entered his thoughts.

"Nothing," murmured Reynolds easily. "You might tell me the owners of the dressing-rooms, Joe, and then I needn't hinder you any more."

Joe obediently indicated the various rooms, and the detective wandered in and out of each one, methodically working up one side of the corridor, remaining only a minute or so in each.

Presently he came to the empty room where Joe was at work on the door.

"I've been doing a bit of papering and painting here, sir," remarked Joe.

"You've made quite a good job of it too," the inspector said approvingly.

Joe surveyed his work from the doorway with some pride. "Not too bad," he pronounced. Nice friendly chap this detective; not at all the pouncing type with hard eyes he'd read of in novels. "The only nuisance is I never can get time to finish a thing, sir. Keep getting called off to do other jobs."

"Papering's difficult," said the inspector. "I once tried to do my attic and it took me nearly two days. Must have taken you some time to hang this paper. It's a largish room. Three or four days, I'll warrant, in odd hours."

Joe scratched his chin.

"No, not so long as that. Let me see. I started Saturday, worked as far as the mantelpiece and finished the rest Monday afternoon. *And* I painted the baseboard too," he added. "But I was able to get on without hindrance."

Reynolds made a mental note. So Joe was here then! "That makes a difference, of course," he replied. "Let me see, Miss Laureen was in her dressing-room on Monday afternoon resting. I expect she finds it's the only quiet place."

"Yes, I saw her, sir. She very rarely comes in if it's not a matinee day. I was working in this room and didn't know she was here then until she called me to get her some cigarettes."

"Well, that was a hindrance you didn't mind, I expect," laughed the inspector.

"Not a bit, sir," agreed Joe fervently, "and anyhow it didn't take me more than ten minutes. Our Miss Laureen's a wonder. The house is packed at every show."

"Yes, she's an extremely clever young woman. Good afternoon," Reynolds said, and left Joe to go on with his job.

He sauntered through two more dressing-rooms before he turned into that of Laureen. A hurried search assured him there was no place to hide anything here. He reverted to the other matter.

It took him less than two minutes to locate a long dark brown coat hanging in a big wardrobe. He carried it to the window, examined the sleeve and smelled it carefully.

Yes, undoubtedly it had had a large stain on it. In two spots he could even detect a trace of red paint which had resisted the amateur efforts to clean it off. He was replacing it in the wardrobe when a hostile voice made him start.

"What d'you think you're doing there?"

He turned round sharply and confronted a hatchet-faced woman who had just entered the dressing-room.

Without a second's hesitation he attacked swiftly.

"I'm a Scotland Yard inspector. Who cleaned that red paint from this sleeve?" he demanded.

The woman's belligerent tone changed at once.

"I did, sir. I'm Miss Laureen's dresser. Of course if I knew I was intruding I wouldn't have come in. I just thought as I was passing I could do some mending for her."

Her eyes flickered around the room restlessly as the inspector scrutinized her face. He was not concerned with her loquacious and cringing explanation. Somewhere he had seen this woman before.

Suddenly she put her hand up to straighten her hat: he noticed the little finger was bent and stiff. In a second he remembered.

"Got a new job, Lily, eh? We've not seen your face for quite a long while. How's George behaving himself?"

The woman started—then shifted from one foot to the other.

"I've not seen him for ages," she lied boldly. "It was always him that got me into trouble, Mr. Reynolds. I'm running straight now, so please don't let them know anything here or I'll lose my place."

"I'm not sure you've any right to be here at all. But let me catch you either stealing or *receiving*," emphasized the detective, "other people's property again and you'll get a longer stretch than you'll like."

"Yes, sir, I'll remember," Lily promised glibly. "Did you want to know anything about Miss Laureen?"

Reynolds did, badly.

"Not about Miss Laureen exactly," he parried. "But I'd like to know something about her visitors."

Lily at once poured out a stream of useless details about the people who called on her mistress.

"Did a young lady—a Miss Valerie Baird—ever call on Miss Laureen?" he asked to stem the flood.

"No, sir. But," she looked over her shoulder and came a little nearer, "a note from some one who signed herself 'Val' came last Saturday evening."

Lily lowered her voice to a confidential whisper and went on: "Minnis brought it up before the interval and I gave it to Miss Laureen when she came off the stage. It seemed funny to me that she tucked it into her dress and actually went on the stage with it during the second act. As if she was afraid to leave it about."

"Which didn't matter at all, considering you had already read the note before you gave it to her," stated the detective sternly.

The woman colored. Then her face assumed a sly expression. "Well, and wasn't it a good thing I did, sir," she argued, "or else I shouldn't have been able to tell you what it was about."

Reynolds rubbed his chin.

"She tried to burn it down here," the woman went on. "We couldn't find any matches and just then the call-boy came and she slipped it into her dress so I shouldn't read it."

"It will save my time if you tell me the contents. No embroidery, mind. I can easily check up the truth of your statement with Miss Laureen," he warned her with uplifted finger. "I want to find this Valerie Baird."

Lily fumbled in her bag and produced a crumpled sheet of paper.

"I copied it as it seemed so queer," she admitted with a shrewd glance at the inspector's face. "Jolly long time it took me too. But I'm glad I did if it's of use to you, Mr. Reynolds."

Any satisfaction she hoped to get proved disappointing. For the inspector cast a quick glance at it, tucked it into his pocket and strode out of the room, his pulse beating a tattoo of excitement.

## XXIV. THE FACE AT THE WINDOW

JUST one little cigarette, Dick," pleaded Laureen from her seat on the dais in the studio that afternoon.

Spencer dabbed some paint on with his thumb and carefully wiped it off again.

"You've done that three times," she teased.

"Can't I have a cigarette?"

"Certainly not," he remarked sternly. "You had one half an hour ago. How can I work? You alter the muscles of your face and neck when you smoke. Heaven knows," he groaned, "it's difficult enough to make you keep still for five minutes."

"Think how boring it is for me to sit here gazing beautifully at nothing."

Dick Spencer ran his fingers through his hair.

"You've got my face to look at," he announced complacently.

Laureen cocked her head on one side and screwed up her nose. "I've seen it. That's what I'm complaining about." She flung up her arms and stretched. "It's no good, Dick. I can't sit still another minute. You're not painting well to-day and you know it. Call it a day and let's make tea and talk."

Dick flung down his palette resignedly.

"Which means I'll make the tea and you'll talk," he retorted.

He filled the kettle and set it on a gas ring.

Flinging himself on the big divan on which she had seated herself, he rested his head against her shoulder.

She picked up a cushion, thereby uncovering a pair of pajamas.

"What's the matter with your bedroom?" she demanded teasingly. "Have you suddenly become so completely artistic that you must sleep in your studio?"

Dick flushed scarlet as he tossed the garments behind the divan.

"Yes—no. Look here, Laureen," he said earnestly, "I'm worried to death about this beastly murder case. Darling, can't you think it over? Let's be married and clear out on a honeymoon."

She looked at his worried face kindly.

"Dear old Dick, one can't run away from the law of England just because you're foolish enough to want to marry me. Indeed that suet-faced inspector would think I'd murdered Delmond and shot Avice into the bargain if I attempted any stunts like that."

"Well, didn't you?" he jested idly, playing with the scarf she wore.

She got up swiftly, shaking him away, her face flaming. "How dare you say that?" she demanded in a low voice.

Dick was by her side in a second, imploring her to forget his clumsy attempt at humor.

"I'm a tactless ass," he groaned. "As if your nerves had not been strained to cracking point already with this tragedy without my teasing you."

Laureen thrust back a thick wave of her hair and pressed her hands to temples that throbbed suddenly.

"Don't worry, Dick. It was foolish of me to mind what you said. I'm tired out with my theater work and the tension of that affair at my flat. And this morning," she shuddered, "on top of all came Avice's accident. I've a queer feeling that shot was meant for me. Maybe next time will be my turn."

Dick caught her hands anxiously. He had never seen Laureen in this mood before.

"My dear, do be careful," he said. "Inspector Reynolds's brother was knifed on Tuesday night, but of course the blow was intended for our lynx-eyed detective."

The girl's eyes widened fearfully.

"I didn't see anything in the newspapers about it," she confessed. "Where did this happen, Dick?"

"In Inspector Reynolds's front garden. Reynolds was away," he smiled as he recalled their meeting in Paris, "and some one who had a grudge against the inspector evidently mistook his brother for him. Rough on the brother, eh? He's getting on all right, I hear."

Laureen caught her breath. If only she could be alone a moment to think undisturbed.

"The kettle's boiling, Dick," she announced.

Spencer obediently vanished to make the tea.

Laureen leaned back against the cushions, staring miserably across the room at the big windows. They nearly covered one half of the wall, one window opening on to a balcony from which a small iron staircase led to the garden.

Her brain reeled with the news of the attack on Reynolds's brother. Was that too mixed up with the Delmond affair? If so, where was it all going to end? Whose turn would it be next?

She felt wearily that she did not care if she were to be the next victim, so long as this lonely terror locked up in her mind could be ended.

Oh, if only she could confide in some one! Almost she had spoken to Lansberg. But now, with a new panic, she feared he also was involved, if not actually guilty.

Dick Spencer as an adviser she rejected from her thoughts. For one thing he was too much in love with her to give unprejudiced advice, and also she could not add a sense of obligation when her feelings for him were merely those of friendship.

Suddenly her eyes dilated as she saw the shadow of a man creep across one end of the window. Before the shadow could materialize she instinctively dived beneath the cushions piled beside her. Leaving a tiny opening between them she crouched, watching.

A man's white face was pressed to the glass. He was trying to peer into the studio. Dark unkempt hair tumbled over his brows, a thin nervous hand shaded his burning eyes.

"Tea's ready," shouted Dick cheerfully from the kitchen. "And I've made some toast."

At the first sound of Spencer's voice the man quickly slid away. Listening intently, Laureen could hear his feet faintly stumbling down the iron staircase.

Trembling, she flung aside the cushions and tried to stand up.

Dick heard a cry and rushed in to find her lying unconscious on the floor. He lifted her on the couch and bent over her anxiously.

"What a fool I am!" she murmured as she opened her gray eyes and gazed round the room. "I've only done that once before in my life, Dick."

"And I've been making you sit in that tiresome position," he reproached himself. "As if all the other worry and strain were not enough to have exhausted you. Let me get you some brandy, darling. Don't move," he begged.

She declined the offer.

"I'm all right now."

"Can you drink a cup of tea?"

"Two, maybe three," she assured him. "You pour it out and don't look like an old hen fussing over her chicken."

She raised herself and made an effort to draw his attention from her fainting attack.

"You'll not act to-night if I have to get Lansberg himself to stop you, Laureen."

"Maybe I shan't," she agreed. But her decision was not based on physical weakness. Was it wiser not to appear to-night?

The tea revived her and a little color drifted back to her pale cheeks. "Please don't interfere in any way, Dick," she urged. "*I* must decide whether I go to the theater or not. I'll go to my hotel and rest now if you'll get me a taxi."

He flung open the French windows as she pulled on her hat. Laureen looked over his shoulder. The balcony and garden were deserted. She noticed that a door in the far end of the garden wall was an inch or two open.

"Where does that lead?" she asked.

"Into a back lane that goes from our street through to the next," Spencer told her.

She surveyed it thoughtfully.

"Makes it easy for burglars, Dick."

"Wonderfully. Only, my sweet one, burglars don't haunt artists' studios—they're nearly all painter folks round here, you see. Come along. I'm going to take you back."

She paused a moment before her portrait standing on the easel.

"Why, it's nearly finished!" she exclaimed. "Dick Spencer, you've brought me here under false pretenses. You didn't need a sitting at all."

"All true artists need dozens of sittings to get the final nuances, whatever that means. Don't deprive me of the only chance I get of seeing you, Laureen," he pleaded.

In spite of her wish he rang up Lansberg after leaving her.

"Laureen's not fit to go on to-night," he said over the wire. "After her sitting this afternoon in my studio she fainted. She told me not to interfere but I felt you'd persuade her better than I."

Lansberg expressed consternation.

"Thanks, old chap," he said. "You did quite right. I'll go to the theater at once and tell the manager to warn the understudy. Of course Laureen mustn't dream of acting to-night."

Dick Spencer grinned sardonically as he came out of the call-box.

"That's being decent, if not noble," he reflected. "She and Lansberg are getting keen about each other, and here am I, the rejected suitor, lending a helping hand. This is where I untie my knot for the day."

He trudged along the hot pavements to his club feeling rather forlorn and despondent. Even inside its doors his gloom did not pass off. Desperately he hated all the publicity that had centered round Laureen since the murder. Every other man he came across developed a sudden desire to be chatty with Spencer, and sooner or later would ask for the latest news of the murder case, knowing he was a friend of Laureen's.

He wandered into the reading-room but it was even worse in that hall of silence. Every newspaper he picked up had some screaming headlines about Laureen, audaciously recounting supposed interviews with her, reprinting photographs of her at different stages of her career. And all of them fiercely demanded news of Valerie Baird.

Flinging them down in disgust he determined to call at Warnham House to ask after Avice.

He arrived hot and irritable. On the steps he met the Countess of Warnham, about to enter. She cast a comprehensive glance over Dick's angry face and with an inward smile divined the symptoms.

"Come in and have a cocktail with me," she invited. Tactfully adding "And don't mention murder cases or this dastardly attack on Avice to-day or I shall become really violent."

Dick Spencer relaxed. He and Lady Warnham were very good friends. A sympathetic amusing old woman, worth nearly all the young ones put together, he decided. Always excepting Laureen and Avice.

All of which Lady Warnham knew perfectly—including the two exceptions.

"Avice is doing very well," she informed him over an artistically mixed "Soul's Ruin." "Slip up and see her for a minute, but don't let her talk. That inspector person has a rendezvous with her to-morrow afternoon and she'll need all her strength for that."

In a few minutes Dick returned. "She's asleep. I didn't disturb her."

Lady Warnham nodded approvingly. "Good child. Stay and have dinner and cheer me up a little."

It was nearly ten o'clock when Dick returned to his flat in a far more peaceful state of mind. He unlocked his door, whistling a tune from Laureen's revue, switched on the light and strolled inside the big studio. For a moment he stood, blinking, dazed, wondering if he had carelessly wandered into the wrong flat.

The entire place was in the wildest disorder: chairs flung over, draperies torn, canvases trodden on. For once, it would seem, burglars had availed themselves of that convenient back lane!

It didn't greatly disturb him. He was insured and anyhow had no valuables. Except that one picture of Laureen. Suppose—

With one quick stride he reached the big easel and stood back aghast. The canvas had been slashed in all directions, with particular savage gashes on the face and golden hair he loved so well.

Spencer was not quite the good-humored fool Reynolds imagined him to be. There was something cruelly malicious in the way Laureen's pictured face had been cut. An unmistakable menace lay there. With shaking hands he picked up the telephone and demanded Scotland Yard.

"I want Inspector Reynolds at once," he said. "Give me his private number if he's not there. It's urgent."

In a moment he recognized a quiet voice replying, and for the first time was thankful to hear it.

"Inspector Reynolds speaking. What's the trouble, Mr. Spencer?"

Breathlessly Spencer explained what he had just discovered, adding that Laureen was probably not at the theater that night.

"I know she's not," replied the detective. "Meet me at her hotel as soon as you can. I want to make sure she's all right. If so, I'll come along with you and see the damage at the studio."

Laureen had reached her hotel at about five thirty and found Bertha anxiously studying a telegram she had just received.

"One of my friends at Clapham is ill, miss, and they've wired to know if I can go down and stay the night," she explained.

"Of course," assented Laureen at once. "Go by all means, Bertha. You've scarcely been outside this hotel since we came. I may not act to-night. If not, I shall go to bed and shan't need you at all."

"Oh, I can't leave you if you're not well, miss," the maid demurred.

"Nonsense. Off you go at once," insisted Laureen. "I'm going to bed, anyhow, for a while."

An hour later, as she was half dozing, the theater manager rang up and told her everything was arranged for her understudy to appear that evening.

"The slips for the programs are being printed. The girl's rehearsing now, delighted to have her chance," he added, mindful of Lansberg's firm instructions—"At all costs I will not allow Miss Laureen to appear to-night." And Lansberg, the manager knew, was not a man to be trifled with.

Laureen laid her head back on the pillow with a sigh of relief. Nothing to do but sleep until morning. Soon she fell into a troubled dream.

She roused with a start to see a tiny flicker of light in the room. It went out as she moved but she could hear some one breathing.

Her heart beating wildly, she instinctively put her hand to the bell over her head and succeeded in ringing it, but as she withdrew her hand she gave a smothered scream, for a pillow was pressed tightly over her mouth and a heavy hand groped for her throat.

There was a sudden banging at the door, a voice shouting "Laureen" and then the pillow was dropped.

She screamed again, and heard a terrific crash. The next moment the lights were switched on and Dick Spencer and Inspector Reynolds stood beside her.

Reynolds stayed only one second to assure himself she was unhurt before he rushed to the open window and leaned out. There was no sound from the courtyard below.

"Which way did he go?" demanded Reynolds hurriedly.

Laureen shook her head. "I don't know. I saw no one but felt something smothering me."

The detective looked at a drawer turned upside-down on the floor and a dressing case beside it.

"Quick, tell me—whose room is that in there? Your maid's?" The door was slightly open.

"My sitting-room. Bertha's room is beyond that. She's away for the night," Laureen gasped.

"Stay with her," the inspector commanded Spencer, and rapidly searched the two communicating rooms, whose doors also opened on the outside corridor. Neither room bore signs of disturbance.

He raced downstairs and startled the night porter.

"Seen any one go out?"

"Only the man who went up to see Miss Laureen half an hour ago," the porter replied. "He said she was expecting him."

"Which way did he go? Quick, it's important."

"He got into a bus that was just passing, going toward Charing Cross."

"His hands—did you see them?"

"Going in he had on yellow chamois gloves. I was on the curb when he ran out and as he caught hold of the bus rail his hand looked as if—"

But before he could finish the sentence, the inspector was on his way.

## XXV. PIERCING THE VEIL

DICK SPENCER bent over Laureen anxiously when Reynolds dashed into the adjoining rooms on his search.

"Are you sure that brute didn't hurt you?" He gently touched the inflamed marks on her neck where those cruel fingers had gripped her.

Laureen scarcely heeded his question.

"Dick, I—I want to see Mr. Lansberg at once. Have you any idea where he is? The theater?" she suggested.

Spencer grinned. Love's young dream must be very real for Laureen to wish to see Lansberg five minutes after she'd had a narrow escape from being murdered! Well, he'd be a father to them both, he decided, and bury his own feelings.

"For once the fool of the family can help you, lady," he replied. "Lansberg is dining at his club to-night with Dr. Tempest as his guest. They're probably still there talking solemnly in that mausoleum. Shall I ring up and ask?"

"Yes. Tell him what's happened and ask him to come immediately. Use the telephone in the next room."

Directly she heard his voice asking for the number she slipped out of bed and drew a loose dressing-gown round her. Taking a towel, she rubbed the rail at the foot of the bed, the door and drawer handles and any woodwork that might have been touched.

Replacing the towel exactly as it was—she was beginning to appreciate the inspector's powers of observation—she walked rather unsteadily into the sitting-room just as Reynolds returned from his inquiries in the hall below.

"No luck," he said in response to Spencer's lifted eyebrows.

"What's the time, Dick?" Laureen asked. She had curled herself up in a deep arm-chair, one hand cupping her chin so that her throat was hidden.

"Twenty past ten," and under his breath Spencer added, "Lansberg's on his way, so cheer up."

She smiled her thanks as Reynolds glanced quickly up from a note he was writing.

"Been telephoning, Mr. Spencer?" the detective asked amiably.

Spencer checked a facetious remark and nodded.

"H'm," Reynolds shot a keen glance at the young man and then turned to Laureen.

"Please tell me all you know about this assault," he said bluntly.

The girl flushed at his tone. "There is very little to tell. I was asleep and awoke frightened by a slight noise. There was, I fancy, a pencil of light in the room. I rang my bell in terror, probably only half awake, thinking I was being smothered by something. I saw no one. And the next minute you and Mr. Spencer had burst open my door. That is all. How did you get here?"

"A bell rang as we came in the hall downstairs," Reynolds explained. "The porter said it was from your room. As we reached the door you screamed. Not knowing the sitting-room door was unlocked, we broke yours open. *Who was your assailant?*" he snapped.

"How can I tell when I didn't see him?" Laureen retorted.

"Has anything been stolen?"

"Not so far as I can see. Certainly my jewels and money are safe. I have just looked."

"The person who searched your room and attacked you was not after money or jewelry, Miss Laureen. Had you any valuable papers or documents?"

Her gray eyes widened and her breathing was uneven.

"No," she replied. "Why do you ask?"

"Because," the detective said deliberately, "the man who searched here to-night is undoubtedly the man who played such havoc in your flat. The same man," his voice dropped to a tenser tone, "who entered Mr. Spencer's studio this evening and having searched wildly and fruitlessly there, slashed your picture to ribbons. *What does he want?*" the C. I. D. official demanded imperatively.

Spencer moved restlessly, tried to speak, but the detective silenced him.

"I can allow no interruption, Mr. Spencer. There has been too much concealment already, with disastrous results. I mean to know the truth now. Answer my question, Miss Laureen. What is this man searching for?"

Laureen gazed at him helplessly, her dry lips incapable of making audible sound. Spencer hurriedly gave her a glass of water.

As she took it from him her hand dropped from her chin. In one stride the detective had reached her and peered at those telltale marks livid now on her white throat.

"So you would even shelter the man who tried to strangle you," Reynolds said sternly. "This man is desperate, remember. Think! He tore your furniture to pieces in his desire to find something. This morning your friend, Lady Avice Garth, was wounded by a shot undoubtedly intended for you, as you accidentally admitted to me. This evening the man ransacked Mr. Spencer's studio, after you had been there this afternoon and possibly hidden what he wants, he must have thought. Again he was baffled, so to-night he comes here and would undoubtedly have murdered you if we had not been in time. The slashed picture gave me the clue that you were in real danger."

The girl raised her eyes and met the detective's glance steadily.

"He must be mad," she answered clearly. "How can I possibly know what he wants? Perhaps now that he has searched every possible place for this imaginary treasure he will give me a little peace."

"Have you deposited anything in your bank?"

"No," she said nervously. "I had no time, even if I'd thought of it."

"Then there remains only one more hiding place, Miss Laureen." The inspector's face was grim and relentless.

She raised her eyebrows in surprise.

"Where?"

"The dressing-rooms at the theater."

Her cheeks were ghastly, her whole body seemed suddenly rigid.

"That may be his next search," Reynolds went on. "Miss Laureen, for the last time, where have you hidden the thing this man is looking for? And what is it?" As he spoke Reynolds saw in a flash many of the separate links fit together, scarcely heeding the girl's murmured reply, "I don't know what you mean."

He had something more than her denials now. This thing—was it not the packet posted in the hall letter-box to Valerie Baird, later collected by Laureen in disguise, and then probably hidden somewhere in the theater?

Working further back, might that packet not have been taken by Laureen from the dead man's pocket last Sunday night? Had the dead man, dressed as a woman, received it from Lansberg earlier? In other words, had Delmond, in woman's clothes, confided that packet to Lansberg for safety years before?

Ah, it was piecing itself together now! And this man with the missing thumb, he had made two attacks on Lansberg in Paris, attacks Lansberg could not account for. Was not this packet the cause?

And again Reynolds came back to the question of its contents.

"For the last time, Miss Laureen, what was in that packet?" He was angry with frustration. He would *make* this woman speak.

"And for the last time, Inspector Reynolds, I again tell you—the truth—I do not know."

Her voice was despairing but definite.

"Where have you hidden it? I insist upon your reply," he demanded loudly, longing to shake her.

From the doorway behind him came in stern, icy tones from Lansberg: "What is the meaning of this inquisition, Inspector Reynolds? Do you realize Miss Laureen is ill and nearly distracted?"

Lansberg walked across the room and took the girl's trembling hands in his. She leaned her head against his arm, the tears running weakly down her cheeks.

"Oh, Ivan," she whispered. "Thank you for coming. I—I can't bear any more."

"It's all right, my child," Lansberg murmured protectingly. "Don't be alarmed." He bent over her a moment, an expression of infinite sadness in his eyes. "By to-morrow, or in a day or two at most, I swear to you that things will have straightened themselves out. I think I understand what you've been trying to do."

He stood up, holding her hands in one of his, an arm round her shoulder.

"Now, Inspector," he said frigidly, "that your ill-timed examination has brought Miss Laureen to the verge of collapse after all she had suffered previously, I suggest you put any vital questions to me or defer them until to-morrow when I have promised to be at your disposal. By the way, I should prefer that interview to be at my apartment at two thirty instead of at the Yard."

Reynolds assented reluctantly.

"I have asked Miss Laureen to say what is in the packet and where it is," the detective stated. "She says she cannot tell me."

Laureen nodded, her eyes half closed.

"That is true, Ivan. Please make him believe it," she implored piteously.

"You have had your answer, Inspector. I think you can go no further in this matter to-night," said Lansberg.

The detective bit his lip. Then he smiled frankly. He knew when he was beaten and was willing to admit it.

"Very well, Mr. Lansberg," he agreed. "Will you tell me one thing, please, that may help me very much? When did this woman who resembled Delmond call at your apartment to reclaim that packet from your care?"

"A week ago," Lansberg replied. "No, this is Thursday. She called last Friday evening just as I was going out to dine."

"Thank you," Reynolds acknowledged with relief. That fitted in perfectly with his theory. "I think I'd better leave you now. I'm sorry to have distressed you, Miss Laureen," he said.

She freed one hand from Lansberg's grasp and extended it to the detective.

"Don't think too badly of me, Inspector," she said in a tremulous voice.

"I don't," replied that man gruffly. "Good night."

He turned back as a thought struck him. "Has your servant returned, Mr. Lansberg?"

Lansberg shook his head.

"No," he replied. "Let me hear at once if you get any news of him."

Reynolds walked back to the Yard surprised at many things, himself included. Was there a soft patch in him that needed hardening?

Or was that the only decent bit of humanity left in his nature, he wondered?

His heart was lighter than it had been for days as he tramped along the street. So many odd bits had fitted in this crazy puzzle to-night.

To-morrow evening he was to have a conference with his chiefs. He had been dreading it, knowing they would require a clear statement of the situation and would not be lulled by a collection of odd clues involving many people and pointing to no one in particular.

To-morrow morning he would be able to talk to Lady Avice and drag out the story of the mysterious Tony. In the afternoon he was to have an interview with Lansberg, and in between he determined somehow to ask Laureen a few vital questions. That she knew of this man with the missing thumb he was fairly sure. And that she knew even more of the elusive Valerie Baird he was positive, the proof being in his pocket-book at the moment.

Late as it was Jenkins was waiting for him in his office. "I've telephoned all the main hospitals," he informed his chief. "There are about five accident cases not quite clear on identity. One, a girl, was knocked down last Monday morning and brought there in a private car. She's still unconscious."

Reynolds noted down the address. "I'll go round there early to-morrow morning," he promised. "It's probably nothing to do with our case, though."

At his ear the telephone bell rang shrilly. He picked up the receiver, listened a moment, asked a few questions and banged it back on the hook.

"Get a taxi, quick," he ordered Jenkins. "You come too."

Jenkins, slightly bewildered, obeyed and got in the car with his preoccupied chief.

In silence they rattled across a bridge over the river and along gloomy streets until they came to a wharf.

Telling the cabman to wait, the inspector got out with Jenkins, and the two men picked their way through bales and kegs to a large shed.

A policeman flashed his lantern on them inquiringly, but at a few words from Reynolds unlocked the shed door, led them inside, and produced an electric lamp.

On a rough table lay something covered with a tarpaulin.

The policeman raised it and Reynolds looked at the still form.

"They got him out of the river an hour ago, sir," the constable explained.

Jenkins stared at the features of the man lying there. "Do you know who it is, sir?" he asked.

Reynolds nodded. "Lansberg's missing servant. The man who stabbed my brother. I expect you'll find his fingerprints tally with those on the knife."

## XXVI. VALERIE

ON that journey from Victoria to Dover, Valerie had ample time to read and reread the whole history of Leslie Delmond's murder. The newspapers of earlier date that she had brought from the hospital linked it all up clearly. Yes, undoubtedly suspicion rested heavily on her and she had no means of proving her innocence.

Who would believe her story of how she passed last Sunday night? And if she could prove it, would not the very publicity tell that other man she so feared where she could be found?

After church last Sunday night she had walked past Laureen's flat and he had seen and followed her. She had run wildly, trying to dodge him. Afraid to go back to her room, lest he was following and even that refuge would be taken from her, she had gone by bus to Richmond Park and slept fitfully hidden in a bank of fern.

Who would believe that story? What witnesses had she?

Next morning she had determined to see Laureen, to warn her, but in crossing the road near her friend's flat a car had knocked her down.

No, she decided, there was only one way. She must hide until this hue and cry had died down and Leslie Delmond's murderer was discovered.

Folding the newspapers mechanically, her glance fell on the "agony" column. One notice stood out, for her, in letters of fire. Tears blinded her eyes as she read the appeal:

*Remember Tuileries Gardens, May 20, 1927.*
*Implore you to write or telephone my number in*
*London directory. Am in terrible anxiety about*
*you. D.*

He remembered then and cared still, this man she loved! Two years of sorrow had divided them, but now that she was alone and in terror he had sent this assurance of his love to comfort her.

Hurriedly she took paper and envelope from her case and wrote:

*My beloved,*
*I have just read the Times personal column. You can never know*
*what comfort your message has brought. Try to believe in me. I*
*cannot extricate myself from these complications. I can only hide. As*
*soon as possible I will let you know where I am. I dare not explain*
*more clearly. Always yours.*

She did not even sign an initial to this letter. Addressing it, she dropped the envelope into the post-box at Dover station.

As she did so, a well-dressed woman, also posting letters, looked at her curiously, but the thick veil hid her features fairly well, and she was sure the woman had not definitely recognized her.

Suddenly she felt faintness creeping over her and realized that only excitement had buoyed her up since her escape from the hospital. Whatever happened, for the moment she could go no further without rest. Checking her luggage she went to a small hotel near the station and asked for a room.

"I've had a long journey and need sleep before going on," she told the proprietor.

The man assured her she should not be disturbed. "A nice cup of tea when you wake up and you'll be all right, ma'am. The sea's a bit choppy to-day. There's plenty of trains to London."

She sank down on the bed and drew the cover over her thankfully. Anyhow she was safe here for a few hours. The hotel proprietor evidently mistook her for a weary passenger *from* France.

It was late afternoon when Valeria awoke and rang for tea. After drinking it she felt much more able to plan out clearly what she must do. Her idea had been to bury herself in Paris in some quarter where tourists and English-speaking visitors did not come. Thanks to ten years spent in a Belgian convent school she could always pass as a Frenchwoman.

It might be safe there, but it would certainly be terribly lonely, and she dreaded solitude now unspeakably.

Then the memory returned of the woman she had encountered at the post-box on Dover platform that morning. What was Mrs. de Groot doing there? Probably going to London. In a flash it came to her that Mary de Groot was going to Avice and Laureen because she knew they were in trouble. It was like Mary, the girl reflected. The American woman was brimming over with kindness and generosity.

Yes, that was it, Valerie decided. Mary de Groot was going to stand by her friends and prove her affection, while she—Valerie—was stealing away to hide, regardless of everything except her own safety. Laureen must be unhappy and anxious, fighting bravely—this much was obvious to her—to keep Valerie's secret. So far she had succeeded wonderfully.

But suppose by this very secrecy Laureen herself should be suspected, perhaps arrested! Her career would be ruined, even if she cleared herself: mud always stuck.

Besides, worse than that in Valerie's mind was the knowledge that she had abandoned Laureen, leaving her defenseless to the attacks of a man who had always hated her, and who would now certainly try to do her harm in some way. Maybe even bodily injury.

Valerie recoiled from the thought of what might happen if she carried out her plan to run away and to hide. She must go back to London at once. No matter what the result might be, that was her plain duty.

First of all, she must see Laureen and warn her of the danger. Suppose after this delay she could not get to her in time! Oh, how unutterably selfish had been this flight!

She rang for a time-table and looked up the trains. The next one arrived in London at eight thirty-five. Laureen would be in the theater then.

"I must go straight there and see her in her dressing-room," she made up her mind. "After that I don't care what they do to me."

Leaving her other luggage in the cloak-room and taking only a suitcase, she entered a compartment, drawing her thick veil carefully over her face. She must run no risk of being discovered before she had seen Laureen.

Disgust at her previous cowardice grew upon her, with every passing mile. How could she have thought of deserting Laureen in such a crisis? Knowing her loyalty, Valerie was well aware that nothing would induce Laureen to protect herself by breaking faith.

There was that note, Valerie remembered, in which she had desperately revealed her fears to Laureen. That, if nothing else, would make Laureen do her utmost to protect her.

The slow train fretted her but at last it arrived almost half an hour late.

In the taxi Valerie wondered how she should get to the dressing-room. That stage-door keeper, with whom she had left her note last Saturday, had looked very stern and forbidding. He would probably refuse to admit her unless she gave her name. And if she did that, she might be arrested before she could speak to Laureen!

Dismissing the taxi she took her bag and walked up the alley. Minnis was in his office talking loudly to two or three men.

Like a shadow she slipped through the doorway and went noiselessly up the stairs.

"Which is Miss Laureen's dressing-room?" she asked as authoritatively as she could of a workman in the corridor. The man indicated an open door and with a beating heart Valerie stepped inside.

Early that morning in London, Inspector Reynolds had telephoned to Lansberg. "I'm afraid your man has been found, sir. He was taken out of the river last night. Will you come along to the Yard now and go with me to identify the body?"

A little later Lansberg stood looking down at the still face of the man he had known as a faithful servant.

Reynolds handed him a note, still damp. "This was tied in his handkerchief," he said. "Can you translate it? It's in a language I don't understand."

Lansberg smoothed out the paper and with difficulty deciphered the smudged words. He read aloud:

*"To my master. Farewell. I have sinned greatly. Forgive thy servant. I make this reparation."*

"Poor Neron!" Lansberg murmured. "It's hard to imagine his committing any sin that could require this penalty."

"He probably thought he had killed me?" said Reynolds, watching Lansberg's face.

"I don't understand, Inspector."

"Yet it's easy if one traces cause and effect, Mr. Lansberg. My brother was stabbed last Tuesday, undoubtedly in mistake for me. The knife found in his shoulder was taken from your safe. You remember finding it open last Tuesday afternoon when you returned from Crowborough with Miss Laureen."

Lansberg assented with a puzzled frown.

"Something else had been taken from your flat—from your servant's room—before that. Something," the detective went on deliberately, "that your servant had hidden fearing it might incriminate you. He naturally imagined I had searched your flat."

"But you were in Paris. Spencer told me so."

"Your man didn't know that. He recalled my questioning of the day before and saw my name and private address on your desk." Reynolds raised his hand. "We know the result."

"Your reasoning is logical, Inspector. It appalls me." He pressed his forehead. "If there is nothing more you need me for, I will go now. I have much to do before we meet this afternoon."

As Lansberg's tall figure vanished Reynolds for one second wondered if he would ever see the man again. But reflection reassured him. Lansberg was being carefully trailed and, short of suicide, could not escape.

At Scotland Yard, Jenkins was waiting for Reynolds with news.

"No need to go to the hospital about that girl, sir. They have just rung up to say she vanished during the night."

"Vanished!" exclaimed his chief. "How could she? You told me she'd been unconscious since the accident."

"The hospital is overcrowded at the moment and apparently this girl's case has not been closely examined. It's all very mysterious."

"Mysterious," snapped the inspector. "It's incredible. Unconscious people don't get up and walk. We should have had her watched. Give me the telephone."

After five minutes of extremely irate questioning the inspector thumped the receiver back on the hook and scowled at his assistant.

"I'll bet a dollar this girl was Valerie Baird. We can try her old address in Bloomsbury. But I'm sure she won't go back there. She was knocked down about twenty yards from Laureen's flat last Monday morning, between eleven and twelve." He swore softly. "I was actually in the flat at the time. Think of it! But for that accident this girl would have walked right into our arms."

"You have proof of that, sir?" queried Jenkins eagerly.

"I've a copy of a note she wrote to Laureen saying she'd call. Here, read it." He passed over the copy given him by Laureen's dresser.

Jenkins read it with great interest.

"Did you notice that bit: 'I've been in England some weeks'?" He put his finger to the phrase as he passed the note back.

"Well, what of it?" demanded the inspector impatiently.

"As so much of this affair has centered in Paris, sir, perhaps Valerie might have come from Paris to England. And if so—"

Reynolds nodded quickly. "Yes, I've got the rest. She might try to go back. We must watch for that. Let me see, she probably aimed for that nine o'clock boat train. Is it Victoria or Charing Cross it starts from? Don't waste any time. And tell the men to use their brains for once."

Jenkins was hurrying from the room when the telephone bell rang.

"You answer," the inspector told Jenkins. "I must get off to my appointment with Lady Avice Garth. Ring me at Warnham House if necessary."

He was half-way down the stairs when Jenkins ran after him, breathless. "It's from Cripps, who's trailing Miss Laureen. He says you told him to ring you if she went to the theater."

"I did. What's the message?"

"Cripps says that Miss Laureen has just gone in by the stage-door of the theater, sir. He telephoned at once."

The inspector took the remaining steps in one leap and jumping in a taxi gave the address of the theater.

"Drive like blazes," he ordered.

## XXVII. LADY AVICE EXPLAINS

WHEN Reynolds arrived at the theater huge placards were already displayed announcing that Laureen would positively appear that day at both performances.

"If not otherwise engaged," Reynolds reflected grimly. He was determined to speed up events to-day whatever happened, his softer mood of the night before gone in his irritation because Valerie had again slipped through his fingers.

He hurried along the alley to the stage-door, brushed past Minnis and ran lightly up the stairs.

The door of Laureen's dressing-room was open, but she was not there. Reynolds was not surprised. He had been sure she would visit the other dressing-rooms and now she had acted more quickly than he had expected.

He tiptoed silently along the stone corridor, stopping every now and then to listen.

Outside the empty room that had been newly papered, he paused. The door was shut but he could detect faint sounds from within.

With the utmost caution his fingers closed on the door handle and began to twist it. It turned without a squeak, and by delicate pressure he found the door was not locked.

Suddenly he flung it open and entered.

Laureen was on her knees near the mantelpiece. She gave a startled cry as she saw who it was and struggled to her feet.

"An early visit, Inspector," she remarked.

"A surprise visit," emphasized Reynolds mildly, strolling toward her. "An ingenious hiding place, Miss Laureen. Don't let me interrupt you."

He bent down and examined a long slit in the wallpaper parallel to the baseboard.

She rested one arm on the mantelpiece to support her shaking limbs, but made no reply.

The inspector opened his pocket knife and slipped the blade into the aperture between the board and the wall.

"Ah, here we are, I think. I was so afraid I should be too late to see this part of the drama." He stuck the blade into something soft and with a little difficulty worked into sight a thick envelop.

He turned it over curiously. It had been through the post but was unopened!

"You have not opened it since—" he stated.

"Of course not," replied Laureen. "I had no right to do so."

"But you know what is inside. You addressed it to Miss Valerie Baird."

"I have my shoes on but I'm not walking," was her swift retort. Her composure was coming back rapidly. There was almost relief in her face.

Inspector Reynolds weighed the packet in his hand reflectively. This girl was either the most consummate actress he had ever encountered, or else she had been shielding some one else desperately and was rather thankful the matter had at last been forced out of her hands.

"Then you still insist on saying you do not know the contents of this packet, Miss Laureen?"

She sighed.

"I don't wish to say anything. I do not know what is in that packet, but I *suspect* there is something there that would injure some one I love very dearly," she replied simply. "There is also a document in it that belongs to a third person. I can't understand why it should be there at all. I have not read it, but I saw the name on it. And neither you nor I have any right to touch *that*, Inspector," she added firmly.

"I take it that you had no time to examine these papers and sort them out to their different owners," the detective remarked.

"That is so," she readily agreed.

"Only the few minutes when Mr. Lansberg was searching your flat last Sunday night."

Her breath came quickly but she made no reply.

"You slipped into the dining-room," he went on slowly, "found Leslie Delmond there dead in the arm-chair and took these papers from his pocket."

"They were not in his pocket," she replied. "His hand was tucked down between the chair arm and the seat. I lifted his hand and found the packet in the lining of the chair. He must have slipped it there when he was dying." She shuddered at the memory.

"Then you went into your bedroom and glanced through the packet before you sealed it in this envelop. Or was it sealed before?"

"I did as you said. The packet was not sealed. I hurriedly looked through it and discovered a paper belonging to—somebody else," Laureen murmured.

"Fearing you and the flat might be searched that night, you addressed and stamped the envelope and, on the pretext of whistling for the policeman, ran down and dropped it in the hall-box. Carter took it from there and posted it next morning," he went on.

"Yes." She was watching him with fascinated eyes as he told the story of her movements.

"The next afternoon you came here ostensibly to rest, disguised yourself as an old lady and called at Valerie Baird's address in Bloomsbury. The red paint from the wet railings has now been cleaned off the brown coat you wear in a sketch each night."

This time Laureen gave a gasp of astonishment.

"That is all perfectly true, Inspector," she admitted, with a touch of admiration in her voice.

His lips twisted in a faint smile. "Not quite such a dull old fool as you imagined, eh, miss!" he thought.

"You then went to the hotel to which you had sent this letter, booked a room in order to get a number and called for this packet at the letter bureau."

"I did. Inspector, you're a wizard."

The inspector waived aside the compliment and went on.

"You returned here, sent Joe for some cigarettes and hid the packet where I have just found it."

"Please don't open it yet," she pleaded earnestly. "I'm sure we have no right until I've spoken to—"

"The owner of the document?" put in Reynolds.

"Yes."

Reynolds took a letter from his pocket and opened it.

"Listen, Miss Laureen, and check me up if at any point in this note it differs from the one you received on Saturday night in your dressing-room. There is neither date nor address on my copy." He read aloud slowly:

*"Laureen darling,*
*I've been in England some weeks, but have not dared to see you and on the telephone I'm always told you're out or engaged because I dare not give my name.*
*L. D. is in London searching for me, and you know who is after him! If they meet it will be terrible. I believe L. is watching you too, to see if we're meeting and find out my address.*
*One night I was at the stage-door waiting to see you come out. He was there, saw me in the crowd and ran after me. He threatens to get me ten years*
*if I won't do what he wishes.* He has those papers. *Oh, if only I could get hold of them! I don't know where he's staying but be careful. My life is one long terror now. I'm afraid of L. D. but far more afraid of—you know who. I'd die rather than see him again.*
*I'm staying at 30 Carisbroke Road, Bloomsbury, but don't write there. I don't trust the landlady.*
*Will call at your flat on Monday morning if I'm sure L. D. is not watching there. I wouldn't bring you into this mess for anything,*

*darling, after all your kindness to me. Have sold a few sketches so am not needing money.*

*Your devoted Val"*

"I think it is absolutely identical with the one I received, but I burned—"

Reynolds smiled casually.

"Yes, you burned the original in the ashtray last Sunday night," he replied. "Your dresser is an old acquaintance of mine. She opened and copied this before giving it to you on Saturday night. She supplied me with this. Beware of her: she's a wily old creature with a streaky past."

Laureen looked at him calmly.

"Probably you know where I went after dinner on Sunday night also," she suggested.

The detective's eyes twinkled.

"I think so," he answered. "You left your friends in the restaurant, strolled out in your pink velvet cloak. Later you reversed it, pulled a small black hat on and called at Valerie Baird's address. After that you walked toward Regent Street and drove to Mr. Spencer's studio." He glanced at his watch. "I have an appointment."

"The packet?" she questioned earnestly.

"I can make no promises," he told her. He felt certain there was a document there belonging to Lansberg. He must consult his chiefs on the matter. He buttoned the packet carefully into an inner pocket.

All that he had reeled off to Laureen had sounded very glib and impressive, but actually he feared that the things which really counted in this case had yet to be discovered. Suddenly he recalled another point on which Laureen might be able to help him.

"Do you ever remember hearing Leslie Delmond speak in a falsetto voice?" he asked.

She seemed a little surprised at what was apparently a trivial question.

"Often," she replied without hesitation. "It was a favorite trick of his."

"Where did you hear him do it?"

Her eyes opened in wonder.

"Why, in Nice, when we were acting in the film. He used to do it for fun, perhaps also to attract attention. I told you I had not seen him since."

"Thank you, Miss Laureen," he replied. "That's all for the present, I think."

At Warnham House he found the countess awaiting him. She met him graciously.

"My niece is much better and quite ready to see you, Inspector."

He was taken up to the darkened room in which he had been on the previous day. Lady Avice was lying on a couch, and after an inquiry concerning her health the inspector sat down facing her, his back to the shaded alcove window.

Buried in a big easy-chair, only his long legs showing, was a man who did not move at the inspector's entrance, and Reynolds made no comment on his presence. But Lady Avice did.

"I have asked Mr. Spencer to be present at our interview, but to take no part in it until I ask him to do so."

Reynolds agreed amiably. Half London could be there as far as he was concerned, as long as he heard Lady Avice's explanation.

"First of all, where were you and Lady Warnham on the night of the murder, Lady Avice?" Reynolds asked.

"We dined here and played chess until it was time for me to go to Mr. Spencer's studio. Then my aunt went to bed and I went to the party. The servants will probably be able to corroborate that."

"Who sent the telegram you received early on Tuesday morning immediately before you rushed off to Paris?"

The girl bit her lip to hide a smile.

"My dressmaker, canceling an appointment. I threw it into my drawer, so mercifully it was saved. Here it is."

"Thank you," said Reynolds, glancing at the telegram and observing that date and hour tallied. "Please give me your account of things in your own way."

"My aunt, Lady Warnham, did not complete her story for two reasons, Inspector," Lady Avice began. "She tried to protect my father's name and, indirectly, mine."

"I gathered that," the detective replied.

"My aunt has already told you that a little more than two years ago she came to my rescue in Nice, of our meeting with Mrs. de Groot, and later with Laureen and Delmond. She, however, did not tell you that Mr. Spencer was with us part of the time, and that he and my father gambled a lot together."

"No, she did not mention Mr. Spencer," said Reynolds. "Before we go any further, Lady Avice, I have an important question to ask you. Was Tony, your brother, I believe, with you also?" He watched her keenly.

Lady Avice's lips twitched.

"No," she said gravely, "Stinker was not there." Then in her cool voice she continued:

"You know of Mary de Groot's infatuation for Delmond. Well, a big fancy-dress ball was to be held in Nice and we decided to go together in various costumes.

"A week before the ball Mr. Spencer came to my aunt and Mrs. de

Groot and casually said they ought to have their jewelry cleaned for the great occasion and that he had heard of a wonderful jeweler who would do it beautifully.

"My aunt and Mary de Groot thought it an excellent plan. Mr. Spencer took their jewels—very valuable in both cases—and four or five days later brought them back, glistening marvelously.

"You understand, Inspector, *Mr. Spencer alone took them and brought them back and was entirely responsible for them.*"

The inspector nodded. "It is quite clear."

"A few days after the ball," went on the girl, "we discovered that my father's debts had been mysteriously paid. But we suspected nothing."

"Naturally, Lady Avice."

"After the film was finished Laureen went to America, and Delmond to Paris, I think. Mrs. de Groot and Mr. Spencer came to London with my aunt and myself. We were trying to cure Mary of her infatuation, you see."

"A difficult task," asserted Reynolds.

"A hopeless one," the girl sighed, "for soon Mrs. de Groot went back to Paris to find Delmond. Occasionally I went over to see her, and once she told me she wanted to marry Delmond but he always made some excuse and that she was sure there was another woman."

"There seem to have been several," commented the detective dryly.

"I must tell you that my aunt very rarely wore her jewels—those she had in Nice, I mean. At times, when we were hard up, she would sell a brooch or a ring, but the more valuable articles were kept at the bank.

"About fifteen months ago I had an agitated letter from Mrs. de Groot, asking me to have my aunt's jewels examined at once but giving no reason. We took them that day to a well-known expert and to our distress found that every alternate stone in a big diamond necklace was an imitation. And the same trick had been performed on the other articles."

"Where was Mr. Spencer at the time?" questioned Reynolds.

"In Paris. I crossed that night and saw him with Mrs. de Groot. At first she tried to protest that her jewels were all right. It was a magnificent gesture on her part to save the honor of my family. In the end she owned that her jewelry had been faked like my aunt's."

"But why should she try to protect Mr. Spencer?"

The girl flushed.

"Because she knew it was he who had given my father the money to pay his debts. And he had given it *after* those jewels had been received back by us in Nice from the cleaner. Remember, Mr. Spencer had been gambling, had lost heavily and was not a rich man."

"Leslie Delmond was at the back of the whole thing, I gather," Reynolds put in. "What was Mr. Spencer's explanation?"

Lady Avice nodded.

"He said Delmond had suggested that the jewels should be taken to the cleaner's, and later on had given Mr. Spencer the money to pay my father's debts, saying it was a gift from Mrs. de Groot, but to be anonymous.

"She was furious to hear this; declared that Spencer was trying to drag Delmond in to save himself, and that she would rather lose all she possessed than allow him to malign Delmond. There was a dreadful scene."

"I can imagine it," murmured the detective. "Meanwhile Mr. Spencer was incriminated unless he had proof against Delmond."

"He had no such proof. Indeed, he was nearly mad with rage, and vowed he'd get those jewels back if he had to wring Delmond's neck to do it."

"Where was Delmond at this time?"

"He had left Mrs. de Groot just before this, and *even then* she believed in him. Mr. Spencer stayed on in Paris to search for Delmond, and at last he traced him."

She hesitated a second. "I remained in Paris too. Just over a year ago Mr. Spencer came to me in great excitement. He had found Delmond, who had owned up after being threatened. Delmond told him where the stolen gems had been pawned and promised Spencer the money the next day."

She paused and glanced toward the figure in the window.

"I didn't like the story at all. Mr. Spencer was very credulous and impulsive, and knowing Delmond, I feared a trick. But Mr. Spencer wouldn't listen to me. Next day he fetched the money and the pawn-tickets."

Again she hesitated.

"A friend insisted on going with him to the pawnshop. He and this friend were arrested on the spot. The bank-notes were all forged. To put it briefly, he was sentenced to one year's imprisonment and his companion to nine months."

She caught her lip as if the memory were painful, but finished firmly: "Mr. Spencer was released a few weeks ago."

The inspector frowned. Spencer, he knew, was in love with Laureen. "But, forgive me, Lady Avice, you ought to have told me all this before."

Lady Avice shook her head and smiled. "I think not, Inspector. You see, when I heard of the murder I feared naturally that Mr. Spencer had committed it."

"Then surely you should have been frank with me earlier. The law demands that," Reynolds asserted.

"The law also makes an exception to that rule, Inspector."

"I'm afraid I don't understand you. Neither do I understand where the mysterious Tony comes in."

Lady Avice laughed softly and beckoned to the man in the window. He rose instantly and came to her side, looking full at the detective.

Reynolds stared blankly. He had never seen this fellow's face before!

The girl twined her soft fingers round the man's hand. "The law concedes that a wife need not give evidence against her husband," she said clearly. "Inspector Reynolds, this is my husband, Tony Spencer. Dick Spencer's twin brother, whom I secretly married in Paris a little more than a year ago—almost against his will too."

## XXVIII. THE LINGERING SHADOW

AUTOMATICALLY Inspector Reynolds took the hand that Tony held out, looking into clear brown eyes which still held a hint of suffering. He could see the strong resemblance now to the artist brother, and began to fathom the reason for Lady Avice's wild rush to Paris. She had feared then that her husband had murdered his enemy. That much was clear.

Lady Avice's voice broke in on his thoughts. "Now you will understand why Delmond blackmailed my aunt, Inspector. He found out I was married to Tony Spencer and threatened to expose the fact that my husband had gone to prison for passing false bank-notes. Delmond wrote me giving his address and demanding money. My aunt courageously went to see him and said he could do his worst. And I wrote him:

> *"If you write or attempt to see either my aunt or myself again, I shall immediately go to Scotland Yard and tell the whole story.*

"That must be the note you found. I never wrote to him before or since. But I telephoned to him twice. The last time was on Sunday afternoon—the day he was murdered."

"Thank you. That clears that up, Lady Avice. And it explains why he was desperate after your message and went to Laureen's flat."

Reynolds was still churning over his surprise about Tony when he heard Laureen's voice in the doorway.

"May I come in?" she asked.

Reynolds assented, still a little bewildered. What new knot would be unraveled now?

Suddenly he turned to Tony. "Where were you, Mr. Spencer, on the night of the murder, Sunday, June thirtieth?"

"Roaming about London, extremely drunk and angry, up to six o'clock looking for Delmond," the young man replied frankly. "Accidentally I met my brother who begged me to come back to his studio and go to bed. I refused and broke away from him. Ten minutes after, in the Berkeley, I met three men I know who were motoring to Dover. They made me go with them and I crossed on the night boat to Paris. I can give you their names and addresses, of course."

Tony paused. "I—I wanted to see my wife, but I was too ashamed of myself then," he went on. "I'd written to her, when I came out of prison, saying I must get that horror off my mind a bit first."

With a glance at the detective, which demanded permission for the interruption, Laureen bent down and kissed her friend.

"Mary de Groot's downstairs, Avice," she said. "She crossed yesterday from Paris but felt so tired that she stayed the night in Dover. This morning on Dover station whom do you think she saw posting a letter?"

"I can't guess," smiled Avice.

"Valerie," said Laureen emphatically, casting a mischievous look at the detective.

Reynolds's lips parted in surprise.

"Valerie!" he repeated in amazement.

"Why not?" asked Laureen lightly. "She has to be somewhere if she's alive, so why not Dover station?"

"She only left the hospital early this morning," the detective almost stammered.

Laureen caught his arm anxiously.

"Hospital? What do you mean? Please tell me quickly."

"I have every reason to believe that Valerie Baird was knocked down and stunned by a car last Monday morning. It happened in Berkeley Street, quite close to your flat."

"I heard the crash and Mr. Lansberg went to the window," cried Laureen. "Oh, to think my poor Valerie was so close and I never knew it. Was she badly hurt?"

"It was thought that she was still unconscious up to ten o'clock last night," Reynolds observed drily. "But during the night she was well enough to get up, dress, and get out of the building unnoticed."

"Don't they have nurses there?" indignantly demanded Laureen. "Poor girl, she was probably delirious at the time."

"Well, for a delirious person she seems to be remarkably capable, Miss Laureen. Posting letters on Dover platform appears very normal."

"Possibly to you," commented Laureen bitterly. "But where is she now?"

"That is what I should very much like to know. May I use your telephone, Lady Warnham?"

Hurriedly he rang up Jenkins and told him to telephone the Dover officials to find and detain the girl. "Hold the line a minute," he added.

"Mrs. de Groot," he said, entering the dining-room and surprising that lady considerably, "how was Valerie Baird dressed when you saw her this morning?"

"In black with a heavy veil," she replied.

He thanked her, gave Jenkins the description and returned to the American woman.

"When Lady Avice arrived at your hotel in Paris last Tuesday did you know Mr. Tony Spencer was her husband?"

"I sure did, Inspector," replied Mary de Groot, lapsing for once into her vernacular.

"Did you telegraph for her to come?"

"I did not. On the contrary she cabled me. Also she cabled my maid telling her to hide the English newspapers so that I should not get a shock."

"About this affair of the jewels being cleaned at Nice. How did Tony Spencer hear of this jeweler?"

A red flush swept over the woman's face and neck.

"Leslie Delmond gave him the address but told Tony not to mention his name in the matter for fear the ladies might imagine he was getting a commission out of the job. Of course Tony promised and, like the good-natured, honorable fool he is, kept the promise."

"Have you any idea who his companion was in the false bank-note arrest, Mrs. de Groot?"

She stared at the detective as if she doubted his sanity.

"Sakes alive! Have I any idea? I should say so."

Reynolds restrained a smile with difficulty. He was getting plain truth from this daughter of God's own country, and the novelty was refreshing.

"There has been so much concealment in this case, Mrs. de Groot, everybody trying to protect somebody else, that my way has been made very difficult. I shall be grateful if you will be frank and tell me what you know," he said tactfully.

The lady extended her bejeweled fingers.

"Well now, isn't that what I've come from Paris for? Judging by the newspapers you're all in an unholy mess through this damfool secrecy. The truth has to come out sooner or later. What do you want to know?"

The inspector repeated his question. "Who was arrested with Tony Spencer?" he asked.

"Valerie, of course."

"Valerie Baird," exclaimed the astonished detective.

"Fiddlesticks!" snapped the American. "Valerie's maiden name was Baird, but it isn't now, worse luck for her."

"What is it?' asked Reynolds, his pulse thumping with eagerness.

"Valerie Delmond. She is Leslie Delmond's widow."

The detective gazed at her, speechless. Never once had he dreamed of this. It explained a thousand things.

"They were married in Nice," Mrs. de Groot went on, pluckily reciting these painful reminiscences, "before I ever knew Delmond. She was a marvelous black and white artist and also did—what do you call it?—they draw with acid on metal."

"Etching," suggested the inspector, recovering a little from this series of surprises.

"Yes, etching, I never can remember that word. I didn't know her in Nice. None of the Warnham party met her, neither did any of us know Delmond was married." She sighed. "Might have saved me from making such a prize idiot of myself."

"But why did none of you meet her as Mrs. Delmond?"

"Because Delmond was at the studio most of the day and she never went near the place. She's a very shy, refined girl, who hates publicity. Poor child, she's having enough of it now, one way and another. And then, Delmond got more fun out of life posing as a bachelor."

"When did you learn of Delmond's marriage?" Reynolds questioned.

"Only when Valerie and Tony were arrested. Leslie had taken good care I shouldn't know before. He vanished at once. He could disguise himself remarkably, so it was easy for him. You see, Leslie Delmond was clever but a coward. When I first found out about the jewels being faked and wrote to Avice, she came to Paris and insisted on marrying Tony first of all, to prove her faith in him. He on his side made her promise to keep the marriage secret until he'd cleared his name. Have you got that straight?"

Reynolds smiled his assent.

"Right, on we go again," snapped Mrs. de Groot briskly. "Tony promptly swore he'd wring Delmond's neck if necessary to get those jewels back. I got angry then—I still loved that scamp, you see. Well, Tony found Delmond and thrashed him, threatening to kill him if the jewels or the money were not given back."

"But some of the money had been spent in paying the Earl of Brentshire's debts, I was told," put in the detective.

"Oh, you do know that much, do you, Inspector? His debts were about thirty thousand francs and Leslie Delmond, working in league with that Nice jeweler, must have cleared at least six hundred thousand francs on the faking of that jewelry. I can't do your crazy English arithmetic, but you can easily see that paying Lord Brentshire's debts didn't make much of a dent in their haul."

Reynolds worked out a calculation on a scrap of paper.

"They got nearly five thousand pounds and paid the Earl of Brentshire about two hundred and forty. And you didn't prosecute Delmond or Tony Spencer?"

"How could I when I cared for Delmond, and Tony was the husband of my best friend. No, I may be a vain and silly woman, but I'm at least half-way human. Besides Delmond had left me. I didn't know where he was, and Tony had only been a tool."

"Yes, I understand," Reynolds replied sympathetically. There was something very likeable in this frank woman. "Please explain to me about the bank-notes. I know nothing about that."

"You don't mean to say so, Inspector," and Mrs. de Groot laughed heartily. "But it's not your fault when they've all conspired to conceal things. I talked to Lady Warnham on the telephone from Dover last night and said I was coming to town to-day and that I meant to open my mouth."

Reynolds's lips twitched. "What did Lady Warnham reply?"

"She said, 'Come along and talk as much as you like. I can't and Avice won't, and soon we'll all be in jail together if this goes on.' She's a wise old lady, I'll tell you, Inspector. What was it you asked?"

"About the bank-notes," prompted Reynolds.

"Oh, yes. Well, Tony frightened Delmond, and at last Delmond said the jewels were pawned, but in a few days he'd give Tony the money to redeem them. It was a lie to begin with, for most of the jewels had been sold, not pawned. He told Tony to call in three days at an address he gave him, when the money and pawn-tickets would be handed to him. Delmond added that he might have to go off on a film job at a moment's notice."

"Very nicely arranged," put in Reynolds. "Delmond could slide out of view easily."

"Tony went to the address and found a girl he'd never seen before. It was Valerie, Delmond's wife, but Tony didn't know and she didn't tell him who she was. She gave him the packet but insisted she must go to the pawnshop with him—she seemed frightened, Tony said. They were both arrested there for having false money.

"Tony sent for me. He told me the story and made me swear not to let Avice know if he was convicted, but to get her back to England. Family honor and all that bunk. I tried everywhere to find Delmond, but it was no use."

"Tony Spencer got a year and the girl nine months," said the inspector.

"Yes. I met Valerie when she came out and made her stay with me. About a month ago she left me to go to London. I believe she'd met Delmond, or some man, and was worried about Laureen."

"Why should she be? Were they such close friends as all that?" asked Reynolds with interest.

"Friends! Why, listen—" She looked up and saw Laureen standing in the doorway. "I say, Laureen, you all have sewed up the facts of this case so tight that what this poor man doesn't know will never hurt him. Think of it! He's just asked me if you and Valerie were friends." Mrs. de Groot laughed heartily at the thought.

Laureen smiled rather pathetically as she walked into the room and stood before the inspector.

"Valerie is my sister; a very dearly loved sister, Inspector," she said.

"You told me you were an only child. You told Mr. Lansberg that also," the detective exploded in irritated tones.

Laureen shook her finger to and fro. "These were my exact words: 'My father and mother believed in a small but good family and I'm it,' " she repeated. "Valerie is my stepsister."

"Yes, those were your exact words. But they deceived me."

"I'm afraid I meant them to," she replied frankly. "You see my father died when I was a few months old and my mother married again very soon. Valerie was born when I was two and a half. We grew up together, went to the same school in Belgium and were only parted when my mother died. Then Valerie went to live with my stepfather, who had always disliked me, and I went on the stage. She came to stay with me at Nice, met Delmond and they were married very soon, greatly against my wish."

"Where were you when she was arrested?"

"In America. I knew nothing of it until my return, when Mrs. de Groot wrote and told me. She said Valerie didn't want to see me yet, fearing Delmond was watching me to find her. It seems incredible but Leslie Delmond loved Valerie, though he was so cruel to her and made her do things that put her in his power."

"Such as what?" Reynolds asked quickly.

The girl pressed her head with a nervous gesture. "Please, Inspector, don't make me say, here. I'm afraid you will know when you open that packet. You can't imagine the torture I'm suffering because of that."

Inspector Reynolds studied her for a moment. "Very well, Miss Laureen. I shouldn't worry too much if I were you. The man is dead," he said in gruff sympathy.

"But his malice is alive," she replied. "Think, if by my words I torture poor Valerie who has already suffered so much!"

"By the way, Miss Laureen, was Mr. Lansberg in Nice that winter?"

"For a day or two only. He was financing the film. One day I heard his yacht was in the harbor and that afternoon I was introduced to him by the manager. We exchanged a few words and I did not see him again until this revue started."

Reynolds turned to Mrs. de Groot.

"You know him, of course."

She raised her hands in surprise. "I know him?" she exclaimed. "Why Mr. Lansberg's a personage. No, I've never met him."

"May I go, please, Inspector?" Laureen asked.

"Certainly," he agreed.

At the door she paused, fidgeting restlessly with the handle. Then she said in a half-frightened whisper:

"Inspector, could you possibly come to the theater to-night? It's stupid of me, but I feel as if something—something horrible may happen."

"Nothing *shall* happen if I can prevent it, Miss Laureen," he assured her. "I will most certainly be there."

"Thank you. I'll have a box reserved for you," she promised.

# XXIX. A CONFESSION

LANSBERG rose from his desk to greet Reynolds as he entered the room that afternoon.

"Sit down, Inspector," he invited courteously. "I have quite a lot to tell you. Dr. Tempest insists on being present." His eyes twinkled. "He and I had a long talk after dinner last night and I think he wishes to protect my interests. I'm expecting him at any moment. Are there any preliminary questions you'd like to ask me?"

"Several," said the detective curtly. He was not going to be swerved from his purpose by this man's calm dignity, nor allow him to be unduly backed up by Dr. Tempest. The doctor was a good chap—didn't he owe his brother's life to the surgeon's prompt and generous action?—but inclined to be fussy over one's methods.

Boiled down, all he had learned this morning brought him no nearer the actual criminal. It merely eliminated certain suspicious characters and explained how and why they had been entangled in the case.

"How and where did you first meet Miss Laureen?" he asked.

"In Nice, when she was acting in the film I was financing. I called at the studios one afternoon, was introduced to her and didn't see her again until this year."

H'm, that agreed with what Laureen had said. Reynolds loved checking up statements.

"Did you meet a Mrs. de Groot then?"

Lansberg smiled. "No, I've not met her yet, but I have heard a lot about her from Lady Avice."

"Did you meet Delmond in Nice?"

"I have never met Delmond," Lansberg asserted.

"Lady Warnham and Lady Avice Garth?" Reynolds queried.

"I've met them many times, of course, in London. Never on the Riviera, which I dislike and rarely visit."

"Do you know Valerie?" Reynolds asked, with emphasis.

Lansberg's eyebrows lifted slightly. "No, Inspector, I do not. But I've read of your search for her in the newspapers this week."

"Tony Spencer. Do you know him?"

"No. But I remember hearing some one say that Dick Spencer had a twin brother whom one never saw nowadays."

"Thank you, Mr. Lansberg. Those points are settled."

The door was opened at that moment and Dr. Tempest came in. Reynolds looked at him anxiously and decided he seemed a shade better than at luncheon yesterday.

"First of all, Inspector," Lansberg said, rising and going toward his safe, "there is something here of which I fancy you have already heard. You had better learn its history now." He smiled humorously over his shoulder as he manipulated the lock and swung the heavy door open. He beckoned Reynolds to his side and pointed to the magnificent collection of jewels glistening on the shelves.

"These are the crown jewels of what was once a tiny kingdom in the Balkans. My eldest brother was the ruling prince. He died and his family was wiped out in the revolution that followed. It is now a republic.

"That," he pointed to the jewels, "is all that is left me of our former rank. I saved them from the wreck. It is quite a healthy, sane republic. Indeed, the president and I are the best of friends. I am godfather to his small son, for whom I am now taking up my old hobby of collecting butterflies. I send him cases of them from time to time."

"You dropped your title, sir?" questioned Reynolds rather deferentially.

"Long ago, and, as I told you, became a naturalized Englishman. But my interest in my old country is strong and I am now negotiating a treaty on its behalf with our government. This information is, of course, for you only and not for the newspapers. Two high officials from the republic were here on Tuesday to see me privately. I motored to a house near Tunbridge Well and met them, leaving Miss Laureen at the golf house for an hour. As you were probably told."

"That is so, sir," Reynolds replied. Most heartily he wished Lansberg had no connection with this murder case. Yet what about that gashed shirt and vest? And the knife in the safe which was later used to stab his brother? Why was Neron alarmed if his master had nothing to do with it?

And what was inside that packet he was half afraid to open? He decided to plunge boldly.

"Could there be any document of yours in the   envelope the mysterious woman brought you to take care of and reclaimed recently?" the detective asked.

"How could there be?" Lansberg replied. "It was brought to me sealed and was returned intact, of course."

Reynolds took it from his inner pocket.

"Is that the same one, Mr. Lansberg?"

Lansberg inspected it closely and handed it back to the detective.

"It appears to be of the same size and weight. But the one I guarded was in a plain envelop. This is addressed to Valerie Baird."

Reynolds tore off the outer cover, revealing a plain white envelop, slit open along its length.

"Yes, that looks like it. Only it's been opened since it left my possession."

The first paper the inspector took out was boldly headed "Lansberg." This must have been what Laureen glanced at and, being startled, replaced it, having no time to investigate.

"It seems to be a description of these jewels and your habits and characteristics." Reynolds thought for a minute. "I've a feeling this was tucked in by accident, a few days ago. Probably Delmond was in with a gang of crooks and, having been here disguised as a woman, he wrote out a description of what he'd seen when you opened your safe to get the packet."

"That's exhibit number one," remarked Lansberg. "Those jewels had better be sent to the bank strong-room, eh, Tempest?"

The inspector was deeply engrossed with a thin sheet of metal he had taken from the mysterious packet. It was finely and delicately etched. An engraved plate of a foreign bank-note! Folded round it was a brief letter to Delmond.

*Dear Leslie,*
*Here is what you asked me to do but I'm not sure it's right even if only for fun to win a bet as you say. I can't send you any money this week but will next, if I can.*
*Yours,*
*Valerie*

So here was the history of Valerie's fears! Delmond had got this and had told her afterward it would get her ten years' imprisonment if found. The poor child had been terrified knowing he had it. No wonder she was afraid, no wonder Laureen had concealed the packet.

Looking further he discovered Tony Spencer's and Avice Garth's marriage certificate, and folded in it Avice's note to Delmond. One or two old letters from Mrs. de Groot were there, but these he only glanced at. There was also a tiny clipping from a French newspaper dealing with the prosecution of Tony and Valerie.

The papers of recent date had evidently been slipped in the envelope after the owner had received it back from Lansberg. Probably to ensure all the valuable articles being kept together.

Reynolds put the packet away safely after showing Lansberg and Dr. Tempest the etching and Valerie's note.

Lansberg drew himself up stiffly, almost as though he were standing at attention. "And now, Inspector," he said slowly and emphatically, "we come to a more serious matter. Dr. Tempest has heard my story and absolutely disagrees with the action I have decided on. He insists on being present at this interview and I in turn insist that he shall be silent until I have spoken."

Dr. Tempest's eyes had something akin to agony in them as he gazed mutely at Lansberg.

"I have agreed under protest," he murmured.

Lansberg faced the detective. "Then, Inspector," he said calmly, "I wish to give myself up for the murder of Leslie Delmond."

The detective forced himself to appear as emotionless as the man who stood before him uttering those amazing words.

"You know I collect butterflies," Lansberg went on, "and realize that I have probably used chloroform to kill them. I have no proof and cannot expect you to believe that I had only a tiny phial of it in my possession last Sunday night. You have a list of my movements—with reservations. I dressed here, dined at my club and having ample time, thought I would walk part of the way to Mr. Spencer's studio."

"Yes, that is correct," Reynolds agreed.

A flicker of sadness crossed Lansberg's face. "For several months I have been deeply attracted to Miss Laureen, and last Sunday night I was looking forward to meeting her at that party. As I neared Beresford Street I suddenly decided to call and see if I might escort her. I walked up the stairs, scanning the doors to see which was her flat."

"You saw nobody loitering near the flats outside?" questioned Reynolds.

"No. I rang her bell, indeed rang twice, because I heard a woman's voice answering the telephone."

"Did you recognize it?" asked Reynolds quickly.

"Impossible through the door," replied Lansberg. "Then I rang a third time. A man—it was Delmond but I didn't know it then—opened the door and asked my business in so curious a fashion that I determined to go inside. He was obviously startled, and was furious at my visit. His first words staggered me. He shouted, 'So you've followed me, have you, you swine!' He sprang at me with a knife and slashed my clothes without hurting me. Then he seemed to go mad and I knew he meant murder. All the time he was shouting about Laureen. He had locked the dining-room door on the inside and was barring the other, brandishing the knife."

Lansberg paused a moment.

"Near me on a low table was a large bottle marked 'Chloroform,' with a handkerchief beside it. Suddenly the fear gripped me that he had attacked Laureen—that he had even already killed her. Unexpectedly my chance came. Delmond dropped a packet he was holding—I now believe it to be the one you have. He stooped down to gather up the papers, as if he had forgotten my presence. I got hold of the chloroform bottle, wrenched out the cork, swamped the handkerchief and sprang on the man's back, pressing the handkerchief over his face. He was quiet so quickly that I thought he was shamming. But as I pulled the wet cloth from his mouth he fell down, limp. I dragged him to the big chair and left him, expecting he would come round almost immediately."

"How long did you hold the handkerchief over his mouth?" questioned the detective.

"A thousand times I've asked myself that, these past days. I was too angry to think clearly. One minute he was struggling and the next still, it seemed to me. Nearly frantic with fear for Laureen I searched the flat. She was not there nor any one else. I gave one more look at Delmond and I will swear that he was breathing heavily when I went away.

"I left the chloroform bottle there, but brought away the knife and also this which I picked up." He took a tiny stone seal from the table and passed it to Reynolds.

"Then, to calm myself a little, I walked to my apartment, locked the knife in my safe, and went on to Victoria where Laureen's maid saw me get on a bus."

"You did not change your shirt at your flat?" the detective asked keenly.

Lansberg shook his head. "I didn't think of it. Only one thing was in my mind, that at all costs I must manage to see Laureen home in case that man was still there. That he was dead never occurred to me.

"When we entered one could smell chloroform, but she thought it was benzine Bertha might have used. I was longing to look in the dining-room but did not want to rouse her fears unduly, as you will easily understand."

"Do you remember closing the door of the flat after you, Mr. Lansberg?"

"That is what I cannot remember. Sometimes I think I must have left it unfastened in my agitation."

"Why didn't you call in the police?"

Lansberg raised his hand with that rare gesture of his. "And draw lurid attention to the woman I cared for!" he exclaimed. "It was quite obvious that Delmond, from his wild remarks, had known Laureen. Do you think I wished to drag some past episode into publicity?"

"You never thought of burglary as his object?" questioned Reynolds.

"Burglars don't behave in that fashion, I imagine. One had not much time for analysis but his visit seemed to be one of malice, not robbery, Inspector."

"How much chloroform was left in the bottle?" the inspector asked.

"I re-corked it after I had dragged the man to the chair and—to me—it seemed that scarcely any had gone. The bottle must have held a pint, and as nearly as I can remember it looked almost full."

"When you went into that room again at one in the morning and discovered Delmond there dead, was that bottle of chloroform still there?"

"No," said Lansberg positively. "I hunted around for it, but it was gone. And I'm certain Miss Laureen could not have taken it," he added eagerly.

Dr. Tempest opened a bag he had brought and lifted out half a dozen bottles of various sizes.

"What size was the bottle containing chloroform, Lansberg," he asked seriously.

Instantly Lansberg selected one and held it out. "I think that size exactly."

The doctor nodded toward Reynolds.

"That," he said, "is a surgery bottle. No chemist would dream of supplying such a quantity except to a medical man. You see my point, Inspector? The quantity Mr. Lansberg would get for killing his butterflies would be given him in this size." He touched a tiny bottle.

"Those small phials might have been emptied into the large one," argued the detective.

Dr. Tempest swept the idea aside. "But," he said, "Mr. Lansberg had never *seen* Delmond and knew nothing against him. My contention is that although every word Mr. Lansberg has uttered may be true, he *did* not kill Delmond. As to Delmond's rapid unconsciousness—at the post-mortem we found practically no food in the stomach, proving the man had not eaten for several hours and so would need less chloroform."

"That's a most important item, doctor. But possibly Mr. Lansberg poured more chloroform than he thought on the handkerchief."

The doctor lifted a carafe of water and carefully filled and corked the large bottle. Taking a handkerchief out of the bag he said:

"Mr. Lansberg, will you please reconstruct your actions of last Sunday night? Tip the bottle as many times as you think you did then and for the same length of time, and then press the handkerchief to my face."

He threw some papers on the floor a little distance from the desk, and stooped down. "I think," he went on, "this was Delmond's attitude, wasn't it? Please act as you did then."

The inspector watched with keen interest as Lansberg grasped the bottle, pulled out the cork, and tipped it three times on to the handkerchief. Making a quick stride he sprang on the doctor's stooping form and held the handkerchief to Tempest's mouth while the inspector counted the seconds.

Then Lansberg withdrew the handkerchief and laid it on the paper.

"I can't be positive," he said, "but it seemed about that length of time."

Reynolds nodded and regarded the bottle. Only a very little of the water had been used in Lansberg's demonstration.

Dr. Tempest rose to his feet.

"Absolutely impossible," he declared, "to have killed Delmond in that short time, Inspector, as I said before. And, *in any case*, remember Mr. Lansberg acted in self-defense. The whole thing lacks motive. Why should a man of Mr. Lansberg's wealth and position wish to murder an unknown film actor?"

"Why did you offer to give yourself up, Mr. Lansberg?" asked Reynolds.

"Because," replied he clearly, "the situation these past few days has been intolerable. I have been spied upon from morning until night, my rooms were entered by a trick last Tuesday afternoon and searched, and my safe was opened presumably by one of your men, Inspector. Miss Laureen's safety has been threatened and her health is at stake if this condition lasts. At first I kept silent believing some one else must have entered that flat, finished what I began, and afterward removed the chloroform bottle. But now I can bear no more. Frankness is infinitely better than this suspense, especially when it is damaging the reputation and strength of the girl I care for. That is my answer."

There was a fineness and sincerity in Lansberg's words that Reynolds did not miss. Added to that, he reflected, was the convincing statement of Dr. Tempest. Who was this other person who entered the flat after Lansberg had gone? A thought struck the detective.

"Could your servant, Neron, not have followed you and killed Delmond?" he asked.

"Impossible," said Lansberg emphatically. "I dined at my club after leaving here. Why should my servant have prowled about watching me? He would not have dared to do so. He had never seen Miss Laureen and did not know her address. No, Neron was afraid after your visit, and I told him roughly the outline of the case, explaining who you were. Don't blame him for a crime he certainly did not commit."

Reynolds summed up the points in his mind. Undoubtedly Delmond had answered Dick Spencer's telephone call in a woman's voice to prevent any suspicion arising of a strange man being there. Then Lansberg had rung the flat bell and Delmond, seeing him, imagined his disguise—as the woman receiving that packet—had been discovered, and he had been followed. He attacked Lansberg in sudden fury. Lansberg went out of the flat and some unknown person entered, and after murdering the unconscious Delmond took away the chloroform bottle.

Who was his assailant? Could it have been Valerie? Everybody else implicated in the case was accounted for on that night.

Then suddenly he remembered there was one other. Where was the man with the missing thumb whose fingerprints had been found on the dining table?

"Mr. Lansberg," Reynolds said firmly, "I have not sufficient evidence to prove that Leslie Delmond died by your hand."

# XXX, A SHOT IN THE THEATER

night, accompanied by Dr. Tempest whom he had invited.

"Laureen's in a highly nervous condition and if she collapses tonight, Doctor, you'd be mighty useful, knowing the cause as you do."

Throughout the first part of the revue, the detective's attention was occupied chiefly by the audience. From the box which Laureen had reserved, he scanned her closely when she first came on. She received a tremendous ovation and her vivacity seemed normal rather than forced.

When the curtain was rung down for the interval Reynolds strolled round the corridors, observing the people.

"Boxes full?" he asked the attendant.

"Two of the parties haven't come yet," was the answer. "That often happens. Especially with young gentlemen who've seen the show several times. They come in after the intermission usually."

Leaving the stage as the curtain fell, Laureen had pushed open the door of her dressing-room. There she saw a girl in black, heard an eager cry of "Laureen, my darling!" and felt arms enfold her.

"I can't believe it's you, Valerie! Oh, my dearest, how ill you look!" She drew her to the couch, holding on to her tightly. "Take off your hat and coat and tell me all about it. I needn't change for ten minutes. I'll send my dresser away."

Rapidly Valerie poured out the history of the past weeks, ending with her encounter of Mrs. de Groot at Dover.

"So you see I had to come back, Laureen. What will they do to me?" she asked pitifully.

Laureen hugged her sister protectingly.

"Nothing, my angel, except over my dead body. Sit there while I dress. I'm so afraid you'll vanish again. Think, darling," she said, stripping off her frock quickly and pulling on the garments needed for the next scene, "it will be like old times to-night. You shall sleep in my bed and we'll talk and talk. Oh, I'm so happy! And you soon will be, too, for at last you are free to marry the man you care for. Does he know you're here?"

"No," she replied firmly. "I won't meet him until this horrible affair has been cleared up. How could I allow his name to be clouded? I'll wait until Leslie Delmond's murderer is discovered."

As she had finished Inspector Reynolds tapped on the door and entered at Laureen's invitation.

"All right, Miss Laureen?" he questioned.

"Thank you, yes, Inspector. I was just a nervous fool, I suppose.

Oh," she laughed suddenly, "shut your eyes. I've a surprise for you."

The detective obeyed, amused at the spectacle of a Scotland Yard officer, intent on a murder case, being led with closed eyes across a revue actress's dressing-room!

"You can look now," Laureen allowed. "Guess who that is!"

Standing before him was a frail slender girl with soft fair hair. Her violet eyes gazed at him sadly but with no hint of fear. He didn't need Laureen's introduction to tell him her name, for she was undoubtedly the original of the snapshot in Delmond's attaché case.

"This is the inspector engaged on the case, Valerie," Laureen explained. "He probably hates me. I've been a mass of prevarication for your sake—until to-day."

"Don't hate Laureen, Inspector," pleaded Valerie. "Hate me if you like. I deserve it for my cowardice in running away. But my sister's the most wonderful being in the world to me."

"I don't hate either of you," said Reynolds. And meant it as he took Valerie's thin fingers in his own big hand.

"Probably you want to ask me hundreds of questions, Inspector. I promise to answer them truthfully," Valerie offered.

"I can only think of one urgent one at the moment. Other people have told me so much that I can trace all your movements, excepting this. Where were you on the night of the murder?"

"After church," Valerie replied, "I was walking in Beresford Street near Laureen's flat before going to my rooms when I saw a man whom I knew. Terrified I ran away and spent the night hidden in the bracken in Richmond Park. I've no proof to give you," she added helplessly. "Next morning, after some breakfast at Charing Cross station, I started to go to Laureen but was knocked down by a motor-car.

Reynolds was about to ask the name of the man who had frightened her when the call boy knocked for Laureen.

"Come, Val, quick. I'm not going to let you out of my sight. You can have a chair in the wings. It's against the rules, but the stage-manager will forgive me this once. Do come up here when the act's over, Inspector," she begged.

The second half was nearly finished when Laureen, her scene ended, darted over to Valerie who was sitting between the wings.

"Val, don't be frightened, dear. *He* is here, in a box immediately over Inspector Reynolds. What am I to do? I'm sure he means murder."

Valerie rose quickly.

"Take me round the other side where I can see him. He won't hurt me, Laureen."

With beating heart Valerie stood in the shadow looking up at the white face and blazing eyes of the man she feared. He was not looking at her. All his gaze was concentrated on Laureen, who was again on the stage for the finale.

Suddenly Valerie saw him raise his arm. Without hesitation she ran across the stage in full view of the audience, and putting herself in front of her sister, looked directly at him.

The man gave a hoarse cry, stared a moment and then slowly turned the glistening thing in his hand toward his own breast. There was a sharp report, and then the curtain descended rapidly.

Upstairs on the floor of the box Reynolds and Dr. Tempest bent over the man lying there.

"Dead?" questioned Reynolds.

"No, but he can't live many minutes."

An attendant brought brandy and the doctor swiftly administered it.

"It may help him to speak," he whispered to Reynolds.

The door opened quietly and Laureen and her sister crept in. Valerie bent over the man while Laureen stayed in the background.

The man's eyelids flickered and then as they opened he saw the face of the girl. "Valerie!" he murmured. "Valerie, you're safe now! I can die in peace. I did it all for you, my beloved girl."

"Quick, ask him if he was in your sister's flat and saw Delmond last Sunday night," urged the detective.

The girl asked the question gently.

"Yes, yes, I was there. I couldn't find those papers. No matter now. Delmond's dead and you're free. You have had all the suffering— Laureen all the money and pleasure. Your turn now, Valerie!"

He muttered inaudibly for a minute and then Reynolds drew the girl away.

"He's gone," said the detective softly. "Who was he?"

"My father," replied Valerie simply. "He had fits of madness at times. He worshiped me but was bitterly jealous of Laureen and her success, for my sake. He was a brilliant artist until that accident to his hand." She was trembling violently.

"Take her back to the dressing-room, Doctor," said Reynolds. "She'll faint in a minute. I shall be here some time."

As the door of the box closed behind them the inspector stooped over the dead man. Yes, undoubtedly this was the same type of pistol as that used in the attack on Lady Avice.

Suddenly he drew back. The pistol was near the dead man's left hand! Reynolds paused a moment, then pulled the right hand into view and gazed at it. Here, he reflected, his task obviously ended. The last link was complete. For this hand lacked a thumb!

## Other Resurrected Press books in Elaine Hamilton's *Inspector Reynolds of Scotland Yard* Series

*The Westminster Mystery  (1930)*
*Peril at Midnight  (1934)*
*Tragedy in the Dark  (1935)*
*The Casino Mystery  (1936)*
*Murder Before Tuesday  (1937)*

## Like us on Facebook to stay up-to-date on all of our latest releases: http://www.facebook.com/ResurrectedPress

# THE CLIFFORD AFFAIR
## BY A. E. FIELDING

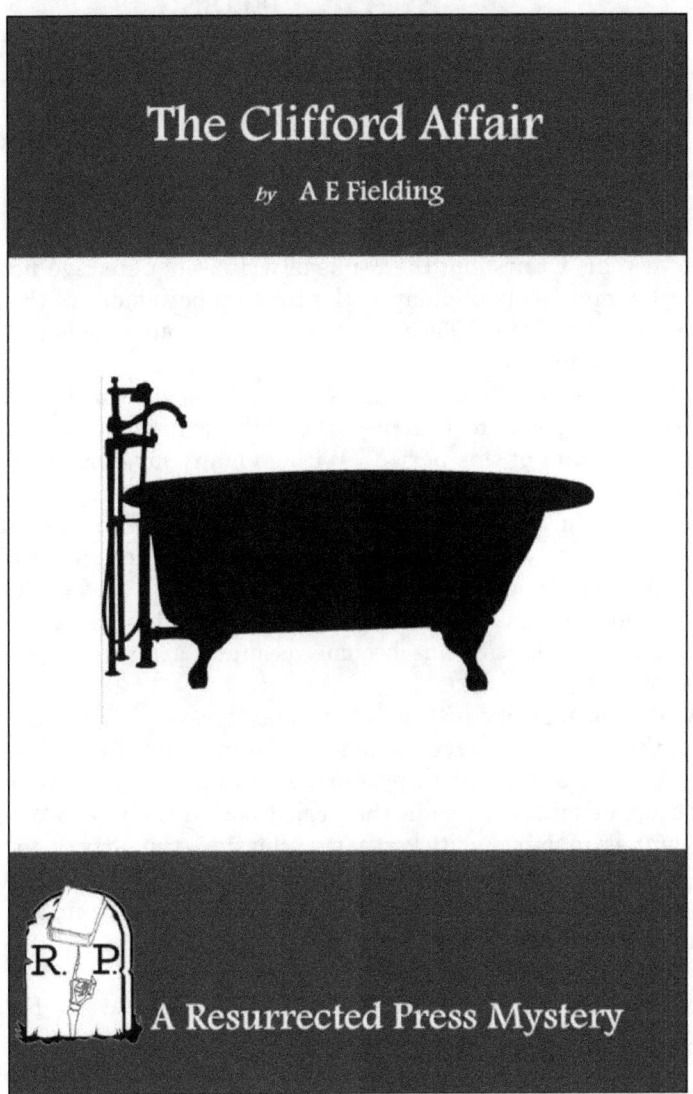

The Clifford Affair

*by* A E Fielding

R. P.

A Resurrected Press Mystery

ORIGINALLY PUBLISHED IN 1927

# The Clifford Affair
## By A. E. Fielding

The period between the First and Second World Wars has rightly been called the "Golden Age of British Mysteries." It was during this period that Agatha Christie, Dorothy L. Sayers, and Margery Allingham first turned their pens to crime. On the male side, the era saw such writers as Anthony Berkeley, John Dickson Carr, and Freeman Wills Crofts join the ranks of writers of detective fiction. The genre was immensely popular at the time on both sides of the Atlantic, and by the end of the 1930's one out of every four novels published in Britain was a mystery.

While Agatha Christie and a few of her peers have remained popular and in print to this day, the same cannot be said of some of the other authors of this period. With so many mysteries published in the period, it is inevitable that many of them would become obscure or worse, forgotten, often with no justification other than changing public tastes. The case of Archibald Fielding is one such, an author, who though popular enough to have a career spanning two decades and two dozen mysteries has become such a cipher that his, or as seems more likely, her real identity has become as much a mystery as the books themselves.

While the identity of the author may forever remain an unsolved puzzle, there are some facts which may be inferred from the texts. It is likely that the author had an upbringing and education typical of the British upper middle class in the period before the Great War with all that implies; a familiarity with the classics, the arts, and music, a working knowledge of French, an appreciation of the finer things in life. The author has also traveled abroad, primarily in the south of France, but probably to Belgium, Spain, and Italy as well, as portions of several of the books are set in those locales.

The books attributed to Archibald Fielding, A. E. Fielding, or Archibald E. Fielding, are quintessential Golden Age British mysteries. They include all the attributes, the country houses, the tangled webs of relationships, the somewhat feckless cast of characters who seem to have nothing better to do with themselves than to murder or be murdered. Their focus is on a middle class and upper class struggling to find themselves in the new realities of the post war era while still trying to live the lifestyle of the Edwardian era. Things are never as they seem, red herrings are distributed liberally through the pages as are the clues that will ultimately lead to the solution of "the puzzle," for the British mysteries of this period are centered on the puzzle element which both the reader and the detective must solve before the last page.

A majority of the Fielding mysteries involve the character of Chief Inspector Pointer. Unlike the eccentric Belgian Hercule Poirot, the flamboyant Lord Peter Wimsey, or the somewhat mysterious Albert Campion, Pointer is merely a competent, sometimes clever, occasionally intuitive policeman. And unlike, as with Inspector French in the stories of Freeman Wills Croft, the emphasis is on the mystery itself, not the process of detection.

Pointer is nearly as much of a mystery as the author. Very little of his personal life is revealed in the books. He is described as being vaguely of Scottish ancestry whose father was a coastguardman in Devon. In his younger days he played for the All-England football team. He is well read and educated, though his duties at Scotland Yard prevent him from enjoying those pursuits. His success as a detective depends on his willingness to "suspect everyone" and to not being tied to any one theory. He is fluent in French and familiar with that country. He is, at least in the first book, unmarried, sharing lodgings with a bookbinder named O'Connor, in much the manner of Holmes and Watson, though O'Connor disappears in the subsequent volumes.

While the early books fall plainly in the "humdrum" school with Pointer appearing almost immediately and much of story revolving on the business of tracking down various clues, the later novels are much more concerned with the lives of the characters surrounding the mystery. Pointer is much less center stage, often arriving instead at mid-book to clean up the pieces and insure that the guilty do not escape justice. It is, perhaps, this lack of focus on the detective, which has caused the works of Fielding to fade away while the likes of Poirot seem to attract the interest of each new generation.

One intriguing feature of the Pointer mysteries is that they all involve an unexpected twist at the end, wherein the mystery finally solved is not the mystery invoked at the beginning of the book. I leave it to the reader to judge whether Fielding is "playing by the rules" in this, but it does keep the books interesting up to the last chapter.

*The Clifford Affair* is the fourth mystery in the series. In it, Pointer finds himself with a headless corpse on his hands. This presents him with some serious difficulties. Not only is the identity of the victim in doubt, but the cause of death, which presumably involved the head, has vanished along with that portion of the body. To this, is added a possible diplomatic complication, as certain clues would seem to point to an infamous Basque Anarchist as either the victim, or possibly the murderer. This latter dimension to the plot shows that international terrorism is not just a recent phenomenon.

Despite their obscurity, the mysteries of Archibald Fielding, whoever he or she might have been, are well written, well crafted examples of the form, worthy of the interest of the fans of the genre. It is with pleasure, then, that Resurrected Press presents this new edition of *The Clifford Affair* and others in the series to its readers.

## About the Author

The identity of the author is as much a mystery as the plots of the novels. Two dozen novels were published from 1924 to 1944 as by Archibald Fielding, A. E. Fielding, or Archibald E. Fielding, yet the only clue as to the real author is a comment by the American publishers, H.C. Kinsey Co. that A. E. Fielding was in reality a "middle-aged English woman by the name of Dorothy Feilding whose peacetime address is Sheffield Terrace, Kensington, London, and who enjoys gardening." Research on the part of John Herrington has uncovered a person by that name living at 2 Sheffield Terrace from 1932-1936. She appears to have moved to Islington in 1937 after which she disappears. To complicate things, some have attributed the authorship to Lady Dorothy Mary Evelyn Moore nee Feilding (1889-1935), however, a grandson of Lady Dorothy has denied any family knowledge of such authorship. The archivist at Collins, the British publisher, reports that any records of A. Fielding were presumably lost during WWII. Birthdates have been given variously as 1884, 1889, and 1900. Unless new information comes to light, it would appear that the real authorship must remain a mystery.

Greg Fowlkes
Editor-In-Chief
Resurrected Press
www.ResurrectedPress.com

.

## Other Resurrected Press books in A. E. Fielding's *The Chief Inspector Pointer Mystery* Series

*The Eames-Erskine Case (1924)*
*The Charteris Mystery (1925)*
*The Footsteps that Stopped (1926)*
*The Clifford Affair (1927)*
*The Cluny Problem (1928)*
*The Net Around Joan Ingilby (1928)*
*The Murder at the Nook (1929)*
*The Mysterious Partner (1929)*
*The Craig Poisoning Mystery (1930)*
*The Wedding Chest Mystery (1930)*
*The Upfold Farm Mystery (1931)*
*Death of John Tait (1932)*
*The Westwood Mystery (1932)*
*The Tall House Mystery (1933)*
*The Cautley Conundrum (1934)*
*The Paper-Chase (1934)*
*The Case of the Missing Diary (1935)*
*Tragedy at Beechcroft (1935)*
*The Case of the Two Pearl Necklaces (1935)*
*Mystery at the Rectory (1936)*
*Black Cats Are Lucky (1937)*
*Scarecrow (1937)*
*Pointer to a Crime (1944)*

# THE CLIFFORD AFFAIR

## CHAPTER 1

The Assistant Commissioner of New Scotland Yard listened for a moment at one of his telephones, told the man at the other end, it happened to be Superintendent Maybrick of Hampstead, to hold on a moment, and sent one of his constable-clerks in search of Chief Inspector Pointer.

It was then just a little before nine of a Tuesday morning. A tall, lithe, lean young man came in with a step that suggested the kilt and the springing heather.

"Look here, Pointer. Suppose you hand over the reins of that case you're on to Clark. He can carry on all right now. Superintendent Maybrick of Hampstead wants help. Or rather, I think he needs it. He's just been called in to a horrid mess, a murder, in one of the flats in his district. From certain things he thinks it's an anarchist plot gone wrong, 'biter bit' sort of thing," Major Pelham said vaguely; "he's got into touch with the Foreign Office already. So by this time there's sure to be some F.O. man sprinting along to have a first look. Go and see what you think of it, will you? If it isn't a foreign spy job, then it should be a fine problem for you to solve. Here's the address." He handed a chit to the Chief Inspector, who left the room with his swift, unhurried stride that covered such an amazing amount of ground.

Pointer drove to the place mentioned—a large block of flats with a view over Hampstead Heath.

The head porter, after a keen glance at the Chief Inspector when the latter asked for "Mr. Maybrick," saluted, and took him up in the lift. The only information which he volunteered was that none of the residents had an idea of what had happened.

"These are all service flats, sir, and news gets around terrible fast unless one's very careful. As a rule illnesses are 'maternity cases' when possible. Deaths are 'measles' to account for the body being took away, but murder—the owners haven't given instructions about that. Not yet." The porter stopped the lift at the third floor, and stepped forward to ring the bell of a flat marked fourteen, which had no card in the little glass case beside the door. Pointer stopped him.

"A moment!" His eye ran over the door and mat and landing, as well as up and down the staircases. Then he nodded. The porter rang. The door opened an inch. The Superintendent inside, in plain clothes too, inspected them both cautiously, then he stood back and Pointer entered.

Maybrick saluted. He was one of Pointer's many policeman admirers. What a pity, he thought, that there was nothing here for the Chief Inspector to get his teeth into, those teeth that never let go.

"A moment!" Pointer said again, as he switched on the light and gave one swift glance around the square hall, a glance that nothing visible escaped. Then he nodded.

"Now lead the way."

"Shall I tell you first what I know, sir?"

"Not if any one from the Foreign Office is on the trail," Pointer said promptly. "They're quick workers. And I like to have my clues untouched, as far as may be."

"No one's come yet, sir. Not even the doctor. And the clues aren't ones that can be disarranged." Maybrick was about to expand into detail, but Pointer stopped him.

"Then this way, sir." Maybrick led down to a door at the farther end of a little passage. Pointer stepped into a tiled bathroom. In the bath-tub—it was not a pleasant sight—lay a man's body, stripped and headless.

"Where's his head?"

"Not on the premises, sir. Gone. Like his clothes. All gone."

Pointer knelt down in the doorway and looked sideways across the floor.

"Rubber-soled shoes. Man's heel marks. Apparently only one pair. What's that?" He advanced now, and bent to a tiny splash of something white on the tiles under the raised china bath.

"Powder they use to clean the tub, sir. Shall I tell you what the head porter"

Again Pointer stopped him.

"Has the body been touched by any one, as far as you know?"

"No, sir. Not the kind of thing to get touched by any sensible man."

"Have you photographed it?"

"Films are being developed at the station now."

Pointer lifted each of the hands in turn.

They were slender, beautiful hands, that looked as though they would be clever at whatever they did. Hard work had never been asked of them.

"Wore a ring on the middle finger of the right hand. Broad, thick ring. Signet ring very likely. Cigarette smoker. Gentleman certainly from the care of the whole body."

There were no marks of blood-stained hands either on the bath, or on the fitted basin beside it, or on any of the taps, nor finger prints of any kind.

Pointer stepped on into a bedroom opening out of the bath-room. Then he returned to Maybrick.

"We can wash our hands in the bedroom. The basin in there's not even been dusted. This one has been used."

A ring came at the door. Maybrick answered it. A small, quick-stepping, alert-eyed, gray-bearded man stepped into the flat. He was of the type to pass easily for English in England, French in France, Spanish, or Eastern, according to where he was met. "Many-tongued Tindall," a great international sleuth or sleuther of sleuths, was an amateur. A man of means attached to the Foreign Office, when he was not on loan to the Home Office. In manner he was very quiet, in speech very direct.

"I've come to see if the dead man's one of our birds," he said, after shaking hands with Pointer. "But you here?" He eyed the Chief Inspector with mock distrust. "No poaching, you know!"

For a second Tindall too stood looking about him with swift, piercing glances.

"Now for the story"—he turned to the Superintendent. First eyes, then ears, was Pointer's way. But Tindall was as high in his branch as Pointer was in the C.I.D., and was, moreover, a much older man. So Maybrick led them into the drawing-room, where the dust lay thick, and where the blinds still shut out the daylight.

The story, as known to Maybrick, was exceedingly simple. The flat belonged to a Mr. Marshall, a senior clerk at Lloyds, who, as usual, wished to let it furnished while he was away on a four weeks' holiday. He had left last Thursday. On Friday, about six, a man had presented himself to the head porter with a view card from the house agents, which gave his name as a Monsieur Tourcoin. The flat was shown him, and a little later the head porter was informed over the telephone by the agents that Mr. Tourcoin had taken the flat for a friend, a Captain Brown. Captain Brown would "take possession" on Tuesday or Wednesday.

On Monday evening something went wrong with the lock of an upstairs flat. The porter thought it a good opportunity, when the locksmith arrived this morning, to have him run his eye over the front door of Number Fourteen as well. Mr. Marshall had complained of its not always catching properly when hastily shut. He also remembered a difficulty with Marshall's bathroom bolt, and took the man in there first. He had his own pass-key, of course.

"They didn't stay to look at any bolts," Maybrick said dryly. "Nasty sight that body in there. They rushed to the telephone and called us in."

"What body in where?" Tindall asked impatiently. He was taken to see it. His face paled as he looked carefully at it and at the room.

"Horrible!" he muttered. "Horrible!"

He turned to Maybrick.

"What made you 'phone to us—made you think the crime political?"

"This, sir." Maybrick passed into a sitting-room, which, like the bedroom, opened out of the bathroom. He pointed to a newspaper on the table. It was a *Times* of Friday, heavily scored at a few passages. Maybrick pointed to these. Tindall read aloud:—

"*Anti-royalist plot suspected in Madrid.* I see he's underscored that '*suspected.*' What's this next? *King Alfonso's yacht Esmeralda to be ready by a certain date.* A question mark is pencilled beside the date. Indeed! Indeed! And here's something about King Boris's coming trip to Sofia heavily marked at the side. Except for that last, the items are only Spanish. . . ." Tindall perched on a chair in a way that suggested flight rather than rest.

"Man's clothes missing. . . . Papers in them gone too, of course. . . . Head taken away. . . . Identity to be concealed, or— Anything else made you think the murder political beyond the marked paper, Superintendent?"

"These." Maybrick lifted up the waste-paper basket. "I screwed them up as nearly as possible as I found them. They're funny reading together with those bits in the paper and that dead body!"

In the basket lay what looked like two crinkly eggs. They were wads of paper that had been crushed into little balls. Opened out, they showed as two sheets of plain letter-paper, headed with the address of the flat. On each were some lines of writing in a pointed, very sloping, foreign hand. The first ran:—

"You have betrayed the change in the crew of the *Esmeralda*. But I give you one chance to explain. Come here to-night and clear yourself if you can. If not—"

The rest of the sheet was blank. Apparently this draft had not pleased the writer. It had been screwed up and tossed away. The second was a complete note. It ran:—

"You are a traitor, but I give you one more chance to explain why you have not carried out the orders I gave you at *Iguski Aide*. Take it. Or it will be the end. Come to this address tonight. If you do not come you know the penalty. Expect it without mercy."

The last two sentences had been scratched out. There was no signature, but a little drawing of the outline of a house with a V inside.

"That scratched out bit about the penalty is why he copied out the note and threw this away," Maybrick explained like a showman.

Tindall's eyes were shining. He stroked his beard with a hand that quivered a little.

"These settle it." He spoke calmly but with the calm of one who forces a layer of composure over a seething mass of red-hot feeling.

"It *was* a political crime! Or an act of justice, if you will."

"You know what that signature stands for?" The Chief Inspector's tone made the remark a statement, not a question.

"The V within the outline of a house? Etcheverrey, Pointer. Yes. Etcheverrey, the great anarchist. Or rather anti-royalist agitator."

Pointer said nothing. Maybrick gave a cluck of delighted amazement. The police of every country knew, and were on the hunt for that name, that man.

"That's his secret signature," Tindall went on. "Only used to his own men. Only known to us at the F.O. And *Iguski Aide!*—'Sunny Corner'! That's Etcheverrey's well-hidden Basque refuge, deep in the heart of some Pyrenees ravine, not yet located. The mere name is only known to a chosen and picked few among his followers. We at the F.O. have only just—only *just* learnt it."

"He's French, isn't he?" Maybrick asked.

"Officially, yes. But there's not a drop of French blood in his veins. Basque father. Catalan mother. Speaks all languages. Brains of the devil. And up till now his luck."

"Do you think Etcheverrey's the killer, or the killed here, sir?" Maybrick asked again.

"The killed. The dead man," Tindall said, after a moment's deep thought. "Etcheverrey would have taken those scraps of paper away. His slayer is not identified by them. I think that the tables were turned on the Basque for the first —and last—time in his life, by the man he summoned here. And I can make a good guess at that man's name. You know my slogan." He turned to Pointer. "What the brain can't see, the eyes can't either. Eyes won't solve this problem. Not even yours. Now what has cost Etcheverrey his head, literally is, I think, his last break."

"His attempt on the Shah of Persia?" Maybrick knew every one of Etcheverrey's unsuccessful efforts by heart. "Pretty near thing for the Shah!"

"And for Etcheverrey," Tindall threw in grimly. "He was all but caught. As it was, they got a good view of him. The only time he's been really seen. And since then there's a fine price on his head at Ispahan. On the real, solid head. Duly delivered. That's why the descriptions we get from there are so vague. All we know of his appearance is that he has unusually small feet, and really beautiful hands."

"First thing I noticed about the corpse." Maybrick was sorting his notes. "Here it is. Par seven."

"Yes," Tindall was talking half under his breath, "Mirza Khan is over here, we know. He's the Shah's secret agent. It's his head or Etcheverrey's, I understand. We know that Etcheverrey is in London again. Sir Edward Clifford rather inclines to the belief that he's been here for years, carefully hidden in some commonplace identity, and that he only leaves London for some swift flight and one of his lightning efforts, and then comes back again and takes up his seemingly everyday existence. I don't agree with him, but that's Sir Edward's view."

Sir Edward Clifford was Permanent Under Secretary of State for Foreign Affairs.

"Every man jack of us has been living on a volcano, with the King of Spain on his way here next month." Maybrick drew a deep breath. "Etcheverrey nearly got him in Spain last year," Tindall went on, "just as he had a hard try for our Prince of Wales in South America." He was examining the room carefully as he talked. There was little to discover. A smallish, still damp splotch of blood on the thick carpet near a little table on which stood a reading-lamp. A few drops of blood had dried on the wooden edge of the table. Smaller ones yet were found on the parchment lamp-shade, and a hint of a trickle down one leg of the arm-chair standing near.

"There's been no struggle?" Tindall looked at Pointer.

"No sign of any," Pointer said cautiously.

"Just so. Yet the man summoned by such a letter as that would have been on the alert and would have struggled. Etcheverrey, on the other hand, would not dream that the tables could be turned on him. He was either shot, or more probably slogged on the head. Dragged to the tub, beheaded, and the head's now on its way to distant Ispahan in the care of that good old hater, Mirza Khan. But all that's for me to find out."

"Well, sir," Maybrick slipped a band over his bulging note-book, "as you're quite sure that the murder was political, I hand it over to you."

The Superintendent was aware that he had done very well. But he knew when he was out of his depth. Nor had he any intention of wasting his time over a case of which the honours would all go to the Foreign Office. They had their own men. It was all very well for the Chief Inspector, who had already, young though he was, risen so high, but he, Maybrick, had more paying matters from the point of view of promotion waiting for him at his police station. And so with a salute, he passed from the scene—to his never dying regret.

"Now for the porters," Tindall continued, when the two were alone. They learnt nothing which could explain the crime itself from them, though they gained a clear idea of how the flat could have been entered and left by any one unobserved. The building had several lifts, the corner ones being automatic and worked by the residents. There were many staircases. There was a restaurant on the ground floor open to the public. There were billiard rooms and reading rooms.

The estate agent for whom they telephoned repeated in fuller detail what Maybrick had already told them about the taking of the flat. Monsieur Tourcoin had paid for the four weeks in twenty-four one-pound notes, and the transaction had been completed on the spot.

"No references asked for?"

"Not in a case of this kind. A furnished flat let for a month. The porters here keep their eyes open. And undesirable people would be asked to leave at once. We find that simpler and better than bothering with references," the house-agent explained.

"Now as to this Mr. Marshall"

"We know all about Mr. Marshall. Our firm has known him and his parents, they lived in one of our houses, for twenty years. Just as we've known the head porter here about that long. There's nothing wrong with Mr. Marshall, I'll go bail, any more than there is with Soulyby, the head porter."

"How did this Mr. Tourcoin learn of the flat?" Pointer asked. . .

"Saw our advertisement in the paper, I suppose."

"When was it advertised?"

"Friday morning for the first time."

"And the paper?"

"*The Times.*"

"And he spoke broken English," Tindall murmured.

The agent laughed. "Rather!" He gave them a very good copy of the man's accent.

"On leaving he nipped into a taxi which some one was just paying off, and called to the chauffeur. 'To the station of Charing Cross. Arrest yourself there for one little minute while I learn what time train for Paris he start.' The driver winked, and said he'd arrest himself all right if need be."

"What clothes was the man wearing?" Pointer asked.

"Motor cap—he apologised very civilly for keeping it on, but he had a bad attack of head neuralgia—big brown and orange check motoring coat. That's all I remember."

"Young man?"

The agent thought so, but as he had seen many men yesterday afternoon he could not be quite sure. The whole affair was so small compared with most of their business that he had not paid much attention.

"Do you remember his hands, when he signed those papers," Pointer went on, "were they large hands?"

The estate agent could not remember anything about them. More details of the conversation were asked, and as far as possible, given. Then the agent took his leave—a very agitated leave.

The head porter had not noticed the appearance of the M. Tourcoin to whom he had shown the flat, except that the man wore a motoring ulster of orange and brown tweed, and a brown silk scarf. He had an impression of a young man, but as he had already on Friday afternoon shown the flat to several friends of Mr. Marshall's, he could not even be sure of that. .

The man had barely glanced over the flat.

"I never thought he meant what he said about taking it, but within half an hour the agents phoned up to me that the flat was gone. Taken by the monseer for a month. As to seeing him again—not unless that's him in there. But the chap I showed the flat to, looked a bigger chap. Bigger and brawnier, though I never saw his face. Not to see it."

"Was he smoking?" Pointer asked.

"Yes, sir. Briarwood pipe. One of these new comfort pipes."

"What kind of tobacco? Any kind you knew?"

"Yes, sir." It was a kind that the head porter particularly liked when he could afford it. A well-known British make. "I says to myself," the man went on, "France is all very well for wines, but when it comes to pipes and baccy—there's nothing like us!"

"Umph," Tindall murmured, when the two were alone. "Tourcoin takes the flat for a Captain Brown. He or this captain Brown can be seen; in it therefore. If need be. One of the two is Etcheverrey. Almost certainly he would be Brown. The Unseen. Now is Tourcoin the man to whom the summoning letters were sent? Is he the man who killed Etcheverrey? Is he, in fact, Mirza Khan, who speaks French—and English too for that matter—like a Frenchman?" There was a short silence broken by the Chief Inspector, who had been standing looking down at the toes of his shoes, hands loosely clasped behind him. He looked up now.

"Those papers found in the basket"—he spoke thoughtfully—"are they in Etcheverrey's writing?"

"He had some thirty different kinds of writing."

"And on the blotter," Pointer went on musingly, "there are no marks except from the two notes we found torn up. . . ."

"None. Why should there be?" Tindall asked, with a faint smile. "You police always want so much for your money."

There was another pause. Tindall eyed Pointer whimsically. Pointer looked back at him with his tranquil, steady gaze. The detective officer had fine dark gray eyes, pleasant, though at times rather enigmatic in expression.

"To stake the effect of a political crime would be a capital red herring, wouldn't it, to drag across the trail of a private murder."

Tindall smiled still more. A smile of real amusement at the doubt on his own reading of the case from a man young enough to be his son.

"We're like two Harley Street specialists, Pointer," he said good-humouredly, "each reading a case according to his own special lines. I say heart. You say liver. You're welcome to treat the case for liver, of course. But it's a heart case. Believe me, it's heart. In other words, I've been studying Etcheverrey so long that I have no hesitation in saying that this murder belongs to me. Don't waste your valuable time in hunting for this poor chap's head. I see that search being organised already."

Pointer laughed a little. Tindall was right. He was already charting his course.

"It's on its way to distant Ispahan," Tindall continued. "Pity Mirza Khan has such a start. Well, he knows my methods. They're lazy, compared with yours, but they're quick."

"They often lead to splendid results," Pointer said honestly. In what might be called society crimes, thefts, stolen letters, the finer shade of blackmail, Tindall had done wonders, besides winning many a triumph in his own field—the political field.

"I leave the details of the flat to you." Tindall despised hunting for clues. "The exact spot where the murder was committed . . . which way the man faced . . . and so on."

Pointer nodded, let him out of the flat, telephoned to Scotland Yard for their expert locksmith, and then rang for the head porter. That worthy was asked to institute a sort of house-clearing. Fortunately he was at one with the Scotland Yard officer in wanting to make sure that the missing head was not hidden somewhere on any premises for which he was responsible.

"I'll see to my part of it. Every nook shall be turned out. Every cupboard moved, or I'll know the reason why," Soulyby promised, "and every parcel opened."

"As soon as the doctor has examined the body we shall have a rough idea of about what time the murder was committed. As it is, we know that it must have taken place between seven on Friday evening, and eight this morning. Ask cautiously about whether any one was seen coming into, or going out of, this flat during that time."

Pointer dismissed him and telephoned to Lloyds. Marshall had been with them for fifteen years, he learnt. Came straight from London

University. His present address was Bastia in Corsica. But as he had spoken of mules and guides. . . . Yes, the man answering the telephone was a friend of his and quite willing to act as his reference if necessary. The firm would act as another. But he believed the flat was taken. The inquiry was about Marshall's furnished flat, of course?

"Just so," Pointer murmured, as he turned away. "Of course!"

He now began his own patient investigations. The bathtubs, he had learnt, were cleaned with Sapolio. The little smear of white under this one seemed to him to be plaster. He scraped it into a stoppered bottle and labelled it before putting it into his attache case. Then he bent over some marks on the tiled floor—marks such as a dull lead pencil might make if it had been rubbed with a broad, circular motion over the spot. Pointer decided that a tin had been placed there, and been pressed hard down while it was moved round and round.

Then he turned his attention to the fitted basin beside the bath. The taps had been turned off and on with a towel he thought. Unfortunately the hall porter could not say, nor could the housekeeper, how many towels had been left in the warm cupboard just by the basin. Pointer looked about him for a pail. But failing that, he took a bronze jar from the living-room and set it beneath the basin. With a spanner he unscrewed the trap in the outflow pipe, and let the contents run into his receptacle. A thickish, reddish mixture came out. Ammonia told him that the reddish colour was blood, the whitish part he took to be more plaster. It looked to him as though the murderer or murderers had washed their hands here. He bottled some of this mixture too, and turned away after replacing the fixture. He started on the bedroom. Here he found nothing except proofs that the room had not been used last night. He passed on to the sitting-room. At that moment the doctor arrived.

"Going to have your work cut out this time, Chief Inspector," he 'grunted. "Even you must be up a tree with this body."

"Any help to give me?"

"The man was probably about forty. Good condition. Nails show he's had no operations, is no victim of any chronic disease. A gentleman, I take it."

"And the head was severed?"

"With two or three hard, downward blows." He gave some medical details. "As to whether the man was dead or alive first—can't be sure till I've examined the lungs, but probably dead."

"Had the man who cut off the head any knowledge of anatomy?"

"None whatever. A sixteenth of an inch lower would have made the job half as easy again. Tremendous violence was used. Must have been a strong chap, and used something on which he got a good purchase which had a very firm edge."

"How long would it have taken, do you think?"

"To cut off the head?" The doctor meditated. "About fifteen minutes, I should say."

"And the death occurred, at a rough guess?"

"Some time last night, I should judge. That cut's about twelve hours old. Certainly not more."

He left at that, and Pointer went on with his work. There were no signs of any bullet having entered a wall or piece of furniture. Nor did the man seem to have been shot in a line with any of the windows, supposing him to have been shot—as Pointer did, partly from the size of the blood stain, chiefly from the fact that the chair down which a rivulet of blood had run was the only one in the room that had a very high, spreading back. It was the last kind of a chair to choose had a blow been intended.

Feeling the carpet, going by the stain, Pointer replaced the chair as it had probably stood. The bedroom door was to one side and a little behind it—an ideal position for a shot. This bedroom door had odd pin-marks in the wood near the handle, two on one side, two on the other, about the same distance apart.

Pointer finally decided that a strip of some thin but strong material such as tape had been fastened with drawing pins taut across the tongue, so as to prevent the rather noisy latch from acting, and let the door be opened by a touch, though it might looked closed.

He drew the curtains and switched on the lights. The side of the door that interested him was then thrown into deep shadow by a Chinese lacquer cabinet. So that, provided that the strip had been white, for the door was white, it might pass undetected by a casual glance, or by a short-sighted person. Pointer thought this last idea very probable. It explained the otherwise venturesome silencing of the door, it was borne out by the position of the reading-lamp that had been drawn to the extreme edge of the little table, and close against the left side of the chair.

Pointer stared at the pin marks. To him they were a very odd detail, one that was quite out of keeping with the rest of the crime as known so far. Primarily they showed that the man who had been murdered was evidently not hard of hearing, since they spelled care that no snap of the catch could be heard. But they meant more than that. Those pin-pricks meant a quick job. Just as they showed that probably there had been no sounds—music, talk—during which the cautious opening of the door could pass unnoticed. It looked as though the victim had been alone. But alone or not. Etcheverrey must be always on the alert, ever suspicious. A man wanted by the police of all the world, a man with a price on his head, a man who had never yet been caught, would not have let any door pass uninvestigated, let alone

one that stood half in shadow. Incongruous in any case, the tape seemed to Pointer doubly so in connection with the much sought-for, wily Basque.

It came to this, he thought, if Etcheverrey had been the man in the flat, he could have taken sufficient time to silence that door in some better way than by means of a hastily fastened-on strip. If the man was not Etcheverrey, then the anarchist would have noticed it.

A search found a bath mat in a hall cupboard. Where, apparently, a loop of tape had been sewn on, now only an end dangled; a roughly cut-off end, cut with a knife, not scissors. The piece that remained was the width indicated by the pin pricks. So the murderer had not come provided with tape. He found a few drawing-pins in a drawer which left just such marks as those on the door. Pointer again tested each object in the room. But still only the carpet, the chair, the table edge, and the lamp-shade showed marks of blood. On none of these, moreover, had there been any effort to clean away the marks. As for the crumpled papers in the waste-paper basket, of which, each promising the other photographic copy, Tindall had kept one, and Pointer one, the Chief Inspector found a few more sheets in a drawer. It looked as though they had been left there by Marshall. The writing had been done with a pointed fountain pen, which, like the ink—Pointer intended to have the latter tested at the Yard—seemed of quite an ordinary kind.

The lock expert arrived from the Yard at this point. A close scrutiny of the Yale lock now taken off the front door told him that though it was old and badly in need of new springs—failing entirely to catch now and then—yet it had not been forced, or picked, or opened with any other but its own rightful key. The house agent had said that he had handed Marshall's two keys to Monsieur Tourcoin.

The ambulance arrived and the body was taken away. Pointer went back to the bath and scrutinised the bottom. With what had those two deep gashes been made? The flat had no kitchen. No suitable knife or weapon hung on any of its walls.

# CHAPTER 2

Pointer strolled down all the stairs and let himself up and down in all the lifts. Finally he stopped beside a couple of workmen who were doing some plastering on the ground floor, near the foot of the stairs that led up to Number Fourteen. He had noticed the bags and the tools when he arrived just now.

"I borrowed some of your plaster last night," he said pleasantly, "how much do I owe you for what I used?"

"That's all right, sir," one of the men said civilly, "me and my mate was just saying that one of the porters must have done it. Quarter of a bag, wasn't it, sir. If you like to call it a shilling, that'll be all right."

Pointer liked a half-crown better, and so apparently did the men.

"Hope I cleaned the spade off all right," Pointer chatted on, lighting a cigarette. A cigarette which he took care not to inhale.

"Lord, sir, there wasn't no call to clean it that-away! Staggered Jim here it did to see it cleaned up. We only uses it for mixin'. Why, you sharpened the thing, didn't you?"

"No. Not beyond cleaning it." Pointer's cigarette was in his hand. He flicked its ash over the handle and stood lookingdown at it while talking. The ash, "finger-print cigarette" ash, showed no marks except those of a gloved hand. The workmen had not touched it. So some one had scraped it and cleaned it since they had used it last.

And, according to the men, some one had sharpened it as certainly was quite sharp enough now to have done what Pointer believed it had done. A couple of blows from it would account for the marks on the bottom of the tub. The murderer must have found his grisly task lightened unexpectedly by the implements left in the building. Or had "Tourcoin" noticed them, and laid his plan accordingly?

"I think I put everything back as it was," he said again; "messy work, plastering. When you aren't used to it. Miss anything else?"

"Nothing, sir."

But Pointer seemed still uncertain.

"Let me see . . . didn't I take a tin?" He was thinking of the marks on the bathroom tiles.

"That old tin isn't no loss, sir. You're more than welcome to it. We found it on the dust-bin, and was going to throw it out again when we was finished."

"Still," Pointer reminded them, "a tin comes in handy, I expect. What size is it? I borrowed another from one of the porters."

"Seven pound biscuit tin, sir. Stove in a bit at one side. It comes in handy for plaster we've sieved and don't want to use immediate, as you say, sir. But there's no hurry!"

"I'll send it down. Did I take its lid too?" he asked, peering about him.

He was told that he must have, as the lid was kept on the box.

Pointer tipped them, "in case the tin shouldn't turn up," and went slowly out of the building, an hour after he had first entered it.

If Tindall was right, and the body found was that of Etcheverrey, then, as far as he was concerned, the case was over. Some Special Branch man at the Yard would be told off to assist the Foreign Office, and Pointer would take up another tangle. But was it Etcheverrey? Was it "political" at all?

Very great care had been taken to dispose of all personal effects. Nothing but those scraps of paper in the basket had been left to tell who the man was. And, supposing the scraps of paper to have been faked, then no clew whatever had been left. For the flat was a furnished flat, shedding no light on the character of its present occupier. As far as identity went, if the papers in the basket were what the Force calls "offers," a trail laid to deceive, then it was as if the police had found a body stripped, and without a head, lying in an empty room.

Each great case, and Pointer nowadays was concerned only with great cases, groups its facts in such a different way from any other, that it becomes an entirely new problem. Pointer had never had one like this before, where all the usual means of identification of murdered man and missile used had been taken away. Of course Tindall might be right. Probably he was. But supposing he were not, how the dickens was he, Pointer, to find out who the man had been? And above all, who the murderer had been? Somewhere there was a weak spot in the crime. There always was. There always would be. Where was it in this case?

The detective officer's every nerve tautened at the idea of a murderer escaping. Pointer never saw his work as a game of brains against brains, where, provided only that the one move was cleverer than the other, it ought to win. He was a soldier, fighting a ceaseless battle where no quarter could be asked or given. The battle of light against darkness. Right against Wrong. If the other side won, it would be all up with the world. Pointer had never failed the side of justice yet. He would not fail it now, if he could help it.

But could he help it? Tindall was working at the case from his end. Pointer was not sure that he wanted to follow the other's track. He must make his own path therefore. If Tindall were right, the Chief

Inspector's road and that of the F.O. man would meet in due course, like the two ends of a well-dug tunnel.

He went up to his rooms at Scotland Yard and did some telephoning. By that time the analyst's report on the bottles which had been sent in was ready. One contained nothing but plaster mixed with water. The plaster was a very coarse kind used by plumbers for certain face-work. The other contained the same plaster, some water, and a mixture of blood.

Pointer walked up and down his room. He was not the Chief Inspector now, but a man who had committed a murder; a man to whom it was absolutely vital that the corpse should not be recognised, or that the weapon used should not be identified. Pointer had an open mind as to which of the two reasons compelled the taking away of the head. The clothes might have been taken for the purpose of confusing the issue.

"Yes," he murmured to himself, "I've put the head in a biscuit tin, mixed and poured in plaster to keep it from rolling around, and now what?"

In the absence of all known hiding-places, he finally, after a short chat over the wire with the Home Office, sent a coded message to every post office throughout the United Kingdom that all wrongly-addressed or uncalled-for parcels were to be reported to him at once. He thought it very possible that the murdered man's clothes, and the towels used by his murderer, had been made into small, convenient parcels, and sent to various fictitious names and non-existent streets in some home-town. Abroad would be out of the question.

All omnibus headquarters, taxi stands, garages, and railway stations were warned to keep an eye out for similar but unmarked parcels which either had been left in vehicles some time last night or might be left in the near future.

Similar instructions reached the L.C.C. dustmen and all parcel deposit offices. The river police were not forgotten. They had found nothing so far which could interest Pointer, but they promised to be even more on the alert than usual, if possible. Then he telephoned to the police surgeon who had first seen the body. He learnt that nothing had been found to explain the cause of death. There were no signs of a struggle. Death had been absolutely instantaneous. The doctor thought that a bullet through the head would account for the facts. "But, of course, as Mr. Tindall suggests, a blow might be equally swift." At any rate, the head had been certainly severed after death. But not long after it. The death itself had taken place somewhere around midnight on Monday night. Pointer put down the telephone and went to the mortuary chapel, a grimly sanitary place.

The finger prints had already been taken, and definitely not identified at Scotland Yard, as those of any known criminal.

Flashed by wireless photographs to the continent, the same answer had come from each capital in turn. So the body was still nameless. And as long as it remained so, the murderer was safe.

Pointer looked the body over very carefully yet once again. Especially the beautifully shaped hands. Hands that in life must surely have done many things well. In whose life? What things had they done?

As he studied them, he remembered their quick examination by the doctor. He knew that on the arrival of an unconscious patient at any hospital, the medical men run their eyes over the nails for any trace of recent operations, illnesses, chronic complaints, or even nerve shocks. Pointer, calling in a constable to help him, scraped the inside of each well-kept nail with his penknife on to a small glass slide. Having carefully covered and marked each slide, he took them back with him to the Yard. There the slides were examined. The result was handed to him almost immediately.

Both hands showed fluff of white paper made from esparto grass of a kind that is usually only sold for very superior typewriting purposes. One nail had lightly scraped a sheet of carbon paper. One—the first of the right hand—showed traces of sugar.

In other words, the dead man was almost certainly a writer, or a typist. But probably a writer who was only in occasional contact with sheets of carbon paper. He might be a secretary. He might be a clerk. But the nails of the feet showed that he had last worn black socks of a most expensive silk. That suggested not a clerk. The sugar on the right hand suggested an investigating finger among lumps in the sugar bowl, which in its turn suggested the free and easy ways of a man's own home. Probably his after-dinner coffee. No china had been used in the flat where the body was found. No sugar-basin filled there. The complete picture as filled in by the police surgeon's and the analyst's reports and Pointer's own reading of the room in which he believed the murder to have taken place, was that of a well-to-do author, possibly a journalist, one used to sudden alarms, who, after his dinner at home, had gone out unsuspectingly to meet his terrible death. A writer of about forty years of age, in good health and circumstances. Not blind, for he had probably drawn that reading lamp towards him, but very likely short-sighted, for he had drawn it close. Not deaf, as the muffled door showed.

Pointer took a turn around his room. It was a step forward. But it looked like being the last step for the moment. Unless— Pointer stared at his shoe-tips. Then he went back to the mortuary chapel.

There was a tiny scar on the sole of one foot, such as might clinch an identification but not suggest one. He studied it afresh. No, that would not help him. There was nothing peculiar about that tiny mark. Again he picked up the hands, looked at the uncalloused palms. The man was no sportsman. Not a hard spot anywhere. Surely there was more to be learned. But how? The hands were the only chance. The only possible chance. . . .

The lines on the palms were singularly clear, and not at all like his own. Apart from palmistry in the sense of prophecy, of charlatanry, some people claimed that you could tell a person's character, even their profession, from the lines in their hands.

Pointer thought of Astra. The police knew all about her.

Astra was the professional name of an American, a Mrs. Jansen, who had amazed London by her skill in reading the character of men and women from their hands. She was no teller of fortunes. But she did tell what lay dormant, or wrongly applied. Parents brought her their children in large numbers, and Astra would examine the little palms, and then give the parents a very truthful, sometimes appallingly truthful, list of their drawbacks and their talents. She would proceed to point out that this must be encouraged, that repressed. In what the child should succeed, in what he was bound to fail. With elder people she was as forthright. "Your gifts are these—your bad qualities this and that." Astra was amazingly honest, and amazingly right. She was no pessimist. "Change your life, use your gifts, keep under the evil in you, and the lines will surely change," was her sermon. "Each of us is our own enemy. Fight that enemy." And she would give clear particulars as to where and how that fight should begin.

The two police inspectors who had been sent to test her, for you must not prophesy for money in England, had come back genuinely impressed. She had not prophesied, but she had hit off each man's character very neatly. Pointer had not much hope in the issue of any interview with her, but she might classify these hands still more narrowly than the microscope had done, and the microscope's testimony would serve to check her statements, if indeed she made any.

He took very careful imprints of the palms on tablets of thick, warmed, modelling wax, brushing a little red powder over them to bring out the lines. He wrapped each tablet in paraffin paper and fastened them side by side in his case. Then he telephoned from a call office for an appointment in the name of Yardly, an immediate appointment. As it was not yet twelve, he was successful. He drove to a house in Sloane Street, and was shown into a cubicle. Mrs. Jansen's clients did not see each other. After a few minutes waiting he was taken into a cheerful room, where, in a window sat a well-dressed woman with a thick mop of curly gray hair held back by combs. A pleasant, keen pair of eyes looked up. A pleasant, firm hand shook his.

Pointer took a seat facing the light, laying his lean brown fingers on two black velvet cushions. He would try her first with his own hands. Her reading of them might end the interview—probably would.

With a magnifying glass the American bent over them, turning them now and then. She nodded her head finally as if satisfied.

"I wish all the hands that have lain there were as pleasant reading," she said, slipping the glass back into its case. "They are the hands of one who, in any walk of life, would go to the top. Your chief characteristic is love of justice. Your dominant quality, penetration."

She went on to give an extraordinary accurate analysis of the Chief Inspector's character. Pointer, who was a thoroughly nice fellow, and very unassuming, actually blushed at the flattering picture drawn.

"I wonder if you can guess the nature of my work? my trade? or my profession?" he said, when she had done. "Or isn't that a fair question?"

"It's a difficult one. But sometimes I hit the nail on the head. I should say that law in some form was your branch. You could be a barrister and a great one—you could be great in any branch that you took up—only that the gift of a flow of words isn't yours. Nor have you that kind of personal magnetism. The friends you win are won by your character. Also, I don't think that you work for money. I mean, I don't think that your income depends on your work. So not a barrister. . . . You're too young to be a judge. Solicitor? . . . No, not solicitor. As I said when I read your hands, you deal with tremendously important issues. Your life is very varied, yet not by your own choosing. The decisions you make are important ones. You're used to constant calls on your physical courage. Used to it, and are going to have plenty more of it. ... I should think the army but for—" She bent closer.

"You know, if you were older and had an ecclesiastical bent, from certain things in your hand I should guess you some Superior in the Jesuit Order. Even Vicar-General . . ."

This did amuse Pointer. He showed it. But it gave him little hope of any good issue from this wildest of forlorn ventures for a Scotland Yard man.

"It's nearer the mark than you think," Mrs. Jansen said shrewdly. "It would have suited one side of your character very well. By your laugh I see that you're not even a Roman Catholic. Then what about—" She frowned, gazing at the erect figure sitting so easily in the chair. Pointer could not slouch.

"Law . . . danger . . . executive ability," she murmured "Police! And since your hands show that you are a man doing work that thoroughly suits your talents, I should say some big man at Scotland Yard. How about the C.I.D.?"

She leant back and looked up inquiringly. Pointer gave a nod.

"You've hit it, and very clever of you indeed! You did that so neatly that I wonder what you'll make of the owner of these hands." He laid down his tablets. "It's to be paid for as a separate visit, of course. Do your best with them, won't you."

She glanced at the tablets. Then she looked a little vexed.

"Really, Mr.—eh—" She paused. "I know the Assistant Commissioner by sight. Are you the Commissioner?"

"No, no! I'm from the ranks. But you were saying?"

"If you take the trouble to glance through my book on Practical Cheirography, you'll see those palms analysed in Chapter Ten. Mr. Julian Clifford kindly let me use his hands in my chapter on authors."

Pointer felt as though he had had a severe punch. For Julian Clifford was England's greatest living author.

"Are you quite sure these tablets are imprints of Julian Clifford's hands?" he asked tranquilly.

"Oh, quite! His are as unforgettable, as unmistakable, as Sarah Bernhardt's. See. Here they are!" She drew a book from under the table and opened it at a couple of plates. Pointer's head was all astir. But he scrutinised them through her magnifying glass. The illustrations seemed identical with his tablets, even to a slight enlargement of the top joint of the left forefinger.

He thanked her and prepared to go. She stopped him with an exclamation. She was bending over his tablets with her glass.

"These were not taken from the hands of a living man! Julian Clifford must be dead!"

"What an idea!" he scoffed.

"A true one! There's a lack of spring, of elasticity about them that's unmistakable. Julian Clifford dead! What a loss to the world! Was it in some accident?"

There was a pause. Mrs. Jansen's reputation was that of an absolutely trustworthy woman. Besides, her face vouched for her. Or rather, her aura. That immense, impalpable Something, woven of our thoughts, our desires, that surrounds each one of us, that never leaves us, that perhaps is most truly "us"—*En nefss*, as the Arabs call it— having its own way of making itself felt, its own warnings, its own dislikes, attractions, and guarantees.

"I wanted you to help us identify a body," he said simply. "Apparently you have. I wonder if there is anything more you can tell me—about Mr. Clifford, I mean."

She interrupted him.

"That's no good with me,—I've seen your palms, remember—I mean that air of a child asking to be helped over the crossing. Besides, why are you here? You weren't in the least interested in your own character. You were keenly interested in those tablets. I don't think it's merely the identification"—her eyes widened—"has something—something criminal—happened to Mr. Clifford? Has he been—killed?" she asked in a low, horrified voice.

"And supposing something 'wrong' has happened to him, Mrs. Jansen?" He gave her back a long, steady stare. "Mind you, all this is in strictest confidence. I'm Chief Inspector Pointer of New Scotland Yard. Of the C.I.D. The whole of this conversation, of my inquiries, must be kept absolutely to yourself, just as the Yard will treat anything you tell me about Mr. Clifford as confidential. Why did the idea come so quickly to you that his death may be due to a crime? You have more to go on than merely my coming to see you."

She looked at him over her horn spectacles for all the world like a modern witch.

"Mr. Clifford came to see me himself a week ago last Thursday," she said finally. "He wanted to know whether I would look in his hands and tell him if any danger threatened him. He was kind enough to say that I had impressed him as truthful when I took the photographs of his hands for my book two years ago. I had only seen him that once before. In Cannes."

"And you?"

"I told him that that was out of my line. Nor could any one have answered that question for him. His hands only showed character and talents. . . . That sort of thing. There are people whose hands do record events. . . . His didn't. Events outside him didn't enter into Julian Clifford. What mattered to him came always from within. Death, for instance, wasn't marked on his palms. Death means very little to him. His personality was quite distinct from his body. With some people it is bound up in it. Even a toothache is marked on their palms."

"What did you tell him? May I know?"

"I told him just that. He seemed rather disappointed. He asked me to look again. 'I'm on the eve of something—well—important.' He hesitated before using that word. I thought he chose it finally rather as a cloak. I don't think 'important' was the word he would have used in writing."

"You think Clifford the man was not so honest as Clifford the writer?"

She did not reply for a moment. Then:—

"I have an idea that he was undecided about something. Or perhaps hesitating before doing something would be a better word."

Again there was a silence.

"Is that all you can tell me about him?"

"Everything," she said, with a frank look into the detective-officer's face.

Pointer stared at his shoes.

"Mrs. Jansen, I wish you'd tell me Mr. Clifford's weak points—as you see them. Suppose something untoward has happened to him. Something that needs investigation. As a rule a man's good qualities don't lead to that necessity. Was there anything in Julian Clifford's character—as shown in his hands—that could have brought about, or led to, or explain—sudden death? Mind you, I ask this in strictest confidence."

She nodded gravely.

"In strictest confidence," she repeated, "nothing in his hands could explain any end other than a happy and honoured one. His was a fine character, noble and generous. He had faults, of course. There was a certain ruthlessness where his work was concerned. He would have sacrificed his all on that altar . . . unconsciously or even consciously."

Still Pointer looked at his shoes.

"Was he a man of high morality, would you say?"

"I don't think he had ever been tempted. He was fastidious by temperament, and his wealth made high standards fairly easy." Mrs. Jansen rose. "And that, Mr. Chief Inspector, is all I can tell you. Mr. Clifford sat a moment there in that chair you're in, peering at his own palms. He was very short-sighted. Then he looked at me half in vexation as he got up. 'What did the ancients do when the oracle wouldn't oracle?' And with that he said good-bye."

"Can I call upon you, in case of need, to identify the hands from which I took these wax impressions as those of Julian Clifford?" Pointer asked, rising.

"I will identify them any time, any where, as his. Hands are to me what faces are to most people—the things I go by."

Pointer paid the moderate fees and drove off. His whole being was in a turmoil under his quiet exterior. Julian Clifford, the great author, younger brother of Sir Edward Clifford of the Foreign Office, to be that headless trunk!

Back at Scotland Yard, within half an hour, the plates in Mrs. Jansen's book were enlarged and compared with quickly-taken photographs of the dead man's palms. Again they seemed to be identical. Every whorl and loop, which showed in both tallied.

Pointer meanwhile looked up Clifford's town address. It was given as Thornbush, Hampstead. A moment more, and he was asking over the telephone if he could speak to Mr. Clifford—Mr. Julian Clifford.

"Mr. Clifford is away, sir," a servant's voice answered.

"Away!" Pointer's tone marked incredulous surprise. "But he had an appointment with the Home Secretary at eleven!"

"He's not here, sir."

"But surely he gave you a message, or a letter when he left? It's Mr. Marbury of the Home Office who is speaking."

Pointer's tone suggested that Mr. Marbury was not accustomed to be slighted.

"I'll inquire, sir," a crushed voice replied.

There was a pause, then the voice came again, very apologetically.

"No, sir. No message was left. Mr. Clifford left early this morning before any one was up."

"Most extraordinary!" Mr. Marbury said stiffly. "I think I'll call and see some one about the matter." He hung up.

So Julian Clifford was supposed to have left his home before any one was up. That probably meant that he had not been seen since last night. Since last night, when a murder had been committed in Heath Mansions.

What about Julian Clifford's brother! He might have some information. But an inquiry at the Foreign Office for Sir Edward told Pointer that the brother was not in town. A few questions to his valet in Pont Street added the information that Sir Edward had left town yesterday, Monday, evening after dining with his brother, Mr. Julian Clifford, at the latter's house. He had gone to his cottage in Surrey, a peaceful spot where the telephone was not.

Pointer opened his *Who's Who*. He reviewed the well-known facts of the novelist and playwright's life. Clifford was a little under forty-five, the younger son of the late Sir James Clifford of Clifford's Bank, long since incorporated in one of the big general banks; he had had a brilliant career at Eton and Oxford, and was the author of an imposing array of novels, poetry, plays, and serious works. He had been twice married, the first time to Catherine Haslar, daughter of Sir William Haslar, High Commissioner of Australia, and, some years after her death, to Alison Willoughby, daughter of Mr. Willoughby of Sefton Park. Clifford had no children.

That was all very well as far as it went. But again it did not go far.

Pointer smoothed his crisp hair which always looked as though it would curl if it dared. Then he pressed a bell. Could Mr. Ward come to his room at once? Apparently Mr. Ward could, for in another moment there appeared in the door a vision to delight a tailor's eye. Ward, sartorially speaking, was It, even in a royal group. His quaint pen-name adorned many a weekly paper. Always up-to-date, invariably correct in all his reports, for two hours of every week-day Ward occupied a small room in one wing next to the Assistant Commissioner's.

"About Julian Clifford—not his literary side, I suppose? Just so. A description of his appearance? Especially of his face?"

Ward gave a very good pen-picture of the great man, after which he repeated briefly what Pointer already knew about Clifford's family.

"Present wife had intended to become a Pusey Sister. Changed her mind and took to divining rods and crystal balls instead. Is on the committees of all the spook societies. People say she's a wonderful clairvoyante. But then they always do say that if the person concerned talks enough to enough people. She usually carries a crystal ball around with her in her bag."

"Supposing," Pointer began, lighting his pipe—that beloved pipe of his which he always denied himself while on the scene of a crime—it might blot out other scents. "Supposing, Mr. Ward, that Julian Clifford had suddenly disappeared from his circle, where would you look for him first?"

"I hardly know. Clifford does this sort of thing every now and then, you know, when he wants some new material for a book. But he always returns to the surface within a week or a month."

"But supposing you had reason to think that something had happened to him—that something was wrong with his disappearance this time?"

"Good God!" Ward's light manner dropped from him. "You don't mean to tell me, Chief Inspector, that anything serious has happened to Julian Clifford?"

Pointer nodded. "I do." He did not insult Scotland Yard nor Ward, by asking him to regard that as confidential. Everything that was said within these walls was always confidential to the men considered sufficiently trustworthy to be consulted there.

"You mean that he's—dead?" Ward asked in a hushed voice. "You think there's been foul play?" He spoke in the tone of a man who asks a monstrous question.

"I'm sorry to say that I'm sure of it. And so, I want you to think whether you've ever heard any talk, any hint, anything that could explain his murder." Pointer gave the few terrible facts. Ward felt that headless body as an additional horror.

"Incredible!" he murmured. "No I know nothing whatever that can explain this crime. It must have been the work of a maniac."

"He was a wealthy man, I always understood?" Pointer asked.

"A very wealthy man apart from his literary work. And a quite sufficiently wealthy man apart from his private fortune."

"Who are the inmates of his household, not counting servants, do you know?" was the next question.

Ward had often been the guest of the Cliffords.

"All of them beyond suspicion. First there's Adrian Hobbs. He's Mrs. Clifford's cousin, and acts as Clifford's literary agent. Clever chap. Thoroughly good business man. Really he's wasted in his present surroundings. Hobbs ought to 've started life with half a crown and a huckster's barrow."

"Straightforward?"

"Perfectly, I should say. That is—eh, well—of course, he's a good business man, as I told you."

Both smiled.

"What's he like to look at?"

"Big, powerful build. Heavyweight." Ward described Hobbs' looks. "Then there's Clifford's regular secretary. A poor fellow who lost his memory during the war. Blown up once too often. Just at the end too. Hard lines, eh? Name of Newman. Clifford ran across him at a base hospital, and gave him a try. He's very good indeed, I believe."

Again, at Pointer's request, he gave a snapshot of the secretary's appearance. Slim, but very strong, he thought him.

"How do these two men and Mrs. Clifford get on? You say they both live with the Cliffords?"

"She bores her cousin, Hobbs, stiff. And I think she secretly bores Newman too. Though he's a chap of whom it's very difficult to know what he thinks."

"Were the Cliffords attached to each other?"

"As far as I know, very much so. But of course—there's that talk about Mrs. Orr, the Merry Widow."

"Widow? Grass or sod, as the Americans say."

Ward laughed. "Oh, a genuine widow. As though you hadn't heard of the beautiful Mrs. Orr. As beautiful and far swifter than the latest eight-cylinder. Julian Clifford is supposed to be—was supposed to be—putting her in his next novel. All I know is he's been haunting her society lately. In season and out of season."

"And what does Mrs. Clifford say to the hauntings? Hasn't she tried to lay the spirit?"

"Mrs. Clifford is quite unperturbed, apparently. She goes on smiling her faint smiles and dreaming her dreams, and hearing her voices and seeing her visions in her crystal. She's one of the few women who haven't begun to cold-shoulder Mrs. Orr of late. Rather the other way."

"More friendly than usual?"

"I saw them driving in the park together only last Friday. Never saw that before."

Pointer hurried off. It was one o'clock. Gossip, even very relevant gossip, must wait until he knew whether it were really wanted or not.

## CHAPTER 3

An elderly-looking, round-shouldered man, whose stoop took from his real height, walked up to the gates of Thornbush half an hour later.

Pointer had looked out the hours of postal deliveries. He had timed himself so as to be on the drive when a postman overtook him. He turned.

"Any letters for me—Marbury?" he asked pleasantly. "And I'll take on any for the household at the same time."

The postman thanked him, told him there were none for him, and handed him four for the house.

Though Pointer looked a typical civil servant from his neatly-trimmed beard to his neatly-adjusted spats, he knocked at the front door with the four letters—three for Julian Clifford, Esq., and one for Mrs. Clifford—in his pocket. He might re-post them after the briefest of delays—or he might not.

"I telephoned to Mr. Clifford just now, and was told that he is not at his home." The very way in which Pointer felt for his card-case suggested near sight and a certain precise fussiness.

"Mr. Clifford is away, sir. But will you see Mr. Hobbs? Mr. Hobbs said he particularly wanted to see you, sir." The butler led the caller into a room near by. A young man rose civilly.

"Mr. Marbury? From the Home Office?"

"I called to inquire why Mr. Clifford failed to keep an appointment he had this morning with the Home Secretary. Can I see him a moment? The matter is connected with the Metropolitan Special Constabulary Reserve, and is very urgent. We are drawing up our lists."

Hobbs seemed puzzled. "Did Mr. Clifford have an appointment? I think there's some mistake."

"Exactly!" Pointer broke in. "I'm sure there is. Kindly let me know where I can reach him on the 'phone."

Hobbs stroked his smooth black hair. Then he stroked his smooth blue chin.

The Chief Inspector was by nature and training a remarkably astute reader of faces, but he was looking at one now which—like his own—hid completely the character behind it. Like himself, Adrian Hobbs looked about thirty, more or less. Like himself, too, he suggested an out-of-door man. Like himself, Hobbs was exceedingly neat in appearance. From his hair to his well-shod feet he satisfied the most fastidious eye. His mind, again like Pointer's, was clearly a tidy mind. But beyond that even Pointer could not size him up. The eyes were large and wide apart. Were they frank or merely bold? The nose was long. Was it predatory or merely self-assertive? Was the large mouth frank? Or was there something just a shade sinister to it when he smiled?

"I really can't understand it," Hobbs said finally. "I had no idea that Mr. Clifford took any interest in the matter—"

"That is precisely why I must trouble you for his address. Or a telephone number that will reach him," Pointer again put in swiftly.

"Sorry," Hobbs smiled slightly, "impossible to give you either. Mr. Clifford has gone off in search of local colour, and where he gets it is always his own closely-kept secret. He left no address. He never does. In good time—a day, a week, two weeks—he'll be back."

"But a man doesn't make an appointment a week ahead with the Home Secretary and not keep it!" Pointer ejaculated," in the tone of a man whose patience is wearing thin.

The truism seemed to worry Hobbs. He nodded, but said nothing.

"I feel sure that he has left some word with some one. He must have!" Pointer urged.

"Mr. Clifford's engagement-book shows nothing for this morning," Hobbs said finally.

"When did he leave?"

"This morning. I got down to breakfast to find that he was gone. There was a note for me to say that he had left to explore some Chinese haunts. Liverpool rather than London, I fancy."

"Incredible!" Pointer murmured. "But"—an idea seemed to strike him—"would you ask Mrs. Clifford to spare me a few minutes? I must try and get this straightened out."

"Do you mind seeing if Mrs. Clifford's in the garden?" Hobbs turned to another man who was writing at the farther end of the large room where he and Pointer were talking. A man whom Pointer knew, by Ward's description, to be Newman, Julian Clifford's private secretary, and whom he had been secretly watching. The Chief Inspector had purposely lowered his voice so that what he was saying should only be partly audible to Newman. He noticed the intent look on the secretary's face, not when he entered the room, but when he spoke of Julian Clifford in a purposely raised voice. The look that came then, was that of a man straining his ears. Ordinary curiosity might explain this with many men. But Pointer did not think that curiosity was a trait of the dark young man with the close-shut mouth, and the deep-set, reserved eyes. Newman's ordinary interest, or he misread him greatly, was concentrated in some inner life of his own. A life so interesting in its close seclusion that he lived there almost exclusively. True, he would, he must, come out into some other court for business purposes, to buy and sell. The many who penetrated thus far, might indeed think that they had the run of all that there was to the man. But Pointer felt sure that there would be walled courtyard within walled courtyard and lock after lock behind which the real man stood on guard.

"Perhaps I'd better go myself," Hobbs said, after a second.

Alone in the room, Pointer thought over the two men, especially the secretary. There were great potentialities in that face. Newman had lost his memory in the last year of the war, Ward had said. But was the face at which the detective officer had just glanced, so apparently casually, the face of one with no memory reaching back beyond 1918?

Pointer had seen men who had lost all recollection of their lives up to a certain point. In the eyes of each had been a look impossible to forget or mistake. A piteous, searching look. The look of those who feel that they are the consequences of days that they cannot remember, that in their characters they are reaping what, as far as their surface intelligence is concerned, they have not sown. But Newman, strange though the effect was that he produced on Pointer's keen scrutiny, had not that look. Those watchful eyes . . . the iron reserve of the face. . . . Nothing could give that last but year on year of rigorous self-control. A self-control that was never set aside for a moment. Great business men sometimes have it, statesmen occasionally. Pointer had invariably seen it on those privileged to attend on royalties.

His thoughts passed on to the effect which his questions about Clifford had had on the men. Hobbs, Clifford's literary agent, had shown no emotion. But Newman? Newman was startled. Pointer knew that as well as though he had been one of these modern instruments which record heart beats. The man's rigid, sudden immobility had but one cause.

Yet, though Pointer could jump to conclusions when he could alter them, he was a very wary man when, as here, his conclusions were fundamental—were the basis on which he must build.

At that moment the door opened. Though Pointer did not know it, it was Julian Clifford's librarian who now looked in. A young man called Richard Straight, who, wandering rather aimlessly about the house, collecting missing volumes from library sets, had just met Hobbs. He had turned and stared after the literary agent. Hobbs' face was strangely set. Straight promptly popped his head into the room which the other had just left. He saw nothing to explain Hobbs' look. A stout, elderly man was trying to disentangle his glasses from his watch-chain. At sight of the librarian, the elderly caller rose.

"Mr. Newman, isn't it?"

"No." Straight came on into the room. "No, but can I be of any use? I'm the new librarian here. Very new, I'm afraid. I only arrived yesterday—from Melbourne."

"I called," Pointer explained wearily, "on a very urgent matter. I must get into touch with Mr. Clifford. I'm from the Home Office, I should mention, and Mr. Clifford was due at a meeting to discuss the lists of the Metropolitan Special Reserve Constabulary. We want him on the committee." He looked questioningly at Straight, who looked questioningly back at him. "Mr. Clifford is absent, it seems. The Home Secretary is waiting!" Pointer's tone was inimitable as he pronounced those five words.

"Where is Mr. Clifford?" Pointer went on irritably, "kindly let me have his address, and I will do what I can to straighten out this most deplorable mistake."

"I haven't it," Straight said promptly. "Mr. Clifford apparently never leaves it when he goes off to collect new material for his work. He only left this morning."

"This morning!" Pointer's tone suggested that here was indeed the last straw. "Why, the appointment was for today!"

Straight merely smiled and shook his head, as though to say that he was not responsible for his employer's habits.

Hobbs returned. He shot a swift glance from Straight to Pointer. An inquiring glance.

"Mrs. Clifford knows no more than I do, but if you feel that you would like to see her, she is willing to give you a few moments, Mr. Marbury."

Hobbs showed Pointer into a large quiet room with bookshelves shoulder-high running around it. A big writing table stood by one window. A Koran stand, various old carved reading-desks, and lecterns, and broad tables such as architects use, were here and there. It was Clifford's own room, and admirably suited to its purpose of writing. The men stood desultorily talking of the weather, which, after having given a selection of winter airs for the past week, had remembered that July was the tune which it was booked to play, and seemed at last endeavouring to provide something suitable.

After a minute or two the door opened. Pointer had never seen any one quite like Alison Clifford. He had expected beauty, for Julian Clifford had written of many a lovely heroine. But this was not beauty as he understood it.

She was very tall, very slender, and very pale. Lint-white the short, soft hair, so fine that, as she turned to shut the door, it stirred above her head like thistledown. With every movement, with her very breathing, it seemed to rise and fall like the hair of a spirit. Her skin was white too. White and smooth, with a sheen as of a lily's petals. Even her lips were but a hint of colour. Her eyes were a clear aquamarine, veiled by lashes so white that they looked as though thickly floured. Something about the face made the Chief Inspector think of a face seen under water, or through a veil.

Pointer explained again about the meeting at the Home Secretary's.

"So sorry to disturb you, Mrs. Clifford, but I thought that perhaps you might remember some trifle which would help to locate Mr. Clifford—"

Mrs. Clifford regretted that she could be of no use. "My husband often disappears for a short time. Generally, of course, he lets me know where he will be, but not always. And I'm afraid he has a very poor memory for engagements."

"Sometimes he's writing, or dictating, and gets to a passage which needs local knowledge," Hobbs put in, "when he'll stop, think a moment, and without a word leave the room, take down his hat and topcoat, and be off. To return with the necessary information and atmosphere perhaps after a week."

Mrs. Clifford smiled acquiescence. "I'm afraid we must possess our souls in patience. He left me a note saying that he might be delayed until Friday."

"Delayed?" Pointer wondered at that word.

"I've heard, of course, of your wonderful powers," he went on politely. "Couldn't you ascertain by means of them where Mr. Clifford really is?" It was a test question. What would the woman's reply be?

"I've been watching him in my crystal off and on all morning," she said at once, smiling faintly with down-dropped lids—lids so thin that Pointer could see the colour of the iris through them.

Even as she spoke she touched the antique silver clasp of a small black velvet bag beside her. Within it Pointer saw a ball of what looked like glass. Bending lower she looked into it. He watched her. Seen like this, with the light on her silvery hair and amber frock, he saw her charm for the first time. There was something very alluring about the picture which she made. She looked like a tree sprite talking for a few moments to a mortal.

"There he is now!" she exclaimed suddenly. "I can always get results quicker if I am with some one who wants to see what I do. Yes, there he is!"

She half turned a shoulder so that both Pointer and Hobbs could look. Pointer saw but the shifting light beautifully reflected in the ball. Hobbs had stalked to the window, and stood with his back to the room, disapproval in every line of his body.

"What is Mr. Clifford doing? Where is he?" Marbury asked, gaping. Was the faint smile that curved her pale mouth mischievous or malicious?

"I'm afraid there's no address given in a crystal. I only see a street ... a very winding street. . . ." She was staring into the ball with what looked like concentrated attention, turning it now and then in its nest of velvet.

"Gables," she went on, "built like steps running up into heaven, are on both sides of him. Now he's lighting a cigarette. He's pulled out his watch. Now he's gone!"

"Gables built like steps running up into heaven?" Pointer echoed. "What sort of houses would they be on?"

Mrs. Clifford shot Hobbs a glance from under her lids as she shut her velvet bag. Pointer fancied that she regretted those words, and hoped that her cousin had not heard them.

"Oh, just irregular gables," she said hurriedly.

"Wonderful!" Marbury fairly gaped; "really wonderful! Thank you so much. And when Mr. Clifford returns, will you ask him to have a message sent me? We may clear up the mystery then. For I confess I find Mr. Clifford's unexpected absence a mystery."

His rather yellow eyeballs—there are drops, very beneficial to the eye, which yellow the balls for the rest of the day—turned vaguely towards the figure of a young woman who had just sauntered down the gravel path towards them past their window. At his words, spoken very clearly, even though in Marbury's little staccato voice, it stopped with the small head a little forward on the long neck, the large eyes glancing into the room at Mrs. Clifford—at Hobbs—at their visitor. Dwelling on each in turn for a length of time that meant uneasiness to Pointer. By what, or by whom, was the uneasiness caused?

"Is that Miss Clifford?" Marbury asked, taking a step towards her, "perhaps she—"

"There is no Miss Clifford," Alison said, while the girl outside stood still. No one made any move towards mentioning her name.

"What! No help towards solving the puzzle of where Mr. Clifford is! Dear, dear!"

Mr. Marbury dropped first one glove then the other. The girl outside in the garden had stiffened where she stood. Now she passed on.

"That's a Miss Haslar, a niece of Mr. Clifford's," Hobbs said quickly, and turned towards the door.

Diana Haslar walked on as though deep in thought—unpleasant thought. Tall and slender, she looked a mere girl, but she was close on thirty. She had a fascinating rather than a pretty face. There were subtle lines in it. There was both mockery and mischief in her smile. And her large eyes looked as though few things would escape them. Had there been a greater warmth in it, her face would have been more universal in its charm. Yet there were hints of fire in the tawny eyes, in the beautiful lustre of her close-clipped, wavy hair, in some tones of her rather deep voice. At last, still apparently lost in thought, still unpleasant thought, she stepped into one of the rooms, and laid a hand on the young librarian's shoulder.

Richard Straight, as he had told Marbury, had only landed yesterday from Australia. He had been head librarian in a large Melbourne civic library. Julian Clifford had met him while on a world's lecturing tour, and had been struck with his original views on how private libraries should be, and could be, run. On his return, the author had offered him the post of his librarian. A small position, but one that could bring Straight into contact with many people worth meeting. Straight had thought it over for a month, and finally accepted it. Had he known what Diana Haslar carefully did not tell him until his decision was made, that the great writer was a connection of hers, Straight would not have hesitated for a day. He had been a constant visitor at the big Haslar house in Melbourne. A friend of Arnold Haslar's, it was not his fault if he was not by this time his brother-in-law. As it was, he still hoped to win Diana.

"Dick!"—the two were about the same age, and Christian names come easily in Australia—"tear yourself away from first editions, isn't a man from the Home Office the same as from the police?"

Richard Straight tore himself away from books very promptly at the tone in which that question was put. He looked at her in surprise.

"You'll be had up for slandering the Force if you mean that benevolent old dear in the morning-room. He certainly can't be the same as a policeman. Why?"

Diana seated herself on the table and ruffled the pages of a book in a way to set a conscientious librarian's teeth on edge. Dick did not seem to mind.

"He came about Uncle Julian. ... I heard him say his absence was a mystery. . . ."

"Well?" Dick asked easily.

Diana looked at him a moment in silence. Then she turned away. Straight knew that a door had been gently shut in his face.

"How do you think you're going to like your work at Thornbush?" she asked, after a moment.

"I think I'm going to like it very much here." This was high praise from Straight. He was an ugly, clever-looking young man with a certain air of quiet self-possession. An air which still annoyed Diana Haslar exceedingly at times. "I should like any place where I could be near you," he added rather fatuously. .

She gave him a rallying smile.

"Any place? I really can't imagine your liking any place, Dick. You're rather a particular young man. Besides, when Uncle Julian has finished his Life of my grandfather, I'm off. It's only the fact I can check the family dates better than any one else can that keeps me here, though I like the work." She finished thoughtfully with a certain critical note in her voice.

"But not the house?" he asked, quickly looking up.

"We're so frank 'down under,'" she said a little wistfully, "dreadfully frank, you used to think when you first came out. And Thornbush—" She seemed to seek for the right word.

"Thornbush isn't?"

"Not frank. No. Not lately. I seem to be always interrupting people in most private conversations. I think I shall be glad when the Life is finished and I'm free once more. Though I love being with Uncle Julian."

"He's a splendid chap, isn't he!" Straight said warmly. "His welcome to me was kindness itself."

"He is kind. Yet he can be hard. When it's a question of his work."

Again there was a tone to her voice that intrigued him. Straight was fond of conundrums.

"Your uncle said in the notes he left each of us this morning that he had gone for local colour. Is it possible that you think 'local colour' should be spelled Mazod Orr?"

This time it was Diana's expression that puzzled Straight as she looked at him. She was far too modern a young woman to be shocked at the suggestion. Yet there was a something in her eye. . . -

"I see that Arnold has been repeating the silly tittle-tattle which is going the round in some quarters," she said scornfully." Why, Alison and Mazod Orr are tremendous friends —she is seeing her off herself for Paris this morning."

There was a pause.

"And how's Arnold?" Straight asked; "was it anything serious?" The name of Mrs. Orr had suggested that of Arnold Haslar to him, for Diana's brother was madly in love with the widow. Straight knew that Diana had had a telephone message early this morning that had made her hurry home, a message about Arnold having been found beside his breakfast table in a state verging on collapse.

"The doctor says it's trying to be 'flu. I wanted to stay, but Arnold's not to see any one. If he remains in bed and keeps absolutely quiet, the doctor thinks he may escape and be up to-morrow."

"Odd if Arnold should catch 'flu," Straight thought. "He always seemed to be immune. He looked all right last night."

"The doctor says he must have had a shock of some kind, or some great excitement. Do you know of anything?" She looked at Straight rather narrowly. He did not, and said so.

"Must have happened when he was called out of town last night," he suggested. "It was a business call, he told me, else we had planned to celebrate my arrival, as you know, by some crimson paint. If it isn't due to business worry, then it may be remorse at his having cut me dead this morning. Absolutely dead."

"Where was this?" she asked sceptically.

"Just outside a huge building on the corner of a main road near here. I got lost trying to take an after-breakfast stroll."

"Heath Mansions." Diana tapped her fingers on the table restlessly. "He didn't see you evidently," she went on in a rather absent-minded, ruminative voice.

"That's just it," he retorted. "Arnold shouldn't moon by daylight. I waved a friendly paw, and he fled as though it held a writ. Probably he was feeling ill. He looked perfectly ghastly."

Once more an odd look crossed Diana's face.

"And he left you early last night?" she asked, as though worried by that fact.

"Nearly as soon as I got there," Straight said, with a smile. "But in response to a telephone call, which made it less of a snub direct."

She did not smile. A silence fell on the room.

Suddenly Diana drew back farther into the shadow. Newman, her uncle's secretary, was walking past the open window outside. He looked up. Their eyes, his and hers, met. Newman's cigarette-case dropped with a sharp tinkle, as though something in her glance had startled him. He retrieved it instantly, and passing on, lit a cigarette rather hastily.

His movements were singularly free from hurry, as a rule. Like his face, they suggested plenty of reserve power. There was something foreign about his appearance: a little in his easy grace, more in his seldom-seen, faintly ironic, smile, most of all in the melancholy of his dark, brooding eyes, which rarely looked up. Newman had a habit of carrying on a whole conversation with his eyes on his cigarette, or looking out of the window. In build he was exceptionally lean and lithe, with small, strong bones.

"I must ask Newman about the Spanish books," Straight murmured. "Mr. Clifford told me in that talk we had last night after dinner, that he's making himself into quite an authority on Spain."

Diana said nothing.

"Mr. Clifford seemed to think him very clever, but—"

Then Straight too decided to say no more.

"Oh, he is!" Diana spoke with a certain grimness, "so clever that one wonders why he remains content with life at Thornbush year after year. There's some reason why he refuses every offer, and he's had some good ones. Just as there's some reason why he cultivates Arnold as he does. Mr. Newman does nothing without a reason."

Diana spoke half under her breath.

"You sound afraid of him!" Straight gave her a very sharp glance.

Diana's laugh failed to achieve carelessness.

"I loathe him. I can't think why he should try so tremendously to ingratiate himself with Arnold, who, unfortunately, has taken the most tremendous fancy to him."

"Perhaps the fact that Arnold's your only brother," Dick suggested.

"Mr. Newman and I feel alike about each other," Diana said shortly, "mutual dislike. On my side, distrust as well. Profound distrust."

"I must keep out of his way," Straight said lightly.

"Oh, he won't bother you! You're of no importance to him. There's nothing to be gained by cultivating you"—she flushed at her own rudeness and added hastily, "except the best of pals. And possibly Mr. Newman may scent the rising man in you that you are, Dick. However, even so, you'll be safe. I can't imagine any one pulling the wool over your eyes."

"I'm done brown quite often," he murmured sadly.

"Not you!" she scoffed. "I always know that if ever any of us gets into a hole you'll get us out.' She bit her lip, as though the words had slipped out. "Edward Clifford thinks the paper you sent in to the Libraries Association a masterpiece. He said he was going to keep an eye on you."

"A benevolent or a watchful eye?"

Both laughed. Straight looked down into her face not so far below his own.

"Were you pleased?" he asked abruptly.

"For your sake—very much." She laughed again, but Straight did not laugh back.

"Can't you manage to love me, Diana?" he asked, with a sudden passion in his voice.

"I thought we talked that over in Melbourne." She turned away, not shyly—Diana was never shy—but with something almost of impatience in her big eyes.

"Love!" she repeated under her breath. "Who does love, really? What is it? How does it come? How do you know when it's real, when it's not? I like you, Dick. I respect your character immensely"

"Then give me a chance! Give me a try-out!" he urged again.

Diana only shook her head. . .

"I'll make you love me"—he spoke as though taking a vow unto himself—"with the real love The love that stands by a man when all else drops away. You have it in you, that I'll swear. You *could* love, Diana!"

Diana was very pale.

"Not with the love that calls the world well lost." There was a note of contempt in her voice. Was it for herself? or for the subject of their talk? It was hard to tell with Diana.

"I haven't that in me. For your own sake, make no mistake! But apart from that, I could be a good helper to an ambitious, rising man. If ever I do agree to marry any one, I'll back him up well."

"But you won't agree to marry—any one—now?" Straight asked in his usual, rather measured voice.

"Not yet. Perhaps I shall never have any better answer. It won't be any loss, believe me. I'm not deep. I'm shallow. Shallow, and pleasure-loving, and greedy for good things." Her tone was trivial again. "And now, let's talk of something else. I mean it." Her eyes warned him not to press her for the present.

"Well, then, let us discuss whether the Foreign Office secret-service men will catch that chap Sir Edward talked about so much yesterday at dinner. The anarchist with the odd name . . ." Straight looked to Diana to help him out. She did not glance up.

"Et—Etch— Sounds as if I were sneezing!" he said crossly. "Etche— What was it?"

She made no suggestion.

The door opened. A girl looked in. It was Maud Gillingham, a great admirer of Alison Clifford's.

"Di—but how white you are! Or is it that frock? Mrs. Clifford has a message for you. A very important one. She's out in the garden."

Maud Gillingham slid an arm through Diana's, and the two sauntered out on to the lawn to where, under a cedar tree, Mrs. Clifford lay in a long garden-chair looking more like the sketch of a woman than actual flesh and blood. She lifted her strange aquamarine eyes as the two came up to her.

"I have a message for you from your grandfather, Diana." She spoke as casually as though she had just met the dead man in the street. "From Sir William Haslar. It spelled itself out on my Ouija board. I would have sent for you at once, only some tiresome person came in about an appointment of Julian's. . . . But this message—'Tell Day' it began. Evidently you are Day."

Diana started. That was her grandfather's name for her, not heard for many a long year, and certainly not known to Alison Clifford.

". . . not to mind whatever it is that you are minding," Mrs. Clifford went on. "That it will all come right. That he could see the end, and it will all come right."

She signalled to Newman, who was standing watching them, to come closer.

"Come along, Maud!" Diana turned to the girl beside her, "let's take a stroll around the rosary. You know"—Diana began when they were out of earshot—"there are times when I can't bear Alison. Spiritualists can be so smug, and generally are!"

"It's like talking to a woman from Mars sometimes," Maud agreed, "but she can be wonderful. With Mr. Newman, for instance. But I forgot—you don't like your uncle's secretary."

"I'm sorry for him," Diana said rather reluctantly.

Maud Gillingham nodded. "Naturally. Anybody would have to be sorry for a man who lost his memory in the war. But instead of pitying him, as we all do, Mrs. Clifford makes him feel that what he's lost is so tiny a thing in the immensity of our eternal life that it really isn't worth while fretting over."

"Yet don't you think she'd fret if she lost her memory?" Diana checked herself. "Maud, I never can quite make up my mind about Alison. Is she posing, or is she quite sincere?"

"Heavens, Di, if she weren't sincere she'd have to be an utter liar. Surely you don't think that of her?" Maud was aghast. She was an honest soul who knew no half-tones. You were white or you were black to Maud.

"N—no. No, of course I don't think that." Diana spoke rather as though dropping a trap-door on something within herself that wanted to peep out. "No, of course not. Every one knows that Alison, however mistaken, has a beautiful mind. But that message from my grandfather . . ." There was a pause.

"*Did* he call you Day?" Maud asked curiously.

"He did. But . . ." There was another pause. "This message from him for me: Maud, doesn't it ever strike you that Alison always gets the messages from the other world that she wants to get? Hears the things she wants to hear?"

Maud reflected a moment.

"I think there's more than that in it, Di. Oh, much more! Look at this last Saturday afternoon. But I don't think you were in the room. Mrs. Orr was here, and was scoffing as usual in her laughing way at something I said about Mrs. Clifford's powers. But I stuck to it that she could 'see'—sometimes—with her hands. Mrs. Orr whipped out a letter from her bag, folded it, and held it folded on Mrs. Clifford's knee, and said, 'Read this, then, Alison darling.' And she did! Mrs. Clifford did! She pressed her hands hard down on the letter and read out a whole sentence. 'If you keep your end up, no one will suspect us.' She would have gone on, only Mrs. Orr put the letter back into her bag. It was from a friend on her honeymoon. Even she looked startled. And no wonder! If that wasn't white magic, what is?"

Now Diana had been in the room; had heard and watched the whole strange little scene. But what had struck her most had been Julian Clifford's face as his wife began slowly— laboriously—like some one reading a distant signpost, to almost spell out the words. If Mazod Orr had looked startled, so had he. Diana thought that his hand had palpably twitched to snatch the envelope with its contents from under his wife's fingers. He and Mrs. Orr had drifted on into his study to look at some new prints which he had bought, and Diana saw again Mrs. Clifford's equable smile as she looked after them. Yet there had been a new element in her expression. Diana's perceptions were very quick. In Alison Clifford's eyes was a look almost of sarcasm. It was the smile with which skill might watch transparent make-believe through which it sees absolutely, but from which, for reasons of its own, it prefers not to tear the cloak away. It was not an unkind smile—Alison never looked unkind—but it had made Diana wonder. The two girls were back again by the cedar tree now. Mrs. Clifford was talking to Newman.

"But even so, why not let me get into touch with your forgotten memories? They're not important, but still, why not have them? I might be able to lift the veil for you."

Newman flicked the ash off his cigarette with an impatient gesture which had something almost of contempt in it. There was a certain haughty, hawk-like look about his whole face.

"I'd rather not. Thank you immensely for caring, Mrs. Clifford. But I have a very definite feeling against having the veil lifted that way. Your powers are very wonderful, but something tells me, warns me, if you like, not to use them for this purpose."

Diana gave him a long, long look. It amounted to a stare.

"I should never be able to resist the chance if I were you!" panted Maud.

"You mean if I were *you*," Newman said looking at her under his heavy, brooding lids—lids that lifted slowly. There was something watchful about his gaze always—not suspicious—just watchful.

Dick Straight joined the group, and when they moved towards the house, sauntered after them with the secretary, of whom he asked a question or two about a couple of old Spanish works on the shelves. They were soon discussing Spanish bindings, and Straight found that his companion was indeed well up in the subject. Diana passed them again.

"I'm off to see how Arnold is, though he hates me to fuss over him." She made her remark exclusively to Dick Straight.

"Interesting girl, Miss Haslar," Dick said casually as she walked on.

"Most girls are," was the equally casual reply. Newman's dark eyes glanced for the barest second at Straight's face; that face was not usually considered a tell-tale one, yet Dick felt certain that the man beside him was aware from it of the state of affairs between himself and Diana.

Straight took an instant dislike to the man.

"Dago blood of some sort," he told himself, as Newman left him with a civil excuse, and turned off into the hall.

# CHAPTER 4

Pointer meanwhile, on his way back to Scotland Yard, had opened the four letters handed him by the postman on the Thornbush drive. The three to Mr. Clifford could have no possible connection with the case. The letter to Mrs. Clifford was different. It was from town, dated yesterday, and ran,

"Dear Alison,—A linelette to say that should you be asked questions, be sure you know nothing. Remember we count on you to put people off. Miles off. Till to-morrow morning.
"In great haste,
"Mazod Orr."

That letter was put back in the Chief Inspector's letter-case. The others were fastened up and dropped in the nearest box.

"We count on you to put people off," he murmured. "Not always so easy, my lady!"

Back at New Scotland Yard, during a belated lightning lunch, Pointer asked Mr. Ward to be good enough to come into his room again for a moment.

"Ever heard of Mr. Clifford's new librarian? A young man called Straight?" he asked briskly.

"Librarian? I thought Newman had that job. But as Hobbs is going for a six months' big game shoot in the autumn, I suppose he's going off duty now—he has some private means, as well as a whacking salary and commission—the new librarian may be a sort of stop-gap. First I've heard of him."

"And who could a tall young woman be with handsome, rather bitter eyes, and a face that should be beautiful but isn't. She looks a lot younger than her years, I fancy." Pointer went on to describe her colouring. He wanted to verify the name that Hobbs had murmured. "I have a snapshot of her in my glove button, but I can't develop it for the moment."

Pointer's glove stud, a thickish stud, furnished a complete minute roll of films, and was a perfect tiny camera by the touch of a nail on the edge.

"That'll be Miss Haslar, Clifford's niece. She's helping Mr. Clifford with his Life of her grandfather, Sir William Haslar."

"Very fond of gossip, isn't she?"

"Diana Haslar? Not half as fond of it as I am," chuckled Ward. "No, she's rather a high-brow."

"Is she attached to her uncle? Mr. Clifford would only be her uncle by marriage, of course."

"Worshipped him. Absolutely worshipped him."

"Is Mr. Arnold Haslar an electrical engineer in a big way, the head of the Wellwyn Company of Melbourne, a relative of hers?"

"Only brother. Only relative, as far as I know. Her father's dead."

"And this brother, was he by way of worshipping Mr. Julian Clifford too?"

"Until he and the widow got so friendly. Mrs. Orr is absolutely ripping, you know. If rumour tells the truth she has ripped through a good deal in a fairly short time, but she's connected with all the peerage that counts, royal god-mother, and so on. So what would you? It'll take a lot to sink her little boat definitely. Haslar is tremendously in love with her. He's of no family, but he's wealthy. She can't do better. Wonder is, she can do as well. For he's the last chap to stand some things. Yet they say it's she who's lately holding off. No one can understand it. Clifford's interest is purely academic. She's a type to him. That's all. But why Mazod the Fair should be apparently turning Haslar down is the mystery. Clifford can't marry her even if he wanted to, which he doesn't. Haslar wants to. Unless she tries him too far. He's not the sort to make a good dupe. The woman can't have lost her very alert wits. . . ." Ward ruminated over the problem.

"What sort of man is this Arnold Haslar?" Pointer finally asked.

Ward pondered.

"Well, not the sort of chap I should select with whom to wipe the floor. Not without a tussle. All correct to the outward eye, of course. But there's wild blood in his background. Botany Bay, in fact. Not for anything terrific. Well-deserved manslaughter we should call it nowadays—at least I should." Ward corrected himself hastily. He and the Chief Inspector had crossed swords on that point before. "You know the retort his grandpa made when Lord Boodle wrote an article during the last election hinting at his family's past? Old Sir William, as he was later, wrote back that it was quite true. His ancestor had been deported for not enduring what his, the honourable writer's, ancestor had been ennobled for standing. To any one who knew the Boodle pedigree it was a bit sledge-hammer, but very amusing. Australia crowed."

"So that there's ill-feeling between him and Clifford over Mrs. Orr?" Pointer repeated meditatively.

Ward nodded. "Said to be."

"Does Miss Haslar know of the attachment between her brother and Mrs. Orr?" This Ward did not know, but he felt certain that if she did so, Diana would very much object.

Pointer stood with bent head, hands deep in his pockets, eyes on his shoes. It was a favourite position of his when deep in thought.

"What about Sir Edward Clifford, Mr. Julian Clifford's brother? What is his reputation among his own set?"

"None better," was the expected reply. "A stickler for conventions, but that's all to the good in a man of his position."

"Were the two brothers on friendly terms?"

"On the very best. Always. Even though both wanted to marry the same young woman, and though Julian Clifford carried off the prize, it made no difference in their friendship. I'm speaking of the present Mrs. Clifford."

And that finished Ward's information.

Pointer pressed a knob. A light shone out on the table of one of his constable clerks in the next room. The man came in.

"Get me the address of the Wellwyn Company's London warehouse. Find out if it has any others in Great Britain."

In a few minutes Pointer had an address in Thames Street. The only warehouse, or office, of the great Australian firm in the United Kingdom.

To it Inspector Watts was sent, to find out by dexterous questions whether any parcel or package had arrived there since last night, except such as were to be handled and opened in the usual way of trade.

Next, a woman detective was sent to call on Mrs. Orr for a subscription to a quite genuine orphanage, and incidentally to find out from whoever would be in the house where that lady had been last night.

That done, an inquiry was put through to Mr. Arnold Haslar at his office in Thames Street. Warehouse and office were in the same building. The inquiry was intended to lead up to a polite request to allow Mr. Marbury to come and see him with a view to adding his name to the same M.S.C. Reserve in which, apparently, Mr. Julian Clifford had been so interested. Pointer learnt that Mr. Haslar had not been at his office all day—that he was down with influenza. And from the butler at his house in Hampstead, Pointer heard that complete quiet had been ordered him and a day in bed. Yes, the attack had been very sudden. Mr. Haslar had been all right yesterday. He had come down ill this morning.

This morning! Pointer was interested. So much so that a plain clothes man was despatched to keep an unobtrusive eye on the invalid's house. And an order was left that the telephones of it and of Mrs. Orr's house, and of Thornbush were to be all connected with New Scotland Yard.

As for Thornbush, just a little over an hour after Mr. Marbury left it, a red-haired, very freckled, lantern-jawed man from the gas company was knocking at the back door. They were installing meters farther down. Something had blown out. The pipes here must be looked to, or there might be trouble. The butler was dazed by a string of the latest bye-laws—so Pointer called them—rattled off at top speed, and promptly let the man make a tour of inspection.

The gas man was very thorough, even though he worked amazingly swiftly. Every cupboard was opened and swiftly scanned. The top glanced over. Every movable article was lifted quickly. Pointer had found out at the Yard, before he started, the average weight of a dead man's head. He had had that weight dropped into a seven-pound biscuit tin, filled with plaster of Paris, and lifted the whole several times, registering the weight.

He found few packages or parcels at Thornbush heavy enough for what he wanted. These few were carefully inspected. He even took one swift turn over the roof. besides being keenly on the watch for biscuit tins ostensibly filled with plaster, he kept a look-out for weapons of any kind. He drew a blank in both respects. But within ten minutes he found what he was primarily after. Finger-prints on a dozen articles of Julian Clifford's were unmistakably the finger-prints of the man in the mortuary.

Pointer was outwardly unmoved, but his pulses beat quicker. He had won the first round. In vain had the head of the murdered man been cut off, the clothes taken away. No longer could a doubter say that the man whose hands Mrs. Jansen had photographed at Cannes, and the man who had come to her office in town, though he called himself Julian Clifford, might be an impostor. Here was the proof that the author and the murdered man were one and the same.

As for the rest, neither Clifford's room, nor his wife's, nor Hobbs', had anything important to tell the Chief Inspector. Nor, strictly speaking, had Newman's. Yet in one way the secretary's room interested Pointer greatly. Newman had lived many years now with Clifford, yet the bedroom and his working room were as bare of personal effects as hotel rooms. There was not so much as a calendar which seemed the personal choice of the secretary. The only books were from a circulating library unless they belonged to Clifford.

Pointer stood looking about him, his bag of tools in his hand—intentionally bare. Intentionally devoid of all marks of individuality was his verdict. Nothing here to help any detective. Choice or necessity? Newman was a conundrum.

A chat in the kitchen told Pointer that Mr. and Mrs. Clifford were considered a most devoted couple by their servants, aid that the latter were not in the least surprised at only one more of their master's many short disappearances.

"It's just his way," one maid said airily. "He goes off like that, all of a sudden, when he gets fed up with writing. Mr. Trimble here he says that Mr. Clifford goes to find out more to write about, but is that likely?"

A few questions about last night, when the gas man thought that he had seen Mr. and Mrs. Clifford at a restaurant in company with Sir Edward Clifford, told Pointer that the dinner at Thornbush, where Edward Clifford and Maud Gillingham had been the only guests, had been a cheery meal; that the two guests had each left immediately after the meal, and that as far as the servants went, Mr. Clifford had not been seen after the butler took him in a glass of iced barley water about ten. Mr. Clifford had told him that "that was all"—his usual words of dismissal for the night. Back on his Yard-bound 'bus, Pointer thought over the household —over Julian Clifford, who had gone to Astra's to have his fortune told, as he might have gone to a gipsy.

He had gone recently. And he had asked the palmist to tell him if danger was marked in his hands. A strange question from a man who apparently within the month had passed to where that word has no more meaning.

Yet if it was his body that Pointer had seen, as the Chief Inspector believed that it was, he had not investigated that flat. He did not seem to have noticed the fastened back lock of that door. It looked as though he had had a definite idea of where the danger lay, and did not expect it to meet him elsewhere.

What was the best course now? Open or secret?

As a rule, an inquirer in a murder benefited by the rare chance of the murderer thinking his crime was still undetected. But here? Dared Pointer let him think himself safe? If that cut-off head was cut off with the idea of blocking the investigation, then it and those carefully laid trails of the Basque anarchist looked, Pointer believed, as though some thing was brewing which the knowledge of Clifford's death would spoil. Some business seemed to be on hand which must stop if it were known who it was that on this last night had been lured to a strange address, there murdered, and stripped and beheaded. They might not all belong together—the murder, the beheading, the stripping. But some vital necessity must have ruled to make a man risk any, or all, of them. No one goes to such terrible lengths unless driven. What was it which necessitated, perhaps the killing of Julian Clifford, but certainly the remaining unknown of the fact that it was he who had been killed?

Back at Scotland Yard, he arranged for a couple of his men to be installed in a road-mender's hut just outside Thornbush—men who understood tapping a telephone wire. They were instructed to do as little damage as possible with the maximum amount of effect. The point was that one or other was to be permanently on guard. And a message was sent to the police stations concerned which would be passed on at once to every constable on his beat, that any oddity noticed at the houses where lived Sir Edward Clifford, Mrs. Orr, Arnold Haslar, and Julian Clifford was to be at once reported directly to the Chief Inspector at New Scotland Yard.

Then he went swiftly to the Assistant Commissioner's rooms. Tindall, to whom he had telephoned, was just entering. Without a word, Pointer laid before the two men a sheet of paper with some red finger-prints on it. He had obtained them by dropping collodium in thin films over the fingerprints on a metal tube of tooth-paste in Clifford's dressing-room, then carefully peeling them off one by one when set, leaving them awhile in a red-tinted hardening solution, and finally pressing each carefully out on to unglazed paper.

"You agree that they're the same as these?" he asked.

"These" were prints taken from the hands of the dead man, and enlarged on squared paper.

"They're identical," Tindall agreed, after very carefully comparing the two. Major Pelham said the same, and the Assistant Commissioner was an authority on finger-prints.

"How on earth—where—whose?" Tindall was all but inarticulate.

"I got these red prints from marks on Mr. Julian Clifford's tube of tooth paste. Equally clear are those there taken off a lamp switch beside his bed. The tube of tooth-paste I have with me. And here's some of Mr. Clifford's manuscript paper. It's esparto grass paper. In other words I'm sorry to say that the murdered man in Heath Mansions is Mr. Julian Clifford the well-known author." Pointer detailed the somewhat odd steps of his investigations.

"Sir Edward's brother!" Tindall murmured, as one half stupefied. There was a long silence. Tindall strode to the window and back. Then he wheeled.

"These prints, of course, absolutely settle the question. So Etcheverrey was the killer this time, and not the killed! But why should Etcheverrey kill Julian Clifford? What took Clifford into that most dangerous man's inner circle? However, let me congratulate you, Chief Inspector. This was good work. Marvellously good. Considering how you at the Yard are so bound by red tape. You need a royal warrant or an Act of Parliament before you dare step an inch off the beaten track. With us, of course, it's different. But frankly, I can't think how you get the results that you do."

"We have to rely more on routine," Pointer agreed sadly, and let it go at that, while Major Pelham wrestled with a refractory cough.

Tindall bent over the finger-prints again.

"And to think of a Scotland Yard man going to a palmist!" he all but chuckled.

"Astra isn't what's generally meant by that word, or we wouldn't let her alone as we do," the Assistant Commissioner reminded him. "She's not a fortune-teller."

"It was a most amazing piece of luck that she had photographed Clifford's hands," Tindall said almost grudgingly.

Pointer nodded. It was.

"It wasn't good luck that made the Chief Inspector go to her," Pelham pointed out.

"What would you have done if she'd never seen Clifford?" the Foreign Office man asked with real curiosity.

"I think she might have been as good at placing him, or his interests, as she was with mine. I tried her with my own hands first. If so, what with her suggestions, and the clue furnished by his fingernails, I think we should have run him to earth in time."

"I wish you were wrong for once," Tindall pushed the sheets of prints away. He spoke with genuine emotion. "Quite apart from my having been a little off the true, I wish with all my heart that you were wrong. Why, his coming novel is said to be one of the finest things even Julian Clifford has ever done! It's not finished yet. I must be the one to break the news to Sir Edward, of course." Suddenly he straightened. "I wonder! Is he the link between Julian Clifford and the Basque? There's no man keener on having Etcheverrey caught than our Chief. And there is a great resemblance between the brothers. But first of all, I must hurry to the French Embassy." He glanced at his watch. "Four o'clock. I've been there until now. Etcheverrey—"

Pelham stopped him.

"Just a moment, Tindall. We must lay this before the Commissioner. I've told him the facts as far as they went."

He took the two into another room. The prints were laid before an elderly, shrewd-faced man with singularly steady, piercing blue eyes.

"You think, Tindall, that Julian Clifford may have been killed because of Sir Edward's inquiries, or because the younger was mistaken for the elder brother?" General Brownlow asked finally.

"I can see no other possible link. No other gap to cross such a bridge as that between a Basque revolutionary and Julian Clifford."

Tindall looked at Pointer. All three looked at Pointer, who looked at his shoe-tips.

A silence fell on the room. Then General Brownlow spoke.

"I don't for a moment doubt your result, Chief Inspector. None of us do, or can. But it rests for identification of the body only on palm and finger-prints. Juries and coroners don't like that kind of evidence. We must go step by step. I think we must keep back from the public our belief, our certainty rather, that the murdered man is Julian Clifford until we get the usual proof. I mean until we get the actual head. As to the family—that must, of course, depend on what Sir Edward says; or on the course of events."

Again there fell a silence.

"'We count on you to put people off. Miles off,'" Pelham murmured suddenly. Pointer had given every fact, as known to him so far, with the most meticulous care. It was only his conclusions that he had kept to himself. "That's a most extraordinary letter under the circumstances!"

"I don't know about Mrs. Orr, but Mrs. Clifford is absolutely incapable of murder," General Brownlow said firmly, "or of being connected with a crime of any kind. I've known her off and on since she was a child. Nor is there the slightest motive here. She has a life interest under her father's will that must bring her in a clear thousand a year. A thousand to Mrs. Clifford is like five thousand to most people. More than ample for her needs. You might as well suspect Sir Edward of having had a hand in Julian Clifford's horrible end."

And with that the conference broke up.

Pointer's next objective was the Hampstead branch of the St. James Bank. Before leaving Scotland Yard a few inquiries over the telephone at all the branches near Thornbush had told him that Mr. Clifford had a town account there. And Pointer was always interested in the banking account of men who died suddenly, let alone of men who were murdered.

The reason for that cut-off head might lie quite near home. Clifford was not a racing man, or Pointer would have thought of a horse. But was there any large cheque outstanding of his which his death, if known of, would have invalidated, or at least held up?

In that case, since Julian Clifford was killed last night, any such cheque would have been presented to-day as soon as the banks opened. This did not oust Etcheverrey from his place in the heart of the mystery surrounding the death of the great writer, but Pointer believed that mystery to be complex, not single.

Pointer had his private doubts as to whether it was quite fair to the bank manager to let him cash a dead man's cheques, for others might be presented, innocently or not. But the Chief Commissioner had decided that nothing should be done for the present which would let the world at large know that England's foremost author was dead. Pointer rather deprecated that decision, but it had been made. Though by now it was past banking hours, a telephone message to the manager had found him still on the premises, and Pointer was shown in at once on his arrival. Detective Inspectors do not ask for appointments every day.

"Do you mind if my chauffeur waits outside in the passage?" Pointer asked, as he shook hands. There was only the one door.

The manager was too full of anxiety to have any room for objections.

"A man's body has just been discovered," Pointer began, "in circumstances that suggest foul play. He was an acquaintance of Mr. Julian Clifford's. We have discovered some notes among his papers which make us think that he had in his possession a large sum of money of Mr. Clifford's. That he was only just in possession of it. A business venture pure and simple, but on a large scale. Mr. Julian Clifford is out at his home. Now this is the point. Was any large sum paid out very recently by Mr. Clifford? We think the payment of which we're speaking was originally by cheque, and probably was presented to you early this morning as soon as the bank opened."

The manager reflected a moment. He had started at the last words.

"It's in strictest confidence, of course?" he asked.

Pointer had to tell him that as the sum might possibly be the motive for an attempt at murder, it was not possible for him to promise secrecy.

The manager reflected a little longer.

"You say Mr. Clifford's away from home?"

"His family tell me he's off on one of those expeditions of his when he leaves no address. Getting up facts for his next book," Pointer said promptly.

More meditation on the part of the manager.

"Well, I'm in rather a difficult position," he murmured.

"Why don't you get into touch with Sir Edward Clifford?"

"He's out of town. Also un-get-at-able."

"A depositor—and such a large depositor as Mr. Julian Clifford," murmured the manager uncertainly.

"Still—murder, you know!" Pointer threw in. And the manager made up his mind.

"Well, a very large cheque of Mr. Clifford's was presented early this morning," he said slowly.

Pointer nodded. "For how much?"

"Seventy thousand pounds."

Having said that much, the manager made up his mind to be quite frank.

"Mr. Clifford had spoken to us of that cheque. About a month ago he had us make the necessary arrangements to pay a hundred thousand into his current account. He told me that he would draw on it by a very large cheque, and that he wished the cheque cashed without any further formalities or delay."

Pointer nodded.

"This morning, as soon as we opened, Mrs. Clifford presented a cheque of Mr. Clifford's drawn to a Mr. Selfe for seventy thousand pounds. It was duly endorsed, and of course we cashed it at once. That is the only large sum which had been paid out of Mr. Clifford's account lately."

"Mrs. Clifford. I see. Was she alone?"

"No. A lady was with her in her car. I happened to be coming in at the moment the car drew up."

"Did you recognise whoever was with her?"

"It was Mrs. Orr."

"You know her?"

The manager hesitated again. "No," he said finally, "but seeing it's you, I don't mind passing on a bit of gossip. My son Gerald is a barrister. Junior to Mr. Robinson. He tells me that they're briefed in a case coming on shortly. Smart society divorce. It's to be heard as soon as the courts open. Mrs. Orr is cited in it by name. No chance of a defence. The wife intends to get her knife into her. Gerald showed me some photographs of Mrs. Orr. That's how I recognised her at once. Odd companion for Mrs. Julian Clifford."

"May I see it? A Selfe is a sort of partner of this man who was shot."

"I see. You think?"

"It's too early to think yet," Pointer returned, as though that were with him always the last resort. "But of course I must have a look at it. If only in the way of routine."

He was shown the cheque. It seemed in perfect order. It was made out to R. Selfe, Esq., and endorsed R. Selfe. The date was last Thursday.

"I must ask you to let me have this for an hour or so."

The manager agreed, provided that it be returned next day.

"I don't want to talk over the finding of this body more than I can help with Mrs. Clifford. It's a harrowing subject, especially if we're wrong, and this money has nothing to do with our case. How did she take the money?"

"In notes of a hundred pounds. Here is the list of the numbers. Mr. Clifford had requested that the money should be held ready for him in just that way. They were handed to Mrs. Clifford in seven packages of a hundred notes. The cashier asked, of course, if she shouldn't send it out to her car by our commissionaire, or lend her the man's services, but she declined both suggestions."

Pointer thanked him and left. He had much to think over. A cheque for a fortune ... an uncrossed cheque ... a cheque to R. Selfe . . . and cashed by Mrs. Clifford as soon after her husband's death as it could be presented . . . with Mrs. Orr waiting in the car outside ... a cheque which Julian Clifford had expected to be presented, and which he wished paid without any trouble being made to the person who should present it.

Not a simple case this . . . complex . . . very.

Pointer had the cheque photographed, and the photograph enlarged. Then he saw what he expected to see. The final e was not continuous with the f of Self, but had been carefully added. So carefully, so exactly, that only the enlarged photograph showed the break and slight overlapping of the strokes. The endorsement on the back presented no breaks. There Selfe was one word, written swiftly and with a dash. Under the camera too the initial R on the face of the cheque showed a certain waviness of line due to slow and careful writing ... so did the Esq. On the back the initial was swiftly penned. In other words, the camera showed that, as Pointer had suspected, the cheque, originally made out by Julian Clifford—for the signature was his without a doubt, hastily and carelessly written—had been to Self ... to Julian Clifford. Some one into whose hands it had fallen, had ingeniously altered it to a not uncommon family name. And the alterations had apparently been made with Julian Clifford's own pen and ink. There was a little peculiarity about the nib used which showed throughout.

Pointer docketed these new and most important facts, then he reached for the telephone. He mentioned to Sir Edward's valet that it was "Mr. Marbury of the Home Office" who was speaking.

"I understood that Sir Edward left yesterday evening to join a commission at Chequers on the Sudan Cotton Areas, but I find he hasn't been there. Do you know where I can reach him over the telephone at once?"

"I am sorry to say, sir, that there is no telephone at Sir Edward's cottage at Weybridge, where he is spending the day."

"His cottage"—Marbury seemed perplexed—"are you sure? When did he leave town?"

"Sir Edward left about nine yesterday evening, sir. He changed into tweeds, and took nothing down with him but a gun and cartridges. That always means the cottage, sir."

"Do you know which gun, and what number cartridges?" Pointer asked in the sudden tone of a man who has a clue.

"He took his old 12-bore gun, sir, and a bag of Numbers 4 and 6 cartridges."

"Did he drive down himself?"

"Yes, sir."

"Well, that certainly seems to settle it," murmured Marbury. "When do you expect him back?"

"In time for dinner, sir. Eight o'clock."

Marbury rang off, after thanking the man. It was now just after five. A wire would be useless. Sir Edward Clifford, Julian's only brother, had taken a gun and a bag of cartridges away with him yesterday about nine o'clock . . . easily identifiable shots in some circumstances . . . under a loose ulster a gun could be strapped to the body with comparative ease, if a man drove his own car. . . .

Pointer hastily got into his gas-man make-up again, looked around for his tool bag that contained other things beside tools, pushed his cap a little farther on one side, touched it to a sergeant coming in at the main entrance, and swung himself on board a Hampstead bus.

The Haslar's house was a bare five minutes' drive from that of Julian Clifford. When the latter had married Catherine Haslar, Sir William Haslar had built the two houses, and given the larger as a present to his new son-in-law. An inquiry of the gas company had told Pointer that on the principle of the shoemaker's barefoot children, the Haslars had gas fires in all their rooms.

Bag on shoulder he lounged up to the basement door.

The butler was appealed to. "Certainly not!" he announced "You can't go making a noise just now. There's illness in the house."

"Well, of course, sir, if you want to be all blown up by a blocked pipe, carry on!" The man spoke nonchalantly.

"You won't make any noise?" The butler was no keener on explosions than are most people.

"Not so much as a mouse nibbling cheese." Pointer came in and looked about him. He chatted as he sorted out his pliers. Chatted of a gas explosion farther down early this morning which he was surprised to learn had not brought in any complaints from Mr. Haslar.

"Ah, well, of course if he came in about four in the morning, he couldn't have heard it. It was at three." Then he went on to tell of Mr. Clifford's house, where he had just been. Mr. Clifford had lost his umbrella. One of the servants at Thornbush had said in Pointer's hearing that he must have left it at Mr. Haslar's house last evening ... an insinuation which was loftily repudiated by Wilkins. Mr. Clifford had not been to the house for a month past.

Pointer, who wore the full uniform of the gas company, was allowed to roam the house by himself. He went first of all to Arnold Haslar's bedroom. There he knelt for the briefest of seconds by the hearth, staring at the bed where lay a young man with his eyes closed. Haslar looked very white. But was he really ill or only keeping out of the way? On the mantelpiece was a much-used New Comfort pipe. In a rubber-lined pocket of a waistcoat hanging in the dressing-room was some tobacco of the kind which the head porter at Heath Mansions had noticed was smoked by Mr. Tourcoin last Friday evening.

Pointer tiptoed to the wardrobe and opened it noiselessly. The man on the bed had not seemed to pay the slightest attention. But he suddenly turned over and barked:—

"What the devil are you doing with my clothes?"

"Gas smell, sir," Pointer said, immediately coming up to the bed and taking a good look at the man in it. "There's a gas leak somewhere. We can't locate it. But if it leaked last night say, and the wardrobe was open, you'd smell it when it was suddenly opened, and think something was wrong again. It smells pretty strong."

He put his head into the wardrobe and sniffed several times. There was an ulster, or some coat of similar texture, hanging on the last hanger. Pointer put out his hand as though to steady himself, and sniffed again. The last coat was an orange and brown check tweed. Without an apparent glance at it, he shut the door and sniffed in a farther corner of the room, working down to the floor in a most convincing way.

Haslar seemed to fall into a heavy slumber. Pointer stood a moment photographing the face on his mind. He noted the big frame, the masterful, rather overbearing jaw, the eyebrows meeting over the bold nose—secretive eyebrows these —and the mouth firm yet passionate. Then he melted from the room and slipped downstairs to the ground floor. Here he found a telephone in what was evidently Haslar's own particular room. One end of the large library shut off by folding doors from the book part proper.

Pointer asked for a number that would have meant nothing to a listener. But it was the secret number used by the officers of New Scotland Yard, and insured instant connection and precedence.

The Chief Inspector murmured a few short sentences. Decoded they meant that one of his men, got up as directed, was to ask the "watcher" outside Haslar's house for a card. It would be one of Arnold Haslar's own cards, that Pointer had just taken from a drawer in the writing table. It was to be used according to instructions.

Pointer wanted that brown and orange ulster at once. If Haslar continued to sleep well, it might be at the Yard by six o'clock.

Then he took up his own work of going swiftly but carefully over the house.

# CHAPTER 5

While the Chief Inspector was roaming Arnold Haslar's house, Julian Clifford's new librarian and Diana had been looking at some rare books at Sotheby's. Straight was expressing his disappointment at Julian Clifford's absence.

"He has left me neither instructions nor a free hand. Hobbs is too busy to question Mr. Clifford's preferences. He certainly is a worker! And Newman, apart from your warnings, dislikes me. Jealousy, I suppose. No man likes to be supplanted."

"Supplanted? Newman?" There was joy in Diana's tone. She had been looking rather bored by Straight's little outburst.

"So Mr. Clifford hinted in our after-dinner talk last night. He's thinking of letting Newman go. But that's in strictest confidence. What concerns me at the moment far more is when he is coming back. I—"

A passing newsboy waved his papers at them.

"French anarchist killed in Hampstead flat! Headless man in Hampstead!" he shouted.

"Hampstead?" Straight bought two papers.

"Why it's Heath Mansions! The building near us!" Diana said, aghast as she caught sight of a photograph on the front page. Straight said nothing. He was reading. Suddenly Diana gave a low cry. She went livid.

"Here! you're ill!" Dick said solicitously.

"A taxi," she murmured. "I'm all right. Don't come with me."

"Certainly I'm coming with you." He signalled to a taxi, gave the man her home address, and jumped in beside her. But Diana sprang to her feet.

"No! I want to be alone. I must be alone." She spoke in a strange, wild voice. She looked around for another taxi. There was none.

"Dick, I want to be alone. You can't come with me." She seemed unable to find other words.

"Sorry to force my society on you," he said quietly, "but I'm coming. You've had a shock."

Diana looked at him with dilated pupils. Her eyes suddenly looked enormous in her pale face.

"You must keep out of this, Dick," she said again in the same firm tone. "You of all men. I know how you would hate to be mixed up in anything disagreeable."

"No more than the next fellow," he assured her. "And when you're in trouble, you don't suppose blows would drive me from you, do you? What frightened you in that paper?"

"You're quick," she said in a low tone; "I'm glad no one else was with me. Dick, something awful has happened. I knew evil was bound to come of— I must go home at once. I must see Arnold—" She pulled herself up.

"Exactly!" Dick reminded her. "What was it the doctor said? He must have no shocks. So Arnold being out of court, suppose you face the fact that you're driven to turn to me?"

Diana passed a hand across her eyes. She shivered.

"Murdered like that! Decoyed, and then butchered!" she said under her breath. "Give me the paper again!" She took it from him hurriedly, and read as though every unnoticed punctuation mark might make a difference.

Straight, too, dipped into his sheet. There was enough and to spare to hold his attention in the columns. When he came to the description of the man who had taken the flat, he gave a start. The house agent had remembered something more than he had told the police. He had now remembered and described to a reporter an unusual ring which the man had been wearing on the little finger of his right hand—a black opal very highly rounded. Two gold snakes were coiled about it, their coils making the ring, their heads apparently holding the stone in place between them as they nearly met across it. The serpents were carved in great detail and in the round.

At first the house agent, though he had remembered the ring, had not placed the man who had worn it. He was now sure that it had been on the hand of the mysterious Tourcoin. His clerk, too, remembered it, as well as the check ulster which the man had worn.

Straight felt Diana sag in the corner beside him as she came to the description of the ring and the overcoat.

"We both know a ring like that, but has Arnold such an ulster by any chance?"

"A ring like that. . . . Such an ulster ...!" she repeated under her breath. "It is Arnold's ring and ulster that are described here. As to the ulster—" She drew in her breath sharply, with a shudder.

"It's a damnable business," Straight said, after a moment's deep thought. "All we can do is to keep our own counsel—as long as we can," he added grimly. "What about the name? The name of Tourcoin?"

"Some one in a French town of that name, or Belgian, I don't know which, asked him to advise them about some new electrical plant not long ago. The name would still be fresh in his mind."

"But why in the world should Arnold have given a false name when looking over the flat? What possible connection is there between him and a Basque communist?" he asked, looking bewildered.

Diana sprang to her feet, rocking with the speed of the taxi.

"I can't stand it! I can't stand it!" She turned a distorted face on Dick. "There's another taxi!" She waved to it. "I can't endure to hear it talked about. To speak of it!" She motioned again. But the cab had it's flag up and passed on. Diana sank back into her seat as though her legs gave under her. Straight bit his lip. The incident showed him how little he counted with her in Diana's inner life. "You saw him yourself this morning coming out of the place—Heath Mansions," woman-like Diana could talk of nothing else. "Others may have seen him too!"

Straight looked at her warningly. "Forget that, Diana! I have—completely!" A newspaper boy with a later edition than the one which they had seen ran past. Straight got a copy.

"Who was the Man who took the Flat?" was now the heading. Diana and Straight, heads together, scanned it. The description, pieced together by an able reporter, fitted Arnold Haslar with appalling closeness.

Neither spoke until they turned into Arnold's garden. Newman, Clifford's secretary, was just being admitted. Diana gave a sudden cry, a cry of sheerest terror, and clutched Dick's arm with fingers that hurt. Her hands were colder than he had imagined living hands could be. He thought that she had fainted. Her face with its eyes closed looked so white. But in a second the lids lifted. She squared her shoulders as the cab stopped. She seemed to pull herself together with a great effort. She looked more like sinking to the ground where she stood than walking up the steps, but she went forward very steadily, refusing help. Wilkins came out hurriedly. "Are you ill, Miss Diana? Let me call Alice. Let me assist you"

She paid no attention to him. Newman had gone on into the hall.

"Mr. Newman?" she asked quickly, imperiously.

"Mr. Newman is here, Miss Diana. He insists on being allowed up to see Mr. Haslar for a moment. I told him that the doctor's orders were to the contrary." Wilkins had obviously not yet heard of the murder, nor of the man with the black opal ring and the check ulster.

Diana stepped in swiftly, and laid a hand on the newel post. She still looked as though she needed its support.

Newman turned at her entrance; he was just mounting the stairs. He, too, was very pale. The eyes were far back in their sockets, but they were still as unreadable as ever. He and Diana faced each other in absolute silence for a long minute.

"I didn't expect to see you," she said in an oddly shaken voice.

"I'd like to go up and speak to Arnold for a moment," was his only reply.

"No one can see him," Diana said in a firmer voice. Newman seemed to hesitate.

"He's feverish, I understand. Is he lightheaded?" he asked in a lower tone, though Wilkins had already gone on down the hall.

Diana did not reply at once. Then she asked:—

"Why should he be? You've seen the evening papers?" Newman nodded.

"Hadn't we better talk in here?" He glanced towards a room.

Diana did not seem to hear him. She was speaking in a very low, very stony voice.

"You saw about the murder in Heath Mansions?" she asked again.

Once more he nodded.

"Did you read the description of the ulster the man was wearing? Of the ring?"

"I read them. Yes." Newman was standing with his head bent. His eyes only were raised and were fastened on Diana. As before, Straight could make nothing of their expression. Was it inimical or merely intentionally blank? Then Straight looked at Diana. Never would he have believed her face capable of showing such passion. The girl seemed to be swept by a fury—a fury that was shaking her where she stood— a fury which was in spate but which she was damming back.

"Why?" Newman asked gravely.

"Because Arnold has a coat and ring exactly like them." Straight frowned. Women were the most imprudent of beings.

"Because coats and rings can be borrowed, Mr. Newman."

"You mean—?" Newman still spoke very quietly, rather thoughtfully.

"That my brother had no interest in murdering anybody. But that might not be true of—Sanz Etcheverrey." She spoke the words in a low, tense whisper.

"The man who was killed?"

"No. *Not* the man who was killed."

Straight looked quickly from Diana to Newman, and back to Diana. What did this scene mean? Newman did not glance at her now. He was looking meditatively at the black and white marble squares of the hall.

Diana swept past him. Her brother's valet came down the stairs.

"Mr. Haslar's asleep, miss. He's been asleep nearly all afternoon."

"Good." Diana hesitated. Straight took a step forward. Could he slip up and get that ulster? He had looked in the cloakroom just now, and it was not there.

"The tailor sent a man for an overcoat of Mr. Haslar's a little while ago, miss. I got it out without waking him," the man continued. "He had a card of Mr. Haslar's, saying that his new check motor coat was to be handed to the bearer, miss. I did quite right, I hope? I didn't wake Mr. Haslar," he repeated.

"Quite right, Smith," Diana said rather faintly. She turned suddenly and came up to Newman, who was moving towards the door.

"A moment! I want to speak to you outside."

When they were clear of the steps she said in a low, bitter voice, "I think it only fair to warn you that I may have to tell all I know to the police."

"Warn me?" Newman asked, as though not understanding her.

"Arnold may have gone to that flat or you may have gone in his things," she went on, "but I am convinced that in some way you are mixed up in the affair. I heard you tell Arnold only last week that that flat was to let. If Arnold gets drawn into the crime I shall speak out. Please don't go on with the farce of having lost your memory." She looked at him with eyes that seemed to scorch what they looked at.

He looked bewildered. "Farce? I only wish it were," he said heavily.

"You have not lost it," she repeated firmly; "I've known it all along."

Now he gave her a measuring look. The look that a fencer gives another when he steps forward, foil in hand.

"Have you told Mr. Straight as much? Not yet? I see. Not yet."

He nodded thoughtfully; almost, Diana felt, as though she, and what she was saying, had retreated into the background of his thought. Almost she could imagine that he was hearing some other voice speak, and was listening to it rather than to her. The feeling chilled her.

Turning towards her, he made a gesture almost of dismissal.

"Do what you feel you must do," he said coldly, and raising his hat, walked on past her.

For a second she stood with clenched hands, then she turned back to the house. She went into the room where Straight stood waiting for her. It occurred to Diana for the first time, that possibly she had not appreciated Dick at his proper value. There was a certain measured, and measuring quality about the young man which had a little amused her, and a little chilled her, out in Australia. Yet she felt suddenly very glad that he was in England, and at Thornbush just now. Dick was never spectacular, but she felt, a little self-reproachfully, that his was the kind of character to which one turns in moments of trouble. If only he were not at other times something so perilously approaching a prig!

He closed the door behind her.

"What in the world?" he began. She raised her hand.

"That ulster has gone—taken—fetched! But by whom?" There was terror in her face now.

"Well test it. Who's your brother's tailor? Rivers of Saville Row?"

He rang up, and after a moment dropped the receiver back.

"No one was sent from there. But, of course, the fact that your brother gave a card looks as though it might have been some local presser . . . some regular man he employs."

"Dick, do you think it could have been Newman whom you mistook for my brother this morning, coming out of Heath Mansions?"

Dick did not answer for a moment, then he said:—

"Why should it be Newman, Di?"

Now it was her turn not to reply.

"Why did you connect him with this dead anarchist?" he asked again.

She shook her head. Her eyes were closed. He had never expected to see Diana look so broken.

"I'm only groping," she said faintly.

"What do you know of your uncle's secretary that makes you link him with this Etcheverrey murder?" he persisted. "You ought to tell me, Di. If there's any chance of helping Arnold out of this unholy mess it will be that you and I pull together."

"I can't tell you, Dick," she said, after another long moment. "I didn't mean to say as much as I did before a third person. But it welled up. Nothing will make Mr. Newman speak out. Nothing! He's like some creature hiding in his lair. He knows that he's safe there, and won't come into the open."

A passion of hate sounded in Diana's voice. Straight gave her a very searching, not over-pleased look. No man cares to hear the woman whom he hopes to marry speak like that of another. It takes too much to explain it. Diana walked to the window and stood drawing a deep breath.

"If things get worse, if suspicion falls on Arnold, I must go to the police and tell them—what I know. But not to you, Dick—not yet. If that's why Newman has seemed so strangely fond of Arnold—" she stood biting her lip and quivering afresh against the sharp light of the window.

"You won't tell me what the secret is between you and him, then?" There was an edge to his voice.

She did not reply. His face flushed.

"I had hoped that I could be of some use to you and Arnold, Di. I am sorry that I overrated your confidence in me."

"Oh, Dick"—she held out a quivering hand—"be generous!"

He took it—a shade stiffly.

"Let me warn you for both your sakes, to think over every step before you take it. In this affair, you can't accuse Newman without involving Arnold. At least, I'm afraid so. The whole affair is really too grave." He went on in a kinder tone, "You see, it was Arnold whom I saw slipping out of what I now know is Heath Mansions this morning. And"—again he hesitated, but the danger of a misunderstanding on her part was too real—"and the doctor thought he had just had a terrible shock, remember. What about the servants? Are they to be trusted?"

"The butler has been with us since father's days. So has the housekeeper. I think they'd stop any of the servants chattering. But of course it's bound to leak out sooner or later. So many people have seen that ring."

She seemed about to leave him, but he detained her.

"Diana," Dick's eyes were very gentle, "I repeat that I think you ought to tell me what you know about Newman. Evidently you know something very important, very much to the point, in this awful affair."

She looked irresolutely at him. Even though she felt sure that Richard Straight was a good man to go to for advice, Diana was terrified of a false step, for the waters were deep. Yet she knew that the very things in his character which kept her from being in love with him, as she thought, his caution, his imperturbability, a certain coldness in his judgment of his fellow men could be an advantage at times—at such a time as now, for instance.

"I must think things over first," she said finally.

He made a gesture of "as you please."

"But be careful!" he warned. When she left him Richard Straight paced the room. Had it merely been Diana who had connected Arnold and that flat, all would have been well. She might have turned to him, and Dick would have had a magnificent chance of winning her enduring love by standing between her brother and the result of whatever it was that he had done.

He had been proud to marry Diana Haslar as things were. . But how long would it take for things to change? It seemed a far cry from Haslar to a Basque anarchist, but that brown and orange check ulster, that snake ring, might yet bring the whole police pack out in full cry after their owner. So Straight feared. It was an intolerable thought, that because Arnold Haslar should have been such an utter fool as to wear them when taking the flat, because he had been such an utter idiot, Diana was to be mixed up in the business, if it ever came out. Why, he too, Richard Straight, might yet be dragged, through them, into the affair.

This idea came like a blow to him. He was as good as engaged to Haslar's sister. He had arrived but a few hours before the crime had been committed. The police said that the man in the flat had been murdered last night. He, Dick, had no alibi for last night. He could tell people that he had been fast asleep from about ten till he was roused next morning, but would they believe it?

Dick did not share Diana's suspicion that possibly it was Newman who had worn her brother's things and taken the flat. Yet it was maddening to think that if only Diana would tell him the whole of what she evidently knew or suspected, about her uncle's secretary, it might be sufficient to free Arnold from all but the blame of a foolish fancy for taking flats under assumed names.

Diana came back into the room.

"Arnold's still asleep. I didn't wake him but I took his ring out of the drawer where he keeps it, and now I'm going to Thornbush. I must speak to Newman again. What's that, Wilkins? Can a gas man come into the room for a moment? Certainly."

They passed a tall, lanky figure with a shock of dark-red hair as they went out. His bag was in their way, so that there was a second's delay as he moved it more hastily than tidily, for half the tools spilled out, and in his very civility to pick them up Pointer blocked the passage still more, and incidentally got two very good photographs. Straight merely looked very worried, very perplexed, and thoughtful, but Diana's face was a travesty of her usual one. Gone was that effect of radiant youth, gone the cool aloofness of her glance. She had recovered a measure of composure, but in her eyes was something desperate, frightened, very nearly cowed. Neither Dick nor Diana spoke on the way to Thornbush, where Diana learnt that Newman had not yet returned. Diana stood a moment thinking deeply, then went on to her own room with a heavy, dragging step. Dick decided that the best thing for him to do would be to try and get some work done.

Outside, a couple of boys—they looked about fourteen—were hunting through the garden. "Sir Raymond Tirrell's nephews," so they had explained to Trimble, had lost a pet dormouse. The little chap, taken for an airing into the garden, had developed an unexpected sprightliness. The tips of his ears had last been seen disappearing through Mr. Julian Clifford's hedge. Might they search the garden? They would be careful of the beds. Sir Raymond was Mr. Clifford's nearest neighbour, so Trimble wished them good luck, and volunteered to keep the cat shut up. The lads must have been very fond of that dormouse. Inch by inch the garden was searched. Two spots where flowers had recently been changed were noted, and reported later on to the two road-menders outside. The boys went off finally with their recaptured pet, so they told a servant.

Pointer meanwhile was looking through some locked drawers in Haslar's study. They yielded nothing of interest to him except some letters of Mrs. Orr's.

Evidently there had been, if there was not now, an engagement between the two. She wrote as though she definitely counted on becoming mistress of the Hampstead house, even though only to have it sold.

Suddenly the telephone bell rang. A servant entered, making towards the instrument at a leisurely gait. But Pointer had reached it at the first tinkle.

"'Alf a tic! It'll be for me. From the boss. Speaking from the head office." He took the receiver and nodded. "It's 'im all right. Yes, sir. This is Mr. 'Aslar's."

"Who's speaking?" called a sharp voice: the voice of a very angry, or a very excited man.

"Me, sir; Long."

"I want your master at once on the 'phone. Is he in?"

"'Alf a mo, sir." Pointer passed a hand over the 'phone. He worked very hard at the trick. Inside the mouthpiece was now another one that blocked it completely so that nothing could pass through to the ears listening at the other end. Nothing showed. The thin rubber mould fitted easily. "It's my boss all right," Pointer turned to the manservant; "wants the foreman." A touch of Pointer's finger and the india-rubber lining to the 'phone disappeared into his palm. "'E's not 'ere now, sir. 'E's out. What number shall I tell 'im to ring up?" was the next best move to asking who was

speaking.

"Westminster 1876? Oh, very good, sir." Pointer heard the receiver slammed down at the other end, and continued, "You'll be at the works, I suppose, sir? And what about those three-quarter fittings? They don't seem to work quite right. Mr. 'Aslar 'ere seems to've made no complaint, but farther down the road the smell is something awful. Very good, sir. Yes, sir. At once!" and Pointer turned away.

"I'll send along my mate to go on 'unting for that escape. I must 'urry. The boss is on his 'ind legs." And Pointer made for the nearest telephone outside the house.

Here he rang tip Westminster 1876. He got the number at once. Pointer was a capital mimic, thanks to hard work and lessons from the best mimic on the London music halls. In a hoarse voice, as like Haslar's as he could make it, he wheezed into the tube.

"Just got back with a damned bad cold. Who's at that end?"

"Me!" came in menacing tones.

"Who the devil's 'me'?" croaked the pseudo Haslar.

"Brown!" came in the same tone. "Now do you understand?"

Pointer coughed into the receiver by way of gaining time. He was doing double-quick thinking.

"I'm in a hurry," he croaked finally.

"What do you suppose I'm in? I want to see you at once. *At once*, understand!" Haslar might have been the mysterious "Brown's" slave. "Same place as before."

"I'm damned if I'll come," Pointer retorted.

"Oh, yes, you will!" There was an ugly menace in the voice. "Oh, yes, you will! I know everything. Understand?"

Pointer did not reply.

"Now do you get me? Come at once. Same place as before."

"Can't. Not to the same place," Pointer said doggedly— and truthfully.

"Why not?"

"Dangerous."

"Where, then?" growled the voice at the other end.

"How about the grill-room of the Savoy?" Pointer asked, as a feeler in that hoarse whisper.

"How about the throne room of Buckingham Palace!" came the retort. "I don't think you quite realise what you're in for, my clever young friend. I've got you in a cleft stick. One shift of a finger and you're crushed."

"I suppose you're aware that this is not an automatic exchange?" Haslar's voice asked roughly, thickly. "Either speak sense, or dry up!"

"I'll talk sense fast enough. Now listen. There's a Spanish feeding place off Shaftesbury Avenue. Fuenta Castellana. I'll be there outside the door at seven to the moment. And look here, Haslar, don't keep me waiting. If I got bored I might stroll into that police station near by. Get me?"

"I've a mind to send Newman," Pointer hoarsely confided to the wire.

"You come yourself!" was the retort, "and don't forget your pocket-book. You'll need it, by God! No cheques, mind."

"I shall get Straight to come too."

"What Straight? Run straight yourself!" The facetiousness did not extend to the voice.

"Oh, all right. But I shall be in disguise. Aged man. Two crutches. Look out for me." Pointer did not dare hang up for fear of the Brown at the other end ringing up the real Haslar. He waited till the other had expressed his burning opinion of such monkey tricks, and repeated the injunction to bring a well-filled note-case with him. Pointer made for his own rooms at the Yard, and turned to his book of disguises.

"Old Gentleman—crutches" was Number Fifteen. In a slit of a cupboard numbered fifteen was the complete outer man of what might have been the Chief Inspector's great-grandfather. Pointer's difficulty was to give himself a touch of Haslar as well. Also his disguise had to look like a disguise. The effect was to be that of an amateur at the game. The bushy white eyebrows palpably put on, the Father Christmas beard obviously added.

He finally took a taxi, driven by one of his own men, and got out at the little bit of Spain indicated by the mysterious "voice."

He could almost have smelled his way thither. Gazpacho of true Iberian strength was evidently one of the dishes of the day.

Outside the door four men were waiting. One was thin. The voice over the telephone had not been that of a thin man. One was young. Nor that of a young man. The third, though stout and getting towards middle-age, was obviously Spanish. The man speaking had not been a foreigner. The fourth was —good Heavens! It was Cory! Major Cory of the Holford Will Case. A case fought out some dozen years before, where the major had been accused by the daughter of undue influence in causing old Mrs. Holford to leave every farthing to him and nothing to her only child, a middle-aged spinster. In spite of his expressed sympathy with the prose- cutrix, the judge, as well as the jury, had had to let the major bear off the spoils. Pointer had heard with great joy that they did the man no good. Racing and Monte Carlo had helped to run through the money in a couple of years.

Cory was one of those men in whom our police take an abiding interest. For the Metropolitan Police have still a great deal to learn when it comes to appreciating those who, like certain rare orchids, seem able to live on air.

So Cory had wanted Haslar on the telephone all morning. Cory gave his name as Brown. Cory knew Newman, but did not seem to know Straight. Humph. . . . Pointer tottered out of the taxi and hobbled up to him.

"Here I am, Cory, where shall we go?"

Cory eyed him, as a dog eyes a man before biting.

"Think yourself clever because you're got up like an organ-grinder? Your voice gives you away, Haslar, though. I'd know you anywhere."

"Would you?" Haslar's voice asked in chagrin.

"Anywhere. But now—" The other, who seemed in a very high and mighty mood, steered Pointer to a table in a corner. He ordered a bottle of 1896 port, mentioning gracefully that there was no point in not having the best that the house kept, as Haslar would foot the bill.

"And now look here, Haslar," Cory began, as soon as they were alone. "I know all! *All*. Get me?" Cory bored a pair of bold eyes into the old gentleman's. "Now, how much is it worth to you not to have me—" Suddenly the "gallant major" stopped, shot one glance at Pointer that made the latter get his right hand ready, and slipped with extraordinary swiftness out of the place.

Pointer looked about him. A man, a police officer by his smart, alert bearing, had entered in company with a companion who looked like a needy artist in search of copy. The two had taken a table not far from Pointer. The Detective Inspector wondered whether ever any of his criminals had more regretted meeting Inspector Bradly than did he at that moment.

Pointer caught his eye and gave the signal of the C.I.D. as he threw a match away. Rising, he handed a bank note to his waiter and said he would be back for the change in a moment. Bradly strolled after him.

"Mr. Gaskell, I believe?" Bradly said politely, touching him on the arm, "Mr. Gaskell from Leeds?"

Pointer shook hands with the air of a countryman overjoyed to see a familiar face in a strange town.

"You saw Cory leaving?" he asked under his breath.

Bradly nodded.

"Saw one of your men after him too, sir. Did I frighten him away? Too bad! Mr. Tindall wanted to see if he couldn't find out something down here about a Spaniard who has been to the mortuary to identify this Etcheverrey who's just been found killed. Thank Heaven, if I may say so! He said he couldn't identify him at all. Might be him, might not. But Mr. Tindall was told that he looked at that foot as though expecting to find a scar on the sole. Mr. Tindall thought he might have come on here. So he might. But 'a tall, slender, dark young man with a big drooping moustache' would fit a dozen chaps in that very room. Still, Mr. Tindall asked me to come along and point out a couple of dagoes who are ready to sell any one to either side."

"You were in that Holford Case, weren't you, Inspector?" Pointer asked presently.

Bradly nodded. "Yes, sir. Before your time, wasn't it?"

"Ever heard the name of Haslar mentioned in connection with it?"

"Haslar?" Bradly thought hard. "I don't remember that name cropping up."

"Nor Clifford?"

"Oh, Clifford was one of the chief witnesses against Cory. He all but dished him. Mr. Julian Clifford, the great author, I mean. He was a friend of old Mrs. Holford's. He maintained that Cory had stolen a later will and burnt it. Knew the very hour he stole it. But he couldn't prove anything. Though he saw to it that every one knew what he thought, so that there should be no hanging on to clubs or society afterwards for Cory. It did me good to hear him in the witness-box."

Suddenly Bradly clicked his fingers. "Mr. Clifford's nephew! Australian boy. Yes, Haslar was his name. It was in the holidays, and he used to come into court with his uncle, Mr. Clifford, and ask me no end of questions in between whiles."

"You're keeping an eye on Cory, I suppose?"

Bradly said that during the twenty-four hours about sixty police orbs were more or less focused on the major.

"He's evidently up to no good," the police officer went on, "he never is, of course. But I mean that he's evidently up to something he can get into trouble over, or he wouldn't have faded away like that when he saw me. I don't deny that I would give a year's pay to jug him, and he knows it! That poor old Miss Holford in an Institute sticks in my crop."

Pointer let Bradly return to Tindall, and walked off. That telephone message from Brown . . . the whole. tone of Cory's conversation with the supposed Haslar ... a previous grudge against Clifford ... a boy, now a man, who knew of that grudge. ...

Pointer walked on deep in thought, leaving his change for some other time.

Clifford—Haslar—Cory. . . . Linked, though but loosely, by the old crime of the stolen will. Clifford as principal witness, Haslar as a young, eager listener, with the retentive memory of a boy for what interests him, Cory as the accused man. Were these three once more linked closely, for all time, by a new crime, by the most terrible of all crimes?

Pointer returned at once to New Scotland Yard where he learnt several things. No one could be found who had seen any stranger entering or leaving flat fourteen, where, according to the head porter, some silver ornaments had been stolen.

Nothing of any importance had been listened to along either Mrs. Orr's, Clifford's or Haslar's telephones, except his own conversation with "Brown."

The woman detective who had been sent to Mrs. Orr's house reported that that lady had an impeccable bill of health as far as last night went. This morning she had left for Paris by the eleven boat train from Victoria, and Mrs. Clifford had been among the little group of friends to see her off.

Inspector Watts sent in word that no packages of any kind had been delivered at Wellwyn and Co.'s warehouse in Thames Street after closing time yesterday, until a vanload of wireless masts had arrived this morning about ten. Detective-Inspector Watts had been assured that no mistake was possible.

Finally came the account of a very pretty bit of wizardry that had been performed in the office of the house-agent while the Chief Inspector had been finishing his investigations among Haslar's effects. Arnold Haslar's voice had been reeled off by a tiny microphone phonograph which had been in the gas man's bag. The house-agent had identified the "What the devil are you doing with my clothes?" as undoubtedly the voice of Monsieur Tourcoin, who had taken Marshall's furnished flat on Friday last. The same performance had obtained the same result from the head porter. So Tourcoin was now fairly well proved to be Arnold Haslar. Was it quite true that no packages whatever had been left at the warehouse? There could be no question of a "burglary" there. Every building in that street had its night watchman. Pointer's ruminations were interrupted by still another piece of information. It was from the man who was trailing Cory. The wily major had taken a bus to some flats, had walked up to the third floor, had shot down in a lift for one storey, and there caught another on its way to the roof garden, while Pointer's man was covering the door nearest to the first shaft. After the roof garden all trace of Cory was lost.

Pointer had given his man very strict instructions to lose him rather than let him see that he was followed. He did not want the major to leave London. The police had half a dozen funk-holes of his on their list, to one of which he was sure to return once he believed that no one was trailing him.

# CHAPTER 6

It was eight o'clock. Pointer began to think that he might waste a few minutes of the case's time in eating a dinner, when a message that reached him along his telephone wire whisked that prospect away once more.

"Is that Chief Inspector Pointer? Police-Constable Caldicott speaking. Acting in accordance with instructions received at the station, I am reporting directly to you, sir, that Mr. Haslar has just been murdered."

Pointer's lips tightened. He had not expected this. Yet, at the same time—

"I was called in by the butler at four minutes past eight, sir. Just two minutes ago"—P.-C. Caldicott was evidently an accurate young man—"Mr. Haslar was shot in his study. Don't know yet how it happened, sir."

It was not many minutes later when Pointer was hurrying with the speaker up the winding drive.

"Left a man in the house, I hope?" the Chief Inspector asked.

"Yes, sir. P.-C. Bacon. I whistled for him at once."

Bacon stood in the hall waiting for them. The servants were evidently battened down below hatches.

"Mr. Haslar isn't quite dead, sir, as we thought at first. The doctor found some signs of life. He insisted on having him carried to his bedroom."

Pointer ran upstairs, and with one constable went thoroughly, but swiftly, over the house and through the garden. No one was in hiding. Then the Chief Inspector turned the handle of Haslar's room very gently.

A young man looked up as he entered without a sound.

"Medical man?"

Pointer laid his card on the table.

"You'll have to be quick, Chief Inspector," the doctor whispered. "We've just sent for Sir Hercules Hawkins. Not that he can do anything. Bullet went in here and is still in." He pointed to a spot just above the right ear. The injured man lay on a table pulled between the windows. Sheets had been spread on it, sheets covered him. Pointer did not waste more than one long look at the head and face. The doctor had cleaned the wound too carefully for him.

"Singed hair?" he asked.

"Singed hair and blackened skin," the doctor assured him. "Revolver must have been fired pressed against the head."

"No hope of his speaking?" Pointer asked.

The doctor shook his head.

"I don't say that for some brief moment consciousness may not come back. It often does just before the end. The final flicker. But that's the merest chance. Ah, here's Sir Hercules, with a couple of nurses!"

A gray-haired man entered hurriedly. Pointer slipped from the room as silently as he had entered it.

"Who's he?" the surgeon muttered; "splendid-looking chap! Knows how to put his feet down. Boxes, I'll bet."

Downstairs Pointer went into the study, the room where the injured man had been found. He stood with his back to the door closely eyeing the whole before he took a step forward.

Suddenly he heard the front door open. Stepping into the hall, he saw Diana come hurrying in. Straight was with her.

Both stopped appalled as they caught sight of the constable who rose from his seat in the hall. Diana's face, already pale, grew ghastly. Then she saw Pointer at the study door. She took a step towards him. Something in its swift motion suggested the pathetic effort of a mother-bird between her nest and a robber. She knew at once that this man with the sun-browned face and the steady, very clear, gray eyes was in command. As she looked at him, she felt a sudden sense of his power, of his ability to surmount difficulties that would stop a smaller man. And with that sense came a sickening knowledge of her brother's danger.

"Miss Haslar? I am Chief Inspector Pointer of New Scotland Yard. Can I have a word with you in the next room? This gentleman is—?" He eyed Straight as though he had never seen him.

"Mr. Straight. My uncle's secretary," Diana said swiftly. "He merely accompanied me to the house when I could not make out a telephone message just now. But please don't wait." She turned to Dick very resolutely. She did not intend to involve him in her brother's disgrace, for she feared that an arrest had been made.

His answer was to open a door. The three stepped in.

"What is wrong?" Diana asked in a toneless voice.

Something in the grave kindness of the face looking at her frightened her more than any words would have done. She read Pointer's look rightly as profound pity. Pity for this young life caught up into the swirl of dark passions, she who should have been a creature of sunshine and happiness. Somehow, Pointer felt that so far the lines had not fallen unto Diana in very pleasant places.

"Miss Haslar," Pointer broke the painful silence, "your brother has met with an accident. The doctor and a surgeon are with him upstairs. He has been shot in the head."

"Shot!" Diana wheeled. She made for the door, but Pointer stopped her.

"No one is allowed to enter his room. They are trying to extricate the bullet."

"He's not dead?"

"Not when I was there a moment before the surgeon came. He's very badly wounded, but he was not dead."

"Who shot him?" Diana asked, putting out a hand and grasping the back of a chair. Whom did she suspect? The dread in her eyes told the keen eyes that barely seemed to glance at her that she suspected some one.

"I know nothing about the case yet," Pointer said quietly. "You probably can tell me who was Mr. Haslar's enemy?"

"He has no enemy. No open enemy," Diana said slowly.

"A so-called friend, then," Pointer said swiftly. He hoped to get some name out of her in her agitation. But she only turned away with a weary, yet resolute, gesture.

"He has a host of friends whom I don't know."

Pointer glanced inquiringly at Straight, who promptly passed the look on to Diana. But she met his eyes stonily.

"Who sent for you?" Pointer asked, after a pause.

"I don't know. A telephone message just reached me at my uncle's, Mr. Julian Clifford's house, saying that something had happened to Mr. Haslar. I couldn't make out what."

She had not tried to. She had guessed an arrest, not a fresh crime. Whose crime?

"If you and Mr. Straight could wait for me in the, drawing-room, I should like to come on up in a few minutes, and ask some questions," Pointer went on.

She looked at him like a creature caught in a snare. Then she nodded, and followed by Dick mounted the stairs as Tindall arrived hot-foot. The Chief Inspector had telephoned him the news before starting out

Tindall, like Pointer, looked keenly about him. There was no sign of a struggle except that one chair had been pushed violently back against the table behind it—a chair on the farther side of the big writing table which only a couple of hours ago had been the object of Pointer's own interest.

The Chief Inspector opened the door and said a word to the constable. A moment later and Wilkins came in. He looked what he was, a dependable, honest man. He was pale now and trembling.

"Who telephoned to Miss Haslar?"

"I did, sir. Just before you arrived. Or rather I got the constable to telephone her something guarded."

"Where did you find your master's body? I see. You heard no shot?"

Wilkins' face twitched. His eyes filled.

"No, sir. But of course with the noise that cars make nowadays, one bang more or less—" Wilkins waggled a shaking hand helplessly. "I've been in service here since Mr. Arnold was a boy at school, and to think that I sat reading the paper! To think that not one of us downstairs raised a hand to help him! Just up from a sick-bed too!" Wilkins quite broke down for a minute or two.

"And Mr. Haslar—was he tidy? careful about cigarette ends, matches, and so on?" Pointer asked to steady him.

"Remarkably so, as a rule, sir."

"Who are Mr. Haslar's enemies?" Tindall asked suddenly.

"Why, he hasn't any, sir." Wilkins spoke with dignity. "Why should he have? At least, he's none in England. I can't, of course, speak for Australia."

That was all that was wanted of Wilkins for the moment. As soon as the door closed behind him, Tindall wheeled.

"So Haslar was remarkably neat and tidy, eh? Just so. And I thought you hadn't yet seen that burnt paper under the desk, while— Hallo!"

Pointer had lifted the flounce of a chair cover and both men now saw a revolver lying under the seat near an open window. Holding it in place with one gloved finger, the Chief Inspector ran a chalk outline around it. Then he lifted it with the greatest care. It was a .25 automatic. From some faint marks in the barrel, Tindall thought that a very light silencer might have been used. They found no finger-prints on the metal. Two shots had been fired.

"Two shots!" Both men looked carefully around the room again. They found no bullet or blood spatters.

"Went wide, probably out through that window, or the other man has the bullet. Carried it away in his body, though that's unlikely, as there's no blood trail. Look here"—Tindall was down on his knees— "that revolver was flung. Flung so as to look as though the murderer had got out into the garden." He pointed to a long streak on the polish of the parquet floor which had stopped at the little snub-nosed thing Pointer was now wrapping in tinfoil.

"It wouldn't have been flung here, from where Haslar was found lying. That disposes of any idea of suicide. Besides, two shots were fired from it. No. Haslar must have fired the first at his opponent, and then had the revolver wrenched from his hand and got the second in his own head, practically killing him. That done, the murderer stepped away from the falling body, and flung the revolver towards the window from about here." Tindall stood "here." "And then left, either by the front door or by the other window. I believe there's a connection between this murder and Julian Clifford's. Uncle and nephew. What do you say, Chief Inspector?"

"A connection? Oh, yes; I, too, think there may be one. Probably a close one."

Tindall joined Pointer, who, after strolling around the room again, touching this, feeling that, even testing the earth around a palm, and lifting the pot up and down in its brass jardiniere, was now bending over a small heap of charred remains of paper which lay under the desk, a match among them. Both stood up after a long scrutiny. Not even the magic of modern science could reconstruct that black dust.

"Some one ground it into the carpet after burning it," Tindall murmured.

"Haslar. His right heel shows it. I looked at his shoes upstairs," Pointer replied. He was down on his knees minutely examining the carpet in front of the pushed-back chair, running a tiny but very powerful vacuum cleaner over it. The gadget was barely the size of his hand, but it did its work well.

Tindall watched him with secret impatience.

"The eyes of the mind, Chief Inspector, are the ones that see farthest. As soon as you've done sweeping, I'd like to question the servants again."

"By all means." Pointer put the little patent back in his case. They called the butler in again and then the valet. The rest of the servants knew nothing.

At half-past six this afternoon Arnold Haslar had rung: said he was fed up with bed, and intended to get up. He was in a very grim mood; but he had been tending that way for a fortnight past, both men agreed.

The butler thought it was due to the coming attack of the 'flu, but the butler, under Tindall's careful pressure, was inclined to connect it with the arrival of a couple of letters by this morning's post. Wilkins had a nephew who collected stamps, and he therefore kept an eye on envelopes from abroad. One of the letters, in a very odd, bold writing, had come from Spain. He had not noticed the other.

"Spain!" Tindall cocked an eye at Pointer. "What place in Spain?"

But Wilkins could not say. The butler connected that Spanish letter with Mr. Haslar's illness because, after breakfast, he had found a letter scattered over the table and floor, torn into tiny shreds, and his master sitting as though stunned beside the table. He had had to be helped into bed, and the doctor summoned. No. The butler had not spoken of this to any one, not even to Miss Diana. He had "thought it better not." The later letters which had come from Mr. Haslar today had been sent down to the office.

The valet had more to tell. About seven, after saying that he would dine out, Mr. Haslar had gone downstairs. About half-past, or perhaps a quarter to eight, he could not be more exact, Smith had heard his master's voice in the north library, which was his own study, raised as though in anger. The words, "You've got to do it, and do it at once!" reached Smith, but he was too far up the stairs to catch anything but that one passionate roar. On that had come what he, as well as Wilkins below, had believed to be a motor-cycle starting up its engine outside with a set of terrific bangs. A few minutes later, Wilkins, coming into the library to see if all was well with his young master, found him slipped to the floor by his writing-table chair apparently dead, a little red wound still trickling blood above his ear. No one had seen or heard any one enter or leave the house. But Haslar's friends generally let themselves in and out with careless ease. The latch of the front door was caught back by day. Questioned as to strangers who had been to the house lately, Major Cory's photograph, among six others, was picked out unhesitatingly by Wilkins as that of a man who, giving no name, had first come to see Arnold Haslar last Thursday evening. He had come on Friday, and also last night, and had then for the first time given the name of Captain Brown. Wilkins' eyes met those of the Chief Inspector and the man from the Foreign Office with a certain dignity.

"I'm telling you the exact truth, sir. Things can't be worse"—which incidentally spoke volumes for Wilkins' idea of the police.

The man had arrived each time at about the same hour on Thursday and Friday and yesterday. Somewhere around nine. Questioned closely, Wilkins said that there had been no signs of any trouble between his master and the man whose photograph he had identified, but he had noticed that on no occasion had Mr. Haslar offered to shake hands with his visitor, who had stayed over an hour on the first two occasions, though but a bare half-hour last night. On the first occasion, at any rate, the conversation must have been of a very private character, because he, Wilkins, had had some business that took him to the library at the same time, and had only caught a low murmur.

"A very unusual thing with Mr. Arnold Haslar talking in his study, sir. As a rule, you have to hear every word, whether you want to or not. It and the library are really only one room, partitioned off."

Pointer referred to some coolness between Mr. Haslar and his uncle, Mr. Julian Clifford. But obviously the butler knew nothing of any such feeling.

Both he and Smith unhesitatingly identified the automatic found by the window as Mr. Haslar's. More important still, the valet swore that it had been in its usual place when his master was having his bath. He had opened the drawer to drop a penknife into it. Smith had an idea that he had heard Mr. Haslar come up and go into his bedroom while he, the valet, was tidying up in the dressing-room. He must have taken the weapon then. As far as Smith knew, Mr. Haslar had never taken the automatic downstairs before.

"So Mr. Haslar expected trouble," Tindall mused. "Knew when it was coming, and got ready for it. Was he a good shot?"

"He was apt to get over-eager, and spoil his aim." And just out of bed, he, Smith, wouldn't be surprised if his master had missed the man entirely, worse luck. Smith knew nothing about any caller last night, but he did know that about ten Mr. Haslar had driven off in a great hurry, telling Wilkins not to let any one sit up, as he would not be back till very late. Smith had an idea, only an idea, that Mr. Haslar had rushed off in answer to a telephone message that had seemed to vex him very much.

"Any one in the house who knows more than you and Wilkins do?" Tindall asked, pulling on a glove.

"No. None of us knows anything really. It's tough! . . . not knowing . . . not being able to do something." And Smith left them.

"Strange case!" Tindall mused; "strange and deep. Etcheverrey like a spider in the middle of the web. I wonder what Sir Edward Clifford will say. He must be back by now. It's close on nine. There's the devil of a lot to do. To bridge the gap between Clifford and Haslar, and link both with Etcheverrey!"

Caldicott, the constable, came in.

"Gentleman of the name of Dance to see you, sir. Mr. Haslar's manager. Said you just telephoned him."

Pointer had.

Dance was a stout, frank-faced man with a strong Australian accent. He was considerably older than Haslar. Just now he looked consternation personified. He was of no help, except that he scoffed at the idea of a business enemy of Arnold Haslar's.

"This has nothing to do with business," he maintained. "Search for the dame! Fortunately at the office Haslar's supposed to be still ill with 'flu. He'll stay ill with it too. We're a good firm. A darned good firm. But shootings—whew!"

"There's a strong-room built into one end of this study," Pointer said finally, "would you open it for us? I want to see inside it." He did—very much indeed.

Dance hesitated.

"You know the code word?"

"Oh, yes, I know it. But"

"The butler told me Mr. Haslar keeps no valuables on the place."

"That's right. Still, you see, after all, a code word"

Pointer and Tindall stood with their backs to Mr. Dance who, even so, held his hat over what he was doing. Finally he called to them.

"Door's open."

The opening showed a fairly large strong-room, large as a big cupboard. Dance glanced at the shelves, on which dusty deed boxes were stacked.

"Nothing's gone. Haslar keeps six-year-back accounts, and papers, and so on, here. Like his grand-dad. The boxes are unlocked. There's nothing else in them."

Pointer found that there was nothing else in them. He looked very, very carefully. So did Tindall, catching his idea.

"And about a package," Pointer went on, after the door had been locked with the same coyness on Mr. Dance's part, "a package that Mr. Haslar, or a friend of his, sent, or brought down, to the warehouse late last night"—Pointer ran over the possible times and sizes—"will you inquire for it and send it along to me?" He gave his name and home address, for Pointer believed that Watts might have been deceived. "We think it will help us, give us a line about this affair. I should expect the parcel to be marked 'to be kept in a cold place.' You haven't a furnace, have you?"

To his relief he learnt that the warehouse was only a between-station for electrical parts and material on its way to or from Australia. There was no furnace.

Mr. Dance would obviously have liked a fuller explanation of many puzzling points, but this was a very busy evening with him, and as all Pointer's hours came under that heading, the meeting quickly broke up. Tindall too shook hands and hurried off.

Pointer looked at his boot-tips for a long second. Then he had Smith in again, and offered him a cigar and a chair.

"There's a confidential question I want to put to you," he said slowly. He waited.

"Confidential it is," the ex-Anzac said cheerfully.

"What was the quarrel about between your master and Mr. Clifford?"

"Mr. Clifford?" For a second Smith stared as a man does who is suddenly, unexpectedly, wrenched around to face another way. Then he looked a little dubious.

"Though you may not see the connection, that quarrel may give us a line on who it was who shot Mr. Haslar," Pointer said very quietly.

Smith eyed him with respect.

"That so?" He straddled his chair and clasped the carved back in a meditative embrace. "That so," he repeated thoughtfully. "Well, I don't know what it was about, but it was a pretty hot affair. You're referring to last Wednesday evening, of course?"

Pointer nodded.

"You didn't hear anything?"

"Nope. I never was much of a listener-in," Smith said carelessly, and Pointer regretfully believed him. He did not look it.

"Only as Mr. Haslar flung the door open he nearly caught my toe, and I had to step back to let Mr. Clifford pass out. Mr. Clifford looked very calm, I must say. Quite unruffled. But Mr. Haslar called after him, 'If you do do it, look out for yourself!' That's all. Not much of a clue there, is there? But it's funny"—Smith sat up straighter—"it's funny that then he threatened 'If you do do it,' and to-day he was shouting that 'You've got to do it!' " He looked keenly at Pointer, who shook his head.

"No, Smith. It wasn't to Mr. Julian Clifford that he spoke  to-day. I wish it had been," he added cryptically.

Smith got up rather sheepishly. "Of course, sleuthing can't be as easy as that, I suppose. And, of course, Mr. Julian Clifford had nothing to do with any shooting."

He went away to make other and more startling combinations yet, of the two sentences, while Pointer went up to the drawing-room where Diana and Straight sat waiting for him.

Straight looked as though he very much wished himself well out of it all. Murders, or shootings, were not at all what he had expected when he had landed in Portsmouth only yesterday as Julian Clifford's librarian. Straight felt that he had a grievance against fate. Here he was, a plain, common-sense sort of young man, only desirous of doing well in the world, of getting on, being drawn into a very black, deep, and dangerous affair. What was the reason for that bullet which had all but killed Arnold Haslar?

"You have no idea who fired that shot at Haslar?" he had just asked Diana.

She only stirred as though in pain.

What did Arnold know? Had he learnt something? Did he guess something? Was it because of some incautiously shown curiosity that— these were the knives at which she was staring, wondering which of them was about to be plunged in her heart.

The door opened and Pointer came in.

"Did you ever hear your brother speak of a man of the name of Cory?"

She shook her head. Straight, too, shook his when Pointer turned to him.

"And you, Mr. Straight, have you by any chance ever heard Mr. Haslar speak as though there were any especial person with whom he is on bad terms?" Straight never had.

Pointer next ostensibly asked each about the other persons at Thornbush this afternoon. In reality he was obtaining from Diana and Straight a time-table of their own actions. They were simple. When

Wilkins had telephoned to Diana they had ostensibly been having tea together. In reality Dick had had the tea, and tried in vain to coax Diana to have some.

After another careful glance in every room, Pointer drove away from the house to stop and question his watcher at the corner—a taxi-driver with a cab that would not go, tinker though he might.

The man had seen no one enter, or leave, Arnold Haslar'?. house, but he was not a picked man. The coming royal visitor kept every good man busy combing through the aliens' quarters of London. Also, nothing is harder than to watch a place for hours on end. Especially if, like this man, he had to pretend to attend to other interests as well. Doubtless he had done his best, yet Pointer knew that at least one person—a man probably—had come, and therefore gone, from Arnold Haslar's house. This person had left a plentiful sprinkling of yellow sand on the carpet in front of that dashed-back chair. Now the paths in Haslar's garden were gravelled with red gravel. The roads and pavements around showed only the usual town dust. At Thornbush, however, the paths were all of yellow sand, rolled for the most part into compact ribbons. But one little walk, cutting off a corner of the drive— a corner that shortened the distance to Haslar's house too, was freshly sanded, and soft as a country lane. It looked, therefore, as though a person from Thornbush had been the man —or woman—who had pushed back that chair.

Diana and Straight had been in each other's company. They were out of the question. Mrs. Clifford was at a Spiritualist meeting. Hobbs was located in the Ritz dining with some South American film magnate. There remained Newman. . . . Newman . . . Pointer had a theory of what had happened in that study. But his theories were always subject to modification, should facts not fit them without having to be twisted. Had Major Cory, after he had given his trailer the slip, made his way to Haslar's house? Pointer thought that he had.

He himself drove to Thornbush and stopped in the garden. In his hand was what appeared to be a stereoscopic camera. It was an uncommonly good binocular. He chose a position against a plane tree and donned dark gray gloves. His cuffs, too, were tucked well up out of sight. A casual eye from the house could hardly notice him at this hour of gloaming against the snake markings of the trunk, as he carefully studied a certain open window facing him.

Newman was bending over a well-lit table on which a paper sprawled, by its ungainly size an English paper. He was reading it avidly. Pointer recognised a picture in it. Newman was reading an account of the "Heath Mansions Mystery," as it was now called. A moment, and he had tossed it to the floor and spread out another from a pile beside him. Suddenly he stopped, turned his head towards the door, and called cheerily, "Come in!" Pointer could hear his voice easily through the open window. As he called, Newman, working with noiseless speed, shoved the several papers into a drawer of his writing table with an amazing stealth. Not a crackle reached Pointer; not a crackle could reach the door of the room.

Newman now called, "Oh, is it locked?" in a tone of great surprise, closing the drawer. All without any noise. Then with an "I'm so sorry, I'd no idea!" he strode to the door. A servant entered. Pointer went around to the front and rang the bell.

He sent in his name as Pointer, without prefixing his position. Newman saw him at once. Pointer introduced himself to him as of Scotland Yard.

"I've come about the accident to Mr. Haslar," he began.

"Accident?" Newman started, or seemed to.

"He was shot at close range just about the time you dropped in to see him this evening."

"Do you mind telling me what happened?" Newman asked coolly, but his lips had a white line around them.

Pointer told him the bare facts.

Newman sat with his head leaning on one hand. He had an unusual power of absolute immobility.

"Miss Haslar must be in great trouble," Newman said, when Pointer had finished.

"She's not so much in trouble as she's keen on getting the man who shot her brother. She thinks he was shot, you see."

"Don't you?"

"Not necessarily. Haslar might have meant to commit suicide. Might have all but succeeded," Pointer said, apparently not looking at the man.

Newman's hand gave a little quiver before it steadied again.

"Why should he do that?" he asked without raising his head.

"Ah, why! Can't you suggest anything?" Pointer asked. "You were the last person seen with Mr. Haslar."

"Was I indeed?" Newman seemed lost in thought. "No, I can suggest nothing."

"What time exactly did you see him?" Pointer went on.

"Somewhere around seven, or a little after."

"Did you see any one coming or going to the house?"

"No one."

Newman did not mention that he had called earlier and had been refused permission by Diana to speak to Arnold.

"How about some one having shot him who has a grudge against him? A man of the name of Cory, for instance?" Pointer suggested idly.

"Cory!" Newman repeated reflectively. "I seem to've heard the name before. But where"

Newman was no fool; Pointer had not thought him one.

"And you think this same Cory—?" Newman queried, as one at sea.

"One or two things were told us that show that he had a grudge against Mr. Haslar. That he felt that he had been drawn into something," Pointer said vaguely. As a boxer, he watched always the feet of the person to whom he spoke. Newman moved no part of his body above the table, but his feet shifted now.

"According to what was told us," Pointer went on in his quiet, ruminative way, "this Major Cory was acting for Mr. Haslar in some way."

"Indeed!" Newman looked politely interested, but no more.

Pointer rose. He had met a wall. For the moment he thought it best to retire. It would be sheer waste of time to ask this man of what he and Haslar had talked, or why he had called on him.

At the nearest telephone he learnt that a message had just reached the Yard asking the Chief Inspector to come to Sir Edward Clifford as soon as possible. He also listened for a minute to the report from one of his men concerning the same gentleman. Then he hurried off in his swift gray car.

# CHAPTER 7

It was close on ten when Pointer was shown into the room where Sir Edward sat talking in low tones to Tindall. The Chief Inspector found a man who, under his surface calm, looked as though he had had a tremendous shock.

For the rest, Sir Edward was a typical diplomat in appearance. That is to say, a man who kept his real self completely out of sight. Urbane, courteous, non-committal, he was a pleasant talker who could speak for hours without betraying one private opinion—a man who never made a positive statement in public in his life.

Pointer's police glance sought the man behind the arras. He seemed to see a gentle and affectionate nature with a strong sense of duty, of right and wrong—not a man of hot blood, nor one given to swift action. Tindall was with Clifford. He had been waiting for Pointer.

"Sir Edward has a very striking theory," the F.O. man began, as soon as Pointer had sat down. "He thinks that though Etcheverrey would not commit an ordinary murder, yet he might if he thought he was being spied on, or if, even more, Mr. Clifford had ever—say for some literary purpose in the future—got into his organisation in some way. You see? You remember that while the Cliffords were at St. Jean de Luz two years ago, Etcheverrey's name was in every paper?"

Pointer nodded. The anti-royalist Basque had given a sort of free pardon to the ex-Empress Zita through the press. And the effrontery of it had amused, or infuriated, the whole of Europe.

"You think Mr. Clifford had some such literary interest in Etcheverrey?" Pointer asked.

"I do"—Sir Edward spoke heavily—"I do. I have for some time past had a very definite idea that my brother was revolving the idea of using Etcheverrey as material, and in the near future."

"Suppose Mr. Clifford had probed deeper than we know?" Tindall struck in. "He had practically unlimited money, a most inquiring brain, invincible courage, or he wouldn't have gone on a whaler as he did once, as one of the crew, too. Suppose he had actually joined some band of Etcheverrey's agents, and been discovered? Betrayed himself in some way, and been murdered; or, as Etcheverrey would consider it, executed. Beheading is the method of execution among the Basques, you know."

Pointer said nothing, he merely listened with close attention.

"And as to Haslar," Tindall went on, "Haslar may have been a go-between between Etcheverrey and Clifford."

"And Major Cory?"

"Also a member of the band, I think," Tindall said slowly.

"Possibly he learnt that Haslar was weakening, might give the show away, and shot him."

Pointer smoked on in silence.

"How do *you* account for Cory?" Tindall asked, with a touch of impatience.

"You F.O. men always want so much for your money," Pointer quoted gravely under his breath, though Clifford was obviously not listening.

"You're working on another line?"

"I intend to to-morrow. We were only called to Heath Mansions this morning. To-morrow will see a big step forward, or all the signs deceive me. I don't think this is a case that can stand still. There's hurry in it, to my thinking. Did Mr. Clifford ever say anything to you, Sir Edward, on which you base your idea of his being particularly interested in Etcheverrey?"

Sir Edward roused himself from a deep reverie which was too deep for Pointer's taste. Men do not usually go off into brown studies when their own theory of their brother's murder is being discussed.

"My brother Julian never referred to Etcheverrey at Thornbush as if he had any personal knowledge of him. Though he seemed, I often thought, amazingly well up in his life story. But then, my brother was well up in so many things." Clifford spoke in a voice of deep regret.

"Who beside Mr. Clifford referred to Etcheverrey at Thornbush?" Pointer asked. "Can you remember any one else who ever questioned you about him?"

"No one but Miss Haslar; and she merely because as a girl she had heard a good deal of him during the war, when she once spent a summer at Hendaye."

There was a short silence.

Tindall rose and took a sympathetic leave. He had many new lines now to follow up. Pointer went with him into the street, and stood a second beside his car.

"How did Sir Edward take the sight of the body in the mortuary? Did he identify it?"

"It was a frightful shock to him. Naturally."

"He recognised the body quite definitely?"

"He did. Quite definitely."

"Did he recognise it quickly?" Pointer persisted.

Tindall pulled at his beard.

"I pretty well insisted at the Commissioner's on being the one to break the news of Julian Clifford's end to Sir Edward, and on taking him to the mortuary afterwards. . . ."

Pointer nodded.

"So I think I owe you the truth. I don't think Edward Clifford particularly wanted to identify that body. I think he wanted to be not quite sure. Natural perhaps. It's a horrible end to the brother you've been good friends with all your life. At any rate, he seemed unable, or unwilling, to be certain that it was the body of Julian Clifford, since the head was missing. But I remembered something he had told me himself apropos of one of my boys hurting himself while diving, that Julian had pierced his foot with a stake once while treading water. I showed him that scar. Either that clinched it, or that decided him to recognise the body. I'm frank with you."

There was a short pause.

"You may not have been the one after all who broke the news of Mr. Julian Clifford's terrible end to Sir Edward Clifford," Pointer said in his turn. "Perhaps Mr. Hobbs did that. At any rate, Mr. Clifford's literary agent was followed into the train at Surbiton, the same train that brought Sir Edward up to town. He travelled up with him in the same compartment. They had it to themselves. That means a long talk. At Waterloo, Mr. Hobbs hurried back to Thornbush without a word or glance at Sir Edward, who got out of the train more slowly. By the way, Sir Edward wasn't apparently expecting any one at Surbiton. He was buried in a pile of papers, so my man says."

"Hobbs! but surely you don't suspect—but I suppose like a good Scotland Yard man you suspect every one!" Tindall was rather bored by such zeal.

"Whatever it was that brought Hobbs flying down to meet Edward Clifford has nothing to do with Etcheverrey, therefore nothing to do with me." He went on "I happen to know that Hobbs hadn't even heard of the man's name, except as Sir Edward talked about him at Thornbush. Of course all of us at the F.O. are full of nothing else these days. No, what brought Hobbs would only be some family worry. Or"—he stopped a moment—"I wonder! Hobbs hinted once to me, not so long ago either, what one might call his suspicions as to Clifford's reasons for leaving home every now and then. But Hobbs had had a glass too much, and I thought nothing of it. But it's possible that he really thinks Clifford is mixed up in some scandal. Or may be mixed up in some. And that would exactly explain Edward Clifford's manner by the coffin. He didn't want to rush things. He wants time to think them over. He does, you know. 'Slow and sure' is said to be his motto. But it's not mine!" And Tindall jumped into a taxi.

Pointer was shown in again.

"When you spoke to Mr. Clifford of Etcheverrey, was any other person present?" Pointer asked after a sympathetic pause.

"Certainly. I often spoke of him when all the Thornbush household was there. And this last time—after dinner yesterday—only yesterday!" His voice shook.

"Who was there then?".

"The whole Thornbush household."

"Did you ever speak of Etcheverrey's diagram-signature, or of the name of his refuge in the Pyrenees?"

"Certainly not."

"Do you think Mr. Clifford knew of it?"

"That I cannot say." Sir Edward seemed to be thinking back. "Tindall has told you, I suppose, of my general impression of my brother being much more up in the facts of Etcheverrey's activities than I should have expected. A word or two here and there—I did not notice them at the time— but by them, and by the questions which he did not ask, I now feel sure that he knew more than one would have expected him to."

"Now about Mr. Clifford's will," Pointer went on, "do you know if he had made one? And if so, where he kept it?"

"He made a will only a couple of years ago. It's at Thornbush. A copy is at his bank, I believe."

"I'd like to see that will. If possible I'd like to have a look at it to-night. My car is outside, may I drive you to Thornbush?"

Sir Edward hesitated.

"It's a terrible position—to know what I know and—However, I believe she is out to-night. Yes, I know she is."

"She?"

"Mrs. Clifford, of course. You shall see the will, Chief Inspector, if it's still there and still addressed to me, and if I can get it without letting Mrs. Clifford know. I understand that she has no idea"

"We've told her nothing," was the guarded reply.

"The shock may kill her. She and my brother were a most devoted couple." He led the way out.

"Have you any idea as to the contents of Mr. Clifford's will?" Pointer asked, when they were off.

"He read it to me. If it's still the one which he made two years ago, as I think it is, I'm sole executor and residuary legatee. There are a few legacies to relatives; ten thousand to Hobbs; nothing to Mrs. Clifford, at her express desire."

"I've been wondering," Pointer said, "whether Mr. Clifford had any unexpected valuables on him. Any large sum of money. ..." ,

Sir Edward seemed to sit rather still for a second. Pointer felt as though in some way he had given the other a jar.

"My brother never mentioned such a thing to me," he said finally, with his eyes now intently fixed on the Chief Inspector.

"Can you hazard a guess as to any dangerous thing that Mr. Clifford was on the eve of doing?" Pointer went on.

"You mean those words of the palmist's—though it's hardly fair to call Mrs. Jansen that. I think Julian referred to something connected with Etcheverrey. Obviously, one might even say."

"I'm always rather distrustful of the obvious," Pointer said quietly. "You didn't see Mr. Clifford yesterday after dinner?"

"No, I left Thornbush about nine and went to my rooms here, where I changed, and drove down to my cottage at Weybridge. The wood pigeons needed thinning out if any of my blue peas were to be saved."

Now Pointer was a country boy. The gun taken, the cartridges chosen, were such as a man would choose for this purpose. But, as a rule, wood pigeons come and go between the hours of five and nine of a July evening.

"Did you shoot many?" he asked carelessly.

"You mean this afternoon? I forgot to take my long-distance glasses down with me. I'm as blind as a bat a couple of yards off. So, though I blazed away for half an hour or so, I only succeeded in hitting one of my own decoys."

"But did you meet any friends at your cottage, Sir Edward?" Pointer did not disguise the fact that he was questioning the other, asking for his alibi.

Sir Edward did not seem to notice what he must have known lay behind the questions.

"No, I never take friends down with me to Weybridge. I only go to my cottage when I want to be alone. Driving down a tyre burst. I had no spare wheel. By jogging along slowly I crawled to the cottage on the rim, getting to Weybridge nearer one than ten. I slipped in without waking my housekeeper or her husband, who acts as my butler-valet. Everything I need is always put up ready for me in the dining-room. Cold supper, electric kettle. So, as so often before, I went to bed without any one in the house being the wiser, after leaving a note on the hall table telling them at what hour to serve breakfast."

"And the car?"

"My chauffeur put on a new wheel."

They drew up at Thornbush. Sir Edward Clifford rang the bell. Mrs. Clifford was out, he was told, with Mr. Hobbs. Mr. Newman was out too; so was Mr. Straight.

"That's all right, Trimble. I shall be in Mr. Clifford's library with this gentleman." Sir Edward led Pointer quickly into the room and tried a drawer. It was unlocked. From the back he drew a sealed envelope addressed to himself. It was marked "The Last Will and Testament of me, Julian Clifford."

"You think I had better open it?"

Pointer looked the envelope over with his glass. It had not been tampered with. He handed it back.

"Please."

Again a quiver passed over Sir Edward's face. It looked like intense emotion as he read the address to himself. In other words, it was just the look that a clever man would assume at such a moment. And Sir Edward was considered clever in a quiet way. He glanced it over.

"This is a new will. Made only some six months ago. I'm still the sole executor and residuary legatee, but the bequest of ten thousand which my brother told me he was leaving to Hobbs is halved. Five thousand goes to Newman. And only five thousand to Hobbs. To Newman 'if still unmarried' is the wording. A thousand pounds he asks Mrs. Clifford to distribute among the servants as she thinks fit. He adds, after some very moving words of gratitude to her, that he leaves her nothing at her express wish, as she strongly objects to inheriting anything from him on his death, and is otherwise amply provided for."

He handed the will to Pointer, who read it through.

So Sir Edward was his brother's heir. And both he and the dead man were believed to have loved the same woman, a woman whom her husband's death would set free. . . .

Pointer did not suspect Sir Edward Clifford, but no position, however worthily won, no reputation for personal integrity, could undo these facts.

"Five thousand seems a lot for Mr. Newman," was his only comment.

"Umm. ... I don't suppose Julian ever expected it would be handed over. There's not so much difference between them in years, you know."

"There was no ill-will between Mr. Clifford and Mr. Hobbs, you think?"

"None whatever. Simply Julian knew that Hobbs is doing uncommonly well out of his literary commissions, and so on."

"May I copy out the gist of the will?" Pointer asked. He wanted to stay on at Thornbush until Mrs. Clifford should return.

Sir Edward nodded and sank heavily into a chair in a dark corner.

Head on hand he sat there, apparently deep in thought. Pointer too was thinking hard. He was busy with the will. So Mrs. Clifford was left out of the will, and knew it. She did not benefit in a monetary sense by her husband's death. Not in the ordinary way. But Mrs. Clifford had cashed a cheque for seventy thousand pounds as soon after her husband's murder as the banks were open. To that extent, merely going by the facts, she had benefited to the tune of a large fortune.

And the will gave Newman as well as Hobbs five thousand pounds. Seeing that that young man was, as far as was known, unmarried.

Curious proviso that. Yet both men lost their legacy, or could not claim it, as long as Clifford's death remained uncertain. Whoever had cut off Julian Clifford's head had believed that he had rendered recognition of the corpse impossible. And Pointer, though he had not an ounce of vanity in his nature, knew that with nine out of ten detectives the ghastly device would have succeeded.

He asked Sir Edward a few questions about the papers in the desk as he looked them over. The other gave rather absent-minded but apparently carefully truthful replies.

It was not far short of eleven when a ring came at the front door. A voice, it sounded like Straight's, but if so it was tense with excitement, asked if by any chance Sir Edward Clifford was at Thornbush. The servant showed him in, Straight's usually impassive face was working. He looked intensely, painfully stirred.

"Can you get a message through to Mr. Clifford, Sir Edward?" he asked in the same eager voice.

"No," Sir Edward said dully; "no, I can't. Why?"

"Miss Haslar wants him fetched if it's humanly possible. She's just had an awful shock. Haslar's spoken. He's recovered consciousness. I've come from his house. I had walked over to find out if anything fresh had been found out. They fetched Diana, who had gone to bed early—" Straight seemed to be unable to continue.

"And what did Mr. Haslar say?" Pointer asked quietly, in that steadying voice of his. He guessed what the injured man had said from the perturbation which Straight showed.

"I was in the room, asking the night-nurse how Haslar was doing, when he suddenly opened his eyes. 'Fetch Diana,' he said quite rationally, only very feebly. The poor girl came on the instant: she thought she was to receive some last word or message of affection. But when she knelt down beside his bed Haslar only gave a fearful cry and struck at her. It was like a ghost trying to strike. And he shrieked out, 'I did it all for nothing! I've killed Julian Clifford! There's his head. Take it away! Bury it!' And with that he fell back dead. At least I think he's dead. I rushed off for you, Sir Edward. They told me at your flat that you were here. Diana insists that Mr. Clifford must come to Arnold at once. She thinks it's the only thing that can save her brother. Heaven knows why!"

Edward Clifford had risen and stood facing this unexpected visitor.

"Arnold Haslar! Arnold Haslar!" There followed a silence short but poignant. "Did *you* know this?" he asked, turning on Pointer. "Did *you* know that it was Haslar who had killed my brother? But what reason? What motive?"

It was Straight now who jumped.

"Mr. Clifford isn't killed. Haslar was delirious." The new librarian at Thornbush looked as though the whole world had gone mad. Pointer eyed his shoe-tips for a full second.

"We believe that the body found with its head cut off early this morning in Heath Mansions is the body not of Etcheverrey, but of Mr. Julian Clifford," he said finally. Straight collapsed into a chair.

"Then—then—!" He stopped and stared first at Pointer, then at Sir Edward. "I *knew* it was delirium!" he said, as though to himself. "For, of course, the man who murdered Mr. Clifford murdered Arnold Haslar too!"

"There is a man who might have tried to kill both men," Pointer agreed, "a Major Cory."

"Cory!" Edward Clifford recognised the name on the instant. "He certainly hated Julian, and with reason. You mean, of course, the Major Cory of the Holford Will case. But where would Haslar come in?"

"We know that Cory and Haslar knew each other," Pointer said cautiously. "Here's his picture." He pulled it out of his pocket and handed it to Straight. "It was taken some years ago, but it's a good likeness. Did you happen to see this man at Mr. Haslar's last night?"

But Straight had not seen whoever it was that had been closeted with Arnold Haslar in his study when he had walked over to Haslar's house after dinner at Thornbush. He explained that Haslar had come out and asked him to wait a few moments, adding that the caller wouldn't stay long. After the man left, Arnold had spoken of going to a music hall and a dance club afterwards, but he, Straight, thought his friend was looking ill, and would be better for a quiet evening. As Haslar was indignantly denying either looking ill, or any intention of staying in, the telephone bell had rung. His friend had gone back into his study—they were in the library—and had listened to a rather long message. He had hung up the receiver after saying grudgingly, "Very well; I'll be there. But it's damned inconvenient." To Straight he had explained that a very urgent business summons would take him out of town for some hours. They arranged to postpone what had been intended as a sort of welcome-back-to-England celebration for himself till to-night.

"And to-night—" Straight began, when he turned to the door. They heard the swish of a car driving up. A minute more and Diana came flying in.

"Uncle Edward, where is Uncle Julian? You must tell me. I must find him. If you don't know, Alison must speak."

"Why, Miss Haslar?" Pointer asked.

"Tell him, Dick." For once Diana was not equal to a task.

"I have told them. They believe with me that the same—" He stopped short.

"Uncle Edward, Arnold's raving! But if we could only find Uncle Julian and bring him to his bedside— There she is. That's Alison!" She ran out of the room again. Those inside, openly listening, heard the front door open, heard Diana's quick, feverish sentences telling Mrs. Clifford of what her brother Arnold had just said.

"Of course Arnold was delirious. He was shot just after reading that awful account in the paper about the headless man found near us, and Uncle Julian being away, he has confused the two all up as one does in a nightmare. But if Uncle Julian comes at once"

"Diana dearest!" Mrs. Clifford was speaking in a very kind tone as she came on into the room.

"You here, Edward? What have you been saying to frighten Diana? Julian's safe and well, thank God. But I can't reach him, Di. He gave no address in that note he left for me. But he said he would be home in time for lunch on Thursday."

Her eyes went to Pointer.

"This is Chief Inspector Pointer of New Scotland Yard," Sir Edward introduced him.

Pointer bowed.

"I'm afraid you must prepare for bad news, Mrs. Clifford," he said very quietly. "We of the police believe that an accident has happened to Mr. Clifford."

"An accident?" For a second her colour, always pale, grew whiter still. Then she recovered.

"Oh, no," she said confidently, "I should have known of it at once. When do you think this—accident—happened to my husband? Why do you think it is to Mr. Clifford?" She spoke with an air of bearing with the stupidity of a child.

"The accident happened last night," Pointer said gravely. "It was a mortal accident." Then he added, after a little pause, "The body has been identified beyond any possibility of doubt, Mrs. Clifford, by the finger-prints."

"But not as my husband's," she said with certainty.

"We believe," Pointer went on, "that a body found near here at Heath Mansions this morning, and taken at first to be that of a Basque anarchist, was really that of Mr. Julian Clifford. There is no possibility of a mistake this time, I am sorry to say."

"Uncle Julian!" Diana gave a cry. "Uncle Julian!"

Mrs. Clifford stared at Pointer, her head held very high.

"A body? Anarchist? You don't mean that headless body of which the evening papers are full?"

Pointer said that he did mean that. Her eyes darkened to green.

"What appalling nonsense!" she said indignantly. "Do you think that I shouldn't have known immediately—felt it at once—if anything had happened to him! How abysmally ignorant you people are of the things of the spirit!" She turned on her brother-in-law.

"You too, Edward! You too think I wouldn't know! Julian will laugh when he gets back on Friday!"

"Mrs. Clifford," Pointer said solemnly, "from where he is, there is no coming back."

Alison flushed a deep rose flush. She drew herself up.

"It's incredible! It's almost as though you all wished—" Then she checked herself. "Forgive me," she turned to Edward Clifford, "poor Edward, you look so worn! But your grief is all for nothing. Julian is alive ... is well ... is happy."

"Where is he?" Pointer asked, with something of sternness in his voice.

She gave a careless twitch of her slender shoulder. "You will know all in good time."

"I am afraid we must take our own measures then," Pointer replied.

"You mustn't do anything that Julian wouldn't approve of when he gets back," she said quickly. "Edward, I trust you to see to that."

"I want to look into his money matters," Pointer said slowly.

Alison Clifford started palpably.

"Certainly not! That is my cousin, Mr. Hobbs', affair. He is my husband's literary agent. Julian would never forgive such a thing. You must wait, Edward"—she spoke with urgency—"Julian will be back by Friday."

"May I see the letter left for you this morning?" Pointer asked. "I understand that a note was left for each person in the house."

"I have destroyed my letter," the answer was instant, and Mrs. Clifford left the room with an air of deep displeasure.

"How about you, Miss Haslar?" Pointer turned to the slender figure shrinking, almost cowering back away from the others.

"I—I don't know where mine is," Diana said in a strangled voice.

"Could you give us an idea of its contents?"

She seemed to force herself with difficulty to speech.

"It was only a line to say that Uncle Julian wanted to verify some topographical point, that he would be back on Friday at latest, and would I meanwhile go on with my grandfather's letters."

"And dated?"

"It was dated yesterday." Diana had turned to Edward Clifford while speaking. He avoided her eye.

So he believed that his brother was dead. He believed that Arnold was responsible, that those wild words . . .

Suddenly she stepped up to Pointer, laid her hands on his arm, and looked dumbly up into his face. An agonised question was in her eyes.

It would have been touching had it been any woman, but from Diana Haslar that mute appeal was very moving.

"I see," she said hoarsely. "There is no hope. He is dead. Oh, God!" It was a prayer, not a mere ejaculation.

Straight stepped forward as she made for the door and took her hand. Sir Edward looked on with no softening lines of his set mouth.

"I'd like a word with you, Mr. Straight, as soon as you've seen Miss Haslar into her car," Pointer suggested.

Straight came back, looking years older than the young man whom Sir Edward had met for the first time only last Saturday.

"Now, Mr. Straight," Pointer began, "we know you've only just landed in England, but it seems that Mr. Julian Clifford had talked with you after dinner last night"—the gas man had learnt that from the butler—"his last dinner. Did he seem to have anything on his mind?"

"Well, I think he had," Straight said judicially. "Of course I thought then that he probably was always a little *distrait*."

"Julian was *distrait* at times," Edward Clifford murmured, with what struck Pointer as a rather wary look at Straight.

"At any rate he was so then. Long silences. Just a word now and then."

"And those words were about?" Pointer asked. And Edward Clifford's face grew blankly inscrutable, as though he were preparing to hear something which he might not like.

Straight did not reply on the instant. He looked as though he were trying to think himself back to yesterday's quiet talk with the man now lying dead.

"About my work. A little. He left an impression on my mind that he would be shortly going away from Thornbush for a while, though he didn't say so in so many words. He said something about working out my own ideas. Especially not continuing exactly along Newman's lines. Newman had been librarian as well as private secretary, you know." Straight paused. "It's awkward to say now that murder's been done, but Mr. Clifford struck me as—" He paused, hesitated.

"Well—as what?" came from Edward Clifford sharply.

"As afraid of Newman," Straight said simply.

"Julian afraid of Newman!" Sir Edward echoed incredulously.

"It wasn't what he said," Straight said slowly, "it was—his face? his voice? I don't know. But I thought so. Yet, as far as I can remember, all he said was, 'I shouldn't go to Newman more than I could help, if I were you.' I said something about Newman seeming very willing to be of help, and he gave me a queer look. A very queer look," Straight repeated solemnly. "Struck me even then as such. 'Let's hope you'll find him so to the end,' he replied, and again it was the tone that was odder than the words. I repeated 'to the end, sir?' And after a long silence he said very curtly, and in a very low voice, 'Mr. Newman is leaving me. But that is strictly confidential. But now you see why I should prefer you to find your own feet?' I forget what I replied. And then he rose and joined Mrs. Clifford in the walled garden. But just as he stepped over the sill, I thought he was going to ask my advice about something—or wanted me to help him in something"

"Julian!" repeated Edward Clifford, in palpable amazement.

"I'm only giving my impressions. And the impressions of a stranger may be all wrong. But that's what I thought. I was going to say something like 'Is there anything I can do?' But of course I thought that if there was, he'd have said so."

Straight stopped. He looked as though half minded to say no more, half inclined to add something to what he had said.

"Well?" Pointer prompted.

Still Straight hesitated. "It's rather difficult to go on. You don't know me. I might be an imaginative chap . . . given to romancing. . . . I'm not. I'm the opposite. But you don't know that."

"Well?" Pointer asked again.

"You'll think I've fear on the brain—but I thought Mr. Clifford not at all keen on the short absence from Thornbush of which he spoke. Or rather, to which he referred. The first time was in the course of some directions as to what he wanted done. He said—as nearly as possible— 'I've a lot of foreign books, most of which I don't care about, yet some of which are quite worth having. Pick out those you would propose to keep. Then leave the rest for me to look over. I may be away for a short time from Thornbush, but I'll glance them over when I get back.' There he stopped. There was a long silence. Then he said to himself, '*when* I come back.' And his face and voice sounded like a man very doubtful of his coming back. That was all then. Another moment came in the course of a few words about Australia, and travels in general. He said—after another long silence— 'Yes travelling is pleasant. If you want to go, and are sure you'll get back safely.' That's all I have to go on. Just those two remarks. But both, and especially the latter, sounded to me as though Mr. Clifford was nervous of something that lay before him. I thought at the time, until just now, in fact, that he must be a poor traveller, bad sailor, and so on."

"Julian! Well, Straight, thank you for telling us this. You certainly have surprised me." Sir Edward sounded genuinely amazed and also a shade relieved, Pointer thought. "It's as unlike my brother as though you had been talking of a stranger. I suppose it really was Julian? You saw his face?"

"Oh, yes." Straight laughed at the idea of a substituted Julian Clifford. "He sat on after dinner and went out into the garden . . . joined you. ... I heard your voices dimly."

There was a little pause.

"And here," Straight rose, "is the note which I received, ostensibly from Mr. Clifford, this morning." He handed a folded piece of paper to Pointer.

"Did you keep it for any especial reason?" the Chief Inspector asked, reading it.

"I—don't—know," Straight said slowly. "I suppose I should have kept it in any case, but—well, the note struck me as odd."

"In what way 'odd'?"

"Well—unlike his words of the evening before. Here he tells me to turn to Hobbs and Newman."

Edward Clifford looked the letter over very carefully. It was dated yesterday.

"Dear Mr. Straight,—A passage in my novel needs verification on the spot. I expect, however, to be back at Thornbush by Friday. I should like you to begin with the subject index as you planned. Newman will give you any help in his power. So will Hobbs, of course.
"Faithfully yours,
"Julian Clifford."

"You think this is Mr. Clifford's writing?" Pointer asked Sir Edward.

"I should say so. Certainly. The very way the punctuation marks are made is his. And that signature. It's on his own paper, too."

It was more than that, thought Pointer. Like the additions to the cheque, it was written with Julian Clifford's own pen, or its exact mate. But as to whether the dead man had written it—

"Did you see Miss Haslar's note?" he asked Straight.

"Yes. She showed it me. Hers and mine were lying on the hall table when I went out for a walk before breakfast. I noticed them lying there along with two for Hobbs and Newman."

"She expressed no surprise at her letter?"

"None." Straight did not add that she had looked very uneasy and had scanned it in silence more than once. Instead he said good-night.

He left a profound silence behind him.

"His conversation with Mr. Straight—the tone of it—was very unusual on Mr. Clifford's part?" Pointer asked.

"My brother must have been deeply disturbed," Edward Clifford replied in the tone of a man taking swift mental soundings. Pointer thought that some little part of what he had heard fitted in, perhaps very badly, with something else. Edward Clifford, supposing him to be honest, had not exclaimed at the idea of Julian Clifford dreading his journey as he had at the idea of his being afraid of his secretary.

"Afraid of Newman," he repeated again. "Amazing! Under ordinary circumstances I should say Straight was romancing, but as it is—!" He sighed profoundly. "Well, I have always known that my brother's secretary is a queer fish. But this throws a new, and a most sinister light on his queerness."

"In what way queer?" Pointer asked, as though Newman had struck him as a type of the commonplace.

"In every way. Of course I know about his lost memory, and so on, but I used to watch him very closely after Julian first took him up, and I came to the conclusion that he didn't want his past to come back to him. There are exercises, founded on the Freudian theories, of getting into touch with the submerged half of the mind. He never would allow them to be tried on him. I— Well—frankly I sometimes doubted whether his memory was entirely gone. And I'll tell you another person who more than doubted, and that's Miss Haslar. She never said so, but I'm sure of it. She distrusted Newman from the first, and insisted that Julian was doing a foolish thing to keep him on. But Julian was one of those men who, when they back a side, can only see that side. He never backed it lightly, I'm bound to say. But once his stand was definitely taken, nothing could shift him."

"Could I speak to Mr. Newman?" Pointer asked. Sir Edward rang the bell. But Mr. Newman was out. When had he left? Directly after "this gentleman" had called to see him. About half-past nine.

"This gentleman," otherwise Chief Inspector Pointer, rose as soon as the door shut behind the servant.

# CHAPTER 8

"I think we had better have a look at Mr. Newman's rooms. Will you show me where they are?" Pointer asked.

Sir Edward took him up. The secretary's bed-room presented a scene of wild disorder. Coats and clothing had been flung here and there. A bag stood half packed, and then abandoned. A gaping suit-case too had been apparently discarded at the last moment as too hampering.

"Flight!" Edward Clifford looked about him with a slow pallor creeping over his face. "Does this mean that we're standing in the room of the man who murdered my brother and mutilated his body so horribly? If so, it'll be"

Pointer said nothing. He was looking intently about him.

"If so"—Edward Clifford's tone changed: it hardened— "if so, Chief Inspector, then that legacy was the motive." He spoke in a quiet but authoritative voice. Pointer wondered what other possibility he was definitely shutting out.

"Five thousand pounds might tempt a poor man," Pointer agreed.

"And, as you know, Newman has a salary of only two hundred and fifty pounds a year. Ample, but not if he were of extravagant tastes. If Newman killed my brother, there is no other motive possible."

"It will be a shock to Mrs. Clifford, I'm afraid," Pointer murmured, "I mean this apparent flight."

"A frightful one. She believed entirely in the man's good faith. So much of a shock that I think it should be kept from her for the present."

"If possible," Pointer said non-committally.

"I think it will be quite possible. But—if Newman is guilty, what are we to think of Haslar's cry?"

"It's a very intricate case this, Sir Edward," Pointer said thoughtfully, as he too glanced all around the room. "One step at a time is all that we can hope for."

"I suppose Newman will be followed if he really has tried, as this room suggests that he has, to escape?"

Pointer set his mind at rest. One of his best men was in charge of Newman. He swiftly made up a parcel of the absent man's clothing—a very complete parcel.

"They give us his measurements," he explained in answer to Edward Clifford's inquiring stare. "Part of the regular routine. You knew Mr. Newman well?"

"I lived at Thornbush for five months after he first came to Mr. Clifford. While Cleave Ford was being fitted with central heating."

"What about his time off? Regular time on which he could count, I mean," Pointer asked.

"His evenings were generally his own. So were Saturdays as a rule. And Sundays always."

"Do you know what he did in the evening, or over the week end?"

"Evenings—I think he never went anywhere except to Arnold Haslar's. He became tremendous friends with him from the first. But on Sundays he vanished utterly and completely. We used to chaff him about it until we saw that he didn't like it much." Sir Edward stopped.

Pointer had stepped to the fireplace. All the grates at Thornbush were concealed by handsome, wrought-iron double doors like small casement windows inset within the marble of the fireplace. It was the neatest way of dealing with small stoves, or grates, that Pointer knew. He believed it to be a Belgian idea. At least, he had often come across it in Brussels. He now opened the little doors and stooping down, felt the bars. Then his eye travelled up the wall. He stepped quickly into the bathroom, and came out with a small nickel shaving-cup in his hand. He detached a water-colour picture from the wall. Then he dragged a table across the fireplace, placed a chair on it, and stepping lightly up, held the picture, glass-side up, as a tray, while he gently blew something on to it off the picture rail—a small wisp of charred paper, so black that no writing showed on its thin film. Then he drew out the cup from his pocket and carefully turned it down over the fragment, holding it all very level as he stepped down on to the floor, and put it on the table.

"Mr. Newman burnt something in that grate. The bar is still warm. Nothing big. He crushed it all into fragments, but this one bit must have escaped his notice and blown up there. I'll send a man with it and Mr. Newman's clothes to the Yard at once. We may learn something from them."

From below came the sound of a banged door. And then another.

"That must be Hobbs." Clifford listened for a moment. "He must be told, of course; about Newman, I mean. But I think Mrs. Clifford should be kept in ignorance of what has happened. After all, Newman may return to the house. It's just possible that this room does not mean what it seems to mean. Don't you think so, Chief Inspector?"

"I don't think he'll come back," Pointer said thoughtfully, following Clifford down the stairs and into the library, after handing his parcel to his chauffeur, and placing the cup and picture with extreme care in an attache case which he strapped over an air cushion on a collapsible table in the car.

Julian Clifford's literary agent was standing with his legs far apart, swaying slightly. He looked savagely up at them as they entered.

"Well, what d'ye want?" was his greeting. "What's up now?"

Clifford looked at him with thinly veiled disgust. The man had been drinking.

"Something has happened to Julian," was Sir Edward's short reply.

Hobbs stared. White streaks like dead fingers showed on his cheeks. He seemed trying to pull himself together.

"What d'ye mean?" he asked a trifle less surlily. "I thought I told you . . ."

"He's been killed—murdered." Edward Clifford could be terse too. "This is Chief Inspector Pointer of New Scotland Yard. He's investigating the case."

Hobbs's dropped jaw all but prevented his nodding to Pointer. He certainly looked an amazed man.

"It was his body that was found near here in Heath Mansions this morning. That headless body." Edward Clifford gulped at those last horrid words.

Hobbs seemed sobered. His face grew mealy white. He was a handsome enough man in a big, burly way. He seemed to shrink a little now.

"I say, this is going too fast! How do you know—if it has no head—how do you know it's Julian?"

"There is no doubt possible," Pointer assured him. "And now Mr. Hobbs, would you mind explaining just where you thought Mr. Clifford was when you assured an official of the Home Office this morning that he was collecting local colour, probably in Liverpool?"

Edward Clifford was looking intently at Hobbs. Hobbs looked back at him. A blank, non-committal look. And yet he sent a message to the other.

"I thought he had gone, as he so often does, for literary material. But I can't grasp this awful news! It's incredible. Surely there's been some mistake. If his head is off, I repeat how can you be sure it's Julian's body?"

Pointer explained about the identified finger-prints.

"And the thickened finger-joint is his. So's the scar on the sole of the foot," Edward Clifford finished.

"You're absolutely certain it's Julian?" Hobbs asked, biting his lip.

"Certain? Absolutely," the dead man's brother assured him.

Hobbs grew paler yet.

"I can't believe it!" he said thickly. "I can't realise it."

Suddenly he straightened up.

"My God! Haslar was all but murdered too!" He turned a white, wild face from one to the other. "What does it mean? Why these two?"

"Mr. Hobbs," Pointer asked again, instead of replying, "where did you think that Julian Clifford was? Have you no idea where he might be expected to be, supposing he had really gone away of his own free will yesterday morning?"

"None whatever," Hobbs said promptly—a shade too promptly. He looked hard at Sir Edward.

There was a silence. Pointer noticed that Edward Clifford did not seem any more anxious to question Hobbs than he had been to question Straight, though he listened with an even more strained attention.

"Have you had any unusual visitors at Thornbush lately?" Pointer asked.

"By Jove!" Hobbs looked this time hard at the detective officer. "There was a man—refused to give his name—asked for Newman. Saturday morning around twelve. Newman was out. He then asked for me by name. I had him shown in, of course. Didn't care for the look of him. Wrong 'un, if ever there was one. Ex-cavalryman type. He talked on about his admiration for Clifford's works and that. I thought he wanted to sell me a typewriter, or get some translation rights for nothing, he was so vague. Finally he asked to see Clifford himself. I said Clifford never saw any one without an appointment. He said, 'Tell him I'm come from Haslar. Mr. Arnold Haslar. Then he'll see me.'"

There was a pause in the narrative. Hobbs looked as though he were trying to be very exact in his account.

"Did Julian see him?" Edward Clifford asked at last.

"What! Disturb him of a morning! I didn't send in any message, of course. I went out into the dining-room and marked time with a sandwich. Then I reported that Mr. Clifford regretted that he was unable to see Mr. I waited for the name. None came. So I went on, 'Unless Mr. '—another pause, but still no name forthcoming— would state his errand. 'Did you say I came from Haslar?' he asked. I assured him I had forgotten nothing. He looked rather taken aback, I thought, gave me a look over as though he was about to propose something shady. If so, he decided against it. Hesitated for another moment, and said sneeringly, '*You* don't seem to be much in Mr. Clifford's confidence,' and left, knocking his hat over one ear."

"Was this the man you saw?" Pointer produced the photograph of Cory.

"That's the man."

"Did he say nothing else?" Pointer asked.

"Nothing of any importance. Nothing I remember. But the emphasis on the 'you' made me wonder if he thought some one else knew more—of whatever his errand was."

"Newman?" asked Edward Clifford sharply. Hobbs said nothing, but his silence was a "yes."

"But you know," he went on, after another pause, during which he stood again jingling some change in his pocket, "I don't think a shady caller had anything to do with Clifford's murder. We have too many of them. I think"—he hesitated, and drummed on the mantel-shelf—"well what I told you in the train, Edward. I met Sir Edward in the train by accident this afternoon," Hobbs explained to Pointer, "and told him that I think Julian Clifford has a separate establishment somewhere."

Edward Clifford looked intensely indignant.

"Impossible! I repeat, quite impossible!"

"Why so?" Hobbs jingled some keys in his pocket. "He was away from home pretty frequently. Why impossible?"

"The idea is quite untenable to any one who knew the plane of life on which Julian lived." Edward Clifford spoke with apparent sincerity.

"And where do you think this establishment was?" Pointer asked quietly.

"Not an earthly," was the prompt reply. "But I've thought it for some time."

"Any reason for the suspicion?"

"Human nature. My cousin Alison would bore any husband stiff," Hobbs said in a contemptuous undertone to Clifford, who looked at him as at a reptile.

"We'll discuss this matter to-morrow when you're more yourself," he said in an icy tone, turning away as though hardly able to trust himself to look at the insolent grin on Hobbs's face.

"Mrs. Orr is a widow, I understand?" Pointer said, apparently out of the blue.

Edward Clifford looked, if possible, more indignant than ever; but he listened for Hobbs's reply. It did not come for a full minute. And then Hobbs said in a thick, low voice, hoarse with passion:—

"What's Mrs. Orr to do with this? I was speaking of a possible separate establishment of Julian's. Not of friends of himself and his wife."

"And now, Mr. Hobbs, one question," Pointer went on coolly, "where were you last night from, say, ten onwards?"

"I went out to post a letter at ten or half-past," Hobbs said easily enough. "I was talking with Mrs. Clifford and writing at the same time, till my cousin went up to bed. Then, as I said, I went out to post a letter, found it a marvellous summer night. Came back and sat on in the garden for a while, then went to bed. It was just short of twelve when I wound up my watch. This morning I found I'd caught a chill out under the trees. When I got down about eleven I found a letter for me from Julian"

"You kept that letter?"

"Don't think so. I'll look, of course; but, as a rule, I never keep any but important letters."

"Did you hear or see anything of Mr. Clifford before you went to bed?"

"Yes, I heard him in his library, I thought. I feel certain I left him there when I went out to post the letter. Afterwards I didn't come through the house at once. By the time I went up to bed all was dark downstairs."

He was not able, or appeared not to be able, to add anything more except just as he was turning away. "Wait a bit—I seem to remember a telephone ringing in the library as I sat talking to Mrs. Clifford. I have a fancy that I heard Clifford reply. That's what made me certain he was there when I went out."

"You can't remember any words of his reply?" Pointer asked.

"Not a syllable. We were talking at the moment."

"Though you may not remember the words, have you no idea of the manner of his reply? Was it friendly? or was it business-like? or was it annoyed at all?"

"Well, I couldn't swear to it, but I have a hazy notion that he was rather impatient. Not like Julian to be that. But I don't think I've mixed it up with any other time." He rubbed his face wearily.

"I think I'll go for a walk now, and see if the fresh air won't help my head. This has been an awful shock. What about Alison?"—he was speaking to Edward Clifford.

"Frightful!" Sir Edward said under his breath. "When she's convinced of the truth it may well kill her."

"What will kill her will be not having known that anything had happened to Julian, when she was seeing him alive and well in her crystal," Hobbs said callously, and turning, left the two together.

Pointer thought that Sir Edward would have liked to follow him out, but if so, the latter checked the impulse.

"I must let Tindall know at once of Newman's flight. He'll be in his rooms at this hour." Sir Edward reached for the telephone and passed on the news.

"He's coming as soon as he can get here." He hung up the receiver. "But a word about Hobbs. You don't suspect him, do you?"

Pointer did not reply.

"Well, I don't," Clifford said firmly. "Hobbs is far too shrewd a business man to be a criminal. As a literary agent my brother considered him unequalled."

He was not too good a business man to drink, nor to have a very dangerous temper, was Pointer's private comment on that. But he said nothing.

"Unfortunately he's developing a habit which will be the ruin of him unless he checks it," Edward Clifford went on, "a habit of taking more than is good for him. But he's not a criminal. On the other hand, he's a man who lives a fast, careless life. That idea of his about my brother's absences"— Edward curled his lip—"put it quite out of your head, Chief Inspector. Anything dishonourable would be impossible to—" And then Edward Clifford came to a full stop. He flushed scarlet. "Er—er—his private life was absolutely exemplary." He finished hastily, and getting up began to walk up and down the room, apparently getting deeper and deeper into a brown study.

Pointer was certain that Julian Clifford was engaged in something not strictly legal when he had met his death. It had seemed a strange thing of which to suspect the great author. But there was his odd question to Astra. There was Hobbs. . . . Hobbs knew something, or thought that he did. So did Mrs. Clifford. Edward Clifford's flush of just now, all bore out the same idea. Besides, though he was apparently grief-stricken at his brother's terrible fate, he also seemed absolutely without any ideas as to how, and where, the search for the murderer should be started. He was as one lost in bewildered helplessness. Pointer had come to the conclusion that Sir Edward did not want the circumstances of Julian Clifford's death probed, except as they concerned Etcheverrey. He either knew, or feared, that any other line of inquiry would open up painful details—painful to the living. He must have some reason for this. It was not one that would have occurred offhand to any reader of Julian Clifford's lofty books. He had turned down Robbs's idea of an intrigue with scorn. But what other idea did he hold himself?

Pointer had believed at first that if he could find the head of Julian Clifford and establish the identity of the murdered man beyond question, that he would get all the members of his family to speak, and so come on the clue to this most strange death. But not if this idea were right. In that case, even then, he could look for no help from the Thornbush circle. Nothing would bring back the dead, they would argue. Pointer knew how egoistic people can be when it is a question of a family scandal. Better, they would think, that ten murderers escaped than that one just man should have cause to wince. Pointer did not agree. But that being the case, the whereabouts of Julian Clifford's head faded into the second place beside the question of what the writer had been doing, what planning, what other interests he had, besides his interest in Etcheverrey?

How could he, Pointer, locate the place where Clifford was supposed to be, if he were honestly supposed to be alive? That vision of him in her crystal which Mrs. Clifford had thought that she saw, or had pretended to see. . . . Houses with "gables like steps" mounting into heaven. He believed that those words had really slipped out. If so, they might help to orient the search. But how could the Chief Inspector get on the track of those gables? Where were such gables? English they were not. Nor Basque. Nor French. Nor Spanish. Pointer ran through a long list of the impossibles. Yet apparently they were in the street where Mrs. Clifford thought that her husband was—supposing her to be innocent.

Tindall was shown in.

"So the secretary's run away! Being trailed, of course."

Pointer said that he sincerely hoped so.

"Can I see his room?" Tindall surveyed the wild scene thoughtfully. Then he returned to the two men in the library. He closed the door carefully, even though a detective was on duty in the hall.

"Sir Edward, a thought has been growing in my mind since you 'phoned. What about Newman being the man we're after? Being Etcheverrey himself? This idea would link Clifford and Haslar for certain, and doubtless Cory. We have learnt that worry and depression were common to both Mr. Clifford and Haslar these last weeks. It was common to both of them, because it sprang from a common cause— from Newman. You know, Sir Edward, you believed that Etcheverrey might be hiding in some quite commonplace identity. How about that identity being your brother's secretary?"

Sir Edward had wheeled, and now stood staring at him.

"What a possibility!" He seemed to consider it. "It's a brilliant guess. What ghastly irony, if so, that I myself should have spoken of my idea before him. Let me see. . . . When Etcheverrey was in Persia, Julian was in Australia. Just he and Mrs. Clifford—over six months away. Hobbs worked on as usual, but Newman took a holiday for the whole time. It was the winter. He was supposed to be in Rome looking up facts for Clifford about the Fascist suppression of newspapers. . . . And then that time when the Prince was in South America . . . that wouldn't fit Newman, but, of course, he may have worked through an agent more often than is believed. The attempt on the King of Spain— yes. Newman was free then. Julian thought him climbing in the Lake district. I must go into this in more detail with Hobbs, and check dates. What do you say, Chief Inspector?"

"'If I thought Newman were really Etcheverrey himself," Pointer said slowly, "I should be inclined to wonder if Mr. Clifford were not trying to bring him into some book of his, and in trying, had not got nearer to the truth than Etcheverrey liked. . . . Nearer to publishing it, I mean. Just now, Sir Edward, you told me that the central drawer of his writing table contained Mr. Clifford's work of the day, the finished chapters being in the left-hand drawers, the notes for the future parts, or for the whole, in the right-hand ones. I took the liberty of glancing at the contents of the middle drawer"—for the second time, he might have added. "Mr. Clifford has apparently stopped at the very last line of a page and in the middle of a sentence. Of course I don't know, but I should have thought that an author would finish a sentence, especially this one. It runs: 'Roberts felt that the'—I can't imagine even a boy in school of a summer day when the bell rang leaving a sentence hung up like that. And Mr. Clifford has a pile of untouched manuscript paper in the same drawer."

"My brother would have finished writing down his thought while the boat sank beneath him!" breathed Edward Clifford tensely. "But the remainder of the sentence—the next page—may be in a blotter." Hurriedly he led the way into the room where he had handed Pointer the will. He pulled open the central drawer.

There, in a neat pile, lay Chapter nine of *The Soul of Ishmael.* There lay the third page with its typing running down to the very margin of the lowest edge. As Pointer had said, it ended with the unfinished sentence. Beside it was a carbon copy. It, too, showed no further pages.

Tindall and Sir Edward hunted skilfully, minutely, as men hunt who are used to searching for papers. Neither they, nor the Chief Inspector, found any completion of the phrase. Apparently Julian Clifford had stopped his typewriter at "the" and never touched it again.

"Some one has taken the page, or pages, following!" Edward Clifford muttered, as he straightened the piles again; "Newman probably."

Pointer was examining a sheet of carbon paper in front of a mirror.

"Here's proof or at least strong presumptive evidence of the fact that there were more pages on that pile. That sheet there is page three. Here are a whole bunch of superimposed numbers, that's certainly an eighteen. Mr. Clifford is hardly likely to have torn up so many pages?"

"Certainly not. He worked page by page, not leaving one until it was perfect in his eyes. I wonder"—Sir Edward tapped the table nervously—"if it was his next chapter for the *Arcturus.* If so, it would be nearly finished by now, I fancy. He was never behind with his work. Where's the last *Arcturus*?" He spun round on his heel and pulled the monthly in question out of a revolving bookstand. "Yes. Chapter eight was the last. What can you make out on the carbon sheet, Chief Inspector?"

Pointer explained that chemicals and photographs would get the full value. As it was, he could only read a few sentences. Tindall, more experienced at such work, did a little better, but he soon flung it down.

"That all takes place in England! That's no good!" Then a moment later he gave an exclamation that brought Pointer and Clifford to his side. He held up a slip of paper with some sentences scribbled on it. They were in Julian Clifford's small, close writing.

He read them aloud.

"'Have Roberts next go to Capvern, and meet E. Join E.'s band— England having become dangerous. Get necessary details as to organisation of E.'s band.' There we are!" Tindall waved the paper in front of Sir Edward, who nearly snatched at it, and then tried to read it upside down. He nodded when he had scanned it.

"Get necessary details as to organisation of E.'-s band," he repeated. "Julian's way, when a thought occurred to him, was to jot it down on the 'first thing that came to hand which he would drop into that drawer. Unfortunately he never made any rough drafts. Still, I think your discovery, Chief Inspector, about the unfinished sentence, is vital. Vital! How did you come to look for it? For, after all, these sheets were under a pile of unused paper."

"It was only natural," Pointer said diffidently. Praise always made him shy. "When a jeweller's been killed, you think at once of jewels in his possession. If it's a banker, you turn to his bank first of all. Or a statesman—you think of state papers. In each case you ask yourself, what was peculiar to the man. In Mr. Julian Clifford's case it was his books, his writing; so, merely as a matter of routine, I looked at his manuscript, or rather his typescript."

"It was a master-inspiration!" Sir Edward repeated. "Let me see," he mused, "I wonder if Bancroft could help us. He's Julian's publisher. I'll see him at once to-morrow. I'll explain that I'm worried about Julian"—Sir Edward's face twitched—"and that I wonder whether in his talks with Bancroft he suggested going to any particular spot."

"Ah! that's where Mrs. Clifford thinks her husband is!" broke in Tindall, with the air of a man who has solved the riddle to his own satisfaction. "Investigating some part of the Basque country. He would, of course, ask her not to speak of his whereabouts. Pointer, well played again!" He turned to the detective officer with the words that used to echo from one side of the football ground to the other in the days before Pointer joined the Force.

"And the gables that I think may have been in Mrs. Clifford's mind, the gables that she therefore 'saw' in the crystal? The gables that climbed into heaven like steps?" Pointer asked.

"Basque houses have so varied an architecture quite apart from their own," Tindall reminded him. "Many of them, they return home, build something in the style of the country where they made their money. But now about this idea of yours. I think we shall score this time. Team work does it. That, of course, was why Mr. Clifford asked Mrs. Jansen the question about possible danger. Playing with dynamite wasn't in it with probing too deeply into Etcheverrey's organisation, or into his past."

There was a pause.

"I wonder if Julian suspected the truth, or what we believe to have been the truth, at the end?" Clifford said, coming out of a deep reverie. "If so, that would explain why he wanted quietly to get rid of his private secretary, why he warned the new librarian of Newman. He might well! Poor Julian, he might well! And if only suspicious, Julian would not speak of it to any one—least of all to me—about a man who might be innocent, who might really have lost his memory."

"That lost memory was a master-stroke," Tindall murmured appreciatively. "Now I'll confess something that's been disturbing me not a little." Clifford shot a glance at Pointer. "Julian asked me about"—he seemed to think a moment—"about two months ago, how one could best make a large payment to a foreigner in such a way that it couldn't be traced back to oneself. I naturally showed surprise. I suggested letters of credit, but he insisted that the money must be untraceable. I couldn't help him with any advice. Bonds to bearer seemed the only way out, since he said that a large sum of money might be in question. But when I pressed him as to what he was up to, he looked at me thoughtfully and finally said that I had better know nothing whatever about the matter.

"I confess I asked no more. I was startled, uneasy. No one likes to hear a member of his own family put questions like those. No one occupying a responsible post in the country, that is. Not with the Labour Party always ready to sling mud at us. I confess I thought of a subsidised paper for distribution in Italy—to be printed in Switzerland, independent of Fascist censure. Julian had some such idea in his mind, I know. I was, of course, strongly opposed to it. But now I see that he was probably thinking of Etcheverrey or some lieutenant of his. Perhaps that was partly in Hobbs's mind when he talked to me this afternoon in the train. He told me that he believed Julian was away on an errand which it might be as well not to investigate. He told me that, apropos of a man from the Home Office who had called at Thornbush this morning. A man called Marbury"

Pointer bowed with a faint smile. "I was Marbury."

"Hobbs said that he hoped he would not insist on investigating where Clifford really was. Warned me that he was afraid that Julian had got mixed up in something—well, something of which it might be as well not to speak in the market-place at the moment. Then he even suggested, as he did again before you, that Julian was mixed up in some vulgar intrigue."

Edward Clifford took a turn up the room and back.

"That discovery of the Chief Inspector's about the page—his idea about the coming revelations in Julian's novel— they do indeed open up vistas. Julian lunched with Bancroft only last week, I know. I know too that he talked very freely with his publishers. Bancroft may have some precious piece of information to give us to-morrow. You'll come with me, of course, Tindall, and you too, I hope, Chief Inspector."

But Pointer could not promise. He arranged for a telephone report in case he were detained.

"Was Mr. Clifford in the habit of talking over what he was writing? In his own home, I mean?"

"As far as I know, never. He liked to get away from his work in his leisure hours. But, of course, to his secretary he would doubtless refer to his work. Probably discuss it—dreadful thought—with him."

"And the person who took the remaining page or pages of the chapter that Clifford was writing"—Tindall was deep in conjectures—"would be that same private secretary, who, if we're right—as we most certainly are—was the very character that Clifford was about to introduce. Newman may have sent that telephone message to Clifford which Hobbs thinks he heard. The message might easily have asked Clifford to come to Fourteen Heath Mansions to meet some one whom Newman might have assured Clifford was an expert Basque scholar. But an invalid, say. Yes, that all fits in quite well into the known facts."

"And Haslar?" Edward Clifford frowned, "what was Haslar's role?"

"Haslar," Tindall replied thoughtfully, "was, we know, or rather is, supposed to be a great friend of Newman's. He may be, instead, merely his tool or his prisoner. But Haslar, we may take it, acting according to his instructions, takes the flat." Tindall paused, evidently getting together some more straw for his next brick. "Cory—like a vulture, his presence with both men means that something's wrong, he's the very emblem of death throughout—Cory who was to figure as Captain Brown ... as the Basque expert, perhaps"—Tindall's cheeks were flushed as he reconstructed his scene—"Cory, we learn from Hobbs, was sent on Saturday morning to Thornbush to get a general idea of Mr. Clifford. Perhaps he was to invite Mr. Clifford to Fourteen Heath Mansions then. At any rate, that fell through. Etcheverrey miscalculated there. Or Cory outran his instructions. But about Haslar—are we to take Haslar's ravings as merely empty words? Or have they a substratum of fact?" He addressed this directly to Pointer.

"Not as empty words, merely," Pointer thought decidedly. "I believe the relations between Mr. Clifford and Mr. Haslar have been a little strained of late?" he asked, turning to Sir Edward.

"They have seen less of each other," Edward Clifford allowed. "Like Hobbs, Haslar is prone to put the worst construction on the most innocent things. My brother was interested as a character in a coming novel, in a friend of the Haslars. In the Mrs. Orr whom you mentioned, and whom, for once, Hobbs had the grace to defend. Arnold Haslar took it upon himself to resent my brother's interest."

"Perhaps Mr. Haslar was in love with the lady," Pointer suggested artlessly.

"Very likely. But as my brother was in love with his own wife, he need have had no fears on that score," Edward Clifford replied curtly.

There was a short silence broken dreamily by Tindall, still at his weaving. "Was Newman's the hand that actually fired the shot at Haslar? What do you say, Chief Inspector?" He wished that Pointer would join a little more freely in the discussion. After all, though not the Foreign Office, the Yard does good work—quite good work.

Pointer told the facts of Newman's probable visit to Haslar's house as revealed by his tiny vacuum sweeper. But he made no comment on them. Instead he seemed to change the subject.

"Apart altogether from his own work, did Mr. Clifford have any papers or letters in his possession which Mr. Haslar wanted, or may have wanted?" he asked unexpectedly.

Sir Edward stared.

"Papers? Letters? I don't quite see. . . . Oh, yes, of course, Cory made you think of that! No, I don't see how there could be any such question here, Chief Inspector," Clifford said decisively. "Certainly I know of none such."

"I think Etcheverrey may have played one of his very clever games. May have got Haslar to choose Cory without explaining why he wanted him," Tindall said now. "Etcheverrey would count on Cory exceeding his instructions. Suppose Clifford were handed over to him, as it were."

Sir Edward made a gesture that looked like uncontrollable anguish.

"Etcheverrey may have counted on Cory taking his revenge," Tindall went on gently but remorselessly, "being a Basque, revenge would be the first thing he himself would take in Cory's place. I think—so far—that Haslar took the flat with no intention of harming Clifford, simply acting under orders. Who knows what trumped-up reason was given him. That of the Basque friend, say. Haslar takes the flat, Etcheverrey as Newman lures Clifford there, Cory is told to kidnap Clifford. He does just what Etcheverrey counts on his doing: he shoots Clifford. Shoots him, as Cory would shoot him, from the back. Haslar falls ill. When he sees the evening papers to-day with the account of Etcheverrey's supposed murder, he guesses the truth. When Newman comes in he knows it. He tells Newman that he must confess. Newman tries to murder him and practically succeeds. I think that is a workable hypothesis. Even those torn-up pieces of paper with Etcheverrey's signature on it which you boggle at"—he turned to Pointer—"fall into line. Etcheverrey, safely ensconced at Thornbush, left them as a true, yet false trail. For they led directly away from Thornbush. As for the head —my new hypothesis may be a trifle weak there yet." Tindall looked almost wistfully at Pointer, who was staring at his own shoe-tips.

"I wonder," Pointer said suddenly, "if you would allow a chartered accountant to go through Mr. Clifford's accounts, Sir Edward?"

Clifford stared. "You think—?"

"I think they ought to be very carefully looked into," Pointer said, rising, "merely as a matter of routine, of course."

"Oh, yes, I see. Of course. I heard my brother say, by the way, that Straight was a chartered accountant before he took up librarian's work."

"Good. Perhaps you would see him about it. I would like it done as soon as possible. The thing can't be done secretly, of course, since the accounts are under Mr. Hobbs, I believe?"

"Entirely. As I told you, Julian was more than satisfied with him. Besides having a splendid knowledge of where to place work, he's a wonder with figures. He was Third Wrangler, you know."

And on that Pointer took his leave.

"Fine fellow, Pointer," Tindall said, as the door closed. "One of the best brains at Scotland Yard. Quite a marvel for his years, but the police routine sets its seal on a man's mind. They can't get away from it." And he plunged into the necessary steps to be taken to follow up and prove his theory.

Pointer meanwhile drove back to his own rooms at Scotland Yard. Night and day were but figures of speech to him when need was. Various men had been routed out of bed and some modern magic as soon as his car had reached Scotland Yard.

When Sir Humphry Davy saved the papyri of Pompeii, he blazed the trail for the treatment of all charred papers, though that trail has turned many a corner since then.

In this instance the paper was heated again and photographed the second before it crumbled to a white ash. Charred paper so heated gives off minute quantities of gas which fog certain specially prepared plates. Ink, however invisible to the  naked eye, acts like a screen between the paper and the camera, shutting off the action of the gases, so that when developed the plate is foggy except in the places marked with ink.

Pointer was finally handed a photograph of that small island of salvaged paper, which a touch would have turned into black dust, on which now he read

I know the danger
discovered your secret
                    wife

The last word was very doubtful. It might have been *knife* or *life*. The writing and the paper and the ink were all those of Julian Clifford.

Pointer sat for a second lost in meditation. Tindall would he pleased to see this. He had a copy sent over to his flat.

Compared with this feat, the deciphering of the carbon paper was child's play. Heated, treated, rolled, photographed, enlarged, one of Pointer's men had typed page after page from it—ten pages in all—with only here and there a blank word. Evidently Clifford used a very good brand of carbon paper. It showed that there had been twenty pages in all, finishing the chapter. As Tindall had thought, they were entirely concerned with England, but copies would none the less be sent to him and Sir Edward, along with the copies of the two sentences extracted from the burnt paper that had flown up on to Newman's picture rail.

Then Pointer turned to another report, concerning Newman's clothes, which he had sent to the Yard at the same time. These had one by one been put into as many paper bags, sealed, beaten, and the dust then microscopically examined.

A certain gray waistcoat had yielded, among other usual trifles such as cigarette dust, lead pencil dust, quite a knob—microscopically speaking—of fiddler's rosin, more properly called colophane; a rosin, that is, which is used by violinists to give their bows more bite on the strings. The analyst had added a note to say that this special rosin was "black rosin," such as is used exclusively by players of the double bass.

The microscope had also found on the knob several bits of very fine quality Wilton carpet wool of a deep, soft blue. In other words, the waistcoat had been worn by some one who played the double bass in a room where there was a blue Wilton pile carpet. The same message came from one of the coat sleeves.

So Newman played the double bass. It suited his grave face, his slender hands and wrists, that Pointer thought looked made of whipcord.

Double bass and blue carpet. . . .

It was not an address, but it was something.

An inquiry over the telephone brought confirmation of the terrible words gasped out by Haslar to his sister. Words heard by the night nurse as well. But Haslar was not yet dead. He still breathed. Pointer's plain-clothes man added that he himself was sitting in the room behind a screen. And finally there came yet another message for the Chief Inspector before he left the Yard.

It was from a very unhappy wight, who explained that he had lost Newman—lost him hopelessly.

"Clever of you, Black," Pointer murmured. "How did you manage it? Or is it a patent process?"

"*I* didn't do it, sir," the man breathed apologetically, "it's not the first time that chap's given a trailer the slip. Not by a long chalk. He left Thornbush immediately after you. I followed him on to a bus. He got off at Charing Cross post office, and posted two letters. Then he went into a cinema."

"Ah," said Pointer, "just so!"

"But he didn't try the usual trick of walking in one door and out another," the detective explained resentfully. "I was prepared for that. No. He must have doubled back on his own tracks in some way. Sat down for a second and then slipped out by the door he came in. All I know is, he has gone. Gone completely."

Pointer was not pleased. But no man, not even a detective, can do more than his best. And after all, the Yard had the blue carpet and the double bass to cling to.

He wrote out a description of Julian Clifford's missing secretary for insertion in the *Gazette*, the police daily paper which no civilian may read. In it, and over the telephone to all police stations, orders were given that the constables were to report any place, where they heard, or had heard in the recent past, stringed music regularly played, especially on a Sunday.

They were told to pass on the request to all milkmen and postmen on their beats or in their neighbourhood. The stringed instrument especially suspicious was given as the double bass, but as Pointer was not sure that a constable's ear could be certain of distinguishing it properly, he also included the whole range of riddles, preferring to sift all information later.

A snapshot of Newman was enlarged for the paper and printed on a grating so that every deviation from the absolutely regular was at once noticed. They were very trifling, very few.

Ordinary enlargements of the snapshot were got ready to be taken to-morrow by detectives to all musical societies, all instrument dealers, and musical supply stores. A double bass presupposes chamber music, or membership of some orchestra, or musical society. A telephone call was sent to all taxi stands and garages asking any men to report at the Yard who had recently carried a double bass. It was barely possible that they had carried one to-night. Newman, even though he thought his home address undetectable, might have changed it, and his instrument, to a fresh place. Here was one of those points that no amount of reasoning could settle. No deductions in the world would discover where that place was. But the dust beaten out of his waistcoat pocket and examined under the microscope might yet find it. Then Pointer called it a day, and went to bed.

But at dawn he was up again, and out at Thornbush, watching with the two road-menders the summer sun wake the garden. Nothing on earth is more lovely. When it grew light enough to see, the men shook off the spell, and fell to work on the places which had been marked by the two "lads after their dormouse," as having been recently disturbed. They found nothing, let alone a tin box with plaster—and a head—in it.

Then Pointer whizzed along to Haslar's garden. The same dormouse had escaped there too, it seemed. Places of disturbed earth had been marked. So the same search took place here too, with the same negative result.

## CHAPTER 9

Pointer was at breakfast at eight o'clock when he received a letter rushed up to him by a motor cyclist from Scotland Yard, where it had just been delivered. It had been posted the previous evening at Charing Cross. It was signed A. Newman, and ran:—

"To Detective Chief Inspector Pointer.
"Dear Sir,—I know that you have had your suspicions of me, and that it is only a question of days before the trap closes if I stay at Thornbush. I prefer to slip away while I can. The headless body found in Fourteen Heath Mansions, and iden-tified—publicly, at any rate—by the police as Etcheverrey, a Basque anarchist, is Mr. Julian Clifford's. I killed him last night for reasons which concern no one but myself. I took the flat for a month, under the name of Tourcoin, and induced Mr. Clifford to come there late last night. The rest you know. Haslar guessed what had happened when he read the description of his coat and ring, borrowed by me; as well as from some things that I let slip. I shot him to prevent his going to the police. I did not intend to hurt him severely. My intention was to inflict a slight wound to disable him until I could make my arrangements.
"Faithfully yours,
"A. Newman."

Pointer had barely finished this when his telephone buzzed. It was one of the men whom he had left at Arnold Haslar's house. He was speaking from a near-by telephone. He read out to the Chief Inspector the letters which he had just taken from the postman. None interested Pointer except one from Newman. Practically a replica of his own letter, informing "Dear Miss Haslar" of the same terrible facts and ending up "yours very truly."

The letters were duly re-fastened and delivered.

Newman evidently believed that he had got clear of the police, or this letter would not have been written—not yet. So Pointer read the situation. But had Newman really escaped? Time alone would tell. As for the telephone message to the taxis, no information was brought in overnight that fitted Newman, nor was his portrait identified by any of the men.

Pointer himself drove at once to Thornbush and had a short talk with Sir Edward, who had spent what remained of the night there. Clifford read Newman's letter with a puckered brow.

"It fits in with our idea of last night, and with that deciphered bit of burnt paper. 'I know the danger,' Julian wrote. But that was evidently just what my brother did not know. Of course the last word on that fragment is either *knife* or *life*. Certainly not *wife*. I see no necessity of even suggesting that third reading."

Pointer agreed that until they knew more, either of the two words might be substituted.

There was a silence.

"This confession of—we will continue to call him Newman —is an extraordinary document. Is it a genuine confession, do you think?"

"Very difficult to say, Sir Edward."

Mrs. Clifford came into the room at that. She looked very composed. Yet Pointer thought that she had not slept well. He handed her the letter from Newman. Sir Edward had decided that that ought to be done. She read it, and let it fall to the ground. For a second she stared at him with eyes dilated by horror, then she sat motionless in the chair which Clifford brought forward. So motionless, that she scarcely seemed to breathe. Finally she looked up, outwardly at any rate quite calm.

"This is all some wild mistake. Arnold began it with his ravings, and now Mr. Newman writes this with some idea of saving him from suspicion. Suspicion of—oh, it's too horribly grotesque! I wish I could make you understand, both of you, that Julian is perfectly well, and never has been in any danger, at least not in danger of his life. I had a letter from him only this morning. I kept it to show you, Edward. Though he expressly asks me to destroy it. I'll get it."

"It's not possible that Julian wrote that letter, Alison," Edward Clifford said sadly. "My dear, there's no doubt whatever that our Julian is dead—none."

Mrs. Clifford bit her lip.

"I'll get his letter. That'll convince you. . . ."

A minute later she returned looked rather flushed. "I must have dropped it somewhere. I thought I had locked it in my bureau, but it's not there."

"What was in it?" Pointer asked bluntly.

"Just vague generalities," Mrs. Clifford said casually, "except that he repeats that he'll be back for certain on Friday at latest."

"Still no address?" Pointer asked, raising an eyebrow.

"Still no address," she said coldly. Pointer stood looking down at her. His face was very grave.

"Mrs. Clifford, I don't think you realise the position at all," he said finally. "We at Scotland Yard believe that your husband was murdered. I believe that he was murdered by some one in, or closely connected with this house. We know that he is dead. I'm sorry to say, we know it. You yourself are not free from suspicion. No one who is in any way connected with Mr. Clifford can be. Yet you persist in an attitude which cannot but be considered suspicious, for it true its best to hold up the search—to put it off. As Sir Edward says, that letter of which you speak is a forgery. We must see it—if it is to be found. It is most unfortunate that it should have been—lost."

Clifford listened as though each word hurt him. He all but interposed once, then he caught the Chief Inspector's warning eye and kept silent.

Mrs. Clifford looked absolutely unmoved. Her rather rabbit-like mouth set itself perhaps A shade firmer.

Clifford leant forward and took her hand.

"Alison, I wish I could spare you. If there were a doubt possible. . . ."

Mrs. Clifford looked at him very pleasantly, but apparently she was not to be shaken from her attitude of absolute conviction that Julian Clifford was well, and would return by Friday evening.

"That's only the day after to-morrow," she pointed out, "do wait till then, Edward, before doing anything. Anything whatever."

Trimble came in. Chief Inspector Pointer was wanted on the telephone. It was Richard Straight's quiet voice this time.

"Is that you, Chief Inspector Pointer? Could you come at once to Mr. Haslar's? I walked over before breakfast to hear how he is. He's still alive. But Miss Haslar is in trouble. She's just had a letter from Newman, and has something to tell you about him that she thinks you ought to know. She may change her mind. I've had a great deal of difficulty. . . ."

Pointer could not fly to the house, but he did his best to get there before Diana should have done anything so unkind.

He was shown at once into her sitting-room. She sat in a big chair looking oddly small and pinched. Her face was very white and still. Before her was an open letter. Straight was pretending to read the morning paper. He jumped up and shook hands.

"Miss Haslar wants me to stay. . . . She has something to tell you"

"Have you had a letter from Mr. Newman too?" Pointer asked her.

"Yes." Diana spoke tonelessly. Her voice was the tired voice of one wearied with a long, long struggle. "Mr. Newman is really Sanz Etcheverrey, Chief Inspector."

Straight jumped.

Pointer only looked at the toes of his shoes.

"You're sure?"

"I was engaged to him. It was a secret engagement. But I was engaged to him."

There was a silence.

"Do you feel like telling me more about it?" Pointer asked. "Except the mere fact of your identification, I think the details can be kept quite confidential."

Diana seemed wrapped in some cloak of remembered sorrow. Even when Straight went over to her and took her hand, she quietly but firmly disengaged her own. Just now she was locked among her memories. No one could enter. "It was the second year of the war," she began again.

"Why, you were only a kid, Diana," Straight interjected.

"I was nineteen. He was twenty-one. I was at Hendaye with some relations called Riply. Mr. Riply enlarged the harlour at Melbourne," she explained to Pointer.

"Sir Karri Riply, the engineer?" he asked.

She nodded. "He was dying. The ship he came over on had been torpedoed and exposure in a boat for three days had given him pneumonia. All the hotels were being used as military hospitals along the coast. But we finally took a villa, his wife and I, at Hendaye. Just this side of the Spanish frontier which was practically unguarded just there. Even long after the Bolo affair, a five-franc or peseta note, as the case might be, would get you over the line and no questions asked. There were lots of Spaniards swarming everywhere as far as Bordeaux. Sanz Etcheverrey was one of them. He called himself Senor Rosa. But he told me in strict confidence that his real name was Sanz Etcheverrey, then an unknown name to me, and to everybody outside a very small circle. Well, he and I—" She gave a half shrug. "I adored him. He seemed to adore me, though he refused to have our engagement made public. He said that as he was on a very private and dangerous mission it would injure him if it became known that he was attending to anything else but his orders. He never pretended—to me— not to be a secret service agent. But I didn't guess that what he was after were the Melbourne Harbour plans which Mr.—he was Sir Karri only the night he died!— Riply always kept with him. Sanz used to ask me all sorts of questions about those plans too. Where Mr. Riply kept them, and so on. I, like a fool, used to consult him as to the best place." Diana gave a hopeless gesture of her hand, then she let it fall back into her lap. "Karri Riply died quite unexpectedly. I hurried home from the hospital where I helped, to find Mildred, his wife, holding him up in her arms while he fought for his last breath. Suddenly I thought of those plans. Sanz Etcheverrey had been talking about them only that day. And at that moment, as though I at last had a ray of sense, I remembered that he had got the password to the safe out of me—oh, very cleverly! But for the first time I had, as I say, a ray of sense. I hurried to the room where the safe stood, opened the door, and there, working with an electric torch, with a beret pulled down over his eyes to his cheek-bones, was Sanz. I knew him at once, though I had never seen him in his Basque dress before. I screamed at him. But he—he hit me!" Diana covered her face with her hands. "I suppose he meant to kill me. He knocked me senseless. He must have picked me up and carried me to my room and locked me in. When I came to I had an awful pain in my head, but I got out through the window. There was no use trying to get help. The servants could not be spared at such a moment. I saw the marks of a car, two cars to be exact, which had just left the villa. They were both going the same way. I knew Sanz's tyres. I got out a motor-bicycle and followed them. I followed them all night until dawn found me in Spain, at Pamplona. There I caught up with him in a sort of locanda—a strange little place. And Etcheverrey was in the midst of the wildest-looking lot of brigands! He was giving them their orders, I think. I asked for the plans back. I still never dreamt that he wouldn't give them to me." Diana's smile told how she judged that action now. "They tied me up and carted—it wasn't carried—me to an upper room. After about an hour Etcheverrey climbed in from the roof. He told me that the others wanted to kill me because I had found out their meeting place, and because they thought I had heard their passwords. He wanted me to come with him. I refused. When I should have distrusted him I had trusted him. Now when, as it happened, he was honest with me, I distrusted every word. He got me out by carrying me on to the roof and letting me down, bound and gagged, to the ground. Then he put me in a car. And at that I did believe him, for some of the men caught sight of us and fired. It wasn't what I should call a car at all. It was a sort of motor float that carried oil to the coast for the submarines. He laid me on the floor and covered me with a rug and drove like mad. How we bumped and swayed! Another car went after us, but Etcheverrey hit its tyres when it gained too much. They only hit one of our petrol tins and set it on fire. We just beat them into France. He had a British passport, it seems—a military passport! And I had mine! It was our papers that got us over the border. Because, after all, when it came to shooting, the French guards turned out to a man in a solid line across the road, on their side of the bridge. Etcheverrey ran me on to Bayonne, where he dropped me at our consul's. Then he turned the car and dashed off. I never saw him again—until I saw him come into the drawing-room at Thornbush in the wake of Uncle Julian, and heard that his name was Algernon Newman, and that he had lost his memory in the last year of the war while fighting on our side in a Surrey regiment at Saint Quentin!"

Again there was a silence.

"Why didn't you tell us this before," Straight asked stiffly, "when first you heard that Etcheverrey was supposed to have been murdered?"

"I don't suppose I can make you understand." And she turned to Pointer as though there was more chance with him than with Richard. "If he *had* really lost his memory, it seemed an awful thing to bring up a past when he was a spy against us. . . . And he saved my life. . . . Whatever he did as well, he saved my life that day at Pamplona. He was wounded saving me."

"Did you ever tell Mr. Clifford about your belief that Mr. Newman was Sanz Etcheverrey the Basque anarchist?" Pointer asked.

"No. If he had really lost his memory—that was the dilemma. Had he lost it, or had he not?"

"You couldn't be sure?" Pointer was looking at her apparently casually but in reality very keenly.

"Not for certain—though I doubted it. But though I tried him over and over again, I could never trip him up. He never gave himself away in all these many years."

"Did you ever tell Mr. Clifford who you thought his secretary was?" Pointer repeated.

"No. I did my best, without telling him, to get him to let Mr. Newman go."

"And Mr. Clifford?"

"He thought I was prejudiced."

"When Sir Edward spoke of Etcheverrey, did you tell him what you have just told us?"

"No. I told no one."

"Did Mr. Newman know you suspected him?"

"Yes. He used to treat it as something funny. I never accused him in so many words of being Sanz Etcheverrey, but I as good as told him that I didn't believe he had lost his memory. Or that he was an Englishman. Or that he had ever fought on our side in the war."

"And he?"

Diana flushed. "He used to jeer at me. It amounted to that. He used to beg me to tell him of his past, not to tantalize him with vague hints. You know Mr. Newman's gibing way. A way that he never had at Hendaye," she ended on a soft note.

"Was Mr. Etcheverrey musical?"

"Very. He could play anything with strings—'Cello, violin, anything with strings."

"Did he ever play the double bass?"

She could not say.

"And Mr. Newman. Was he musical?"

"No. He always insisted that he couldn't tell whether they were playing Wagner or Blackpool."

"Was Mr. Clifford interested in Etcheverrey—I mean, of course, as distinct from Mr. Newman, his secretary?" Pointer asked next.

"I thought so. Lately it seemed to me that he was always talking of him, to Mr. Newman of all men! Uncle Julian spoke as though he got all sorts of ideas about him from Mr. Newman."

"Do you think Mr. Clifford intended to make any literary use of the knowledge. Expected to put Etcheverrey himself in a book?"

Diana stared in horror.

"That thought would have been the last straw!" she said in a low voice. "Reckless as Sanz Etcheverrey—as Mr. Newman is, he wouldn't dare to chance that! Yet—" She bit her lip.

"You think it would appeal to him?" Pointer finished.

"It might," Diana agreed, "he loved to play with danger."

"But you yourself had no idea of any such intention on Mr. Clifford's part?"

"None whatever. Nor have I now, I'm thankful to say." The answer came with convincing sincerity. So she had not taken those missing pages of Mr. Clifford's unfinished chapter. A suspicion that had crossed Pointer's mind just now.

Pointer turned to ask Straight the same question, but the look of absolute stupefaction on that young man's face was answer enough. Obviously he had not heard of any idea of introducing the anarchist into the author's work.

"Good Lord!" he breathed, "what a coincidence that Mr. Clifford should have been murdered by the man! I suppose it *is* a coincidence?"

"More probably Mr. Clifford stumbled on some truth," Pointer explained.

"I see," Straight still looked amazed, "and Etcheverrey, finding himself discovered, killed him."

This was Tindall's and Sir Edward Clifford's suggestion too. And like a warning notice not to keep to the wrong side of the road, two sentences stood out before Pointer's mental eye. Two sentences that had been burnt to a brittle cinder: "I know the danger"; "discovered your secret."

"Oh, no, no, no!" Diana burst out, with a sound to her voice as though it came tearing from her very heart itself, "not that! Etcheverrey would never have killed Uncle Julian for any personal reason. If it's true that he killed him, then it was for some other, some political end."

"I believe you love him still," Straight said harshly, looking at her in open indignation.

"And if I do—can I help myself?" she asked passionately. "Can you cure yourself of cancer by wanting to be cured? Don't you suppose I've told myself all the facts over and over again? Of *course* it's glamour and only glamour. Of *course* I've had a lucky escape—but I can't tear it out." She was all but whispering. Tears stood in her eyes as in a child's, but these were the tears that scald.

"And I thought you loathed the chap!" Straight looked bewildered and hurt. "You always said you loathed him," he repeated accusingly.

"Of course I said so, because I didn't," Diana retorted indignantly.

"Well—women are the devil," was the morose and very feeling reply. "And only now that he has murdered Mr. Clifford and tried to murder your brother, you think the time has come to speak out?" Straight snorted. "And I thought it was love of justice! To tell me to my face that you still love this murderer—"

"He's not a murderer." Diana was white but decided. "He's a man acting for his government. If he—if he—had anything to do with Uncle Julian's death it was as an agent; as a secret service agent"—she hid her face in her hands—"obeying orders as a soldier does."

There was a pause.

"And now, Miss Haslar, to pass on to another point"—the Chief Inspector looked very grave. "It was not Mr. Newman who took that flat, 14 Heath Mansions; it was your brother, Mr. Haslar. He has been identified beyond any doubt."

"He was all muffled up," Diana began quickly.

"Mr. Haslar has been identified by his voice—an unusual voice," Pointer said quietly, inexorably.

Diana gazed in dumb misery out of the window. A lovely day seemed to mock human suffering. A thrush, even though it was July, the month of flowers, not of birds, tried a few notes. Then he fell silent, as suddenly as though he were a friend and had seen her face. But the calls of the gold-finches flashed to and fro across the roses; and on a sudden, sweet and clear, a wren's song rang out like a silver bugle, as gay, as spiritually alive, as in spring. The little brown singer popped back into its shady nook, but something in the gallant strain had helped Diana. She turned around.

"When you first read in the papers of the murder of Etcheverrey, what did you think?" Pointer went on. "You could not then have thought that it was Mr. Newman who had taken the flat, since you say that Mr. Newman is Etcheverrey?"

"I thought it was Arnold then, of course, who had taken it," she agreed. "I thought—he had learnt of Sanz's treachery —and had— killed him."

"Because of you?" Pointer asked gently.

"Because of me, and because of the taking of the Melbourne Harbour plans."

Straight understood that drive back to Arnold's house now. That cry of fright when she had seen the man, of whose terrible death she had just read, standing on the steps."

"And when you saw Mr. Newman?" Pointer pressed.

"I knew then that it was he who had killed—not been killed. I thought that he had taken Arnold's ulster and ring. But I never guessed that the unknown, murdered man was Uncle Julian! And in spite of what he writes in those letters, I can't believe it. I can't!" Diana ended on a strangled cry.

Straight jumped as though something had stung him.

"I can't stand your grief for this anarchist," he said hotly. "You're not even pretending to—to cast him off. If you were disgusted with him, it would be different. But, as it is—I told you that I loved you. I told you that I wanted nothing better than to make you my wife. That I would wait years for you to say yes." He paused dramatically.

"Well?" Diana—it is regrettable to record the fact—snapped at him.

"I won't trouble you any more," he said coldly. "I withdraw any pretensions to winning your affections. I could hardly hope to carry the day against such a rival as this Basque murderer evidently is."

He stalked from the room. Diana burst into an unmirthful, cackling laugh.

"Jilted by the second man," she murmured. "Really I seem to be most unfortunate!" But her laughter died out as suddenly as it had come. Her head resting against her folded hands, she lay quite still in the chair, looking very forlorn all of a sudden. She had counted on Dick Straight. She had not loved him. She had known he could be severe, but she had counted on him.

The door opened again. Straight held it shut behind him.

"But if ever you should need me—" he began a little sheepishly.

"I don't need you. I never have, and never shall," Diana retorted. And this time Straight banged the front door behind him in earnest.

Diana turned to Pointer, who had apparently been looking at his shoes as a man does when two people forget that they are not alone.

"You had no idea that your brother and this Mr. Newman were concocting any scheme together in which your uncle, Mr. Clifford, figured?" Pointer asked.

The blood seemed to leave Diana's face.

"I—I—knew they were together a good deal," she temporised.

"Did Mr. Newman ever seem to you to take a high hand with Mr. Haslar?"

"With Arnold? On the contrary, he always fell in with everything—" Diana started. She had spoken too quickly.

"I couldn't say what went on when the two were alone together," she corrected herself.

"You had no idea of anything being planned which concerned Mr. Clifford?"

"No." It was an obvious lie. So something was on foot which she had noticed!

"Miss Haslar, your brother is in a most dangerous position," Pointer said in a low and gentle but very decided voice. "I'm not trying to trap you into some admission. During this interview I'm really only trying to see if he might not have taken that flat for some other reason—for a quite different purpose—than what seems the obvious one."

She was silent.

"You know of none? You can think of no reason?"

"None," Diana said firmly—much too firmly. Real ignorance would have hesitated, have cast about. ... So the reason of which she knew, or at which she guessed, told against her brother, and probably did concern Julian Clifford, her uncle.

"What papers were they which Mr. Haslar wanted taken from Mr. Clifford?" Pointer asked immediately.

He had hit some mark. Diana's eyes widened, as do the eyes of a man before he drops, who has been struck over the heart.

"I don't know what you mean?" She was gone, before Pointer could intercept her, slipping out of her chair and through a door like swift running water.

Pointer had had an outline of the Holford Will case hunted up at Scotland Yard, and had read it through— once. What was there in it which had made Haslar pick out Major Cory? What purpose could such a man serve? Supposing always that Haslar had selected him of his own free will—and Cory, in the few minutes when he talked to Pointer, had not spoken of any common master. He had, indeed, seemed to feel for Haslar the resentment a man feels for one who has personally tried to dupe him, to entangle him.

Why, then, had Haslar selected Cory? All that was shown of the major by the evidence at the trial, was that he was an unscrupulous blackguard who would have sold his grandmother to make glue were he offered a good price for her. He had stolen a will very cleverly though—for that Cory had stolen old Mrs. Holford's will Pointer did not doubt after he had read the inside police information—and he had stolen it so cleverly that the best brains in England had not been able to bring the crime home to him. He had done it by a trick. He had returned what purported to be the new will to the family solicitor, but when the envelope was opened, it showed quite another, relatively unimportant paper.

Yes, Pointer had decided, Cory was the last man whom any one who had sat through that trial would pick out for a capable assassin. He had shown up as a white-livered whelp. But if any one wanted a paper stolen . . . Clifford's missing manuscript pages did not affect this. They were taken to be destroyed, not preserved. They were not stolen in Pointer's sense; nor, if it was anything to do with Clifford's work, would Haslar have had need of an outside thief or furnished flat, so that if, as he believed, Haslar had deliberately chosen Cory, Pointer thought that he held one end of the very tangled coil which surrounded the murder of Julian Clifford.

Back at Scotland Yard, Pointer had not finished his swift notes on the latest development of the Clifford Case when yet another telephone message reached him.

Thirty-three constables, five milkmen, and seven postmen had already reported stringed enthusiasts along their usual beats. One postman even claimed that the instrument in question had been most certainly a double bass. It proved to have been a piccolo, but at one of the addresses—a block of chambers off Gray's Inn—Newman's portrait was recognised as that of a Mr. Pollock, Mr. Algernon Pollock, who had had rooms in the building for some five years now. Mr. Pollock was a country gentleman, the porter said, who only came up to town now and then, about once a week it might be, and always over the Sunday. Great musician, in the sense that he was very fond of music. Many a ticket for a concert, or the opera, had been bestowed on the porter. Pointer had arranged that each of his men should represent himself as a buyer of old stringed instruments, who was trying to locate the contrabasso used by the great Domenico Dragonetti, which was believed to be in private hands in London. Each of the detectives went on to say that a gentleman had been described to him by a musical-instrument mender as the possessor of this particular treasure. And he in his turn described Newman. In this case the description fitted— fitted perfectly. Could the collector of musical instruments see Mr. Pollock? Mr. Pollock was away; he had telephoned up yesterday evening late to say that he would be out of England for a few weeks.

Pointer had a very curious volume in his library at Scotland Yard. He turned to a chapter headed Window-cleaners. Every reputable firm supplied him with a list of the houses for which they worked. A little later, and the head porter of the chambers was called up by a man who told him over the wire that he was the manager of the particular window-cleaners company who had a contract for the building. There was talk of a strike. Rather than incommode their most valued customers, the Window Association were sending out a couple of their best men to do the windows this week, so that, should there be any question of trouble, the Gray's Inn flats at any rate would not suffer.

The hall porter told them to send the men along, and within a quarter of an hour a tall, lanky, bearded man, with another smaller companion in the well-known uniforms, carrying the proper appliances, arrived. The one had been a regular window-cleaner, at least for a while. Pointer had picked up tips from him as they came along—the best of which was a bottle of methylated spirit. Even so, he was no speed-fiend at the work. A glance at the board told him that Mr. Pollock had one of the top flats. Pointer promptly left his assistants to begin with the ground floor, and started up the stairs. A maid unlocked the little suite. There were three rooms. The gray music room had a harebell blue Wilton carpet; a fine piano was in one corner, a double bass stood against one end.

The bedroom, the next room into which Pointer stepped, was painted to represent an opening in a beech forest. It was beautiful in colour, but it told Pointer nothing. The third room, the living-room, was furnished with a luxury which made him stand a few minutes considering it very carefully. Those Heppelwhite chairs with their carved wheat ears, and shaped rail backs were genuine. They were not to be picked up for a song; nor that sideboard to match; nor those Waterford tumblers; nor the Spengler Chelsea figures standing on both sides of an early Worcester jar, whose green tinge spoke for its honesty. A rare old Pretender goblet faced Pointer. Its crowned cypher I.R. had an Amen engraved below it. Behind it was a beautiful piece of Beauvais tapestry. Or was it from Mortlake? In either case, it was a lovely though sombre thing, and far beyond most purses. Pointer stepped to some candlesticks on a superbly carved writing-table, and looked at the hall mark. York silver, and a Paul Lamerie tray, on the table of a man whose salary was £250 a year! And then Pointer saw something coiled on the wall over the writing-table which kept even him rigid in his place for a second. It was a hangman's noose. . .

# CHAPTER 10

Pointer knew that especial twist of rope, and knew that knot. He stared at it fascinated. What was its meaning? He examined the top of the rope with his lens. Its dust suggested many months in the same position. An ice-axe had been thrust through the loop. On each side were snapshots of glacier climbing, but that was not a climber's rope. Nor a knot used for any other purpose in the world. Nor in any prison but a British prison. What did it mean? Placed where the eyes of the man at the desk would always see it—must always see it— in that room where everything else was a joy to look at.

Pointer went over the many books. Mr. Pollock had not come back here to "tidy up" last night. Evidently he was afraid of his hiding place being discovered, and preferred to make yet another.

One whole wall was given over to Spanish works alone. Many of these were political. The books were mostly blank as far as name went, but here and there was an Algernon Pollock in Newman's very characteristic writing.

Pointer found three names in an address book, which skilful telephone inquiries soon showed were the names of the other members of a musical quartet which met every Sunday afternoon at Pollock's flat for chamber music. Each had known his host for a varying length of time, but all only since the end of the war. A few more well-planted questions showed that Mr. Pollock had by no means lost his memory of what went on during, or before, that great event. The Chief Inspector next unlocked the drawers of the writing-table. He found nothing that bore on his hunt, until he fished a roll of pink tape out of a drawer. It was wound around a postcard to serve as a core. Unrolling the tape, Pointer smoothed out the card. The top had been cut off at some time to permit of its going into a frame. So at least Pointer thought from the little marks on the edges. At the back, one line of writing alone survived the shears. A rather faded "you an idea of the place." The words were in Mrs. Clifford's

writing, but that was not why Pointer stared at the card.

"Gables like steps running up into heaven," that was how these roofs were built. The picture was of a street in some town—not an English town—and those peculiar gables.

Pointer put the card carefully into his letter-case. Then he glanced over the bathroom, and went out into the hall, told the porter that he was feeling ill and that his mate would carry on, and hurried back to New Scotland Yard. Here he changed and went in his own person to interview the proprietor of the flats, and to explain to him that Scotland Yard feared, "from information which had come to hand," that a robbery was being planned on some of the rooms in the chambers. He wanted, therefore, to introduce two of his men in the guise of a night and a day porter. They would require no pay. The proprietor was enchanted with this proof of the wide-awake attitude of our great detective force, and Pointer's men were accepted on the spot. Only the proprietor and the head porter were to know the truth.

In his car he studied the little picture postcard again—studied it through his glass. The architecture, all brick, was new to him, and was quite charming. It was a definite style, Pointer saw, and an old style— one that had grown. A house or two showed it in its entirety, but all of them in some particular. In every case the gables were high, and rose in steps, generally seven or nine, on a side to the peak, another step. The windows were high. Some of the houses showed each window enclosed in vertical mouldings crowned with arches, which were again enclosed in one large moulding carried up into the gable. The doors were many of them of slatted wood. Some were studded. Pointer the man quite forgot Pointer the detective-officer as he came on item after item of charming design and work. Where was this place where the builder was still a craftsman? He studied each detail anew. The houses were all of brick—small Tudor bricks, and all the courses— Pointer got his first clue.

"Flemish bond," he muttered to himself.

That is to say, the rows did not, as in "English bond," consist of bricks laid alternately longways and endways, "stretchers and headers," as a builder would call them. But each row was alternatively composed of all headers or all stretchers. And the whole of every house all down the side of the curving street which the postcard showed, was built in this way. Only Flemish bond . . . those fireplaces at Thornbush had told Pointer that probably some one there knew Belgium.

Pointer took the postcard and went to see one of his many friends. He had them in all walks of life. It was to a priest that he turned now. Father Warbury had given a lantern lecture to some of the young plain-clothesmen only a little while ago, which Pointer had attended. He had lectured on the architecture of Holland, and at one point in his very interesting address, he had made a little leap into Flemish styles before pulling himself up, and saying that that was a subject in itself, and a most fascinating subject.

Pointer found the priest in, and showed him the postcard. He looked at it for a bare second.

"Bruges. Charming town. Don't know it? I'm pained. I thought you knew all that we ordinary mortals do 'and then some,' as the boys say. Yes, Bruges." He looked again at the little piece of cardboard. This time the word seemed a talisman. Bruges to the good father meant but the fifteenth and sixteenth-centuries, and stood, not for a town of misery and horrors, but only for a little square which, running from the Pont des Augustins to the Pont Flamand and the Porte d'Ostend enclosed a world of art and genius the like of which could not be matched then, or later. To him it meant van Eyck painting in the Main d'Or, Menlinc in the rue St. Georges, with Bourbus and Gerard David near by; and Caxton bending over his presses. At any other time Pointer would have been delighted to be conducted into this submerged city of old, but now he was only anxious to get away. The priest noticing this, picked up the card again and turned to modern times.

"Yes. This is a picture of the rue de l'Aiguille in Bruges. There's no other architecture in the world quite like it—not even in Belgium. Leopold II. had sense when he wouldn't let the modern mason spoil his Nuremberg . . . 'the Venice of the North,' as some call it . . . ridiculous, of course. Bruges hasn't the colours of Venice, but neither has Venice such skylines."

Father Warbury again lost himself in a disquisition. Beginning cheerily this time with broken, redented bows, to pass on over perpendicular string courses, brick lace work, decorated key stones, and relieving arches, to the gloom of disappearing timpans, rounded frontons, and plastered door cases.

Pointer hurried away as soon as the last word was said.

Bruges? What could be supposed to be taking Julian Clifford to that town? . . . supposing that Mrs. Clifford's slip about the gables that climbed into heaven was a genuine slip, and it was so slight that Pointer believed it to be genuine. He got a guide-book, and soon saw that had she wanted to direct his attention to Bruges, she would have described the beffroi, or the cathedral, or the canals. Yes, Pointer believed the slip to have been a true one. What illegal action then could Clifford have been, or have been supposed to be, engaged in at Bruges? Bruges is very near Ostend—a few minutes by train or car. Could Ostend be the real objective? But Ostend has no streets where the gables climb into heaven in converging sets of steps that meet at the gable point.

Pointer called Ward in again.

"Anything going on in Bruges to draw such a man as Julian Clifford there, and have him want his presence kept secret?" he asked.

Ward pondered.

"Plenty to draw any lover of the beautiful to Bruges. In spite of its trippers, and its drinking water that may, or may not, be typhoid. But to have Julian Clifford want his presence kept secret"—his face lightened—"of course! Mrs. Orr! Her mother, Lady Winter, married a Belgian. Baron van der Bracht. They live just outside Bruges."

"Family respected? The van der Brachts, I mean?"

"Very much so. Tremendously hit by the war, but he's one of the Court Chamberlains. Mrs. Orr is supposed to be over there, I've heard to-day."

Pointer pondered over the idea after Ward had gone. Mrs. Orr? Mrs. Orr and Julian Clifford? That idea might conceivably be stretched to explain Clifford's murder by some one, Haslar or another, who was in love with Mrs. Orr. But it would not explain Mrs. Clifford's attitude. There were plenty of things to take an artist or a collector to Bruges. Collectors walk in very dark places sometimes. Did Julian Clifford collect? His house did not show any such taste. His wife, so Ward had told him, professed a dislike of most old things.

Still—Pointer decided to try another "friend." Mr. Aronstein was back in town to-day, and Aronstein was the buyer for the great American millionaire and collector, Wallend Seaborn.

"To a collector," Pointer began over a lunch to which the other had insisted on carrying him off, and whose amplitude made the abstemious Chief Inspector shudder, "is there anything now going in Bruges which is really worth while— worth while on a large scale, I mean?"

"Bruges," Aronstein toyed with some more foie gras, "relic of the Holy Blood, of course. That's unique. Brought back from the Holy Land by a crusader, but apart from the money to buy it, which would run into several fortunes, the town would rise as a man if the authorities even hinted at such a sacrilege, and tear buyer and sellers to pieces. The same is more or less true of the crystal shrine in which it's shown. Diamonds and sapphires and solid gold figurines. Then, of course, there's the Chimney of the Frank. Marvellous piece of carving. That, too, the town would never sell."

"Anything it would sell?" Pointer persisted, "in some roundabout, secret way?"

Aronstein shot a long, lazy but very keen glance at Pointer. "You're far from being a *little* pitcher, but you certainly have the longest ears of any man I know."

Pointer looked very astute.

"One hears things," he murmured modestly.

"This talk is strictly confidential, of course? Oh, I know you, Chief Inspector; I haven't forgotten the Josephine necklace. Still, I'd like your word."

"Would anonymous be sufficient?" Pointer pleaded, "any information I get will be for use, not show. That do?"

"Perfectly. Now what do you want to know? Open out."

"Is there anything buyable in Bruges that would take, say, three or four days to get hold of, would cost a pot of money, would be risky to get out of the country, or at least get the purchaser into serious trouble if he were found out?"

"There is. More properly there are. Several things. Bruges, like many another Belgian town, wishes to sell a few of its treasures—but you know all this, of course."

"Just assume that I know nothing whatever. Why shouldn't the town sell?"

"The government doesn't want the nation's treasures cast out wholesale. It's passed a very stiff law to that effect, and it's very much on the alert. I've had several things offered me, from this very town we're speaking of, provided I would take all responsibility if things went wrong."

"All responsibility if things went wrong," murmured Pointer thoughtfully. "How wrong could they go?"

"Prison. Long term. Theft. And theft of church property," Aronstein said briefly. "The agent who approached me, made it quite clear that the town council would disown all part in the affair—would never have heard of any offer. But privately I would be put into touch with the right people who would let me have the various articles—at a price, mind you— if I would take all risk of the government getting on the track of what was going on. It wasn't good enough for me. I don't need to do things in that style. *Caveat emptor* in an ordinary way, yes. But prison! Though I don't say that if *l'agneau mystique* from Ghent—"

"Could you tell me in detail what was offered from, or by, Bruges?"

"Several pictures. . . ."

Pointer shook his head. He did not think that pictures would account for the mystery at Thornbush. Mr. and Mrs. Clifford had sent a large number away to homes, and down to their brother's place at Cleave Ford.

"A couple of tapestries well worth having from the cathedral. A gold monstrance. Possibly—doubtful that—but possibly the St. Ursula shrine. A missal. . . ."

Pointer shook his head at each item.

"And, low be it spoken, the Charlemagne Crystal."

"The Charlemagne Crystal?" Pointer pricked up his ears.

Aronstein lit a cigar nearly as fat as himself. He loved to lecture.

"Genuine Charlemagne. Genuine crystal. Supposed to have been the reason for Charlemagne's successes . . . saw things' in it. Saw Ronceval, but too late. Eginhard, his secretary, mentions it. So do all the *Romans de geste*. Charlemagne willed it to Luis of Aquitaine, his third son, who took it to Aquitaine. The legend runs that Joan of Arc is supposed to have consulted it at Rheims and seen her awful end, and that was why she tried to give up politics. Unfortunately for the legend, before her day it had left France. How did it get to Bruges? Well, after the *Bruges Matins*, when the town rose against the French, and the gutters ran red with his soldiers' blood, Philippe-le-bel, the then King of France, took the crystal with him as a talisman to aid him in the great reprisal against the city. Though one would have thought three to one would have been sufficient preparation without magical aid. Anyway, when he was defeated at the Battle of the Golden Spurs, the crystal fell into the citizens' hands and became Church property. So did the king, pretty nearly. The crystal has remained in Bruges to this day. Unless it's been sold secretly, since it was offered to me for Mr. Seaborn. The town took charge of it after they dissolved a Dominican monastery. But, mind you, it would still rank as Church-owned."

"When was it offered to you?"

"Nearly two months ago, on June first or second."

"How would any one set about purchasing the crystal?" Pointer asked.

"Very cautiously, if he were wise," laughed Aronstein. "But Bruges at last has built a splendid new museum. The great West Flanders Museum, and appointed a new director. A Mr. de Coninck. He's willing to deal, if the purchaser can get the stuff out of the country, and will take the risk of prosecution should he be caught. Some men might be tempted. I'm not."

"How much is the crystal worth?"

"You'd have to pay something around sixty, or possibly seventy thousand. Even I should have to fork out fifty."

"Mr. Julian Clifford collects, doesn't he?"

"Not that I know of. But Sir Edward attends a sale now and then. He has some good things down at Cleave Ford."

"Ah, yes, I understand that Mr. Julian Clifford's secretary, a man called Newman, buys for him."

"Newman? I've met Newman. Wonderful chap on Spanish bindings. But I've never seen him at a big sale."

"Would Julian Clifford be likely to hear of these things on offer at Bruges?"

Aronstein laughed.

"I wondered how much of this you already knew!"

"The agent's name?" Pointer suggested trying to look omniscient.

"Mrs. Orr. Ah! I thought you knew it. Yes, she's a sister-in-law of Coninck's—or at least her half sister is Madame de Coninck."

As soon as the lunch was over, Pointer wirelessed an inquiry to Bruges as to the Charlemagne crystal. The reply came back at once. The crystal was very well, thank you, Why shouldn't it be? Could the Chief Inspector have a look at it? Was it on view? It was. Case number sixteen. First room on your right as you entered the museum. Yes, that fitted quite nicely into Pointer's mosaic. It was the answer that he expected.

So there was a great prize to be bought at Bruges. Did Julian Clifford's mysterious secretary know this too? Did the collector in him—for the chambers near Gray's Inn were those of a real collector—covet that crystal as well?—for himself? Or as a gift to some one who would prize it highly?

A complex case this.

By hurrying up his work, Pointer was able, after all, to accompany Sir Edward and Tindall to Julian Clifford's publisher. On the way he told them of the alteration in the cheque cashed by Mrs. Clifford early yesterday morning.

Sir Edward hurried on for a moment in silence.

"I'll look the matter up, of course. Thanks for mentioning it, Chief Inspector. I'll look it up. But I have an idea as to what it refers. In strict confidence I was told something last night which explains that cheque. In any case it had nothing whatever to do with my poor brother's awful end. It was a purely family matter."

"Of seventy thousand pounds?" Pointer echoed in a surprise which he made very obvious.

Clifford changed his step.

"And what about the fact that the cheque was made out originally to Self? That the e and R and Esq. were added afterwards?"

"I understand your natural anxiety to clear up every point," Sir Edward spoke soothingly, "but in this case there is no need to worry. I can assure you that the cheque was altered by Mr. Clifford himself, and that it, and the reason for it, have nothing whatever to do with his death."

"But have they nothing to do with his head having been cut off?" Pointer asked, without apparently glancing at Sir Edward.

The man he was questioning almost tripped.

"I—how could it be connected with mat terrible mystery?"

"If the cheque were not yet presented when Mr. Clifford was murdered, his death would delay, or prevent, its being cashed. The only way to get that money quickly would be to avoid any suspicion arising until after the money was paid out by the bank, that the man killed was Julian Clifford. Given certain circumstances, it is not easy to think of a better way of preventing that identity being known than the one taken here. Given the circumstances of a murder, for instance, or a death in town, where a body is hard to dispose of."

They were in the empty, quiet Temple Gardens, and Clifford stood still. Tindall, too, stopped and tugged at his beard.

"A very natural thought, Chief Inspector," Sir Edward said at last, "But one which does not apply here. I can assure you that the money was not needed in any particular hurry. On the contrary, had those at Thornbush had any idea that my brother was dead, it would never have been presented at all, and a great deal of trouble would have been saved." Pointer looked unconvinced.

"I should like to hear the explanation given you of that cheque," he said finally. Pointer generally got his own way. His was a compelling personality, perhaps because it was so quiet as a rule.

"Suppose we take a cab for a few minutes' talk. We're before our time." Clifford lifted his stick to one passing on the embankment. As they settled themselves, Pointer asked: "I suppose that Mr. Straight is at work on Mr. Clifford's accounts?"

"Well—not to-day. No. I think I must talk the matter over with Hobbs first. In fact—in fact the accounts are rather connected with the affair of which I was informed last night."

"By Mr. Hobbs, Mr. Clifford's literary agent?"

"By his cousin, Mrs. Clifford, in the first place. She confided to me her belief that my brother has got himself into some trouble—abroad. I can't be more precise. She would not give names of places, even supposing that she knew them. It's not exactly an illegal thing which he intended to do, and which, therefore, she and Hobbs believed he was actually doing over there this week. But, on the other hand, it's one which would perfectly explain her and Hobbs's attitude. You see they thought, and she still thinks, that in Julian's own interest, by his own express commands, nothing must be said of where he is. She told me enough to let me see that we must go very carefully indeed. For unfortunately certain negotiations have already been opened up. It's a question of the purchase of something which is not allowed to leave the country —openly. Hobbs, whom I immediately tackled, assured me that he is putting things right, and that by the end of this week, all danger will be over of my brother's name being mixed up in any scandal, provided we do nothing to make a scandal inevitable. That cheque is quite in order, Chief Inspector. It's for the purchase of this—object; a huge sum, but I understand not beyond the worth of the object, and after all, Mr. Clifford could afford to gratify the only request of the sort that his wife has ever made. Hobbs cabled last night to stop the deal. He thinks he was in time to prevent its actually leaving its own country, and that being so, he has every expectation, certainty almost, of having the money refunded—in time. The money was sent off to an intermediary yesterday morning. But any investigation on our part, Chief Inspector, would do irreparable mischief just now. Quite irreparable. My brother's name would be brought  into a most deplorable prominence. Hobbs went so far as to assure me solemnly that were he alive—and were the facts to become known—my brother, Julian Clifford, would be liable to imprisonment! Of course, I myself would have to resign at once at the mere whisper of such a thing. Now, this whole affair has nothing whatever to do with Julian's death, nor with the terrible taking away of his head. As I say, Hobbs believes that he sees his way to put things back exactly as they were. Mrs. Clifford will not get her wish—for the moment. But if only matters can be adjusted, she, when she knows the facts, as she must very soon, will look at the matter exactly as we do."

"And the alteration on the cheque?" Pointer asked rather dryly.

"Hobbs spoke of it to me. The cheque was first drawn out to Self. Then, when Mr. Clifford decided not to appear so directly in the matter, and learnt that one of the—ah—intermediaries was called Selfe, he himself merely added an e, and so on. The alterations did not show, and Julian did not initial them."

"I see," Pointer said. "Mr. Hobbs seems to've thought of everything." He spoke in a tone of real appreciation.

"Our aim now," Sir Edward went on, "is to uncover the reason for Etcheverrey's murder of my poor brother, and how far Haslar was guilty, or accessory to the fact. It's a hard enough task without adding other tangles to it. That discovery of yours points to the only solution of this riddle, I do believe—the discovery that my brother was going to write something which Etcheverrey felt that he must stop. Add to that Mr. Tindall's remarkable guess as to the identity of Etcheverrey, and I think we may safely feel that we are on the right road."

There was a little silence.

"What was it, what *could* it have been that my brother was going to write which caused his death?" Edward Clifford repeated ruminatingly.

"I've a notion that only a betrayal, real or fancied, would have made Etcheverrey kill a man," Tindall said, "unless it was all a ghastly mistake."

Mr. Bancroft proved to be a pleasant, business-like man, an old acquaintance of both Tindall and Sir Edward.

"Necessary to reach Clifford at once . . . and you think . . . yes, I see the idea. I know he is away from home. Mrs. Clifford told me as much when I 'phoned to her yesterday.

For Clifford had made an appointment. He was going to bring us in the next chapter of *The Soul of Ishmael* himself some time during yesterday morning. We had been discussing it last time he and I lunched together. We're bringing it out in parts in our monthly magazine as you know. We suggested a little more—eh—well, adventure—incidents—"

Bancroft looked apologetic at having to mention such words. "The public taste is so depraved nowadays that it insists on high seasoning. Over-seasoning. And even such a giant as Julian Clifford who leads the masses, has to take account of it."

"'I *must* follow the mob, because I lead them.'" Tindall quoted the French revolutionary's words.

"Ex—actly! As it happens, Clifford was turning over in his mind a very dramatic idea. His—I really cannot call William Roberts a hero— his chief character, let us say, being forced to leave England, was to go abroad and find an outlet for a quite unsuspected side of his character with a notorious Basque anarchist. The anarchist was to be drawn from life if possible. Clifford gave me an outline of what was to come." Bancroft here unlocked a drawer. "I think he meant to take these notes with him, but he jotted them down at my house and left them behind him, and I confess I could not resist the temptation to keep them. They are so exceedingly interesting—so clear. But possibly you may find in them some suggestion as to where he would be likely to go first. He refers to Capvern once or twice. And to a place called Guizep— really these Basque names are worse than the Welsh."

Bancroft laid an envelope in front of Sir Edward, who took it gladly.

"Let me have it back when you've done with it. Cliffordiana, you know," the publisher said smilingly, "and Clifford may yet ask me for it. By the way, when, or if, you do reach him, ask him to let us have the next instalment as soon as he can, will you? Newman says that no chapter was handed to him to be sent on, so he prefers not to risk a mistake. So do we! And as Clifford is expected back by Friday—Mrs. Clifford seemed certain of the day—at a pinch we can wait till then."

"When did Mr. Clifford leave the notes behind him?" Pointer asked.

"When? About a fortnight ago. Week ago last Friday." Bancroft flipped some pages over in his engagement pad.

Finally, after nearly an hour, the three took their leave.

"Well," Sir Edward said, as they stood a moment before the house. "Bancroft has been very helpful. Some of those suggestions he remembered—and that precious envelope with Julian's own notes. They, I think, had better be photographed at once. Three copies, please, Tindall, tell the clerk. And let each of us have one to pore over as soon as possible. There may be nothing in them. But one can but hope."

Pointer shook hands. He had left his gloves in the publisher's private room. Mr. Bancroft was still alone. Pointer found his gloves, and stood a moment chatting.

"You're bringing out a life of William Haslar shortly, I understand?" he asked.

"We hope to. But the proofs are still at Thornbush. As a rule, Mr. Clifford is most prompt in returning them."

"Interesting book to write," Pointer rambled on in the tone of a lover of books, which he was. "Still, for even a distant connection, there must have been some difficulties. What letters to leave out . . . what incidents to suppress. . . ."

Mr. Bancroft agreed. But he only agreed. He added nothing to Pointer's knowledge.

"Miss Haslar is helping him with them," Pointer went on. Mr. Bancroft again agreed.

"Arnold Haslar came down with flu yesterday," Pointer went on. "High fever. Odd thing is, he keeps calling out to Julian Clifford to let him have 'the paper.' Implores us to 'take the paper' from him. We don't know what paper. No one knows what to make of it or what to do. The doctors seem to think we're keeping something back. But how on earth can any one tell what paper, or what letter it is, which Haslar wants to get away, or get back, from Clifford?"

Mr. Bancroft was interested, but he could not help. He could only instance a distant relative who had also behaved in an eccentric manner during a high temperature. So a disappointed fisherman had to leave, with no fish, large or small, of the kind that Pointer thought would alone explain the choice of Major Cory by Arnold Haslar.

The photographed copies of Julian Clifford's notes were quickly sent on to him, and Pointer glanced them over. Then he went on with his telephoning—telephoning that took him all the rest of the afternoon and evening.

It was past midnight when he was disturbed by a report from one of his road-menders.

"Hobbs has just left, sir. Walking. Direction of Haslar's house. Wright's following."

Pointer was off in his car within a few minutes. He stopped it a little to one side of the house and went on on foot. Outside the gate he lit a match, and tossed it away in a peculiar curve.

A second later a hand touched his arm.

"Wright speaking, sir. He's inside. Came straight here."

Wright melted away, to return to his post outside Thornbush, and Pointer let himself into the house with a latchkey which he had slipped off Arnold Haslar's own key ring. Below the door of the library a light showed. The room was locked. The key blocked the key-hole completely. Even with his sound accumulator on, Pointer could only hear low voices —a man's and a woman's voice. At last they came nearer. The door was very cautiously opened. Diana Haslar put her head out and looked up and down the hall. Pointer stood just inside the door of the next room, which he held ajar.

"Weren't you seen coming here?" she asked fearfully.

"No. No one's on the look-out at Thornbush, and I crept in too quietly here to be heard. I'll leave you to shut the front door after me.

Till day after to-morrow then, at Thornbush. If the boat's in on time, you'll be back by half- past five at latest."

She nodded, and closed the door with infinite caution behind the man, looking like an Eastern page in her short cherry silk dressing-gown and slippers. Pointer followed her upstairs at a safe distance. She went into her brother's room. The door was shut, but he found another door leading into the bathroom open, and peeping in he saw Diana sitting by her brother's bed with a book on her lap. But she was not reading. On her face was a look of intense excitement, intense joy. One of Pointer's men was in a distant arm-chair by the window, ostensibly as an assistant nurse. Round the leg of his chair was a cord, the colour of the wood, which ran through eyelets in the wainscoting to each of the doors. In the day-time it was taken away, but slipped on at night by the man on duty.

Pointer stooped down and gave it two quick tugs.

A minute later, and the man stepped out with an empty glass. He followed Pointer to his own room and closed the door.

"Has Miss Haslar left the room at all?" Pointer asked.

"Yes, sir. She went down about twelve for a snack. She's taking the watch till two, as I reported to you, sir. She came back just now, at ten to one. I suppose she dosed off a bit."

"You didn't hear any sounds at all just before she went down?"

"No, sir. No sound at all."

Pointer melted away. Merely as a matter of routine, genuinely so this time, he stepped into the library, shut the door, and switched on the light.

Sometimes people in a very engrossing conversation left odd things behind them, and the low voices which he had heard had sounded very absorbed.

The room looked as usual, except that a couple of chairs had been moved from one side to the centre of the room. They were not very near each other. Neither they, nor their position, suggested intimacy.

Pointer looked beyond them at the place where they had stood. Moving them had left free an old knee-hole writing-table, which, so Pointer had found yesterday, was used as a hold-all for odds and ends. Just now the table too stood a little away from the wall at one end. Pointer eyed it curiously —closely. Something caught that keen eye of his lying between one of the feet of the table and the wall—something that had prevented that end of the table being rolled back true as it had stood yesterday and this morning.

It was the ferrule of an umbrella—rather new-looking. Now umbrellas are not much used in libraries at any time, let alone in a dry July. Pointer turned it over very thoughtfully. Hobbs had not carried an umbrella when he left here just now, nor when he left Thornbush. His trailer had told Pointer that he was carrying nothing in his hands.

But Julian Clifford had taken his umbrella with him when he left his home night before last. The butler was certain of this, for on going up to bed he had noted its absence as well as that of his master's soft felt hat. Besides, Clifford was one of those men who always carry an umbrella. Pointer had sent one of his men to the house with a gamp this morning which purported to be one that Mr. Clifford had left in the post office. The butler had rejected it promptly. The detective, by clever doubts and beliefs, had obtained a close description of the author's umbrella—a fairly new one, a recent present —among other more praiseworthy peculiarities it had a loose ferrule, one that threatened to drop off at any moment. Mr. Clifford had caught it in tram points the first day of carrying it. Trimble mentioned that Hawkins meant to have it seen to, but Hawkins never saw to anything before he had to.

Pointer laid the little thimble down on the writing-table and studied that piece of furniture intently. The chairs moved away from it meant that the whole table had been swung out. He swung it out. Behind it, the papered wall showed no opening, nor did the carpeted floor. The wainscoting ran unjointed past the spot. There remained the table itself. But to open any of its drawers it would not have been necessary to move the chairs away. Pointer took out the drawers and laid them on one side. Then he examined the remaining skeleton. Yes, there was a place running the width of his hand all along the back. Pointer promptly up-ended the table. There are not many ways of opening secret places in such pieces. He finally found that by screwing one of the feet around twice out jumped the back of a panel like the door of a cuckoo clock. He put his hand in and pulled out an umbrella, and then its handle, then a couple of letters tied with red tape and addressed in a faded handwriting to a Mrs. Walton in Yorkshire. The date was nearly thirty years ago.

The umbrella handle exactly tallied with the description of Julian Clifford's which had been given to Pointer's man. The umbrella looked as if it had been violently treated—possibly in the effort to cut off the handle—possibly before. The handle had been hacked off with some blunt instrument, the cane crushed and splintered.

Yes, with such an instrument, for instance, as a sharpened spade.

He took his finds away with him, and but for them, left everything as he had found it. Then he went home.

So Miss Haslar and Hobbs were to meet the day after tomorrow at Thornbush after a boat got in, and had met tonight in the library of Arnold Haslar's house!

Intricate case this! He decided to watch Diana Haslar himself to-morrow, for the hour of the rendezvous and some- thing in the tone of

Hobbs suggested that it was to be the finale, or the wind-up of, or, at any rate, the report on some piece of business on which Diana would be engaged. Mrs. Clifford's cousin, Julian Clifford's literary agent, had spoken in the tone of a man who would be waiting, but the look on the face of the dead man's niece was that of one who has promised another that he can count on her, of one who is to do something.

Pointer was sorry. He had planned a very busy and very early morning at her brother's warehouse as a rat-catcher, with a wiry-haired marvel from the Yard—a champion ratter. No night watchman and no warehouseman in Britain could resist the offer that he intended to make.

However, after due reflection, he decided on "ladies first."

## CHAPTER 11

And that was why, on the morrow, when Diana got down at Bruges, a chauffeur followed her out of the train and into the town—a chauffeur who had crossed to Ostend with her, had taken a ticket to Bruges just after her, who had arranged with the Bruges police to have a taxi-cab waiting for him outside the station. But Diana was walking, so he made a sign to the man at the wheel and walked on after her.

Bruges, ringed and intersected by canals, is interesting, and can be charming; but not in July, when it is crowded with British trippers who surge noisily in serried ranks along its main streets, avoiding its art treasures but crowding its cake shops.

As it happened to be a saint's day, or a wedding, or a funeral, the bells of all the churches, above all the great bell of Saint Sauveur, the massive cathedral, were shattering the air with swift, jarring peals. The bells of Bruges are now rung by electricity, and need not even pause for tired muscles.

It was the half-hour. And the *beffroi*, that beautiful tower that lifts its coronet high into the air above Bruges' big *place*, was giving one of its quarter-hour selections of carillons. Melodies may sometimes be suitable for being played on bells; this one certainly was not. Barrel organs were grinding merrily within a few feet of each other. Trams banged their gongs all down the curving street.

Diana, who looked a little dizzy with the clamour of Bruges-la-morte, turned into the rue Sud de Sablon. Being July, her English ears did not miss the songs of birds in this country that eats them.

The roof lines of the constantly winding streets were enchanting. Dentellated, crenellated, they rose against a sky whose colours told that the waves of Zeebrugge, the harbour of Bruges, or Brugge, as the Flamand calls it, were very near. She walked on, glad of the exercise.

"*Pas op, mejuffrouw!* (Look out, miss!)" a white-hatted gendarme, who was regulating the traffic, said quietly.

Mistaking the Flemish word for the equivalent of "Pass on," Diana stepped forward. She nearly "passed on" altogether. A car, dashing around the corner, taught her the perils of ignorance. But a long arm swept her back into safety. A chauffeur, a tanned man in a trim uniform, with a pleasant flash of white teeth below his drooping moustache, touched his cap with a "Pardon, Madame!"

She turned at the French, for Bruges is Flemish speaking. She saw him step towards a taxi from which a man had just slipped, and take the wheel.

"Is that your taxi? Can you drive me to the Beguinage?" she asked in the same language.

"Certainly, Madame!" and shutting her in the cab, he drove off into a side street, where he pulled up, and got off, apparently to do something to the back of the hood; in reality to open a map of Bruges and take a long look at *Ten Wyngaerde*, The Vineyard, as the town calls its Beguinage.

The Beguinages of Belgium are peculiar to this corner of Europe. From the thirteenth century on, women solved the question of domestic difficulties and dangers by living a community life which gave them all the protection of a convent, but where they could have almost the liberty of the world. The Beguines, who dress at a glance like other nuns, in white and black, sometimes take no vows, sometimes all but that of poverty. Their money is their own to use and leave. They dwell, not in narrow cells under one roof, with every hour of the day mapped out for them, but live, if they so prefer, in little houses, alone, or with another Beguine friend, set in the encircling, protecting wall of the Beguinage. In the centre of the Beguinage at Bruges—a small affair compared with that of Ghent—is a quiet green. Tall elms, elms that saw men set out on the last crusade, give it a thin, elderly shade. Orchards and vegetable gardens lie behind it. Inside the little houses a simple austerity must nowadays reign, just as all the inmates are women of the highest character. For the rest, they live pious lives under their chosen Superior beloved by the poor, given over to good works. The chauffeur drove the car to the arched entrance over a bridge that spanned one of the canals. Here he had to stop. Before them, like a city within a city, lay the Beguinage, its little red roofs dotted among the greenery. In front the water mirrored the curve of its gray wall. Artists sat sketching it. To one side was the Minnewater, Bruges' much overrated beauty spot. For though the town has charming corners, they lie in quiet nooks, off the main roads. But here at least was peace. Softly the carillon floated down, melodious sounded Saint Sauveur's tireless majestic bells.

Diana got out. No carriage may mar the silence of the Sister's home. She made to pay her driver.

"I'll wait for Madame," he said promptly.

But Diana told him that she had no further need of his services, paid him, and walked on quickly under the domed gate, past the crucifix where the Beguines kneel, coming and going. A sister met her going swiftly towards their church.

"Mademoiselle van Bracht?" Diana asked.

"Over there. The white house with the geraniums in the green windows, Mademoiselle," and the Beguine hurried on.

"But she's at service just now," she added over her shoulder.

Diana did not seem to be put off her intended call. The chauffeur, who had lounged in after her, with the vacuous air of a man staring at unfamiliar sights, saw her step on as swiftly as before. He saw her rap at a little green-painted door.

"Baronesse van Bracht? Sœur Therese?" Diana asked.

"I am Sister Therese. Won't you come into my sitting-room?" the sister said in French. Diana followed her into a little back room on the ground floor, furnished plainly but comfortably, and so dark that the light had to be kept switched on beneath a statue of Sainte Begge.

The chauffeur tried the latch of the door. It opened under his careful hand without a sound. In his rubber-soled deck shoes he passed into a tiled passage with two doors on either hand. A door at the end of the passage showed the canal, quiet and deserted. He turned, and softly opened the first door on his left. He stood in a neat kitchen. As he hoped, a door led into the next room, where he could hear the two women. Noiselessly he drew the curtains shut over the window, then he cautiously opened the communicating door. Diana was just handing an envelope to the Beguine, who was saying:—

"I will see that it is passed on at once to my sister, Madame de Coninck. She will do the rest. By this evening all will be put right. I will give you a receipt if you will step into this balcony"

At that instant the light went out. Sœur Therese called out in English, and in English English too.

"Who's that? Who's holding my hand?" Then she screamed.

"What's wrong?" Diana called quickly. "I'm here, Sister. What's wrong?"

There came a knock on the door leading into the passage. The same moment the Beguine switched up the light. She glared at Diana like a mad woman. The knock came again. Her white headdress awry, the sister tried to pull it straight; she tugged at the black veil which shadowed her face and which, as a rule, is laid aside indoors.

The door opened, and the chauffeur looked in shyly.

"Pardon, Mesdames, but is anything wrong? I was knocking to ask the young lady whether she left this scarf in the cab, when I heard a cry—"

The sister looked from him to Diana and back to him with the swift, ferocious look of a panther.

"It's a plot, is it?" she said in a low, dangerous voice. "I see!"

Diana stared at her. The chauffeur stared too. His hair seemed to stand up with surprise. His mouth open, he looked from the sister to the English girl.

"She's mad," he said in French. "Come with me, Madame. She's quite mad, eh?"

"Stop!" The Beguine held out her hand. In it was something that glittered.

"Make a move either of you, and I shall shoot. I want that package back. I intend to have it back, so—"

Diana was quick of eye, but just what happened she did not see. The chauffeur did not seem to move a finger. Yet something shot across the room full into the sister's face. It was his cap. The man sprang after it. He seemed to use no force whatever. He only put out one hand, but the automatic fell with a smack against the opposite wall.

"We must go for help. She is evidently quite mad." He spoke pityingly as the woman turned and twisted in his arm.

"Go on to the car below, Mademoiselle. I will follow in a little minute. *Pardieu, la pauvre sœur!* I will notify the police on the way to the station."

"No," Diana said quietly, "I don't leave her like this. What package is it you miss, sister? The one I brought?"

For a second the sister stared at her, then she said, "I thought you were in it. I see you're not. This man has that letter you brought. I'm sure of it. I'm certain he opened the door from that next room, switched out the light, and twisted the package from my hand before he pretended to knock at the other door. It's only a step between them."

She spoke in English. The man goggled stupidly.

"*Quoi?* She says?"

Diana translated all that was necessary.

"A letter has been lost? Then why not telephone to the gendarmerie at once? There is a telephone at the portress's lodge. I saw the wires as I passed it. We can all three go there if the sister doubts me. But she is mad. The poor lady!"

Diana looked at the sister, whose face was white with red circles on the cheek-bones—circles of fury. She looked like a horrible clown.

Diana, with an odd look of uncertainty in her usually self-possessed glance, did not move.

"If you will be so good as to open that wooden shutter over there we could see better," the chauffeur said again. "I do not like to let her go. She may do herself a mischief. Throw herself out of that window, for instance." He gave the sister a look in which there was something mocking and something very stern. "The window that is open," he went on, "the window of the little balcony. A slip, and one would be in the canal. And the canal just here is choked with weeds, and quite deep enough to drown the sister, especially if by any chance that sort of iron raft were to fall down which I see is only stood against the window just below, so that a push from an outstretched hand would send it in too. It could so easily pin any one who had fallen in down among the weeds; and it is quite a deserted stretch."

Diana did not stir, but her jaw tightened.

"This man is a government spy," the sister said fiercely. "We must get that letter back. We must act!"

"You are acting, Mrs. Orr," the chauffeur answered blandly, "and acting very well. But I don't think you'll get that package back."

Diana jumped. It was the voice of the Chief Inspector from Scotland Yard. And what was that about "Mrs. Orr"?

"I am Sister Therese," the Beguine said very calmly now. "Mrs. Orr is my half sister. We are rather alike. Miss Haslar, you know what hangs on recovering that envelope."

Diana seated herself.

"I'm going to understand this," she said, and she meant it.

"I'm afraid that would take longer than you think. But this"— Pointer dived into an inner pocket and held out something—"is what you brought, isn't it?"

"Why should you take that?" Diana asked indignantly. She looked prepared to snatch it from Pointer herself.

He gave her an apparently swift but very searching glance. "Miss Haslar, I think you know that I'm not tricking you when I assure you— *assure* you—that it is where it should be. Who gave it to you?"

Diana did not answer. She looked at him. She looked at the Beguine whom Pointer still held by one hand on her arm. It was unlike Diana to let things drift. But she made no move, and she turned very pale.

Again he looked at her, with a rather enigmatic look.

"A train back to Ostend leaves in half an hour. I want you to take that, Miss Haslar."

She intended, he knew, to spend the night in that flamboyant resort. Her telegram to the Royal Hotel there for a room had been read this morning at Victoria before it was sent off. Two rooms, adjoining, and with a communicating door between had been engaged instead. Though this she would never know. A woman detective, who had accompanied Pointer, would be beside her. New Scotland Yard was doing its best to watch over Diana.

"I suppose you are crossing back to-morrow?"

She was.

"When you get back to town go straight to your brother's house. Don't go to Thornbush until I have had a talk with you. And don't telephone to any one there that you are back in London." She started. He looked her squarely in the eye. "Don't, on any account, go to or communicate with Thornbush, Miss Haslar," he repeated, "until I have called. I will try to get to you as soon after you reach home as I can. You have been in greater danger to-day than you quite realise." His eyes went to the window overlooking the canal, to the Beguine, and back to Diana.

"Danger—to me? I don't understand." She didn't.

"When a murder has been committed, and a head cut off, those who have gone as far as that are not likely to be playing for low stakes. You mustn't come between a tiger and his kill, and expect mercy," was the Chief Inspector's only explanation. His manner was very grave.

Diana shivered. She was looking very different now from the girl who had taken the cab.

"Will you tell me the truth when you come to-morrow?" she asked, not as one making a bargain, but desperately.

"What I tell you will be strictly the truth. And I expect from you strictly the truth," he said quietly. "And now, I think you had better start."

"But this—this sister"

"Ah!" Pointer gave a queer little smile, "this lady and I have a few things to say to one another."

Diana left the little cottage where all should have been peace, and where she had just spent a most violent few minutes. Something seemed to have given way in Diana. She looked as though something vital had been taken from her.

After an uneventful but sleepless night she left by the boat next morning, quite unaware that the rather severe-looking young woman beside her on the deck had anything to do with her. Her train was to the minute. She had nothing but a suitcase for the Customs, and five o'clock found her quietly letting herself into her brother's house. She peeped into his room, and saw with infinite relief that he was drawing deeper breaths than when she had left him yesterday morning.

She decided to have tea in the library. Its doors were practically sound-proof. No sound from there could possibly disturb the sick man. The room was empty, but from the other end, Arnold's study, she heard a stir.

She stepped towards the communicating door. As she did so, she accidentally clicked her bag against a chair. Instantly all was silent. Opening the door, she saw to her surprise that, though she could see no one, yet the strong-room was open. Had some one been tampering with the deed-boxes ranged along its shelves? She had a vague idea of their number and position. She stepped into it to look closer. On the instant the door slammed shut. She heard the click of the locks falling into position. She was a prisoner in a sound-proof, all but air-tight metal safe.

It was at that precise moment that Mrs. Clifford was very much bored. She was at a concert. The Albert Hall was stuffed from stall to roof. A great violinist had given of his best, and the enthusiasm had been delirious. Encore after encore had been demanded and generously given. It was long past the usual time when the last item was started. It was a Vivaldi Concerto. Mrs. Clifford disliked Vivaldi, even when played by a master.

The concert room was quiet and not too bright. Idly she pulled out her crystal ball and sat looking into it, her arm pressed against her neighbour's, for a voluminous lady overflowed from the other seat. Suddenly she gave a little gasp, and leaning still more to the right, got a better view of the crystal. The players were attacking the Rondon. Mrs. Clifford turned to the man beside her, a man who had twisted around in his seat when she had taken the one beside him, and buried himself still deeper in his music folios, so that his back was practically turned to her.

"Mr. Newman! Something is happening to Diana Haslar! She's in danger. Can you telephone to Mr. Straight? I can't use telephones, you know."

"Sh-h-sh!" hissed the music-lovers around them indignantly.

The man beside her flung his music books on to his seat, and swiftly, with a hand under her arm, led her out into the corridor outside.

"Go at once! Or telephone to Mr. Straight, he's nearer." Mrs. Clifford seemed quite unmoved by Newman's presence, as he was by the fact that she had known her husband's secretary in spite of a very remarkably good disguise—a very professionally made-up disguise.

"What did you see? Where is she?" he asked swiftly. Mrs. Clifford sank on a settee and went on staring at her ball.

"I've lost her! No, there she is!" Newman was behind Mrs. Clifford. He, too, was bending over the ball, his arms on either side of her.

"She's locked in an iron cell. There's very little air. She's pounding on the wall. She seems to be calling for help. It's all dark. Outside some one is standing listening. He's in the shadow, yet he seems familiar. Why, it's Arnold's study! Then that cell must be his strong room. And the word that opens the door must be lost. But what—" Newman had gone.

Pointer came over on the same boat and train with Diana, heard her give her taxi driver her brother's address, and then turned into the buffet for a hasty sandwich. He telephoned to the Yard for the day's reports. There were several. From parcels addressed to non-existent streets and people Mr. Clifford's clothes had practically all been retrieved. Along with them was a blood-stained and beplastered hand towel. The clothes had been identified by Mr. Clifford's tailor.

Pointer felt as though his boat were drawing in, drawing in all the time.

Last of all he learnt that ten minutes ago Hobbs, Mr. Clifford's literary agent, had left Thornbush and had been followed to Haslar's house. He was still there.

On the instant Pointer was out of the telephone booth, and speaking to the sergeant in charge of the station-police. In another he was on one of their motor-bicycles which are fitted with silencers as perfect as expense can make them.

He whizzed off for the Haslar's house at a speed which only his steering made possible. Even so, one tabby never returned to its home.

Arrived at the house, Pointer looked at the gravel of the drive. It showed that a car had just turned at the front door a car with the same tyres as the taxi which Diana had finally captured at Victoria. Driving away, the car had been lighter than when coming. Probably, therefore, it was empty and all was in order. He let himself in with his annexed latchkey. Noiselessly he ran up to her bedroom and listened. All was silent. He tried the door. It was unlocked. The room was empty. So was her boudoir.

He glanced in at the sick room in passing, through the door into the bathroom, but he gave his man no signal. Diana was not there, nor in either drawing-room. On the ground floor, dining-room and morning-room and library were all empty. Remained only the study. As he jumped for the communicating door, it opened, and Hobbs came out.

"Miss Haslar's in there," Pointer said swiftly but very easily. "I've followed her here from the station. I must have a word with her."

Hobbs fell back. His face turned green, his jaw slackened. Pointer's unexpected appearance, his swift yet casual words, his absolute certainty as to where Diana was, seemed to rattle Hobbs.

"I—eh—"

Pointer did not wait. He stepped in and glanced once around the room. Then he was at the safe door. He knew the password, thank God. Pointer had connected up the safe dial with a certain well-hidden burglar's dial before sending for Haslar's manager last night. It had marked every letter he set. The word had been Visit. Pointer now turned the five letters—tried the word. The door refused to budge. So some one, Hobbs probably, had changed the password.

Pointer, his ear to the safe, tapped with the end of his watch chain, sharp swinging blows. He caught a faint tap-tap from the inside.

"She's in there! Good heavens, man, you must have locked the door on her, never guessing that she was inside. Quick, Mr. Hobbs, the password!"

Pointer was throwing the man a rope. But the colour was coming back into Hobb's face.

"Miss Haslar's upstairs in bed, I take it. I haven't seen her, nor do I know anything about the safe or the combination lock. I dropped in to look up a technical point in one of Haslar's electrical books. I was in the library when I heard a tremendous thud. It took me a second to realise that it was the door of the strong room that I heard. At least, I suppose it was. I'm not certain even of that much."

He rattled off the speech at top-speed. His words were not exactly blurred, but there was a thickness about them that made Pointer's heart sink. Hobbs was the worst for drink, and the only chance for the girl locked in would have been a clear-headed, shrewd Hobbs, a Hobbs who would have known when he must cut his losses. Pointer knew from yesterday what Hobbs could be like when he was not sober, and to-day he was more nearly drunk than yesterday—much more nearly.

Pointer gave a whistle like a blackbird's when a poacher blunders too close at night. A man clambered in through the open window. He said a word to him. The man moved to Hobb's side, who looked as though he were watching something awful come up to him.

Pointer jumped to the telephone. He was taking no chances. He might yet get the password out of Hobbs, but meanwhile he was telephoning the Yard to send him the safe-expert with his most up-to-date tools to open a strong room door, which was—Pointer gave the makers' name and the size of the door. But the master-cracksman was away. No one knew when he would be in. Another man would, of course, be sent, but there was no second Cockerell.

Pointer felt certain that it was Hobbs who had altered the code word, but he might be wrong. He tried for Haslar's manager, but Mr. Dance was out. Then he got Thornbush. No one there was in. Mrs. Clifford was out. Mr. Straight was out; it was believed that he had gone to Sir Edward Clifford's. Mr. Hobbs was out.

Pointer turned again to Hobbs.

"Come, Mr. Hobbs, try and think if you can't remember the code word. It would mean a lot," Pointer's eyes dwelt on the other. "I was over in Bruges yesterday with Miss Haslar. I have the letter, by the way, safe and sound, which you gave her to take to Mrs. Orr."

Hobbs's face twitched as though an electric shock had passed through him.

"She might have had a bad time in Bruges. . . . But a good turn cancels a bad one—sometimes. I'm sure she wouldn't remember Bruges if she got out of that strong room at once. . . . Nor would I!"

Pointer was exceeding the law, and doing it most unwillingly, but the need of the entombed girl was paramount. Hobbs looked as if a terrible struggle was going on within him. The sweat stood out on his white face. But he set his teeth.

Pointer turned away. Was Hobbs gambling on the chance that Diana Haslar would never speak? But Hobbs was no fool. Whatever Diana knew could not be equivalent to rejecting the life-line that the

Chief Inspector had thrown him. There was a greater reason than fear of what she might say, might suspect. Suddenly Pointer guessed it.

He turned and gave the man in the chair a long look. Hobbs caught it, read it, leapt in his seat, and then sat rigid, his eyes staring glassily.

The door burst open and Straight rushed in. Behind him, hesitating, as though disliking to set foot in Arnold Haslar's house, came Sir Edward.

"What's this about Haslar's strong room and Miss Haslar?" Straight asked.

"Know the password?" Pointer asked, but without any hope. Straight only shook his head with a look of horror.

"You mean to say it's true? That she's been locked in there?" he asked under his breath. "Isn't there a way of telling the right word by listening to the fall of the tumblers?"

"Not with this safe," Pointer said gravely, "but there's still time." His eyes rested for a fraction of a second on Hobbs— "Still time."

Hobbs half stepped forward. Almost, Pointer thought, his hand went towards the dial, but the neat brandy that he had drunk made him wheel about and return to a chair in the shadow by the window.

The safe-breaker arrived from the Yard. He set to work at once with a pneumatic drill. Chemicals were out of the question because of the girl inside.

"How did you hear of what had happened?" Pointer asked Straight above the roar of the drill.

"Mrs. Clifford got some one to telephone me. A commissionaire at a concert hall, I understand. She seemed quite certain of what had happened. . . . But surely Miss Haslar can be got out all right?"

"We must hope for the best," Pointer said none too encouragingly. "If the safe had been standing wide open for a little time before it was closed, she may have a better chance. Our man is quite good as a rule. Sir Edward was with you, I suppose?" Pointer finished.

"No, I ran into him in the garden outside," Straight explained absently.

"I had something very important to say to Miss Haslar," Sir Edward explained at once, retreating with Pointer to the farthest end of the room; "I will tell you about it later, Chief Inspector. A fact has come to my knowledge which makes me wonder. . . . However, Miss Haslar had not returned when I asked for her at half-past four."

"You waited in for Miss Haslar?" Pointer asked, watching his man try another way of tackling those immovable tumblers.

"No, I decided to call again later."

"Did you think the servant who let you out looked as though he had just come in from outside?" Pointer asked next.

"I let myself out, so I cannot say. Looked as if he had come in—?" Sir Edward began to repeat Pointer's odd question, a question which had served its turn of learning that Clifford had not been shown out.

Sir Edward looked round. Hobbs was out of earshot if he spoke low.

"Hobbs is under arrest? So you know?"

"Know what, Sir Edward?"

"Straight came to me about it. It seems he *did* go through the books yesterday and to-day. Straight suspected Hobbs's accounts from something that Diana told him about a letter which she opened by mistake. Straight says the books are cooked: cleverly done, but he's certain they're cooked. He wants another chartered accountant to go through them with him. He speaks of something like fifty or sixty thousand not

accounted for. Of course in ten years. . . ."

The man from the Yard approached Pointer.

"I'm beaten, sir. This latest pattern is beyond me. There's a chap in Bermondsey, Silly Billy, he might do it. He's just out of a stretch. Not a bad sort."

Bermondsey! From Hampstead to Bermondsey and back! And to find Silly Billy. Meanwhile what of Diana? Pointer too was very pale. It was an awful thing to be standing there helpless and think of the agony just beginning so close beside them. Must they chance gray powder, and the effects of it? Death by chemicals was no worse than death by suffocation.

Suddenly a bookish, gray-haired, spectacled man, a typical musician from his appearance, stood in the room. So swiftly, so silently had Newman come in that only Pointer had seen him enter.

# CHAPTER TWELVE

Mrs. Clifford hurried in after Newman. For once she looked in great distress.

"Is Diana still locked in?" she asked before she was in the room.

Straight jumped for her.

"The word, Mrs. Clifford! The new code-word. Do you, by any chance, know another word than *Visit?*"

She shook her head in silent horror, then she turned to Newman.

"Do you?"

"I don't know any other code-word than *Visit*." Newman had flung down a box that was all but beyond even his wiry strength. He tore it open, and began to lay out strange, bulky things on the carpet with desperate speed.

"That word won't open it now." Pointer alone had not shown any surprise at the return of the secretary—disguised —accompanied by Mrs. Clifford. "I can't reach Haslar's manager, nor could he help. The word has been deliberately changed. Going to use electricity?"

Newman nodded. His eyes were unmistakably those of the master of the situation.

Mrs. Clifford had turned to her brother-in-law and Straight.

"Mr. Newman telephoned to you? Oh, Edward, what shall we do? What can we do? If only Julian were here, as he will be shortly now, for this is Friday. Adrian, don't look so terrible," she glanced at her cousin's awful face, "I'm sure we'll get her out yet."

"Clear the room, please." Newman jerked out a box full of an odd, gritty powder with a strong rust smell.

"You want no help? Our man, Burton, is a trained engineer," Pointer asked.

"I want the room cleared, that's all."

"Burton," Pointer turned to the man who had tried his hand at the door and been beaten, "go below and stand by the main switch." Pointer wanted no tampering. "Sinclair, you and Mr. Hobbs go into the room opposite. Mrs. Clifford, if you and Sir Edward—"

"We'll wait upstairs. I'll concentrate, and send down my spirit to help."

"Thank you so much," Pointer said gravely, "and I'm sorry, Mr. Straight, but—"

Straight lingered.

"*Can* you do it?" he asked Newman imploringly, "a blunder would only make it harder for the right man. ..."

"I shall not blunder. I was in the Secret Service, Mr. Straight. You will see Miss Haslar out very soon, I hope." Newman was already running his hands over the door.

"Mind if I watch you?" Pointer asked, when they were alone.

Newman lifted his heavy lids and let them drop. "Rather you didn't. I'm a nervous chap."

Pointer stood with his back to him and did not use a mirror. But Newman did not sound nervous. Quick and sure, Pointer could hear his movements at the safe. Burton had already knocked out the spindle, Newman now began plugging the hole with desperate speed, using the powder which he had brought with him. Then he tested something with an electric apparatus which he put on the table and connected with a wall-plug. It looked like some sort of dwarf thermo-generator.

Next, after some calculations which he made swiftly but very carefully on a little machine in his odd box, Newman started work of a kind that Pointer could not follow. The expert from the Yard arrived breathless.

"Am I too late? Can I do anything?"

Pointer indicated Newman.

"He thinks he can open that door. The code word's lost. Evidently he's not trying to drill holes. What about it? It's beyond me."

Cockerell stepped forward. He asked a few questions. Newman, without slackening his lightning work, answered curtly enough. By this time strange blue flashes were crackling around the dial box, and forked lightning seemed to answer from the edges of the closely-fitting door.

Cockerell looked excited.

"I've never seen this before—or have I? Wait a bit. . . . Where did I see work like this . . . that must have been done on some such method—ordinary electricity was used then, of course, but where . . . when?" . . . The safe-breaking expert went off into a deep study.

"Does he know his job?" Pointer asked.

"Rather! And yet—I should say better theoretically than practically. Where did I once see something that reminds me of this? . . ."

Suddenly Newman gave a little exclamation. His *crickle, crackle* stopped. The blue and the yellow flashes no longer seemed to fight each other. In the air was still the strange electric smell of an X-ray room, but Newman was now pulling at the door with cloths over his hands. It opened. Diana lay huddled on the floor. Newman darted forward and picked her up. His disguise had gone by this time. Wig and beard had been pulled off in the heat of the work, and the sweat had washed the make-up from his hands and face.

Diana clung to him.

"Sanz!" her arms went round his neck, "I called you, and you came! I called you the whole time . . . with all my heart and all my soul."

Her face was transfigured. Her beautiful hair clung in damp curls to her finely-shaped head as a baby's does. She was pale. Under her lids were purple shadows, but her eyes were like stars.

"If you won't hold me fast, I shall you." She spoke with a strange solemnity.

This was no laughing meeting of lovers. Diana knew what the hand to which she clung might have done. Yet she clung to it.

"In spite of—everything?" he asked her gravely.

"In spite of—beyond—through—everything. Don't put me down, Sanz. Don't let me go again."

He only looked at her—a searching look to which the foreign sharpness of his features gave something rapier-like. Standing there still holding her, he had a dark, virile beauty which struck those watching him afresh.

Suddenly her eyes fell on Pointer. A look of terror swept down upon her face, putting out the light in it.

"I forgot; I betrayed you!" she stepped back from him, "and then I called you and you came! Oh, Sanz, I've lured you into their hands!"

"How do you mean that you betrayed me?" he asked quietly.

"I told them who you are. After your letter I—I thought it was a love of justice, but I couldn't bear that they should think you—it—a murder!" She whispered the last words, her face gray again.

"But supposing it was one?" he interrupted in a hard voice.

Diana made a helpless gesture.

"It's no use. I've tried to hate you for these years past, I've fought till I'm tired. Life wasn't worth living. In there, when the door banged shut, and I thought I should never see it open again, I've learnt the truth."

He stopped her. He was as pale as she under all his dark colouring.

"You forget that I'm wanted for murder. You forget the murder of your uncle—the shooting of your brother." He spoke almost roughly.

And at that Diana broke down.

He came across to her and took her face for a second between his slender dark hands, gently, as one takes a flower. Then he turned away.

Diana looked at Pointer.

"I must see him before he goes."

"You shall."

"Alone?"

"Alone." Pointer passed her and went on into the strong-room, carefully scrutinizing the boxes. It was dark inside here, except for his lamp. The work on the door had put the lights inside out of action. But there was something in here which he expected to find. . . . Suddenly his hand actually trembled for a second, when his long, lean fingers felt over a well wrapped-up tin marked in a scrawl:—

A. Haslar.
Not wanted forward. To be stored in a cold place.

There was a dent in one side. It was heavy for its size, and the size was that of a seven-pound tin.

Pointer carried it out. Then he saw that Mrs. Clifford was back in the room, her arms around Diana. Pointer put the tin on a table behind him, but his thoughts did not leave it. Inside it was, he knew . . .

Alison Clifford would have helped the girl up to her room, but Diana refused any help. Mrs. Clifford, smiling a little, moved back. She caught her foot in a rug. To steady herself she laid a hand on the tin which Pointer had just set down. There came the oddest sound from her—a gasp, followed by a sort of strangled cry. She fell forward across the table grasping the tin in her arms.

"Julian! Oh, Julian!" She gave a frightful scream and tore at the wrappings with her fingers, shrieking like a demented woman.

"Hush, Mrs. Clifford," Pointer said firmly but very gently, "for the sake of the sick man overhead, for your own sake, you must not scream like that."

She had her hands still on the box, and the look in her eyes frightened Diana, who had run to her. She thought that her reason had gone.

"It's Julian's head!" Mrs. Clifford said in a strange, horrible whisper to Sir Edward, who had come in hastily. "In there! In that tin! His!"

This time Diana screamed—a low, horrified cry. "Is she mad?" she whispered in mingled terror and pity.

"Mrs. Clifford," Pointer said gravely, "I'm so sorry for this horrible shock—"

"His eyes are closed," Mrs. Clifford was murmuring now in a wild whisper.

Pointer forcibly lifted the box out of her grasp. He could not let her continue to "see" what that face must look like now. Not yet earth—no longer flesh.

"You know the truth now," he said gently.

Alison knelt on trembling violently.

"Mrs. Clifford," Pointer said again, "I must take this away for a little while. You shall see your husband's body shortly, believe me. But not like this! Not—" She did not seem to heed him. Pointer thought that she had fainted. He would have left her to the care of Diana and

Sir Edward, but when he turned away she clutched his sleeve. She almost tore the stout cloth of his cuff.

"Give me that back! It's mine! Mine by every law of God and man!"

"It is yours," Pointer said with real emotion, "but you must let me put it where it belongs. You must give us"—he glanced at the clock then at Sir Edward—"just one hour. Then you shall see your husband's body, if you still wish to do so, to-night."

She let him go at that and sat staring in front of her with a terrible expression on her face. At once wild and lost, as of a woman who felt the very foundations of her soul rocking within her.

"I'll bring her. To the mortuary chapel, I suppose? Where exactly is it?" Clifford asked. He himself was a ghastly white.

"I'll leave my car. My man will know." Again Pointer turned towards the door, that precious tin clasped in his arm. This time it was Newman who stopped him.

"Aren't you forgetting me?" he asked shakily, "your prisoner?" Like every one else in the room, whether they understood it or not, he looked profoundly moved by what had just happened.

"No," Pointer said easily, "oh, no, Mr. Newman, I'm not forgetting you. I must ask you to return to your old rooms at Thornbush until I have an interview with you." Newman would be better watched this time, Pointer knew.

Outside he saw Diana talking to Wilkins, her face convulsed. He motioned to her to come into an empty room. She all but refused.

"How did that tin come to be in this house at all?" he asked her.

"It came from the warehouse early this afternoon," she replied in a quiet, dull voice. There are points beyond which sensation becomes numb. "Wilkins put it on the hall table thinking it was sent up by mistake, or that I had asked for it. That is all he knows about it. And all I know about it."

The Chief Inspector gave a few more directions to the man in charge of Hobbs. Then he drove off with his precious tin—the tin for the sake of hiding which, so he believed, a half-sober Hobbs had been willing to let Diana Haslar die a frightful death.

The Commissioner and Major Pelham were present when the tin was opened. The plaster was carefully sprayed away until that appeared which they had expected to see, and which Mrs. Clifford had apparently already seen in some strange way—the head of Julian Clifford.

It had a bullet mark behind one ear.

An hour later, Mrs. Clifford followed with Sir Edward. The head had been carefully joined to the severed neck, and a cloth laid over the juncture. The face itself was made as little repulsive as possible. The plaster had done much to preserve it, and the warehouse chill had helped.

Sir Edward brought her in finally when word was sent out. She tottered to the coffin, and stood bending over it for a long time in silence. Then she dropped to her knees beside it.

"Ferryman, take me across? Oh, Ferryman, take me across!" The choking cry brought tears to the eyes of a very stolid-looking young policeman who was on duty in an unobtrusive corner.

"Poor soul! Mad, quite mad!" he said to himself; "talking about ferries here."

Pointer could not let this tormented soul gather itself up in peace, if tormented it really were. For Duse could have acted as Alison Clifford had done here and at Haslar's house. Sarah Bernhardt equalled that cry of pent-up passion bursting all efforts at control. Gently he touched her arm.

"Mrs. Clifford, who fired that shot?" he said insistently. "Who killed your husband from behind—without giving him a chance to save himself?"

She did not seem to hear him.

"I was wrong," she murmured under her breath, adjusting the sheet with what seemed like loving fingers. "'For here rolls the sea, and even here lies the other shore. Not distant. Not anywhere else.' " She turned and faced Pointer as though he had not spoken, looking at him as at a strange and rather meddlesome stranger.

"Mrs. Clifford," Pointer repeated quietly, "no one admires Tagore more than I do. But he would be the first to say that here lies duty as well. 'Here in this everlasting present.' And duty, your duty to your dead husband, to the civilisation which has sheltered you, which gave him the chance to become what he was, is to aid us—or rather Justice"

The widow sank into her chair. She covered her face with hands that looked almost translucent. Edward Clifford watched her, his own face drawn and haggard. When she finally showed hers again, it was serene.

"I cannot help you, Chief Inspector. Please don't misunderstand me." Her eyes on him, she paused. Keen, searching, were the last words to apply to their gaze. Yet Pointer felt as though she could see far—were seeing far. But he knew his own face to be an impenetrable mask when he chose. It was so now.

"I cannot help you," she said again, almost as to a child. "Or rather what you stand for—the law, man-made law— man-made and therefore to me blind and cruel. My husband has passed into another phase of life. Had he 'died,' to use your expression, by what is called an act of God, you would not have me try and avenge his death. Then why now? The result is the same. All your efforts cannot light the empty lantern. The light is shining where you cannot see it—for the moment. Julian would say the same."

"And the man who killed him?" Pointer asked coldly.

"The man who did it will suffer—will pay in another way. I will not help you to make him pay in your way."

"Then the next murder he commits will be on your soul, Mrs. Clifford," Pointer said very gravely.

Sir Edward started as though to speak, but checked himself. "Justice is necessary," the Chief Inspector went on, "and human punishment is necessary. Or we should be back among the head-hunters in no time. The wheel won't turn forward unless we put our shoulders to it." He spoke intentionally in a matter-of-fact voice: "Your husband was murdered, remember. Slaughtered as a beast is slaughtered."

He paused. Her lids flickered and her eyes widened. She drew in her breath sharply.

"He lies there crying to you for justice," Pointer ended passionately.

"His body lies there, Chief Inspector," she corrected, but apparently with an effort. "Julian Clifford *is* as much as ever he was; as near! as dear!" Suddenly two large drops rose and hung on her lashes. They gave the finishing touch to her face. Even Pointer felt his anger melt within him. Surely this woman was what she seemed.

"What was the reason for which Mr. Clifford left his home on Monday night? Why were you so sure he was in safety?" he continued.

She gave a cry at that and wrung her hands.

"Did you think he was in Bruges buying the Charlemagne crystal?" he persisted.

She interrupted him. "To think I believed him safe! To think I thought I saw him in the crystal! Then what did I see? How did I see?" She stared wild-eyed at Pointer.

She looked shaken to the heart. Pointer said nothing. If this were not acting, then he realised that the woman must have had such a shock as to be near the confines of what could be borne.

"I who thought I could see further than others!" she murmured. "But I *did* see Julian in the crystal . . . just as I saw Diana a little while ago. She was there where I saw her. Then why not Julian? Why not my husband?" she asked wildly.

"You have very wonderful gifts, Mrs. Clifford," he said quietly, "but you could not see what was not there, the dead among the living. I think your own imagination, your own belief as to where your husband was, projected itself into that crystal."

She was, or seemed to be, too exhausted to be questioned further, and he helped Sir Edward put her into her car and take her home to where a "nurse" from Scotland Yard was waiting to look after her—with a most vigilant eye.

Her objections to helping him find the criminal, were they solely as she represented them?

Pointer's profession, one he greatly respected, led along so many dark and twisted paths of the human heart. As a doctor spends his days at sick beds beside diseased bodies, so did the Chief Inspector's work take him among diseased minds. It was inevitable that he should distrust appearances as much as any mystic. Given hesitation on the part of the angel Gabriel, Pointer would have distrusted him. What, then, of Mrs. Clifford? She had cashed that cheque for notes, some of which Diana Haslar had taken to Mrs. Orr. Pointer believed that Diana had been given them by Edward Hobbs, Mrs. Clifford's cousin.

Tindall came hurrying in. The telephone had brought him the news. Both men were waiting for the police surgeon to make a summary examination of what had been hidden in the tin.

"Amazing about Mrs. Clifford," the F.O. man said tensely. "Did she know beforehand what the tin contained? Or did she 'see' into it? If the former, she knew that it would be opened within a very few minutes."

"She may have seen what I was seeing, and seeing tremendously keenly," Pointer suggested. "My mind was full of what I felt sure was inside that tin, what I guessed I should find on the shelf in that strong room. Just as sitting close beside Mr. Newman at a concert she got the message which Miss Haslar says she was sending him. Certainly she could not have known by any ordinary means that Miss Haslar was locked in that safe. I shouldn't wonder if whenever she reads a sealed letter, as they tell me she can do at times, or sees into a locked box, if there were some one in the room who knew what the letter or the box contained. She saw through Newman's disguise apparently, but then Newman would have recognised her at once, and must have been very conscious of her presence beside him."

"Thought-reading, in short?" Tindall asked dubiously.

"Always supposing it's not guilty knowledge," Pointer agreed. "I noticed her cousin Hobbs walked away to the window while she looked into the crystal, and 'saw' the stepped gables—saw her own thoughts, I take it, supposing she's innocent."

"This is going to be a slow, intricate case," Tindall said thoughtfully.

Intricate, certainly, but Pointer did not think it would be slow. He made no reply.

"How did Miss Haslar come to be locked into the safe, and who in the world put the head there?" Tindall asked, almost tearing his hair.

Pointer only turned to take the doctor's report which a man had just brought in.

The bullet had just failed to pass entirely through the lower part of the back of the head from left to right and was easily taken out. It was the kind to fit a .25 automatic, and had been fired from too far off to singe or blacken the skin.

"It fits Haslar's automatic," Pointer murmured. "No one else at Thornbush seems to own a weapon of any kind, except Sir Edward Clifford. He, too, has a .25—a common enough type."

"Haslar's warehouse—Haslar's revolver!" murmured Tindall. "I've taken the liberty, by the way, of putting one of our men as well on guard outside Thornbush. I confess I expected Etcheverrey to be detained. Or are you leaving him to me?"

"I'd like nothing done about him till to-morrow," Pointer said thoughtfully, "just as I want to keep my own counsel for that time."

"After his accomplices, eh? Good! So Etcheverrey's under our hands again. Rather fine of him coming back to save Miss Haslar, after that confession of his. Sort of thing he might be expected to do, though. Twisted nature his, with odd streaks of generosity in it."

Tindall accompanied Pointer to his rooms in Scotland Yard. Sir Edward had spoken of going there as soon as he had seen Mrs. Clifford home. Evidently he had something important to say, and something important to ask. He did not keep them waiting long.

"Now Chief Inspector, how did you learn about the Charlemagne crystal and Bruges?" Edward Clifford began at once. "Mrs. Clifford only told me that in strict confidence last night. Hobbs had hinted at it in the train, and obviously Julian had had it in his mind when he questioned me about paying over large sums so that they could not be traced. But how did you learn of it?"

"In the course of some routine work," Pointer said evasively. "I expect, however, to get fuller details from Mr. Hobbs presently."

"Hobbs!" Sir Edward made a wry face. "You certainly let no grass grow under your feet in his case either. Straight had only just told me of the defalcation. Straight found"— Sir Edward now turned to Tindall—"Straight found that Hobbs has cooked the books for the last ten years or so. And to the tune of a large fortune. He wants a first-class man to go through the books with him. The Chief Inspector was right in his suspicions of Hobbs."

They had not been suspicions with Pointer. The belief in the existence of heavy defalcations was the bed-rock of one half of Pointer's theory as to what had happened to Julian Clifford.

"And what about that cheque?" Sir Edward again addressed himself exclusively to Pointer. "Did Hobbs pay it over? He handed it to Mrs. Clifford to cash yesterday morning, telling her that Julian had enclosed it in the note which he had left for him. Hobbs's story is that in that letter Julian wrote that he had received word too late of some urgent necessity, some hitch, which only his own presence over in Bruges would smooth out, and that he was leaving at once, shortly after midnight on a returning fruit-cargo boat. Julian had all sorts of odd friends. The boat would get to Zeebrugge at eight Tuesday morning, and my brother would be at de Coninck's house by ten. He had to leave the cheque for Hobbs to cash and forward the money. Hobbs had a very busy morning ahead of him yesterday, and asked Mrs. Clifford to go to the bank for the money. She knew what was on foot. My brother intended the crystal as a surprise for her, but she had, it seems, overheard some words of his to Mrs. Orr which had told her what he was about. But as he had set his heart on surprising her, she kept up, before him, the pretence of knowing nothing. So Mrs. Clifford cashed her husband's cheque at once on Tuesday morning, and handed Hobbs the money. He assures me that there really is a Selfe assisting Mrs. Orr at the Bruges end, and that the cheque is perfectly in order. Mrs. Clifford, when I asked her a few questions, she cannot talk much about it yet, confirmed all this. She added that Mrs. Orr pressed her very hard to let her take the money over. She, too, was going to Bruges, and was, as I suppose you know too, acting in the affair for her sister, the wife of the newly-appointed director of the West Flanders Museum, that great building that's just been built outside Bruges. The director was not to appear in the affair at all. But Mrs. Clifford preferred to carry out what she believed to be Julian's instructions. Were they his instructions?" Sir Edward looked hard at Pointer, who only stirred his tea thoughtfully.

"If not," Clifford's hand shook a little, "the murderer must be— But I confess I find Julian's death a deeper and deeper mystery the more I study it. I, too, found out a piece of evidence yesterday—not bearing on Hobbs, however, but on Haslar. Mrs. Clifford handed me Julian's diary when I pressed her for dates and hours. In that diary there's an entry about the discovery in an old bureau that belonged to Sir William Haslar's private secretary, or at least was always used by him, of two copies of letters which had been sent to the writer's wife, some thirty years ago now. He was killed in a carriage accident. She died shortly afterwards. In them this man, Walton was his name, accuses Sir William of very terrible things. Subversion of party funds, and what practically amounts to blackmail. They're poisonous imputation though there have been whispers at times that Sir William did sail very close to the wind now and then. My brother makes a note to say that he intends in fairness to the public to have these letters inserted as an appendix in his coming Life. He notes down the indignation of Diana, but especially of her brother Arnold. Diana, according to Julian, was certain after the first shock, that no one would credit the allegations. But Arnold Haslar took it differently. There is an entry only this last

Thursday in which Julian records that Arnold practically threatened him with violence if he dared to defame a dead man by printing those libels. My brother apparently was quoting Arnold's exact words. I have no idea where the letters are. I asked Hobbs, and he told me the very disquieting fact that Julian had had them on him when he left Thornbush—carried them on his person. He distrusted Miss Haslar, believed that in spite of her apparent acquiescence, she might steal the letters. And after all, family pride is a very strong chain. Now, Chief Inspector, where do we stand? I confess I am puzzled. Here are the defalcations—not yet proven, it is true—but Straight says he'll go bail that he's right, and believes it's not far short of a hundred thousand pounds has gone. Julian never lived up to his income, I knew. Here's the fact of these Haslar letters with the fury of Arnold Haslar at the idea of their being published—Arnold Haslar, who called out that he 'did it for nothing!' Arnold Haslar, who knew about the missing head, and who the murdered man was, when the only printed information was that the corpse was Etcheverrey! But then, what about Etcheverrey himself?"

Still Pointer did not reply. He only nodded thoughtfully.

"Are we wrong about those destroyed pages in my brother's manuscript: the pages pointing straight to Etcheverrey—to Newman?"

This time Pointer did look up.

"It's a very intricate case," he agreed, "but I think—I think —that the pages of Mr. Julian Clifford's coming novel were taken and destroyed because of what was in them. And I think that because of the information shortly to be published through them, Mr. Clifford was murdered." And Pointer inhospitably rose and with an apology ended the few minutes' talk. He was at work before the door closed behind them. The paper in which the tin box had been wrapped was of an unusually good quality. It matched some which Pointer had seen at Thornbush—paper in which his publishers sent Julian Clifford his proofs. Who would open Mr. Clifford's proofs? Newman probably. And the string . . . Pointer found within the half-hour that the string was the same as the ball on Newman's writing table.

Pointer drove on to the warehouse. He found the night watchman just closing shutters and gates. From him he learnt that the box had been handed to a pensioned-off night watchman very early Tuesday morning. The man was only called in for extra duty when, as then, the regular man was busy on some especial job. This extra watchman had put the box in the cellar, but had forgotten to mention the fact to any one. It was only by chance that to-day, Friday, he had learnt of Mr. Dance's inquiry, and by that time, unfortunately, the foreman had mislaid the address given him by the manager to which any such parcel was to be sent. The men preferred not to mention this fact to

Dance, but sent the package to Mr. Haslar's house, believing that though down with the flu, he could still see about his own parcels.

Pointer went to interview the ex-night watchman. He left him not much the wiser. A car had driven up to the gates of the warehouse about three on Tuesday morning. The driver had got down and handed him a parcel, saying that Mr. Haslar wanted it taken care of according to instructions which he had written on it. But he did not want it entered on the books, as it would not be left for long. With that the man had clambered back into his seat, turned the car, and driven off. Stanley, the man who took the tin, had marked it K for the cold storage, and, after putting it in the appropriate cellar, had forgotten all about it until to-day. His belief that it was Mr. Haslar's chauffeur who had called in the car rested on mere assumption. He had too little to do with the warehouse nowadays to know Arnold Haslar's car or driver. He could not even describe the latter. He might have been Arnold Haslar himself, and he might not.

# CHAPTER 13

Pointer drove to the police station where Hobbs was lodged in a comfortable enough room. The shock of the arrest had cleared his brain. He was quite himself again now, and had ordered, and eaten, a very good dinner.

"Why am I being detained here? Why is bail refused, if it's on any charge for which you have a right to detain me? Why am I not allowed to communicate with my solicitor?" he began in the tone of a man who had determined to take the upper hand.

"Bail is never allowed on a murder charge, Mr. Hobbs." Pointer took a chair.

Hobbs was holding himself in with some difficulty. "Murder? Whose murder? What murder?"

"The murder of Julian Clifford. And, if we see fit, the attempted murder of Miss Haslar through a plan concocted together with Mrs. Orr in Bruges where she posed as her unmarried half-sister, a Beguine there called Soeur Therese. Mrs. Orr was really quite talkative when I explained how things stood over here. She had no idea Julian Clifford was dead."

Hobbs's face twitched.

"You don't think you can get away with this sort of stuff with me, do you?" he asked.

"It's the truth, Mr. Hobbs. Mrs. Orr is not the kind to throw good money after bad. She gave us every help, like the sensible woman that she is. We have, as I told you, the money you sent her by Miss Haslar. Five thousand pounds."

"Ay, yes, the money that was sent to straighten things out, if necessary. Sir Edward told you about Mr. Clifford's proposed purchase of the Charlemagne crystal. Needless to say, the money I sent her, except her own promised rake-off of one thousand, was only deposited with Mrs. Orr, so to speak. She was expected to account for it very strictly. As to her own commission, I saw no reason why she should be the loser because Mr. Clifford's terrible end had cut short the negotiations."

"Especially after she had inserted that personal in the *Times* of yesterday, Tuesday? 'Hobby. Five needed instantly as promised. No letters. May.' She says a small official in the new museum had heard something about the proposed sale. And the money found on you when you were searched just now! A nice sum, Mr. Hobbs. The remainder of the cheque for seventy thousand, as well as some bearer bonds."

"I was carrying that sum according to Julian Clifford's instructions," Hobbs retorted. "It now returns to his estate, of course. Now that I know, what I did not believe until this afternoon, that he is dead. You know why that cheque was cashed. Whatever happened to Mr. Clifford after he wrote those notes which each of us at Thornbush got Tuesday morning, I was only carrying out instructions."

Pointer shook his head. "It won't do, Mr. Hobbs. We've had an accountant looking into the books. According to him you've had altogether not far short of a hundred thousand pounds already out of Mr. Clifford's fortune."

Hobbs did not question the figure.

"The new librarian, Straight, was the accountant, I suppose? I thought that was his game! But you'll have to have reasonable proof, better proof than that before arresting me for murder."

"We have ample proof of motive," Pointer said tranquilly. "Really quite good. Just let me run the facts over to you, Mr. Hobbs. There is the systematic robbery extending over many years—about ten, Straight thinks. Mr. Clifford evidently made some discovery—you determined to kill him at once. You were already getting ready to leave England with Mrs. Orr. She had determined to throw in her lot with you when she found that her name must be published in a coming divorce suit. But before you both went off to subsist quite pleasantly on the money you had accumulated, you thought that the Charlemange crystal would give you the opportunity for additional loot. You never intended Mr. Clifford to get the crystal. What you did intend was to see that Mr. Hobbs got the seventy thousand which you and Mrs. Orr claimed was being asked by the town for it. You have no alibi for Monday night. You lured Mr. Clifford to Fourteen Heath Mansions, or you took advantage of some one else's having lured him there, followed him, and murdered him. You cut off his head, packed it in plaster in a biscuit tin, wrapped it in some paper in which Mr. Clifford's proofs had been sent home, tied it with string from Mr. Newman's ball, and took it to Mr. Haslar's warehouse, rightly thinking that in the ordinary course it would not be detected there for a long time —long after you had left England. How much chance will you have in the dock against that story, Mr. Hobbs? Remember your palm prints on the spade handle through the opening in the gloves you carefully wore."

That last improvised touch did it. Hobbs sagged down in his chair, his mouth working.

"I'm innocent!" he said at last in a hoarse voice, "innocent of all the charges."

"You *can't* be innocent of both the charge of embezzlement and the charge of murder, Mr. Hobbs. Your one chance to clear yourself of the capital charge is to prove to me that Mr. Clifford's death absolutely disarranged your plans."

Hobbs sat a moment, then he straightened up. He had feared as much from the beginning of the interview, but had hoped to avoid a confession.

"I warn you, of course," Pointer went on, "that anything you say about Mr. Clifford's death may have to be used in evidence, whether against you or another, but anything that you tell me about other matters will be considered as confidential, except where it touches on the murder."

"What does Edward Clifford say?"

"I haven't discussed the matter with him. The only bargain I can make with you, Mr. Hobbs," Pointer said with steel in his voice, "is that one lie, and you may find yourself arrested on a capital charge. But, on the other hand, if you tell frankly all that you know, we may waive the accusation of attempted murder. I can make no promises, of course."

There was a long silence.

"I'll tell you exactly what happened," Hobbs said finally, "it's my best chance with you, I see. It may help—I think it will. Monday night I sat out in the garden till about ten. When I came in, I found a note on the telephone pad for me from Mr. Clifford asking me to go on after him to Fourteen Heath Mansions, where he would wait for me. No name was given of the flat's owner. I was rather surprised, for I had no idea that he knew any one there. But I went to the address, used an automatic corner lift—I had a friend who lived there once, so I knew my way about. As I stepped out of the lift on to the landing, my scarf caught in the lift door. I stopped to put it right. Had to peel off my gloves, and stepped over to the window ledge to lay them down. That brought me to one side of the landing in the shadow. While I was rewinding the scarf, the door of Number Fourteen opened suddenly, and a man thrust his head out, looked around, and then slipped out and closed the door, standing still again for a moment to listen. I was just going to move towards him when he ran down the stairs as light as a cat. Well, I was startled. I stepped to the door and caught hold of the little brass knocker. It gave—the door was open. Apparently the lock hadn't caught. I couldn't understand the affair at all. But I knew that Clifford had the Haslar letters with him in a letter-case. I called his name. No one answered. I walked into the first room to my right and there I found him—dead—shot—sitting with his head sunk forward on his breast ... he was quite warm. There was no weapon to be seen. Well,"—Hobbs stopped and lit a cigar with a match that quivered—"I was appalled. There's no use pretending that Julian Clifford's death wasn't the end of things for me. Edward Clifford, or any other executor, would run a very careful eye over accounts. I couldn't cover my tracks under a couple of days' intensive work, and I wasn't ready to fly at once—I daren't with a murdered man. Then there was the cheque for seventy thousand pounds which Clifford carried ready to cash when necessary, and which, as you know, we'd been working for. I thought of taking his body off with me, but you can't carry dead people around town. I thought of all sorts of things. Then I remembered that on coming in, I had come by a corner door—I had noticed some workmen's tools and sacking. I thought of a sack, and of dumping the body into the river somewhere. I went downstairs and found that there was no empty sack. But there was an empty tin, a tin large enough to contain a head. I went back to Thornbush, got my car out —by some lucky chance the chauffeur had the evening off—took along with me some paper and string, left the car not far from Heath Mansions, walked in by the same way, still without meeting any one. The porters and people were all in the big, central, well-lit part. I took the tin and a spade up with me. The spade went under a loose topcoat which I had put on at Thornbush when I went back for the wrapping material. I had left the door with the latch caught back. I went in, took off Clifford's clothes, did them up into two parcels, and addressed them to fictitious names—I've forgotten what names, or where, for then I took the head . . His voice shook. "I don't need any punishment for having done that. It's punishment enough. I see it night and day. Shall see it. . . . You can't do a thing like that and be the same man afterwards. However ... I poured plaster into the tin, and so on, as you already know. And after some thought I decided that the best place for it would be Haslar's warehouse. He had once told me how things got snowed under in the cellars, do what they would. Besides, I thought then that there was a poetic justice about it, for I believed that Haslar had killed Julian Clifford."

"But we found the tin on a shelf in Mr. Haslar's strong room," Pointer said doubtfully.

Hobbs swore at himself. "Like a fool I put it there when I went to Arnold Haslar's this afternoon and found it on the hall table."

"And what took you to Mr. Haslar's house?"

Hobbs kept sullen silence for a moment. Then, "I had found the Haslar letters Wednesday night which had been on Mr. Clifford before his death, and for which I had been looking everywhere, letters which only interested Haslar, in a secret drawer in his library along with Clifford's umbrella. I forgot the letters while talking to Miss Haslar, and getting her to take some money across for me to Mrs. Orr. I knew quite well that I was watched by day, but I thought I could slip across at night and get them. They were better destroyed."

"That version won't do, Mr. Hobbs," Pointer said decidedly. "You took those letters from Mr. Clifford's body—from his dead body you maintain—when you took the cheque. Just as you—not Haslar—took the umbrella, hacked it into pieces to get it into a parcel with the clothes, and then found after all that it was too awkward to manage."

This was only the sounding of a pilot going carefully in difficult waters.

"You went out for a walk on Tuesday morning as soon as you came down. You walked over to Mr. Haslar's house, let yourself in, or found the door open and walked in, and put the umbrella in that secret partition. You could easily hide the umbrella on you, or carry it in a roll of maps or papers. . . . Then when the whole affair began to get unpleasantly hot, you decided that the letters which you were carrying on you must be hidden somewhere. Somewhere known only to yourself. Some hiding-place, moreover, that would tell against the person in whose presumed possession they were found, should they be found. Mr. Haslar is not likely to open any of his drawers for a long time, so to Mr. Haslar's old bureau you carried them Wednesday night. Miss Haslar caught you with them in your hand. You pretended, of course, that you had just taken them out of the place where her brother had hidden them."

That Diana had actually seen Hobbs with letters in his hand which it was known that Julian Clifford had been carrying on Monday night, the night when he was murdered, was one of the things that explained why she ran so much danger in going to the Beguinage. Why, once her help was no longer needed, it was not intended that she should return to England.

Pointer reasoned—rightly—that when Hobbs had to send the money to Mrs. Orr by some carrier who he believed was not being watched, he was in a quandary. Whoever was taken into his counsel, however slightly, would be a permanent danger to him and to Mrs. Orr. That person had therefore better be silenced. Hobbs, so Pointer believed, chose Diana both because she could be easily induced to take the letter, and because she would be as well out of the way. She knew too much. She had opened a letter meant for Hobbs, Sir Edward said. One that had made her suspect that the literary agent's entries were not accurate. She was a grave menace. Once let the idea that Hobbs had been robbing his brother take root in Sir Edward's mind, and—supposing that he himself knew nothing of the crime—then, in spite of Newman's confession, Hobbs's chance of getting away with, or without, the money for the crystal would be small.

"You decided this afternoon to get back those letters in order to frighten her into silence if things went wrong," Pointer continued, "that is, if she should by any chance return from Bruges. And that was why you went to Mr. Haslar's house when you fancied yourself unwatched. You evidently have a latchkey. You let yourself in this afternoon, and the first thing you saw was that tin in the hall. You put it in the strong room whose password you knew, like most of Mr. Haslar's friends. And because it was there, Miss Haslar had been locked in by you when you thought she had gone in after it—you refused to say to what word you had set the dial." Pointer bit back with difficulty his comments on what had happened.

"I forgot the word." But Hobb's eyes did not meet the other's. "Besides, I'd had a glass of brandy. Neat too. Who wouldn't, when they found that damned tin resurrected, and staring at them from a hall table? Ever since that night in the flat I've only kept going by—" He pulled himself up and sat biting at his cigarette.

"And the crystal was never intended to be really a sale?"

Hobbs set his teeth for a second. "No, just a plant. We had decided to burn our boats, Mrs. Orr and I. As soon as we got hold of the notes for the cheque, I was to leave England and join her. But I couldn't get off at once, things had come too much in a rush for that. And by Tuesday evening I was told by Edward Clifford and you that the body had been identified."

"Did Newman know about the crystal?"

"Certainly not! He was our greatest danger. Of course had I had an idea of the truth"

"What truth?" Pointer asked casually.

"Why, the reason for which he killed Julian Clifford. That he was in love with my cousin. Mrs. Orr had long suspected as much. I had always laughed at the idea."

"It was Mrs. Orr's notion to get Mrs. Clifford into things too? So that if they went wrong there would be your cousin to fall back on?" Pointer asked in his most colourless voice.

"That was the idea," Hobbs said shortly.

"Mrs. Clifford believed the crystal was to be genuinely bought?"

"Oh, lord, yes! Only thing she had ever wanted. She had seen it in Bruges some years ago, and told Julian then that she would give her eyes to possess it. That was quite enough for him. He wanted it as a sort of peace-offering for his frequent absences, I think."

"And Mrs. Clifford believed that Mr. Julian Clifford left for Bruges on Monday night?"

Hobbs nodded.

"And the letters left in Julian Clifford's name?"

Hobbs hesitated. "It's a bad business. But it's not murder. I wrote the letters, of course, the letters signed by Clifford's name. There's nothing easier than what's called forgery. No one ever thinks of doubting a letter when they see a familiar name at the foot. I had to do something to keep people from suspecting what had happened. I knew about what to say in each, of course. Fondest love to Alison. Poor girl.

General directions to Newman to carry on. Same to Diana. Straight was to start on the subject-index I'd heard Clifford speak of. I wrote the notes Tuesday morning after leaving the tin."

"You think Mrs. Clifford had no doubts throughout as to the genuineness of the two she got?"

"None whatever. A baby in swaddling clothes could deceive my cousin."

"And was it usual with Mr. Clifford to leave her like that —with only a written note for good-bye?'

"He had done it at least once before, I knew, when he was at work on a serial. He never worked out his serials before-hand. I remembered that on that occasion he had scribbled her a line, poked it under her door, and been out of the house when she got up."

Pointer nodded. "I see. Now, as to the cheque? We know, of course, that you altered the name to Selfe. But how did you account for the name to Mrs. Clifford, I mean?"

"I told her Selfe was the man through whom the crystal would actually be purchased."

"And the second letter, also in Mr. Clifford's writing, the letter which Mrs. Clifford received Wednesday morning at breakfast? The letter posted in Bruges by Mrs. Orr?"

Hobbs grinned sarcastically.

"Well, naturally, I had to take it from her desk and destroy it. It wouldn't have deceived either of you. It wasn't meant to. It was meant to do what it did. Keep my cousin, Mrs. Clifford, quiet."

Again here was a silence.

"Now about the man whom you saw coming out of the flat at Heath Mansions. Did you recognise him?"

Hobbs gave him a long look. "You're clever, Chief Inspector, damned clever. But you'll get a surprise. The man I saw was Straight."

"The new librarian? The man who has just found out the defalcations?" Pointer murmured equably. "Indeed. You saw him clearly enough to swear to?"

"Quite."

"It couldn't have been any one else? Any one of about his height and general appearance?"

"You mean Edward Clifford? It might easily have been. He's always been in love with my cousin. But as it happened, it was Straight."

Pointer sat on a moment, looking at his shoes.

"One thing more, Mr. Hobbs. Mr. Clifford made some notes on his novel, the novel that is coming out in the *Arcturus*. They're not among his papers. Do you know where they are?"

"I've nothing to do with any notes of Clifford's," Hobbs said impatiently, "if they're lost, it's no use coming to me."

"Would Newman know about them?" Pointer asked.

"He might. But Clifford, as a rule, saw to everything to do with his writing himself. Newman's work was social. Clifford, of course, got invitations and letters by the ton."

"But I suppose Mr. Newman typed out Mr. Clifford's manuscript?"

"No. Clifford did his typing himself. He revised too, constantly. As a rule his work went straight from him to his publishers. Though Newman would have the actual sending or taking of it, after I had settled about terms."

"Would Newman know beforehand what was coming in a novel?"

Hobbs yawned. His face was lined with weariness—nerve weariness.

"Couldn't say. Clifford had taken to discussing his coming book *The Soul of Ishmael* with him lately."

Again there was a silence ... of utter fatigue on Hobbs's part. Pointer rose.

"Well, Mr. Hobbs, of course I must verify your statements as far as possible. Meantime you're at liberty to return to Thornbush. Sorry, but I must insist on its being Thornbush. Sir Edward has not spoken. Straight can be trusted not to speak when he's asked not to. Until to-morrow, when other arrangements can be made, the household at Thornbush must remain as it is. No restrictions will be put on any reasonable outings."

Pointer saw Hobbs off, and then telephoned to Thornbush. Was Straight there? He was. So was Miss Haslar, who had not yet returned to her brother's house.

Pointer found them deep in talk.

"Maud Gillingham would be just the wife for you," Diana was saying as Pointer stopped for a second outside the door.

"I want you two to see more of each other. I shall never marry. I shall wait for Sanz and another life. But Maud is ever so much sweeter tempered than I am, and she's biddable, which I should never have been. Also she's got pots more money."

"Diana!" Straight protested, without any over-vehemence. After all, Diana had openly chosen the Basque anarchist. Pointer entered and asked Straight for an interview. Diana turned to Richard.

"Please let me stay! Oh, Dick, please let me hear the worst. I know—I know that—that it may be hard hearing, but I can't be kept out of this. For Arnold and Sanz both keep me in it. In its heart. Please, Chief Inspector, let me stay."

"It rests with Mr. Straight," Pointer said at once; "if he has no objection, I have none."

"Stay, then, Diana, but you mustn't mind if I have to say things, and say them in a way that may hurt you," Straight warned her.

"Mr. Straight," Pointer began promptly, "we have just had a piece of information which concerns you."

Straight had not expected this. He sat up.

"You were seen last Monday night leaving Fourteen Heath Mansions after Mr. Clifford was shot, and leaving it in a hasty, almost furtive manner. Can you explain this?"

Diana gave a gasp of resentment, but Straight silenced her with a smile.

"Patience, Di!" He turned to the detective officer. "I left Heath Mansions after Mr. Clifford arrived, but not after he was shot. Your witness is lying there. It's an odd story; but it won't help the case forward at all."

"It should have been told me," Pointer said stiffly.

"And it would have been told you. But I like to think things over. Also, it implicates a friend."

"Arnold?" breathed Diana.

"Arnold," the name came reluctantly.

"And the story?" Pointer asked. Still Straight hesitated. "I'll try not to jump to conclusions," Pointer promised.

"Well, as I told you, I dropped in at Haslar's on Monday after dinner, but found that he was unexpectedly called out of town."

Straight paused.

"Did he give you any idea of why and where?"

Pointer had asked this before. Then Straight had given an evasive reply, now he said, "None. I think he was inclined to, but he finally said, 'You're too straightlaced a chap, Dick, my son. We will not blacken your innocent soul with the night's dark deeds.' I decided to go for a walk, it was a heavenly evening, and turn in early. I had only landed that morning. I walked about the heath at random, and then made for Thornbush. Passing what I now know to be Heath Mansions, I ran into Mr. Clifford. He stopped me, asked me if I'd mind dropping a couple of letters in a pillar-box for him, and then coming on after him to flat Fourteen in the building to which he pointed. He added"— Straight looked at Diana as though asking her to forgive him—"he added that he expected to have rather an unpleasant interview with Arnold Haslar. Would I mind coming up? He had left a message for Hobbs, but Hobbs mightn't get it in time. I wasn't very keen on an unpleasant interview between my friend and my employer. Mr. Clifford evidently read as much in my face, for he said, 'It's all right. I only want to borrow your eyes. Haslar has just telephoned me that he has a friend who lives there and who can prove that certain letters which I believe to be genuine are forgeries.' With that he turned in at the gates of the flats. I didn't find a letter-box at once. Doubtless I passed several. When I got back, I walked up the stairs and to my surprise found the door of Number Fourteen ajar. I rang, and then, as no one came, I walked in. The door of a room on my right was open. There sat Mr. Clifford at a little side table beside a lamp, reading a letter. He glanced up and said, 'It's all right, Straight. I shan't need you after all. Sorry to've given you the trouble of coming up here for nothing.' I murmured something and went out. As I closed the door, Mr. Clifford said something which I didn't quite catch. But I think—I only *think*, mind you, Chief Inspector, that it was 'Newman's here. I shall be quite all right.'"

"Newman!" Diana echoed in a little gasp.

"I may have heard him incorrectly. His back was to me and he spoke hurriedly. At any rate, I went on out. In the doorway I heard"— again he glanced at Diana—"I heard a sound like Haslar's cough. I stopped to listen. I wasn't sure whether it came from behind me—from inside the flat, that is—or from outside the flat—from the stairs. I looked out of the door, up and down the landing and stairs. I couldn't see any one. I went to the lift-shaft to press the button for the lift, and as I did so, I thought I caught sight of Haslar's ulster below me"

"Going down or coming up?" Pointer asked.

"I couldn't say. I thought I saw it on a landing. I ran on down, but I saw nothing of Haslar. So I returned to Thornbush and bed. Next morning I heard that Mr. Clifford had left. I saw nothing improbable in that. Next I heard of the Etcheverrey murder in flat Fourteen. That did stagger me. But obviously there could be no connection between Mr. Clifford and a murder. It wasn't as if he had been announced as murdered. I should have come forward at once then, of course. Next, I learn that Etcheverrey's body was claimed by you and Sir Edward to be that of Mr. Clifford, but that Mrs. Clifford and Hobbs denied that it was he, and were certain that he was safe and sound. Obviously I had to think things over. I decided that my tale would add nothing to the facts. I found Mr. Clifford alive, and I left him alive. I confess that the thought of being mixed up in a crime— It was a terrible position. ... I would have had to bring in my friend Arnold Haslar. Altogether I decided to wait a little while longer and see."

There was a little silence.

"And one thing more," Straight went on, "I stood outside the door listening, as I said, to see if I had really heard Haslar, and how I could not have seen any one if they had been standing outside the flat, or on the landing—" Straight shook his head.

"You think whoever saw you was inside the flat, not outside?" Pointer asked.

"I don't know what to think," Straight replied, "it's too terrible a case to decide on quickly."

There was another silence. Diana sat with her head resting on her hand, her face shaded, her lips tightly pressed together.

"And you, Miss Haslar, you knew of this meeting on Monday night between your brother and Mr. Clifford?"

She looked at Pointer, tightening her lips still more.

"I'd like a word alone with you if you would let me have it," Pointer said.

Straight rose reluctantly at her glance. He stepped up to Pointer before opening the door.

"Be gentle with her," he murmured under his breath, "she's going through a frightful ordeal."

When the door closed behind him Pointer began again.

"Suppose you chance it, Miss Haslar, and trust me to see the truth through all the maze of misleading events and side issues. I don't see how you can do any harm by speaking out. Nothing can make matters worse for Mr. Haslar, and knowing that, suppose you take heart."

"Then you don't believe in Mr. Newman's confession?" she asked eagerly and yet with dread in her voice.

"Until all the facts are cleared up, it's not possible to be certain who was an accomplice and who not," Pointer said truthfully. "We know your brother took the flat. But it's possible that he may have taken it simply as the first step in a rather elaborate plan to get back those letters blackening your grandfather's character which Mr. Clifford intended to include in his coming biography of Sir William Haslar. We have the letters themselves."

Diana looked sceptical. But her look changed as Pointer drew a note-case from his pocket and took out of an envelope photographic copies of the two fateful notes. She was startled. Yet, oddly enough, it gave her courage. Here was a man who wanted but the truth. A man who had the knack of getting it, moreover. Diana searched his face again. It was the face of a man of high personal character. There were brains in it. But it could be an absolutely unyielding face. She sat through another agonised moment of silence. There was danger whatever she did or said.

"I think he may have taken it in order to lay a trap for Mr. Julian Clifford," Pointer said again, "a trap to get possession of those letters. Am I right? I've thought so all along. But it wasn't easy to get the proof, to find out what he wanted."

Diana surrendered the position.

"I think so too," she said slowly. "I know nothing definite. But I think he meant to—well, keep Mr. Clifford there for a few days."

"Against his will?"

Diana nodded.

"That, at least, was what I feared when I heard on Tuesday morning that Mr. Clifford had left Thornbush so suddenly before breakfast. And when a man from the Home Office called during the morning, and spoke of Uncle Julian's absence as such a riddle. Seemed so amazed at it! But Mrs. Clifford and her cousin appeared so certain that they knew where Uncle Julian was, that I thought how silly I had been. . . But you see Arnold had just been taken ill that morning, at the breakfast table, and the doctor had spoken of some excitement or shock." She bit her lip.

"Suppose you tell me everything you know about your brother's taking that flat," Pointer suggested. "How did he learn of it?"

Diana hesitated. Pale, she grew whiter still. So it probably was, as Pointer thought, through Newman.

"I really *know* nothing. Not even that he had a plan," she said finally. "It was only that when Uncle Julian refused to promise not to use the letters, when Arnold could not budge him from his intention of adding them to the Life which was already being proof-read, I felt sure that Arnold would try something. He got the position he holds because of his daring plans, and the absolute fearlessness with which he goes ahead and carries them out. You see, I know him so well that I can guess a good deal of what's going on in his mind. Besides, one day when I said I'd steal the letters if I could—and so I would have"—Diana's eyes flashed—"they were cruel lies about one of the best and kindest men that ever lived. And lies about him when he was dead and could no longer defend himself—Arnold told me not to worry. Just that."

"When did he say that?"

"Last Friday."

"You two were alone?"

She nodded.

"You had no idea of what his plan was?"

"Well, Uncle Edward—Sir Edward Clifford, I mean— was chaffing a friend that night at a dance club where Arnold and I were. He accused the boy of having kidnapped the examiner and taken the exam papers from him. Arnold started, and gave Sir Edward the look of some one who thought for half a moment that his secret had been guessed. I knew then what his scheme was, or at least suspected something of it. There weren't many things you *could* do to get those letters." She spoke with an unconscious irritation which would have amused Pointer at another time.

"You were on his side, of course? You thought anything fair under the circumstances?

She shook her head.

"Not towards Uncle Julian, no. I wasn't on Arnold's side at all. Uncle Julian hated publishing those letters. But he thought it the right thing to do. When people have to do dreadful things because they think them right, what is there one can do?" Diana's tone was infinitely sad and hopeless. "However dreadful, what can one do? Besides"—her voice changed—"besides, I was afraid that Arnold would overreach himself. You could no more bully or frighten Uncle Julian than you could Arnold himself."

"Did you attempt to dissuade him?"

"Oh, yes. Coming home from the Havana. But he only got impatient, and told me I was all wrong. That there was no question of personal violence in his mind, nor of bullying. He told me to be quite sure of that; said he wasn't an absolute idiot."

"You think he meant what he said?"

"Arnold always means what he says."

"Did you ever hear the flat referred to?"

She did not reply.

"I wish I could spare you these questions," Pointer said regretfully, "but truth is your best course, believe me. The very best course—for every one."

She flashed him an eager look. There was a sparkle of almost painful hope in it.

"You—you mean?"

Something in Pointer's eyes encouraged her.

"I think I must have heard Arnold refer to it over the telephone last Saturday evening. I heard him say, 'He can't come till Tuesday, but the flat's taken for a month, so that's all right.'"

"Do you know to whom he was talking?"

Diana hesitated.

"Was it to Mr. Newman?"

Her silence was answer in itself.

"Mr. Straight is a great friend of yours and your brother's, I believe?"

"Very great."

"Did he know about the letters—I mean about their existence?"

"Not in the least," she said earnestly. "Mr. Straight is the last man to permit himself to be drawn into a family squabble."

"And Mr. Newman?"

"Mr. Newman was with Uncle Julian when they were found. He and Adrian Hobbs both knew of them."

"And Sir Edward Clifford?"

"I begged Uncle Julian not to tell him. Sir Edward has always been most unjustly critical of my grandfather's policy about the Australian navy."

"And now—how did you come to go to Bruges, Miss Haslar? You found Mr. Hobbs at that desk in your brother's study, didn't you—at the secret drawer?"

"He had the letters you've shown me in his hand. And Uncle Julian's umbrella too. He told me that he had only just found them in that old concealed double back, after hunting for them all day. But I hardly cared about the letters, for he told me something else. I thought it too good to be true, and yet, I believed it!"

"That Mr. Julian Clifford was alive after all?"

"Yes, that you had made a mistake about identifying the body found in Heath Mansions as his; that Alison was right, that Uncle Julian was safe and sound only in a most awkward position. I would rather not tell you about that," Diana said, pausing.

Pointer assured her that the police knew it already.

"And you? Did you know that the nun was Mrs. Orr?" Diana asked. "Or did you just suspect it?"

"I suspected it so strongly that I knew it," Pointer said, a trifle grimly, "chiefly from her manicured nails. They positively glittered. And a little from the marks of having worn rings very recently on her fingers, especially the dent of a wedding ring."

"And was it really her intention to—or was that about the window and the canal only to frighten her?"

Pointer did not answer. He thought that the less said about that the better. He had practically had to promise as much to Mrs. Orr before she would speak. He had only his suspicions on which to go.

"And did Adrian Hobbs intentionally shut me in that strong room?"

Pointer did not answer that either.

"And about Sanz," she said, after a pause, in a low voice; "what is going to be done with him?"

A door had just opened in the east library. Pointer had heard it and recognised the step. Not so Diana.

"You would never have known that he was Etcheverrey, but for me!" Suddenly she sprang up. Diana's spirit was ever for action, weary though her body might be. "Chief Inspector, I feel as though somehow you were my one hope. Sanz Etcheverrey *couldn't* have killed Uncle Julian. I know he traded on my love for him to take those Melbourne plans, but that was different—that was political. He was against us all during the war, and I thought I hated him. I told myself I did. I lost my only other brother though he was a chaplain, in the war. But this is quite different. In spite of all, I know he didn't kill Uncle Julian."

Pointer looked at her. She read his look.

"You mean that I think that because I love him?" She seemed to think over that possibility. "I do. And in that awful strong room last night I learnt that nothing in the world is more worth while than being able to love. It's a miracle. To be loved is nothing—that's easy; that's chance. But to be able to love! And I had been trying to crush it out of me all these years. I thought hatred finer. For years I've been trying to think that Sanz was playing some deep game of his own here at Thornbush. But he didn't play a game when he came back, in spite of his confession, to get me out last night. He offered up his life for mine. Has he—has he given up his life for mine?"

Diana asked the dreadful question with indescribable anguish.

"That coming back to rescue you stands to his credit whatever the issue." Pointer would not say more.

"And that confession?" Diana was in an awful position. Her brother stood on the one side, her lover on the other.

"It's a good thing to doubt everybody and everything in a case of this kind," Pointer said vaguely but kindly.

Diana looked at him imploringly. A very strange look to see on Diana's face. But nothing of the thoughts behind them were mirrored in the Chief Inspector's inscrutable gray eyes. He was as usual aloof, remote, and tranquil.

"But if he didn't kill Uncle Julian, then he must have written that letter to save some one. To save Arnold. Not that Arnold needs saving," Diana added hastily, "but I've wondered whether Sanz didn't think he did, and so jump in to the rescue. I was mad to think Sanz could have tried to shoot Arnold. I wanted to think anything bad of him, so as to—" She seemed to recollect herself. "Forgive me ranting like an Adelphi heroine. I'm not taken that way often. But what's his fate to be? Mind you," she came a step nearer, "nothing will alter my feelings towards Sanz. Imprison him for life, hang him—I shall always love him, always wait for him! For no matter what his ideas of duty force him to do, however horrible his political opinions, he himself—Sanz Etcheverrey the man, not the anarchist—is a hero!"

The communicating door between the two libraries opened sharply with a jerk. Algernon Newman, as he still signed himself, came in very gravely. He hardly glanced at Diana.

"Chief Inspector, I've come to clear up a few things—no, not directly concerned with what interests you, but only personal matters. No, please stay, Miss Haslar!"

"Miss Haslar? It wasn't 'Miss Haslar' whom you got out of the safe last night, Sanz," Diana threw back at him. There is no confidence in the world greater, no power surer than that of a woman who is talking to the man whom she knows loves her. And Diana had looked deep into the eyes of her rescuer last night. She knew his heart.

"It wasn't Sanz Etcheverrey who opened the safe," Newman said heavily. "Sanz Etcheverrey is a more or less romantic figure, at least in a woman's eyes. There's nothing romantic about me." He paused. Diana said nothing, but she was obviously with him in any change of name or personality which he might be going to make.

Newman looked ill and very tired. Evidently some fierce fighting had gone on within him. "I'm only a crook's son. Worse—a murderer's son."

Diana half rose. He stopped her with a weary lift of his eyes.

"You mustn't sacrifice your life to a sham romantic personage. You are romantic, you know. There's no romance about being the son of Henry Cadby, embezzler, forger, thief, and finally murderer. That was where I learnt how to open safes —at home." He turned to Pointer. "Oh, I know Cockerell recognised my father's invention of packing with powdered aluminum and iron oxides and then using electricity in a totally new way. But it wasn't because of Cockerell I'm telling the truth now. I could have pretended that I'd caught Cadby once, and so on. . . . But you, mustn't go on thinking me anything but what I am: mud; the scourings of the street." He was talking only to Diana now. He came up to her chair. "Thank you for saying what you did just now. It was what Padre Haslar's sister would say. It helped me to do—what's lot harder than coming back last night." He finished with a half smile, an unconscious flicker of his lips that lent the foreign leanness of his face a touch of ironic vividness. In it was experience, suffering, and bitter wisdom. "Then you were in danger," he went on softly. He stopped as though struck by the phrase. "Perhaps, after all, the danger was as great just now. Anyway, you know the truth—the reason why I would never let you become engaged to me. *You* engaged to *me!*"

"How can I know the truth when I don't understand it?" Diana spoke with unexpected coolness. "Why did you tell me you were Sanz Etcheverrey long ago at Hendaye? And those men at Pamplona, they called you by that name."

Newman sat down.

"I'll begin at the beginning. I learnt to speak Spanish as a baby, for I was born at Barcelona, where my father was a rather well-to-do mining engineer. Cadby and Penfold was the firm. My mother died when I was born. My father had spent several years in the tin mines of Cornwall. That's where he and Penfold decided to start together in the Catalan capital. When the firm got into difficulties after Penfold's death, my father came to England. I believe there was a fire, and he started with the insurance money as manager in a biggish firm. Anyway he began to speculate, lost, and borrowed the firm's money; to conceal these he forged entries stole more money, and so on—the usual thing. He was convicted and sent to prison. Meanwhile he had married a woman in the set into which he had by this time sunk. Crooks, all of them. My father came out of prison—I was twelve by that time—and went from bad to worse. He now made his living as a safe breaker, a cracksman. He invented a wonderful way of opening safes; had he been honest he might have risen high, I sometimes think. He made a great deal of money, stole it, in other words. Lived in great style. Called himself Baron de Ribiera from Argentina. Then came the war. I was just short of eighteen, but I joined up, thankful to get free. I had tried several times to earn my own living, but something always gave me away. My father would find out where I was, or some friends of his recognised me, or the police warned my employers whose son I was"

"But you weren't a thief!" Diana said with confidence.

"Not I! I'd have starved first. I hated the life, the whole horrible family life—I enlisted under the name of Pollock, my mother's name. Then came the news that my father had murdered one of his accomplices who was about to give him away. He was caught red-handed, and hanged. You remember the case, I suppose?"

Pointer had been looking it up. Cockerell had finally remembered where he had seen a safe that had been opened on lines similar to those followed for that strong room door last night.

"Man called Strachey?" he asked gently.

"Just so. Well, I slogged away at soldiering. They put me into the quartermaster's office because I was quick at figures. No chance to do more than jog along. . . . And then in 1917 I got hold of some information through a friend in the Foreign Legion, a chap who came from Malaga, about Sanz Etcheverrey, a Basque who at that time was rather on the German side. He was against all the countries of the war, but now he would help one, now the other, for his own reasons, his own price. This information was that a certain official high in the Spanish Government had promised Etcheverrey an amnesty for some followers of his who were dying in Spanish prisons, if he would get hold of details about the Anzac troops and troopships. The official's wife was a von Buck, by the way. They had heard of Riply's escape from the torpedoed ship, and they knew of those plans. Etcheverrey had agreed. The chap from Malaga didn't tell me all this, of course. I had to piece things together. I worked out a plan for catching Etcheverrey and laid it before the quartermaster-general. It was turned down. I was told to stick to figures. I deserted. When I went off in 1914 my father—he was always a generous man with money, and always kind to me, put a thousand pounds to my credit in Cox's bank as a parting gift. I told him I was leaving home for good. I hadn't touched the money, and didn't mean to. But I drew on it now, brushed up my Spanish, came down to Hendaye, and started in great style. I let it be known that I belonged to the Spanish Secret Service. I got into touch with two of Etcheverrey's men and more or less induced them to think that I was Etcheverrey himself. He's double my age, but looked only half his years. I looked a lot older than I was. Besides, they'd never seen him. He kept himself absolutely in the background. I didn't claim to be him, of course. I merely didn't deny it. Little by little I guessed that the Melbourne Harbour plans were the objective of these two. But it was only that night, the night that Riply died, that I was certain. I had just half an hour to forestall them. I couldn't trust two women to guard those papers from these Catalans. They'd have cut you both into strips to make you give them up." Newman threw this to Diana over his shoulder. He was talking to Pointer, but he included Diana from now on.

"I had to get you out of the way before they could come. Once let them see you in that room, and they'd suspect that you had the papers. I stunned you and got you into your room. The two Catalans came along before I got clear. I called out that I was off for Pamplona, Etcheverrey's supposed headquarters. I knew Etcheverrey was expected there. Well, the two hung on to me. But they had an accident with their car at a turning when we were almost in Pamplona. I had to go on. As it chanced Etcheverrey was working in Nice, and the rumour that he was coming was spurious. I passed myself off as him with the crew I found there, supplying U-boats with petrol, they were part of a sort of pipe line that ran to the coast. Then you blew in." He looked ruefully at Diana. "However, we got clear. Only unfortunately they hit a petrol tin on our car over which my coat sleeve hung down. Tin and coat went up in a blaze together. You got the fire under, but the Melbourne Harbour plans were smoke. They were in a pocket of that coat. That meant that I had nothing to show for my absence but a very thin tale of adventure; but I gave myself up and decided to tell it, leaving out the purely personal part, of course. There was a court-martial, but—well, the news was just out of my father's execution. They were very decent. They decided to believe me. I asked for a front line job, and this time I got it. I chose a Surrey regiment, because your brother was chaplain to their division, so you had told me at Hendaye." He was speaking only to Diana now. This might be his last talk to the girl, except the tragic leave-taking that the Chief Inspector had promised her.

"That's what you meant by Padre Haslar?" Diana had hardly noticed the reference before. He nodded.

"It was next best to being with you. Life was a bit grim those days. Your brother was a man in a million. He"— Newman made a gesture of inability—"but what's the good, you can't describe a man like him!"

"He was a dear!" Diana said, with a catch in her voice; "he loved the whole world."

"He loved God," Newman said seriously. "It takes a very good man to be able to love God. But he did. You knew he was killed trying to get a couple of wounded soldiers out of a shell-hole that was filling with water? Hit just after he got them through our barbed wire."

Diana nodded. She guessed what was coming.

"I was one of the two. We had been three days in that shell-hole."

There was a long pause.

"When I woke up in hospital—I had collapsed at the wire —I found that no one knew who I was. My identity disc had been cut off when they dressed my arm at a clearing station. So had my few remaining rags. We had all to be evacuated quickly and my things were left behind. I was too weak to be questioned. And I didn't care to talk. I had heard the Padre had been shot helping poor Wingate to make a last effort. Wingate was much worse wounded than I was. I didn't want to live. But in the ward was a chap who had lost his memory. It struck me that he was a lucky devil. And then I pretended to've lost mine. Only to be left in peace, at first. But I began to think what a wonderful thing it would be if I really had lost it—for ever. The memory of that circle of crooks, of the underworld, of all I loathed, of my father whom I secretly loathed too. Though, as I say, he was always kind to me— kind and forbearing. To be rid of it all! To drop it off like a dirty shirt. It seemed a heavenly thought. I played it. It worked. No one suspected me. You see, I had been studying the poor fellow in the ward who really had lost his memory. He wanted it back. Lucky man! Then Mr. Clifford came along, and spoke of Padre Haslar. Spoke of him as a friend. I couldn't claim to've known him, but that made me accept Mr. Clifford's offer to see what he could do for me. What I could do for myself was how he put it. Well—the rest you know. Any one of the name of Haslar could wipe their boots on me for"—he pulled himself up—"for Peter Haslar's sake," he finished hastily. But he had intended to bracket another name with the dead chaplain's.

"And now, Chief Inspector, what are you going to do about me? Nothing of this alters my confession. Diana, Miss Haslar, is going too far there. I give myself up for the murder of Julian Clifford and the shooting of Arnold Haslar." Newman spoke in a steady, firm tone. "I stand to that."

Pointer said nothing. He seemed lost in a profound conviction that his bootmaker had sent him two rights or two lefts, and that a closer scrutiny of his shoes would reveal the mistake.

"What are you going to do with me?" Newman asked again.

"Have a word in private, I think, first of all," Pointer suggested.

Diana got up. She looked as though she felt the need for thought. This Newman was another man. Son of a crook, son of a murderer, and yet . . . Diana felt that life could be extraordinary difficult. Suddenly she wheeled.

"Then if you're not Etcheverrey, why did you kill Uncle Julian? If it's not political, if you're not—" She did not finish either sentence.

Newman's face hardened. His jaw line showed more clearly. He said nothing, only stared with expressionless eyes out of the window as she left the two men together.

# CHAPTER 14

"What about Mr. Pollock's flat?" Pointer asked. "Where did Mr. Newman get the money for such furnishing?"

Newman looked fixedly at him.

"Quick work! Yet I haven't gone near the place since all this. I thought you were more than usually clever when I first saw you. Or have I been under surveillance all these years?"

"No, the address was only discovered in the course of some routine work on this case. But about the things there?"

"Ah!" Newman's smile was bitterness itself. "Family traits proving too strong for me might explain them, mightn't it '—to a Chief Inspector? Just as what I might call Home Hints made it easy for me to get away from your men, and to disguise myself afterwards. If you're a criminal it's handy to know the ropes from childhood."

Pointer's eyes were apparently on his shoes.

"I see. Yet with that explanation of your furniture, how was it you worked on with Mr. Clifford as his secretary so long?"

"Thornbush was home to me, Chief Inspector. At least, let us put it that the motive for murder kept me there."

"Mrs. Clifford?" Pointer asked bluntly.

Newman leapt from his chair.

"Who dares say that?"

"It's what people always wonder when a man kills a married man for no apparent reason. And in your case, it was suspected for some time before."

The iron self-control broke in Newman's face.

"It's a lie! A foul, infamous lie! Mrs. Clifford? She's a saint! Perhaps that's why, to my shame be it said, Chief Inspector; and though she has been kindness itself to me, she bores me even more than she does Hobbs. And that's saying something! Mrs. Clifford wasn't the reason why I—killed Julian Clifford."

"Then what was the reason?"

Newman lifted his dark eyes for a second to the window. "Neither to you, nor to any one else, will I give the reason, Chief Inspector." He spoke with absolute finality.

"The prosecution will be based on a clandestine love affair between you and the lady. There's no other motive possible."

Newman looked darkly at him.

"The reason I killed Julian Clifford was because he had stumbled on the truth about me," he said slowly; "and on something disgraceful in my past as well. Something which he intended to tell." The sentences, came out slowly, as steel is drawn out inch by inch. Newman's face was impassive as ever. The words rose before Pointer, "I know the danger"—"discovered your secret." Words in the murdered man's handwriting found burnt in this man's room.

Pointer said nothing for a while.

"And about Mr. Clifford's general knowledge of Etcheverrey? And his special knowledge of his signature and the name of his home?"

"I learnt all I could while planning to get hold of him at Hendaye. 'The plan that failed!'"

"Because of Miss Haslar?"

"Well, obviously it tore it when she and I fled together." Newman's swift, sardonic smile came and went, leaving his face as grave as ever.

"And you told Mr. Clifford what you knew?"

Newman looked at him thoughtfully. "Little by little. When he began to be so interested in the fellow, I let him think I had a Spanish anti-revolutionary friend with whom I talked over week-ends. Mr. Clifford liked to get hold of something that Sir Edward didn't know. I think he wanted his book to surprise him."

"Was this information confidential?"

"Not in the least. But I'd rather not discuss Mr. Clifford. Not with you, Chief Inspector. Not with anybody, but least of all with you. Your questions aren't always what they seem on the surface." Newman's voice was dry. "I had hoped, of course, to get clear away and stay clear away, after my confession."

"I see. And now, Mr. Newman, Mr. Clifford made some notes on that novel of his that is coming out in the *Arcturus*. They're not among his papers. Do you know where they are?"

Unlike Hobbs, Newman did.

"The only notes I know of were some he left by an oversight about two weeks ago at his publisher's house. But as he afterwards decided to shift Etcheverrey's headquarters to the Spanish side of the Pyrenees, he decided that they would be of no use to him."

"And about the novel itself? You know, I suppose, what he planned to do? You have an idea of how the story would have run?"

"I have an idea of the main outlines. But—" Newman checked himself. "I refuse to discuss Mr. Clifford, as I have already said once before."

"Pity. Well, should you decide to make a clean breast of everything, though I shall not be available, the Assistant Commissioner will always be there. I may have to go away on an investigation at once. As long as you confine your strolls to this neighbourhood, not farther than Haslar's house say, you can come and go as you like—for the present. Of course you'll be followed, and by a good man. I needn't say what any attempt to shake him off would entail."

Newman gave a short and very bitter laugh.

"There are a few more questions I must have answered if Mr. Haslar is really to be cleared." Pointer went on. "First, who was in the room when you spoke to Mr. Clifford of the diagram signature of Etcheverrey's and of the name of the Basque's home?"

Newman seemed to think. "No one but Hobbs. But he wasn't paying any attention. He was hunting out some mistake in royalties that he'd just found out."

"And when was this?"

Newman could not say for certain. Some time the latter half of last week.

"And now about Mr. Haslar himself. We know, of course, all about his connection with the flat. But was it you who first mentioned the flat to him?" Newman thought a moment. Pointer felt sure that he was going to give an evasive reply, or refuse to answer.

"I hope we can clear Miss Haslar," he said sadly. "Unfortunately, she seems mixed up in that business of the flat."

"Miss Haslar?"

"She was heard talking of it to her brother before he took it. We are sure that he had some helper there. I'm afraid that that helper could only have been his sister. He wanted her to get the letters away from Mr. Clifford, we think, or rather we are fairly certain."

"I told Haslar of that," Newman said briskly.

"Is Marshall a friend of yours?"

"No, a mere acquaintance. But he happened to mention to me when I met him by chance in the tube last week, that he wished to let his flat furnished. So, as I say, when there was a question of a furnished flat being wanted"

"By Miss Haslar, I suppose."

"By Haslar himself," Newman corrected shortly. "Miss Haslar knows nothing of the flat. Or, if she knows of it, it's only been after the event."

"But she was to help her brother about the letters. It's no use, Mr. Newman, attempting to shield her, we know that Mr. Haslar had a helper. Had a plan to get those letters of his grandfather's away from Mr. Clifford. No one but Miss Haslar could have helped him."

"I take back about having thought you more than usually brilliant," Newman said curtly. "There are other people in the world, Chief Inspector, than this little circle here and around Thornbush. There is, or was, for instance, a man called Captain Cory. You asked me about him yourself once. He's a man who has a grudge against Clifford. He's also a man who had showed himself uncommonly skilful at getting hold of papers. Haslar had been present at his trial. When he concocted the plan of the flat, or rather—" Newman waited a moment. Then he said:

"I think absolute frankness is best here. I don't want you to think that there was any mix-up between the taking of that flat and Haslar's arrangements about the letters and my part in the matter; that is, the death of Mr. Clifford. Haslar took the flat for one single purpose only— that of getting back the letters with Captain Cory's assistance. I used the flat for my own purpose. That clear?"

"Did you meet this Cory yourself?"

"No, Haslar telephoned me Friday evening that Cory wouldn't get to the flat till Tuesday, but on Saturday morning Cory himself came to Thornbush. He asked for me, but I was out. I rather think he came to find out if Mr. Clifford carried the letters on him. always. Or possibly he intended to double-cross Haslar in some way. Get hold of the letters and sell them at a stiff price. He only saw Hobbs, as it happened."

"Was Haslar going to be present in the flat when the letters were taken?" .

"We both were. We didn't trust Cory an inch further than we could see him."

"The plan was not one that included violence?"

"Haslar's plan? Certainly not. We were to be there to prevent anything of that sort. That at least is what Haslar thought." Newman gave his unmirthful smile. "The taking of the papers was to be entirely Cory's part. I believe the idea was that Haslar would telephone to Mr. Clifford that he had met a man who could prove that the Haslar letters were forgeries, if Mr. Clifford would bring them to Fourteen Heath Mansions. Then Cory, made up a little as Major Brown, would receive him, look at the letters, and—the rest was left to him, as to how he intended to trick Mr. Clifford into thinking he returned the same letters to him."

"When was this plan arranged?"

"I don't exactly know. Thursday and Friday, I think. I wasn't present."

There was a pause.

"I suppose you know that the doctors are as hopeful this morning about Haslar as they were pessimistic up till now?" Pointer asked. "You know they think that he took a most unexpected turn down the right road to-day?"

Newman said nothing.

"They're trying the latest craze, no nurses to-day," Pointer went on half-absent-mindedly. "Once an hour a nurse slips into his room and gives him a capsule. Strychnine. For the rest of the hour he's left in absolute stillness and darkness. Funny thing medicine. One capsule an hour makes for recovery, while three would kill him before he could swallow them. He'll be able to speak to-morrow. To tell us the real story. For, of course, Mr. Newman, until he does that, it's hard to believe that he was not more implicated in the murder than you represent him."

Newman's face had darkened at the good report of Haslar.

"And that rope on your sitting-room wall," Pointer went on; "I recognised it as one of ours, of course. From inquiries I find that the rope that hung Cadby is missing. They are always kept, as you know, together with a death mask of each man. You tipped some out-going sergeant of police a little too freely, I'm afraid. But it belongs to us, Mr. Newman. You must let us have it back."

"You can have it any time you like," Newman said through his teeth. "It's served its turn. I put it there to remind me of who I am. But as Miss Haslar knows the truth now, it can go. She'll be wise and take the respectable side of the road. Oh, life is damnation!" The sudden outburst was repressed as soon as it flashed out.

Pointer looked at his shoes for some moments.

"That rope belongs to us," he repeated slowly. "I suggest that you have a talk with a Superintendent of Police whom I've asked to come here as soon as he can. He's a man who was sent over to Barcelona in connection with the Strachey case."

Newman's face grew more sombre still.

"I don't want any last messages," he said hoarsely.

"You'll want this one. You'd have had it long ago but for your change of name. Pollock was posted as missing, of course. The man who murdered Strachey was not your father. Your father, so Cadby swore in a duly witnessed statement which he made to the governor the day before his execution, was Penfold. The statement was investigated and found to be correct."

'Penfold? His partner?" Newman could hardly speak articulately.

"His partner—a civil engineer—a man of the highest character; of whose integrity there never was any question. You are John Penfold, only child of Henry Penfold, a very honest gentleman, and of Isabelle Treherne, daughter of a solicitor. Both of them of Penzance, Cornwall. She had Armada blood in her, which I think accounts for something in yourself which puzzled us all a bit—though as a Devon man I know a Cornish man when I see one. However, to go on—that fire in Barcelona was Cadby's doing, to cover up some falsifications in the books as well as to get the insurance money. Unfortunately your father, to whom he was sincerely attached, had gone to the office. Cadby thinks he must have suspected him, and gone to have a quiet look at the books. He was burnt to death. With all his bad qualities Cadby was never the same man again, or so he said in his confession. You were an orphan, your mother had died when you were born. Penfold's money was lost with the firm's smash. Lost by Cadby. Cadby took you back with him to England, passing you off as his son. He thought that if people knew that he was bringing up the son of his late partner, some suspicion might arise that he felt himself in some way responsible for your father's death.

"Also, he had a sort of feeling that though you, to you, he might atone. It wasn't a feeling that kept him straight, but it prevented his ever willingly letting you want for anything, or letting you go.

"You never thought of inquiring in the Barcelona records whose son it was that was born there. We did, of course. Cadby had no son. Penfold had one boy who is duly entered on the registers, was duly baptized at the English Church there. Your sins are on your own head. Whatever you have done, now that you know the truth, you will not be able to plead that it was your father's blood that was too much for you, family traits too strong for you. Copies of the papers concerning your parentage will be handed you by the Superintendent when he comes."

Newman stood staring at him. All the colour had drained from his face. Before his mind's eye passed his miserable, desperate, hate-filled boyhood in surroundings from which his honest fibre revolted. He thought of his efforts to get out of them, of the years at Thornbush, happy years had he been leading a true life. And now! He shut his eyes for a second.

"But for your confession you could walk out of this house with a lighter heart than I dare swear you've known before," Pointer went on.

"You're a devil!" Newman said passionately. "What you've told me alters nothing." There was something desperate in the tense voice and in the eyes that stared out at the sunshine. "Alters nothing! I *did* kill Julian Clifford and shoot Haslar. But not a word of this news of yours about myself to Miss Haslar, nor to any one."

"Oh, certainly. It's entirely your own affair," Pointer agreed.

Newman, very pale, stood biting his lip, swallowing hard.

"It was Mr. Clifford I understand who wished Hobbs to leave him?" Pointer asked suddenly.

Newman stared for a second as though he could hardly hear the other through the tumult in his head.

"The other way around," he said absent-mindedly.

"I asked, because, but for your confession, Mr. Newman—since you wish me to continue calling you that—we at the Yard would wonder whether he might not have just found out that Hobbs had been systematically robbing him. We could go on to wonder whether Hobbs had not murdered Mr. Clifford to save himself from prosecution, and all that that would mean. Mr. Hobbs, we might say, had learnt of Arnold Haslar's plan about the flat on Saturday morning from Major Cory, who sold him the information, and had gone to the flat Monday night—Cory had been given a key which he might have handed over— and there Hobbs murdered Mr. Clifford after luring him to Heath

Mansions. He would have a dozen pretexts. That is what the police might think. They might look on Mr. Haslar's injury as an accident. In fact, but for your confession, the whole case might assume a very simple aspect."

The skin on Newman's face seemed to tighten as a wet drum tightens, till it stretched taut across his high cheekbones—the cheekbones of a man of action. For the first time Pointer saw his hands shake as he clenched them.

"You're the devil himself!" Newman said hoarsely, in a tone of anguish, and turning, he stumbled from the room as though the floor were pitching and tossing beneath his feet.

Sir Edward looked in. Straight was with him. Seeing Pointer alone, they came on in.

"I suppose you are arresting Newman?" Sir Edward asked. "It's very trying meeting him face to face—at liberty— around this house. The house of his victim."

"Mr. Newman won't be here to-morrow, I fancy. But, Sir Edward, I thought you were doubtful of his confession?"

"I'm doubtful of everything," Clifford said wearily. "This news about Hobbs, frightful! A cousin of Mrs. Clifford's. A member of my brother's family, so to say. He cannot be prosecuted, of course. Mrs. Clifford would refuse to do so in any case and my hands are tied. Why, he would only too gladly broadcast my brother's unfortunate idea of purchasing the Bruges Crystal. My sister-in-law believes that he will surely be punished in some esoteric way. I'm afraid I should find jail more satisfactory."

"It may come to that yet, Sir Edward, and more," Pointer said slowly. Then he changed the subject, and told Clifford the good news of Haslar's expected, or at least hoped-for recovery. Sir Edward seemed delighted at the prospect of hearing from the injured man exactly what had happened.

"He'll at least be able to name his assailant, it was broad daylight when he was shot." Straight said that according to the latest bulletin, Arnold Haslar was expected to be able to both speak and answer a few questions by to-morrow morning. Until then the doctors wanted him kept in silence and absolute stillness. Straight was beginning to look himself again. Diana had known best all along. He did not claim to be heartbroken at her definite turning-down of any idea of marriage between them. After all, there was something to be said for not being engaged to a girl who had a love affair with a Basque bandit, and a brother who, wearing flamboyant coats, took a flat in which people were afterwards found murdered.

About nine o'clock another and a startling bulletin came from the sick room. It stated that Arnold Haslar had recovered consciousness and asked for Chief Inspector Pointer. Unfortunately Pointer was not to be found at the Yard, nor in any of the places suggested by his clerks. So the sick man had contented himself with a few laboured words only, but these were startling enough.

Haslar had been in the flat at the moment when the murder was committed. He had actually seen Julian Clifford shot.

The bulletin finished with the news that he had just fallen back again into a profound sleep which must on no account be broken.

An hour went by. Then another. There was no sound or stir in that darkened bedroom where on a narrow white bed it took keen sight to make out a shape lying motionless. A head so bandaged that it was scarcely distinguishable from the pillows into which it sank. A chalk-white hand lay inert on the metal brocade of the blanket. Light, and slow, and faint, came the breaths from between lips but a few degrees less colourless than the bandages, than the linen.

The nurse had come and gone, the patient had had his hourly capsule, and had immediately seemed to slumber on— if slumber it could be called.

It was past midnight when the door opened slowly—slowly but not furtively. In came a man. He stood a second to get his bearings in the dimness of the one light that shone like a large pearl above the table on which stood the medicine. He stepped up to the bed. Then he moved to the little table and looked at the box of capsules—read the label, the directions, and stood a second quite still. He switched off the light and crossed to the window. Looked out. Rearranged the curtains and turned up the light. Then he went to a huge walnut wardrobe—opened it and felt inside. Once more he came back to the bed. Something in his circling suggested a vulture about to settle. His hand went out to the box. He opened it and counted oat six of the little objects inside. From an envelope in his pocket he shook out six other capsules into the box, the same as the others in appearance. Now he paused, listening intently. Then bending over the bed, he pressed shut the nostrils which a bandage loosely covered. The mouth under Haslar's toothbrush moustache opened. Into it the man swiftly dropped the capsules taken from the box. Instantly the breathing stopped half-way. A faint shudder ran through the body. The hand drew down in a spasm beneath the sheet. The whole body seemed to straighten itself. The head slipped sideways off the pillows' on the farther side. The man waited a second. Then he laid his hand on the man's heart. There is an elementary trick in Ju-Jitsu by which a hand so placed is held by a grip above the elbow, while the body on which it rests bends forward all but breaking the wrist. This happened now. The man screamed like what he was—a trapped animal.

"Take it quietly," said the man whom he thought dead. "Tindall, Doctor Evans, and an Inspector are in the next room watching you.

"Richard Straight, I arrest you for the murder of Mr. Julian Clifford last Monday night." The usual warning was given by Chief Inspector Pointer—in bandages, lavish chalk make-up, and a shirt which fastened up his back by tapes.

"Inspector Watts, you can take away the Japanese cinematographic camera from the top of the wardrobe. It's a camera that works in the dark, Mr. Straight."

"Rubbish!" Straight had some difficulty in getting his lips to shape the words. "Why, I had only met Mr. Clifford an hour or so before— what earthly motive would I have had for killing him?" He tried for a note of derision.

"Motive? His novel The Soul of Ishamel is coming out in monthly parts in the *Arcturus* magazine. Either you had met Mr. Clifford before, or he had come on your story by some chance, without knowing your name. You might have met without either of you recognising the other again for he often dressed in a disguise when he was on his investigations, and he was very near-sighted. At any rate, in *The Soul of Ishmael*, the reason why the chief character has to leave England, is the same as that which made you leave England. Only you went to Australia, while the man in the book was to go to the Pyrenees and join Etcheverrey's band. And that reason was appropriation of money which the town council thought was properly invested. With a swindle to cover the tracks—a clever swindle. Your tracks were carefully covered, I admit— so carefully that another man went to prison for what you did. But the tracks are there—down in Bedford. And the tale as told in Mr. Clifford's novel is so exact, the steps so carefully given, that any acquaintance on reading it, knowing you of old, knowing about the money which you claimed had been left you as a legacy, could not but link you with the story, had it gone on for but one more chapter. And that linking up by an intelligent reader would have meant prison for you, Mr. Straight—a long term—prison and an end to all your ambitions. You were quite safe so long as the little connecting link could not be brought home to you. Mr. Clifford's novel showed how this could be done."

"Preposterous!" But Straight looked as though his spine were crumbling inside him. "What about Newman's confession? What about his being the anarchist of whom Clifford was writing? And how should I have known anything about the flat at Heath Mansions? Your tale's a tissue of absurdities."

"That flat? You were sitting in the south library downstairs here after dinner at Thornbush, while Mr. Haslar was talking to Captain Cory on Monday in his study. Every word they said must have been heard by you through the communicating door. The whole plot was gone over for the last time. How Mr. Clifford could be lured to the flat by the message about the Haslar letters, of how Cory was to steal the letters, and so on. You heard Cory say that he could do nothing until Tuesday."

Pointer was guessing the unknown by the known facts. But the trial of Richard Straight for Julian Clifford's murder proved that he was right.

"But this is lunacy!" broke in the man under arrest. "I had only parted from Mr. Clifford after my first dinner with him, and on the best of terms, as the servants, as every one at Thornbush can testify."

"Quite so. Therefore it was probably after that dinner that you read the current number of the *Arcturus*. A number in  which the story breaks off just before the crucial point—for you. A few more pages and it would be too late. An *Arcturus* was lying on the table in the library where you sat while waiting for Mr. Haslar's visitor to go. You read it, saw your danger, it's imminence, and heard a plan being finally run through beside you which you thought would save you. That was why you shot Mr. Clifford in the flat to which you lured him by just such a telephone message as you had heard suggested. You doubtless imitated Haslar's voice, or claimed to be speaking for him. And afterwards you took away from his writing-table drawer the typescript pages which would have betrayed your story.

"It was you, not Mr. Haslar, who postponed the planned gaieties of last Monday night. You probably alleged some work for, or talk to, Mr. Clifford. Or your own fatigue after your journey. That telephone call that you told us arrived after you got to the house and which hurried Mr. Haslar into the country, came from you yourself as soon as you left him. You sent another to Mr. Newman. So that neither man could stray into the flat. And also so that if things went wrong, neither man could have an alibi. I think you used Cory's name for that purpose, and let them think they were to meet him for some urgent reason. After the murder, Mr. Haslar would of course think those bogus appointments confirmed Cory's guilt. To Mr. Newman it would look like Haslar's doing. The key to flat Fourteen you took from Mr. Haslar's ulster hanging in the hall before you left the house. You also took his automatic which you know from his habits in Australia he kept beside his bed. You were friends enough to chance being found upstairs. Then you went to the flat. You thought it might be as well to leave some sort of a trail. Little dreaming how Mr. Hobbs would help you by taking away everything that would ordinarily identify Mr. Julian Clifford. You remembered hearing at dinner about Etcheverrey and the hunt for him. You passed the time until Mr. Clifford could get to you by writing a couple of notes which you crumpled up in a way that you always do

crumple your thrown away paper, a tight, egg-shaped ball. You could
not know, that they would bring the trail looping back to Thornbush,
and Mr. Clifford. When Mr. Clifford came, you let him in, doubtless
saying that Haslar or the supposed owner of the flat would be back in a
moment. You left Mr. Clifford seated by the lamp looking at some book
placed there to catch his eye. You went into the bedroom, pushed the
door open, and shot him with Mr. Haslar's pistol to which you had
fitted a cardboard silencer—an Australian dodge which you had
evidently learned out there. Hobbs saw you leaving the flat after the
murder. In your agitation you forgot to notice whether the defective
catch of the front door shut properly. Your account of meeting Mr.
Clifford, of leaving him alive, is of course pure invention. Just as was
your tale of Mr. Clifford's fears of Newman, and his dread of his coming
journey. You were careful not to overdo it. You only thought you heard
Mr. Haslar's cough. But to run on, after you left the flat, you put Mr.
Haslar's revolver back in his room. And then went quietly to bed under
the roof of the man whom you had just murdered. To-day, when you
heard that Arnold Haslar had been present in the flat, and claimed to
have seen the murderer, you decided to silence him."

Straight made no further remark except to swear that he was
innocent and that this was but the invention of Scotland Yard.

He maintained this at his trial, but when his appeal against the
death sentence passed on him was disallowed, he wrote a letter to the
Chief Inspector, one of those long, detailed letters that men of his
temperament often do write at such a time. In it he confessed that
Pointer's theory of the motive; a theory proved up to the hilt at the trial
was right; that Mr. Clifford in the course of talking to him after dinner
on Monday about his work had let fall that he was going to take the
coming instalment of *The Soul of Ishmael* to his publisher's next
morning. This was an item which had meant nothing to Straight at the
time but which had spelled disaster, full and complete, when he had
read while waiting in Haslar's library the last published chapters of
the novel. Straight knew then that he had only a few hours in which to
avert discovery —practically only Monday night.

After many digressions, Straight went on to say, in this final
confession, that he had probably himself given Julian Clifford one half
of his own story long ago,—on a boat going to Corfu,—when he,
Straight, had met a man who claimed to be a commercial traveller in
dried fruits. It was after a dinner at which Straight had taken too
much to drink. The drink and a gorgeous night unloosed his tongue,
and half the tale of a clever swindle on the council funds was told to the
commercial traveller as a good yarn.

Next morning a very sober Straight found that the commercial had
left the ship at dawn. Straight never touched stimulants again. He

hoped, and believed, that the part told by him would be forgotten. In any case it was fairly harmless as long as the man to whom it was told did not come upon the other half and put two and two together to make a most unpleasant four—a four that could mean prison. Unfortunately for himself this was what had happened. Julian Clifford had come upon the other half of the story which had been told him by a stranger in the dusk of that Mediterranean night, an unseen stranger who stood to him merely for a base, but intriguing tale. And Julian Clifford, with the flair of the true artist, had welded the two stories together in his yarn as they had been welded in fact. He had even given the swindler a character strangely like Richard Straight's. As to Straight's knowledge of Etcheverrey's signature and home,—Julian Clifford, during the after-dinner talk, had jotted down a few suggestions for some minor headings in the subject index which was to be the new librarian's first task. On the back, as Straight was putting it away in his pocket-book, he called the writer's attention to a V in a tiny outline of a house, and two incomprehensible words.

Clifford had peered at them, mentioned that he was very short-sighted, and explained them with a laugh as Etcheverrey's code signature, and the name of his home in the Pyrenees, something that even Sir Edward did not know.

Straight had the paper in his pocket, when the idea of using Etcheverrey as a trail occurred to him in the flat. A trail that as Pointer had said, he imagined would lead far afield.

"Any time you have another case like this on, let me know, and you're welcome to sign my name again to whatever bulletins you like," Doctor Evans assured Pointer before he hurried off to see to Haslar. The sick man's bed had been secretly rolled into another room. The only truth in the last bulletins, which Pointer had written, was that Haslar was making a wonderful recovery.

On the stairs the Chief Inspector met Tindall hurrying up. Telephone messages had been trying to reach him for hours. Unfortunately the F.O. man had come upon a most promising short cut to Etcheverrey and had taken his Chief with him on a fruitless excursion into the suburbs.

"Straight instead of Etcheverrey!" Tindall could not read just his ideas for a moment. "By the way, you telephoned us that you had absolute certainty that Newman was after all not Etcheverrey. You're sure of that?"

"Absolutely."

"Why?"

"I'm afraid the reasons are confidential."

"Humph—well—he had a most amazing knowledge of Etcheverrey's secrets if it's true that he was Julian Clifford's source of information on the Basque."

"Mr. Newman checkmated Etcheverrey once during the war." The door opened. Sir Edward came in slowly. Heavily.

"I've just told Mrs. Clifford the news," he sank into a chair.

"And how does she take it?" Tindall asked sympathetically.

"She—she thinks that my brother is giving her a message from the other world to his slayer. A message of forgiveness. A promise that expiation in this world will wipe the slate clean, and that Julian will be there ready to greet him as a friend when he 'passes over.'"

"By Jove!" was all Tindall could murmur.

"It must be a wonderful help to be able to believe that sort of thing," Sir Edward said a little wearily, a little wistfully, and a little impatiently. "I confess I found it for once hard to empathise."

There was a short silence. Then Tindall turned to Pointer.

"I've heard you say, Chief Inspector, that the game's never lost until it's won. You've certainly won this one. And won it well. Clues versus deduction, eh? Well, for once they have scored."

"I never knew a case where deductions alone could have gone much further afield," Pointer said thoughtfully. "Only clues, pure and simple, could get one out of such a labyrinth."

"So Julian's notes, which to us, seemed to point full to Etcheverrey, to you pointed to Straight? Odd!" It was Sir Edward speaking.

Tindall made a grimace.

"His carbon sheet, rather? Eh, Pointer? The sheet I turned down."

Pointer nodded.

"Still, that phrase in the notes about 'England dangerous' struck me very much. Seeing that I had Straight in my mind as the probable criminal. I wondered if Roberts's past, instead of his future association with Etcheverrey, might not be the danger, the cause of the murder. And the five pages on the carbon sheet gave us just the clue we needed. On the very last page of the chapter as it was meant to be.

"We have two men who are very good at that sort of an investigation. By the help of it, they soon worked back to the truth. Incidentally Newman, who I found knew about the notes left nearly a fortnight ago with Mr. Bancroft, had made no effort to get hold of them."

"You suspected Straight from the first!" Clifford asked, "On what grounds?"

"I suspected everybody," Pointer said a little dryly. Tindall smoothed away a grin under cover of stroking his beard. He knew quite well whom Pointer had included in his suspicions.

"Of course Hobbs' telling you that you saw Straight come out of the flat was a plain enough tip," he murmured, "but I imagined you didn't believe the tale. Hobbs himself thought so."

"Hobbs had to think so. He was going to be under the same roof as Straight, and had a tremendous grudge against him. Which was why I had to question Straight about the incident, for if he had learnt from Hobbs that I knew of it, he would have known by my silence, that he was suspected."

Tindall nodded to each point in turn. "But what set you on Straight's trail in the beginning?" he pressed. "You talk of clues. Surely it was reasoning rather. Reasoning from the facts, not to them. Pointer too preferred the latter way when possible, but it had not been possible in the Clifford affair. In other words reasoning from a clue I found."

"Which clue? Where?"

"The tape pinned across the door catch. If the murderer was one of the narrow circle at Thornbush, in which circle I included the Haslars, that pointed to some very hurried, very improvised, plan.

"Whoever did that, knew that only a short time could elapse between the arrival of the victim and his death. Else so clumsy a precaution would have aroused suspicion. But evidently the man who came was not, and was not expected to be, suspicious. Here was where the oddity lay. For apparently, too, he did not know the flat well enough to roam about it. That tape looked to me very unlike the work of whoever had taken the flat. Let alone the work of Etcheverrey. For, they would have had ample time to silence the lock invisibly. It certainly did not look like the work of an engineer, let alone an electrical engineer of Arnold Haslar's standing. It looked to me like some sudden arrival to the Thornbush circle, and the choosing of Monday night, also made the crime seem the work of a newcomer. For if the criminal knew of the flat, he would probably know that Cory, who never runs two enterprises simultaneously—he had some pigeon-plucking to finish might come in by Tuesday. But why should any one wait until the last night when the flat would be free unless he couldn't help himself? Unless that was his first opportunity? Or Mr. Clifford might have refused to come to Heath Mansions, or some hitch might have occurred. On the other hand, if a new arrival, it must be one who knew that Mr. Clifford is short-sighted, or he would never have chanced that tape. Also, supposing I was right, and those paper scraps in the basket were the work of the murderer, he would have to be some one who could have heard of Etcheverrey. Straight fitted all these provisos. In short all this pointed so directly to him, as the only newcomer to Thornbush, that I very carefully investigated all other possibles for fear lest I had got an idea into my head. Getting an idea into one's head is a detective's nightmare."

Pointer did not add that he had also suspected—in the absence of any other known motive—the new librarian of having known and loved Mrs. Clifford in the past, and that, therefore, he had been very doubtful of her too, for it was only in the last few hours that his men had been able to prove his own idea right, and working by the clues on the carbon sheet, get hold of the real reason for the murder, and so free all the other inmates of Thornbush, except Straight, from suspicion.

"Yet, otherwise, after the crime, Straight never gave himself away?" Tindall thought. "Until just now. When he fell into your trap."

"That trap was the only thing that could catch him. The only thing that would prove who the murderer of Mr. Julian Clifford had been. He had left no clue behind. It might be Newman, after all, or Hobbs, or any one. I might be all wrong. But Straight gave himself away once—badly. When he described to me how Mr. Clifford was sitting beside the little table in the flat. Unless his story was true, the mere fact of his knowledge of Mr. Clifford's real position marked him as the probable murderer. And, too, I think, I should have suspected him anyway after a little scene which I witnessed between him and Miss Haslar. It was a sort of lover's quarrel. At least that was the impression at which Straight med. He acted like an impetuous, quick-tempered young Fellow who was jealous, and intensely hurt by a girl's preference for another. Now impetuous and quick-tempered :hard Straight certainly is not. Even without any previous suspicions, I should have asked myself why Straight should take the trouble to act—before me."

"And why did he?" Sir Edward demanded.

"He wanted to get free. From the man who had worn that ulster and taken that flat. Free because of him even from Miss Haslar in spite of her large fortune. Then came the news that the truth was out. That we knew that the dead man was Mr. Clifford. After that, Straight wanted to be known to be in love with Mr. Clifford's devoted niece and about to enter his family circle. But when he found finally that she definitely turned him down, he was quite willing that she should smother in that strong room. He told me that he didn't know the code-word. Yet when Mrs. Clifford came, he hastened to ask her if she knew of no other word but Visit. No one had mentioned Visit. That was a bad slip."

"He would have let her die? Good God! Why?"

"If she wouldn't marry him she was a possible hindrance—a restraint. Straight knew that he might yet be pushed into tight corner. Hobbs suspected him. And with Miss Haslar and Arnold Haslar both out of the way, he could be free to do what he liked. Just as Mr. Clifford's death left him free to give us that extraordinary improvisation about his after-dinner talk with him. Straight had no intention of murdering either Miss Haslar or her brother, of course.

Murder is dangerous. Its advantages must be great, therefore. But Straight could have stood by and let things run their course this afternoon."

"Straight!" Tindall muttered again as one mutters a rid die's unexpected solution. "That little rat! I always wondered what Miss Haslar could see in Straight, even for a short time."

"I think she never saw anything in him but a steady, reliable character, a good guide through life! I think she did her best to like him, and never succeeded because of an inward voice that refused to be told how sterling a character was his."

"Straight must have been slightly bewildered when he heard of Clifford's head being missing." Tindall said under his breath to Pointer.

"When he was told that Newman was Etcheverrey, I fancy he thought that he had only forestalled another criminal by a few minutes."

"You never suspected Haslar at any time?" Edward Clifford asked coming out of a revery.

"If murder were Mr. Haslar's object, I couldn't see why he took a flat. Took it in a way that he might fancy would throw any ordinary inquiries off the track, but which he would know as well as any other man would not put a detective off. That coat! Also like you, Mr. Tindall, I couldn't see why the murderer should set himself the horrible task of cutting off a head, when there were so many easier ways of concealing the body's identity. That looked to me only the desperate resort of some one who found the man dead, and to whom it was of the most vital importance that the death should not be suspected, at least for a time. Once granted that Julian Clifford was the murdered man, then, if not an outsider, Mr. Hobbs was clearly marked as the probable disguiser of the identity, provided there were heavy defalcations in his books—so heavy that the death of Mr. Clifford and the subsequent looking into his affairs would spell ruin for him—a ruin far beyond any legacy of five thousand pounds to put right. The cheque was confusing, of course. So was the effect of Mr. Clifford's supposed endeavour to purchase the Charlemagne Crystal. Then there was always the question of collusion—of helpers. Altogether, it's been a most puzzling case."

"Yet Newman never puzzled you?" Tindall wondered.

"As a personality he did indeed. And also as to what, or how much, he knew. But apart from suspecting Straight at once, I soon saw that Mr. Newman knew too much to have left that Etcheverrey trail behind him on the scene of the murder. For he alone of the Thornbush circle was aware that Mr. Clifford intended using the anarchist in his work, and had talked the idea over with Mr. Bancroft. To Straight that news came as a fine shock. He thought he had been so clever!"

"When did he hear of it?"

"When Miss Haslar told me that she believed Mr. Newman to be really Etcheverrey. A belief that seemed to me to rest on a very shaky foundation."

"Chief Inspector!" It was Diana who burst in on them. "Who shot Arnold? It wasn't Mr. Straight, for he was in the library at Thornbush with me at the time! Horrible, horrible thought!" Her face blanched.

"No, it wasn't Straight. He of course insisted that the same man who killed Mr. Clifford had tried to kill your brother, because he had an absolute alibi during the time when Mr. Haslar was shot."

"But who did try to kill him?" she demanded frantically.

"Suppose you had done what your brother had done," Pointer began gently; "taken a flat for one purpose. Made your arrangements for that purpose. Suppose some one else used those arrangements for quite another purpose. For murder. And you learnt the awful truth. Not the report in the papers. Saw yourself implicated very deeply. Believed that you could not clear yourself. Knew that you had opened the door to life-long blackmail. Suppose you were suffering from an illness which peculiarly affects people's nerve. Couldn't you imagine yourself going up to your room, getting your revolver, and telling yourself that you must use it, and use it at once. 'Do it' were the words Mr. Haslar used. 'Do it, and do it at once!'"

"Arnold does talk to himself when he's very much stirred." Diana was half dazed. "You mean that Arnold shot himself?" There was horror, and there was boundless relief, in her voice.

"Just so. With the second bullet in his revolver. The first had been fired by Straight, who used a silencer. The faint mark is on the revolver still. I think that your brother had but that moment come downstairs and learnt from Mr. Newman, who had rushed in to tell him the terrible truth—the truth he had to know—of who it was that had really been murdered in Heath Mansions. Then Mr. Newman had to leave him for fear lest through his presence that truth be suspected, and Thornbush be connected with the brown and orange ulster. Probably your brother let Mr. Newman out. In the letter-box he saw a letter which Major Cory had just dropped in. I've had a chat, rather unwillingly and one-sided, perhaps, with that gentleman. It was a peculiarly menacing letter from a man who felt that he had been intended for a scapegoat. It was, I fancy, the little heap of charred paper that Mr. Tindall and I found under Mr. Haslar's writing-table."

"But how did Mr. Newman know who the dead man was?"

"When Mr. Clifford left his home so abruptly, Mr. Newman, I think, suspected that Mr. Haslar had had a hand in his absence. And even on being told by your brother that he had nothing to do with that absence, I think he still had his doubts, and had tipped a porter at Heath Mansions to let him know when the new, temporary tenant of Mr.

Marshall's flat arrived. The man let out the truth that a murdered man hid been found there, and told him of the taking away by the police of the body. Mr. Newman, I think, stuck on a big black moustache, and going to the mortuary chapel posed as a Spaniard who might be able to identify Etcheverrey. We know that such a man called. I think Mr. Newman recognised Mr. Clifford's very remarkable hands, and recognising them, hurried at once to your brother's house—was met by you and left. Returned again, and had a word with Mr. Haslar. We shall soon learn if my ideas are fairly right."

They proved to be absolutely correct.

"But how do you know—did you suspect from the first—mean, that no one had shot Arnold but himself?"

Pointer looked across Diana at Tindall.

"There was a palm in a pot. The palm had been watered that morning—it was all wet. The brass pot, in which the earthenware one stood, was dry and even dusty. Yet when I tried to lift the inner one out, it couldn't be done because of a deep dent in the jardiniere, a dent that obviously could not have been there when the maid last took out the palm, a dent caused by that revolver crashing against it when it fell from Mr. Haslar's hand. Deflected by the brass pot, the weapon skidded along the floor to near the window. I think Mr. Haslar utilised a moment to fire when a motorcycle outside his house was starting up its engine."

"But those awful words of Arnold's," Diana broke out: "'I did it for nothing!'"

"He had shot, but not killed himself. And when he said he had killed Mr. Clifford I think he believed that by devising that plan for Cory to get the Haslar letters away from Mr. Clifford, he had handed Julian Clifford over to a man who had killed him in revenge for what had happened years ago, —happened and never been forgotten by Cory. The rest was but the effect of the shock of the lurid descriptions in the papers, and of his knowledge of whose that missing head was."

"Straight seemed shocked enough at what happened to Haslar," Tindall pointed out.

"Because he guessed the truth—that Mr. Haslar shot himself. Straight *knew* that there was no murderer at large but himself. And that meant that Mr. Haslar had learnt who it was that had been killed in Heath Mansions, and did not believe in the Etcheverrey trail. And if Mr. Haslar, then why not others? When Mr. Haslar called out those words that night, Straight saw that his best chance—there was no question of concealing them—was to take his stand beside Miss Haslar. For a while."

Again came one of the short pauses which people need when they are trying to keep up with information that quite upsets their own ideas.

"Then it wasn't my brother whom Mr. Straight had seen near Heath Mansions?"

"I should say not, Miss Haslar. I think that was part of a plan of Straight's to frighten you about your brother's connection with the murder for his own ends. To play the part of the faithful friend."

"But Arnold must have had some shock, so the doctor thought, to account for his state that morning."

"That was probably administered by Mrs. Orr. In our talk at Bruges after you left, I learnt from her that she had written—well—a farewell little note to Mr. Haslar from Paris. It reached Hampstead Tuesday morning. He found it lying on the breakfast table for him. It was a very cruel little note. A definite break. Mrs. Orr did not want your brother coming on after her, and interfering with her quite well-laid plans."

At any other time Diana would have made a scathing comment on Mazod Orr giving up her brother, but now all she cared for was that Arnold was cleared, and that Newman was cleared. Tindall and Sir Edward left the room.

Diana took a deep breath. Her eyes were softly luminous. No one could say that her face was cold now.

"And Mr. Newman took everything on himself!" There was a little pause. "Oh, if only I dared! Does blood—even such blood matter really. After all, we Haslars—he is all that's fine. Surely if he could come unscathed from out of such a home, others could. Under better, happier circumstances."

"Come along and let's see what Mr. Newman has to say," Pointer's tone had something boyish in it, as he led her into a room where Newman was standing, his face like the face of a crusader who has won through to Jerusalem.

"Well, Chief Inspector, I take off my hat to you! Especially after I— I'm glad you know now that I didn't kill Julian Clifford. A man I place second only to Peter Haslar. To whom I owe—all that I do owe him. You are right all along the line. Even as to my being the man who called to see Etcheverrey's body. I never imagined any one could unravel this tangle!"

"Especially"—Pointer spoke grimly—"after you had twisted it up still more by that so-called confession of yours. Oh, I know why you did it. To pay back the debt you owed to the dead brother. For Miss Haslar's sake, too, probably. But I hope the thought that you might easily have gone to the gallows instead of Richard Straight, will keep you from ever doing such a thing again. Your improvised motive to me this evening was really alarmingly pat."

It was a very official eye that looked frostily at the other man.

"I—at the time it seemed the only chance. I knew Arnold would never have done it in cold blood, of course. But I was afraid that some discussion about his grandfather's letters— And when you nearly broke me down with what the police might think but for my confession, I didn't dare speak without thinking it all over. I—well, frankly I thought it might be a trap. Though there was the ghastly chance that it might all be true. It was—it was—"

With a deep sigh, Newman tossed what it had been, away from him for ever.

"It was my duty to break down what I firmly believed to be a spurious confession," Pointer said, inwardly a little amused at the positively ferocious glare that Diana was fixing on him. "Now I really would like to hear your explanation of two things. First, Mr. Pollock's furniture."

Diana stared. But Newman looked faintly self-conscious. "Ever heard of *The Knight's Dream?*" he asked.

"You mean the musical comedy that's been running for a couple of years?"

"I wrote it—words and music. It's a gold-mine apparently. I'm working on another. My agents only know me as Pollock, of course. And the only address they have are my bankers and the Musicians' Club in Wigmore Street. And your second question, Chief Inspector?"

"We found a charred piece of a letter in your room at Thornbush on which we deciphered in Mr. Clifford's writing, 'I know the danger,' 'discovered your secret,' 'wife.' At least I believe the word to be wife. Now those sentences looked rather damning, but wasn't the secret that Mr. Clifford thought he had discovered your love for Miss Haslar?"

Diana gave a gasp. "What a dreadful scrap of paper to find!"

"It was puzzling!" Pointer agreed.

"Yes," Newman said, screwing up his eyes in thought. "Yes, the whole sentence ran somewhat after this fashion. I know that letter by heart," he added turning round with a look new to Pointer—a look that changed him into the lad Diana had loved at Hendaye.

"I know the danger of jumping to conclusions, but I feel sure that I have discovered your secret of hoping to make Diana some day your wife.' And Mr. Clifford went on in the kindest way to tell me, that in justice to Diana herself, that must not be. I might be married already."

"When did he write this?"

"Two years ago."

Two years ago was the time when Julian Clifford had altered his will so as to leave Newman, if still unmarried, a competency.

"And you replied?" Pointer thought it as well to take advantage of this moment to know all that there was to be known.

"I told him he was utterly mistaken in my feeling for you," Newman flashed a grim, yet fond smile at Diana, whose eyes were brimming. "I kept the letter as an additional help to—stick to my guns. But I wonder that such a sentence, found in such a case, didn't hang me," he threw at Pointer interrogatively.

"You were so careful to make your flight look suspicious," Pointer said with a half unwilling smile in reply. "You had gone to so much time and trouble in your bedroom to take down a suitcase, and get a bag off your wardrobe top, and strew so many garments, each of which you had to take from its place, around the room, that it seemed odd you should have burnt this letter if it really was incriminating.

"But Miss Haslar is waiting to hear what it was that Superintendent told you. My best wishes, Mr. Penfold."

And Pointer closed the door behind him.

THE END

# Other Resurrected Press books in A. E. Fielding's *The Chief Inspector Pointer Mystery* Series

*The Eames-Erskine Case (1924)*
*The Charteris Mystery (1925)*
*The Footsteps that Stopped (1926)*
*The Clifford Affair (1927)*
*The Cluny Problem (1928)*
*The Net Around Joan Ingilby (1928)*
*The Murder at the Nook (1929)*
*The Mysterious Partner (1929)*
*The Craig Poisoning Mystery (1930)*
*The Wedding Chest Mystery (1930)*
*The Upfold Farm Mystery (1931)*
*Death of John Tait (1932)*
*The Westwood Mystery (1932)*
*The Tall House Mystery (1933)*
*The Cautley Conundrum (1934)*
*The Paper-Chase (1934)*

*The Case of the Missing Diary (1935)*
*Tragedy at Beechcroft (1935)*
*The Case of the Two Pearl Necklaces (1935)*
*Mystery at the Rectory (1936)*
*Black Cats Are Lucky (1937)*
*Scarecrow (1937)*
*Pointer to a Crime (1944)*

**Like us on Facebook to stay up-to-date on all of our latest releases: http://www.facebook.com/ResurrectedPress**

# AVAILABLE FROM RESURRECTED PRESS!

## GEMS OF MYSTERY
### LOST JEWELS FROM A MORE ELEGANT AGE

Three wonderful tales of mystery from some of the best known writers of the period before the First World War --

A foggy London night, a Russian princess who steals jewels, a corpse; a mysterious murder, an opera singer, and stolen pearls; two young people who crash a masked ball only to find themselves caught up in a daring theft of jewels; these are the subjects of this collection of entertaining tales of love, jewels, and mystery. This collection includes:

In the Fog - by Richard Harding Davis's
The Affair at the Hotel Semiramis - by A.E.W. Mason
Hearts and Masks - Harold MacGrath

## JOURNEYS INTO MYSTERY

A collection of three novels of travel and mystery from some of the best known writers of the Edwardian Age

A man is mysteriously murdered on the night express from Rome to Paris. Which one of the passengers is the murderer. The Countess? The General? The clergyman? The maid who disappeared?

A sapphire necklace stolen from a cab in the London fog. A ship's steward who is either more or less than he appears to be. A jewel thief who criss-crosses the Atlantic in search of victims.

A grand London hotel. A missing German prince. A murdered man whose body disappears from the hotel. These are the challenges facing an American millionaire and his daughter after he buys The Grand Babylon Hotel.

*The Rome Express* – Arthur Griffiths
*The Voice in the Fog* – Harold MacGrath
*The Grand Babylon Hotel* – Arnold Bennett

# RESURRECTED PRESS CLASSIC MYSTERY CATALOGUE

### E. C. Bentley
*Trent's Last Case: The Woman in Black*

### Ernest Bramah
*Max Carrados Resurrected:*
*The Detective Stories of Max Carrados*

### Agatha Christie
*The Secret Adversary*
*The Mysterious Affair at Styles*

### Octavus Roy Cohen
*Midnight*

### Freeman Wills Croft
*The Ponson Case*
*The Pit Prop Syndicate*

### J. S. Fletcher
*The Herapath Property*
*The Rayner-Slade Amalgamation*
*The Chestermarke Instinct*
*The Paradise Mystery*
*Dead Men's Money*
*The Middle of Things*
*Ravensdene Court*
*Scarhaven Keep*
*The Orange-Yellow Diamond*
*The Middle Temple Murder*
*The Tallyrand Maxim*
*The Borough Treasurer*
*In the Mayor's Parlour*
*The Saftey Pin*

## R. Austin Freeman
*The Mystery of 31 New Inn from the Dr. Thorndyke Series*
*John Thorndyke's Cases from the Dr. Thorndyke Series*
*The Red Thumb Mark from The Dr. Thorndyke Series*
*The Eye of Osiris from The Dr. Thorndyke Series*
*A Silent Witness from the Dr. John Thorndyke Series*
*The Cat's Eye from the Dr. John Thorndyke Series*
*Helen Vardon's Confession: A Dr. John Thorndyke Story*
*As a Thief in the Night: A Dr. John Thorndyke Story*
*Mr. Pottermack's Oversight: A Dr. John Thorndyke Story*
*Dr. Thorndyke Intervenes: A Dr. John Thorndyke Story*
*The Singing Bone: The Adventures of Dr. Thorndyke*
*The Stoneware Monkey: A Dr. John Thorndyke Story*
*The Great Portrait Mystery, and Other Stories: A Collection of*
*Dr. John Thorndyke and Other Stories*
*The Penrose Mystery: A Dr. John Thorndyke Story*
*The Uttermost Farthing: A Savant's Vendetta*

## Arthur Griffiths
*The Passenger From Calais*
*The Rome Express*

## Fergus Hume
*The Mystery of a Hansom Cab*
*The Green Mummy*
*The Silent House*
*The Secret Passage*

## Edgar Jepson
*The Loudwater Mystery*

## A. E. W. Mason
*At the Villa Rose*

## A. A. Milne
*The Red House Mystery*

## Baroness Emma Orczy
*The Old Man in the Corner*

**Edgar Allan Poe**
*The Detective Stories of Edgar Allan Poe*

**Arthur J. Rees**
*The Hampstead Mystery*
*The Shrieking Pit*
*The Hand In The Dark*
*The Moon Rock*
*The Mystery of the Downs*

**Mary Roberts Rinehart**
*Sight Unseen and The Confession*

**Dorothy L. Sayers**
*Whose Body?*

**Sir William Magnay**
*The Hunt Ball Mystery*

**Mabel and Paul Thorne**
*The Sheridan Road Mystery*

**Louis Tracy**
*The Strange Case of Mortimer Fenley*
*The Albert Gate Mystery*
*The Bartlett Mystery*
*The Postmaster's Daughter*
*The House of Peril*
*The Sandling Case: What Would You Have Done?*

**John R. Watson**
*The Mystery of the Downs*
*The Hampstead Mystery*

**Edgar Wallace**
*The Daffodil Mystery*
*The Crimson Circle*

**Carolyn Wells**
*Vicky Van*

*The Man Who Fell Through the Earth*
*In the Onyx Lobby*
*Raspberry Jam*
*The Clue*
*The Room with the Tassels*
*The Vanishing of Betty Varian*
*The Mystery Girl*
*The White Alley*
*The Curved Blades*
*Anybody but Anne*
*The Bride of a Moment*
*Faulkner's Folly*
*The Diamond Pin*
*The Gold Bag*
*The Mystery of the Sycamore*
*The Come Back*

**Raoul Whitfield**
*Death in a Bowl*

**Mildred A. Wirt**
*The Clock Strikes Thirteen*
*Clue of the Silken Ladder*
*The Cry at Midnight*
*Ghost Beyond the Gate*
*Guilt of the Brass Thieves*
*Hoofbeats on the Turnpike*
*The Secret Pact*
*Saboteurs on the River*
*Signal in the Dark*
*Voice from the Cave*
*Whispering Walls*
*The Wishing Well*

*And much more!*
*Visit ResurrectedPress.com for our complete catalogue*

## About Resurrected Press

A division of Intrepid Ink, LLC, Resurrected Press is dedicated to bringing high quality, vintage books back into publication. See our entire catalogue and find out more at www.ResurrectedPress.com.

## About Intrepid Ink, LLC

Intrepid Ink, LLC provides full publishing services to authors of fiction and non-fiction books, eBooks and websites. From editing to formatting, from publishing to marketing, Intrepid Ink gets your creative works into the hands of the people who want to read them. Find out more at www.IntrepidInk.com.

www.ingramcontent.com/pod-product-compliance
Lightning Source LLC
Chambersburg PA
CBHW052345020726
47503CB00001B/114